DRAGON HUNTER
THE SKYSTONE CHRONICLES BOOK 3
BLAKE & RAVEN PENN

GOOD LUX CREATIVE

Dedication

For Our Parents

Thanks for supporting/enabling us throughout our lifelong fiction addiction.

Contents

Dear reader,

In our travels across worlds,
we've gathered many stories of
heroes. Those heroes always face
an unseen enemy.
May this book help you face yours.

Sincerely,

Blake Penn

Raven Penn

the skystone chronicles

The Land of
EVGARD

the skystone chronicles

The Land of EVYNDARA

the skystone chronicles

The
EthereaL TriaD

The chart below shows the nine types of etherarchy common among worlds. Your world tends to call these effects "magic" or "supernatural." We use the term etherarchy because it is the command of ether that accomplishes these mythic effects.

Any person who can command etherarchy is a magi. They fall into one of three groups.

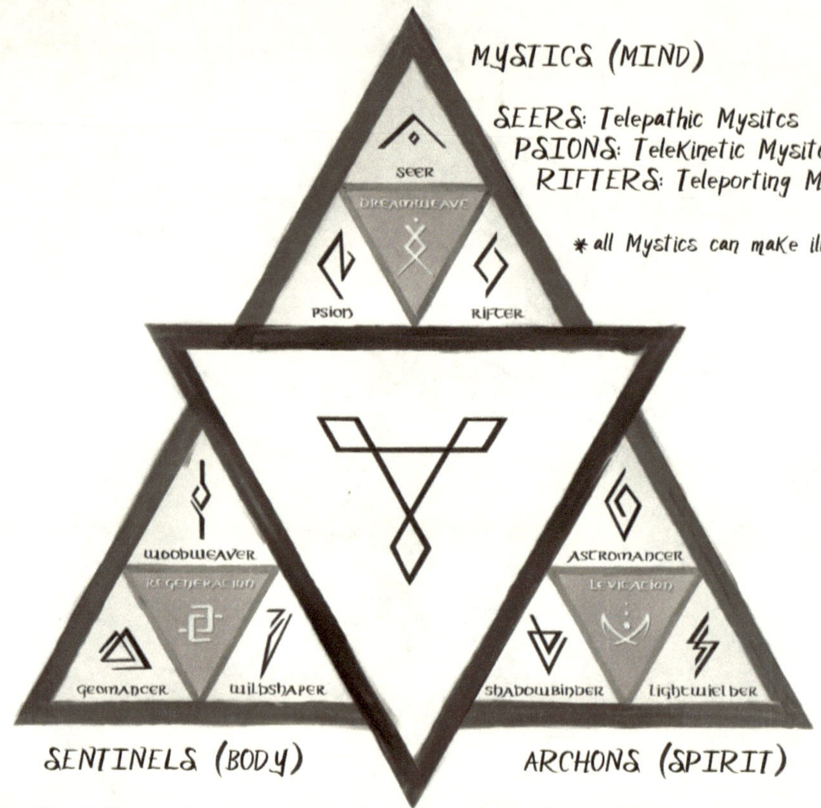

MYSTICS (MIND)

SEERS: Telepathic Mysitcs
PSIONS: Telekinetic Mysitcs
RIFTERS: Teleporting Mysitc

*all Mystics can make illusion

SENTINELS (BODY)

GEOMANCERS: Earth-based Sentinels
WILDSHAPERS: Fauna-based Sentinels
WOODWEAVERS: Flora-based Sentinels

*all Sentinels can regenerate

ARCHONS (SPIRIT)

LIGHTWIELDERS: Light Archons
SHADOWBINDERS: Dark Archons
ASTROMANCERS: Ether Archons

*all Archons can levitate

*A note on silver: It is common knowledge that all etherarchy is nullified on contact with silver. This is why Mage Hunters wield silver weapons, and why Evgardian Keeps have silver lined cells designed to hold magi.

the skystone chronicles

Preface

A Brief Guide to Evgard is included in the back of the book, or you can check out skystonechronicles.com for more information on the world.

Also, signing up for our mailing list will even get you a free short-story set in the world of Evgard!

Now, without further ado, we hope you enjoy *Dragon Hunter*!

On the night of Keep Rengard's Winter Solstice Ball, Meleya and the rest of Squad Reckless help the Black Valkyrie defeat the leader of a dark magi coven. Because of their bravery, the Black Valkyrie invites Meleya, Jax, and the others to enroll at the Mage Hunter Academy in Evyndara. At first, Meleya balks at the prospect, but with her mother having gone to Evyndara to receive the magi cure, she feels she has no choice but to accept.

As a Knight of the Torch and sworn enemy of the Hunters, Jax has his doubts about going to the Academy. But his desire to help Meleya and prove himself to Solrac convinces him to don the dusky blue cloak as a spy.

Back at the Knights of the Torch's headquarters in Orothion, there is division amongst the leadership. When Vesta's faction seizes control and begins preparations for war with Evgard over their mistreatment of magi, Solrac and the other dissidents are labeled Rebels and are forced to flee Orothion.

Elsewhere, the Drekai find themselves engaged in an unwanted conflict with the Canyonlands. Empress Khaisa struggles to quell the attacks while her thoughts are occupied with the brewing darkness in the spirit plane, Etheria.

Meanwhile, Asher, Kai, and Elle make their way across Evgard in order to get Elle to one of the realm's last surviving trainers for true dragon riders. The Mirror Forest of the Ridgeback Mountains makes for the perfect training grounds... both for dragon riders and for Mage Hunters.

With danger rising from all sides, the Rebel Knights are growing nervous. But the Farseer fears the Drekai may be right—the greatest threat to the realm may not be one from the physical plane. It seems that voidarchy has crept its way into the souls of some of Evgard's most elite, and the Gray Ones are preparing to make their move.

MEMORY I

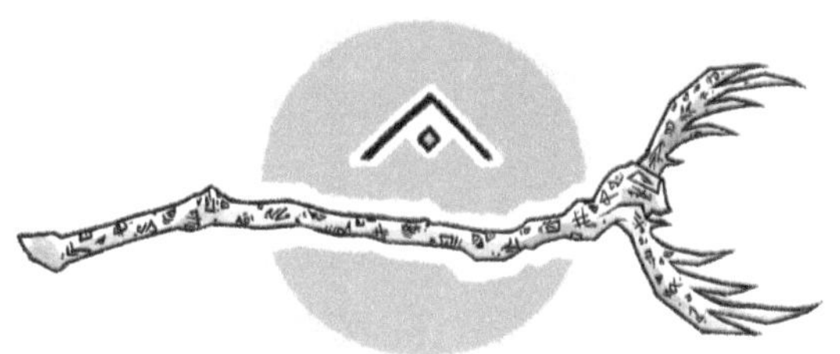

P ure ether.

Solrac knew that the iced-over river at the base of a frozen water-fall wasn't the ideal spot to set up a tent. Especially this high in the Ridge-back Mountains where the wind blew faster than a darting drakalope.

But the omens had led him here because of its high concentration of ether. Even without using the Sight to see into the ethereal plane, Solrac noted the white layer of faintly glowing ether cascading over the frozen surface of Veil Falls. The raw power source flowed into his tent to fuel his blazing omenfire.

Golden runes pulsed over Solrac's forehead, and he wore the rich, deep red robes of the Farseer as he sat before the golden flames. The flames weren't hot, so at least he didn't have to worry about them melting the icy river below.

All he had to worry about were the terrifying, life-shattering omens that predicted the imminent doom of the entire realm.

Set on the ground between Solrac and the fire were three objects. The first, a snow white drake's talon. The second, a Drekai scimitar. The third, a diamond-shaped, wooden hand mirror.

The last was the one that Solrac feared the most.

"Let's start with something easier, shall we?" Solrac muttered to himself, turning away from the mirror and reaching for the drake's talon.

The moment his fingers closed around the talon, a vision of the past began to coalesce within the omenfire.

A blizzard raged around the mouth of a cave. Solrac heard the sounds of rushing wind mingling with low, protective growls. A mighty frostdrake appeared within the mouth of the cave, its icy white jaws opening skyward with an earth-shaking roar.

Facing the drake was a man in his mid-twenties. He wore elegant blue-scaled armor and wielded a jeweled greataxe as he tossed his fair curls.

"Mason Drakeslayer," Solrac said when he recognized the High Prince over all of Evgard.

Flashes of an epic fight between the drake and the High Prince played within the omenfire. Claws clashed against armor until at last, coppery dragon's blood dripped from Mason's greataxe.

Through the vivid memory, Solrac could feel the drake's agony as it lay dying. Feelings of failure pierced through the pain as the exhausted, wounded High Prince moved to get past the dying drake and into the cave it guarded.

Woosh!

With the last of its ebbing strength, the drake clamped its jaws onto Mason's leg. The young man cried out, falling to the cave floor alongside the frostdrake.

As the drake closed its eyes for the last time, the last thing it saw was a mass of strange, gray shadows descending on the High Prince.

Then the vision vanished from the flames.

"Yikes," Solrac said as he gingerly set down the drake's talon. Typically, Solrac sought out omens of the future, or they simply came to him unexpectedly. But memories... memories were far clearer, since the past was much more certain than the future. Still, Solrac was uncertain about whether or not those gray shadows were meant to be literal or symbolic.

Solrac wiped sweat from his brow. Omen reading always left him feeling drained, but at least he didn't have to keep up the epic Farseer presentation side of things too. Being alone liberated him to focus all his energy—and all of this raw ether—on discovering what was in store for the land of Evgard.

"Perhaps this next one will be a little less ominous," Solrac mused, trying to stay positive as he reached for the Drekai scimitar's long, teal handle.

At once, a new vision unfolded within the golden flames. Solrac saw this very blade in action, moving faster than lightning as it clashed against another of similar build.

Two fierce warriors dueled in a clearing surrounded by enormous, gnarled cedar trees covered in thick, green moss. Though he'd never been to the Dragon Isles himself, Solrac spotted the Drekai palace in the background, and it looked like the entire nation of part-dragon people had gathered to watch the fight.

However, Solrac knew firsthand that this was no mere fight. This was a Drekai honor duel to the death.

The two female swordfighters dueled ferociously. Solrac wasn't surprised to see that one of them, the woman wielding the teal-handled scimitar, was none other than his old acquaintance, Zerana. Her husband, Akayto, had hesitated at Solrac's request to take his late wife's sword, but Akayto trusted Solrac. At least, he trusted the Farseer, which—though nobody knew it—was essentially the same thing.

This vision was of the distant past, showing Zerana at no more than eighteen or nineteen years old, wearing fine Drekai clothing with light chest armor and loose pants that tightened at the ankles. A fine turquoise scarf stood out around her neck, clashing with the green clothing of her opponent.

"Empress Khaisa," Solrac murmured as he recognized the other fighter. He'd seen the empress of the Dragon Isles before in vision, though he knew that currently, the empress was around twenty years older. This memory must've been from long before she'd ascended the throne.

"*Ehta nii ikaata!*" Khaisa cried. One of the runes over Solrac's forehead pulsed as he expended a little extra ether to make the translation from Drekai to Evgardian play over the vision.

"Don't hold back!" the vision translated. "Use your powers, Zerana!"

"Not until you use yours, true dragon rider," Zerana shot back, weaving her way through Khaisa's guard and knocking her weapon out of her hand.

As the duel continued, the throng of Drekai watching the fight stomped their feet. Some shouted in support of Zerana while others favored Khaisa. Zerana's dragonfire green eyes stormed all the while.

Overlaying the vision, the fight seemed to take on a sort of glow—purple light appeared to dance around the warriors while sparks of black frustration and deep green rivalry accented each strike.

"Thank you, symbolism," Solrac mumbled to his omenfire.

Finally, with a cry, Zerana pushed in on Khaisa and sent her sword flying. A second later, Zerana had her opponent pinned to the ground, scimitar over her neck. Zerana was the superior warrior. The crowd roared.

Khaisa set her jaw, bravely bracing for the killing blow. "End it," she said.

Zerana froze. From the sidelines, a booming male voice called, "You must finish this, Zerana!"

The vision flashed to the man's pained face. He wore an ornate crown with blue and green jewels that matched the scales along his hairline, cheekbones, and shoulders. It was immediately clear to Solrac that he was looking at the Drekai Emperor, who didn't want to see Khaisa dead, but whose customs dictated that an honor duel like this ended only at death.

The flames burned brighter as the vision closed in on Zerana and Khaisa's faces. Zerana's betrayed a thousand emotions, ranging from fear to indecision to guilt.

Zerana closed her eyes, slowly raising her blade over Khaisa. Too slowly. Solrac frowned.

In the time it took Zerana to prepare her fatal strike, Khaisa whipped out her emerald heartscale from a cord around her neck. Khaisa moved like an ashviper, eyes glowing gold as she accessed the power of her bonded true dragon.

A golden rune appeared over Khaisa's forehead as she telekinetically threw Zerana backward.

Zerana landed with a thud, but she was smiling. This was more like it.

Zerana dodged a blast of emerald green dragonfire from Khaisa's hand, her own eyes glowing gold as Zerana hover-dashed to close the distance between them. The crowd roared, as did Khaisa's vibrant green dragon who was watching from the sidelines.

Khaisa reached out a hand to telekinetically summon her fallen blade, and the real battle began.

Zerana lashed out with her blades, drawing blood on Khaisa's arm. Golden patterns traced along Khaisa's skin to heal the wound as she responded with a series of slashes of her own. But Zerana's body took on the element of shadow, and Khaisa's blades passed straight through her with no effect.

Zerana remained untouchable throughout the battle, and both the crowd and Solrac could tell that she was toying with her opponent.

Despite Khaisa's ability to access many kinds of etherarchy through her true dragon's heartscale, Zerana was clearly the better warrior.

The odd, symbolic colors from the omenfire still swirled around the duel as it played out in the flames. Frowning, Solrac noted yellow clouds forming around Zerana. He wasn't quite sure what that meant... hesitancy? Fear, perhaps? But Zerana was clearly going to win the fight, so what could she be afraid of? Suddenly, the cautious yellow changed to stiff, iron-gray resolve.

Meanwhile, frustration mounted on Khaisa's face. Zerana took a step backward as if to catch her breath, leaving herself vulnerable for only a split second. Solrac's brows furrowed.

At once, Khaisa gathered a massive torrent of emerald green dragonfire all around her. Zerana gasped as Khaisa thrust her hands forward, completely engulfing her in the flames.

The fire blast seemed to stretch into eternity. When Khaisa finally pulled back, the crowd was silent as they stared at the pile of ash where Zerana once stood.

For a few moments, there was nothing. Then cheers for Khaisa erupted, echoing throughout the lush forest empire.

The Drekai people swarmed Khaisa to congratulate her on her epic victory, but all Solrac saw were swirling sparks of pale orange confusion surrounding her troubled face.

Solrac's expression matched Khaisa's. He'd known Zerana many years after this vision had occurred, which meant that despite what he'd just seen, Zerana had not died that day in the Dragon Isles.

"More of that drakking symbolism, perhaps," Solrac muttered. But what did it mean?

Still reeling from his vision of the Dragon Isles, Solrac turned to the wooden hand mirror lying in wait in the final place on the floor.

He wasn't yet touching the mirror to learn what dark secrets it held, but still, memories filled Solrac's mind at the mere sight of it. He remembered too well the day he'd given the mirror to his new wife after carving the original poem into the back. He knew the lines by heart:

Look to each skyfall that flares through the night
And know that my love burns even more bright

Everything had changed since then. Solrac had become the Farseer. Vidya had become the Farseer's bane, the Black Valkyrie. It was ironic, especially since Vidya had no idea why Solrac had been forced to leave her so soon after their ill-conceived wedding day—as far as she knew, the Farseer was an almighty legend, while Solrac was nothing more than the man who'd broken her heart.

Solrac sighed, turning away from the mirror. Even after all these years, Vidya still possessed a dangerous amount of Solrac's heart.

He couldn't bring himself to touch the mirror to see what vital memory it held. Not yet.

Suddenly, a surge of ether from the ley lines caused the omenfire to burn higher. Solrac faced the flames and saw a vast, yellowed map of Evgard within them.

Two symbols hung above the map. One he knew well: the fiery beacon of the Knights of the Torch. As for the other... it could only be the triangular icon of the ethereal triad, the symbol of etherarchy.

But wait—A silver sword materialized to stab the triad, causing bright red blood to drip from its center. Screams echoed from within the flames, and Solrac shuddered as he comprehended the symbolism. That was the mark of the Mage Hunters.

Suddenly, both symbols came together, bursting with pearlescent white light before ending in a flaming explosion. From that explosion was born an image that made Solrac jump.

An enormous, shadowy dragon seemed to leap out of the omenfire, jaws wide as they clamped around Solrac's head. As the dragon's maw closed, the beast vanished into smoke and the omenfire returned to its neutral golden color.

For a second, Solrac just sat there, frozen in place.

Then, just as quickly as it had appeared, the dragon was gone. Solrac swallowed hard—He was fairly certain the flames had shown him this strange dragon before. Though, to be fair, this *was* the first time that an omen had tried to bite his head off.

But what does it mean? Solrac wondered. *More wild dragons coming in from the Dragon Mists? Perhaps it represents the Drekai, or even the Gray Ones?* Whatever the symbolism of the marks and the dragon, Solrac feared for the future of the realm. He'd need to consult the omens further, but first, he could use a rest.

Solrac sighed, letting his runes go out. It had been a long, lonely journey into the High Ridgebacks, and it appeared that he wasn't going home anytime soon.

"It's alright," Solrac said to himself. "Some alone time in a dismal, wintery forest with nothing but mysterious symbolism and heatless golden fires just might be the greatest thing that could've possibly happened."

Solrac chuckled, then sat up straighter before accessing his illusion powers to change his regular, lightly accented voice to the deep, excessively grandiose voice of the Farseer.

"Focus, Solrac, Duke of Glacia," he told himself. "There is no time to waste. You must discern the meaning of these omens, and quickly. The future of Evgard depends on it."

Chapter I: Thief

ASHER

Even I'd had doubts about stealth-diving into the Mage Hunter Academy in broad daylight.

But as my bonded dragon, Thorn, and I cut through the sunny winter sky above the Mirror Forest, I couldn't help but feel those same excited nerves that always accompany a risky heist.

Thorn made a low, rumbling roar of agreement. He tossed back his scaly, black-and-bronze head, and I had to duck to avoid getting hit by his majestic, staglike antlers. Through our bond, he sent me a feeling like a blazing bonfire—Thorn loved adventure as much as I did.

I laughed, leaning forward to encourage my dragon to fly faster.

Much faster, Thorn replied through our bond as he obliged.

"Asher! Slow down!" Kai called out. "We're about to come into view of the Academy and I haven't got the illusions up on our dragons yet."

Not far behind Thorn and me, my cautious best friend soared atop his own dragon bond. Kai's stone-colored four-winged evren, Flint, was smaller than my wyvern, but that hadn't stopped Kai from wearing about every piece of heavy plate armor he could find. From helmet to chestplate to leg-guarding tassets, Kai was—as always—prepared for the worst.

Against my nature, I urged Thorn to slow down. Within moments, a detailed golden rune glowed to life over Kai's forehead. As he completed the rune, the air ahead of and below us seemed to shimmer, then blur ever so slightly. The blur stayed a consistent distance ahead of us as we flew.

"There," Kai said over the rushing wind. "That illusion should mask us from below. Anyone who looks up will only see clear skies. Still, try not to stay in one place too long, since I'm not sure how consistent it will be. The angle should technically be constantly changing relative to our position—"

I didn't *stop* listening to Kai's explanation at that point... My brain just *started* focusing on something else. Anything but Kai's long-winded explanation of the intricacies of his etherarchy. He was a Mystic, the most intellectual of the three magi types. I was never more grateful to be an Archon—When I wanted to use my powers, I didn't have to trace intricate runes I'd memorized beforehand. All I had to do was will it.

Suddenly, I spotted something nestled in the foothills over the next ridge. "There it is!" I called, pointing.

Sure enough, the Mage Hunter Academy had just come into view. Even from here, I could tell magi like Kai and me weren't welcome there. Three gleaming towers shot into the sky, their silver plating accenting the gray stone like a warning. Silver was costly, but I had no doubt they'd spared no expense when it came to showing magi just how much of the anti-ether metal they had at their disposal. The Academy itself was shaped like an enormous triangle with a sword cutting through it—the iconic symbol every Mage Hunter wore on their silver pauldron.

More structures stood imposingly along the mountain to the north, ending with a sharp, black tower that overlooked the entire valley. The tower was tall and thin, with an ornamental design on top that curved elegantly to one side before tapering off to a sharp, upward-facing point. The shape reminded me of a pair of dark swan wings.

Our enemy sure liked to stick with a theme.

"There's Swan Spire," I called back to Kai.

"That's where we need to go," Kai confirmed. "But we need to be cautious in our approach. Don't stray from the plan, okay Asher?"

"Who, me? When have I ever strayed from the plan?"

Below me, Thorn let out the wyvern equivalent of a chuckle. Silence emitted from Kai's helmet, and I could tell he wasn't about to dignify that with a response. That was fair. In fact, I found myself struggling to recall a time when I *hadn't* strayed from my best friend's meticulously crafted plans.

As Kai and I shot toward the distinct black tower, I noticed a few additional glowing golden runes had joined Kai's first, forming a row across his forehead.

Asher, can you hear me? This time, Kai's voice didn't come from beside me. Rather, I heard him inside my head, a clear signal that it was time to switch from talking in person to communicating over the mindlink.

On cue, I felt a little wiggle from inside my boot. Kai's ethereal pet mirror gecko, Glint—or at least one of Kai's many copies of her—was hiding in there. Through her, Kai was able to connect with my mind.

Clear as crystal, I thought back. *Then again, I've seen a lot of crystals that aren't clear at all. They're more clouded, you know? Hmm... that phrase is pretty flawed. How about 'clear as water'?*

Asher... Kai started.

You're right, same problem, I cut in. *Maybe 'clear as glass?'*

Thorn chimed in through our bond, *'Clear as air?'*

Chuckling, I relayed his suggestion over the mindlink, then continued, *How about 'clear as my flawless skin'?*

Asher... Even in my head, I could practically feel Kai rolling his eyes.

Right again, Kai, I thought. *But to be fair, that pimple has been gone for days now. You don't have to keep bringing it up.*

ASHER.

Sorry. Focusing now.

If only, Kai's thought was resigned, but I could tell he was smiling. On the inside.

We were now close enough to make out six terrifying black starswans circling Swan Spire. They didn't seem to notice us, which meant Kai's illusion was working. So far, so good. We were almost within striking distance of that sinister gaggle.

I knew those swans all too well. They belonged to the woman whom I'd hated above all others for nearly five years.

The Black Valkyrie.

I shuddered as we approached her tower. When I'd learned our mission was to rob the Black Valkyrie herself, I'd jumped at the chance. Higher than most, since, as an Archon, I could levitate.

Step one, Kai thought over the mindlink. *Take out the starswans. I've got this one.*

Beside me, I saw Kai point a finger at the nearest black swan. Purple energy swirled together into a focused point at his fingertip before he sent it shooting through the air, straight at the starswan's head. As the energy hit, I noticed a subtle shift in the watchbird's flight pattern. Its wing beats became more rhythmic, its eyes glazing over and glowing purple.

I could sense Kai's satisfaction in my mind. *There. Now, all it will see is the same repeated visual of the forest. You could fly right in front of its beak and it wouldn't see you.*

So, you're saying I—

Kai mentally cut me off. *No, Asher, that doesn't mean you should fly right in front of its beak.*

Stars, you're no fun.

Kai shot more purple energy at the remaining five starswans, complaining all the while about how much more efficient his channeling would be if he used a device like a wand or staff, then gave me the go-ahead to proceed to step two.

Ready, Thorn? I asked, giving my dragon a pat on the neck.

Hatched ready, he replied eagerly.

Then, I jumped from his back.

The chilly air rushed in my ears, only somewhat muted by the small, dark teal scales along their tips. As a half-born, my scaled, pointed ears were one of my most distinct features and, despite the disapproving looks I often got for my Drekai ancestry, I liked to show them off. It was why I kept my jet black hair short on the sides but longer on top.

As I fell, I could feel my hair coming loose from its fangknot hairstyle. The icy wind contrasted with the warm rays of sunlight on my golden-brown skin.

I enjoyed the freefall for slightly longer than I probably should have as the ground rose to greet me. Long enough that Kai sent a panicked warning over the mindlink.

Asher!

I grinned, my eyes flashing from their regular dragonfire green to gold as I burned ether. My archonic levitation abilities kicked in, and all at once, the air stopped rushing around me so quickly.

My hair whipped into my face. Barely resisting the urge to let out a whoop, I threw in a double flip before landing in a crouch on the ground.

I channeled my thoughts through the mindlink. *That. Was. Awesome! Kai, did you* see *that? Tell me that wasn't the most epic thing you've ever seen!*

Through my bond with Thorn, I felt a flame of agreement, along with a single word: *Epic!*

Kai was less enthused. *Did you have to add the flip? There must be a lot of silver in Swan Spire, so my illusion was weakened. That stupid flip increased the likelihood of your being seen by nearly fifteen percent!*

Thorn is so much more supportive than you, I mentally grumbled. *Nobody's trained a crossbow on me, so it looks like that fifteen percent can eat soot.*

Moving on, I turned to face the black stone of the building towering before me. I spotted one open window beneath its swan wing-like crown. That would be the simplest way in.

I took a few steps back for extra momentum, then burned more ether, my eyes flashing gold once more as I hover-dashed straight at the wall.

My levitation powers sent me running straight up, my feet all but flying over the stony surface. Again, I fought the urge to whoop as I landed perfectly on the window sill.

Careful, Kai warned, though his voice sounded faint. He must've been right about the silver in the tower stifling his powers.

Relax, I thought back. *I was fast. There's no way anybody saw that.* Still, I did a quick check to my left and right, just in case.

Now hurry, Kai thought, his voice phasing in and out, loud to quiet, in my head. *Next step: Find that key, and fast. I'd estimate that the Black Valkyrie will be back in her tower somewhere in the realm of twenty-one to thirty-five minutes.*

How in the void do you know when that woman will be back? I questioned.

Kai's reply felt strained. *Do you really want me to explain? Because I could tell you every last detail of what combination of runes allows me to run a low ether-signature reverse mindreading hack via contact between her astral familiars—*

No no, I rushed to stop him. *Don't trouble yourself. I beg you.*

Anyway, the bottom line is you should have plenty of time to find the key. It will be the one with the crystal on it. I want you out of there in ten minutes just to be safe.

I only need nine.

With that, I stepped inside the tower.

I hadn't been rummaging through the Black Valkyrie's stuff for long before I was staring at a strange, white-haired young woman in an orange cloak who—for the second time in our lives—had drawn her long seaxe-style sword on me.

I was annoyed with her for interrupting my search for the key, but also kind of intrigued. The last time I'd seen her had been miles and miles south in Keep Rengard. She was the last person I'd have expected to find here at the Academy.

There must've been a decent amount of silver in the room, because I hadn't heard Kai through the mindlink at all since coming inside. Even my bond with Thorn felt weak in here. I was on my own.

I'd been trying to stall the snowhead girl, engaging her in somewhat useless banter for the past few minutes while I looked through some of the Black Valkyrie's endless drawers and trunks. No key—so far. First, I'd claimed to be from the 'local tower inspection society,' and when that hadn't worked, I'd pretended not to remember her at all. Her cheeks had grown red with frustration, and she'd only gotten more and more annoyed with every word.

Soot. I'd been hoping to charm this girl into cutting me some slack, but that was clearly not going to work this time.

"Enough of this stupid game, thief," the girl said. She leveled her seaxe my way as I tossed aside a book in my search for the crystal key. Stars, was she always this uptight? I needed to let her know I remembered exactly who she was.

"Oh! That's right!" I put a hand to my forehead and looked her dead in the eye. "You're that snowheaded guard who tried to run me through back on the Rise."

The tension between us was strong as she narrowed her dark brown eyes. "What are you really doing here?"

My fingers twitched as I glanced toward her sword. Was she really going to use it?

"Oh, you know. Normal things," I replied as the two of us slowly began circling one another. "Enjoying the mountain views, getting some cool winter air… robbing the Black Valkyrie."

If Kai's mindlink had been working, I was certain I'd have heard him yelling at me for flat out telling the truth. But I still wasn't certain whether this girl was my enemy or not.

Time to find out.

"But tell me, snowhead," I said, "What are *you* doing here?"

Her response came fast. "I'm a new member of the Black Valkyrie's entourage."

Time froze as her words echoed inside my head. The Black Valkyrie's entourage. For the better part of last summer, that group of good-for-nothing Mage Hunters had relentlessly pursued my friends and me. That confirmed it.

She was *definitely* my enemy.

Without another moment's hesitation, I dug deep to access more ether.

My eyes burned gold as I summoned a weapon of my own. Misty ether coalesced around my hands, turning from glowing, wispy white essense to its solid, super-crystal form. Within moments, I was holding my long, double-bladed dragonhook spear in my hands.

In response to my etherarchy, the young woman raised a finger to runetrace. At once, a round, gold-rimmed portal spun to life just over her arm. Soot—she was a Rifter, a teleportation-based magi. She wielded the portal like a shield as she assumed a perfect battle stance.

For the first time, I noticed the gleaming Rifter's silvermark on her left cheekbone. A symbol carved with silver ink to brand known magi, which certainly hadn't been there the last time we'd encountered each other.

"Huh," I said. "That's new."

The snowhead set her jaw. "So, are we gonna do this?"

I matched her determination. "Absolutely."

And, without further ado, we raced to meet each other in the middle of the room, weapons clashing.

My starglass spear didn't shatter on contact with her seaxe-style longsword. That was good. That meant that this would-be Mage Hunter wasn't fighting with a silver weapon. I wouldn't need to resort to fighting with my dad's old skyseeker dagger, or breaking out my small stash of silverbane.

We both tried a few more swipes, testing each other out. The snowhead was quick, and clearly well-trained with that sword. She knew exactly how to block, even against my longer weapon.

She kept her eyes fixed on me, but mine wandered to the nearest shelf of books. Would the Black Valkyrie have stashed the key somewhere in there?

"I know who you are," she said, her tone serious. She made a quick offensive swing toward my side, and I jumped backward, both to avoid a hit and to get closer to that shelf.

"Aww, don't tell me I have another stalker." I rolled my eyes. "Helga won't be happy about that—she likes feeling unique."

I jabbed at her with my spear, but she intercepted it with her arm-portal. Before I knew it, my spear's blade had materialized out of a new portal at my side, and I was barely able to hover-dodge out of the way of my own stab.

"Impressive," I said.

"Thanks," she replied.

"Oh, sorry—I meant that was an impressive stab I just made." I winked, which made her scowl deepen.

I leaned into her rifting, dropping my spear with one hand and yanking it the rest of the way through her exit portal with my off hand. She hadn't seen that coming, and it bought me the split second I needed to hover-dash over to that bookshelf. I immediately began pulling out books to see if any were hiding crystal-adorned keys.

"So," I began as I worked, "you got a name, or should I just keep calling you snowhead?"

One by one, I tossed books to the ground. My foe made a frustrated grunt, dashing toward me. I prepared to block her next move, but rather than come at me, she bent low to catch the book I'd just dropped.

Brows furrowed, she locked eyes with me. Then, she pointedly shoved the book back into its place on the shelf before swinging her seaxe my way once more.

I blocked, cocking my head. "Passionate about books, are we, snowhead?"

She grit her teeth. "My name's Meleya."

"Meleya," I repeated.

Meleya plowed on, "You can't just mess up all of someone's things like this." Pressing her blade into my spear, she reached down to clean up two of the other books I'd chucked.

I snorted. As if I was about to give the Black Valkyrie any courtesy. She was the person I'd spent the greater part of my teenage years so far hoping to kill.

To make my point, I used my off hand to deliberately grab another book. The snowhead—Meleya—gave me a warning look, and I raised one eyebrow in defiance as I dropped the book to the ground.

She cried out, something between a warrior's yell and that of a babysitter fed up with a disobedient child. One portal ripped to life to catch the falling book, and another tore open to replace it on the shelf.

One look at her told me it was on.

Our fight continued in full force, only now I found myself racing around the room, overturning boxes and throwing cloaks from their hooks on the wall. Naturally, I told myself it was all in search of the key.

Meanwhile, between strikes from her seaxe, Meleya was trailing right behind me, opening portal after portal to try to clean up the havoc I was wreaking on the room. Her mad tidying escapades were working to my advantage, giving me more time to rummage through drawers and shelves, but there was still no sign of that drakking key.

"I know you're a Knight of the Torch," Meleya said as she caught a framed painting before it could crash to the floor. She followed up with a swipe at me as I came racing by.

I hover-dashed out of reach on my way to a rack of black armor in the corner. "Oh! That explains why you keep trying to kill me. Us Knights don't exactly mix well with Mage Hunters."

For good measure, I bumped against a cabinet, causing a glass bottle to roll off the top of it. Meleya sent a portal racing across the floor to catch the bottle and return it to its place.

"Soot! You have problems," she cursed, training her seaxe on me once more. Her ability to multitask was objectively impressive.

"*I* have problems?" I scoffed, batting away her seaxe as I scanned the area for another place to search. "You're the one who can't help but compulsively clean up after me. It's like you're a middle-aged librarian trapped in a seventeen-something's body."

"Immature son of a dragonmutt." Meleya swung, and I blocked.

"Stuffy scale-in-the mud." I swung, and she blocked.

"Scarfity scarf-wearer... person," she faltered.

"Wow," I feigned horror. "You always been this good at insults? You really got me there."

She roared and kicked me hard in the chest. I yelped when I stumbled backward directly through a me-sized portal.

Flailing, I reappeared across the room, where I fell over one of the few unopened trunks left in Swan Spire. Both me and the trunk's contents spilled all over the floor.

I gasped when I realized that I was sitting in a huge pile of miscellaneous junk—including dozens of keys.

Large keys, rusty keys, shiny silvery keys... and several with crystals embedded in them.

Perfect.

I could hear Meleya rushing across the room toward me, and I knew I only had a few seconds. I rapidly sifted through random junk, pocketing each key that had any sort of crystal attached.

I was just reaching for one under a small stack of yellowed envelopes when my heart stopped. One of those letters was simply labeled, with smooth handwriting bearing a single name:

Zerana of Moss Falls.

I froze, my lips forming the word before I could stop them. "Mom."

I reached for the letter, but at the same moment, a certain infuriating, orange-cloaked, snowheaded Mage Hunter skidded to a stop in front of me, sending most of the junk, including the envelope with Mom's name on it, flying.

Meleya's long seaxe came slicing my way, and I burned ether to hover-launch myself straight upward. I floated there, expertly avoiding her swinging sword.

"Get down here and fight me like a normal person!" Meleya ordered.

"I don't think I'm capable of 'normal'," I chuckled, casually dodging her every attempt as I scanned the floor. I no longer gave a flying scale about any old key—I had to get that letter. Years ago, the Black Valkyrie had brought Mom to the Mage Hunter Academy... and her ultimate doom. What if that letter contained more information regarding Mom's death? I had to know.

Suddenly, I felt a sharp tug on my leg. I burned even more ether to keep aloft as I looked down to see that Meleya had dropped her sword and was now clinging to my leg, trying to pull me back to the ground.

"I said, *get down*," she growled, dark eyebrows lowered over angry brown eyes.

"But it's so much more fun up here!" I gave her an unapologetically childish grin as I dropped my weapon as well, then shot a little higher toward the ceiling, hoping to both ditch Meleya and get a better view of where that letter had gone.

Unfortunately, Meleya's grip was tighter than I'd expected. Her legs flailed as we both hovered in mid-air.

"Anyone ever told you you're stubborn?" I grumbled.

"Anyone ever told *you* you're obnoxious?" she countered.

I made the mistake of trying to shake her off, which only made her start climbing up my leg like it was some kind of rope. Soot, she was stronger than she looked. I levitated back and forth to see if I could shake her off, but Meleya held fast.

Meleya gave another frustrated yelp as her hand flew through the air. Gold light trailed after her finger as a new golden Mystic rune shone over the center of her forehead.

Suddenly, a gold-rimmed Rifter's tear ripped open above me. Meleya made a yanking motion with her hand, and the portal dropped downward to encompass my head, shoulders, and torso.

Meleya had placed the exit portal flush with the ground below her feet. My upper half popped out of the floor like I was some kind of gopherdrake.

"Oh, so that's how you're playing it," I laughed. "Maybe you're not as stuffy and dull as I thought!"

"What do you mean stuffy and—hey!" Meleya protested as I reached up to grab hold of her boot. She kicked to try and shake me off, still somehow holding fast to my leg as my lower half hung suspended halfway through her portal.

The whole scene was absurd, but I didn't care. With a start, I realized I'd popped out right near that overturned trunk, beside which I spotted a certain yellowed envelope bearing my mother's name.

I strained, reaching for the letter. I could just feel the bottom corner with my fingertips...

That's when the door burst open, freezing both of us in place.

Meleya and I turned to see a group of stunned people standing in the doorway. Gleaming weapons hung from their belts, and I recognized at least a couple silver pauldrons with the Mage Hunters' symbol etched into them.

Oh stars.

The rest of the Black Valkyrie's entourage had arrived.

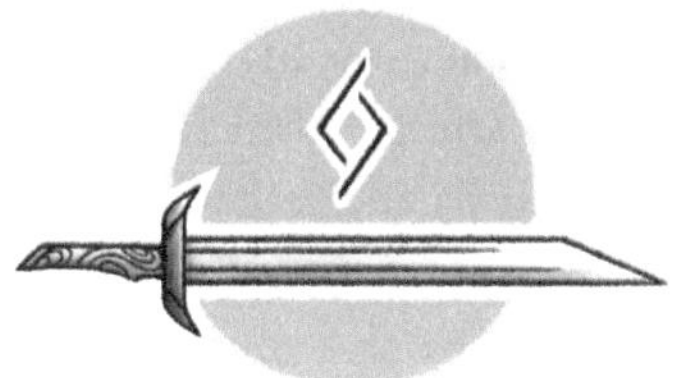

MELEYA

It was hard to tell if my face was so red out of intense frustration or pure embarrassment. Probably both.

"Meleya?" came a chorus of voices from my fellow Mage Hunters as they spilled into the Black Valkyrie's tower, their expressions ranging from shocked to befuddled to amused as they took in the sight of the trashed room. Despite my best efforts, my scuffle with Asher had left the tower in shambles.

Not only did the group seem astounded by the mess, but for whatever reason they were all staring at me. Sure, I was still suspended in the air as I clung to Asher's leg, while his top half sprouted through the floor below me to grab *my* leg, so I guess that wasn't something they saw every day. Worst of all was my boyfriend, Jax, who looked downright angry to see Asher and me like this. Drak.

Our group leader cried out in anger as she pointed to Asher.

"*You!*" Jaira's intense eyebrows hardened at the sight of him.

Asher gave an obnoxiously casual wave and spoke melodramatically. "This isn't what it looks like, dearest Helga! I swear."

Apparently Jaira didn't find Asher's joke—whatever it was—funny.

"Get him!" she roared.

At her word, the others rushed us. Four surrounded Asher in a strategic quadrilateral formation, while Bjorn, my wild-eyed, mohawked ex-squad-mate, shot across the room like a bolt from a crossbow. He gave a horrible, maniacal yell that sent shivers up my arms and made Asher's eyes pop.

In an understandable act of self-preservation, Asher let go of my leg and scrambled through the floor portal at high speed.

I lost my grip on his leg as it vanished through the portal. I fell, dropping straight through that same portal only to come out falling again through the one above. After looping through both portals twice more, I finally had the brilliant idea of turning off my rune. The portals dissolved into etherdust and I landed on the ground in a crouch.

I noticed Jax was still frozen in place by the doorway, unsure what to do. He certainly stood out, what with his muscular build and the wild, steely gray hair sticking out from the maroon bandana he always wore wrapped across his forehead. Jax's dark, midnight blue eyes were wide, staring at Asher like he was seeing a ghost. That made sense... I knew they'd worked together before, with a group of outlawed freedom fighters called the Knights of the Torch.

Not that I'd found Asher's behavior particularly knightly.

Meanwhile, the rest of the entourage was engaged in what appeared to be some kind of insane game of drake and drakalope. Excluding Jax and myself, six Mage Hunters were all after one hyper-fast, swaggering, teenage Astromancer.

Asher's spear still sat abandoned on the ground, but he used his levitation powers to dart all around the room, gold light warping the air behind him like he was some kind of spastic shooting star. Even maniac Bjorn with his long legs couldn't hope to keep up.

I was puzzled. Asher was clearly outnumbered, so why wasn't he making a break for the window? What could possibly be worth sticking around for?

As I wondered this, Asher strategically zipped past his four pursuers and channeled more etherarchy to form rough starglass weights all along their boots. Lothar, Brigan, Solvai and Shaya... they were all trapped, just like that. I couldn't help but notice Asher do a double take upon seeing Shaya, a redheaded fellow Mage Hunter, but I supposed that I was just seeing things. After all, why would Lothar offer a discreet bow to the young man who'd just incapacitated him?

Whatever the case, Asher shook it off, then tried to snare Bjorn in starglass as well. But Bjorn didn't slow down at all as he chased his target.

"Fear not, my mohawked friend," Asher said, just barely levitating out of the way of Bjorn's pure silver dagger. "I have something special for you, too."

With that, Asher whipped two tiny crystal vials out of his pocket. Each was filled with a vaguely familiar greenish-gold liquid.

"Eat silverbane!" Asher cried as he chucked one vial at Bjorn's weapon. On contact, the vial shattered and, with a puff of orange smoke, the substance began eating away at his silver dagger.

"Scorch!" Bjorn cried out, frantically wiping the silverbane from the dagger with his pant leg. "Drak you, ethercursed!"

"Language!" Asher gasped as he formed a starglass muzzle over Bjorn's scowling mouth. He dove to the ground close to where I stood, and I automatically assumed a defensive position.

But Asher wasn't after me. Rather, he was reaching for something on the ground near my feet... That envelope that had fallen out of the Black Valkyrie's trunk during our earlier skirmish.

But Asher wasn't the only one taking advantage of his foe's distraction. Jaira's silver Mage Hunter's whip moved like lightning—In fact, it even *had* lightning crackling up and down its length. Jaira was a lightwielding magi, though unlike most, her powers didn't bow to silver, nor did they manifest in the usual gold.

Bright blue lightning ran down the length of her whip as she snapped it at Asher's wrist. He recoiled, yelping in pain, both from the sparking lightning and the silver in her whip.

"There's more where that came from," Jaira warned, preparing for a second strike. As she did, her eyes narrowed. "What are you after, half-born?"

Her gaze traveled along the ground, searching. But just before it landed on that envelope, I stepped to the side to hide it beneath my boot.

Asher cast me a grateful, somewhat confused look. I was a little confused myself. I wasn't entirely sure why I'd done it, I only knew that if Jaira found that envelope, she'd do everything in her power to either destroy it or lock it up forever. Whatever was in that letter was valuable enough to Asher for him to risk his life, and I had a faint idea why. After all, I'd heard what he'd involuntarily said when he'd first spotted the envelope.

Mom.

If there was one thing I understood, it was wanting to protect one's mother.

That's when Asher chucked his second crystal vial, this time at Jaira. With a puff of orange smoke, the odd substance began disintegrating the silvery armor of her Mage Hunter's uniform, from her oversized shoulder pauldron to the very buckles on her overtunic.

Jaira cried out. The substance didn't harm her skin, but she had to drop her whip to hold her shirt together. A few people snickered, and even I couldn't hold back a small snort.

With all of his active pursuers at least somewhat incapacitated, Asher scrambled to his feet. He leaped into the open window, turning around for one last look about the room.

First he locked eyes with Jax, who was still frozen near the tower's entrance. Next, Asher's bright, dragonfire green eyes settled on me, and he gave me an over-the-top salute.

Then, he jumped out the window.

For a ridiculous second, I wondered how he could survive a fall from this high up. Then I remembered that he didn't have to.

Poking my head through the open window, I could see Asher already racing westward into the Mirror Forest, sitting astride a large, black-and-copper wyvern. Within seconds, they'd disappeared into the thick foliage.

Inside Swan Spire, there was a moment of silence as we watched the thief get away. Then suddenly, Jaira screamed with rage.

"Chase him down!" she roared. "We can still nab him if we're fast. Riders, call your scorching dragons and let's—"

"No."

We all jumped at the sound of the smooth, even voice in the doorway. Standing proudly and wearing an all black Mage Hunter's uniform, her cape adorned with inky swan feathers, was the Black Valkyrie herself.

She tossed her ash-colored hair over one shoulder as she calmly strode into the room. Aloofly, she observed the sorry state of her sanctuary. Despite my efforts to keep it intact, Asher's mad search and the subsequent brawl with the other Mage Hunters had left Swan Spire in chaos.

The Black Valkyrie held our silent attention as she moved about the space. When she passed the Hunters still weighed down by Asher's starglass, she casually used her silver-tipped spear to shatter it and free them.

I caught sight of Jax's expression as he stood across the room. His brow was knit, and I noted tension in his sharp jawline as he watched the Black Valkyrie.

The Black Valkyrie had barely glanced his way upon entering the tower. She hadn't given him any more attention than the rest of us, but then again, how could she? Jax's relationship with the legendary leader of the

Mage Hunters was a secret—Out of everyone here, I alone knew that Jax was the Black Valkyrie's son.

"Did the thief take anything?" the Black Valkyrie finally asked.

I jumped when all eyes turned on me.

"Uh…" I began, "just a handful of keys from that chest over there." I pointed to the overturned junk trunk. "And… that's all."

A tiny bead of sweat formed on my temple as I kept my foot solidly rooted in place over that envelope. The Black Valkyrie's lower eyelids squinted slightly, but she didn't question me.

I breathed a sigh of relief as she turned away, continuing to observe the room. I felt an inexplicable obligation to keep that letter about Asher's mom safe.

Maybe it was because my own mother was the reason I was here at the Academy in the first place.

Mom's words from the note she'd left for me still rang in my ears:

Dear Meli… I spoke with the Black Valkyrie… Asked her if I could receive the magi cure. Once I'm free from this curse, I'll find you and Dad.

It was common knowledge throughout Evgard that the Academy was where they were working on perfecting the magi cure—the cure I'd once longed to receive myself. Now, the idea of someone stripping me of my etherarchy filled me with dread.

I had to find Mom. Even if I was too late to stop her from giving up her powers, I had to get her out of here and back to Dad.

"We have far more important things to worry about than a silly thief," the Black Valkyrie declared. She dramatically raised both hands into the air, using one to trace a rune. Like Jaira, her etherarchy appeared sapphire blue rather than the typical gold.

At once, dozens of scattered items began telekinetically rushing back to their places. Overturned trunks righted themselves as picture frames straightened. Within seconds, the room had returned to perfect order. I liked that rune.

Then I felt the envelope under my foot trying to zip back to its trunk as well. Rather than letting it go, I ducked to grab it, crumpling it slightly as I stuffed it securely into my tunic pocket.

Only Jax seemed to notice anything out of the ordinary, and I winced when he gave me a suspicious look. Soot, we needed to talk.

"Now, on to business," the Black Valkyrie announced. "Welcome, new members, to my team of elites. Despite this most recent failure, you've proven your excellent potential as Hunters, and I'm glad to have you join me on our noble quest to protect the realm."

The Black Valkyrie made her way to the doorway once more as she went on. "I don't know what news you all have heard as of yet, so allow me get you all up to speed."

She turned to face us all, her posture impeccable and her expression proud. It made me want to stand up straighter myself.

"Evgard is on the brink of chaos," the Black Valkyrie grandly asserted, as if she were performing for a large crowd "As you well know, the increase in skyfalls has not abated. Wild dragonkind are a greater threat to the realm than ever before, yet rather than pursue a common goal in unity as true Evgardians ought to, some have seen fit to form their own factions."

She nodded toward where Solvai, Brigan, Jax, and I stood. "I know those of you from Squad Reckless are all too familiar with the Coven of the Gray Ones." A shiver went down my spine as I thought of the gray-masked, hooded magi we'd battled multiple times over the past several months.

The Black Valkyrie looked down the bridge of her nose at each of us in turn. "They have come to the conclusion that magi are superior to the regular citizens of Evgard."

Bjorn growled, narrowing his eyes at me and the other magi in the room. I tensed, ready to grab my weapon. I doubted he'd actually try anything right now, but Bjorn had long hated me for my etherarchy.

"In a way, they are right," the Black Valkyrie ignored Bjorn. "Magi do have something that others do not. Etherarchy."

With that, the Black Valkyrie's irises flashed bright blue. As she accessed her Archonic powers, black shadowfire rippled along the blade of her spear and she levitated just above the ground, her black cloak fluttering. The spectators, myself included, were fixated on her display of power.

"Etherarchy is a tool," she continued, "to be allowed only to the few strong and deserving enough to use it. We are among these few."

"And the rest?" Jax asked darkly.

The Black Valkyrie frowned, as if contemplating how she wanted to answer. In the end, she shook her head, then dismissed her shadowfire and landed back on the ground before us.

"But the Coven is not the only magi threat Evgard faces in its hour of need," the Black Valkyrie went on, ignoring her secret son's question. "The Knights of the Torch are equally dangerous." Jax bristled but didn't contradict her.

"The Coven of the Gray Ones and the Knights of the Torch are two sides of the same coin," she said. She traced a new rune, then flourished her hand to produce a shimmering, translucent illusion of a coin floating just in front of her. One side of the coin depicted a blank mask with glowing blue eyes—the symbol of the Coven. The Black Valkyrie rotated her hand and the coin followed the motion to reveal another symbol on its back: A beacon of light.

The Black Valkyrie went on, "The Knights see the plight of the magi as an opportunity to usurp power, rather than an opportunity to aid their fellow Evgardians. In a flagrant act of war, they have attacked and pillaged three towns along the shores of the Capital Keepdom of Evgard itself just this past week."

"That's a sooty lie..." Jax mumbled under his breath, so quietly I doubted anyone but me heard him.

"It seems the Knights are finally bold enough to emerge from the shadows," the Black Valkyrie said, ignoring him. "For too long, they've hidden behind the smokescreen of myth, hiding out in Skygard as their beloved patron, the Farseer, appears every now and again to show off his power. But now... well, see for yourselves."

With that, she made another dramatic flourish with her hand, and her coin illusion grew larger. Its surface changed to show a scene of a scowling woman with a Geomancer's silvermark on her left cheek. An army of men and women surrounded her, wearing red cloaks bearing that same beacon of light symbol I'd seen on the Black Valkyrie's illusory coin. The woman led her troops into battle, hurling shards of geomantic slate at the innocent people of the city as they tried to flee.

A fiery lump instantly formed in my throat as I watched the horror unfold. As a soldier, I'd been taught above all else that our job was to protect the citizens of Evgard. I hated what I was seeing, and tried to make eye contact with Jax. Could this be true? But even as an undercover Knight of the Torch himself, Jax seemed taken aback.

The Black Valkyrie's voice held the perfect amount of sorrow. "Even now, the Knights prepare to launch more brutal attacks such as this."

She let the illusion play out a little longer to drive home her point, then cut it off with a flourish of her hand.

"I hope you each can see the importance of our mission," the Black Valkyrie said, taking the time to make eye contact with each person present. When she got to me, she gave an understanding nod.

"Now, it's time we got you into your new uniforms. Jaira, it looks like you need one the most." The Black Valkyrie raised an eyebrow and I realized poor Jaira was still holding the collar of her newly buttonless tunic together with her hands. Jaira shot the rest of us a glare, effectively getting everyone to look away.

"Come along," the Black Valkyrie beckoned for us to follow her out of Swan Spire. "It's time to turn you all into official Mage Hunters."

Like the rest of the grounds and the buildings, the Mage Hunter Academy's armory was imposing, grand, and positively jam-packed with silver.

Silver armor lined one wall while silver weapons lay on racks set up throughout the vast space. And of course, there was the ever-present silver in the mortar between the bricks of the walls.

I shuddered. As a magi, the presence of so much silver sent chills up my arms and made the whole place feel frigid and isolating.

The Black Valkyrie had told us to pick out our uniforms and new weapons, and I already saw Jaira, Bjorn, and the others eagerly selecting theirs. Jaira very much needed a new tunic after her brush with Asher's silverbane, while Bjorn had already selected a shiny silver pauldron from the racks and had moved on to weapons. Though Asher's vial of silverbane had damaged Bjorn's dagger earlier, I saw him proudly clip the blade to his belt alongside his new long, silver seaxe. The silver dagger looked even more terrifying now, with rugged, jagged points lining one side.

For a moment, I just stood there, looking over the wall of armor. According to the Black Valkyrie, there were a few shoulder pauldrons set aside for Hunters that were magi. Thankfully, they weren't forged from silver, but rather, from shiny steel.

Unfortunately, it wasn't easy to tell the difference visually, and I didn't exactly feel like touching each painful piece of silver armor to find out.

Suddenly, a strong hand touched my back, and I turned to see Jax at my side. When he looked down at me, dragonflies hummed to life in my stomach.

"You okay, M?" he asked, his voice low.

"I could ask you the same thing," I replied.

"Wanna tell me what really happened in Swan Spire?"

"What do you mean?"

Jax grimaced. "I mean, uh, you know. With Asher. You remember who he is, right? That he and I are both..." He looked around to ensure nobody was eavesdropping. "That Asher and I are both Knights of the Torch?"

I nodded.

Jax went on. "So, what was he really up to? What mission was he on?"

I swallowed, sidestepping Jax and heading for the rack of tunics. He followed, and together we looked for uniforms in our respective sizes.

"Like I told the others, he was looking for a key," I said as I sifted through the rack to find the women's tunics. "And I don't know much more, since I was too busy fighting him."

"Fighting him?" Jax scoffed. "You knew I worked with him and you still fought him?"

"He was asking for it," I grumbled. "Just thoughtlessly messing up the tower like he *wanted* to be a jerk. And he was so... so annoyingly casual, I just panicked. I don't know." I pulled a tunic off the rack and held it against me to see if it fit.

"Drak," Jax cursed. He had a tunic in his hands too, and I watched as he whipped out one of the twin axes he always kept strapped to his back. He used the fanged point on the blade to cut at the seam where the sleeve connected to the shoulder. Once he'd torn through, he put away the axe and ripped the rest of the sleeve off with his hands.

The sound of tearing fabric drew some attention from our fellow Hunters, particularly my two best friends, Solvai and Brigan. Solvai chuckled and shook her head, brown waves falling around her freckled face. She'd been one of Jax's squadmates as well, and knew that his trademark look involved going sleeveless to show off his incredibly toned, muscular shoulders and arms.

On the opposite scale, my other best friend, Brigan, pressed his lips together in annoyance. As a proper nobleman, Brigan always wore his uniform exactly as intended, and even kept his dark hair perfectly smooth each day, other than the single corkscrew curl over one side of his forehead. Meanwhile, Jax's gray hair always stuck out of his maroon bandana at wild angles.

Brigan gave me a searching, almost longing look, and I found myself blushing and looking away. In more ways than one, Brigan and Jax were at odds.

Meanwhile, Jax had slipped out of his guard's overtunic and was pulling on his new Mage Hunter's tunic. He was clearly flustered, and his large, rough fingers struggled with the smallish buckles.

Wordlessly, I put my hands on his. Then I began doing up the buckles for him. Luckily, they weren't silver like Jaira's had been.

"I'm sorry," Jax muttered. "I just hate feeling so disconnected from the other Knights. There's so much going on while I'm here undercover."

"You mean the schism?" I whispered.

Jax nodded. "I don't know who's with Solrac and who isn't. I'd try asking Kai through the gecko mindlink, but..." Jax trailed off, squeezing his eyes shut. He seemed conflicted as he went on. "But I'm not entirely sure if Kai and Asher are on the right side, either. M, we have to get your mom and get the void out of here. Then we can find Solrac and join the rest of the Rebel Knights."

My fingers froze as I was latching the last strap on Jax's tunic. I looked up at his earnest expression, guilt washing over me.

I knew being at the Academy, so close to his estranged mother, was the last thing Jax wanted to be doing right now. But as far as his plans for *after* the Academy...

"Jax," I started, finishing with the buckle before gently laying my hands on his broad chest. "You know I'm not a Knight of the Torch."

"For now," Jax replied, looking deeply into my dark brown eyes. It might've been my imagination, but I could've sworn I felt his heartbeat pick up through his tunic. "But you will be soon."

"I'm not so sure," I said. "You heard what the Black Valkyrie said about those cities near the capital. You saw the Knights of the Torch slaughtering innocent people."

"Who gives a scorching scale about what that woman says?" Jax set his jaw.

"So you think she lied?" My dark brows knit. "Or you think it wasn't really the Knights of the Torch who killed all those people?"

"Solrac wouldn't allow that," Jax said, trying to convince both me and himself.

"Maybe not," I granted. "But I'm not ready to choose a side just yet. I've always thought the Mage Hunters were the enemy, but I saw what the Black Valkyrie did to help us stop the Coven in Rengard. And if she's right about what the Knights are doing… I just don't know what to believe right now. Besides, Jax, all I want is to bring my family back together after years and years apart. I'm only here to find my mother."

Jax took a step backward, and my hands fell from his chest. There was a storm in his midnight blue eyes as he replied.

"And I'm only here for you."

I opened my mouth to respond, but before I got the chance, the Black Valkyrie's voice rolled throughout the armory.

"Finish up quickly, then gather around," she ordered.

Jax and I gave each other one last look, then hurried to gather the rest of our new uniforms. We found the steel pauldrons then chose our weapons. Every long seaxe was made from an alloy of silver, but most had a leather-wrapped handle so I could wield mine while still accessing my etherarchy.

Once the group had assembled, the Black Valkyrie gestured to a row of pegs along the wall. Hanging from each peg was a crisp, new Mage Hunter's cloak.

As I swapped out my orange guard's cloak for the dusky blue Hunter's cloak, I felt my chest constrict. I had to force myself to breathe evenly as I latched it on, and I couldn't help but feel as if I was merely trading one form of servitude for another.

First, I'd been forced to join the guard in order to keep my magi parents from execution. Then, the Black Valkyrie had given me little choice but to join the Mage Hunters. Meanwhile, Jax wanted me to join the Knights of the Torch, and I still didn't know which side was right. Would my choices ever be my own?

At the thought, a cold wave flowed through my veins like ice. Darkness filled my chest, and faint blue light played at the edges of my vision.

Oh no. Please, not now—

Meleya… a raspy voice whispered in my mind, and my breath caught. I hadn't told anyone about the wraith—At least, I hadn't told anyone that I'd been feeling a dark presence following me ever since that night on watch duty in Rengard Canyon's North Tower.

"Meleya?" Solvai's voice pierced my reverie as she put a hand on my shoulder. The shadows rapidly fled my mind, the coldness dissipating.

For now.

"You okay?" Brigan appeared on my other side, his familiar brown eyes filled with worry. I realized my anxiety must've been showing through my face.

I swallowed the lump in my throat. "Fine," I lied. I hated how powerless I was against the mysterious spirit demon, and for whatever reason, it made me feel ashamed. Besides, I cared too much about my friends to share this burden with them. Jax, Solvai, and Brigan… I had to protect them.

That was the other reason I wanted to stay at the Academy—The wraith wasn't the only dark weight I'd been carrying around. I needed answers, and I had a hunch that the one person who could answer them was standing right in front of me.

"Very good," the Black Valkyrie said, looking over our new uniforms. "As members of my entourage, you'll spend each morning training with me or Jaira in Swan Spire. In the afternoons, you'll join the other new cadets in regular classes. For now, take your old things back to the dorm and get settled. It's been a long day, and you'll need your rest before training begins tomorrow at dawn."

She dismissed the group, and I was about to return to the dorm with the others when the Black Valkyrie called for me.

"Snowstorm," she said, using the title she'd given me after we'd fought in tandem at Keep Rengard's Winter Solstice Ball. "If you'll stay behind, I'd like a word."

I immediately glanced at Jax, who had been about to leave the armory. He stopped in his tracks, then turned around with a look that made me think he'd rather don real, pure silver armor from head to toe than leave me with his mother for five minutes.

"Alone, please," the Black Valkyrie said, not looking at her son. I watched Jax's expression crumble at her words, and my heart ached for him as he hurried out the door.

The Black Valkyrie telekinetically shut the door to the armory behind Jax, and I sensed a hint of pain in her face too. I got the feeling it wasn't easy for her to treat her son like just another Hunter, but she felt she had no choice if she wanted to protect him.

As quickly as the crack in the Black Valkyrie's proud demeanor had appeared, it vanished as she turned to me. "I know it's only your first day here at the Academy," she said, "but I'd like to ask a favor, Snowstorm.

You see, with your particular abilities, you're the only one suitable for the job."

A bundle of nerves jumped into my stomach. One look at the Black Valkyrie's determined expression told me she wasn't likely to take no for an answer.

"What do you need?" I asked.

Her midnight blue eyes blazed with an inner fire. "I'd like you to join me on a highly classified mission. The Farseer has been spotted in the High Ridgebacks, and I need you to help me capture him once and for all."

I inhaled sharply, eyes growing wide as the Black Valkyrie continued.

"We leave at first light."

CHAPTER 3: THE SAFEHOUSE

ASHER

"**F**or the record, that was *way* longer than nine minutes, Asher."

Kai's tone was furious as the two of us wove across the canopies of the tall cindercone pines, heading deeper into the Mirror Forest. Our dragon mounts flew quickly—The sooner we returned to the safehouse, the better.

Kai went on. "This entire mission was an absolute disaster!"

"Are you kidding?" I replied more positively. "The Black Valkyrie's entire entourage came after me and I'm still alive! That sounds like a major success to me."

Below me, Thorn gave a roar of agreement.

Kai shook his head. "It was way too risky, with too many variables at play. What if you'd been overpowered? Caught in a silvered net, or one of Jaira's chains? What if they'd tried to follow you? Not to mention Jax—What if you'd blown his cover?"

"To be fair, I didn't know Jax was infiltrating the Academy." I put my hands up. "I'm not exactly in the loop on Mister Muscle Man's assignments. But speaking of the unexpected..."

I trailed off, and Kai gave me a quizzical look.

I grimaced. "Just... activate the mindlink for a second."

Kai obliged, and I began to share my memory of being in the Black Valkyrie's tower. Normally when I replayed memories of our crazy endeavors, I liked to mess with Kai by embellishing the way I remembered things. Not this time.

Her face was hazy, since I'd been so distracted by what was going on. But I could've sworn I recognized the face of a certain redheaded young woman who'd shown up as part of the Black Valkyrie's entourage.

Kai gasped aloud when he saw the girl's pretty face and long, red hair tied up in a high draketail style.

"That can't be..." Kai started.

"Shaya?" I finished.

Even as I said the name, a wave of memories washed over me. Watching Shaya dance in the rain atop Kaliiko Mountain in the Scar. Spending hours sparring together in the Knights of the Torch's hideouts. Forging our own trail as we hiked outside Keep Drakfell, and our false kiss in the chaotic city streets. Every memory pierced my heart like a dagger.

Yet the girl in Swan Spire had looked at me like I was a total stranger. And it was true. We'd never met before, not really. The person I'd met last summer may have worn Shaya's face, but it had all been a lie. A cruel, sinister trick: The Black Valkyrie herself in disguise as she infiltrated the Knights of the Torch.

As I'd trained my etherarchy with Boone over the past several months, he'd helped me accept that not seeing through the ruse hadn't been my fault. None of us had recognized the Black Valkyrie in Shaya, not even Solrac, and while I'd been able to move past it, it was still strange seeing her face.

When I looked back at Kai, he was taking notes in the black leather journal he always kept on hand. "That can't be good," he said under his breath.

Kai closed the notebook and looked back at me with concern. I gave him a nod to let him know I was okay.

"There's something else," I said. "Shaya's not the only new member of the Black Valkyrie's entourage."

The mindlink was still active, so I quickly showed Kai another memory of the recent fight in Swan Spire. Meleya's seaxe arced toward me, her long, white braid flying out behind her. The mere sight of her was enough to prompt a string of curses from Kai.

"Scorching soot and scales!" he called over the wind. "Meleya of Misthaven's a Mage Hunter now? That does not bode well."

"Yeah." I cocked my head. "How'd you know her name?"

Kai didn't respond, his expression deeply troubled.

"Kai?" I prompted.

Kai shook his head. "We've sort of met before over the Glint network. But that's not what has me worried—You know how I've been practicing with omens lately?"

I laughed. "Do I ever. Your omen reading is what got me executed in Skullheim. Shouldn't have really needed omens to know that place was bad news."

"I know my prophecies have been unreliable at best so far," Kai admitted. "But still. Solrac wants me practicing them more, and from what I've seen… just stay away from Meleya."

"Why?"

"Just promise me you'll stay away, okay?"

I could tell Kai wasn't going to offer any more details, so I shrugged before promising I would. Mage Hunters were among my least favorite people in the eight keepdoms. Avoiding one especially annoying, compulsively tidy one wasn't going to be a problem.

Anyhow, Kai may have declared the mission a disaster, but even he admitted there was at least a seventy-three-to-eighty-six-percent chance I'd gotten away from Swan Spire with the right key. He'd finally be able to unlock that case we'd stolen back in Rengard, just as soon as we got to the safehouse.

Right on cue, we soared over the next ridge and the safehouse burst into view.

At least, it did for Kai and me. Anyone just passing through would see nothing more than a large, foreboding expanse of the Mirror Forest featuring a swampy lake and more cindercone pines.

But the illusion no longer worked on us. Not now that the mystical illusion-wards surrounding the safehouse recognized our ether signatures.

It was a complex, rather obscure style of etherarchy that I didn't understand. Even Kai was baffled by the ancient, Guardian-era security system that kept the safehouse, well, *safe*. The illusion-wards were just part of it. Rhana's land also held a series of etherlocks—gold devices, shaped like triangles with long diamond shapes sprouting from each point. I'd seen them a few times while exploring the property, set at intervals around the massive swath of forest, and knew that each one was about as big as a serving tray. I may not've understood the underlying etherarchy, but I knew it all kept the secret base secure—more than just the illusions to keep intruders from seeing the safehouse.

As if the word 'safehouse' did this place justice—Rhana's cabin was *incredible*.

Even 'cabin' was the wrong word. As we descended toward the structure, I couldn't help but think it was more like an extreme, military-grade ultra-cabin complex.

The main building was nearly the size of a citadel, with dozens of large starglass panels covering the south side of its slanted roof. When we'd first arrived a few months ago, Rhana had explained that the starglass gathered ether from sunlight in order to power the series of Lightwielder's torches both inside and outside her cabin, along with some of the cabin's mechanical defenses. She wouldn't tell anyone just how extensive they were... and kept alluding to some kind of mine we might trigger if we weren't careful on her property.

As if that weren't enough, what the illusion masked as a swamp was really a gorgeous lake. There was a boathouse and dock, and the lake even bore its own small, lush island in its center. Thorn and I had explored most of the little island, though besides the numerous waterbirds, the only thing the island boasted was a dazzling glass-walled chapel dedicated to the three goddesses. The chapel was pretty, but I'd never been much for praying myself.

The safehouse had a deep basement, a substantial library, and the most luxurious dragon stables I'd ever seen. Rhana had at least a dozen bonded dragons, each of whom took turns patrolling the borders of the safehouse property.

When they'd called this place a hovel back in Orothion, I'd pictured a run-down cottage covered in vines. Now, I was beginning to wonder if the leaders of the Knights had signed some sort of contract promising to conceal the cabin's true dimensions.

But even more epic than the cabin itself was the sight of the true dragon rider cutting toward us through the skies.

Her dark hair streamed out behind her like a flag, contrasting against the pearlescent white scales of the true dragon she rode. She was one of the only riders I knew who preferred long skirts to pants, and soot if she didn't look like a goddess in her white, lightly armored dress.

Elle.

Just the sight of her practically got my pulse hover-dashing. And then, to top it all off, she swooped in front of us, leaning back in her saddle to call out:

"Bet you can't catch me!"

Elle gave her trademark mischievous grin, her amber eyes flashing a challenge at me before she zoomed toward a thicket of trees near the cabin.

"Oh, it's on!" I cried, then turned to Kai. "Let's go!"

Kai rolled his eyes, stalling his dragon in mid air. "Uh... no."

"Come on," I replied. "It's for Elle's own good—If we let her win, her ego might never recover. Do you want that on your conscience?"

"I'll live," Kai replied, giving his evren a pat on the flank before veering off toward the stables. He turned over his shoulder and called, "Bring me those crystal keys when you're done being an idiot."

"You mispronounced 'being awesome'!" I leaned forward in Thorn's saddle, and we were off, tailing that majestic white true dragon and her even more majestic rider.

My dragon bond was larger and faster than Aurora, but the latter was more nimble. It was impressive, considering she'd only gotten large enough for Elle to ride in the last month or so. Right when we were just about to catch up to them, she and Elle did a barrel roll over us, changed direction, and zipped off again.

Elle whooped with glee.

I echoed the whoop, holding extra tight to Thorn as he turned a tight spiral of his own.

Come on buddy, you're not gonna let them outfly us that easily, are you? I teased my wyvern through our bond.

You blame me? Thorn teased back. *You try something then.*

Alright then.

I dug deep, focusing on my ether well. I felt a thrum in my chest, and my irises flashed gold as I put a hand to Thorn's neck. I'd been training hard with my powers since last summer, and I was getting good. Like, *really* good. Good enough that sharing my levitation abilities with a full-grown dragon was no longer a stretch for me.

White ether mist began to form around us, and Thorn took off like a shot, hover-flying through the air and catching up to Elle and Aurora in a split second.

"Catch *this!*" I called as we left them behind. Elle's indignant face was enough to nearly get me falling out of my saddle with laughter.

As I looked back, that face instantly shifted to one of confidence. Elle leaned toward her mount, and I was sure she was communicating with Aurora through their bond.

The white true dragon spread her wings to expose her four elegant claws. Then I saw Aurora's eyes burn gold with archonic power of their own.

In a flash, Aurora was cutting through the air as fast as we just had. She was like a graceful white meteor, and a rippling trail of green and purple light trailed behind her. My jaw dropped at the sight of it.

That was *fast* for a breakthrough.

Aurora and Elle threw in a double spiral as they passed us, hover-flew a loop, then came to a stop in front of Thorn and me, cutting off our flight path. Thorn beat his wings to pause in the air too, close enough that I could clearly see Elle's face. She wore a wide grin, and one dark brow was arched over her sparkling amber eyes.

"Consider yourself caught, Asher of Steel Rim," she said, putting a hand on her hip.

"Aurora can hover-dash now?" I asked, both impressed and excited.

"She's a quick learner." Elle beamed, stroking Aurora's white scales. The young true dragon blinked shyly.

As a true dragon, Aurora—and, by extension, Elle—were technically able to access all nine types of magi powers. Every day they were getting better with levitation, the power shared by all archonic magi. For such a lithe, feminine dragon, Aurora was also remarkably good with certain aspects of geomancy, a Sentinel power. Using the aspect of stone, Aurora was far stronger than she looked. Still, I'd noticed the pair struggling to master any of the Mystic powers. Despite the long weeks of training, they'd yet to access any psionic, seer, or rifting abilities at all.

Elle and Aurora's training was the main reason we were here at the cabin—Rhana was one of the last true dragon rider trainers in the realm. Plus, she'd bonded enough dragons to understand all kinds of etherarchy.

Speaking of Rhana, a loud, long whistle summoned us back to the ground. We landed, dismounting our dragons to stand before our hostess.

Like the safehouse itself, Rhana was nothing like how I'd pictured her back in Orothion. The leaders of the Knights had mentioned that this woman hadn't left her home in over two decades, which my brain had interpreted to mean we were on our way to meet some hunched, scraggly-haired, old witch-lady.

I couldn't have been more wrong. Rhana was old, yes, but every strand of gray and white hair was tucked into a tight, perfectly smooth bun at the base of her neck. She always stood with her back straight, feet apart, and hands clasped behind her back. Even if she hadn't always worn the guard-issue boots and dragonleather chest armor, I would've known without a doubt she was a former soldier.

Not only that but, up to this point, I couldn't remember a single conversation with Rhana that hadn't included her mentioning her time serving in the Dragon Wars.

"Very good form, Eliana." Rhana gave Elle a stiff nod. "Remember, as a true dragon rider, you're an icon of strength and leadership. Many will view you as such religiously."

Rhana nodded to the side and, for the first time, I noticed the small throng of spectators. At least twenty or so people—more Rebel Knights of the Torch who'd recently been welcomed into the safehouse themselves—were watching Elle with reverence.

Elle cleared her throat and stood taller at the sight of them. Her expression was serious as Rhana went on.

"I've never seen a more natural rider, even back when I fought in the Dragon Wars."

And there it was. I couldn't hide my grin and Elle noticed, giving me a subtle look.

At that, Rhana turned her attention from Elle to me, her expression in turn going from approving to skeptical.

"Like I said," Rhana continued, "Eliana flew well and the breakthrough in levitation was impressive, *despite* the distraction."

"That's me," I said with a quick, two-fingered salute. "Asher of Steel Rim, distraction extraordinaire."

"Hmph," was Rhana's joyless reply. The old woman tried to hide it, but as usual, I noticed her eyes flick to the dark teal scales on the tips of my pointed ears.

I understood why she didn't like or trust me. As a veteran of the wars between Evgard, the Dragon Isles, and colonies of third ascension dragons, Rhana had her reservations about anyone with even a hint of Drekai blood. I automatically held my head high the way Mom had taught me. If there was one thing Mom had left me with, it was a sense of pride in my Drekai heritage. That, and my teal scarf. Still, living with Rhana's constant disapproval wasn't exactly easy.

Rhana grunted. "I trust your mission to Swan Spire was successful, scale-skin?"

Inwardly, I cringed at her choice of words, but I gave a crooked grin to cover it up. "According to Kai, there's a seventy-something percent chance that's a yes."

Rhana gave one of her signature curt nods before reminding Elle about their next training session later that evening and retreating toward the cabin. The second she was gone, Elle turned to me, eyes bright.

"So, that's another point for me for hover-flying up there, right?"

"Whoa," I replied. "If anything, we should take away a point for that. Stealing my signature move? Rude."

Elle laughed, lightly shoving my upper arm. Her hand lingered, then traveled down my sleeve toward my hand. This time, I didn't need to use any etherarchy to feel like I was flying.

"Aurora learned it from watching you," Elle said. "You're quite the Astromancer these days."

"Am I?" I asked. Out of the corner of my eye, I saw that the throng of spectators was approaching fast. Elle noticed too, and simultaneously we pulled our hands away from one another. She cleared her throat once more, and I took a hasty step backward.

"Stars!" I said. "You're right, Thorn, I still have to get those keys to Kai. Good seeing you, Elle. Have a good chat with your fans. Congratulations on being so... opulent."

Opulent? I thought, fighting the urge to smack myself on the forehead. *What does that even mean?*

To add soot to scorchmarks, I tripped on Thorn's tail in my hasty escape, narrowly missing his tailblade. I heard Elle give a light chuckle from behind, which—stars—only made me like her even more. That exit had deserved mockery.

Thorn and I arrived at the stables where my dragon reached out to me through our bond. He didn't send any warm notes of comfort, though, only fiery frustration.

Moron, he thought.

"I know!" I cried as I led him past a few of Rhana's dozing dragons to his stall. I began undoing Thorn's saddle as he went on jabbering through our bond.

You've been avoiding Elle. For months.

"You noticed?" I snorted, hefting the saddle onto its hook on the wall.

Why hold back? Thorn's dragonfire green eyes bore into mine. *Still afraid? Not ready?*

"No," I grumbled. "It's not that anymore."

You like her a lot. She wants to be with you too.

"Exactly!" I said earnestly. "That's the problem. You saw her flying. You heard what Rhana said about her, and you saw all those people. They're here for *her*. Elle is an icon, a true dragon rider, and not just a noble—a scorching princess!" I gulped. "I'm just some distraction. A lowly half-born thief from the outlands."

I leaned against the rough wood of the stable wall, closing my eyes. I didn't like to admit just how hard it was to endure Rhana's constant disdain. I knew as well as anyone that the Knights of the Torch had only wanted me on their team in the first place because they'd thought I'd make a good 'distraction' during their heist. And sure, people had always treated me badly for being a half-born, and 'scale-skin' was actually among the least offensive things I'd been called in my life. Soot, Baron Eidan back in Steel Rim had been far worse, constantly antagonizing me for what I was, and in more populous towns, total strangers had often spat at me when I walked past.

Mom had trained me to never let any of it get me down.

But Mom wasn't here anymore.

My mind went instantly to that letter in Swan Spire. Why had Mom's name been on it? What secrets did it hold? I wished I could've gotten away with it.

I reached up and felt my turquoise scarf, the one she'd given me. Her simple gift always seemed to keep the darkness at bay.

Thorn carefully crept up to me, nudging me with his scaly black nose. *You are more than some thief from the outlands,* he said through our bond.

"Thanks, Thorn," I replied quietly, rubbing the black and bronze-marked scales along his neck.

We shared the silence for several minutes. Then suddenly, Kai skidded into the stables.

"Asher!" Kai was very much out of breath.

"Right," I said. "Sorry, I was just about to bring you the keys—"

"Not that!" Kai shook his head. He gestured for me to follow him, and I had to jog just to keep up with his intense speedwalking.

"What's going on?" I asked as we made a beeline toward the southern border of Rhana's property.

"New arrivals at the safehouse!" Kai huffed.

"More people looking to join up because they heard we've got a true dragon rider?" I asked, trying to keep any bitterness out of my voice. It wasn't fair for me to be frustrated like this.

"Maybe some." Kai shrugged. "But you're going to want to see this group."

"Why?"

Kai's response was a wide grin from ear to ear as he pointed southward. Just through the trees along the edge of the property, I saw Rhana greeting a large group of people.

At their head was a massive, furry, red bloodhusky. I suddenly realized why Kai had been so excited. The dog barked, then bounded toward Kai and me.

"Why hello there, His Majesty!" I recalled the bloodhusky's unique name as he licked at my hand. I knew what he was after, and luckily I found a leftover piece of drakalope jerky in one of my pockets. I tossed it to His Majesty, who licked his lips with glee.

I patted the giant dog on the head. "Where's Solrac?"

"Ya mean that good-for-nothin' son of a dragonmutt ain't here?" said a familiar, gravelly voice with a strong northern accent. "Sorry sap's later'n a drakkin' Behrfellian summer."

"Boone!" I grinned at the sight of the wiry older man with his snow white hair and deeply tanned, leathery skin. When he saw Rhana, he stood at attention and gave the guard's salute, raising his right fist to his left shoulder.

"Captain Rhana." Boone nodded. Rhana saluted back before continuing her conversation with another new arrival.

"You two know each other?" I asked.

"Captain Rhana 'n I served together back durin' the Dragon Wars," Boone explained.

"Did I hear you say Solrac still wasn't here?" said the woman who appeared at Boone's side. She was in her thirties, with black hair and chronically skeptical almond-shaped eyes. As usual, I couldn't tell whether Valla had more scars or weapons on her person. She had a seaxe on each hip, a warsword on her back, and countless daggers strapped to her thighs, sticking out of her boots, and only the goddesses knew where else.

"You done heard right," Boone replied. "That scorchin' scalebrain Solrac better drakkin' get here soon."

I had to admit, I was getting worried about Solrac myself. He and Kai had spoken a few days earlier regarding our mission to Swan Spire, but we hadn't heard from him since. Kai had reached out through the Glint mindlink a few times, but had received no response.

We had good reason to worry, too. I wasn't as well-informed as Kai, but even I knew that things were not right among the leaders of the Knights of the Torch. Solrac and the other two heads disagreed about going to war with Evgard. But Solrac had been outvoted. Consequently, Solrac and the others who'd wanted peace had been branded Rebels and were chased out of Orothion. We still had spies on the inside—like my father—but Solrac had needed to run for his life. Many of us in Solrac's faction had come here to the safehouse, with more making their way to the Mirror Forest from other places in Evgard. Discontent abounded, and it was hard to know who to trust. Boone was right—We needed Solrac.

"Who are all these others?" Kai asked, gesturing to the throng of nearly twenty people chatting amongst themselves as they stared, awestruck, at Rhana's cabin.

"Ain't it clear as a ridgerat's mud puddle?" Boone replied. Kai and I exchanged perplexed glances. I didn't spend much time examining ridgerat's mud puddles, but I was fairly confident they were not particularly clear.

Boone plowed forward. "These 'ere folks are new recruits for our little band of Rebel Knights of the Torch. Ex-prisoner magi from the Canyonlands, mostly. Good thing too. As magi, I seen 'em in action, an' I tell you what: This lot fights better'n a craghopper 'neath a full moon on a sleepy summer ev'nin'. Thank the goddesses for that."

I was used to Boone's somewhat nonsensical anecdotes at this point, and responded, "Why?"

Boone's face was serious as he locked eyes with me. "Because, son. We're gonna need as many fighters as we can get. Drakked-good 'uns, with a knack for stavin' off the supernatural."

Valla gave a frustrated sigh. "Boone, we defeated the Coven back in Rengard."

"Don't mean a drakkin' thing! The Coven of the Gray Ones in the south is only the beginning." Boone looked first to the group, then to Kai and me.

"Best be preparin' for the worst, boys," Boone said. "Won't be long now."

"Before what?" Kai asked nervously.

Boone's expression turned grave. "'Fore them dark murder spirits, the Gray Ones, come for us, too."

CHAPTER 4: THE FARSEER

MELEYA

Frigid water droplets beaded along my skin. White and gray mists swirled together all around me, reminding me of the deadly Dragon Mists that had once held me captive. Above me in the dark sky, blue lightning flashed, but I heard no thunder. Everything was eerily still.

Suddenly, a shape darted through the mists. I whirled on whatever it was, ready to fight, but to my horror I had no weapon sheathed at my hip. The figure rushed by once more, this time closer, before the fog swallowed them up.

Cautiously stepping backward, I prayed they hadn't seen me. Then all at once, there they were, standing mere feet away.

I gasped at the sight of the hooded gray figure. Other than two darkened eye holes, its face was blank. A masked member of the Coven of the Gray Ones.

I ran.

Within moments, I came to the edge of a lake. I barely stopped in time, teetering forward and seeing my own reflection in the mirror-smooth water.

When I saw myself, my stomach twisted with horror.

The masked coven member I'd been running from in the mist... was me.

Vivid blue light shone through the eye holes in my mask. Just like many members of the Coven, there was a title scratched into my mask in bone-white lettering:

Snowstorm.

I shuddered, stumbling backward away from the stillwater lake.

When I turned to run, I found myself face to face with a man. At least, sort of face to face. His features were shadowed so that I couldn't make out any details other than his glowing sapphire eyes. I could tell he was watching me, and that filled me with dread.

Who are you, thief? the figure asked, his doubled voice piercing straight to my core.

I screamed.

My eyes shot open and the nightmare evaporated into the light of early morning. I was covered in sweat, and I couldn't move. I wanted to scream the way I'd done in the dream, but no sound came out.

That was good, I realized, since the Black Valkyrie was probably still sleeping on her bedroll in the tent across from mine, and I didn't want to wake her.

I could hear the winter wind rushing outside, and blue light reflected upon the walls of the simple dragonhide laavu-style tent. My heart still threatening to thud out of my chest, I glanced at the small, bright blue crystal lying on my bedroll.

Once again, the Soul Reaper's voidshard had burned through my rift hold. This was happening more and more often. Why couldn't my etherarchy contain it?

I squeezed my eyes shut, wishing the shard would just disappear. Back in the Dragon Mists, a friend had died trying to get this thing so she could destroy it. I wanted to destroy it myself, but I had no idea how.

I forced myself to move. I needed to hide the voidshard before the Black Valkyrie saw it.

Gold light trailed from my trembling finger as the corresponding symbol appeared over my forehead. A small gold crack tore through the air in front of me, and I made a prying motion with one hand to reopen my rift hold, a small space in the spirit plane that Rifters could use to store things. My old mentor had once drunkenly described it as a 'one-way personal portal pocket.'

When I'd first created my rift hold, I'd used it as a sort of spice cabinet. I could still see my little canisters of paprika and cornflour sitting beside some vanilla bean and a few sprigs of dried sage.

But in the center of the white, faintly glowing spirit pocket was a space dedicated to holding the voidshard.

I grabbed the crystal, ready to shove it back inside my rift hold.

Just before I got the chance, however, a voice pricked my mind. Not the voice from my dream, but the raspy, feminine voice that was constantly slipping into my head.

Wait, it said.

I froze, my reply a whisper so quiet I could scarcely hear it myself. "Why?"

The voice laughed, adding to my fear from the nightmare. The voice went on. *I know you feel like your choices aren't your own. Think of what you could do if you were the one with the power.*

I swallowed. Those were more words than my wraith had ever spoken to me before. She was getting stronger.

Indeed, the voice agreed. *Each time we defeat a fellow Gray One, we absorb their strength. When we defeated the Liberator on the night of the Winter Solstice, we sent Skapa's essence back to the void. But her power remained, along with the power of every wraith she'd ever conquered.*

"Wh-what?" I murmured, my heart racing. "I didn't mean to do that. I just wanted to stop the Coven from taking the Rise and hurting my friends."

Coldness swirled inside me, and I could feel my wraith expanding, reaching deeper into my mind.

Stop that, I thought, and she recoiled.

Her voice was quieter now. *Think of the good we could do for the realm—for your family—if we used even a fraction of the power held within that crystal.*

A tingle of energy ran through my body from my core to my fingertips as I remembered what it felt like to access the voidshard's power while battling the Liberator.

It felt powerful. *I* felt powerful.

What is this thing, really? I thought.

The raspy voice began to laugh again, and the sound made every hair on my body stand on end. Looking down at the dark crystal, I couldn't keep from reading the names etched into either side:

Kjell and *Agnai.*

I had no idea what the names meant. All I knew was that they were dangerous. Besides myself, the only one who knew about the names was a man named Zoren, a Drekai Mage Hunter and my former captain of the guard. Zoren had admitted to me that he was really an undercover agent of the Drekai empress, and I'd told him the names back in Keep Rengard just before he'd disappeared. I'd asked around, but not even the Black Valkyrie knew what had happened to him.

Gritting my teeth, I shoved the crystal back inside my rift hold, closing it as quickly as I could. The wraith's presence retreated, but I didn't feel much relief.

I didn't realize I was breathing heavily until I saw the Black Valkyrie stir on her bedroll across the tent. When she saw that I was already up, she figured we might as well make the most of it and continue along our journey, so we packed up our supplies and set our course due north through the Mirror Forest.

We'd spent most of yesterday hiking, then camped for the night in the relative warmth of a circle of cindercones. A pair of the Black Valkyrie's best Hunters, a Geomancer named Shaw and a Seer named Ilyan, had tipped their leader off that the Farseer was in the High Ridgebacks in the northern Mirror Forest. According to the Black Valkyrie, we'd reach the spot in a matter of hours.

When the Black Valkyrie approached me about helping her capture the Farseer, I didn't know what to think. The Farseer had once saved my life and Jax's, and his remedy had saved King Axel of Rengard, despite the horrible fate the king had met shortly afterward. He'd also given my parents a shot at freedom, even if my mother hadn't taken it.

But when the Black Valkyrie had promised to take me to see my mother upon our return, I'd had no choice. Not a real one, anyway. Had that been what my wraith meant when she talked about my choices not being my own?

The hike was long and quiet but for the crunching of snow beneath our boots. I'd grown up in the desert canyons of Rengard, where snow this thick was unheard of. My nose was red, and the tips of my ears stung. I carried a toasty, lightly smoking cindercone in my gloved hands, but despite that, I'd forgotten what it was like to feel warm.

The trees were too thick to see through in most places along our path, and even when they weren't, the Black Valkyrie had ordered me to refrain from using my teleportation to speed up our journey. She had plans for my powers later, but she said the Farseer would be able to sense any use of ether in the vicinity. We didn't want to scare him off before we even arrived.

We trekked on in silence until finally the towering crest of the mountain came into view through the snow-laden pines.

"Not much longer," the Black Valkyrie said, glancing over her shoulder at me. "We should reach the spot by nightfall. We'll need your rifting soon, Snowstorm."

After last night's dream, her use of the moniker made me wince. "I prefer Meleya," I admitted.

"As you wish," she replied. I could sense she had more to say on the subject, but remained silent as she hiked on.

I took a deep breath, then exhaled into a babble of words: "Why are we doing this? Is it so the Farseer can heal the High King's son from the shadow wasting? If so, do we have to capture him? Why not just ask for his help?"

The Black Valkyrie seemed amused by my onslaught of questions, and slowed her pace slightly. She still walked ahead of me, but only by a stride or so.

"It's true that the High King once commissioned me to capture the Farseer in an effort to save his son," the Black Valkyrie spoke carefully, "but while we still need the Farseer in custody—and for good reason; the Knights of the Torch are a threat to the realm—that's not what motivates me to seek him now."

I waited for her to elaborate, but after a minute or so I pressed. "Why then?"

The Black Valkyrie slowed her pace so that she fell into step beside me.

"So I can prove to someone I *can*," she said.

When I turned, I could see sincerity in her dark blue eyes. I suddenly realized why she didn't want to bring the entire entourage on this mission. It was personal.

"Who?" I asked boldly.

She surprised me with another honest answer. "Solrac." When she said the name, a look of longing crossed her face.

"Jax has mentioned that name before," I said. "He's one of the Knights of the Torch?"

"One of them," the Black Valkyrie scoffed. "Solrac is so embroiled in the Knights he's incapable of seeing anything else. The Knights of the Torch are Solrac's first and only love."

"And Solrac is yours," I muttered, putting pieces together. One look at the pain and anger in the Black Valkyrie's expression made me instantly regret musing that out loud.

"You're wrong," she replied coolly. "I have loved again. The one I love now is everything. He's the reason behind all that I do. Because of him, I made a vow to change this cruel realm forever."

I raised an eyebrow. I had a hard time believing that the Black Valkyrie would speak so passionately about the other man from her past, my drunken mentor, Torsten.

The Black Valkyrie looked me in the eye, and I thought I noticed a tiny tear glistening in the dim sunlight streaming through the trees.

"He's someone we now share," she said.

My breath caught as I understood. "Jax."

The Black Valkyrie nodded as we searched for the easiest path through the snow.

"Why don't you tell the truth about who Jax really is?" I asked.

The Black Valkyrie stopped abruptly, her dark brows furrowed. There was a dangerous light in her eyes that caught me off guard. And… was that a third silvermark on her left cheek? It was difficult to tell with her hair.

"What do you know about that?" the Black Valkyrie asked harshly.

Subconsciously, I paused to let her pass ahead of me, but she halted as well until my legs remembered how to move. "Nothing. I only meant it's hard for him when you hide the fact that you're his mother."

She breathed a sigh. "Of course."

I frowned. "I understand that the more people who know, the more danger he would be in. But he really cares about you, and it would mean so much if…"

The Black Valkyrie shook her head. "He doesn't care for me. Not anymore. He did once, perhaps, but not now that Solrac and the Knights have poisoned him against me. Besides, no son could love a mother after all I've done. And he's right—I'm not worthy of his affection."

We carried on in silence for several minutes, but she continued keeping pace with me rather than walking ahead. I wondered if she had many people in her life to speak with openly, and sensed some relief in her normally tense, aloof expression.

After another hour, we paused to eat lunch. Normally, I was the one to pack meals for myself and my traveling companions, but the Academy's cook had sent us with nothing but a bland loaf of bread, a hunk of cheese, and some strips of dried dragonhog ham.

The Black Valkyrie was set to dig in, but with her permission, I swiped her rations and laid them on a cloth I'd set atop a nearby log. I rubbed my hands together, my mind already working on a solution to our lunchtime woes.

We may not have been able to use etherarchy without drawing unwanted attention, but apparently I was welcome to start a small fire by shredding one cindercone into tinder, then crushing together two firemaple leaves over it. First, I gathered a few hard-shelled black walnuts from the snowy forest floor and set them at the edge of the fire to dry out. I also collected a few wild winter onions I'd seen growing near the cindercone roots throughout our hike.

I finely chopped the onions, then looked around. I didn't have anything to cook on, but I did have a brand new steel Mage Hunter's pauldron on my shoulder.

The Black Valkyrie watched with amusement as I sauteed the wild onions in my impromptu skillet. I added a little water from melted snow and a few sprinkles of cornflour as a thickener from the stores within my rift hold. That was a use of etherarchy so small we decided it was acceptable.

Her smile grew when I flipped open the small, worn-out, waterproof pouch I always kept clipped to my belt and pulled out my salt shaker. Throughout my childhood, there were two things I'd never wanted to be caught without: a backup weapon and my salt shaker. After all, salt was the backup weapon of spices.

I sliced the bread and cheese, then assembled two hefty sandwiches, using the sauteed onion mixture as a sort of spread and finishing with the strips of dragonhog ham.

The Black Valkyrie's eyes lit up at the first bite of the savory sandwich. She declared that bringing me along was the best decision she'd ever made for a whole new reason.

But I wasn't finished. While I ate my sandwich, I rinsed my pauldron skillet and set it back on the fire. Next, I used my seaxe to tap into the nearest firemaple tree. Long ago when I'd roamed the Canyonlands with the nomads, a woman from the Duststorm Caravan had taught me how to extract sap from canyon maples. I assumed the process also worked for the firemaples of the Ridgeback Mountains.

Indeed, I soon found myself with a sort-of-skillet full of sweet sap. I carefully shelled the black walnuts and crumbled them in with the sap, then added a pinch of salt.

Just as the Black Valkyrie and I finished our sandwiches, our candied walnut dessert was ready. Salted sweetness crunched pleasantly in our mouths, with just the right amount of maple flavor.

Cooking put me in a much better mood as I rinsed out my pauldron, replaced it on my shoulder, and put out the fire. We continued our trek north up the mountain with an extra spring in our step.

The Black Valkyrie and I walked side by side, and I was surprised when she struck up another conversation almost right away.

"I used to get nightmares too."

I spun to face her so fast that my long, white braid nearly whipped me in the face. She knew about my nightmares? Maybe she hadn't been asleep this morning like I'd thought. My heart stilled—She hadn't seen the Soul Reaper's voidshard, had she?

"The Gray Ones that follow us aggravate even our dreams," she said. "I know one has chosen you."

"You do?" I whispered. It seemed she was only talking about the Gray One, not the shard.

"Yes, and I can help."

Hope flooded my entire body.

The Black Valkyrie went on. "I can teach you how to harness the Gray One's power for good. How to *use* the darkness to keep it at bay."

"But what if I want to get rid of it?" I asked, brows knitting.

"You can't get rid of your wraith—You can either succumb to it, or learn to control it as I have mine. The wraiths are what will grant us the ability to salvage this land. I'll begin your training the moment we return to the Academy."

"Oh." I didn't like the sound of that, but anything was better than living in constant fear of the shadow on my back. "Thank you, Black Valkyrie," I said sincerely.

She gave a half-smile. "I prefer Vidya."

"Vidya," I repeated.

As I said her name, the corner of Vidya's lip twitched, and I couldn't tell if she was pleased or frustrated.

"Not when we're with the others, of course," she clarified. I nodded with understanding, and we continued our hike northward.

The Farseer's hut was exactly the kind of thing a legendary, possibly immortal, folk hero *would* hide out in. While it was made from stretched dragonhide and was triangular in shape like any other nomadic tent, plumes of mystical gold smoke rose from the top. A red symbol that reminded me of a torch or beacon had been painted in red over the doorway. The sun had recently set, and white moonlight shone onto the tent.

But the tent wasn't what made my mouth hang open. It was *where* the Farseer had placed it.

For whatever reason, the Farseer's hut sat directly atop the smooth ice at the base of a towering frozen waterfall.

There was something different about this waterfall. Though the water was clearly iced over so that it no longer moved, I could swear I still saw it flowing. Only instead of water flowing downriver, it looked like white wisps of pure, faintly glowing ether rushing gracefully upward over the ice.

"Veil Falls," Vidya whispered. "Stand by, Meleya. If he runs, it's up to you to rift him back to me."

"Okay," I said, reminding myself that, if I did this, Vidya would take me to see my mother. I didn't like it, but what else could I do? Besides, Vidya had promised me that our goal wasn't to harm the Farseer, just to capture him.

Nerves and adrenaline coursed through me as Vidya and I crept toward the tent. A layer of hoarfrost had glazed over the ice so it wasn't too slippery.

We stood on either side of the tent door as it flapped gently in the breeze. Vidya drew her blackened, silver dragonhook spear, while I drew my new silver seaxe with the leather-wrapped handle. I wielded it one-handed, the other ready to runetrace.

Then, at the same moment, we ducked inside the tent.

The Farseer was sitting smack in the middle of the tent before a bed of coals that emitted a strange, golden fire. A woody smell hung in the air, and I could tell his glowing eyes were closed within the darkness of his hood, while a single white skystone hung suspended over the center of his forehead.

Just like when I'd met him before, the Farseer wore deep red robes and red-scaled gauntlets on his hands. Laid beside him on the ground was his gnarled, antlered staff, covered in at least a hundred runes. Some of them glowed as he sat in his meditative state.

Vidya and I cast each other perplexed looks. He hadn't even flinched at our entrance. He must've been deep in a trance.

Skeptically, Vidya pulled out a pair of silver manacles as we approached. She skirted the bed of coals and was about to ensnare the Farseer in the silver when both our gazes shot toward the back of the tent. Had a flap there just moved?

Vidya's expression hardened and she rapidly swirled the butt of her silver spear—right through the Farseer's sitting frame.

I gasped as her weapon passed directly through him, dissipating the Farseer as if he were nothing more than starry, ethereal smoke.

"Illusion," she seethed. "Go!"

She pointed her spear toward the back of the tent, and I didn't waste a second before obeying her command. I darted to where I thought I'd seen the tent move, and though an illusion must've been cloaking the seam, when I pushed against it, a flap folded out to reveal a secret exit.

I dashed through into the chilly, moonlit night. There, racing across the snowy landscape was another red-robed Farseer, identical to the illusion we'd seen in the tent.

My rune was up and glowing instantly. As the Farseer bolted away, I caught him in a portal so that he emerged right in front of me.

Vidya joined me outside just in time to intercept him. Spear clashed against staff as he moved to block.

He immediately disengaged and dashed away again. He moved faster than should've been possible, and I quickly realized how. The rune over his forehead was a variation of one I'd seen my father use dozens of times—one that allowed Psions to telekinetically push on inanimate objects.

In this case, the Farseer was pushing on his own clothing to propel himself forward.

"Meleya!" Vidya called to me, and I reacted.

My next portal deposited the Farseer right back in front of Vidya once more. When he tried to flee again, my next portal did the same. Again and again, no matter what direction he turned, the Farseer couldn't escape my flurry of portals.

"I'm so sorry," I muttered, grimacing.

"No way out this time." Vidya looked smug as she whipped her spear against the Farseer's staff.

Parrying her strike, the Farseer turned my way, his eyes aglow from within his hood. He yanked his staff away from Vidya's silver blade, then trained it on me. Another psionic rune I recognized as one of Jax's favorites glowed over his forehead.

Oh soot.

Suddenly, it felt like my new blue cloak weighed a thousand pounds. It dropped me to the ground, pinning me beneath it as my Rifter's rune vanished into golden etherdust.

Meanwhile, a whole string of runes glowed from the Farseer's forehead. He fired a series of dream darts at Vidya, forcing her to disengage, then thrust his staff into the ice beneath his feet. It began to crack.

The crack raced all around him in a circle. Then he made a raising motion with one hand, and the whole sheet of pure ice beneath him rose into the air, carrying him along with it.

He stood majestically as his ice took him at least thirty feet into the air, with no sign of stopping.

Vidya noted my incapacitated state and took matters into her own hands.

Or rather, her own *wings.*

With a cry, Vidya leapt upward. Angular, sapphire blue Wildshaper markings glowed from her skin as a pair of wide, glorious swan wings sprouted from her back.

My eyes widened. That was new. When we'd last fought together, Vidya had been able to access the power sets of two of the nine magi types: Psion and Shadowbinder. Now, it seemed she was a Wildshaper too. That explained the third silvermark, though once again, her angular Sentinel markings glowed blue light rather than with the regular gold of etherarchy.

Vidya soared upward, and I craned my neck to see her meet the Farseer on his ice platform in the air. It was hard to maneuver beneath this lead-like cloak, but I managed to get to an angle where I could see the action. Before such legendary figures, I felt insignificant anyway.

The winged Black Valkyrie and the mighty Farseer clashed in the sky, silhouetted against the bright white moon. He seemed able to anticipate where her every strike would land and dodged them easily. Meanwhile, she intercepted his flurries of dream darts using either her silver weapon or flashy counter-dreamblasts of her own.

Both fought with equal skill and equal drama, opting for—largely unnecessary—dives and flourishes that only added to the spectacle. I got the feeling they'd performed this dangerous dance before, with neither of them able to gain the upper hand.

That was, until blue-tinged black fire ripped along the edge of Vidya's silvery blade. Shadowbinding ether. The flames ate away at the Farseer's staff, weakening him with their disintegrating power.

Even from down here, I could see the sapphire blue light glowing from Vidya's eyes. She fought with a vengeance, each strike empowered with otherworldly might. It was difficult to tell in the darkened night, but it seemed that the color had drained from her skin and clothing. She appeared gray, and emitted a powerful dark glow, as if she were sucking away all surrounding light.

I instantly knew that she was accessing power granted to her by her wraith. With mixed feelings, I realized she wanted to train me to do the same.

With a warrior's cry, Vidya thrust her spear toward the Farseer. The silver and shadowfire caused the Farseer to lose his grip on his weapon, and Vidya's blow sent the staff flying through the air before plummeting toward the snowy earth below.

Before the Farseer could recover, Vidya shoved him hard with the butt end of her spear, a torrent of vivid blue dream energy pulsing into him. The Farseer slipped from his icy platform, robes fluttering as he fell. Vidya dove after him, her graceful black wings cutting through the air.

The Farseer looked exhausted. Whatever he'd been doing up here in his tent must have drained him of his ether even before our arrival.

Without his concentration, the weight of my cloak returned to normal, freeing me and my hands. Desperately, I traced a new rifting rune and extended my hand toward the falling Farseer.

My portal caught him just before he hit the deadly, rock-solid ice below. I sent him as gently as I could through an exit portal, where he landed with a soft thud in a nearby snowbank.

He didn't move. I scrambled to my feet, meeting Vidya where the Farseer lay in the snow.

Vidya's swan wings vanished in a blue cloud as she approached the Farseer. His chest moved shallowly up and down, so at least he was alive.

"Finally," Vidya said with a laugh. "After all this time, you're mine." She reached over, taking hold of the man's deep, red hood.

With a flourish, she whipped back the hood to reveal a man's face. He was dark-haired with a trim goatee, and was probably somewhere in his forties. A Psion's silvermark, the same one Vidya and Jax wore, stood out on his cheek.

For a legend, the Farseer looked surprisingly... normal.

Vidya, on the other hand, reacted as if she'd been slapped across the face. Color returned to her form and her eyes stopped glowing bright blue. She stumbled backward, falling into the snow.

"No," her voice shook. "S-Solrac?"

Wait.

Solrac? This was Solrac?

As in, *Solrac?* The man Jax admired so much? The Knight of the Torch Vidya once loved?

Solrac was the Farseer?

"Vidya," Solrac replied. He had a light, pleasant eastern accent, and his deep brown eyes shone with a thousand different emotions. His sharp jaw flexed, similar to the way Jax's did when he was stressed. "I should have told you long ago."

Slowly, both Solrac and Vidya got to their feet, their eyes not leaving each other's faces even for one moment. I felt like I was imposing on a very personal moment, and awkwardly averted my gaze.

Soon, Solrac took a single step backward, then another. Then, with one last pain-filled gaze, he took off running across the snowy plain to the north, a final burst of psionics propelling him swiftly through the snow.

Vidya watched him go, still rooted to the spot.

"Should we go after him?" I cautiously asked.

Vidya swallowed. She was clearly shaken, but I saw resolve in her eyes as she replied.

"No. Let him go, Meleya. We're going home."

FRAGMENT: TRUE DRAGON RIDER

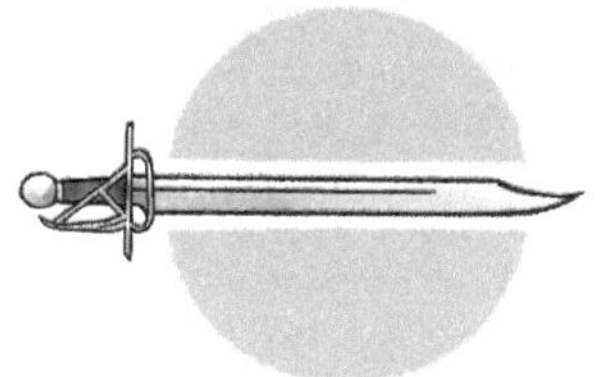

ELLE

Shouting. Swords clanging. The beating of dragon's wings. Crisp, black-and-white uniforms formed a backdrop against flashes of gold etherlight while emerald dragonfire sprayed at blood red cloaks.

Elle's heart thudded as she watched the fierce battle between the armies of Evgard's capital keepdom and Skygard's Knights of the Torch. Watching the action was part of her training. Elle wasn't *really* on the battlefield in person, of course. Rather, her trainer, Rhana, stood with her on the edge of the forest surrounding the cabin, and was using an etheric relic called a dreamweb to project what was happening hundreds of miles away on the western shores of the Capital Keepdom of Evgard. One of Rhana's dragon bonds was actually there in the flesh, using her Seer powers to cast the fight in real time through the dreamweb Rhana had made using her ascension scales.

Beside Elle, Aurora gave a whimpering growl. Through their bond, Elle felt her dragon's sorrow as she watched the battle unfold. Elle, too, felt sick. Like the rest of the Rebel Knights, Elle felt that the war between Evgard and the Knights of the Torch was one huge mistake. But Lady Vesta was determined as she sent platoon after platoon against the High Throne. The mistreatment of magi had to stop, and she felt violence was the only way to achieve it.

The battlefield, a winding river leading to a roaring waterfall on the western edge of the Keepdom of Evgard, was ablaze with action. The glowing, extra sharp edges of Lightwielder Knights' blades hacked straight through the Evgardians' shields. Black-and-white-clad soldiers swooped in on fully ascended wyverns and evren to take down Knights in red cloaks. The third ascension dragons's scales gleamed, their wings as wide as the river.

"The dragons are gorgeous," Elle couldn't help but quietly note.

"Yes, and powerful," Rhana added, as rigid as ever. "Even the most skilled warriors are found wanting when faced with the weakest of fully ascended dragonkind. You're too young to remember the era before the Dragon Wars, when third ascension dragonkind helped true dragons maintain large swaths of territory throughout the north, the Badlands, and the Canyonlands. Now, the Capital Riders are some of the greatest warriors the realm over. Watch carefully."

Elle jumped as the illusory form of an enormous wyvern with powerful hind legs and sprawling wings appeared to land directly beside her. The wyvern's bloodthirsty roar—and his rider's—may have been happening leagues away, but to her etherarchy-enhanced senses it sounded both real and eminently close.

Just then, a squad of seven red-cloaked soldiers from the Knights of the Torch banded together. One among them was a magi—an Astromancer, judging by the comet-like darts of ether he sent flying toward the great wyvern from the end of his long seaxe.

The ether blasts sent white marks spiraling out across the dragon's scales. But this wyvern was on its third ascension. With its extra-thick hide, the ether darts weren't enough to faze it. At its rider's word, the wyvern opened its wide, ferocious maw to spray the Astromancer's squadmates with emerald dragonfire. The Knights screamed as they retreated, many diving into the river to douse the flames. Elle's hand flew to her face. Yes, she was a trained swordswoman, but as far as actual battle, she hadn't seen much.

"Scorch," Elle cursed. "We have to do something!"

"The only thing you can do is watch and learn."

Rhana observed with grim acceptance. "The Capital Riders are well-trained, united, and ruthless. Still, it is vital to note that had this wyvern's bond not been forced, its fire would have been enough to finish every one of those soldiers. A forced bond robs both dragon and rider of their full might."

"Are all of the Capital Riders bonded to their dragons by force?" Elle asked.

"Almost all of them, yes," Rhana replied.

Elle's heart was heavy as she knelt beside Aurora, wrapping her arms around her neck. Aurora nuzzled Elle contentedly.

As the illusory battle raged on, Elle frowned. "How are the Knights of the Torch able to mobilize so many squads?" she asked. "This battle is taking place hundreds of miles from Orothion, yet they seem to have caught the Capital soldiers by surprise."

"Now you're thinking." Rhana nodded her approval. "Though as to the answer, I couldn't say. Lady Vesta seems to have a couple tricks up her sleeve. She's a geomancer, so she may have tunneled, but in a location so near the sea, such is unlikely. Ah—" Rhana took a step forward and pointed at the northeastern sky. "This is what we've been waiting for."

A mighty blue dragon as deep as night shot majestically through the pale winter sky. Beams of sunlight shone through two wide wings and highlighted the creature's four claws. It wore brilliant black and white armor on its head and chest to match the ornate cloak of its rider.

Equally impressive was High King Magnus as he rode the rare true dragon with his spear held high. His gleaming ascension armor was adorned with the dark blue scales of his mount, and he had a jeweled crown of dragonforged steel built into his helmet. Eight gems in different colors—one for each of Evgard's keepdoms that Magnus had at long last united.

The true dragon and his rider may have only been an illusion projected by the dreamweb, but seeing the pair still gave Elle chills. Young Aurora's eyes shone with wonder.

"Magnus and Noctus," Rhana said. "Historically, those who bonded true dragons were regarded as something beyond even a king or a queen, but a leader chosen by the goddesses themselves. Many years ago, I trained dozens of these noble riders. But during the Dragon Wars, High Queen Frida had nearly every true dragon in Evgard killed. For a long time, there were no true dragon riders at all. None, until Magnus."

Rhana's tone, normally stiff and monotonous, betrayed her deep sorrow. Elle knew Rhana was the last true dragon rider trainer in the realm, and while she'd suspected Rhana had trained the High King, now she was certain.

"Magnus's bond with Noctus," Elle began slowly. "Was it forced?"

Rhana pressed her aged lips together. "Not at first. His power was unmatched, his right to rule undisputed."

"And now?"

Rhana paused. Without answering, she motioned for Elle to keep watching the illusion of the battle.

Already, Magnus and Noctus's mere presence had sent the Knights of the Torch scattering. The former swooped over the battlefield along the river, and a few bold Knights shot crossbows toward the pair. But the true dragon's power manifested in the form of geomancy to block the bolts with stone skin wherever his armor didn't cover. Lightwielder Knights tried to blast them with bolts of lightning, only to have them rebound when Magnus blocked them with a shield of pure light energy.

"Magnus is no magi," Elle observed, impressed. "Yet through his dragon, he's able to fully access lightwielding as if he were one."

"Not fully," Rhana corrected. " But to a degree, yes. Lightwielding, Geomancy, and Psionics are some of Noctus's favored types of etherarchy. As a true dragon, he has the potential to access all nine, as the Guardians of old once could. But that doesn't mean they all come naturally."

Next, Magnus went on the offensive. His dragonforged steel ascension spear arced through the air, ablaze with green dragonfire. He swirled the glorious blade and sent a ripple of emerald fire outward in a circle.

With remarkable precision, the stream of green flames left at least six red-cloaked Knights screaming. A golden rune glowed over Noctus's head to psionically tear off their armor, leaving them vulnerable to Magnus's follow-up attack. Two Knights took spears to the chest while the other four were subject to the true dragon's raking claws. Already, many Knights began to flee.

Rhana sent a message to her Seer dragon bond to let her know they were finished. All around them, the illusion of the battle disappeared.

"Stars," Eliana muttered, stroking Aurora's head. "I hate not being able to step in and put a stop to all this needless bloodshed."

"Soon you will," Rhana said. "You will be strong and capable. A true leader, united with your dragon bond and blessed by the goddesses. Revered by those who choose to follow you. You are an icon, like Magnus. But unlike him, you will be a symbol of what a *true* Knight of the Torch should be. Remember, the first tenet is to choose light, and there can be no choice in forced bonds."

Eliana spoke boldly. "When you trained the High King, you wanted him to become a Knight of the Torch, didn't you?"

Rhana's expression hardened. For a moment, Elle thought she was going to order Elle to run through their flight patterns twenty times while she pondered her own impertinence.

Instead, Rhana barked a different order. "Implore your dragon to make fire."

"But why—"

"Fire," Rhana repeated.

Eliana bit her lip, wanting to protest further just to prove she couldn't be controlled. Rhana herself taught that true dragons only ever choose to bond those with strong spirits.

But in Rhana's expression Elle saw both challenge and pain. Elle realized that even more than digging in her heels, she had to prove that she wasn't like Magnus.

Elle took hold of the shimmering white heartscale hanging from her neck, and the lithe white true dragon beside her happily extended her neck.

A wavy line of dragonfire shot from Aurora's mouth. Elle loved the unique flame, with hints of vibrant purple radiating off of the dragonfire green light. It reminded Elle of the wondrous ribbons of light that she'd seen dancing across the northern sky while visiting northern Drakfell with her parents.

"Now you, Eliana," Rhana ordered.

Elle drew her elegant Skygardian saber. She concentrated on the blade, and dancing emerald and violet flames engulfed it. She swung the sword, casting the fire in an arc at the ground before her, much like Magnus had done with his own dragonfire.

Rhana gave a curt nod of approval. "Notice how pure, smokeless flame glows the brightest," Rhana said. She gestured toward the swath of bright flame, swirling upward from the grass. Then she shifted her finger to point at a dimmer patch of the fire that had caught on a dried, withered clump of smokesage. As the brush burned, gray smoke rose into the chilly air.

"But where there are impurities, there is smoke," Rhana continued. "If you aren't free of impurities, you can't burn bright. If you can't burn bright, you can't drive out darkness. This is where other riders have gone wrong. In the chaos of this realm, they'll do anything to achieve their goals—even if it means sacrificing his moral code."

"His?" Elle said, arching an eyebrow.

Rhana sighed. "Magnus was one of the most talented riders I ever trained. He and his mount, Noctus, were the ideal pair. Skilled, driven, loyal to each other... that dragon would do anything for his bond."

At that, Aurora nuzzled Eliana, who in turn wrapped an affectionate arm around her head.

Rhana glanced down at the dying flame on the smokesage. The last few remaining coils of smoke rose and vanished.

Rhana went on. "In his haste to achieve stability, Magnus allowed his once-strict moral code to slip. He convinced himself that the Knights' code—and the unspoken code between dragon and rider—wasn't as important as uniting the realm. He needed an army."

"The Capital Riders," Elle said as she put the pieces together.

Rhana nodded. "He only got it by forcing the dragons into bonds with riders they did not choose. Forced bonds are inherently weaker, but with enough new riders on his side..."

"Magnus became the great uniter," Elle said.

Rhana nodded. "He achieved peace. Or at least, stability. His once-pure bond with Noctus became forced as well. Magnus believes it was worth the price, but as for me, through the eyes of my dragons, I've seen the darkness that has begun to fester in Evgard under Magnus's rule..."

Rhana looked Elle squarely in the eyes. "When Solrac asked me to train you, I said no. But that drakked scoundrel convinced me you were different. You, Princess Eliana, won't let any impurities keep you from becoming the leader who burns bright. As a true dragon rider, you must stay focused. You are a beacon lighting the way for others. You forget that, and you not only let them down, but you let yourself down. Do you understand?"

"I think so," Elle said.

"Magnus let himself become distracted. I hope you won't do the same."

At that, Elle couldn't stop the image of Asher's face from appearing in her mind. His carefree, crooked smile. The way his dragonfire eyes lit up when she walked in the room.

But Rhana's words gave Elle pause. Elle knew that bonding Aurora meant giving up her freedom. She couldn't ask Asher to give up his.

Aurora sensed the pang of sorrow in Elle at the thought, and nuzzled her snout against Elle's hand.

Elle held her head high and raised a hand as if she were holding a torch.

"Light the way," Elle said proudly.

Rhana never beamed, but if she did, she would've been now. She gave a solemn nod as she mimicked the gesture.

"Light the way," she echoed.

Then Rhana continued, warning in her tone. "War is coming. The Farseer knows it, and I can feel it. Between that and the skyfalls, we don't have time to take things slow."

At that, Rhana produced a glowing skystone. "Aurora is ready to enter her second ascension. Then, we can make you some proper ascension armor."

The sun was just setting after the long day of training, and Elle was looking forward to washing up, changing into a fresh dress, and brushing out the tangles in her long dark hair. But first, she planned to walk Aurora back to her stall in the dragon stables and sing her to sleep. It was Aurora's favorite part of the day.

Stars, Aurora looked magnificent as a second ascension dragon, with her elegant, curving horns and larger size. When Elle looked closely, she could see gorgeous, swooping spiral patterns curling along her flank. Elle couldn't have been prouder of her bond's progress.

Meanwhile, thoughts of the day's training ran through Elle's mind. Rhana had such high expectations for her, as did many of the people of Evgard. Could Elle live up to their preconceived image of the picture-perfect true dragon rider?

Elle was so deep in thought that she almost didn't notice that Aurora was no longer walking beside her toward the stables. She whirled around to spot white scales disappearing into the cindercone treeline.

"Aurora?" Elle said. The true dragon turned toward Elle, a jovial light in her dragonfire green eyes. She was excited about something.

"Come in, Aurora!" Elle waved for Aurora to rejoin her. But Aurora shook her graceful head. Through their bond, Elle felt a sensation like eager rays of sunshine. Aurora continued into the thick trees toward the edge of Rhana's property.

Elle didn't like the idea of leaving the safehouse boundary, but what could she do? She would never use Aurora's heartscale to compel her to do something against her will. That left only one option.

Elle followed.

Not too far past the protective barrier surrounding Rhana's land, Elle heard the sound that must've been the thing drawing Aurora. A soft, melodic whistle floated through the snow-laden trees in the dying light of day. It was mesmerizing.

Elle was barely able to keep up with Aurora as they approached the source of the sound. Then, all at once, Aurora darted out of view.

"Aurora!" Elle called. She pushed through the thick cindercone boughs, causing the snow resting on them to sprinkle onto the forest floor as she burst into a small clearing.

What Elle saw there stopped her dead in her tracks.

It was him. Tall, and strong as he leaned against a cindercone tree. His dark hair was streaked with ruby red to match the scales growing along his hairline and cheekbones. A pair of jet black wings were tucked behind him, his eyes closed as he lost himself in the sweet, haunting music of the ocarina he played.

It was Kheradok, the young general of the Dragon Isles army. Beside him was Aurora, contentedly humming along as the Drekai warrior stroked her scales.

Stars. Elle's heart began to pound. What was he doing here?

Not one to cower in the shadows, Elle stepped closer. General Kheradok opened his eyes just enough to note her presence before closing them again as he continued his song.

Elle folded her arms and waited. Soon the last notes of his song finally faded, and he tucked the ocarina away. Still, Elle could sense lingering contentment from Aurora through their bond, and her dragon didn't leave Kheradok's side as he continued stroking the scales along her neck.

Silence stretched across the clearing as Elle waited for Kheradok to speak.

The young Drekai general locked eyes with her.

"To think," he began, his accented voice low. "All the while when I was tracking the half-born, Asher, the woman I thought was a mere dragon keeper with an uncanny skill with a blade was really Eliana, the crown princess of Drakfell and rider of the white true dragon."

Elle hardly ever got nervous. But the way Kheradok spoke set dragonflies buzzing in her stomach. This man was honor-bent on dueling Asher, and had pursued him—and, by extension, Elle and Kai—throughout much of their journey across Rengard on their way to the Mirror Forest. Ultimately, thanks to the Canyonlands' queen declaring war on the Dragon Isles, General Kheradok had abandoned the chase in order to fulfill his duties. Kheradok hadn't been the wiser about Aurora's true nature, since Kai had done his best to use illusions to make Aurora look like a fluffy, white jetsand lynx most of the time.

Until now.

"Your Rebel Knight safehouse is well guarded." Kheradok grinned. "It took me a long time to find you."

"How did you?" Elle put a hand on her hip.

"Aura tracking," he said, holding up an intricately marked crystal. "Using Sight runes you Evgardians have lost to time."

Elle inclined her chin. "I'm guessing you're hoping to force me to take you to Asher so you can finally have your foolish duel?"

Kheradok's expression hardened. "I *will* duel Asher of Steel Rim. My honor demands it. But I will respect the deal Asher and I made while fighting those dragon slayers at Longhorn Hill. He and I will face one another after the close of the summer. But that is not why I have come today."

A gentle roar from Aurora pulled both her and Kheradok's attention. The dragon nuzzled against Kheradok's side. She seemed to like the sound of his voice as well as his music.

Elle bit her lower lip. Then, in a clear invitation to explain why, she said, "Aurora seems to like you."

"Aurora," Kheradok repeated, scratching her white scales more vigorously. "Is that your name then, little one? Though you're not so little anymore, my second ascension friend."

Elle tapped a toe, waiting.

Kheradok spoke carefully. "I used to spend a lot of time in the hatchery at Zolehiinu, the capital city of the Dragon Isles. Aurora... I've been playing for her since before she hatched."

That took Elle by surprise. "Really?"

Kheradok nodded. "I was careful to never touch the egg those many months I visited the hatchery. Still, the Seers predicted it—the white true dragon and I were meant to bond."

"What?" Elle could hardly believe her ears. But through her bond with Aurora, she felt peace like starlight and knew that it was true.

Kheradok began slowly crossing the small clearing toward where Elle stood. Aurora seemed to trust him implicitly, but Elle still wasn't so sure. Kheradok continued.

"I'm sure you know by now that true dragons only bond with those meant to be great leaders. Rulers of nations. As Empress Khaisa's heir, surely I was meant to be Aurora's rider."

Elle's mouth fell open. "You're the... the future emperor of the Dragon Isles? There's no way—I would have learned that in my lessons on politics."

"My situation is unique," Kheradok explained, stalking ever-closer while Elle held her ground. "Khaisa is my aunt, and since she has not—and never will have—any children, I am the sole heir to the Drekai throne."

He pressed his lips together. "Admittedly, my claim to the throne is contested. But the true dragon's bond would have solidified my right to rule."

"Then why wouldn't you touch the true dragon egg?" Elle challenged. "If you were so sure she would've chosen you?"

Kheradok was almost to where Elle stood now, still speaking calmly. Reassuringly. Part of Elle wanted to draw her sword, but she knew better than to provoke his attack.

"A Seer watched over the dragon hatchery. She was skilled in omen reading, and predicted the future of many of the eggs. Some dragons were destined to be warriors, watchers, or protectors. But the white true dragon egg, one of the last of its kind after the Dragon Wars wiped so many out, had a very special destiny."

Behind Kheradok, Aurora gave a soft growl.

Kheradok continued. "'*Destined to restore the Guardian's fire,*' the Seer said. Both Empress Khaisa and I are certain: Aurora is fated to save our people from our war with the *khaamu.* The wraiths."

He was only a foot away from Elle now. Elle shoved down the jumble of increasingly wild dragonflies in her stomach.

"You still haven't answered my question," she pressed. "Why wouldn't you bond the egg before?"

Kheradok looked Elle deeply in the eyes. For the first time, his confident demeanor wavered as he replied.

"Because the Seer also predicted Aurora's death."

Elle paled. "What?"

"I will never forget the Seer's omen," Kheradok said somberly. "*She will be trapped... sent to the great beyond of* Etiirika *before her time.*"

Elle's heart grew heavier with each word. She glanced toward the innocent, beautiful true dragon perched sweetly in the clearing, the warm, rosy embers of daylight reflecting onto her scales. It couldn't be true.

"I loved that little egg," Kheradok said, genuine sorrow in his tone. "Fearing her terrible fate, I sought to delay things for as long as I could. I wanted to give her more time. Then your father, King Rodan, stole her egg from Zolehiinu, and she chose you as her bond instead. But now... now I have to make things right. No one else is strong enough to do what must be done. I will accept her fate along with my own as her rider."

Elle wasn't quite sure when he'd closed the gap between them. She took a startled step backward, only to find that Kheradok had her backed against a thick cindercone trunk.

Pulse racing, Elle held her head proudly, eyes set in determination. "If you think I'm going to just hand over Aurora's heartscale, you've got another thing coming."

"I figured you'd say that." He calmly placed a gauntleted hand against the tree beside her head. Elle suddenly realized she was trapped.

"Why are you here, General?" Elle asked, summoning every ounce of poise she could muster. Scorch, his eyes were like emeralds.

For a tense moment, Kheradok didn't answer. But his silence was enough of an answer for Elle. She reached for her saber—too late.

Panic shot through Elle as she felt something press menacingly against her. She glanced down, and sure enough, Kheradok held a long, thin dagger in the perfect position to pierce her heart.

Kheradok's voice was a low whisper that sent chills up Elle's spine.

"I'm sorry, princess, but I'm here to kill you."

Behind Kheradok, Aurora let out a whimper. Through their bond, Elle could feel her fear. Confusion. Conflict.

"I'm sorry to you too, Aurora." Kheradok sounded genuinely saddened. "I know the breaking of the bond will be hard for you, but I can see no other way. I will help you heal."

Aurora lowered her head, as if pleading with Kheradok.

"Neither of you deserve this," Kheradok continued, his face inches from Elle's. "Princess Eliana, it was you yourself who once taught me never to underestimate an opponent. You are a skilled warrior with a strong sense of duty. Truly a worthy rider for the white true dragon."

Elle swallowed her own fear, determined to maintain her dignity. She mentally scolded herself for not drawing her sword sooner. She needed to stall him, not just to save herself, but Aurora as well. "Why kill me then?"

"I do not relish taking a life. Each life is precious beyond measure. But what I want above all else is peace for my nation. One of the greatest threats to that end is allowing High King Magnus the chance to take that heartscale around your neck for himself. That is why I must take it first. Restore Aurora to the Dragon Isles where she belongs so that she and I can fulfill her great destiny and save my nation from the Gray."

Elle knew she should've been quaking in her boots. Kheradok was stronger than her and he had her trapped. This was it. There was no way out of this.

Unless...

"Huh," Elle said, her tone markedly casual. "Interesting."

Kheradok frowned. "What's interesting?"

Elle shrugged. "Oh. I guess I just thought you were an honorable guy. My mistake."

"I value honor above all else," Kheradok said, looking deeply offended. "I will honor the peace of my nation, no matter the cost."

"See? That's the problem." Elle shook her head. "How can you claim to be honorable, a proponent of peace, when you're willing to toss aside your principles the second they conflict with your goals?"

Kheradok bristled at her words. "Nothing is more important than achieving peace. Sometimes the cost is high."

"And apparently, sometimes that cost is your own soul," Elle replied fiercely, unfazed by the pressure of the blade against her ribcage. "Who you are at your core. That's something I would never sacrifice. That is why Aurora chose *me*."

A low warning growl from Aurora punctuated Elle's claim. Kheradok's eyes betrayed just how unsettled he was. He didn't move a muscle, his eyes boring into Elle. She stared proudly back.

"Go ahead," Elle challenged. "Kill me."

For a moment, Elle thought he would do it.

But then, rather than a dagger stabbing through her side, Kheradok's lips were pressing against her mouth.

Elle was completely stunned. She had *not* seen that coming.

Instinct told her to kiss him back. This was far preferable to him ending her life, and maybe even key to saving herself. Besides, Elle wasn't afraid to admit that Kheradok was attractive, and in possession of no shortage of admirable qualities, at least if one overlooked his—so far unacted on—willingness to murder. Plus, wasn't she always saying a kiss wasn't a proposal?

But, Elle realized, to kiss Kheradok back would be a betrayal of who *she* was at her core.

For the second time that day, Asher's face appeared in Elle's mind. His dragonfire irises were only a few shades lighter than Kheradok's, yet the depth held within each man's eyes was more different than day and night. Asher held her heart. He valued it enough to admit he wasn't ready for anything more between them. But then… would he ever be ready?

Even more importantly, could Elle ever let him sacrifice his freedom by choosing her?

Hours seemed to have passed in that one second. Elle somehow maintained even composure as Kheradok pulled back, releasing his hold over her.

"Eliana of Drakfell," Kheradok said, sheathing the dagger once more. "Maybe you are strong enough for what's to come… I believe you have taught me yet another lesson."

Elle gripped her sword. "And maybe there's hope for your honor yet."

CHAPTER 5: TRAINING

ASHER

"You call that an offensive strike, scale-skin?" Rhana bellowed at me from just outside the training circle. As usual, she stood like an army officer, with her feet apart and hands behind her back. Her wrinkled face was extra creased as she frowned with disapproval at my apparently lackluster performance.

"Why, yes I do!" I called back, wiping the sweat on my forehead with the back of my hand. "You seem pretty offended by it, at least."

Rhana ignored my hilarious joke, but I could've sworn I heard a low, growling chuckle from a couple of the large dragons standing beside her. For today's training, Rhana had invited three of her own dragon bonds to assist.

"Drekai move fast, like ashvipers," Rhana said. "Strike that slow again and that general is going to take you out in half a move. You of all people should know that. Do the move again, but do it right."

I bit my lip as I tried to remember the pre-strike battle forms Rhana had been drilling into my head. They were supposed to be good for fighting multiple opponents, or fighting someone who could teleport. For the past few weeks, she and Boone had been working together to prepare me for my *zhaku* this summer.

My honor duel—to the death—with Kheradok, the general of the Drekai army.

When Rhana had found out I'd had the nerve to interrupt an honor duel between the King of Drakfell and the Drekai general, she hadn't hesitated to let me know just how idiotic that was. Though I'd briefly considered the advantages of ridding the world of one more noble, at the time, all I'd been thinking about was saving the king's life. Now, the powerful Drekai magi-warrior was planning to face *me* in just a few short months. I wondered what he was doing right now. Was he running around the Dragon Isles, training as hard as I was?

I'd tried to get out of the honor duel with Kheradok a few times already, but if there was one thing I'd learned about Drekai culture—both from the determined General Kheradok and my strong-willed mother—it was that Drekai valued honor above all else.

Yep. There was no getting out of the fight to the death. I was just lucky the general had agreed to postpone our duel after dragon slayers had unceremoniously interrupted his attempts to fight me while on our way to Rhana's cabin. Between that and the Dragon Isles needing Kheradok's leadership in their war with the Canyonlands, I'd earned more time to prepare before facing him.

For months, I'd been long-distance training with Boone in a strange sort of Astral-pocket dream arena using a dreamweb that I'd unfortunately broken during the journey here. But despite all those training sessions—according to Rhana and Boone, anyway—I needed all the further practice I could get.

Apparently, that meant summoning up my starglass armor and parading around for Rhana to judge my worth as she sicked three of her third ascension dragons on me.

For the umpteenth time today, Rhana's dragons made their respective moves. Two drakes used their lashing tails to attack me from either side, supposedly to mimic the Drekai general's ability to use portals to be in multiple places at once. Meanwhile, the massive, mighty wyvern in the middle was a black-scaled Wildshaper named Wiley. She gave a quirky little cock of her head—something she always did when accessing her powers.

Oh dear.

Wiley breathed a series of emerald green fireballs my way, a wildshaping power borrowed from spitfires, the winged serpents native to the Dragon Isles. According to Rhana, these were an excellent substitute for the fireballs the General could throw with his gauntlet, and were likely connected to how he had gained that power in the first place. Wiley was an expert, and toned down her fireballs so that they were mostly smoking soot and wouldn't actually harm me through my starglass armor when—I mean, *if* I failed.

I put all of my training I'd done with Boone into practice, using my favorite of the breakthrough techniques he'd helped me discover. My eyes glowed brighter gold as I flared liquid ether into a mist around me to augment my levitation abilities. It made me faster than a shooting star.

Leaving a trail of ether mist behind me, I dodged the first drake's tail strike. Then I focused on countering the fireballs. With a somewhat lackluster yell, I whirled my starglass spear, blocking each one in turn.

That's when I saw the second drake's tail coming at me from the side. I burned more ether, but my heart wasn't in it and my last-second hover-jump turned out more like a hover-hop. Still, it was enough to get me out of range of the drake's tail.

As I continued the training, dust puffed up around my fast-moving feet from within the sparring circle. The circle perfectly matched the standard Evgardian guard specifications, and stood right next to the safehouse's training grounds. I was really starting to wish this extreme military survival cabin had turned out to be the cozy grandmother's hovel I'd originally pictured.

My mind wandered to the sidelines as both my body and spirit continued forcing themselves through Rhana's exercises. At that moment, the grounds were where at least two dozen people chatted after their recent battle preparation session. Most were Rebel recruits Boone and some others had picked up from other safehouses and brought back here for training. It was still up in the air whether Boone was right about fighting more Gray Ones followers, but he and Rhana had set to work getting every able-bodied fighter into shape just in case.

The recruits were eager, and had spent the morning trying out drills and practicing with silverbane under Boone's direction. While Boone had done an excellent job training me one on one, it was clear he wasn't exactly cut out to be a drill sergeant. When a couple recruits had misinterpreted his order to 'make like a buckin' kirin rider gettin' throwed from the saddle,' valuable silverbane had ended up all over the dirt.

While a few would-be soldiers were still cleaning up that mess, most of them were now watching me practice. I'd been at this for over an hour, and none of them seemed particularly impressed. The ether mist surrounding me began to waver, and my eyes glowed a little less brightly.

After taking a fireball to the leg and a simultaneous *whack* from a drake's tail, I dared to look Rhana in the eye. She barked with disappointment, "Put in a performance like that, and you're dead, soldier! Streya's crown. This scorched duel is about more than your precious life, and it's high time you started acting like it."

Part of me wanted to get frustrated or even angry at her harsh attitude, but how could I when I knew she was right?

Grunting, I started the drill over with renewed effort. I flared the mist of liquid ether around me to achieve the 'snake-like speed' Rhana seemed to think my Drekai blood should give me. I felt like a fool, and, to no one's surprise, Rhana agreed.

The bystanders watched on as Rhana stepped inside the circle to yell at me once more. "You want to show me those pointy ears know how to listen on their own, or should I find a way to *make* you listen?"

I pressed my lips together, my chest feeling hollow at her harshness. Did this kind of instruction really work on soldiers? Besides that, did she really think I wasn't trying here? I almost wanted to ask for another trainer—Stars, I'd even take the unimpressible Valla over this, but she was off tracking down Solrac. Even Sven, my rigid captain from Squad Nimble, had never been this exacting.

The last thing I wanted to do was keep practicing right now. I longed to go find Thorn and fly far, far away from all of this. Through our bond, I felt a spark of worry from my dragon.

I come back? Thorn asked in my heart.

No, I rushed to reply. Thorn was out on a hunt well outside Rhana's property line, and I didn't want him cutting it short on my account.

I'm fine, I promised as I nearly skidded outside of the practice ring. Another blow from one of Rhana's drake's tails hit me in the back, cracking my starglass armor.

I braced myself to take the next round of Rhana's disparagement, but a gravelly voice cut her off.

"Wait just one li'l minute there," Boone stepped into the circle as well. He gripped his scale-adorned belt with both hands, and his leathery face showed knit brows and a deep frown. "Why don't the lot of us make like a scorchapple twig just got snapped underfoot by a big ol' daddy craghopper's hoof?"

Befuddled silence greeted Boone's request. Rhana tilted her head at him.

"And that means...?"

"Break," Boone explained. "Make like that drakkin' twig an' break—least for the day. Likes of me believes we all could use a bit o' rest."

I cast Boone a look of gratitude, and he nodded back as if tipping a hat that wasn't there.

"It's still early afternoon, Boone," Rhana protested. "You were a soldier in the Dragon Wars same as me—You know it's not right to quit before getting something right."

"Ain't nobody quittin'," Boone said seriously. "Just time for a li'l interim is all."

"But Boone, I don't think you understand—"

"Rhana," Boone's already low voice went even lower as he stared daggers at her. "Ain't me not understandin' here. I been trainin' with this boy a lot longer'n you—Ain't Asher's ears that are havin' a hard time listenin'."

Rhana shut her mouth, her brows lowered as she and Boone engaged in an extremely intense, wrinkly staring contest. In the end, Rhana backed off, leading her three dragons back to the stables.

I dismissed my starglass armor and the ether mist as Boone turned to the rest of the enthralled spectators. "As for y'all, ain't you got somethin' better to do than standin' agape like a pack of cud-chewin', busy-body aldrakas? Trainin's done for the day. I don't wanna see y'all's hineys back here until tomorrow mornin'."

The group immediately dispersed, ducking their heads. Nobody looked at my sorry, sweaty excuse for a soldier as I stood alone in the sparring circle.

That is, except for one pair of amber eyes near the back.

Soot. Elle saw all that?

She looked at me with concern as well as a healthy dose of pity. Great.

It looked like she wanted to come over and talk with me, and my heart jumped. I was conflicted over whether I wanted to see her right now or whether I'd rather just go hide under a rock for a few hours. But stars, Elle looked stunning in her new, brilliant white ascension armor. She'd have looked like a princess even without the matching tiara. Since Aurora's ascension, she was almost as big as Thorn. The white true dragon perched there next to Elle, looking more regal than ever.

Elle had finally taken a step my way when a cluster of the cabin's newcomers surrounded her. Their expressions were eager as they spoke to her, and I caught a couple fragments of their words:

"Can't believe it."

"True dragon rider."

"…honor to be in your presence."

Of course. These days, Elle was a beacon. People were drawn to her, her position as a true dragon rider making them see her as more than royalty. More people came to the cabin each day, hoping to train alongside the powerful rider and fight for her noble cause. They truly believed that she'd been chosen by the goddesses to lead them, and stars, maybe they were right. I just missed the days when I didn't have to fight so hard for her noble attention.

I had no idea how so many people had heard of her already. Rhana's cabin was now hosting people from Rengard, Evyndara, Skygard, Drakfell… even some from the northern keepdom of Behrfell had come yesterday. Rhana had grumbled about how her cabin was becoming more crowded than a roadside tavern, but she'd clearly built it to house an army. And that's exactly what Elle was drawing here.

Elle cast me a quick, apologetic glance as the crowd swept her away. The beautiful, charming noblewoman rider couldn't just ignore the attentions of her subjects.

That was fair.

I sighed as I stood alone in the circle. I saw less of Elle each day, and part of me was afraid she was avoiding me.

My starglass spear was still clutched in my hand. Staring at it, my eyes flashed gold as I channeled ether to change its shape. The long haft shrunk into a shorter handle with a small hand guard. The blade went from the multi-pointed dragonhook style to a long, curved single-edged sword.

I examined my new creation: a Dragon Isles standard scimitar, just like the one my mother used to wield. Obviously, hers wasn't made from starglass, but battleworn Drekai bronze with a teal-wrapped handle.

I'd seen my half-born mother fight with her scimitar a hundred times, mostly against wild dreklings or dragons that came to our little outlander home in hopes of getting a taste of our ether. But once, I'd watched her battle another person—a rogue Drekai raider.

I replayed the memory in my head. Dad had been working in the mines when the raider came, and as a lanky, mighty ten-year-old, I'd felt it was my solemn duty to step up as the man of the house.

The burly Drekai had golden yellow scales covering his hairline, cheek-bones, shoulders, and knuckles. Deep gold horns sprouted from his head, just a few shades lighter than his layered, battleworn bronze chestplate.

"...supposed to be dead right now," the man seethed, clutching a *raskalaata,* an oversized, bladed war boomerang, in his hand. He stood menacingly in the doorway, towering over my mother.

"Get out of my home," she replied, her voice harsh and firm.

"I'm not going anywhere." The Drekai bared his teeth. "Not unless I take you with me."

The Drekai raider took a step toward my mother, and I cried out, running across the room from my hiding place in the hallway. My irises burned with etherlight as I summoned a kid-sized version of my usual starglass spear.

The Drekai man stumbled back through the doorway, surprised by my sudden approach. He looked me over, eyes growing wide.

"Stay away from her!" I demanded, training my blade on him. Even at ten, I knew from stories that Drekai raiders were merciless, taking whatever they wanted and fleeing back to the Dragon Isles with their spoils.

My mom's face blanched when she saw me. Then, without hesitation, she seized her bronze scimitar from its hook upon the wall.

"*Zhatehlu ji voiima,*" she challenged, and even with the limited Drekai vocabulary I had then, I understood the phrase 'duel of wills.'

Mom pulled up her sleeve to brandish the collection of interlocking, diamond-shaped tattoos on the inside of her arm. At the sight of it, the man seemed to hesitate. But then he revealed his own set of tattoos—not as many diamonds as Mom, but still a lot. I hadn't known what they meant at the time, but now I realized those were Drekai 'honor marks.' A new diamond for every duel they'd ever won.

The man brandished his *raskalaata,* and the fight was on.

He and Mom dueled fiercely in the dusty clearing just outside our front door near our cactus garden. I hurried onto the porch, ready to spring into the fight myself.

"*Nii!*" Mom called to me. "No, Asher. Never interrupt a Drekai's duel!"

"But—" I protested.

"Asher..." Mom said my name the way only a mother can.

I hated it, but I stayed put while she crossed blades with the raider. Their fight was incredible, Mom hover-dashing to keep ahead of his enormous, bladed boomerang, which he wielded like a longsword. Mom was a shadowbinder, which meant she could levitate like me. It also meant she could phase-shift—Anytime her foe's *raskalaata* got past her guard, she turned her body to shadow so the blade passed straight through her. Fighting her was like trying to catch smoke.

Despite the raider's size and skill, Mom overcame him, ultimately training her scimitar on his chest. The green dragonfire in his eyes was intense and his breathing was heavy, but he dropped his weapon in surrender.

"*Ena, ja iskaan laata,*" Mom's tone was fierce. "*Khet ka taan ji min laaksi. Vaana.*"

My limited Drekai language skills kept me from understanding all of what she'd said. *Ena* meant 'go,' *laaksi* meant 'child,' and *vaana...* Was she telling him to swear to never tell anyone about me?

The Drekai agreed to Mom's terms, whatever they were, then left our humble home. I'd tried for hours to get her to tell me what the man had wanted, but she told me to forget about the whole thing. But how could I forget my brave mother standing up to a raider twice her size? I wanted to be just like her someday.

Back in the sparring circle at the safehouse, I was struck by a pang of sadness and longing. Things would've been so different if Mom were still here. Dad swore he could still see her in the spirit plane sometimes but... well, I couldn't exactly trust Dad's sight to be reliable. The Black Valkyrie had blinded him the same day she'd taken Mom, which meant Dad had to rely exclusively on his Rifter's ability to see the spirit world in order to get around. They said Etheria was a wild, unpredictable place, filled with strange, sometimes dark, ether, and it was hard to believe his communications with Mom were anything beyond the frantic hallucinations of a poor, grieving widower. Even Kai had his doubts about Dad's claims. But still... I'd thought I'd seen my mom once before for myself: When I'd been initiated into the Knights of the Torch and walked through the omenfires at Orothion.

I closed my eyes and tried to relax as a light breeze blew across the training grounds, carrying the smoky scent of cindercone pine. It cooled the sweat off of me, and almost seemed to whisper through the nearby trees.

Asher, a feminine voice seemed to say. I frowned. Mom?

I straightened, looking sharply to my left and right, but there was nobody around. Well, nobody but a beefy, elderly man dressed in furs standing near the lakefront. He startled when I suddenly locked eyes with him, then gave me a wave along with a cheesy grin that revealed several gaps in his teeth.

I waved back, chiding myself. My emotions were clearly messing with my head.

Turning my starglass scimitar over in my hand, I chewed the inside of my cheek. Since Mom's death, things between my father and me had been pretty strained. I couldn't blame him for becoming overly cautious. After all, he'd lost his wife, his sight, and his ability to work all in one day. But still... He'd never approved of Kai and me going out thieving to earn money, even though we only ever stole from nobles. It seemed all I ever heard from him was a stern 'be careful.'

For the umpteenth time since our mission to Swan Spire, I wished I'd gotten away with that envelope with Mom's name on it. I'd spent a dangerous amount of time thinking about going back for it, but Kai had vehemently forbade me from doing something so risky.

Then again, Kai had been incredibly distracted with that case we'd picked up back in Keep Rengard. That seventy-three-to-eighty-six-percent chance had come through, and with a little lightwielding assistance from one of the magi ex-prisoners Boone had rescued, Kai had been able to use one of the crystal keys to open the case. It was full of information gathered by an undercover Knight named Cenrik regarding the Coven of the Gray Ones. The dark cult knew a lot about those creepy, gray spirit monsters Boone called ghosts, which fed into Boone's urgent need to prepare the Rebel Knights to face them.

The only problem was... nobody knew how to fight 'ghosts.' As for me, I was still on the fence about whether or not these mysterious Gray Ones were even real. More likely, the Black Valkyrie and her devoted Mage Hunters were using the illusory monsters as a scare tactic. That sounded like just the sort of messed-up thing that my mother's killer would try.

With one last look around the empty training area, I let the starglass scimitar in my hands dissolve into shimmering etherdust.

The sun had long since set, leaving me alone and worn out in my room in the cabin. After today's training session, I wasn't in the mood to talk to anyone.

Nobody but Thorn, at least. He'd returned from his hunt, and I was planning to sneak out and meet him for a quick flight before bed.

Rhana was pretty strict on curfews, so I made my escape via window. The brisk night air got me to buckle up my dragon buffalo leather jacket and secure my turquoise dust scarf more tightly around my neck.

The roof was covered in Rhana's starglass panels. She had to be using some kind of skystone to keep them from dissipating. There was ample space for me to walk safely around the panels, but I was careful to give them a wide berth just in case. Rhana already didn't like me, and the last thing I wanted to do was mess up her cabin. I made my way toward the north side of the rooftop near the dragon stables.

I crouched, ready to hover-leap off the roof.

Then something assaulted me.

A gray and black mass of scales and fur about the size of my face launched toward my chest. I yelped, falling backward onto the rooftop as an angry, chittering, ring-tailed draccoon clung to my jacket.

"Stars!" I exclaimed as the dragon-raccoon shook his tiny, black fist before my face. "I'm so sorry, Sir Draccoon. I didn't realize this rooftop was your domain." The draccoon was still squeaking with apparent rage, so I went on.

"I'll come bearing gifts next time?" I promised.

The draccoon seemed to accept this, and scurried down my leg. I bid him farewell, and was just about to jump off the roof when I noticed the creature's expression. He wore a sly grin, and both hands were tucked behind his back.

"Wait a second," I muttered, hand flying to my neck. My turquoise scarf was gone.

"Hey!" I cried. "That's not a gift for you!" The draccoon squealed, revealing my scarf wadded up in his little claws. Then he turned and darted back across the roof in the opposite direction.

I felt a glow of alarm from Thorn letting me know he was on his way. I told him there was no rush. This draccoon was just an annoyance.

"Get back here!" I whisper-yelled as I dashed after the draccoon, but he was a fast little bugger. While I'd been extra cautious the first time I'd crossed the roof, this time, I activated my ether to hover-dash around the large panels like a shooting star.

I dove at the feet of the draccoon. He let out a long, panicked squeak just as I was about to seize him by the tail.

That's when he stretched his arms out wide. Thin flaps of skin extended from his wrists down along the sides of his body, like makeshift wings for gliding. Then the little thief leaped from the roof.

"Soot!" I cried, preparing to jump after him.

I stopped short when I heard a grunt. Confused, I looked down to see that the draccoon had landed atop the shoulder of a snowheaded man in the midst of clambering onto the rooftop.

At first, his white hair almost made me think he was Boone, but this man was at least twenty years younger, closer to my dad's age. Additionally, Boone was an Astromancer like me, whereas this man wore a Psion's silvermark on his left cheek. A telekinetic rune hung over his forehead for just a second longer as he pushed on his nomad-style armor to hoist himself onto the roof.

"Well drak, Dusty," the man said, shaking his head at the draccoon. He had a much lighter northern accent than Boone did. "Ain't right stealin' from our fellow cabin guests. Give 'im his scarf back, will ya?"

The draccoon—Dusty, apparently—vigorously shook his head. The man's dark eyebrows raised over smiling eyes, his scruffy face displaying clear, but unsurprised, disapproval. The draccoon let out a melodramatic sigh before passing me my scarf.

"That's right." I narrowed my eyes at the wily draccoon and tied the scarf back around my neck a little more securely than before.

Then Thorn arrived, carefully landing on the roof and crouching protectively next to me. He narrowed his eyes at Dusty, who stuck out his tongue.

"Thanks," I said, turning to the man.

"Don't mention it." The stranger broke into a smile, giving my large, black and bronze wyvern a quick nod. "Dusty's a good little ethereal familiar, but he just can't help himself. Don't tell anyone, but..." The man leaned closer and cupped a hand around his mouth. "...Dusty and I used to be highwaymen up north."

I grinned back. "Oh, don't worry. Thorn and I have dabbled in the 'repossession of valuable goods' market ourselves."

The man laughed. "I like that. Your name's Asher, ain't it?"

I nodded and the man stuck out his hand. I grasped his forearm and he did the same.

"I'm Ivar," he said. "What you doin' up here at this hour?"

"I know, I know," I said with a sigh. "I should be in bed. Rhana's curfew, I need to be well-rested for another day of training, etcetera."

"Saw you trainin' earlier today," Ivar said.

I looked down. "Who didn't?"

"I know what your problem is."

I furrowed my brow. "What?"

Ivar grinned, extending his arm so that Dusty the draccoon could slink down to the ground, keeping a healthy distance from Thorn and his bladed tail. Then, Ivar unsheathed the long seaxe at his belt.

He stepped to the side, giving his weapon a practice twirl. "Lesson one in trainin': Ain't nobody gonna learn the same way. You don't strike me as much of a rigid soldier type. That right, Asher?"

I shook my head so hard most of the hair in my warrior's fangknot came loose. I pulled the loop out of my hair altogether just to save time.

Ivar grinned even wider. "In that case..."

Without another word, Ivar lunged toward me with his seaxe. I didn't think, I just reacted, summoning my starglass spear almost instantly.

And with Thorn and Dusty eagerly watching from the sidelines, our sparring session began.

Ivar was unlike anyone I'd ever sparred with before. It turned out this man was an absolute menace with telekinesis. He wore a crisscrossed, nomad-style harness-slash-pauldron across his chest and shoulders, which he used to telekinetically push and pull himself around. He leaped over starglass panels like they were nothing, and was one of the only people I'd met who could keep up with my hover-jumping.

Well, almost.

We zipped back and forth in a wild game of tag but with weapons. It was so fun, I wondered if it could even count as training at all. This was *so* much better than trudging around slashing at the air for no reason.

Dusty and Thorn watched on. Eventually, Dusty climbed onto Thorn's antlers to get a better view. Thorn seemed to enjoy providing a perch for our scrappy new friend.

Throughout the rooftop spar, Ivar offered up more tips in the form of 'lessons.' Lesson two involved staying relaxed and not overthinking the upcoming fight, something Rhana's training had done the opposite of.

Lesson three was about keeping a list of moves in my arsenal so that I could draw on them at the right moments. That way, I could lean on muscle memory rather than second guessing myself when I faced the Drekai General.

Ivar suggested naming each move, not only so I'd remember them better, but so that I could communicate with other members of my team should the need ever arise. Kind of like how Kai and I used moves like 'double trouble,' an illusion trick.

Next, Ivar showed me a couple of the moves in his own arsenal, from the 'flop 'n' drop,' which involved telekinetically lifting his enemy into the air and then suddenly dropping them, to the 'ring-tailed fury,' which was mostly just Dusty going straight for the face. The demonstration of that one wasn't something I wanted to experience twice.

My favorite of Ivar's moves was one he called the 'psi-clone.' He lit up a variation on a telekinesis rune, then spun his seaxe rapidly like a windmill. I remembered Solrac doing something similar once while we were crossing Drakfell's harshest desert, the Scar. With his sword moving that quickly, it was nearly impossible to get inside Ivar's guard.

"Heh," I chuckled as the rapidly spinning blade blew my hair. "Psi-clone." I liked this guy's style. Thorn chuckled.

"Your turn," Ivar said, daring me to come at him.

Without hesitation, I stabbed straight at Ivar's psi-clone with my drag-onhook spear. The starglass grated against the blade, and for a second, it looked and sounded like my weapon was going to shatter.

But I wasn't finished. I flared my ether, sending a pulse down the length of my spear, then another, and another. Each pulse carried a layer of ether which formed a layer of starglass along Ivar's seaxe. With a few more pulses, the weight and clunkiness of the extra starglass dropped Ivar's blade to the ground with a resounding thud.

"Excellent strategy!" Ivar beamed. "What do you call that one?"

I grinned. "The 'just encase.'"

Ivar snorted, and we named a few more of my moves from there. There was the 'comet,' where I hover-dashed so quickly no foe could hope to keep up, the 'fake-then-take,' where I feinted to one side with my blade before disarming my opponent with its hook, and the classic 'hey look, a distraction!' In that one, I just screamed while maniacally pointing off to the side, confusing my enemy long enough to land a hit.

I figured I should try incorporating more ether into my moves, like Boone had been training me to do. But when I tried to make a big burst of it to blast at Ivar, it fizzled out. The 'astro-nova' was going to have to wait.

Lesson four was about technique, lesson five covered knowing my enemy, and lesson six was all about defense. After an hour or so, Ivar and I were both covered in sweat, but this time I was smiling from ear to ear.

"And finally," Ivar said, using telekinesis on his dragonleather harness to launch himself right over the top of my incoming stab, "ain't nobody ever learned nothin' by makin' themselves miserable. Lesson seven: Life's supposed to be happy, and if you ain't happy, you better figure out why and fix it up right quick. Even while trainin' with Rhana. She's got experience neither of us have, and I know you're tough enough to weather storms—'specially ones'll make you stronger. Got it?"

"Got it!" I grunted, hover-jumping higher to catch Ivar by the harness using the hook of my dragonhook spear. It was a perfect hook—though I may have added a little extra starglass to it to make sure I snagged him just right.

Ivar's etherarchy faltered as I yanked him down. His sword clattered out of his hands, landing blade-down on the nearest starglass panel. A crack split the panel right down the middle, and Ivar and I looked at each other with wide eyes.

"Oops," Ivar muttered. "By now I've learned that Rhana ain't never truly in a good mood, but this sure as the void ain't gonna improve things."

"Don't worry," I said. I pulled out Ivar's sword and handed it to him, then leaned down and touched the panel. For some reason, a fractured starglass panel didn't seem like such a big deal to me anymore. Burning more ether, I filled in the crack with some starglass of my own. I'd always been pretty good with starglass precision, and when I finished, we could hardly tell the difference.

Ivar and I sat down on the edge of the roof, and he complimented me on my skill. He said if our fight had gone on even a minute more, he'd have run out of ether and ended up with an ether overuse headache. Meanwhile, my ether well was still only about a quarter drained. Before coming here, Ivar had been one of the prisoners in the Canyonlands, and he explained that three years in a silver prison cell had shrunk his ether well. He was working on expanding it back to its proper size, but it would take some time.

"It's too bad the Drekai general I'll be facing isn't a Psion," I said, dangling my legs in the open air. "Between you and another guy back on our old heist crew, I've got a lot of experience fighting Psions."

"What kind of magi is the general?" Ivar asked as Dusty the draccoon curled up at his side. Thorn perched beside me, his tail curving around our group.

"Rifter," I replied.

"Well, voids. What you need is to spar with my daughter. She's a Rifter—about your age, and she ain't no general, but she served in the Canyonlands army, so she'd have some military moves up her sleeve. And the way I seen her fight... Soot, that little storm would give you a run for your marks!"

"Where's your daughter?" I asked, curious.

Ivar sighed, looking up into the starry night. "Wish to the skies I knew. We got separated back durin' an attack on the Rise in Keep Rengard. My wife, Freya, made me run off with Boone and the others before the Mage Hunters could take me in, but my daughter stayed behind with the guard. I sent Dusty back to check on her not long after, but by the time he arrived, li'l Mels was gone."

"Mels?" I said, my mind suddenly racing. "Wait... Your daughter's a snowhead like you, isn't she?"

"Sure is."

"Dark brown eyes, long braid, fights with a seaxe, and a little finicky when it comes to neatness?"

Ivar cocked his head at me. "That's Mels alright. How'd you know all that?"

"Stars," I exhaled, getting to my feet. "Ivar, I know where your daughter is."

CHAPTER 6: THE HIGH PRINCE

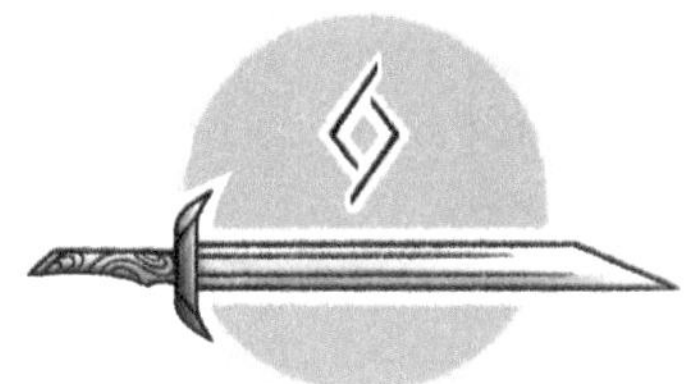

MELEYA

"**G**auntlet down: Snow should absolutely and unequivocally be outlawed." Brigan pulled his heavy cloak more tightly around him. "Point one—nobody wants a dry, reddish icicle for a nose, or ears so cold they feel hot. Point two—these bulky winter clothes are in no way conducive to agility. And finally, point three—and I'll fight all of you on this—snow isn't even that nice to look at."

My squad erupted with protests, and I had to agree with them. I grew up in the same desert keepdom as Brigan and was no fan of the cold, but to say it wasn't pretty?

"You're crazy!" Our burly squadmate, Cam, shook his head, showing off the dragon tattoo on his neck.

"Just look around," Solvai said, gesturing to the white-dusted field where we stood alongside this year's other Mage Hunter cadets. The snowy boughs of the cindercones surrounding the field were picturesque, the adjacent, iced-over mirror lake smooth like glass.

"It's true," another squadmate, Erik, agreed. "There's something magical about capturing a wintery landscape. I just want to paint all of it. I've never seen anything so lovely."

Erik pointed to the series of peaks surrounding the valley. They stood in a wide half circle, partially enclosing the field, lake, and trees on the north side. To the southeast, the towers of the Mage Hunter Academy rose gracefully into the clouds.

"You call *this* lovely?" Brigan lifted a mud-caked boot. Mucky footprints covered the ground where dozens of cadets milled about nearby.

"Give me a seashore over snow any day," Brigan insisted.

One of my other squadmates, a dark-haired girl named Edrea, added her two marks to the conversation. "Brigan's right, snow is far uglier than people give it credit for. It's almost tolerable up until the yuletide holiday, but after that? We're just biding our time waiting for it to scorch off."

Edrea blinked at Brigan a few times as if hoping he'd praise her for agreeing with him. Brigan didn't seem to notice, but Cam, Edrea's stepbrother, gave her a quizzical look.

"There something in your eye, sis?" he asked. Edrea glared at him.

"And another thing," Edrea doubled down. "Cold weather only adds to the struggle of all the skyfall refugees. Think about all those camps we passed on our journey here. How do you think they're holding up?"

I frowned. Edrea made a good point. It was common knowledge that more and more skyfalls—falling stars that brought both valuable skystone and wild, ether-hungry dragonkind to Evgard—were uprooting families, forcing them from their homes and into shabby camps where they were more likely to contract the shadow wasting. Umbral creatures lurked around these camps, spreading their strange, numbing sickness. As someone who'd grown up without a real home, my heart went out to the refugees.

Brigan snapped his fingers. "I just got a letter about that from my parents. They say Keep Kolbohr has offered to take in every refugee realm-wide who's been afflicted with the shadow wasting."

"All of them?" Erik's eyes widened.

"That's good of them," I said. Still, I couldn't help but wonder why the King and Queen of the Mining Keepdom would be willing to take on such a huge task.

As Brigan threw down a few more 'gauntlets' about the refugee situation, I looked around the circle. It was good to have my old squad surrounding me. We'd been through a lot together, and with Solvai, Brigan, Jax, and myself being part of the Black Valkyrie's entourage while the others were in the regular cadet program, we hadn't reunited since arriving at the Mage Hunter Academy until today.

I frowned as I realized our squad was missing one very important member.

"Where's Jax?" Cam asked, scanning the throng of other cadets. Everyone turned to me.

"I was about to ask the same thing," I said.

"Probably got held up doing push-ups somewhere," Brigan mumbled. The squad chuckled—they were all as aware as I was of Jax's vigorous workout habits and impressive muscles.

Well... maybe not *quite* as aware as I was.

"I'm sure he'll be along soon," Solvai put in. "He was in class with us this morning in Swan Spire."

Solvai was right. While Jax had been there for Jaira's lecture on the nine different magi types and how to spot them, this was the second week in a row that Vidya hadn't been present. In fact, ever since we returned to the Academy together after our discovery about the Farseer, I hadn't seen her even once.

I couldn't blame her for being upset and confused. Solrac was the Farseer... It was almost too much for me to take in, and I hadn't even known Solrac firsthand prior to our skirmish. Unsure what to do, I hadn't told another soul about what we'd learned in the High Ridgebacks. Not even Jax.

Still, I was getting anxious. I was worried about Vidya, of course, but there was also the matter of my mother. Vidya had promised to let me see her as soon as we returned. I didn't want to be insensitive, but I also didn't want to let her off the hook.

Suddenly, three of my squadmates broke into wide grins, and I did too. Looking around, I knew the other dragon riders on my squad had felt the shift in the air.

Musical, flute-like notes played in my heart. An ascending melody that was dangerously energetic.

That could only mean one thing.

I took hold of the golden-yellow heartscale hanging from a cord around my neck. Turning around, I saw a cluster of brightly colored dragons approaching from the direction of the Academy. Wingless drakes walked along the snowy ground, while the flying dragons, wyverns and evren, flew just above them. Against the white landscape, they looked striking and dignified.

That was, all but one.

I barely had time to put some distance between myself and the other cadets before the most blindingly bright dragon in the group barreled directly into me. My evren, Sniff, and I both went tumbling, leaving skid marks in the snow.

Despite the cold winter breeze, I couldn't help but laugh as Sniff joyfully licked my face. His fox-like features were eager, his four wings practically buzzing with excitement.

"Of course I missed you, boy." I rubbed him behind the ears and his expression went adorably slack, his tongue hanging out in contentment. The melody in my heart swelled through our bond.

Accompanying Sniff's flute-like communication, I felt a deep, resonant thrumming like a drum line. My smile widened. Sniff wasn't the only dragon I'd bonded.

Blink, I thought through the bond. I couldn't help myself—I runetraced.

A golden rune glowed over my forehead and the Sight promptly bloomed to life before my eyes.

As beautiful as the snowy scenery had been before, it dulled by comparison to what I could see now. Everything glowed with a brilliant misty aura, from the trees to the birds to the pale sky. Even the mountains themselves seemed to pulse with a stony gray light.

My squadmates' auras were even more dynamic. Each was so unique, from Edrea's proud royal purple cloud, or the regal red mist flowing around Brigan like a waterfall, to the gorgeous, feather-like cerulean encompassing Solvai. Near Solvai's core, I could even make out the white crystalline outline of her ether well, the source of her magi power.

But I was more focused on the exquisite silvery aura hovering just off to my side. The misty shape of a dragon, an evren like Sniff, was as clear to me as any living being. That was the thing about Blink—She was Sniff's twin sister who'd passed away. Still, her silvery spirit remained as my devoted companion in the ethereal plane. Likewise, her heartscale now hung around my neck, though I kept it on a longer cord than Sniff's so no one would notice it. Not even my best friends knew about Blink.

I laughed with contentment, feeling grateful for the ability to use my powers openly like this. Now that I was silvermarked, it didn't matter if I hid them. As a Rifter, my powers centered around various types of teleportation. This form of teleportation, like tiny portals for my eyes that let me view the spirit world, was the one I loved most. There was just so much going on all around us that we couldn't normally see.

"Cadets!" Our instructor's call resounded from across the field. "The new combat trainer will be here shortly. In the meantime, form up for your first training exercise! There are twenty-eight new cadets this cycle, so everyone needs to be part of a group of seven."

Chatter started up immediately as cadets scrambled to form groups. I let my rune dissolve into etherdust as my squadmates looked at one another.

"Seven," Solvai said. "Just like a squad. That's perfect."

"Sure is."

I stiffened at the sound of the unwelcome voice. The whole squad turned to the newcomer with skepticism, and more than one of us subconsciously reached toward our weapons.

Bjorn of Skullheim lumbered over to us, crossing his arms over his chest. His mohawk was as wild as the look in his eyes.

"Been far too long since I was part of old Squad Reckless." Bjorn smiled wickedly. "Last I checked, the lot of you were hurling mud and picking fights at every turn, barely able to hold your own seaxes. Look at you now."

"Our team's full, Bjorn," Solvai said, almost keeping the shake out of her voice. Bjorn fake lunged toward her, baring his teeth like some kind of animal. Solvai squeaked as she instinctively jumped backward.

"Works every time, eh, mighty squad captain?" Bjorn laughed cruelly. Solvai pressed her lips together, probably in an attempt to keep from tearing up. I balled my hands into fists.

"Solvai's twice the leader you'll ever be," Brigan said.

"Twice as defective of a human, you mean," Bjorn replied, pointing his jagged silver dagger toward Solvai's new Wildshaper silvermark. "Just like you, Misthaven. Sooty ethercursed."

Bjorn spat at the ground between Solvai and me. I grit my teeth—Experience had taught me to avoid provoking a dragonbull like Bjorn, but I couldn't help it.

"Solvai told you our team was full," Brigan said, more forcefully this time.

Bjorn's fingers tapped the hilt of his seaxe. "I always knew magi were less intelligent. They said to form groups of seven, and I only count six of you."

"Make that seven."

The whole squad breathed a major sigh of relief to see Jax approaching. Jax crossed his muscular arms, which were accentuated by his sleeveless tunic. He glared at Bjorn, clearly reminding him of the last time they'd brawled on our first day here at the Academy. Bjorn was fast and strong, but Jax was more than enough of a match for him.

For a moment, it looked like Bjorn was going to fight Jax again. Instead, he scoffed.

"None of you dirty magi are worth your weight in scales, anyhow." With that, Bjorn disappeared into the crowd of cadets to find another group.

The squad beamed at Jax, and Cam gave him a friendly punch on the arm.

"Where you been all morning?" Cam asked. "You missed our morning workout."

"Tell you later," Jax said to Cam. Meanwhile, I was already closing the distance to wrap my arms around my strapping sort-of boyfriend.

"Warning, I'm kind of—" Jax started. Too late, I realized it wasn't the sparse sunlight reflecting off of Jax's skin making him look shiny. Jax was covered in sweat, and now, so was I.

"Told you he was working out," Brigan said.

"Working out?" Jax cocked his head. Then he seemed to reconsider. "Uh, yeah. That's what I was doing. Working out."

I narrowed my eyes. Hadn't Cam just said Jax had missed their normal workout session? Despite the sweaty evidence, I wondered what Jax had really been up to.

Before I could ask, Erik piped up. "Jax, you've got to weigh in on Brigan's latest 'gauntlet down.' Snow—Do you find it pretty or forgettable?"

Everyone turned to Jax, but he didn't seem to be aware of any of them. His eyes were completely focused on me as he tucked a stray lock of stark white hair behind my ear.

"I think snow is absolutely beautiful," he said.

"Aww," Solvai cooed.

"Nicely done," Cam said with a nod of respect.

"Scorch," Brigan mumbled under his breath.

I was blushing something furious, but then a long whistle cut the moment short. A hush fell over the crowd as the newly formed groups of recruits turned their attention toward the south.

A dragon rider approached, proudly seated atop the stately back of a wingless, navy blue drake. The dragon wore regal black and white armor and was twice as large as most drakes, a clear indication he was already on his third and final ascension.

The rider was equally distinguished, wearing the finest ascension armor I had ever seen. Hundreds of navy and white scales had been worked directly into the dragonforged steel plate, the wide pauldrons cutting a majestic figure. The rider had a lethal-looking greataxe strapped to his back, and his chin-length blond curls and dignified gait made it clear he was some kind of noble.

At the sight of him, everyone in the field took a knee. Murmurs started up, and I kept hearing one name repeated over and over:

Mason Drakeslayer.

My eyes widened. Everyone across the realm had heard of High Prince Mason Drakeslayer, killer of some of the most dangerous wild dragons Evgard had to offer. Last I'd heard, he lay dying from some strange form of the deadly shadow wasting disease. What was he doing here at the Academy?

It was plain to see just how much the High Prince enjoyed everyone's adoration. He and his drake parted the crowd to stand at the edge of the frozen lake, facing the cadets.

He flashed a bright, confident smile, then held up a hand for silence. Not that anyone had been talking.

Once he'd paused sufficiently for effect, High Prince Mason finally spoke.

"Friends of the realm, come, gather 'round.
Let joy, great awe, and charm abound!
'Tis a pleasure to meet with you here near these lakes,
Now you all have met Mason, slayer of drakes."

I found the poem cheesy, but he delivered it with enough confidence that I applauded along with the rest of the cadets. Mason Drakeslayer blew a couple of over-the-top kisses to the crowd and I couldn't keep from raising an eyebrow. I made eye contact with Solvai, who was making the same face I was. We shared a chuckle.

"Silence, please, contain your adoration," Mason said. "What an honor it must be for you to be here in the Valley of the King's Rest standing before me. As some of you might've guessed, I, Mason Drakeslayer, son of High King Magnus and crown prince of Evgard, am here at the illustrious Mage Hunter Academy to be your new combat instructor."

More murmurs rippled through the applauding crowd. I could hardly believe my ears. Why would the High Prince want to teach at the Academy? Didn't he have... I don't know, 'matters of state' to attend to?

As if in response to my thoughts, Mason went on, "Some of you may find it odd that I would see to such things myself, but there's nothing more important to my noble father and myself than the well-being and protection of the people of Evgard. Besides, I daresay my reputation as a warrior precedes me."

With that, Mason slung his greataxe from his back and began to swing it in grand strokes. He and his dragon executed a turn so that we could all get the best view of Mason's agile display of skill. Then, still twirling his gleaming weapon, he expertly leaped from his drake's saddle to land in a mighty fighting pose. He lingered there as the group cheered once again, then an extra moment or two, as if hoping someone would carve his likeness in stone.

Finally, he straightened up.

"Well, what are you waiting for?" Mason tossed his fair curls. "Riders, mount your dragons! Everyone else, to the field! Let our first training exercise begin!"

The training exercise was simple enough. Three teams, dubbed 'Hunters,' chased the fourth team, dubbed 'magi,' in an attempt to corner and trap them in the field's central 'jail', marked by a circle of stones. It was a tricky, but surprisingly fun drill, especially since those of us who were dragon riders were allowed to ride, while those of us who were magi were allowed to use our etherarchy. Sniff and I swooped through the air in pursuit of our opponents.

They'd traded out our usual weapons for dulled practice blades, but other than that, we were practicing with the Mage Hunter's signature tool: silver. This gave every actual magi extra incentive not to get caught.

Rounding up the 'magi' team occasionally resulted in a quick spar, and with our high number of magi and our military background, Squad Reckless was a force to be reckoned with on the field. Between Jax's psionics and my rifting, people just couldn't get away, and Solvai's wings afforded her a better view of the field than anyone else.

With our captain, Solvai, calling the shots, we were able to round up the 'magi' team more quickly than any other. As a magi myself, I felt mildly uncomfortable about the concept of the game, but I played along, trying not to think too hard about its implications. Then again, maybe knowing how to catch other magi would actually come in handy, particularly when I considered people like those in the Coven of the Gray Ones.

Throughout the exercise, I couldn't help but cast the occasional glance toward the sidelines where High Prince Mason and his third ascension drake observed the field. The prince stroked his smooth chin thoughtfully, and I suddenly got the eerie feeling that he was watching me specifically.

I shook it off. That was ridiculous.

Finally, it was our turn to be the 'magi' team. Sniff and I raced all over the field as we dodged other riders and the odd dragon-less cadet whenever we flew close to the ground. I did my best to rift any of my squadmates out of danger when I could.

Prrring-a-ling! Sniff trilled happily through our bond. This was the perfect exercise for getting all of my evren's excess energy out.

I clung hard to the saddle as Sniff threw in a little double twist near the field's boundary. Solvai had landed nearby, doing battle with another cadet. She jabbed with her spear, the extra reach allowing her to disarm the swordfighter fairly easily.

Unfortunately, there was another foe sneaking up on her from behind—one with a mohawk and a set of wild, murderous eyes.

Bjorn loomed behind Solvai, ready to attack. The silver chain-whip in his hand gleamed.

Before I could react, he swung the silver whip forward, and as it wrapped around Solvai's leg. She fell to the ground, her wings disappearing into golden etherdust.

I felt bad that my friend had been captured, but then I noticed that Bjorn wasn't taking her to the jail. Instead, he stepped toward her, clutching his old silver dagger at the ready, now damaged from the encounter with Asher of Steel Rim back in Swan Spire. The ragged blade looked sharper and more painful than ever.

"Solvai!" I cried, sliding from Sniff's saddle as he coasted above the field. I landed hard on the ground, but remained on my feet as Solvai whirled to face Bjorn.

Bjorn was already almost within Solvai's guard. She tried to shake free of his silver chain whip, but he was strong and tall enough to easily grab her spear and wrench it from her grasp. A wicked grin on his face, Bjorn tossed the spear to the side.

"Hi there, dirty magi," Bjorn said. I ground my teeth and Solvai's eyes widened.

"Shift, Solvai!" I called. If Solvai could just wildshape into full falcon-drake form, I knew Bjorn wouldn't stand a chance.

"The silver," I barely heard Solvai mumble as she tried to free her leg. My blood was boiling—scorch Bjorn. He was clearly keeping her tied up as long as possible just to put her in pain.

I runetraced, opening a portal to try and disarm Bjorn. Bjorn saw it coming, and elbowed me hard in the face through my own portal, knocking me to the ground as a swipe from his silver dagger dissolved my portal into dust.

Drak, I thought as pain bloomed across my cheek. I hated feeling powerless against Bjorn's silver.

You do not have to be powerless, my wraith's voice rasped in my head.

Dizzy from the hard hit, I tried to get to my feet and dash to Solvai's side. Bjorn had returned his attention to my friend, who was now weaponless. He dragged her by the silver chain he had tied around her leg, yanking her closer as he tauntingly held the dagger over her.

"Let's see," Bjorn said cruelly. "Each type of magi keeps their sooty ether well in a different place. Mystic wells are in their heads, and Archon wells are in their chest. But you're a Sentinel, aren't you? Your power comes from your core. So to maximize how much this hurts, why don't I just put this here?"

Solvai screamed as Bjorn pressed the flat of his silver blade against her stomach. He wasn't stabbing flesh, but I knew firsthand what kind of icy agony Bjorn was putting my best friend through.

All while sadistically smiling.

Something snapped inside me. Overruling my cautious nature, I stretched my hand toward Bjorn, the other flying to runetrace. He snarled as he shoved Solvai away, his silver blade ready to stop my newly forming portal.

At once, the gold-rimmed tear ripped to life before him. But as Bjorn slashed at my portal to dissolve it once more, it changed. The gold suddenly shifted to a bright, sapphire blue, preserving the portal against the silver.

I felt my wraith flash through my mind—she was augmenting my power.

My fury fueled me as I reached through my blue portal to seize Bjorn's dagger. The silver didn't hurt me the way it should have as I tossed his sooty weapon as far as I could throw—right into the nearby lake.

Bjorn's jaw dropped almost as far as mine. What was I *doing*? Panic flooded me, and I rapidly shut down my portal and the corresponding rune. The blue vanished and, with a degree of difficulty, I pushed my wraith from my mind once more.

My heart was thudding wildly, my adrenaline out of control. Though she was no longer channeling her power through me, I could hear my Gray One's raspy laughter reverberating inside my head.

See? That wasn't so bad, now was it? Untold power lies at your fingertips, Meleya. Next time, you need not fear using it.

Bjorn was still looking at me in stunned silence. I set my jaw, gripping my seaxe as I prepared for him to make another move.

Instead, his lip curled into a smile as he turned toward the sidelines. I followed his gaze to where Mason Drakeslayer was standing, watching my every move.

My heart leaped. My dark portal had been so small and insignificant, but had the High Prince seen what I'd done?

"M-Meleya?" Solvai croaked from the ground. She was blinking in confusion, which made me hopeful that she'd at least missed my display. In the distance, I saw a few other members of my squad heading our way to assist her.

"Bye bye, skymage," Bjorn said with a dark smile before hurrying away.

Skymage? I wondered. Where had I heard that word before?

Soon after that, Mason wrapped up the training exercise. Our squadmates fretted over Solvai and me, but we assured them we were fine. Jax was furious when he saw the bruise on my head, and I was afraid he planned to find and take down Bjorn then and there.

But the idea of Bjorn telling Jax about my use of blue etherarchy filled me with dread, so I kept reassuring Jax that my head was fine and that we should let the instructors choose how to discipline Bjorn. He didn't like it, but agreed to not make a big deal about it as long as I promised to go see the Academy healer right away.

The squad somewhat pacified, we headed back to the dorm for a break before our evening class. I still felt raw and a little afraid after what had happened on the field, and found myself gravitating toward the triangular room's comforting fireplace.

I was just beginning to warm up when I realized I wasn't alone.

"Afternoon, Meleya!" called a chipper, lightly accented voice. Shaya sat on the rug with her legs crossed, beaming up at me. "Solei's blade! You look like you just saw a ghost!"

Maybe I did, I thought. At least, I might've *heard* one.

Shaya patted the ground beside her and I took a seat, curious as to what she was up to. The redheaded girl had a large wicker basket in front of her filled with thick, slightly shimmery black thread. One string trailed from a large ball of silky yarn and onto a pair of needles. The needles seemed to be made of crystal, and they shone in the flickering firelight.

"What are you making?" I asked.

Shaya grinned. "A shawl for a friend. Like it so far?"

I examined the delicate black design that'd been produced by her quick-moving needles. The pattern seemed to contain hundreds of tiny falling stars.

"Very much," I said. As Shaya worked, I noticed for the first time her pair of lacy black gloves.

"Did you make your gloves as well?" I asked.

"Oh." Shaya paused momentarily as she looked at the gloves. "Uh, yes I did. Not entirely on purpose, but yes."

I raised an eyebrow by way of an invitation for Shaya to elaborate, but instead, she breezed ahead.

"How was combat class with the other new cadets? I heard they've brought in Mason Drakeslayer himself as the instructor. Can you believe that? What's he like? Is he as handsome as they say?"

"Uh," I started, "he's fine, I guess. If you like the fair-haired, self-important type."

Shaya laughed like I'd just said the funniest thing in the world. "I suppose you prefer the muscular, smirking type."

"Smirking?" I turned to look at Jax, who was on the other side of the room doing hanging sit-ups. He'd telekinetically charged the two handles of his axes in order to use them as a bar, suspended in mid air. Jax counted the reps under his breath, and I noticed Jaira watching his impressive form out of the corner of her eye.

When Jax saw me looking, he gave me a cocky little half-smile before continuing his workout.

Shaya giggled. "Smirking."

My cheeks reddened as I forced myself to stop watching Jax, returning my gaze to Shaya and her knitting.

"Where were you during combat class?" I asked. "You're a new cadet too, right? Same as the rest of us."

"I ditched on principle," Shaya said. "I refuse to participate in silly games that promote more anti-magi propaganda."

"Really?" I said, my mouth falling open.

Shaya sighed. "Not really, no. Though I wish I was that brave. Someone ought to teach these sooty Mage Hunters their place. Or better yet, the sooty High King." Shaya knitted with extra vigor.

My eyes widened and I couldn't help but glance to my left and right to make sure nobody had overheard Shaya's rebellious outburst. Obviously, part of me agreed with her, but still. People like us got executed for saying less than that.

"No, I only missed the training because I have a sort of... on-campus job." Shaya shrugged.

Before I could ask anything further, Shaya paused her knitting and shut her eyes. A soft smile appeared on her face, then she continued weaving the threads.

"What were you doing?" I asked.

"Oh." Shaya blushed. "You might laugh at me."

I cocked my head.

"It's just... I like to imagine I'm weaving happy memories into every piece I make. I was picturing the time I bonded my wyvern."

I noted the reddish-gold heartscale hanging from Shaya's neck and smiled.

That's when I felt a tap on my shoulder. I looked up to see a timid, ruddy-haired young man.

"Lothar?" I asked, recognizing Jaira's Hunting partner.

"Hello, Meleya," Lothar said, shuffling his feet. "I have a message for you from the High Prince." Shaya cocked her head at that.

My muscles tensed as I recalled a conversation between Lothar and me after the Winter Solstice battle. While visiting me in the medical sanctuary, Lothar had told me about how he'd been the personal servant to High Prince Mason before the shadow wasting had taken his lord. Now that he was well again, it seemed that Lothar had gotten his old job back.

Lothar went on, sounding a little nervous. "If you'll just come with me."

Shaya waved and returned to her knitting as I followed Lothar out of our dorm.

High Prince Mason's office was twice the size of any other instructor's, excluding the Black Valkyrie's tower, of course. Rich, navy blue drapes trimmed with white that matched the High Prince's ascension armor covered the walls, as did fancy paintings of Mason and his father, High King Magnus. The finely carved, cushioned chair I sat on probably cost three times as much as the entirety of my family's possessions back during our days traveling with the nomadic caravans.

Mason sat across from me at a grand diamondoak desk, leaning on his armrest as if posing for a portrait. He looked at me with knit brows, presumably thinking he looked handsome and officious that way. A long, uncomfortable silence stretched between us as he pursed his lips, trying to stare into my soul or something. I kept glancing off to the sides, my hands sweaty as I gripped my chair. I'd never had a meeting with a High Prince before. Was I supposed to talk first? Bow every once in a while?

Finally, the High Prince spoke.

"Sorry about that head wound," he said. "What a bother. I find Bjorn incredibly driven, but a bit on the manic side, don't you think?"

"Uh, yeah," I replied. Was I legally allowed to disagree with a High Prince?

Mason Drakeslayer continued. "I'll get right down to business. I'm sure you're more than a little curious as to why someone like myself would be here at the Academy, especially in light of my recent condition."

I nodded. "I heard you were sick."

"I was. Very sick, with an… *intense* case of the shadow wasting after my quest to slay the fearsome northern frostdrake went awry. But, despite this, my quest was successful!"

He paused as if waiting for me to applaud or throw myself at his feet in awe. I awkwardly smiled and clasped my hands together as I gave another nod.

High Prince Mason seemed to accept this. He leaned forward over the desk, his brows knit in that ridiculous way of his as he whispered to me.

"You are part of the reason I'm here, Meleya of Misthaven. You see, I know what you want most."

Swallowing, I said, "You do?"

Mason chuckled before launching into another poem.

"The thing you crave, fair Snowstorm, more than any other
Is to reunite yourself with your dear father and sweet mother."

My mouth fell open as Mason produced a pair of official-looking pieces of folded paper. He dropped them onto the desk, gesturing for me to take a look.

A quick scan of the pages sent my pulse racing. I didn't comprehend all of the elaborate phrasing, but a few words stuck out to me:

Ivar of Stonekeep
Freya of Ash Flats
Known magi
Charges dropped
Freedom

"Freedom," I said aloud. "These... these are freedom papers for my parents."

"They're yours," Mason said with a brilliant grin. "Registration for both your parents. Once I sign these, they'll be free to roam the realm without question, living wherever and however they desire. There's even a clause about a bit of monetary compensation for time lost in prison."

I could hardly believe my ears. Freedom and stability for my parents—a real life, without fear—was all I'd ever wanted.

"And it's yours," Mason went on. "That is, if you give me what I want in return."

"Anything," I found myself saying.

"I thought you'd say that. Now—" Mason paused for dramatic effect, "tell me, Meleya of Misthaven. I work with someone who some call 'the Soul Reaper.' But those of use who understand his true mission call him the Surgeon. Ever heard of him?"

At the sound of the name, the lavish office seemed to get a few degrees colder.

The wraith in my head hissed, and I could tell she knew about this man as well. Besides that, the weight of the voidshard sitting inside my rift hold seemed to burn. It was as if the voidshard had heard its master's name and wanted to get to him.

My wraith whispered in my head, *No. The shard is ours.*

"I can see that you have." Mason's lip quirked up. "Good. Soon, all of Evgard will know him. The Surgeon is a very powerful man—perhaps the most powerful in the realm, second only to myself and my father. The Gray Ones themselves revere him. I trust I don't need to explain who the Gray Ones are to you... Isn't that right, Snowstorm?"

I swallowed. Mason had definitely seen my display of dark ether on the field today. Soot. Had he asked Bjorn to provoke me?

My voice came out very small. "Why are you telling me this?"

Mason leaned onto his elbows, his brows knit in what felt like a pretense of concern. "The Surgeon has lost something incredibly valuable to him. Something personal. A certain shard of crystal: long, thin, and glowing with powerful blue light."

My blood ran cold.

"It's called a voidshard, the token of his bond with his Gray One," Mason went on, staring directly into my eyes. "This voidshard was taken from the Soul Reaper, and he wants it back."

Soot.

Soot.

My heart was thundering so loudly I was certain Mason could hear it. Did he know?

Mason plowed ahead. "The voidshard's last known location was an extremely well-guarded cavern within an old, hidden lava tube in the Dragon Mists. Theft from such a venue should've been impossible."

I exhaled, realizing I must've imagined the accusatory light in Mason's eyes. Maybe he *didn't* know I had the very voidshard he was referencing.

In my rift hold.

Right now.

In my head, my wraith laughed.

I, on the other hand, did everything in my power to keep my expression as neutral as possible.

Mason explained, "We—that is, the Surgeon, has already sent a few servants to the cavern to do some digging. They tried to pull memories from the umbral creatures that once protected the shard, but dumb umbral minds are unreliable at best. Broken. Borderline feral. Meanwhile, the Gray One in whose custody the shard was entrusted was somehow destroyed. His essence is so scattered throughout the ethereal plane that it will likely take decades for him to reform."

I shuddered as I remembered watching the wraith do battle with the Farseer in the very cavern Mason was referring to. Those umbral creatures and that wraith would've killed Jax and me if the Farseer hadn't come.

"We did, however, find a clue." Mason put a hand to his chin. "The bodies of two Drekai men were found in the cavern. We've long known that the people of the Dragon Isles have sought the Surgeon's voidshard, but it appears that one may have finally succeeded. These two Drekai had a third companion—a woman. In fact, this is part of why your insight will be so valuable. According to reports, you and your squad encountered this same Drekai woman while on patrol at Outcast Outpost's North Tower."

I furrowed my brow as I realized what Mason was saying.

"She has beige-colored scales on her face and the tips of her ears," Mason said, "and wields a boomerang—a Drekai *kalaata*—with an edge of lightwielding ether. She goes by the name Zyri."

"Z-Zyri?" I repeated. Sweat beaded along my temples as I fought to keep my face even, my mind replaying Zyri's death. The woman who'd saved Jax and me multiple times, and whom I'd come to think of as a friend, sinking beneath the still, black water in that desolate cavern at the hand of that wraith—That was why they hadn't found her body.

Drak, I suddenly realized. *Mason and the Soul Reaper don't know Zyri is dead.* Nobody knew—Well, nobody but Jax and me.

Mason was looking to me for a response. Desperate to come across as casually curious, I stammered, "The Surgeon thinks uh... that this Zyri woman has his voidshard then?"

Mason nodded. "She seems the most likely suspect. The shard is still connected to the Soul Reaper's consciousness, though the visions it shows him are shrouded in mist. He is quite certain that a woman possesses the shard, though he cannot see her face. For now, your only lead is the Drekai Zyri."

"*My* only lead?"

Mason chuckled again. "Yes. See, if you want these..." He plucked the two folded pieces of official-looking paper from my hands, "...we first need *you* to locate the Soul Reaper's voidshard."

"Me?" I protested. "Why me? I'm no tracker, I'm a soldier."

"And one of the only Rifters in the realm, thanks to my mad grandmother's Rifter purge. Thanks to her, we find ourselves in need of someone proficient in the Sight."

Mason stood, then slowly began pacing alongside his desk. He held my full attention as if he were a prowling cougardrake; I had to fight the urge to reach for my seaxe.

Then Mason did something totally unexpected. He raised a finger, then carefully traced the rune for the Sight himself. To my shock, blue light trailed from his finger and the rune soon shone upon his forehead.

"What in the..." I started. "You're a Rifter too?"

Mason shrugged, clearly enjoying my stunned response. "Only recently. Becoming a skymage was part of my recovery from my illness."

"What do you mean recently?" I cocked my head. "You don't *choose* to be a magi, you're either born with an ether well or you're not."

Mason gave a dark half-smile. "Or you *acquire* an ether well. Ascend your soul, similar to how a dragon does."

I could hardly comprehend that. Mason had chosen to become a magi by somehow obtaining an ether well? It suddenly occurred to me that maybe this was how the Black Valkyrie had been able to channel three different kinds of power. She, like Mason, was the very thing Bjorn had called me on the field today when he'd seen me use blue etherarchy.

"Skymage," I said, my voice practically inaudible. I remembered what Lothar had told me back in Keep Rengard: that skymages were ancient magi with multiple or augmented powers. I'd assumed they were born that way, but apparently it was more like dragon ascension.

And somehow, it was all tied to the Gray Ones.

I frowned at Mason, speaking slowly. "If you're a Rifter now, then why don't you use the Sight yourself to find Zy—the Drekai woman?"

Mason's countenance grew disappointed. "The Surgeon had hoped for this, but alas, the ether well now tethered to my soul is weak. Shriveled to a husk from years of underuse. I can hardly access my powers without becoming exhausted, not to mention this scorching headache you Mystics always seem to get."

Mason put a hand to his head, wincing as he let his rune dissolve.

Despite the ominous nature of our conversation, I felt a pang of sympathy. After a quick scan of the room, I spotted a pitcher of water and a few goblets beside it. I probably should've asked first, but without thinking, I got up and poured the High Prince a drink.

"Try this," I said, passing him the goblet. "Drinking more water and taking a bit of a rest always helps with ether overuse headaches. You could also look into getting a quartz crystal to store extra ether for moments of need."

I showed Mason the glowing, white quartz tied to my belt. It had been a gift from Jax when I was first learning about my powers, and had saved my life more than once on the battlefield.

"Thank you," Mason said, taking a drink. His brows knit again, only this time, his expression seemed genuine. For a moment, it even looked like he was confused as to what he was doing here.

Then, just as quickly, he shook his head, his gaze hardening. His brows furrowed with anger, and I took a cautious step backward.

"Focus," Mason half-muttered, half-snarled to himself, his voice lower than before. He roughly set down the goblet as he squeezed his eyes shut.

"Are you okay?" I asked.

Then Mason straightened, blinking at me as if nothing strange had happened.

"As I said, the Sight can be a unique tool for spying," Mason said, pursing his lips once again. I was concerned, but listened intently as he went on. "As the son of Magnus, the Great Uniter, the greatest king this realm has ever known, I ask you: Will you help us restore the voidshard to its proper owner?"

I glanced longingly at the freedom papers Mason had set back down on the desk. A real life for my parents was all I'd ever wanted. I'd joined the guard at thirteen for the chance to free them. When that hadn't worked, I'd relied on the Knights of the Torch, but that had failed too.

Now, the key to solving all my troubles was hidden within my rift hold... Still, I hated the idea of someone blackmailing me for my powers. Not to mention, I knew that Zyri wasn't the woman the Soul Reaper was looking for.

I was.

As much as I hated to admit it to myself, the thought of returning the voidshard seemed relieving. The nightmares, the burden, the fear... it would all go away.

It would take some fancy storytelling to explain to Mason why I had it, but between that and my parents' freedom, it was hard to see a good reason *not* to give up the shard right now.

Keep the shard, my wraith rasped. *The power is ours.*

For a terrible second, the power tempted me. It had felt good being able to channel etherarchy despite Bjorn's silver.

But the real reason I couldn't give up the voidshard was the simple fact that Zyri had died for this. She'd given her life trying to get this thing to the Drekai empress, and soot, I couldn't let her sacrifice be in vain. No, I couldn't give the shard back to the Soul Reaper, the very person Zyri said was the Gray Ones' most dangerous weapon. The realm might depend on it.

Mason was still waiting for a response. He leaned forward, speaking in an almost comforting way. "We all need to do our part in these trying times, as even more skyfalls threaten our peace and safety. Your home keepdom, the Canyonlands, holds out in their war against the Drekai. The northern Keepdom of Kolbohr is accepting refugees with the shadow wasting. This is your part to play, Meleya. Help the Surgeon. Find his voidshard and return it to him so that we can finally stand against the perils we face."

I cautiously opened my mouth. "What happens if I refuse to help?"

Mason shrugged, nonchalantly picking up my parents' freedom papers in one hand and slinging his greataxe off his back with the other.

"As you ponder which path you wish to choose
Think of what—or who—you stand to lose."

High Prince Mason couldn't have been more clear if he'd threatened my parents with execution at his own hand.

Heart pounding, I replied, "When do I start?"

Mason broke into another winning smile. "We were hoping you'd say that."

Fragment: The Apprentice

JAIRA

The moment the new ether well connected to her soul, Jaira could feel the ascension of her power coursing through her. Normally, the Surgeon used dreamweave etherarchy to put his patients to sleep during soul surgery, but not Jaira. She'd opted to remain fully conscious. That way, she could glean every bit of information possible from the Surgeon's process.

She was glad she had. She could feel her Gray companion working to fuse the new ether well into place. The rush was sublime—even more so than when she had received her first ether well.

Captain Cenrik, the undercover Knight of the Torch, had been a powerful Lightwielder. Thanks to the Surgeon, all of Cenrik's power belonged to Jaira. And now, she'd doubled that power. She had a second ether well, taken from an Astromancer Knight of the Torch who'd been captured on the field of battle.

Jaira thought gleefully, *Everyone who said this outlander girl would never amount to anything can eat soot.*

If only they could see us now, Shisya thought from deep within Jaira's mind.

Shisya had found Jaira and spoken to her for the first time back in Ghost Lake last year. While some feared the Gray Ones, Jaira had welcomed Shisya's presence, accepting her voidshard, the token of their bond, very soon after they'd met.

"There, our eager apprentice," the Surgeon's doubled voice echoed. "It is time to try out your new abilities."

Tingling with energy, Jaira let Shisya into her mind as she sat up. She dug deep, her irises already flashing bright blue. A blast of blue-tinged pure ether shot from her fingertips. The pulse hit the nearest wall, sending spiraling marks spreading out in every direction.

Astromancy. Now Jaira would be more than enough of a match for that arrogant, dragon-eyed Knight of the Torch, Asher.

Together, Jaira and Shisya inhaled deeply. A rush of giddiness flooded them at the feeling, and Shisya's laughter was enough to get Jaira chuckling under her breath as well.

Ah, what it is to feel *alive,* Shisya mused.

"We are glad to see that the surgery was a success," the Surgeon said. The great Soul Reaper—or rather, the Surgeon—stood above Jaira. He had many names and titles, but they all described this man. His thin face was blank as always, his eyes glittering with a fragmented, sapphire blue glow. His gray robes trailed to the ground, where they ended in tattered threads.

"Tell us," the Surgeon continued, "can you channel voidglass?"

Eager to please, Jaira and Shisya focused together. But while they'd been able to produce ether blasts with ease, their ability to turn pure ether into concrete, crystalline, blue starglass was limited. All they could manage was to create little glass shards that fell to the floor, dissolving into etherdust on impact.

"It is just as well," the Surgeon said with clear disappointment. "Skill with voidglass is not necessary for you, my apprentice."

From there, the Surgeon put away his tools—sharp blades forged from the most delicate voidglass Jaira had ever seen. They were enchanted so that they did not cut flesh, but spirit.

"Walk with me," the Surgeon said. Jaira eagerly slid from the operating table and fell into step beside her master.

Together, they strode along the upper balcony, leaving the laboratory portion of the Surgeon's lair behind. The soul surgery lab was in a loft, overlooking the rest of the lair: the observatory.

The high, curved glass panels of the observatory ceiling let in the light of billions of stars. An enormous telescope dominated the room, but there was still plenty of room for the Surgeon's hoard of skystone.

Jaira was impressed every time she saw it—the largest stockpile of skystone the realm over. From shelves to tables to large swaths of the floor, everything was covered with the brilliant, ether-generating crystals.

Some were large, nearly half as long as Jaira was tall. Others were as tiny as Jaira's pinkie nail.

All pulsed with pure, untapped ether.

The nobility of Evgard believed the skystone tribute they paid to the capital went to the High King. But Jaira knew the High King had given it all to the Surgeon as payment for reviving his son, Mason. The Surgeon was the one with the real power.

The Surgeon took his place at the base of the telescope. He adjusted it, then squinted through the eyepiece. Jaira monitored his every action.

"See anything?" she asked.

"The Dire Wolf and Dragon networks grow closer," the Surgeon said. "Soon, the Phoenix constellation will join them. The time for the convergence draws near. We must be prepared when it comes. This opportunity comes but once a millennium."

Jaira was dying to ask for more information regarding the convergence. Why was it so important? And more importantly, what did the Surgeon plan to do when it came?

But she knew better than to press him for information. The fewer who knew of the Surgeon's plans, the better chance they had of succeeding. Besides, even Shisya feared the Surgeon, calling him a Guardian. But Jaira knew that the Surgeon—while powerful—was no Guardian. Not yet. There was still one ether well he lacked: A Seer's well.

Once, Jaira had asked why the Surgeon didn't simply pluck a Seer from anywhere throughout the realm and take his or her ether well for his own. Surely, with the Mage Hunters and even the High King under his thumb, the Surgeon could find one easily. But the Surgeon had scoffed. He would not allow just any Seer's well to complete his set of nine.

Jaira recalled the Surgeon's words: "That was our mistake last time," he'd said, angry fire in his double-toned voice. "But not even the great Farseer can stand against us without his own ether well."

That was the real reason the Black Valkyrie and her entourage, including Jaira, had spent months pursuing the Farseer across the Badlands. Oh, the High King had thought the legendary Farseer's ether well was destined for his son, Mason. But that had merely been a ploy to get High King Magnus to allow the Mage Hunters' most elite to take on the job of capturing him.

"A pity the Black Valkyrie was unable to overcome the Farseer when she had the chance in Keep Drakfell," the Surgeon mused. "She seems oddly unmotivated of late, do you not agree?"

"Yes," Jaira said. "She's different. Ever since returning from the High Ridgebacks she's been... unstable. Confused. Something strange happened up there, I'm sure of it."

It was true. The Black Valkyrie had once been Jaira's hero. She'd wanted to become just like her. But now... now Jaira wanted *more*.

"The Black Valkyrie will remember where her priorities lie," the Surgeon said, continuing to gaze at the night sky through the telescope. "We are certain of it. Her hate is strong. It will fuel her to destroy the Knights of the Torch, and then, once our poetic little High Prince and his Gray One find and return our voidshard, nothing will stop us."

A scream made Jaira jump. She'd nearly forgotten someone else was up here in the laboratory. A man lay partially unconscious, strapped to an operating table with silver manacles. He had a silvermark on his left cheek, and wore a distinct red cloak—another Knight of the Torch they'd brought in after a battle with the Capital Riders.

"Do not worry, friend," the Surgeon said. "We have not forgotten you."

His long gray robes swept behind him as he and Jaira returned to the lab.

Jaira watched with fascination, noting every detail, just as she had with her own soul surgeries.

First, the Surgeon's skin glowed with vivid blue Sentinel markings. The magi struggled against his silver bonds, but the Surgeon used woodweaving etherarchy to produce a gas that paralyzed him once more. Jaira noted the way the Surgeon's iris grew to fill his eye as wildshaping strengthened his vision. He accessed Geomancy as well, flattening small bits of silver into thin-plated mirrors so that he could work with more precision.

Runes in blue light strung out across his forehead as the Rifter's Sight allowed him to see the patient's ether well in the spirit plane. His tools floated to and from his hands telekinetically using his psionic abilities. They were made of voidglass, something Jaira would learn to make herself soon. The Surgeon then lined the blades of the tools with an edge of forged light—lightwielding ether to make them sharp enough to cut the patient's very soul. She watched closely as another rune lit up over his forehead, infusing his tools with dream energy and somehow causing them to become ghostly.

There was no blood as the Surgeon worked, of course. Souls didn't bleed, and his patients' physical bodies remained fully intact throughout the process. The Surgeon was bent over the man's chest. This magi was an Archon, which meant his ether well was tethered to his spirit at his heart.

As the Surgeon made a particularly deep incision to the man's soul, Jaira saw the Knight twitch.

"Voids," the Surgeon cursed. A set of metal-and-light-ether tongs psionically floated to the Surgeon's hand, and he used the tool to reach into the man's chest.

When he withdrew the tongs, they held a misty, translucent object. It looked like a plum-sized crystal, filled with glowing white energy. The magi's ether well.

With a flourish of his hand, the Surgeon used Astromancy to produce a blue-tinted starglass jar. He hurriedly placed the ether well inside, then sealed it shut.

While the well itself was white with raw ether, Jaira noted a few pale green clouds surrounding it. Remnants of the magi's aura. But more interesting than that was the long crack running from the top of the crystal to its bottom.

The Surgeon cursed again. "Another broken well. Do you know what this means?"

"Its power will be divided," Jaira said, hungry to prove she'd paid attention to previous lessons.

The Surgeon nodded his approval. Then, he and Jaira watched as the man on the table took one final, ragged breath before going still. Even with all the Surgeon's experience, Jaira knew that the process of soul surgery was tenuous at best, and that one mistake could result in the death of the patient. Those who survived the process were sent to the Asylum hidden beneath the Mage Hunter Academy. Those who didn't...

Tapping into his shadowbinding, the Surgeon used the disintegrating power of black shadowfire to dispose of the man's body.

Jaira knew she should've felt sorry for the dead man, but she was just so awestruck by the sheer power of the Surgeon. That kind of power could rewrite the rules of their society.

To think we ever admired the Black Valkyrie, Jaira's wraith, Shisya, thought. *The Surgeon is infinitely stronger.*

"Such a busy night." The Surgeon sighed, gazing through the glass panels to the star-studded night sky as the hissing black shadowfire slowly ebbed away. "We must visit our mines. And you, Lightbane, ought to return to the Academy."

"Let me come with you," Jaira pleaded, desperate to learn everything she could.

The Surgeon put a hand to his chin. "Hmm... Not even the Black Valkyrie has been to the mines. We have feared the sight of them would be too much for her."

"I'm stronger than she is," Jaira rushed to promise. "She hasn't fully accepted the Gray the way I have. You know it's true."

The Surgeon stared at Jaira a moment more, as if reading her soul. Jaira's wraith made her fingers tingle.

"Very well, our eager apprentice." With that, the Surgeon opened a portal and beckoned for Jaira to accompany him through.

The mines of Keep Kolbohr were deep and dim.

The miners worked in silence but for the clinking of their tools echoing up and down the wide, cavernous shaft. They moved slowly but consistently, going about their work without so much as turning their heads when Jaira and the Surgeon arrived.

It didn't take long for Jaira to see why the sight of the mines would put off even the Black Valkyrie. The workers looked like veritable ghosts. Their hair, skin, even their eyes... everything was gray.

Victims of the shadow wasting, Jaira realized with a degree of bitterness. Their weakness was what led them to this fate, doomed to never amount to anything.

Jaira felt a stab of hatred for the miners as they pushed wheelbarrows full of glowing stone upward and out of the caverns. More skystone for the Surgeon. Skystone that must've fallen thousands of years ago and become buried deep within the earth.

"Ah," the Surgeon said. "Right on time, as usual."

Jaira turned to see a pair of people approaching. The two of them wore long, gray robes and indistinct, featureless masks. Masks Jaira recognized as the mark of members of the Coven of the Gray Ones.

It was true, Jaira had fought alongside the Black Valkyrie against the Coven in Rengard. But that was only because their leader, the Liberator, had been overzealous, accumulating power in hopes of displacing the Wraith King—the Surgeon's bond.

The very thought had made Shisya laugh. *None is greater than the Wraith King,* she always said. Jaira had to agree.

Once the masked pair reached Jaira and the Surgeon they removed their gray hoods and masks, revealing the jeweled crowns they wore. Jaira knew they were in the Mining Keepdom of Kolbohr, which meant this could only be that keepdom's king and queen.

Jaira couldn't stop the smile from spreading across her face. This girl from small-town Whitestone Hall was now among the realm's most powerful players, in on conversations with kings and queens.

"Your majesties," the Surgeon said, though Jaira noticed he didn't bow. Neither did Jaira.

The king of Kolbohr gave a nod. "More skyfall refugees with the shadow wasting arrived this morning as expected. We've already put them to work in the deep tunnels. It's dangerous, but there were many new arrivals, so we can stand to lose a few."

"What a great service you are providing the realm." The Surgeon gave a vacant smile. "Giving these poor, suffering people a purpose."

Suddenly, a violent roar split the air. Jaira jumped at the sight of a wild, feral wyvern clawing its way into the cavern. It was clearly hungry for the ether in the skystone.

The wyvern thrashed, and several shadow-wasted miners fell down the long, empty shaft without so much as a scream. Within moments, Kolbohr soldiers in brown cloaks and Coven masks used crossbows to shoot the wild dragon down.

To Jaira's surprise, the emotionless, gray laborers resumed their work without missing a beat.

"Everything is under control," the king went on as if nothing had happened. "The odd wild dragon, but nothing we can't handle. The workers bring in more skystone every day."

"This pleases us," the Surgeon said, his doubled voice echoing down the mineshaft. "When the comet comes, we will be ready. At long last, the Gray Age is nearly upon us."

ASHER

Riding a kirin was nothing like riding Thorn. With Thorn, I felt like we were one as we soared through the skies. But with these dragon horses, there was no bond, no thrill, and no sky. These particular kirin were wingless, and it was tricky getting used to riding my dappled gray through the winding paths of the Ridgeback Mountains.

Gripping the reins, I followed Boone's lead through the snowy woods toward Aura Ridge. His stark white hair made for the perfect camouflage here, and even his multi-hued, tan dragonscale cloak blended in with the tree trunks. It was a good thing he was riding a black dragon horse, otherwise I'd never have been able to follow him.

Meanwhile, Ivar rode up beside me, tugging on the reins of his chestnut brown kirin. Behind him rode at least two dozen more kirin from Rhana's stables, saddled and ready to transport any new Rebel Knight recruits we might get today.

Boone and Ivar had already been out on a few of these recruiting missions, but this was my first time. At first, I'd been hesitant about coming along. They didn't need my help assessing potential Rebel Knight soldiers and bringing them to the safehouse; that was for more experienced people with a knack for leadership. Still, for whatever reason, Boone had insisted I come, saying it's what Solrac wanted. Apparently, before he disappeared, Solrac had been strangely invested in having me take on a more serious role among the Rebel Knights of the Torch. He said the Farseer himself requested it, though I couldn't imagine why. I was put on the team as 'the distraction.' Besides, with ears and eyes like mine, I didn't exactly inspire trust.

Beside me, Ivar let out a heaving sigh.

"Can't believe Mels is just over that ridge and through the Valley of the King's Rest," he said, "and I can't do nothin' 'bout it."

I followed Ivar's gaze, and sure enough, I recognized the mountains surrounding the Mage Hunter Academy.

"Sure as scales you can't!" Boone called over his shoulder. "Ain't no one allowed outta the safehouse without a cleared mission from Rhana. Such is for the best, what with your li'l girl bein' with them scorched Mage Hunters. Rhana hates them Hunters drak near as much as I do."

"Still..." Ivar cast another longing gaze eastward.

Boone's demeanor softened. "Ain't no need to worry about your girl. From what I've seen, she's tougher'na fang tortoise under the desert sun. 'Sides, she's got Jax workin' undercover in there with her, and I'd bet my most prized possession—this 'ere dragonscale cloak—that he'll keep her safe."

Ivar gave a small smile. "I've only met Jax once, but I get the feelin' you're right about that."

"Why?" I asked, genuinely baffled as to why any father would think his daughter was safe with someone as careless as Jax.

Ivar chuckled. "'Cause Mels and Jax are—"

"Scorchin' scat-beetles!" Boone suddenly cried out. "That there's the last cairn! We'll be at the Aura Ridge safehouse in less'n two shakes of a craghopper's tail!"

Boone gave a whistle, causing the group of dragon horses to pick up the pace. I was about to spur mine forward as well when I noticed Ivar give one last wistful glance toward the Mage Hunter Academy.

I could hardly blame him. After all, I found my thoughts wandering to the Academy more and more often these days myself.

I couldn't seem to get that envelope out of my head—the one with Mom's name written on it. The more I thought about it, the more certain I felt that it held answers regarding her untimely death. The curiosity was killing me, and more than once I'd not-so-casually brought up the idea of going back for it to Kai.

Every time, Kai had shut the idea down. Obtaining the letter didn't make logical sense, Rhana's rules specifically forbade it, and it would be better for me to forget all about it anyway. Each conversation ended with Kai saying the same thing: Don't go back to that tower.

I shook my head. Both Ivar and I needed to get our minds off of the Academy.

"So Ivar," I said as the two of us followed Boone and the dragon horses. "You and Boone seem pretty close."

Ivar nodded. "Boone and I traversed the realm from Keep Rengard to the safehouse, all the while keepin' wild dragons from torchin' our little group of former prisoners, every one of 'em magi. We must've attracted every dragon from the Scorchwind Desert through to the Southern Ridgebacks. I was glad to have a skilled dragon slayer like Boone at my side."

"You're both snowheads from the north," I said. "Any relation?"

"Nah," Ivar said. "But I never really knew my father—ditched when he learned I was a magi. 'S'why I've been thinkin' of adoptin' Boone there as my unofficial dad.

"Hey Boone!" Ivar called out, hands cupped around his mouth. "My li'l Mels could use an honorary grandpa! You in?"
Boone let out a loud, long whoop. "Done always wanted a family! Now come on, you two poky li'l dragonpups! Safehouse is just 'round this 'ere bend!"

Right on cue, the snow-covered trees parted to reveal a large, wooden structure built atop a majestic mountain peak. The peak overlooked a gorgeous valley, with the building perched precariously on the edge. In fact, it looked like half of the lodge extended over the empty space.

I grinned. This was my kind of safehouse.

In black paint over the door I read the words 'The Gallant Gopherdrake,' accompanied by an image of the most dapper-looking little gopherdrake I'd ever seen.

"It's a tavern," I muttered, recollecting that most, if not all, of the Knights's safehouses I'd been to had all been taverns as well: 'The Drunken Drake', 'The Drowsy Drekling', 'The Dreamy Drakalope—'

"Hey," I said, "shouldn't this place be named something with two D's?"

Boone looked at me as if I were insane. "You think the Knights of the Torch're that predictable, do ya? Two D's."

With that, Boone ordered us to tie off the kirin. Then, together, the three of us went inside.

Things were quiet in The Gallant Gopherdrake. A few travelers clad in aldraka wool populated the dimly lit main floor, sipping steaming mugs of cider. But the tired, elderly barkeep straightened right up when he caught sight of Boone and Ivar.

The barkeep adjusted his spectacles and cleared his throat. "What can I get you?"

Rather than order a drink, Boone leaned over the bar.

"New Rebel passphrase," he whispered. I raised an eyebrow, but Boone winked at me.

"Solrac said they'll never guess that one," he said. Ivar chuckled.

The barkeep nodded, beckoning for us to follow him behind the bar toward a secret door out back. Boone explained that we Rebel Knights could no longer use the same passphrase we'd used when we were with the mainstream Knights of the Torch, not since Vesta took charge of Orothion, anyway. That meant The Gallant Gopherdrake and dozens of other safehouses throughout the realm had been forced to pick a side as well.

I was glad to have this particular tavern on our side. The secret Rebel-Knights-only area was *awesome.*

Vast, clear starglass windows gave us a perfect view of the striking wintery landscape outside. Windows that covered every wall...

...as well as the floor.

A thrill ran through me as I stepped out onto the see-through floor. Through it, I could see rocky cliffs, cindercone pines, and a frozen lake hundreds of feet below. Crisscrossed inlays of iron ran throughout the floor amidst the starglass—probably to keep any misplaced silver from dropping half the tavern over the cliffside.

From her place in my boot, I felt my copy of Glint squirming as she peeked out. She immediately ducked back in—Kai's ethereal mirror gecko had never been a fan of heights.

"Drakkin' drakefish," Boone muttered as he braved the translucent floor. Ivar grimaced as he joined us as well.

"This is fantastic," I said, dropping to my knees to get a better look. "Like levitating but without burning any ether!"

"I'd've been inclined to agree with you back when I was your age," Ivar said. "But soot if becomin' a parent don't change your perspective on everythin'."

"Don't y'all worry," Boone said. "If this 'ere floor can support that lot of chonkin' torradons, it sure as scales'll support us."

Boone gestured to the huge gathering of people near the far corner. Where the public section of the tavern had been quiet, back here was booming. They all seemed to be thronging one person standing near the back.

One dark-haired, beautiful person and one majestic, white-scaled true dragon.

Elle's sparking smile radiated genuine care as she spoke to each person in the lineup individually. It was clear from their expressions that they revered her, almost like a goddess, and Elle had ensured she looked the part. She wore her gleaming tiara and white ascension armored dress, which perfectly matched Aurora's scales.

Some people reverently touched the second-ascension true dragon as they spoke with her noble rider, and I even saw someone pass Elle their swaddled baby. Elle gently cradled the child before giving them a light kiss on the forehead.

I was staring, and Elle must've somehow felt it. Through the crowd, we locked eyes.

It was strange—The mischievous spark I'd grown to expect in her amber eyes seemed... distant. Muted somehow. Swallowed up in the burden of performing her duties as a true dragon rider and icon of the realm.

The group surrounding her quickly pulled her attention, and I shook my head to break the trance. Boone was talking again, inviting Ivar and me to join him at a table at the far end of the room. Elle wasn't the only one with a job to do.

With rumors about Elle and Aurora drawing people from all over the realm to the Rebel Knights' cause, we had a fleet of eager new recruits lined up within minutes. Boone ordered a round of golden boltbrews for the three of us, then we got started.

I watched with interest as Boone and Ivar conducted the interviews. We needed to ensure each person was trustworthy and loyal, and soot, there was such a variety. I tried to keep their names and faces straight, but after an hour, they all began to blur together. But through it all, their individual reasons for wanting to join up struck me.

"My father was a magi," said one bright-eyed young man not much younger than I was. "I want to fight for magi freedom."

"I wish to dedicate my life to the service of Eliana, the true dragon rider," said a determined outlander woman.

"We've been Knights of the Torch for years," said another man, nodding to his wife. "But we never wanted this foolish, needless war with Evgard. We stand with the Knight's Code and the Rebel Knights."

"May you always choose light," Boone gave the couple a solemn nod before adding their names to his list.

Later, the grumpiest old coot I'd ever seen took his place at the table. His scruffy black beard was long enough to braid into a tail that reached his belt buckle.

"I'm just here to send as many Mage Hunters as I can back to the void where they belong," he said menacingly. Then he squinted my way. "Even if it means associating with half-borns."

I ignored the handful of potential recruits who took issue with my Drekai heritage. Actually, I had more trouble accepting some of the nobles who wanted to join the Rebels. It was the noble class who was causing most of the realm's problems, after all. I was tempted to ask a couple of extra questions to all nobility just to ensure they were sincere.

The interviews got me thinking about what I'd say if I were sitting across from Boone, Ivar, and me at this very table. What reason would I give for wanting to join the Rebel Knights? When I'd met Solrac, Valla, and the rest, I'd wanted to go with them not because I believed in the cause or any of that. I'd gone hoping for revenge on the Black Valkyrie for killing my mother.

That was what had gotten me here in the first place.

But what was the reason I stayed?

I glanced once more toward where Elle and Aurora still charmed the masses. Elle appeared so confident as she advocated for the Rebel Knights and a better Evgard for all. Her parents, the king and queen of Drak-fell, may've been politically trapped into an alliance with Vesta and the mainstream Knights in Orothion, but that didn't stop Elle from fighting for what she felt was right. She was a born leader, with no doubts in her beliefs.

Or herself.

After a few more hours of conversation and recruiting, Boone and Ivar told Elle it was time to get going. But Elle had other ideas.

"I promised my friends here a light show," Elle said. There it was—the mischievous spark in her amber eyes.

Boone and Ivar hadn't been so sure, but Elle insisted. Within a few minutes, she was riding across the darkening sky on Aurora's back as brilliant purple-and-green ribbons of light trailed behind her. Aurora breathed the unique fire while Elle somehow channeled it through her sword. I watched in awe along with the rest of the guests as their performance lit up Aura Ridge.

Afterward, Elle had seemed happier. Still, she regained some of her rigid noble-ness as she led the new members of her Rebel army back down the snowy path toward Rhana's mega-cabin-slash-military base. Solrac would've been proud of how many we'd gathered. The new recruits rode the many kirin we'd brought along, but there were still several who had to double up. I gave up my dappled gray dragon horse to the grumpy, Mage Hunter-hating old man, and instead of riding, I took to the tree branches. My eyes burning with gold etherlight, I hover-jumped from bough to bough above the group. It was a fun sort of game, trying to make myself as light as possible so as not to drop snow onto anyone riding below.

I had to keep reminding myself to slow down and stay with the group, and soon found myself hover-leaping just above Elle as she rode at the head. Aurora walked gracefully on her four legs through the snow with Elle astride her back, her white wings tucked carefully at her sides.

I jumped down and fell into hover-step beside them.

"Good evening, Princess Eliana," I said with a little over-the-top bow. "You did well today."

Elle nodded in gratitude. Her voice was a little hoarse from overuse as she responded. "Boone, Ivar, and you did as well. What a fine group of recruits."

"We both know most of them are here for you," I replied. I hovered a little higher so I could give her my best crooked grin. "I suppose you'll be wanting at least three or four points for that."

To my surprise, that didn't get a laugh, wink, or teasing response from Elle. Instead, she tensed, looking over her shoulder at the lengthy procession.

"I won't let them down," she said, mostly to herself. Then she raised a hand high above her head, her fingers wrapped together in a fist as if she were raising an invisible torch.

"Light the way!" she called to the group.

They responded with enthusiasm, holding up fists of their own. "Light the way!"

I hovered near her side as we continued our trek down the mountain. I probably should've left her alone—she was clearly too exhausted for conversation—but I couldn't get myself to hover-dash back up to the treetops.

I watched as Elle's head nodded, her eyes heavy. She kept catching herself and straightening back up, and I noticed Aurora doing her best to keep her bond from falling asleep in the dragon saddle.

Stars, she was so tired.

With so many people to look after, this journey wasn't going to be over for another hour or more. Part of me wanted to pull Elle down and hover-dash her right back to the cabin and a warm, cozy rest for the night. But I knew Elle would never allow that. She had to stay right where she was as an icon for the people who looked up to her. She had to light the way.

I squinted into the setting sun. It was getting harder to see in the darkness, and Elle was several feet ahead of the closest rider. I wondered...

Ensuring nobody saw me, I burned a little more ether. I channeled my power to make the finest, clearest starglass I could—at least as clear as the cliffside floor of the Gallant Gopherdrake had been.

Within moments, I'd conjured a simple starglass apparatus that molded perfectly to Aurora's saddle and up along her proud neck. The frame was enough to hold Elle perfectly upright within her ascension armor as she rode.

And not a moment too soon, either. Elle's eyes had just drifted closed, only this time, rather than jolt herself awake again, she settled into my impromptu starglass supports.

Aurora glanced my way, gratitude shining in her vibrant dragonfire green eyes. I felt a warm feeling like shimmering, comforting light, accompanied by an almost musical, *Thank you, Asher.* I could tell she was also letting me know she could take care of Elle from here.

Of course. It would be far better for appearances if I left Elle to lead on her own. No reason to get people asking questions about Elle's random half-born friend.

I gave Aurora one last nod, then returned to the obscurity of the tree-tops.

After three straight days of nothing but rain, I was bored out of my mind.

The first couple of days had been totally fine. Despite the bad weather of early spring, I took to the skies on dragonback. Thorn and I had woven through the raindrops, bursting clouds and chasing lightning. It was the perfect distraction.

But after the fifth time coming back inside the cabin dripping all over the floor, Rhana had banned me from going outside until the storm let up, and the one time I tried sneaking out ended with my receiving both the reprimand of my life as well as extra kitchen duty for a week. I'd started seeing dirty pots and pans in my sleep.

After that, Rhana had stiffly informed me that if I broke any of her rules again, she'd throw me straight into a solitary confinement cell for the night.

"Your cabin has a jail?" I'd asked.

"Of course my cabin has a jail," Rhana had scoffed. "Twenty cells make up the deepest underground floor of the safehouse."

I'd already spent more than my fair share of time in prison. I didn't want to invoke Rhana's wrath, which meant I was stuck in the house for the foreseeable future.

Hence the sprawling, miniature starglass city taking up half the safehouse library.

Spread across three tables, several shelves, and even a large swath of floor, the newly founded city of Astrovale was a monumental masterpiece of starglass. Then again, I may have been biased since I'd poured most of my morning into creating intricate details on every citadel brick, smooth fountain, and cobblestone pathway, not to mention the epic starglass bridges connecting each table and shelf.

"Careful, Kai!" I yelped, hover-dashing from the place where I was working on Astrovale's local seedy saloon. "Your elbow almost obliterated the nomad camp! The poor Ridgerat Caravan can only take so much."

"You said I could have this side of the table to work," Kai huffed.

"And you can," I said, "once the nomads move on."

Kai mumbled something incoherent under his breath before replying, "Well, tell them to hurry it up. I need to get some omen-reading practice in."

I shrugged. "The nomads come and go as they please, Kai. It's completely out of my hands—"

"*Asher.*"

"Hey, look at that. Big duststorm's heading into west Astrovale—better get a move on, nomads."

The sounds of thunder and heavy raindrops drummed in the background while Kai and I worked on our—equally important—projects. I relocated an entire miniature starglass caravan while Kai pored over the books he'd piled on the library desk. Seer stuff with boring titles like *Eltosira's Guide to Omen Reading*, *Understanding Visions of the Past, Present, and Future*, and *Symbolic Interpretation: Science or Art?*

Beneath the thick stack of reading material, I saw a familiar, rectangular wooden box: the case of intel we'd recovered from the office of the undercover Knight of the Torch, Cenrik, back in Keep Rengard. It turned out that one of those crystal keys I'd filched from Swan Spire had indeed opened the case, which was bursting with more dull, wordy intel for Kai and the others to sift through.

Cenrik had been captured by Mage Hunters, leaving behind a lot of information regarding a group of dark magi called the Coven of the Gray Ones. Apparently, this Cenrik fellow had been looking into a plot to overthrow Keep Rengard, which, according to Boone and Valla, had taken place the night of the Winter Solstice. They'd defeated the Coven with the help of the Black Valkyrie's Mage Hunters—ugh. But according to Cenrik's information, the Coven wasn't only operating out of Rengard. He had reason to believe that several of the northern Keeps, Kolbohr in particular, housed more Gray followers.

The sight of the case gave me dragonbumps. I averted my gaze to the small, roundish rock Kai was holding as he read.

"Is that your seer stone?" I asked, though Kai was focusing so hard he didn't hear me. Just before leaving the Knights of the Torch headquarters in Orothion, the Farseer had given Kai the intricately carved stone in hopes that it would help him improve his skill as an omen reader.

I peeked over Kai's shoulder to get a better look at the seer stone. He was still so absorbed in his reading that he didn't realize I was there.

I took advantage of the opportunity, leaning even closer to whisper directly in Kai's ear.

"I am the ghost of Karl the craghopper—"

Before I got the chance to say more, Kai jumped and nearly fell out of his chair. I doubled over with laughter.

"I swear, Asher, you will put me in my burial ship," Kai said, holding his seer stone up like a weapon.

"Whoa whoa whoa," I held up my hands in surrender. "If you're hearing the voice of deceased dragon goats, that's hardly my fault. I was just wondering if your seer stone has been working. How goes the omen reading?"

Kai sighed. "Not so well. My visions are largely useless, with way too many possible meanings. I can show you if you like."

"Sure."

"Here's one from this morning." Kai raised a finger to trace a mind-linking rune and the corresponding symbol glowed to life over his forehead. As the mindlink activated, I could feel a slight wiggle from my copy of Glint, Kai's ethereal mirror gecko pet, from inside my boot.

Meanwhile, Kai placed the seer stone ceremoniously on the library desk, then rested his hand on top of it. At once, he flooded my mind with the vision he was seeing.

Golden fire surrounded the entire vision. It reminded me of the wall of strange, heatless golden flame they'd invited us to walk through as part of our initiation into the Knights of the Torch.

Within the ring of omenfire, a glorious, shining city appeared. It was so bright that it was hard to see, but I could tell the citadel was grand and tall, and the surrounding buildings were white and shimmery, like raw skystone.

Through Kai's mind, I saw a vast shadow descend over the city as if the sun had been blocked out. Then the earth began to shake and the city shattered, revealing a shimmering curtain that held back a horde of glowing blue eyes and a multitude of sparks in muted colors, all trapped in roiling white and gray smoke. Then a glimmering blade slashed through the curtain, and the smoke poured out, along with the eyes and the colors, which grew brighter and brighter.

Then the vision went black.

Kai gave an exasperated sigh as he dissolved the mindlink.

"Ugh!" he said, giving the seer stone a shove. Then he pulled out his black notebook and jotted down what we'd just seen:

"Mighty city, earthquake, curtain, blue eyes, colorful sparks," he said aloud as he wrote. "What does it all mean? It's going to take me hours to sift through omen guides trying to figure this one out on top of everything else."

Peering over Kai's shoulder, I caught a glimpse of the page across from the one Kai had just written on. The poor page had been assaulted by black ink, Kai's tiny handwriting filling every cranny with possible interpretations for other visions he'd been having. Three headings stood out among the mess of words:

"Tree, Tower, Moon," I read. "What are those about?"

Kai's face screwed up with annoyance, and without another word, he reignited the mindlink to show me.

"Brace yourself for the ending," he warned. Then, the vision opened.

Once again, golden omenfire surrounded the action in my mind.

A cold white torch floated, rotating slowly though empty black space. A tiny spark burned within it, which grew taller and wider. The fire was gold, splitting off into every direction like the branches of a tree.

"There's the tree," Kai narrated as we watched. "Now, naturally, I've assumed that the torch is a symbol of the Knights of the Torch. I believe it's a symbol of the Rebel Knights rather than the mainstream Knights, since the torch is white, the same color as Aurora's scales."

"Genius," I commented. "So, the torch is… a torch."

"Shut up." Kai clearly didn't appreciate my sarcasm. "The fire grows, which likely symbolizes the growth we've been experiencing due to Elle's successful recruitment missions. As for why it morphs into a tree, there are several possible interpretations."

"Ooh, please share them with me. In alphabetical order, if you don't mind."

From across the table, Kai glared, but did ultimately launch into a well-researched tirade about typical interpretations of trees in seership. Everything from the goddess Selene, to fertility and genealogy, to something called the 'Everflame.'

"This one intrigues me most," Kai said. "Historically, the Everflame is occasionally depicted as a fiery tree. Philosophers like Eltosira claim the Knights of the Torch actually drew from these old pieces of art to come up with their torch symbol in the first place."

"So you think the vision is showing you this... everember thing?" I asked.

"Ever*flame*," Kai corrected.

"Semantics," I replied.

"Maybe," Kai said. "According to the books here in Rhana's library, the Everflame was said to be an ancient flame breathed by the first dragon and brought to our land by our ancestors when they came here on the skyboats. They believed it had the power to purge darkness, and... well..."

Kai trailed off, and the fire-tree vision dimmed as he lost focus on the mindlink. I watched as Kai turned his notebook to get a look at the front cover. It was black leather, with a design pressed into it. For the first time, I realized it depicted a tree.

Kai went on. "My parents gave me this right before they left. The more I research the Everflame, I can't help but wonder if this, their last gift, has something to do with it."

"Wait," I said, "are you saying you think your parents' top secret Knights of the Torch mission has something to do with the Everflame?"

"No," Kai replied too fast. Then he knit his brows. "Maybe? I don't know what to think about the vision. Like I said, omens aren't my strong suit."

"Tree, Tower, Moon?" I said, repeating the words I'd read on Kai's omen page.

"Exactly. Here's the next part."

The mindlink re-solidified, and Kai's vision continued. Now the fiery torch-tree gave way to a glass tower floating over what looked to be a map of Evgard. The tower was bright blue, and grayish mists swirled eerily beneath it. Hanging in the darkened sky above the tower were dozens of stars.

Kai spoke with exasperation as we stared at the stars. "I've spent literal *days* combing through texts on lunar activity and charting, both astronomical *and* astrological. After replaying my memories of the vision several times, I was able to identify each of the three constellations as those involved in the upcoming convergence of mythic stars."

"Convergence?" I asked. I'd been all set to tease my friend about his star studies, but those last words gave me pause. Elle had mentioned the convergence last summer, and a Seer dragon friend of ours had mentioned I'd play a role in it, whatever that meant. I paid closer attention as Kai continued.

"The Dragon, Phoenix, and Dire Wolf networks will align for the first time in a thousand years this coming spring, about one year from now. That's gotta mean something."

"But what?"

"That's the whole point," Kai said. "I don't know. Now, keep watching."

Next came a round red moon. The vision focused on the moon, and... Soot. It was red with blood.

A drop fell from the moon to water the steps of a vast stronghold. I thought I recognized the castle's powerful silhouette, like the spines of a dragon ascending toward a seaside cliff. It was Orothion—the Knights of the Torch headquarters in Skygard.

Above the castle, the moon had turned to crystal. It looked like there was a name etched onto the surface, but it was too blurred to make it out. Then suddenly, a green-tailed skyfall came shooting toward the moon, shattering it. For the briefest second before the vision closed, it looked like shards of crystal were flying straight for my eyes.

Despite the vision playing in my head, I yelped and hover-leaped backward.

"Stars!" I cried. "You weren't kidding about bracing myself for the ending."

Kai closed the vision. He breathed an exasperated sigh, putting a hand to his head. "I can't figure out what *any* of this means. The tower, for example, could be referencing the Mage Hunters. After all, their Academy has numerous towers, including Swan Spire. But why was it glass? A symbol of fragility, perhaps?"

The Mage Hunters are fragile," I summed up. "That sounds like a good omen if I ever heard one."

"Unless the glass isn't glass at all, but rather, crystal. Specifically skystone. But why blue?"

"Evil skystone?" I suggested.

"Corrupted, maybe," Kai muttered.

"Semantics," I said again. I still wasn't quite sure if I was using that word right, but Kai kept going.

"And then there's that drakking blood moon over Orothion," Kai said, his tone growing more exasperated as he flipped through his notebook once more. "What in the scorching stars am I supposed to glean from that?

I shrugged, trying to calm him. "I'm sure it's no big deal."

My efforts did not succeed.

"No big deal?" Kai practically shouted. "Solrac has told me time and again that he *needs* me to figure this stuff out! A Seer is only as good as his ability to read the future. But what I can't understand is *why.*"

In frustration, Kai slammed his black notebook shut. I silently began putting up a protective wall around the parts of Astrovale nearest him, just in case, as Kai plowed on without so much as pausing to take a breath.

"We have the Farseer himself on our side, for Streya's sake! He's a legendary master of omens, so having me waste my time failing at them is redundant. *Why* am I wasting my time failing?"

"Semantics?" I suggested.

"You can't just say 'semantics,' at random times and expect it to make sense, Asher!" Kai cried. "Do you even know what it means?"

Before I could answer, Kai buried his face in his hands, his voice coming out muffled as he went on. "I'm a logical person, and everyone knows that. Omen reading is among the *least* logical aspects in all of my etherarchy! It's like trying to teach a fish to fly!"

Kai finally went silent. I gave him a few seconds to breathe before approaching with caution.

I patted my best friend on the back and he looked up at me with somewhat shiny eyes. He was clearly hoping I'd have something encouraging to say.

I took a deep breath, choosing my next words carefully.

"Boo hoo."

The fire that burst to life in Kai's dark eyes tipped me off that he did not appreciate my mocking tone. When he launched himself at me and started wrestling me to the ground, that confirmed it.

"Hey!" I cried, wrestling him right back. "You're destroying Astrovale!"

"Good."

Kai and I rolled right through main street, demolishing delicate taverns, general stores, and residences and leaving a trail of etherdust from dissolving starglass in our wake. I pinned Kai by the arms, in the process crushing what was once Astrovale's proud, sprawling cactus garden.

Below me, I saw Kai's gaze flash downward and to the right. Following his line of sight, I realized he was looking at the grand, starglass citadel.

"You wouldn't dare..." I warned, tightening my grip on his arms.

Kai narrowed his eyes, then used his foot to kick down the entire structure in one defiant blow.

I roared with melodramatic rage, getting to my feet and channeling more etherarchy. Misty white ether swirled together, solidifying as I trapped Kai in a tight starglass cage. Sturdier, more opaque starglass this time.

Kai grabbed the bars with his hands. Then, to my complete surprise, he slipped right through them as if his body were a mere...

"Illusion?" I scoffed in disbelief. I felt a tap on my shoulder, then turned around to see the real Kai standing behind me, shaking his head. The illusory Kai dissolved into etherdust.

"Nice try," Kai smirked. "I pulled the switch while you were looking back at your precious Keep Astro-land citadel."

I raised an eyebrow, barely able to keep the smile off my lips. "It's Keep *Astrovale* and you know it."

"Don't you mean it *was* Keep Astrovale?"

That did it. Kai and I burst into laughter, both feeling an incredible sense of release. We'd been cooped up for too long, stuck with nothing but to-do's and stresses.

I formed a pair of starglass clubs, handing one to Kai. The translucent white starglass in the clubs was much denser and stronger than the starglass I'd used to build my city.

Then, together, Kai and I completely demolished the rest of Astrovale.

Sending each structure dissolving upward into etherdust was even more fun than building it in the first place. And the best part was: absolutely no cleanup whatsoever.

By the time we'd destroyed the last starglass tree, Kai and I were grinning from ear to ear. We'd needed that.

Then, as Kai overlooked the starglass city-free room, he suddenly put a hand to his forehead.

"Oh. *Oh.*"

"What?" I asked.

"The first vision," he said. "The one from this morning. It foretold the destruction of a great city."

My mouth fell open in delight. "You foresaw the destruction of Astrovale!"

"Of course I did." Kai slumped with a sigh.

He then turned his gaze to the floor and gasped "Oh soot! Cenrik's case!"

At once, Kai dropped to the floor where his stack of books, including the wooden case, had fallen from the table. The case was cracked, the stacks of papers inside scattered.

"Oops," I said, bending down to help. I gingerly lifted the case, only to have the bottom panel split further.

"Careful," Kai said, reaching to take it from my hands.

"Wait," I replied, examining the case more closely. Carefully, I shifted the cracked panel to reveal a tiny extra space hidden at the bottom of the case.

"A false bottom," Kai said, eyes widening.

There, crouched on the floor, Kai and I pried open the secret compartment. Inside was a carefully folded piece of cloth with a note laying on top. Kai and I exchanged glances.

"Maybe we should tell the others—"

Before Kai could finish his protest, I seized the note and began to read aloud.

My fellow Knights of the Torch,

While most of my research to date has been compiled using facts, here I disclose my personal speculation regarding the matter of the Gray Ones.

They are hungry, dark spirit beings. I have heard whispers. Whispers from beyond this plane from a wraith that I believe has chosen me. I am ashamed to admit it, but this Gray being tempts me, telling me things I long to hear, regarding the ability to connect their plane, Etheria, with ours. He preys on my desire to bring my beloved brother back from beyond the grave. I know this is not possible, but the Gray One speaks of tearing the veil between the worlds.

Knights of the Torch of old spoke of this veil with reverence. A barrier, protecting both our world and Etheria, only penetrable by the ancient veilblade, kept safe by the mind goddess, Streya.

"Veilblade?" Kai interjected. "I've heard of that. It's a relic from the Guardian Era, said to have once belonged to the mind goddess herself. Religious people like the Sisters and Sons of Streya use its likeness in their sanctuaries I think."

"Now ghosts want to get it so they can break into Evgard?" I said, shivers creeping down my spine. "That's not great."

I didn't really want to know more, but I kept reading.

Additionally, my spying efforts regarding the Coven of the Gray Ones led me to a certain crystal. My dragon, Luster, discovered this odd, blue crystal in a well-hidden cave beneath the dragon stables here in Keep Rengard. I sensed the shard's dark power, and I was careful not to handle the crystal for any longer than necessary. I believe the crystal belongs to the Coven's leader, the Liberator. It is their source of power, granted to them by the Gray Ones themselves, and I worry they plan to use these in order to achieve their dark purposes.

I have reason to believe the Drekai are interested in obtaining this crystal and maybe others like it. As Captain of the Guard here, I've received reports of Drekai scouring the south in search of what they call a 'voidshard.' I can only assume those monsters are after the power of this crystal, same as the Liberator.

Stars be with you,

Cenrik

When I looked up at Kai, he seemed as perplexed as I was. Cautiously, I flipped back the wrapped cloth that had been under the note. Sure enough, inside was a thin shard of crystal.

I frowned. After reading Cenrik's note, I'd expected it to be blue. But this one was white, glowing with fresh ether like a skystone. In fact, I was pretty sure this *was* a skystone. I wondered what had happened to it since Cenrik had tucked it into the case.

I squinted, just able to make out two names etched onto the crystal: *Skapa* and *Lorelai.*

"Who's Lorelai?" I asked.

"Probably the Liberator of the Coven," Kai murmured with fascination. "Soot. This isn't good. If the Coven was using these to obtain more power, and the Drekai are looking at using them too—"

"I don't think the Drekai are after the same thing as the Coven," I jumped in without thinking.

Kai looked doubtful. "But Cenrik's reports said they were searching for these voidshards in the south. Why else would they be doing that?"

"Maybe because they're trying to *stop* people from using them," I replied, folding my arms. "Think about it—Kheradok, the general of the Drekai army, was chasing us down, bent on dueling me at the end of last summer. The only thing that had stopped him was Elle convincing him to give me more time. That, and the Drekai empress calling him back to help with their war effort."

"Right," Kai said. "Their war with the Canyonlands."

"Or—" I put up a finger, "their war with *voidarchy*."

Kai pressed his lips together as he mulled over my theory.

"What if Boone is right about the Gray Ones coming for Evgard?" I said. "If so, our solution is simple: We talk to the Drekai. Find out what they know, and maybe even talk about an alliance—"

"I have to stop you there." Kai put up a hand.

"Why? You have to admit, it would make sense."

"Maybe," Kai said, "but even if you're right, it wouldn't matter. Drekai and Evgardian... They just don't mix."

My heart sank at the words I'd heard many times before. From people like the rude Baron Eidan, to allies like Rhana. From leaders like Solrac to friends like Kai.

Drekai and Evgardian don't mix.

So, what did that make me?

Kai scanned the note Cenrik had left once more. "We need to get this information to Solrac. He'll know what to do."

"Valla's still searching for him."

"Maybe we should check in with her," Kai said, already flipping through his black notebook. He stopped when he got to a page with a list of colors, numbers, and names. At the top of the page, he'd written 'Glint Network.'

Kai ran his finger down the list until he reached 'Glint Six,' the mirror gecko copy that was assigned to Valla. At my request, Kai activated the copy of his mirror gecko that was still in my boot so I could listen in as well.

A couple of complicated-looking runes shone over Kai's forehead. "Alright," Kai said out loud, "Valla's Glint should be glowing now. She'll know to—"

Kai? That you? Valla's voice suddenly sounded over the mindlink.

Yes! Valla, we've got some information we need to get to Solrac. Any luck on your search? Where are you?

I felt a string of mental grunts and groans from Valla's end, as if she was lifting something heavy. Grunts and groans, along with... elation?

I'm heading west over the high ridgebacks, Valla thought over the mindlink. *I found him.* Her thoughts betrayed joy, excitement, and relief.

You found him? Kai repeated, a thrilled note sneaking into his thoughts as well. Through Valla's thoughts, I could've sworn I heard a bloodhusky bark. I got to my feet in anticipation.

I found Solrac, Valla confirmed. *I found him, and I'm bringing him home.*

CHAPTER 8: THE GLADE

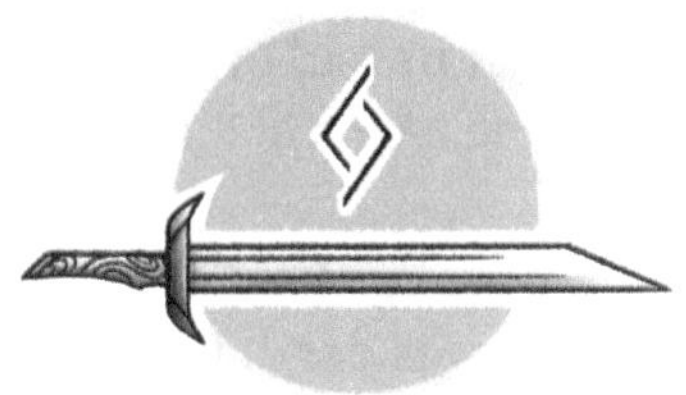

MELEYA

High Prince Mason called this place 'Scryer's Grotto.'

I called it the void.

I sat on the cold, rocky floor of a darkened cove. The sound of constantly dripping water echoed off of the damp, slimy walls. Surrounding me were nine enormous crystals, each one larger than I was, jutting across the small space at haphazard angles.

Among the few sources of light in the grotto were the sporadic bursts of glowing blue steam from the vents in the ground. Cool mist shot from one of these every few minutes, making me jump and leaving me constantly on edge.

Then, there were the creatures. I could hear slithering and low growls almost constantly as mysterious monsters lurked just beyond my series of alcoves. I'd never seen one, but I could've sworn a tentacle had crept out from one of the numerous tide pools around here.

Still, it was hard to tell if it was all in my head. Maybe the isolation was getting to me.

For two to three hours every day, I'd been sitting inside Scryer's Grotto, the rune for the Sight aglow over my forehead. That was the amount of time it took my ether well to drain almost to nothing, leaving me exhausted before I returned to the dorm each night. I wished going to the dorm at the end of every evening was more of a respite, but with my nightmares getting worse, sleep evaded me. Though I tried to hide it, my friends were starting to notice how tired I looked. As far as they knew, I was just taking an extra evening class from our new combat instructor. I didn't dare tell them anything else.

Scryer's Grotto was strange, its very air radiating dark power. When I'd asked why the all-powerful Surgeon didn't just track Zyri and his voidshard himself, Mason had vaguely informed me that the Surgeon not only had no time for this task, but he had other talents with his etherarchy than the Sight. They needed me. And if I wanted to free my parents, I needed them.

I had no choice but to play along. I was on a mission to find Zyri, a Drekai woman I knew for a fact was dead. So, really, I was just biding my time, praying Mason Drakeslayer didn't catch on and take away my final chance to free my parents once and for all.

With the Sight activated, I could see into Etheria. Flashes of brilliant colors danced before my eyes all across the planes of the nine giant crystals. Auras.

The crystals were carved with dozens of powerful ancient Rifter's runes. Various labels adorned the crystals: Evyndara, Behrfell, Drakfell, Rengard... Each crystal corresponded with one of Evgard's eight keepdoms, with the ninth marked for the Dragon Isles.

I now knew exactly why Mason had needed a Rifter, and as he'd called me, one with a particularly strong affinity for the Sight. Through the spirit world, I could see the auras of hundreds of people currently going about their lives throughout the entire realm.

Scarlet, cream, emerald, aquamarine... At first, I thought Mason Drakeslayer was crazy to expect me to happen upon Zyri's exact shade of beige.

"You can't be serious," I'd said that first day he'd shown me the grotto a few weeks earlier. "You want me to use these things to scour the entire realm in search of one specific beige aura? This uh... Zyri person can't be the only one out there."

"You know as well as I do that no two auras are alike," Mason had said, challenge in his gaze. "Drekai are much like dragons—their scales match their ethereal aura. You saw this woman's scales that night in the canyon, did you not?"

"Yes," I'd replied.

"If you're having trouble remembering, I can always call in one of your squadmates who was there that night to help you. Jax, or Brigan, perhaps, or maybe your captain, Solvai—"

"No," I'd cut him off. The last thing I wanted to do was put any of my squadmates in danger by getting them tangled up in this mess. "I remember."

The first place Mason had told me to look was the Dragon Isles, but of course, I hadn't found anything useful there. The hours passed slowly within Scryer's Grotto. My eyes burned from staring at all the flashing colors for so long, and my back ached from sitting on the hard, uneven stone floor. I saw plenty of beige-colored auras flash by throughout the various keepdoms, though naturally, none matched that of my deceased Drekai friend.

You can end this anytime you wish, my wraith's familiar voice rasped in my ear. I pulled my knees closer to my chest as the gray being's wispy tendrils smoldered beside me.

While using the Sight, I could see her as clear as my own hand in front of my face. Shaped vaguely like a human woman from the waist up, her lower half spilled over the grotto's damp floor in ever-curling gray smoke. Her narrow face was blank and featureless other than a pair of glowing, lightning blue eyes. Something about the voidish power of the grotto seemed to make her presence stronger here than it was anywhere else.

With the Surgeon's voidshard, we can overcome any foe, she said.

"What is a voidshard, anyway?" I found myself asking.

Finally curious, are we? The wraith laughed, then sat down on a rock to face me. *A voidshard is what the most powerful wraiths give to the person they have chosen to bond. Much like your precious dragon heartscales.*

"So why haven't you given one to me?" I asked.

You have not yet earned my trust.

I shuddered at that. This whole conversation set my teeth on edge.

Let me in, the wraith said. *I can show you how to really use the shard. We will use its power to force them to free your parents. To free all magi, if you wish.*

"No," I said.

Why not? Do you not tire of resisting?

"Yes," I whispered, a single tear sliding from each of my dry, over-worked eyes. My head was splitting as my ether overuse headache inten-sified.

Ba-doom.

Tring!

I could feel Blink's drumbeats and Sniff's fluting through our bond, but even my bonds felt distant. I didn't know where I was, but I was fairly certain I was no longer in the Ridgeback Mountains. Mason dropped me off here each evening by way of a rift anchor, powered by the biggest skystone I'd ever seen.

Relief filled me when at long last a blue-rimmed tear ripped open near the rift anchor by the wall. It startled me, and the Sight rune dissipated from over my forehead so that I could no longer see my wraith.

Mason Drakeslayer stepped through the portal. Today's session was over.

"Find anything?" the High Prince asked, an aloof light in his eyes.

I shook my head.

For a moment, Mason's eyes flashed with frustration. "She's not trying hard enough," Mason said harshly, turning his head slightly to one side. I took a cautious step backward.

Then Mason righted himself once more. "I hope you're not wasting time down here," he said, shifting back to his usual smooth tone.

"I'm not wasting time." I could feel Mason glaring at me and didn't dare make eye contact. I'd been told on more than one occasion that I wasn't very good at lying.

Mason didn't seem fully convinced. Still, he beckoned for me to step through the rift that would take us back to the Academy. It wasn't a rift Mason had made himself, but one baked into the rift anchor stone on the grotto wall. I thought of how exhausted Mason had gotten while using the Sight that first day and frowned. The way he'd spoken of 'recently' becoming a Rifter didn't sit well with me; frankly, I didn't even understand how such a thing was possible.

But I was too exhausted to dwell on it. A long night of voidish nightmares lay ahead of me.

The next morning, I woke up feeling cold. Last night's nightmare had been worse than ever, with the same gray-cloaked figure following me, appearing before me no matter where I tried to run. I knew now that it was the Soul Reaper, watching me through his connection with his voidshard. How long would it be before he figured out I wasn't Zyri?

Blink was in my dream this time. My spirit dragon bond had appeared to chase away the hooded figure, her silvery dragonfire making him disappear.

When I woke, I found the voidshard lying on my pillow once again. The thin blue crystal stared back at me, the names written on either side making me feel hollow. *Kjell* and *Agnai.*

Kjell was an old Evgardian name. But the name Agnai was one I'd never heard before.

Where I'd once felt cold at the sight of the voidshard, I now felt a sort of numbness. As with every other morning these days, I rapidly runetraced to hide my dark secret within the confines of my rift hold before my dormmates, Solvai, Jaira, and Shaya, could see it.

I dressed quietly in the dark so I wouldn't wake any of them, then headed out into the common area. The bare, triangular room offered little comfort.

Well, the room didn't.

But the sight of a certain Psion did.

"Jax?" I said.

"M!" Jax hurried over to me from where he sat at the desk near a bookshelf. He had a scrap of paper and a pen in his hand.

"What're you doing up this early?" he asked.

"Just... trouble sleeping."

He paused, looking at me in the low morning candlelight. His gaze lingered on the dark circles beneath my eyes, and I looked away, ashamed. Too many times this week he'd asked me why I looked so tired, and each time I'd blamed my mysterious late evening 'class' with the High Prince. I couldn't tell Jax the truth—It would put him in danger. I now had a whole new understanding of why Vidya didn't want anyone to know that Jax was her son.

"What were you writing?" I asked, eyeing the paper and pen.

Jax gave me one of his classic smirks. "You really want to know?"

I raised an eyebrow. "That's why I asked."

"You really *really* want to know?" he teased.

"Does it have something to do with all your early-morning working out?"

"Maybe."

I bit my lip. Jax had been late to class almost every day for weeks. Jaira, who was still leading our classes, never called him out on it, either. I got the feeling she found Jax handsome. I wished Vidya would go back to leading the classes, but I'd hardly seen her since our journey to the Ridgebacks. And whenever I did, she seemed more and more unsure of herself. I wondered if the other Hunters were starting to notice the Black Valkyrie was losing her edge.

I turned back to Jax, reaching for the paper.

"Show me."

"Make me," Jax replied, holding his arm up so that the scrap was out of reach. I jumped, trying to get to it, but he only held it higher. I shot Jax a furious look, which made him grin as he held the paper up as high as he could.

I tried to pull his arm down, but it was no use. I had to resort to rifting.

Using a pair of small gold-rimmed portals, I plucked the folded note from Jax's hand and waved it in his face. He laughed as I proudly unfolded it.

There on the page in Jax's hurried handwriting were four words:

Run away with me.

When I looked back up, Jax's teasing demeanor had completely shifted. His eyes were intense as he stepped closer to me, then traced his thumb along my cheek. Shivers displaced any nerves I'd been feeling before.

"Run away with me," Jax said, his voice low. "Just for today."

"What about class?" I whispered.

"Drak class. I wanna show you something. You in?"

When he looked at me like that, I knew there was only one answer.

"Yes."

"So when are you gonna tell me where we're going?" I called over the sound of rushing wind.

Jax's laughter was the only response as he sat in front of me in his dragon's saddle. We flew east through a heavy cloudbank on the back of his deep green evren, Jade. Mist from the damp air lightly sprayed my face.

Finally, we broke through the cloudbank, and the sun's warm, golden rays were like a glorious reunion with a long-lost friend. I instantly felt lighter as I watched its beams bathe the nearest mountainside.

Jax directed his evren to drop us off in a sunny glade where the winter snow had almost completely melted away. Warm leaves sprouted from tangled smokesage plants and a circle of large boulders surrounded the glade, keeping out the chill wind.

Jax slid out of the saddle, then turned around to offer me a hand. Once my feet were on the ground, Jax's evren gave him a knowing nod, then launched back into the skies, leaving the two of us completely alone for the first time in weeks.

"How did you find this place?" I asked, breathing in the pleasant, slightly campfire-y scent from the smokesage. The desert plants and the jagged, irregular boulders reminded me of home in the canyonlands.

"I built it," Jax said, squeezing my hand. "Moved the rocks in to make it cozy and keep the wind out."

Understanding dawned in my eyes. "All those times you were late to class..."

"I was up here." Jax shrugged, subtly flexing his biceps. "I really *was* working out. Even with telekinesis, those boulders are drakking heavy. But that's not even the best part."

Jax eagerly pulled me to a big, almost perfectly rectangular stone about the height of my waist. It looked like he'd painstakingly carved a square chunk out of the rock on one side, and another cavity in the stone beneath it. The lower one had charred coals inside.

I cocked my head as Jax hurried to the other side of the rock, where he produced an enormous, cloth-covered basket

"M," Jax said with mock ceremony. "I give you your very own kitchen."

He pulled the cloth from the basket to reveal a tantalizing array of ingredients, from vegetables to butter to eggs. There was even some drakalope meat wrapped in brown paper.

I instantly realized that he'd used his psionics to telekinetically carve the large stone into a countertop. The hollowed-out portion was his attempt to build an oven, and he'd somehow managed to gather up all of those ingredients—probably swiped from the Academy kitchens—just for me.

Soot. I kept my cool demeanor for about half a second before tears sprang to my eyes.

I couldn't be bothered with running all the way around Jax's creation, so I just scrambled right over the top to tackle him with the tightest embrace in the history of Evgard.

Jax laughed as he wrapped his muscular arms around me. "I'll never forget the look on your face when I found you a kitchen back at Outcast Outpost. I talked to the cook here at the Academy, but he turned out to be a real jerk who didn't want to share his space with anyone. That left only one option: sneaking up here to build you a kitchen of your own."

I could barely speak, but I somehow managed, "I love it."

It didn't take long for me to coax a big pot of tender drakalope and vegetable stew out of my new psionically-made kitchen. I made sure to prepare a large amount so that we could bring some down to the rest of Squad Reckless later.

As the hours passed, I completely forgot about the classes we were missing and the trouble we were going to be in when we returned. I felt like we'd entered a secret world outside of time itself. Nothing existed outside of this glade and this moment.

Jax smacked himself on the forehead when he realized he'd forgotten to make a table and chairs to eat at. He offered to try carving one now the same way he'd carved the countertop.

"How *did* you carve everything so perfectly?" I asked.

"With this," Jax said, reaching for the axe holsters he usually kept strapped to his back. He'd taken them off when we'd gotten up here, and for the first time, I noticed a third sheath hidden behind them. This one was curved, made to fit a...

"Is that a *kalaata*?" I asked as Jax pulled out the thin, curved piece of metal. He passed me the Drekai-style boomerang with a bladed edge lined with faintly glowing gold light.

"Careful, it's super sharp," Jax warned as he passed it to me.

My breathing became faster and more shallow as I instantly recognized the boomerang as the one that had belonged to Zyri. I hadn't realized Jax had kept it, but soot. If Mason ever saw Jax carrying this around, he'd be in terrible danger.

"I just didn't have the heart to get rid of it," Jax said. "It's all that's left of Zyri, you know?"

I nodded. "I don't think she'd mind. But I wonder... should you really be carrying it around?"

Jax looked a little puzzled, but he could tell seeing the boomerang bothered me. After a moment, he took me by the hand and led me to a little alcove formed by two of the large boulders he'd moved into the glade. It was a quiet, peaceful spot with a little red-orange wildflower growing right in the center.

Tears filled my eyes as Jax and I carefully dug a hole in front of the flower and buried our friend's weapon there. I felt both closure and relief—now Mason would have no reason to suspect Jax.

I leaned against Jax as we remembered Zyri, the Drekai woman we barely knew, who'd saved our lives and given her own in service of her empress and country. My resolve to keep her secret grew.

After the memorial, Jax and I shared a marvelous, picnic-style meal. The savory flavors of my warm drakalope stew melted in our mouths. Then, I used the flour, butter, and a few sprinkles of salt from the pouch I always kept clipped to my belt to throw together a simple crust. I shelled some of the scaleberries Jax had provided and reduced them over the heat to make a filling. My mouth watered at the thought of flaky, scaleberry hand pies as I slid them into the hot oven.

The warmth from the smokesage roused the glade's spring grasses from their long winter's sleep. While we waited for dessert to bake, Jax lay down on his back in the grass, one hand on his abdomen and the other behind his head as he basked in the sunlight. He looked so good with his toned arms and V-shaped torso, I nearly started drooling over *him* instead of the pies. I got down beside him on my stomach, propped up on my elbows so that I could see his face.

"Thank you, Jax," I sighed. "I can't imagine a better surprise."

"Thank *you*, M," Jax replied. "I can't imagine a better meal. You're really the most amazing woman I've ever met."

"And you've met your fair share of women," I teased.

"Hey!" Jax glared, turning his gaze from the sky to my face. As his midnight blue eyes met mine, his glare melted instantly.

"Hey," he repeated. This time, his voice was low and a little gruff. My cheeks grew warm, and my gaze darted to the thin, pale scar on Jax's lower lip. Suddenly, he was runetracing, a familiar golden symbol glowing from his forehead.

I felt a tug from my belt as Jax telekinetically pulled me to him. Not that I'd been far away.

I met him halfway, closing the distance between our lips. It was a hungry, ardent kiss that sent my heartbeat flying.

Boom-boom, I felt my spirit dragon Blink's approval through our bond. She liked Jax.

Brrring! Sniff chimed in. To my surprise, his high-pitched note sounded positive as well. Sniff had always been a little wary of the hotheaded Psion. But his intention was clear: Sniff was happy to see me happy.

I felt a rush of glee. I hadn't realized how much I'd been craving my dragon's endorsement. After that, both Sniff and Blink kindly bowed out of my heart and mind.

And it was just Jax and me.

We shared more kisses, each one more earnest than the last. My whole body felt like it was on fire as I ran my fingers along the back of his neck, over his collarbone, and onto his chest. Meanwhile, Jax's hand on my back sent chills running up and down my spine. I'd never known I could feel this way about someone.

Before we got too carried away, Jax suddenly pulled back and looked past my shoulder, sniffing the air.

"Is something burning?" he asked.

"The pies!" I cried, scrambling to get up. When I pulled out the dessert, I was relieved to see that most of the scaleberry hand pies were still edible. Only the two closest to the back had caught, their crusts blackened on the corners and top.

"Drak," I muttered. "Everything was so perfect."

Jax materialized behind me, slipping his arms around my waist and resting his head on my shoulder.

"Everything still *is* perfect," he said. "Come on—These'll have to cool."

Part of me wanted to get right back to kissing Jax again, but we both decided the burning pies were probably a good warning to slow down. We sat together, Jax with his back against one of the large boulders and me on the ground in his lap, leaning back against him.

"What's a secret about yourself nobody else knows?" I asked. I craned my neck to look up at Jax, and I could tell he couldn't fight his smile any more than I could fight mine.

"Whoa, you want my secrets? Those are... you know. *Secrets.*"

"You don't say," I laughed. Then I sighed. "I want all your secrets, Jax."

His eyes swam with profound energy. He looked almost ready to answer, but then he faltered at the last second.

"You first," he said, dodging the question as he leaned his head back against the boulder.

"Okay," I replied. "I know this sounds crazy, but someday, I want a vegetable garden."

Jax chuckled. "M... that's *so* edgy."

"Hey," I insisted. "I've been stuck in the guard for years, trying to free my parents from prison. And now, I'm stuck at the Academy, still fighting to bring my family back together. The cloak I wear might be a different color, but I'm always wearing one I didn't get to choose. Who knows what soot will come next?"

Jax pulled me closer. "I'm going to help you save your mom, M. I promised you that before we came here, and drak if I'm not going to keep that promise."

I leaned against him and in response, Jax lightly kissed the crown of my head. He lingered there, breathing in, then gave a contented sigh. Shivers danced along my skin as we stayed that way for almost a full, silent minute.

I'd nearly forgotten all about my original question until Jax took another long, deep breath, speaking carefully on the exhale. "As for my secret... One day, I want to build something great."

"Like what?" I asked. "A tower? A castle?"

"Maybe," Jax hesitantly began before plowing ahead. "It's like there's something in me that's... I don't know. Afraid. Afraid of being forgotten, maybe? But if I can just build something important enough—whatever it is—then maybe I'll stop... uh, maybe I'll stop being the guy who gets lost in the crowd and left behind. I want whatever I build to be something that matters. Something that'll last through the ages. I know that sounds dumb."

I broke into a smile. There was something endearing and sweet about the way Jax rambled whenever he was nervous.

"It sounds wonderful," I said. "And you'll never be the guy who gets left behind. Not by me."

At that, Jax's embrace tightened. I never wanted to leave the glade.

When the pies had cooled, Jax and I continued talking over dessert. We laughed long into the afternoon, and it wasn't until the sun was low in the sky that Jax finally called for his evren to come and get us.

Jax carried the leftovers and I held to his waist as we flew back into the cloudbank toward the Academy. The peaceful feeling from the sunny glade lingered, and I smiled softly. With so much darkness surrounding me, I'd never been more grateful that someone cared enough about me to take me above the clouds, at least for a day.

"You are my sunlight," I murmured, resting my head against Jax's upper back. I doubted he'd heard me, but he tilted his head backward and to the side so that it touched mine.

Too soon, the last rays of sun gave way to gray, misty rain.

VALLA

Valla's gaze was sharp as she used her Wildshaping powers to strengthen it. Glowing gold wildmarks traced out around her eyes. Her normally black irises were icy white, like those of a polar wolf. Additional wildmarks traced her ears, amplifying her hearing.

She constantly scanned the treeline, keeping watch. Valla wished she could douse the low orange campfire to stay invisible to predators or enemies, but Solrac needed the warmth.

Through the crackling flames, Valla could see Solrac lying on their only bedroll, their only aldraka wool blanket tucked around his shoulders. Valla had forced him to eat from their dwindling supply of dry bread and drakalope jerky before he fell asleep, but despite her care, he remained dangerously thin and pale after his time alone in the High Ridgebacks. And, as if that weren't enough, minor bruises and cuts decorated his body as if he'd survived an intense fight. Valla had used some of her regenerative Sentinel powers to heal his most pressing wounds, but she didn't dare drain her ether well too much out here in the wilds. Her enhanced hearing made it clear that his breathing was more shallow than she would have liked.

"What were you doing up there," Valla murmured to Solrac, "and why in the void didn't you let me come to protect you?"

Valla spoke quietly, but still, at the sound of her voice, Solrac stirred. Valla cursed herself for waking him, but her annoyance quickly melted when Solrac broke into a grin at the sight of her.

"Valla," he said, sitting up with effort. He blinked up at the dark night sky. Or rather, the pale violet sky of the hours just before daybreak.

"How dare you." Solrac rubbed his eyes. "Did I not specifically tell you to wake me so that I could take over the watch while you slept?"

"You did," Valla replied.

"Get over here immediately." Solrac vacated the bedroll to stand above Valla with his arms crossed.

"I don't need rest," Valla said stubbornly. "If you're able to walk, we should continue down the mountain toward Rhana's safehouse."

"I cannot believe this!" Solrac melodramatically put a hand to his forehead. "How could you do this to me?"

Valla frowned. "Do what?"

"Deprive me of an opportunity to practice traditional masculine chivalry!"

Valla rolled her eyes. "You'll survive."

"You don't know that." Solrac's eyes went wide. He stuck out his lower lip, then looked from Valla to the bedroll.

Valla grimaced as her resolve dissolved. Scowling all the way, Valla crawled under the blanket. She let her polar wolf senses revert to normal, but she didn't need heightened senses to smell the hint of oakmoss and fine leather. Solrac's scent.

Valla closed her eyes, but she didn't dare sleep. These woods were full of wild dragons and dragonkind, not to mention umbral creatures. Rumor had it that the umbrals in the Mirror Forest were stronger than most. And more plentiful. Valla had to be ready to protect Solrac at any moment.

After a solid half-hour of pretending to sleep, Valla thought she heard rustling. She tightened her grip on the hilt of her seaxe and cracked one eye.

She didn't see any creatures prepared to pounce—but she did see a very disapproving Solrac staring her down.

"As one of the most competent people I've ever met," Solrac said, "I did not think I would have to explain to you a concept as simple as sleep."

Then Valla said something she immediately regretted.

"Maybe if you were to kiss me goodnight."

Soot. Valla must've been more tired than she thought.

Still, the way Solrac's gaze softened... He seemed to be studying her face, taking in each individual scar with tender admiration. It was enough to get Valla's heart racing.

For a moment Valla thought he was really going to kiss her.

Then Solrac looked down at his feet. Valla's heart sank just as quickly.

"You know I cannot do that, Valla," Solrac said.

"Why?"

"You know why."

Valla's reply was terse as she sat up. "No, I don't. You say you're not free of Vidya, but Solrac, what will it take? The woman you once loved is gone."

Solrac's deep brown eyes shone with unfathomable sadness. "I know."

"She might as well be dead. Worse than dead—She despises you!"

"I know, I know." Solrac brought his hands to his temples.

"Why not choose me, then?" Valla clenched both her fists and her teeth. "You know how I feel. Why I've stayed by your side all these years."

Long pent-up emotion bubbled up inside Valla. This wasn't the first time she'd spoken to Solrac about her feelings for him, but this was the first time she'd been so bold. Perhaps it was a result of the worry she'd felt while searching for him in the icy mountains. Or the mounting tension Valla, Boone, Rhana, and the others all felt regarding the looming threat of the Gray Ones. Maybe it was simply the lack of sleep, or the fact that she and Solrac never seemed to get enough alone time. Whatever the case, Valla was laying it all on the line.

"You never had to stay," Solrac said. "In fact, I asked for your transfer many times, only to be told you'd refused."

Valla got to her feet. "How could I leave you when you needed me? Even now, I was the only one who didn't give up searching for you. The one who tracked you all the way up here in this sky-forsaken wasteland."

Solrac stood as well. "And I'm forever in your debt, but Valla, I—"

"Don't pretend you don't care for me."

"Of course I care for you! I care for you so much it pains me!" For a moment they both stood in silence, then Valla dropped her eyes. When she next spoke, her angry tone had been replaced by one of longing.

"Then why not move on with me? Isn't nineteen years long enough to get over someone?"

"No amount of time will erase the vow I made." Solrac's gaze darkened. "She wasn't a mere fling. Vidya... She was my wife."

"So what?" Valla bit.

"A bond like that is not lightly broken."

"It is for some."

"But not for me." Sorlac rose to his full height, and Valla knew him well enough to sense the raw pain flaring up behind his eyes. His jaw tightened. "I let Vidya down all those years ago. I cannot help but feel partially responsible for all that has transpired since."

"So it's guilt then? Here I was thinking it was love," Valla spat, and Solrac's expression crumbled. His vulnerability made Valla's heart ache, but she couldn't back down now.

Solrac exhaled, physical and emotional exhaustion driving him to sit back down. He cracked his knuckles, eyes shut.

"Valla," he started, "this is who I am. If you are dissatisfied, then please, I beg of you, leave. There are plenty of worthy assignments for skilled Knights of the Torch like you."

Valla grimaced. "Not with Vesta running Orothion. Besides, you're not the only one who swore a vow. I promised to protect you, and scorch if that's not what I'm going to do."

Solrac looked up at Valla, eyes shining in the embers of the fire. "Even if I can never give you what you want?"

Valla paused, internally cursing her lower lip for trembling. When she spoke, her voice was quiet.

"Do you want me to go?"

Solrac gulped. "I only want you to feel as though you're free to—"

"Do you want me to go?" Valla repeated, this time with force.

Solrac didn't respond. The crackling of the coals and the distant hooting of evren-owls punctuated the silence.

Valla held her head high with pride. "Then I'm not going anywhere."

Solrac winced. Valla stubbornly began to pack up the bedroll.

"Come on," she said. "Sun's up. If we leave now, maybe we can cover enough ground to make it to the safehouse by nightfall."

Solrac silently helped Valla douse the fire and gather their belongings. He remained uncharacteristically quiet as they headed down the mountain.

Valla couldn't help but be grateful for the silence.

Where there's silence, she thought, *there's hope.*

CHAPTER 9: RAKAAI

ASHER

"**I**f this 'ere scorchapple cider ain't the warmin'est drakked thing in the eight keepdoms, I ain't a snowheaded scoundrel!"

Boone's folksy comments weren't the only thing giving me intensely familiar vibes. Surrounding the campfire at sunset were almost all the members of our old heist crew.

Solrac was finally back, and he sat on a log at the head of the group. He had his lute out, the rune glowing over his forehead allowing him to play the lute telekinetically so that he could sip his cider. The lute floated at shoulder level, plucking a lighthearted melody that seemed to match the dancing of the flames.

His Majesty the bloodhusky was curled up at Solrac's feet, lazily swaying to the music. At Solrac's side, Valla looked as grumpy as ever, but Boone, Kai, and I were enjoying the tune, and Kai's dragon, Flint, contentedly tapped his tail as my own dragon bond, Thorn, seemed to hum along as he crouched at the edge of the lake.

The lake just outside Rhana's cabin was covered by a thick layer of mirror-like ice, but Thorn had burned a hole through it using his dragonfire. He'd wait for unsuspecting drakefish to swim by under the ice, then rapidly stab through the hole using his tail spike. Each time he caught a fish, he'd proudly show off his tail-spike-skewer before digging in.

As we sat together near the edge of the small lake island, I couldn't help but feel the absence of our missing crewmates. Solrac must've been feeling the same way, because he suddenly burst into song.

Our crew has crossed the sea and sky
Since last we shared a drink
Each one of us embarked on tasks
That brought us to the brink
Valla, Boone, His Majesty
They took to Rengard's canyons
And there entangled with the Gray
And their wildshaping dragon!

Meanwhile, Asher, Kai, and Elle
Faced dragonslayers grim
To reach this safehouse swiftly so
Elle's training could begin
I, Solrac, became entrapped
When Vesta turned, you see
I fled to the Ridgeback's icy peaks
'Til Valla rescued me

But nay, our crew is not complete
While Kari forges on
And Jax, while decked in dusky blue
Spies on the darkest swan
But surely fate will once again
Having changed our lives forever
Will at last, through storm or haze
Bring us all back together

As the lute finished the song with a final flourish, His Majesty added a longing howl that echoed into the twilit sky.

"And of course," Solrac said with a smile, "we cannot forget the new friends we have made along the way. Who could have guessed that the lovely Princess of Drakfell would bond the very dragon egg we'd set out to steal?"

"Speaking of Elle," I said, "she should be here. I invited her and Aurora earlier today."

"She's probably busy packing," said Kai, using Flint's scaly back as a desk as he absently took notes in his journal. "She and Aurora are traveling to the Rebel Knight safehouse just south of Diamondback Fork first thing tomorrow."

"Ivar and a couple'a others are plannin' to accompany her," Boone said. "Should be a whole lotta new recruits down there a-waitin' for her arrival."

"Well then," Valla said, frowning. "They'll have to be disappointed. Rhana's orders: Eliana won't be going anywhere."

Kai looked up from his notebook. I raised an eyebrow.

"Why not?" I asked.

Valla exchanged glances with Solrac. "The Gallant Gopherdrake tavern was just ransacked by Capital soldiers. The whole thing is in shambles."

Surprised reactions broke out around the circle.

"What?" my voice rose above the others. "When did this happen?"

"Last night," Solrac solemnly confirmed. "We received word this morning."

"Along with the news that more Capital soldiers were spotted lurking near a few of our other safehouses in the area," Valla added. "Rebel Knight safehouses specifically."

Solrac sighed. "It seems our safehouses are no longer living up to their names."

"Why'n the stars would them black'n'whites spend time tryna smoke out the likes of us Rebels instead of focusin' on fightin' Orothion folks?" Boone asked.

"That is what I wondered as well," Solrac said. "Because of this, I sent Valla out in dragonhawk form this afternoon to spy on them." Solrac nodded to Valla before he continued.

"It seems that the news of a true dragon rider to rival High King Magnus is spreading through the realm like wildfire. Turns out, the High King does not like that. He's put out a bounty on young Eliana's head—one hundred gold marks to the person who can bring in the true dragon and her rider."

At that, Solrac produced a folded sheet of paper. The page depicted Elle's face, with Aurora's likeness standing just behind her. The bounty was listed, as well as a description of the two of them. It even depicted a few ribbons of light that looked like Aurora's dragonfire. Across the top of the page was the word 'Wanted'.

"One *hundred* gold marks?" Kai's eyes popped as he took the wanted poster from Solrac to get a closer look. I immediately swiped it from his hands.

"Soot," I cursed. The thought of people trying to capture Elle made me sick.

"So we're all in agreement then," Valla said. "For her own safety, no more baby-kissing for our true dragon rider. Boone and Ivar and the others can handle the recruitment missions."

"This is Elle we're talking about," I said. "I want to keep her safe more than anyone, but you're crazy if you think she's just going to stand by."

"She's not going to have a choice." Valla narrowed her eyes.

"Oh, isn't she?" came a disembodied voice, and I turned just in time to see Elle and Aurora landing on the shore. Landing just behind her were Rhana and Ivar astride two of Rhana's dragons. They must've heard we were gathering with Solrac tonight and didn't want to miss out on any important decisions. They made themselves welcome in the circle, and Boone ladled them each a cup of scorchapple cider from the pot hanging over the fire.

"I have an important role to play," Elle said once they'd settled in. "I won't cower here when I can make a difference. The people of this land deserve a true dragon rider with their best interests at heart, whether they're magi, half-born, or anything else."

I perked up at the words 'half-born.' Rhana, on the opposite scale, grumbled something about scale-skins under her breath before shooting me a subconscious look.

Ivar was looking at a folded, weatherworn map, a troubled look on his face. "Fact is, the High King's declaration that Elle's an enemy don't bode well for us on a number of levels. Essentially, he's tellin' every keep and every keepdom it's time to pick a side."

"Where do the keepdoms stand, then?" Boone asked.

Ivar laid out his map flat in the dirt, and several of us leaned toward it for a better look.

"The Capital Keepdom is with Magnus, obviously," Ivar said, pointing to a narrow strip in the map's center. The Capital Keepdom of Evgard was set along the Ridgeback River, and within its boundary was the majority of the Ridgeback Mountain range.

Next, Ivar dragged his finger to the southeast. "Evyndara—where we're at now—is divided. The leadership's pledged loyalty to the High Throne, though we've managed to poach a few smaller keeps out here on the west side. Still, we can't count on much."

"What about Evyndale?" Valla asked, using her sword to point to the realm's easternmost keepdom. "Solrac said the Farseer was hoping to meet with the king and queen there."

"Evyndale's just a bunch of low-life, pompous, Capital scale-suckers," Rhana said. "That's what the Dragon Wars taught me. Too many half-borns on the coast, too."

I shot her a look, but she pointedly ignored me. A few others looked uncomfortably away, too. I held my tongue, but only barely.

"Rengard isn't in a position to back either side," Ivar moved on, directing our attention to the massive Canyonlands Keepdom that filled the southern portion of the map. "Not with their war with the Dragon Isles."

"A war perpetuated by a scalehead of a widowed queen," Valla grumbled.

"Nevertheless, we hope to visit and sway Queen Ilona and the other Rengardian leaders in time as well," Solrac said.

"Kolbohr's no good neither," said Boone, withdrawing one of his starglass daggers and shooting a tiny blast of ether from the end to land smack onto a smaller keepdom in the northeast.

"Too many ghosts a-lurkin' 'round those parts, believe you me," Boone said ominously.

"Isn't there anyone on our side?" Kai asked. He was taking notes in his journal, clearly worried about the growing number in the 'enemies' category.

"Drakfell," Elle said. "At least, I'm certain my parents would take our side were it not for the Knights' schism. They risked a lot, turning their back on the High King to join the Knights, and abandoning Skygard now would leave them vulnerable."

"My meetings with the queen of Behrfell resulted in similar sentiments," Solrac said. "She is unwilling to support us while the Knights remain divided. If we want the northern armies, we must first find a way to put a stop to Vesta's march on Evgard."

"My dragons have been keeping an eye on her armies' movement," Rhana said. "She continues to match the Capital Riders by catching them by surprise. Eliana and I have wondered how she's so mobile."

"What do you mean by 'mobile'?" Ivar asked.

"A few days ago, she launched an attack on Cascadia," Rhana said, "but only this morning her armies showed up in Scaledeer Pass."

We all bent over Ivar's map as he pointed out each location. One was on the Capital Keepdom's southwestern shore, while the other was in the center near the Capital city.

"Well I'll be a diamondback's dead uncle!" Boone exclaimed. "How in Solei's blue sky are they doin' that?"

"I think I've got an idea." Ivar's expression turned solemn. He took a long swig from his drink, then exhaled before saying one word: "Riftin'."

"Rifting entire armies across the land?" I asked in disbelief.

"Impossible," Kai said. "The ether supply versus use ratio is too high even for the most skilled Rifter."

"Unless…" Solrac trailed off. We all turned to him as he stroked his goatee. I could tell a part of him very much enjoyed holding our attention.

"Unless what?" I finally asked.

"Skystone," Solrac said.

Valla nodded, brows lowered. "With enough skystone, a Rifter would never run out of ether. They could rift leagues of soldiers as far as they wanted, as long as they had an anchor there."

"But wouldn't that much skystone draw every wild dragon from miles around?" I asked.

Rhana scoffed. "Not if they're operating out of Orothion. Use your head."

I felt my frustration rise again, but Solrac was suddenly runetracing. A golden illusion symbol appeared over his forehead.

"Rhana's right," Solrac said with an air of drama. With a flourish of his hand, Solrac produced a miniature, translucent illusion of the Orothion citadel. I'd only been there once, but I recognized the iconic ascending turrets that ended with the highest peak overlooking the cliffside and the ocean.

"Orothion is one of the oldest remaining strongholds built during the Guardian Era," Solrac said, his tone becoming showmanlike. "The Guardians are most prominently remembered for their ability to access all nine types of etherarchy, but besides that, they were incredibly skilled builders. History says that the last Guardian and one of the founders of the Knights of the Torch, the great philosopher Theok, wanted to protect the base. Under Theok's direction, the Knights built many safeguards into their castle."

Solrac made a swiping motion with his hand, and the illusion focused in on a small portion of the castle. We watched, captivated as he showed us a triangular piece of golden metal with three diamonds coming off each point.

"Etherlocks," Rhana said. "The three I've got here at the cabin came from Orothion."

"Them etherlocks're what keep the ghosts away!" Boone put in. I nearly chuckled, but based on Solrac and Rhana's serious nods, Boone wasn't just being superstitious.

"They're also what cloak both this place and Orothion from forces that would harm those who seek refuge inside," Solrac went on. "Including wild dragons. It's how Skygard has been able to remain a safe refuge for magi. The secret to building etherlocks died with the Guardians, and no one has ever been able to replicate—or decrypt—the ancient technology."

"Of course," Kai said. "If Vesta had a large hoard of skystone *inside* the Orothion castle, the etherlocks would keep its ether signature from drawing wild dragons.

"It would also explain how she's moving so many soldiers so far across the realm," Elle added. "All she'd have to do is deliver rift anchors to various locations, then let the skystone power every jump."

I suddenly sat straight up. "Soot—but she still needs a Rifter to make the portals."

Understanding dawned in Valla's eyes too. "Akayto," she said.

"Who's Akayto?" Ivar asked.

I gulped. "My dad."

Solrac grimaced as he, too, realized we were right. "Ever since the purge, Rifters are scarce. They are too often kept as prisoners and used for their power."

Ivar clearly didn't like that. Neither did I.

"Are you saying my father is a prisoner?" I asked as adrenaline began to flow within me.

"I cannot say for certain," Solrac replied. "The mirror copy of Glint Kai left with Kari has not been able to provide us with clear information. Is that correct, Kai?"

Kai nodded solemnly. "Glint Two is down. At first, I figured Kari must've gotten busy and forgotten to ensure she gets enough sunlight to properly maintain our connection. But now... I'm not so sure. I'm worried someone might've found her Glint and used silver to destroy her."

"Oh stars," Elle said, putting a hand over her heart.

"Scorchin' scaleshrews," Boone agreed. "You think Vesta's stooped to offin' li'l geckos?"

"She's out of control," Valla said. "Why doesn't Zel stand up to her?"

I recalled Zel, the cheery, elderly half-born man who was part of the Knights' leadership council. I doubted he could stand up to a scalefly, let alone fierce Vesta.

"You saw what happened to me when I went against her," Solrac said. "Vesta sent us fleeing the keepdom on pain of death."

"Well we can't just sit here!" I leaped to my feet. "We have to send someone back to Orothion to find out if Kari and my dad are okay. I'll go myself!"

Rhana stood as she barked at me, "Nobody leaves this cabin without my say so."

"But we're taking about my fa—"

Rhana cut me off. "Sit down, scale-skin!"

I snapped back without thinking. "You sit down, you geriatric Drekai-hater."

"Asher, show some respect!" Boone warned.

Valla narrowed her eyes at me too. "Rhana has more experience in her pinkie finger than you do in your entire body."

Anger rose inside me and words were tumbling out of my mouth before I could stop them. "She hasn't left her property in decades. What does she know about the real world? I don't care if she was the High Queen back in the day—that doesn't make her the authority now!"

"Asher, I'm warnin' you…" Boone said.

"He's right about one thing," Rhana said, crossing her arms. "I'm not the authority here. That responsibility falls to the true dragon rider."

"Right," I said sarcastically. "The true dragon rider you want to quarantine here. This isn't what she wants."

"I can speak for myself, Asher," Elle shot back.

"Then do so, Eliana," Ivar said diplomatically, trying to ease the tension. "What say you regarding a quest to Orothion to rescue Asher's father and the others?"

Elle stiffened as all eyes turned on her. Rhana and I sat down as slowly as Elle stood, smoothing her long skirt. The tiara on her head glinted in the firelight.

When she replied, her tone was formal. "I will consider all the possibilities and propose a befitting plan within a reasonable time frame."

Rhana gave a proud nod. She must've approved of Elle's vague, diplomatic response.

I, on the opposite scale, did not. I ground my back teeth together in frustration. Elle had never struck me as one of the stiff, unfeeling noble types before. This wasn't her.

Solrac cleared his throat. "Eliana is correct. We need a well-thought-out plan. Akayto will be alright for now, as Vesta would not let any harm come to her only Rifter. But acting in haste will only put him, Kari, and ourselves in danger. We must consult the Farseer further before we make our decision. Oy. There is much to discuss with him…"

Solrac put a hand to his head, wincing. Valla was on her guard immediately, checking him over to ensure he was alright. I'd nearly forgotten that he'd almost died up there in the Ridgebacks.

"You mean the Black Valkyrie, don't you?" Valla said. "You mentioned the Farseer spoke with you about her while you were in the mountains."

"Yes," Solrac replied with a sigh. "The Farseer has been seeing concerning images in his omenfires. Ones that include the Black Valkyrie and the other… skymages."

"Skymages," Kai repeated. "That's what someone from the Black Valkyrie's entourage mentioned last year too. I've been doing some reading since then, and I've learned that, long ago, skymages were special servants to the all-powerful Guardians. Magi the Guardians blessed with multiple types of etherarchy."

"Like the Black Valkyrie," Ivar said. "Saw her fight back in Keep Rengard and saw her silvermarks myself. She's got both psionics and shadowbindin'."

Solrac was subconsciously rubbing his back as he added, "And Wildshaping."

Protests erupted at that. Valla looked especially disturbed.

"I'm afraid it's true," Solrac said. "The Farseer is quite certain of it. And Vidya is just the beginning. More of these so-called skymages are surfacing by the day. The Mage Hunter, Jaira, for instance, has magi abilities now as well."

"That's true," I said. "I saw her lightning whip myself in Swan Spire. I just assumed she was using some kind of relic."

Ivar shook his head. "Nah, that's her own power alright."

"It's them ghosts, I tell you," Boone muttered.

"I fear Boone is right," Solrac said. "Chaos is brewing from all sides. Vesta's Knights, the Mage Hunters, the war between the Canyonlands and the Dragon Isles, threats against Eliana from the Capital... They are all signs of what's to come. Voidarchy—dark ether. That is the real threat our realm faces." Solrac ran his hands through his hair. "But that is one problem I do not know how to prepare for."

I snapped my fingers. "But the Drekai do."

"What?" Valla raised her eyebrow. Most people were looking at me with confusion. Rhana was shooting me another glare.

Kai was the only one who seemed to know where I was going with this. "Asher, no," he said.

I ignored him. "The Drekai know way more than we do about voidarchy. They've been fighting it already themselves. You all saw what was in Cenrik's case. All that stuff about the Drekai looking for voidshards?"

Solrac put a hand to his chin. "That is true, I suppose."

"It's the perfect opportunity," I said, growing animated as the idea took root. I grabbed Ivar's map and pointed to the Dragon Isles in the far west. "You all said yourselves we're desperate for allies. I have that duel with General Kheradok coming up. Why not swing it into a bid for an alliance? As a half-born, I could help lead our—"

"You're no more fit to lead than a child." Rhana cut me off. "You're impulsive and foolish, just like your plan. Ally with the Drekai..." She shook her head.

My gut twisted at her harsh words. Part of me wanted to yell at her again while another part wanted to cry.

Instead, I bit my lip, looking out at the rest of the group. "Is that how all of you feel?"

Silence met me. Not even Elle would look me in the eye.

Kai put a hand on my shoulder. "Asher, in another world, it would be a good plan. But there are too many factors at play. Too many wild cards."

"By that, you mean me," I said. It wasn't a question.

The tension was thick, the only sound the crackling of the campfire.

Finally, Boone took a long swig from his drink. I took that as my cue to leave.

Thorn was ready and waiting at the lakeside.

The next morning, I woke up before anyone else and headed straight for the dragon stables. Thorn felt me coming through our bond, and was ready and waiting at the entrance.

The mixing warm and cold air of early spring at sunrise rushed across my face. My hair loop slipped, leaving my bangs to whip in the wind, and I felt like I could breathe again. Flying with Thorn always cleared my head.

From up here, I could see the Mirror Forest's cindercones outside the property line, sloping down and endlessly eastward. That was the direction of the Mage Hunter Academy, one of the many places I wasn't allowed to go. I felt like a prisoner—like my dad was back at Orothion.

To the west, a break in the trees outside the property line made way for a grassy field. A few early-blooming wildflowers stood out with vibrant shades of yellow, purple, and scarlet.

I felt a pang of nostalgia as I noticed a small lake near the field. A lone dragon buffalo lapped at the water's edge, and the sight of it suddenly transported my mind to another mountain lake.

Mom's valley was a lush paradise nestled between the dry, craggy cliffs just north of Steel Rim. She and I, along with Dad, had spent many wonderful days there watching the dragon buffalo drink from the crystal clear water. We had a favorite perch: a little outcropping in the cliff face Mom had called '*Kiivi Zariika*,' which she'd taught me was Drekai for 'cozy rock.'

I couldn't help but let my mind slip into memory as I recalled one spring afternoon sitting with Mom on the ledge at *Kiivi Zariika*. It seemed so long ago, before I'd gotten caught up in the Knights of the Torch or honor duels—I hadn't even started cragchasing with Kai yet. It was my fourteenth birthday, just a few months before the Black Valkyrie had come for her.

To celebrate, Mom made *anuukas*, Drekai rolled pancakes—my all-time favorite breakfast. Each pancake was cooked extra thin with crispy edges, then filled with cream and sweet cinderberries.

"Cinderberries as sweet as my *laaksi-rakaai*," Mom said with an embarrassingly affectionate tap to my nose.

"Mom," I said, melodramatically batting her hand away. "I'm fourteen—not very *laaksi* anymore."

"You don't want to be called my little love?" she brought a hand to her chest in mock shock. "So, you'd rather I called you my *khomaala taiin-ikaani-rakaai*?"

My Drekai language skills weren't perfect, but I knew enough to recognize that she was calling me an 'awkward teenager.'

I snorted. "Let's stick with *laaksi*."

Mom chuckled, her teasing expression melting. I noticed a hint of sadness in her dragonfire green eyes. "You're right, though. You really aren't little at all anymore. Asher..."

Before I knew it, she was untying the turquoise dust scarf she'd always worn around her neck. She'd replaced almost all of her possessions from her former life in the Dragon Isles, but not her scimitar or her scarf.

"Have I ever told you what the markings mean?" Mom asked, passing me the scarf. I flattened it to a square and held it on my lap where I could better see the tiny, intricate pattern running all across it in faintly gold threads. To most, it just looked like a cool design, but Mom had always told me that amidst the triangles and diamonds there was also draconic writing. Not the Drekai language as it currently stood, but an older version.

"It's the lyrics to a song," Mom explained. Her usual joking tone had turned serious. "I used to only know them in Drekai, but a few months ago I translated them for you. I... I want you to understand the words as fully as possible."

With that, Mom began to sing, her voice sweet and clear.

You are a link in a legacy of light
A chain that spans the ages
Sent to tend with wisdom and might
Through bright or darkened stages

We will guide you
Ever beside you
We who've come before
Do not fear
Your time draws near
Share light forevermore

There was a short silence after Mom finished the song before I gave her a nod.

"Nice song, Mom," I said, holding out the scarf to her. My mind was already wandering, wanting to climb down the cliff face and play down in the lake. I wondered if Mom would declare it warm enough to let me swim.

Mom could tell I was distracted and let out a sigh before ruffling my hair. Several black strands fell over my eyes, and she smiled as she pushed them out of the way.

"Yes, you can go swimming," Mom read my mind. "But I want you to keep the scarf."

"What?" My eyes widened. "But this is *your* scarf."

"And it was my father's before that," Mom said. "Now, it's yours, Asher."

I grinned widely, tying the bandana around my neck. I'd long admired Mom's scarf—It was brightly colored, and I liked to stand out.

Then, Mom and I both channeled etherarchy, our eyes glowing gold. She was a Shadowbinder magi while I was an Astromancer, but both of us were spirit-focused magi, or Archons. That meant we could both levitate.

We hover-jumped from *Kiivi Zariika*, then raced to the gorgeous, clear lake within the valley. She leaped extra high, turning back to call out to me as she fell.

"You've got this, Asher!"

You've got this, Asher.

My eyes snapped open. They were filled with tears as my mind returned to reality... but... that voice. That had definitely been Mom's voice, and not just in my mind.

But, of course, when I looked around, all I saw was open sky and a bright break in the clouds. It was just Thorn and me up here.

You okay, Asher? my wyvern asked through our bond. He must've sensed my rapidly beating heart.

"Fine," I replied out loud. Mom was gone. My dad claimed he could still see her in the spirit plane, but I'd long known he was letting the Sight play tricks on his mind.

Right?

I felt at the scarf around my neck, feeling grateful that I still had a piece of her. *I only wish this piece was enough,* I thought as my mind—for the millionth time—wandered to that envelope I'd seen in Swan Spire.

But Kai's perpetual warning echoed in my head: *Don't go back to that tower.* I let out a frustrated sigh.

Finally, Thorn and I circled back toward the cabin. Thorn landed at the entrance to Rhana's dragon stables, where I took off his saddle and led him inside toward his stall.

The last thing I'd expected to hear inside those stables was a frustrated, feminine grunt, accompanied by the sound of a shovel angrily thrusting into dirt.

Thorn sniffed the air and a blooming ember of a smile glowed through our bond as he turned and left me, slinking off to his stall with a quiet wyvern chuckle.

Confused, I rounded the corner to find...

"Elle?" My mouth fell open as I took in the sight of the Princess of Drakfell, dressed in a dingy brown work dress. Her crown was gone, her long hair piled into a messy bun atop her head. Dirt smudged her cheeks and forearms where she'd rolled up the sleeves of her dress.

She was probably unrecognizable to most of the people here, but seeing her like this immediately transported me back to the dragon stables at Keep Drakfell. Before I'd learned who she really was, Elle and I had spent a lot of time together working as stablehands. Above all, Elle loved dragons, and was more than willing to go in disguise to spend more time with them.

"Asher?" Elle looked just as surprised to see me. Surprised, but not upset.

"What are you doing out here?" I asked.

"What do you think?" she replied, grunting once more as she vigorously thrust her shovel into the mud. "After last night's campfire meeting, I needed to release some steam." Elle looked me over.

"What are *you* doing out here?" she echoed my question.

"Nothing," I replied.

"Nothing?" Elle arced a smooth eyebrow. "Well, in that case..." She broke into a mischievous grin, then reached toward a row of tools hanging on a nearby wall.

Oh soot. I knew what was coming. I crinkled my nose, as I knowingly removed my jacket and rolled up my shirt sleeves as well.

Elle laughed and tossed me a shovel of my own. "Just like old times, Asher of Steel Rim. Looks like you and I are on stable-mucking duty."

Elle and I spent the next couple of hours scooping dragon dung. At first, I wasn't sure this was how I wanted to voluntarily spend the rest of my afternoon, but soon a wonderful, familiar feeling settled over the two of us. I remembered just how much I'd looked forward to long days mucking out stalls back in Keep Drakfell, just the pair of us, laughing and singing to pass the time.

Elle must've felt the same way, and a new verse to her old dung-scooping song soon rang throughout the stables:

Cabin dragons eat a lot
And leave a ton behind
But Ash and I, we'll clean it up
And we won't even mind
Rhana's dragons, though well-meaning
Certainly could learn self-cleaning

As usual, Elle's improvised lyrics had me in stitches. By the end of her song, I was laughing so hard I dropped my shovel.

The handle fell, landing with a splash in a puddle of mud for the wyvernhogs who shared the stables to wallow in. Thankfully, their wallowing mud was kept separate from their defecation area, because I watched a few rogue drops splatter onto Elle's dress, arms, and face.

She gasped, amber eyes storming as she turned my way. I couldn't help but double over.

Glaring, Elle used her own shovel to scoop up some miry sludge of her own. Without giving me time to react, she launched it toward me, and brown instantly speckled my shirt.

My jaw dropped, and for one last moment, Elle and I stared at each other in silence.

Then, battle commenced.

It was disgusting, of course. But more than that, it was insanely fun.

Elle and I were laughing so hard our sides ached by the time we slumped to the ground, sitting back to back, splattered with mud from head to toe. We were both in desperate need of a wash, but I somehow felt more refreshed than I had in a long time.

"So, since you're clearly dirtier than I am, I'd say that's three points for me, at least," I said with a grin.

In response, Elle grabbed one last handful of mud and wiped it directly across my cheek.

"Three for you, and four for me." Now it was her turn to grin.

Stars. Even messy with muck, Elle was beautiful.

We sighed, leaning against each other's backs and looking up at the stable's strong, wooden rafters.

Elle sighed. "You're right, you know."

"Right about what?" I asked.

"About the Drekai. I... I think they have the answers we need about voidarchy too."

"You do?" My heart skipped. At least someone had given my apparent insanity a second thought.

"Yes. And now that I've had time to think, I believe your idea to parlay the duel with General Kheradok into an alliance is a good one. I plan to bring it up to Solrac and the other Rebel Knight leaders again when the time is right."

"Stars," I said, both grateful and suddenly nervous.

Elle seemed to sense my tension through my back. "I know that puts a lot of pressure on you, but don't worry. I've seen you training with Rhana, Boone, and Ivar over the past several weeks."

"You think I can beat an experienced, older Drekai warrior? A general no less?"

"He's not *that* much older than us," Elle said quickly. Was that an almost defensive tone?

When Elle didn't elaborate, I pushed against her back.

"You okay?" I asked.

"Huh?" She straightened with a start. "Oh, yes. And yes, I think you stand a very good chance of beating Kheradok—*General* Kheradok, I mean. You're both incredibly driven and determined, but you... There's something special about you, Asher. You've always stood out. Not just to me, but to everyone."

I chuckled. "It's the nose. Say what you will about the rest of me—messy hair, easily distracted, and personality flaws all over the place, but I've always thought I had a very nice nose."

Now it was Elle's turn to press against my back.

"Right. I was definitely talking about your nose. Exclusively."

"I knew it."

We laughed, and I felt another wave of release. It felt good to just talk with Elle like this. In this chaotic time, she put me at ease.

"Elle?" I started. "Do you remember what you said back in Orothion at the end of last summer? Before we left for Rengard?"

Elle measured her words. "Yes. I called you stupid."

I grinned. "True. But you also said you wanted to kiss me."

"And you said you weren't ready." Elle jabbed me with her elbow.

I took a deep breath, reaching behind me to take her mud-smeared hand in mine. "Well, I think I'm ready now."

I heard Elle's breath catch as her fingers closed around my own.

I went on. "Over these past months, I've watched you become one of the greatest, most inspiring, beautiful leaders this realm has ever seen. And as I've watched you from the sidelines, I've realized just how much I missed you."

"Missed me?" she asked. "I've been right here."

"*Eliana* has been here," I said. "The noble princess and true dragon rider, icon of Evgard. But today, I was lucky enough to spend time with *Elle*. Elle, the clever, dragon-loving girl I first started falling for last summer."

For a long time, Elle didn't respond. After a while, the silence became heavy enough that a small sense of dread began to stir inside my chest.

"Oh, Asher," she finally said. "I've wanted you to come around for months. But..."

Uh oh. 'But' just became my least favorite word.

"But," she continued, "I think you're right again. About the two sides of me, Elle and Eliana."

Elle swallowed, and I felt her grip on my hand slipping as she went on.

"I have a duty to perform. As much as I want to spend my days running around free, spending all my time with dragons, I can't. It's not in my stars."

My heart sank further as I searched for something to say. For once, I was speechless.

"You need an 'Elle,'" she said. "But I need to be an 'Eliana.' That's why I think it's better if for now—and maybe forever—we just stay friends."

She let go of my hand completely then, getting to her feet.

"I should get cleaned up before anyone sees me like this," Elle muttered. "Goodbye, Asher."

"Bye, Elle," I replied dumbly, unsure what else there was to say.

Then she ran from the stables. I wasn't sure if it was because rejecting me had been painful or if she couldn't wait to get away from me. I felt sick to my stomach. But something in me knew she was right.

Eliana and I were from two different worlds, and there was no way I'd ever belong in hers. She deserved to have someone by her side who could match her intellect and grace in court.

Not someone who got her into mud-flinging matches.

CHAPTER 10: THE ASYLUM

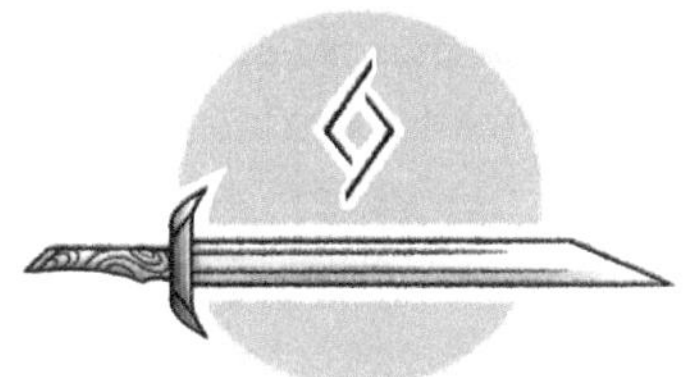

MELEYA

The illusion of a wraith shimmering just above the tip of the Black Valkyrie's psionically floating shadowspear may have been small, but the depiction still set my teeth on edge. The Black Valkyrie's illusion perfectly captured the ever-churning smokiness of the Gray Ones, with its upper half more fully formed into human shape. The face was featureless but for its glowing blue eyes, and from within its chest I saw the same faintly glowing blue core I'd noticed when I'd seen the creatures in Etheria.

After a long day of regular Mage Hunter instruction, Vidya and I were now alone in Swan Spire. She'd finally felt well enough to resume teaching the odd class, though Jaira ran most of them. Still, at my request, Vidya had finally agreed to fulfill the promise she'd made me in the High Ridgebacks and teach me how to control my wraith.

"Wraiths are nothing more than a power source," Vidya explained as she slowly paced around her floating spear. "Like your ether well or seaxe. You can use her like you would any other tool."

"How?" I asked, feeling uneasy about this entire conversation.

"It takes time and practice. At first, I fought my wraith, but I eventually found peace. But only once I accepted that the Gray Ones, in exchange for a taste of our humanity, will grant us access to power long lost to our generation."

"Power's not what I'm after," I said. "All I've ever wanted is my mom and dad's safety. For them, and me, to have a real home."

"Ah, but power breeds security," Vidya said. "Think of your parents, trapped by those in power. But if you were the one in control...well. That would change everything."

I pressed my lips together at that. Vidya had promised me the chance to see my mother. I knew she was here somewhere. But when I'd asked again, Vidya had regretfully informed me that such matters were now out of her hands. Mason Drakeslayer had taken charge of handling enemies of the realm, and he'd denied her access to the place where my mother was being held after receiving the cure. That had filled me with dread. Not only had my mother already lost her etherarchy, but Mason's leverage over me was even stronger than I'd realized.

"That's just it," I said. "What if I'm not the one in control?"

"Wraiths only have as much power as we give them," Vidya said. "That was the Liberator's problem. She and the Coven granted the Gray Ones too much dominion. Worshiped them, even. But as you and I both saw on the night of Keep Rengard's Winter Solstice Ball, that can only lead to chaos."

"That's an understatement," I said, remembering the madness that had taken place that night. There had been umbral creatures, gray hoods, and more bloodshed than I ever wanted to see again.

"Chaos is what the Gray Ones crave," Vidya went on. "And our task, Meleya, is to harness that chaos. Make the Gray serve you."

"That's what you've done?" I asked.

Vidya paused. "The Gray is what allowed me to fight the Liberator and... others."

I got the feeling that by 'others,' Vidya meant the Farseer. Or rather, Solrac.

"But at times I question why," Vidya said quietly, her aloof expression faltering. The illusory wraith flickered, and the telekinetically floating spear briefly dipped toward the floor.

"Why?" I repeated the word. "Why us?"

Vidya bit her lip. "Because wraiths always choose those with the most potential. We have no choice but to embrace it."

No choice, my wraith rasped in my ear.

A loud pounding at the door got Vidya to stand up straight again. She dismissed the rune over her forehead and the wraith illusion vanished as she grabbed her spear.

"Come in," she called.

A pair of Mage Hunters entered the tower, and I was surprised when I recognized them. One was a thin man with a Seer's silvermark on his cheek and a large, shiny snake familiar draped over his shoulders. The other was his Hunting partner, a burly Geomancer whom I could've sworn I'd seen die at the Winter Solstice ball. He looked completely fine now as the two swept into the room.

"Ilyan, Shaw," the Black Valkyrie nodded first to the Seer and then to the Geomancer.

"Black Valkyrie." The Seer, Ilyan, nodded back. "We come with a message from Mason Drakeslayer. He says the Snowstorm is late for her evening combat class with him."

At the mention of my so-called class with Mason, my blood ran cold. Scryer's Grotto was waiting.

Vidya frowned as she turned to me "What's this?"

"Uh," I started, then did my best to give the response Mason had made me swear to give whenever anyone asked. "The High Prince has been having me study spying techniques. As a Rifter, my ability to use the Sight makes me the ideal choice. I... I'm eager to serve the realm in this capacity."

Vidya's frown deepened at that, and for a second, I worried she could see straight through the half-lie. The last thing I wanted to do was to make a scene and put my mom in even more danger.

Finally, Vidya turned back to Ilyan. "Tell Mason Drakeslayer I'm not finished with her yet."

Ilyan narrowed his eyes, and the ethereal snake on his shoulders hissed. "The High Prince doesn't like to be kept waiting."

There was a bit of a standoff. I could tell that Vidya was waiting to see whose side Ilyan and Shaw would choose: Hers, or Mason Drakeslayer's.

At last, Ilyan broke the silence by repeating his earlier statement. "The High Prince will see the Snowstorm now."

"Actually," Shaw piped up. "I think we can let the Black Valkyrie finish first."

The two men glared at each other. It seemed the power struggle between Mason and Vidya ran deeper than I realized.

Desperate not to cause any trouble for my mom, I got to my feet.

"It's alright," I said. "I'll go." Without another word, I hurried from the room.

My ether well was low, and my headache was growing, which meant that Mason would be here soon to take me away from Scryer's Grotto and back to the dorm.

Time passed slowly as I pretended to search the ever-flashing crystals for the aura of a dead woman. By now, I'd been bold enough to explore the caverns a little deeper. More tidepools hid amongst the craggy stone, and in some places seawater ebbed and flowed. But when I'd found a pair of thick, rusted chains hanging from the ceiling, I'd retreated back to where the crystals grew. I wasn't interested in finding out what those chains were for.

Curious as to where in the realm Scryer's Grotto actually was, I spent a long time casually looking for my own aura. It took a few nights, but I finally spotted it on the very edge of the crystal labeled 'Kolbohr.' When I focused on the spot, I could sort of see misty shapes indicating a seaside. That would explain why it was so damp here.

Looking at the Kolbohr crystal, I saw groups of auras that appeared muted, somehow grayed out as they milled about what appeared to be a mountainside. I spent a while pondering why so many auras in the same place would all be grayish like that, then I remembered what Brigan had said the other day about the Keepdom of Kolbohr welcoming any skyfall refugees who'd been stricken with the shadow wasting. Could all these auras belong to shadow wasting victims? And what were they all doing here?

I might have been losing my mind as I stared, but I could've sworn I also saw the caramel-colored aura of my old mentor, Torsten, in the Capital city of Evgard in the Waterfall Keepdom. Later, I wondered if the deep purple aura wandering the northern border between Behrfell and Kolbohr belonged to Zoren, the Drekai Mage Hunter who'd captured my parents.

Eventually, I found a particularly strange group of auras that seemed half as bright as the rest. These were different from the possible shadow wasting refugee auras—those had been muted in color. These seemed muted in, I don't know, intensity?

Upon closer inspection, the dimmed auras appeared to be floating along together in some kind of fleet. Longships perhaps? But from what

I could tell, they didn't stick to rivers or seas. For a while, I wondered if I was watching a strange nomadic caravan, but they weren't necessarily land-bound either.

I tracked the cluster of auras over the course of a couple of days, but only found myself getting more confused by them. This whole place was confusing. Confusing, and lonely.

As if on cue, a voice resounded in my head.

I am here, Meleya, my wraith said.

"Get out of my head," I said, squeezing my eyes shut.

Is that really what you want? the wraith replied. *Is it not comforting knowing I am here, just in case you need access to my power? Twice voidarchy has saved the people you love. It is like the Black Valkyrie says, Meleya. Use the Gray. Some are not strong enough to control it, but* you *are.*

"Augh!" I cried into the darkness, slamming my fists against the nearest giant crystal. I didn't know what to think.

I focused on the crystal before me as more meaningless colors danced along its edge. It was the Evyndara crystal, which was the keepdom the Academy was in now. Desperate for something to do, I scanned the crystal until I found a feather-like cerulean aura. That was Solvai in the dorm at the Academy. Beside her was Brigan's vivid red, and not far from theirs I saw the brilliant tangerine color of Jax's aura. I stared at it for several minutes, my fingers following Jax as he moved about the dorm.

I was about to start looking for my other squadmates' auras nearby when a flash of vibrant turquoise pulled my attention. Two turquoise auras stuck close together. One was darker, but the other...

I frowned. It was the exact hue I'd seen on the scale-tipped ears of...

"Asher of Steel Rim," I said under my breath, putting a finger on the aura. It had to be him—It was like Mason had said: no two auras were alike. It even had the same sort of erratic, playful—and obnoxious—energy I'd sensed in Asher that day we'd fought in Swan Spire.

Thinking of my tangle with Asher reminded me of that envelope he'd wanted badly enough to take on the Black Valkyrie's entire entourage at once, and of the gratitude in his eyes when I'd hidden it from Jaira. Unsure what else to do, I'd later tucked the envelope safely away into Sniff's saddlebag and forgotten all about it.

My frown deepened as I noted a certain other aura floating beside Asher's. It was another shade I recognized; a strong, determined sage green.

"Dad?" I said, my voice echoing throughout the grotto. I hurriedly clapped my hand over my mouth. Yes, I knew I was alone here, but I still... something about this place put me on edge.

My head was spinning. Asher and my dad were together. Right now. Somewhere in...

I glanced at the keepdom name carved into the crystal: Evyndara—the same keepdom I was in now.

I focused the Sight harder on that spot on the crystal and more details came into view. Cindercone pine tree auras... a clear, smooth lake, mountains... They were in the Mirror Forest! And not far from them, I could see the auras associated with the Academy. They weren't all that far away, maybe a few dozen miles.

I knew Dad had gone with the Rebel Knights after the battle on the Winter Solstice. If he and Asher were there...

Soot. Had I just discovered a Rebel Knight camp?

"You found something."

Mason's voice made me jump so high my head thumped against the massive crystal above me. My Sight rune dissolved as I lost concentration.

"What did you find?" Mason pressed, stalking closer as the portal he'd come through disappeared.

"No," I replied defensively. Then, realizing that my answer didn't match his original question I quickly tried to remedy it. "I mean nothing. I found nothing. Nothing is what I meant to say."

"You're not a very good liar, are you?" the High Prince said, pushing me aside to get a look at the Evyndara crystal shard I'd been examining. He traced a Sight rune of his own, the symbol shining over his forehead in blue.

He squinted at the crystal, but I could tell his ability to use the Sight wasn't anywhere near good enough to see what I'd seen. After a moment, Mason cursed.

"Scorch this weak ether well!" He put a hand to his head.

Mason blinked a few times, his expression shifting from angry to something more darkly sinister. I bit my lip.

"Perhaps," he began, "you need another reminder of why you're here." Mason reached into his tailored navy-colored jacket and pulled out those same two folded sheets of parchment he'd flaunted on the first day we'd met: the freedom papers for my mother and father.

"What did you see?" he repeated, this time more menacingly.

"My father," I replied. It was true—partially.

At that, Mason's expression softened, and it was like he was actually seeing me. The blue rune over his head flickered out.

"I need you to focus on the mission," Mason said. "I'd hate to have to get the Surgeon involved. Do you understand?"

"Yes, your highness," I said, inclining my head.

"Very good," Mason said, pushing past me to get to the rift anchor that would take us back to the Academy. He activated the stone, and I moved to follow him through the portal.

"What do you think you're doing?" Mason snapped.

"Aren't we going back?" I cocked my head. He was giving me emotional whiplash.

"*I* am," Mason said. "As for you, I thought I made myself clear. I need results on the search for the voidshard, and until I get them, your so-called 'evening class' with me just doubled in length. I'll be back in another two hours."

"Wha-what?" I stammered, anxiety bubbling up inside my chest. "But... please, High Prince Mason, don't make me stay here. This place... the voices and the darkness..." I suddenly felt like I couldn't breathe.

For the briefest second, it looked like Mason felt for my plight again. But then, in a dark flash, his expression hardened once more.

"Then we suggest you perform your task with extra vigor."

With that, Mason left me alone with my demon in the dark, damp cove.

I had no idea how late it was when I returned from Scryer's Grotto that night, only that I'd never felt more exhausted in my life. My eyes were heavy, my lungs still felt tight, and my ether well was down to its last dregs, leaving me with a splitting headache.

I snuck into the darkened dorm, still debating whether or not to go to sleep. More nightmares about the Soul Reaper awaited me, I was certain of it.

That was when I saw a head of brown hair and a face full of freckles look up at me from the rug. Solvai was sitting before the dim hearth, but she got to her feet when she saw me.

"Meleya," Solvai said. "Thank the goddesses."

171

"Solvai?" I asked, my voice dry. "Why are you still up? You need rest before class tomorrow."

"I was waiting for you," she replied, her brows knit with worry. "Where were you?"

"My evening combat class went late," I said.

Solvai shook her head. "That sooty class. I don't care if he's the High Prince over the realm—This isn't right. I've seen you fight, and you sure as scales don't need extra training."

I pressed my lips together, hardly daring to make eye contact with my best friend. She was obviously waiting for some kind of explanation, but I knew the second I opened my mouth I'd inevitably burst into tears.

"Ugh!" Solvai tossed her hands. "Again with this tight-lipped attitude. Ever since we got here, I feel like you haven't been yourself. You're not sleeping well and you hardly eat. That's not like you *at all*. Brigan and I are both worried."

Solvai's hazel eyes were rimmed with concern. I suddenly wanted to break down, sit with her on the rug before the fire, and tell her everything.

You would put your dearest friend in danger like that? My wraith's voice stopped me in my tracks. The raspy voice suddenly bombarded me with thoughts that seemed to come at me from all directions.

Telling Solvai means admitting that you are weak.

Should you not be strong enough to bear this alone?

What if Solvai were to take action against the High Prince? That will not end well for the daughter of the Liberator, one of the most notorious magi outlaws in recent history. It would not take much for the High Prince to have her imprisoned—or worse.

I bit the inside of my cheek so hard I tasted blood. Then I looked my friend dead in the eyes and told the biggest lie of my life.

"I'm fine."

Disengaging from our silent standoff, I went to enter the women's sleeping quarters, but Solvai caught my arm as I passed.

"I don't believe you," she whispered.

"That's too bad," was my lame reply.

Solvai grew frustrated. "Enough of this idiotic victim game you're playing. I stayed up so I could find out if you're okay."

"Maybe you shouldn't have!" I snapped back, immediately hating myself for raising my voice at her. But it was too late to stop now. "Why do you drakking care?"

"Because I'm your friend!"

"If you're such a good friend, then get off my back already!"

"If I can't talk to you, then who can?" Solvai asked. "Are you at least talking with Jax about whatever's bothering you?"

I set my jaw. "There's nothing to talk about."

"Meleya," Solvai pleaded. "You're exhausted. You're not thinking clearly—"

"Maybe it's you who isn't listening clearly! I don't want you to say another word to me."

I'd expected—more than that, I'd *wanted* Solvai to match my anger. Instead, she shut her mouth tight, then silently turned around and walked back into the dorm, quietly shutting the door behind her.

Better the two of you keep your distance anyway, my wraith whispered. *This way, she will be safe. Very well done.*

I was careful not to make any noise since I didn't want to draw attention from any of my dorm mates—I didn't know how thin these walls were. But I couldn't stop the tears from flowing down my cheeks.

Jaira's lecture barely registered as she stood before our group in Swan Spire. The members of the entourage were seated in a half circle, with the Black Valkyrie standing near the back of the room, observing.

Vidya had started attending classes again, telling the others that she'd been down with some kind of flu. But I was certain she'd been reeling from our discovery about the Farseer, unsure what to think or how to process the new information. She was still having Jaira take the lead on teaching classes, and I was worried about Vidya as she watched on from the back of the black room.

On one end of our row, I saw Brigan and Solvai sitting together. When Solvai caught me looking, she pointedly returned her attention to the lecture. We hadn't spoken in the days since our fight.

In that time, the solitude had grown even more stifling. Mason was having me spend hours each evening in Scryer's Grotto, and my wraith was constantly in my head. Vidya had promised me back in the High Ridgebacks that she'd teach me how to deal with the Gray, but that didn't seem like that was going to happen anytime soon. The nightmares were intensifying as well, which was why I spent every waking hour desperately trying not to drift off.

"...and that's why it's vital to ensure unregistered magi aren't able to band together. Isolation is the key to breaking them," Jaira spoke with enthusiasm. Bjorn was eating up every word, of course. The others watched with varying degrees of skepticism, from Solvai's stone face to Brigan's troubled demeanor as he took notes on the lecture.

The bubbly redheaded girl, Shaya, was somehow still smiling, though one look told me she was daydreaming rather than truly listening. As usual, her hands were busy in her lap, a ball of black thread on the floor beside her as her pair of knitting needles flew endlessly back and forth.

"Therefore," Jaira went on, "like the branch of the Coven of the Gray Ones we soundly eradicated last winter, one of the greatest threats the realm faces in our day are the Knights of the Torch and the Farseer."

Jaira swept her gaze to the back of the room, as if checking to see how Vidya would react to her claim. When Vidya didn't move, Jaira pressed.

"Isn't that right, Black Valkyrie?"

Vidya gave a curt almost-nod, but apparently that wasn't good enough for Jaira.

"That's what you always taught me," Jaira said. "That until the Knights are destroyed, Evgard will never have peace. You still believe that, right? Just making sure I'm getting the lesson right."

Vidya grit her teeth. "That is correct. The Knights... must be eliminated at all costs. For the... for the good of the realm."

"That's right. It is good to see that you haven't forgotten our shared goal." Jaira gave a sinister grin before continuing the lecture.

From his chair beside me, I noticed Jax wincing. I leaned closer to him, putting my hand on his.

"What's wrong?" I whispered quietly enough not to draw attention.

Jax stared at my hand, then switched to my tired eyes. After a too-long pause, he responded.

"You first."

Now it was my turn to pause. Solvai's words from the other night came to mind: *Are you at least talking with Jax about whatever's bothering you?*

"One tactic to try when hunting a potential magi," Jaira's lesson pierced my thoughts, "is to learn all you can about the subject's family. Use their siblings, parents, or anyone they love as leverage to get them to confess."

She spoke so coldly it made me sick. Meanwhile, I saw Jax's gaze flick to the back of the room where Vidya stood. For a second, I saw her looking back at him before her expression hardened again.

Jax turned his gaze forward once more, and I sensed tension in his jaw. My hand was still on his as his fist clenched.

"She really does love you, you know," I muttered.

"You don't know that," he replied so quietly I had to lean closer to hear.

"I know that she'd do anything to keep you safe. I... I can understand that."

"She'd do anything, alright," Jax spoke with his teeth clenched. "Including abandoning me and messing up my entire life. Some kind of love that is."

I swallowed. "Is your life really so terrible?"

"Yes, scorch it. Growing up with Torsten as a father was a nightmare. That woman literally ruined my childhood."

"Maybe she was wrong to do what she did," I began, "but I'm sure she was just caring for you the best way she knew how."

I suddenly realized I wasn't just talking about Vidya, but myself. I had no idea if I was making the right decision by not confiding in Jax or my other friends. *Was* there even a 'right' decision?

"Maybe she was right to leave," Jax mumbled almost incoherently. "She didn't think I was worth staying for."

"Jax." I frowned. "What are you—"

"Just shut up," he cut me off, then withdrew his hand and put it to his head.

My reply came fast and frustrated. "Fine then."

When I looked at Jax, his eyes were closed. All at once, I wondered if he'd been telling me to shut up... or if he'd been telling someone else. After all, I knew from our first day here that I wasn't the only one with a wraith following me.

I shuddered as I recalled the hulking, burly creature I'd seen looming over Jax that day while using the Sight. My old mentor, Jax's estranged father, Torsten, had once said the Gray Ones used magi as their 'chosen vessels', whatever that was supposed to mean. Had Jax been 'chosen' as well?

The idea of Jax suffering from an unwanted voice in his head put me even more on edge. The Gray was everywhere. Unstoppable. Was anyone

I cared about safe? Maybe Vidya was right—The only way to deal with the Gray was to use their power.

I tried to take a deep, full breath but found I couldn't. My hands shook, my chest tight. I felt dizzy.

Beside me, Jax noticed.

"Drak," he said, "not this again."

He was right. It wasn't fair for him to have to deal with me when anxiety claimed me like this.

I got to my feet, and the whole class turned my way.

Jaira stopped lecturing to put a hand on her hip. "Did you have something to say, Snowstorm?"

"Need some air," I managed.

"M!" Jax called out to me, but I didn't listen as I practically flew from the room.

Sunlight. After so many nights trapped in the darkness of Scryer's Grotto, I wanted sunlight. I needed it.

But of course, it was another cloudy day in the Ridgeback Mountains. My breathing remained ragged as I walked through the Academy's central outdoor courtyard. It was springtime, yet I still felt as cold as I had all winter long. There was no reprieve. No hope.

Piercing my existential haze, I felt a faint, flute-like melody in my heart, accompanied by drum beats.

Sniff and Blink. My bond with my dragons had felt fainter than ever. I wanted to spend more time with them, but with so much going on, there hadn't been time.

Brrring! Sniff trilled.

I can't come now, buddy, I emoted back.

Ting-a-ling?

Why? I... I don't know.

For whatever reason, I felt like I needed to be alone. I *had* to figure out how to bear this alone. Not even my dragons should be burdened by my problems. I longed to run away to a kitchen of some kind. Baking always put me at ease.

But the chef here at the Academy was territorial, and besides, I didn't want to see anyone right now. I briefly thought of the wonderful, perfect kitchen Jax had made for me in the mountain glade. Just thinking of that day brought tears to my eyes. Would I ever be that happy again?

"Ah, just the Rifter I was looking for." The sound of High Prince Mason's voice made my heart sink. Still, I turned around, inclining my head.

"Please," I started. "If you want me to go to the Grotto now—"

"That's not why I'm here," Mason said. His face was kinder than usual. "Rather, we were thinking—I mean, *I* was thinking you could use some... well, some inspiration."

I cocked my head.

Mason sighed, looking around to make sure nobody was around to overhear. He leaned closer.

"I think it's time I let you visit your mother."

My eyes grew wide.

"That's right," Mason said. "You're free to visit the Asylum."

I certainly didn't expect to see my old Mage Hunter friend at the front door of the underground Asylum.

"Trickshot?" I said, hurrying down the dimly lit hallway. The auburn-haired woman was just coming through a heavily bolted door at the corridor's end.

"Meleya," Trickshot said, securing her medic's pouch more securely over her shoulder. She didn't seem all that surprised to see me. She tossed her thick braid behind her, and I caught sight of the white streak in it—the one she'd gotten during the battle at the Rise on the Winter Solstice. Both Trickshot and her Hunting partner had taken life-threatening ether-blasts that had left them scarred.

"I suppose it was only a matter of time before I saw you here," Trickshot said. "Makes me wish I didn't have a healing class to teach right now so I could stay."

"You mean you work here?" I gestured to the sign above the door.

Trickshot nodded. "I take care of the patients' physical needs while my—"

"Hi!" a bubbly voice echoed from the end of the hall where I'd just come from. Shaya's red ponytail swung as she bounded toward us. "Sorry I'm late, Sis," she said to Trickshot. "And Meleya! I'm *so* glad you're here!"

"That 'on-campus job' you mentioned," I said. "You work here?"

"That's right!" Shaya grinned.

"Like I was saying," Trickshot said, "I take care of the patients' physical ailments while my sister—"

"I make them happy!" Shaya said, pulling something black and satiny from a satchel. She proudly held up a pair of knitted socks. "Just finished these as a gift for Fidan! He's going to love them."

"I'm sure he will," Trickshot said. "For whatever reason, the patients show marked improvement after receiving one of Shaya's gifts."

I noticed Shaya's hands as she passed me her latest creation. The lacy black gloves she always wore seemed to be thinner and more sparse than they'd been the other day.

As I examined the well-made socks, I noticed the thread's extra shimmer. Looking up at Shaya, my gaze darted to the Shadowbinder's silver-mark cut into her left cheek.

"Is this... shadowsilk?" I asked.

"Solei's blade—*yes!*" Shaya replied eagerly. "It's my signature touch. The shadowsilk in my knitting lasts indefinitely because I infuse the *teeniest* pinch of skystone into the threads as I weave them."

I nodded to her hands. "Are your gloves shadowsilk as well?"
Shaya froze at the mention of her gloves. She and Trickshot exchanged glances.

"Uh..." Shaya started

Trickshot jumped in. "Meleya, I think it's time we got you into the Asylum. There's someone I know will want to see you."

Gloves forgotten, I felt a sudden tangle of dragonflies jump to my stomach. Trickshot was absolutely right. It was time to face my mother.

The inside of the Asylum was just as dim as the hallway had been. Low-burning torches lined the walls, which were decorated with twig wreaths and mounted dragonelk heads.

A few dozen people sat in comfortable chairs or milled around the main living room. None of them spoke, but I noticed several wearing shimmering black knitted things— Scarves, hats, and socks. One woman even held a lovely, Shaya-made black doily on her lap.

But I hardly paid attention to any of them. My focus was on the delicate, feminine profile of a woman sitting in a chair near the hearth. She had long, smooth hair and big brown eyes like mine.

"Mom!" I exclaimed, crossing the room to get to her. She was turned so that I could only see the right side of her face, but as I approached, she turned to face me.

I gasped.

Mom's face… It was perfect. Not a blemish on it.

Gone was the angry, red scar covering the left side where she'd tried to burn away her silvermark when I was seven. Without it, I hardly recognized her.

I stopped in my tracks.

Meanwhile, Mom's face lit up. "Meli!" she cried, leaping from her chair to throw her arms around me. Still dazed, I returned her embrace, feeling smooth shadowsilk draped over Mom's shoulders. She wore a lovely, lacy black shawl from Shaya. I recognized the pattern that looked like tiny falling stars from the threads Shaya had been knitting that day we'd sat together before the fire in the dorm.

"Thank the goddesses you're home!" Mom said, pulling back to cup my face in her hands. I noticed she pointedly used one hand to cover up the Rifter's silvermark on my left cheek so she couldn't see it. That frustrated me, but I didn't move her hand.

"Please tell me you remembered to bring it," Mom said with a sparkling smile.

"Bring what?" I asked lamely, still recovering from seeing her face healed. Why did the sight of it make me so sad?

"The game, of course!" Mom said, pulling me closer to the fire where she sat the pair of us down on a rug. "I could've sworn I left the game with you, didn't I? Don't you have it?"

"Oh," I said. "Right. Sure." I was mentally a few steps behind as I pulled out the little drawstring bag containing the deck that had traveled with my family from caravan to caravan for as long as I could remember. Mom had left it with me along with the note letting me know she was on her way to receive the magi cure.

"Perfect!" Mom seized the cards and began to shuffle as if this was the most natural thing in the world. As if we hadn't seen each other for a mere afternoon rather than months.

"Is that Fallen Stars?" Shaya said, pointing to the deck. She'd just finished giving a resident the newly knitted socks. "I *love* that game! Deal me in!"

"Of course," Mom agreed, passing out a short stack of cards for the three of us.

Shaya joined us on the rug and the game began. It was a full two rounds before I stopped being too dumbfounded to speak.

"Shaya," I began. "Was everyone here once a magi?"

Shaya nodded as she played a card. "This is where they send them after giving them the..." Shaya leaned closer to me, whispering so that Mom couldn't hear. "...*alleged* magi cure."

"Why do they keep them here instead of setting them free?" I asked. "If their ether no longer draws wild dragons, they're no longer a threat to the realm, so what's the point? Why not send them back to their families?"

"They say it's because they need time to assimilate to their new and improved state," Shaya whispered, "but I think it's so the high nobles can use them however they please. As leverage or examples. Maybe so the High King can parade them around as evidence of his so-called benevolence." Again, Shaya's casual revolutionary attitude took me by surprise.

"So, Mom," I started as I watched her begin the next round, "your ether well is gone then. And you're... happy?"

"Yes! Isn't it wonderful?" Mom tossed back her long, silky hair as she took the round. She started another round, then beamed at me. "I'm finally free. Everything's going to be perfect now, little Meli, I promise."

I looked to Shaya for... I don't know, some kind of explanation. Mom had always been very serious, chronically looking over her shoulder. The slightest thing could set her off, and Dad and I had spent so much time and energy emotionally guarding her. Shaya gave me a sympathetic look as she opened her mouth to say something.

Mom cut her off. "You were gone far too long this time, little Meli. I keep telling your father you're too young to go out hunting with him, but does he listen? That Ivar."

"Too young to go out hunting with Dad?" I repeated. I hadn't done that in years. Certainly not since my parents went to prison when I was thirteen.

"Meleya," Shaya started, but Mom jumped in once more.

"Keep up like this, I told your father, and she'll have visions of battle glory dancing in her head. Too young for such nonsense."

Shaya tried to speak again, but this time it was me who stopped her as I addressed Mom.

"I don't have visions of glory, Mom, but I have seen battle," I said. "You know that."

Mom gave an uncomfortable, borderline manic laugh. "Silly Meli. Daydreaming again? They don't allow children in the guard."

I frowned, the dragonflies in my stomach buzzing up a storm. "How old do you think I am?"

Mom gave me a too-energetic smile as she put her hand on my face again, her fingers covering my silvermarked cheek. "Oh sweetie. You just turned seven last autumn, of course."

I just stared at her, openmouthed.

"Your turn, Meli." Mom nodded to the cards fanned out in my hands.

"Actually, Freya," Shaya said, putting a gentle hand on Mom's arm, "I need to speak with Meleya for a few minutes. You stay here, alright?"

Mom agreed, and I let Shaya pull me aside.

"What in the void is going on with her?" I said the second we were out of earshot. "She thinks I'm seven years old? Do I *look* seven?"

"Of course not," Shaya said calmly. "I was afraid this would happen. See, the cure affects different people in different ways. Losing one's powers is like losing a major part of oneself. Most victims of the cure respond by becoming sad and reserved, though the gifts I knit seem to help with that. Freya's case is one of the more extreme. Her mind is reverting to a time before she learned that you, her only daughter, had etherarchy. It's the only way she can cope."

"No," I protested, fighting the lump forming in my throat. "No, it isn't. That's not fair—She shouldn't just get to erase who I am."

"I know it's hard to process," Shaya said. "But if there's one thing I know about mental trauma, it's that healing takes time."

"I have to get her out of here," I said, already feeling my lungs growing tighter. "This... *asylum* can't be the best place for her. For any of these people. Mom... she needs my dad."

"I'm inclined to agree," Shaya said, her usual cheerful expression growing as serious as I'd ever seen it. "If it were up to me, none of these wonderful people would be trapped here, underground and isolated. It's the opposite of the sort of care they actually need."

Her fingers twitched as if she were just itching to do something about it. Was it just me, or had her lacy black gloves gotten thicker since I'd first gotten here? Shaya's eyes flashed, and I thought I noticed little flecks of glimmering gold mingling with their light brown color.

Shaya sighed, resigned. "But by Solei's blade, there's nothing we can do—nowhere we could take them to get them the help they need. That precious nobleman High Prince Mason oversees the Asylum now."

"And he'd never in a million years give up his leverage over me," I muttered under my breath. I inhaled as deeply as I could, but my chest felt constricted.

"What was that?" Shaya asked with a frown.

It was taking everything in my power not to hyperventilate. I could barely open my mouth to speak.

"I—I have to go," I managed.

"But your mom—" Shaya started.

"I can't stay here," I said. I didn't even turn around to give Mom a second look as I headed straight for the exit.

Yes, Meleya, my wraith's voice suddenly penetrated my thoughts. *Run away.*

What do you want from me? I mentally cried.

I sensed the wraith's pity. *Only to ease your burden. Let me in. Let me help you.*

I didn't answer as I hurried back down the dark hallway, tears cutting across my cheeks.

Chapter 11: Don't Go Back to That Tower

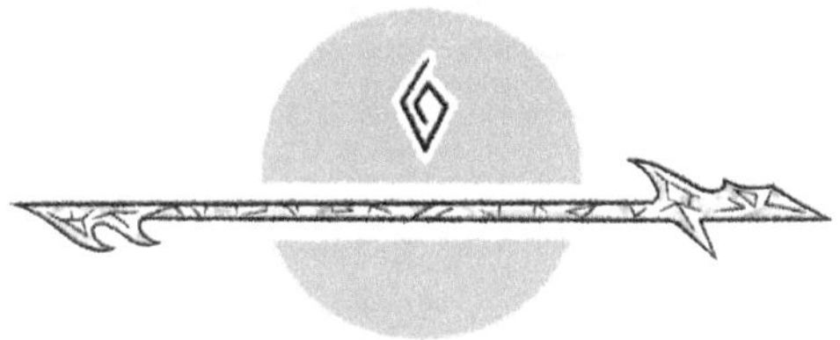

Asher

For possibly the first time in my life, I'd actually written down a plan.

I felt like a total nerd, clutching the paper in my hands as I scanned my own barely legible notes—Someone really needed to make me improve my handwriting. A few days ago, perhaps in an effort to take my mind off of Elle, I'd secretly torn out a page from Kai's notebook, then spent an embarrassing amount of time brainstorming, outlining, and scheming. My brain hurt. Was this what Kai felt like all the time?

The thing was, I knew that this time, wild improvisation wasn't going to cut it. I had to time everything perfectly if I was going to succeed. Slip out like a shadow on a moonless night.

Technically, I'd be slipping out in broad daylight in the middle of a sunny afternoon, so that comparison didn't really work. For one thing, I knew Rhana's bonded dragons were extra vigilant at night, patrolling the property line for intruders. It was also harder to avoid her psionic traps in the dark.

Besides, I really didn't want to get caught. I had no doubt of the legitimacy of Rhana's threat to let me spend several days in her jail. But even more serious were the numerous concerns Kai had listed the other day—If the Mage Hunters caught me, it would endanger the entire Rebel Knight army.

But I had to do it. I needed to know what was in that envelope with Mom's name on it.

I *had* to go back to that tower.

According to my humiliating piece of paper, most of Rhana's dragons took a short afternoon nap, leaving only two on guard. The Rebel Knight army was training in the field out in front of the cabin with Rhana, Boone, and Valla. Solrac was resting. Kai was in the library poring over more omen books. Elle and Aurora were with the soldiers too, making sure they were available to all the people who practically worshiped them.

That meant nobody was specifically watching the woods behind the cabin.

Thorn and I crept silently across the clearing between the safehouse and the cindercones. Once we got to the trees, I knew of an area where Thorn and I could take off without any traps. We'd have to fly slowly and stick close to the trees, at least until we were out of range for Rhana's dragons to sense us.

We were mere strides away from the cover of the cindercones when I jumped at the chitter of a familiar, obnoxious pet draccoon.

"Stars," I whispered, putting a hand to my chest. Thorn cocked his head as Dusty wagged a tiny black finger at us, clearly chastising us for sneaking around.

"Go with haste, Dusty." I put a solemn finger to my lips. "Tell no one of what you've seen, and I shall not feed thee to Thorn for dinner."

Thorn whirled on me with narrowed eyes. Through our bond, he let me know he found the draccoon meat-to-bone ratio less than pleasing. I informed him that Dusty was only an ethereal familiar, so his 'meat' would probably taste like dreams and imagination or something vague like that anyway.

With an annoyed sigh, I glanced down at my relatively meticulous plans. 'Get past Dusty the meddlesome, loud draccoon' was not listed here. Ugh. Again, I felt a wave of sympathy for Kai. It must've sucked soot trying to plan for someone like me.

"Goin' somewhere, Asher?" I wasn't surprised to see Ivar crossing the clearing. He scooped up Dusty, who perched on his shoulder and crossed his furry arms with satisfaction. I stuck my tongue out at the little menace.

"Just taking Thorn for an afternoon ride." I shrugged casually. "A wyvern's gotta stretch his wings."

"Saw you out flyin' this mornin'," Ivar said, putting a hand on his hip. "A wyvern don't gotta stretch his wings that much."

"But he does have to eat. Just going for a quick hunt, then we'll be back in time for the evening meal."

"Thorn ain't hungry. Can always tell if a dragon's eaten recently or not by the squint of their eyes. 'Sides, Thorn don't usually take you along when he's huntin'."

"Sure, but it's *because* Thorn's not all that hungry that he's okay taking it slower by bringing me along. We don't spend nearly enough time together, Thorn and me, and—"

"Asher..." Ivar raised an eyebrow.

"No, you see—"

"*Asher*—All that soot and nonsense may work on the rest of 'em, but you and I, we're alike. Used to be a thief myself up north, remember? I can spot a load of dragonbull dung a mile away. So, you wanna tell me what you're really up to?"

Beside me, Thorn let out a chuckle. I glared back at him.

I sighed. "Ivar, please, you have to let me go. And you can't tell anybody where I'm going either."

"I'm listenin'."

Ivar listened intently as I explained the situation. I told him about the Black Valkyrie taking Mom away from us, and how if there was even the slightest chance I could find out what had happened to her, I had to take it. That envelope might be the only closure I'd ever get.

"Where's the envelope?" Ivar asked.

"The Mage Hunter Academy," I admitted. "The last time I saw it, it was hidden under your daughter's boot."

"Mels?" Ivar's dark eyebrows knit.

I nodded. "There's a chance she's still got it. Please, Ivar. I have to know."

Ivar didn't respond for several long seconds. Meanwhile, I cast a nervous glance down at my page of plans. We needed to hurry before more of Rhana's dragons joined the watch along the property line.

Finally, Ivar spoke. "Check up on Mels for me, alright Asher? Bring her home to me if you can."

His reply took me aback. "You mean you'll let me go?"

Ivar nodded. "Like I said, I've done my fair share of sneakin' around. 'Sides, I trust you not to get caught. You're a smart guy, and you know what's at stake. You wouldn't do somethin' to endanger your team."

Ivar looked at me seriously, and I knew his remark was more of a warning than an observation. I gave him a nod back to let him know I understood.

Then, with one last squeak from Dusty, Thorn and I darted into the cindercones.

The last time I'd snuck into Swan Spire, I'd had a skilled Mystic named Kai to help me take out the flock of starswans circling the tower. Then, I'd been able to hover-waltz right on in.

This time, I knew I'd need to be more careful. Besides, there was a strong possibility Meleya herself still had that envelope, which meant I needed to find her, not just sneak around Swan Spire, rifling through trunks and hoping for the best.

I needed a disguise.

After my not-so-encouraging meeting with the other Rebel Knights, I'd filched the map of the Mage Hunter Academy that Kai had used when devising our original break-in. One building set along the slope near the dragon stables was labeled 'armory,' which I was willing to bet was the perfect place to pick up a dusky cloak and silvery pauldron. Maybe I could even snag an enforcer's helmet to ward off would-be onlookers.

Thorn stuck close behind me as we slunk through the trees within the Academy walls. There it was—the armory, nestled just down the mountain from where we stood, between Swan Spire and the main Academy building where all the classrooms were.

"Stick near the dragon stables, Thorn," I told my wyvern. "You'll blend in, and that way you'll be close enough to help out if something goes wrong at the armory."

Thorn sent a spark of agreement, casually approaching the stables while I took a deep breath, accessing my ether. My eyes flashed gold as I hover-dashed down the slope to reach the armory in seconds.

I was just creeping along the armory wall toward the door when I felt Thorn reach out to me through our bond.

Wait, he said, sending a feeling like a fiery blockade to stop me in my tracks.

What is it? I replied. *I'm almost to the door—*

No armory, Thorn emoted. *Come to stables.*

Why?

Trust me. Come.

With a twinge of annoyance and a rush of curiosity, I quickly reversed my recent hover-dash trek.

I took in the Academy stables alongside Thorn. Most of the stalls here belonged to kirin—lithe draconic horses—which the Hunters probably used for long journeys. One kirin snorted at me with mild annoyance, her front claw padding the ground as she tossed her chestnut mane. I threw her a scorchapple from a bucket and she gave a little whinny of appreciation.

"You're welcome, Lucky," I said with a mock tip of my hat." The dragon horse seemed to roll her eyes at her new name. But I needed all the luck I could get, so—

Focus, Thorn reminded me, directing my gaze past the kirin stalls.

All the stalls near the back of the stables were dedicated to bonded dragons. I spotted a couple of wingless drakes eating from troughs, a pale blue wyvern watching Thorn with curiosity, and a very hard-to-miss evren with gleaming, bright gold scales curled up on the ground near the back wall.

I instantly understood why Thorn had called me back. Leaning against the golden-yellow, four-winged dragon was a white-haired girl with a long braid.

She had her back to me, but there was no mistaking Meleya.

With only the smallest degree of hesitation, I strode toward the back of the stables, Thorn close behind.

"Fancy meeting you here," I boldly exclaimed, fully expecting Meleya to spin around, seaxe at the ready.

She did spin around, just slowly. When I saw her face, I noted dark circles under red-rimmed, wet eyes.

Oh soot. She'd definitely just been bawling her eyes out.

She halfheartedly wiped her eyes as if she could hide her tears, her voice hoarse. "What in the stars are you doing here, thief?"

Rather than answer her question, I asked one of my own. "Are you okay?"

It was a stupid question. I knew that the second it left my mouth.

"I'm great," Meleya said, her sarcasm strong despite everything. "Just steal whatever random thing you're here for, I don't care," She turned away from me again, slumping to the straw-covered stable floor as she leaned her back against the golden dragon. The dragon gave a sniffle of sympathy, then nuzzled closer and curled up to rest his head near her feet.

Thorn and I exchanged hopeless glances. Thorn's eyes darted back and forth between me and Meleya's defeated form.

Go over there, Thorn ordered through our bond.

Me? I protested. *Why don't you go over there?*

I'm a dragon. Weird.

Well, I don't know what to do in this situation.

And I do?

Thorn and I glared at each other in a brief standoff before I reluctantly began tiptoeing toward Meleya. She was crying again, clearly at the point where she literally didn't give a flying scale if I witnessed it.

Unsure what else to try, I sat down at Meleya's side. Cautiously, I put a hand on her shoulder.

She immediately jabbed me in the arm with her surprisingly sharp elbow.

"Um, ouch." I pulled back to rub my arm, glaring back at Thorn. My dragon was chuckling at my pathetic attempt to comfort my... enemy? Possible Knight of the Torch comrade? My trainer, Ivar's, Mage Hunter daughter? I wasn't exactly sure what Meleya and I were to each other.

Nevertheless, I couldn't just leave her here. For one thing, I needed to see if she had my mom's envelope. For another, she was crying alone in the dragon stables.

"So," I started, "if you could live in either the desert, the mountains, or on the beach, which would you choose?"

My out-of-the-sky question took her off guard, and Meleya looked at me like I was a crazy person.

I plowed ahead. "I love the desert myself, but as far as living goes, nothing beats the view from my favorite mountain back home in Steel Rim. I'm not much of a beach guy, though."

Meleya didn't respond for a while. She was still giving me the stink-eye, but hey, at least her tears had stopped flowing.

"What about you?" I pressed. "You a beach kind of girl? You love that salty sea air and riding the waves, don't you?"

"I've never been to the beach," Meleya said, probably just to shut me up.

I grinned. "Well, that's not a fair question then. You'll have to let me know once you've experienced all three. Now, tell me about the first time you rode a dragon."

Meleya raised an eyebrow.

I laughed. "You don't mean to tell me that you've never flown with this golden boy?" I gave the brightly-colored evren beside us a little rub on the flank, and he began panting excitedly. "He's your bond, right? What was it like riding the first time?"

Meleya hesitated a second longer before replying. "I fell off his back."

"Well, that's embarrassing."

Meleya shot me a glare. "You're embarrassing."

I glared back. "I'm not the one hiding out in the dragon stables crying."

She looked away, and I couldn't tell if it was because she thought I was a jerk or because she was fighting a smile. Maybe both.

I sighed. "Look, I don't know why you were crazy enough to join the Mage Hunters. Soot, I don't know you at all. But obviously you're not happy here."

"What's it to you, thief?"

"I just think life's supposed to be happy. And if you aren't happy, you'd better figure out why and fix it up right quick."

Meleya straightened, then turned to me with dark, furrowed brows. "Where did you hear that?"

"Lesson seven, if I remember right," I said. "Your father taught it to me."

"You know my father," Meleya said. It didn't look like she was surprised.

I nodded. "Tall, scruffy snowhead named Ivar. Carries an opinionated ethereal draccoon around. Asked me to bring you home to him."

It took Meleya a moment to take that in. She swallowed. "I don't have a home."

"So I should tell him you prefer the company of magi-killing Mage Hunters to that of him and the other Knights of the Torch?"

"The Knights of the Torch are just as bad as some Hunters," Meleya retorted. "I don't know how either of you could be a part of it."

"The Knights aren't like that," I said. "Not the real Knights, at least."

"Real Knights?"

"They call us the Rebel Knights. Vesta and the others in Skygard kicked us out because we didn't want their war. We're building a force of true freedom fighters on our own."

Meleya chewed her lip, clearly still unsure. To my side, Thorn was getting restless.

"Thanks, but Knights of the Torch don't mix well with Mage Hunters," Meleya said, shaking her head.

I set my jaw. I was getting tired of being told certain groups didn't mix.

Still, I remembered why I had come here in the first place, and didn't want to waste more time.

"Meleya," I started, "the other day in Swan Spire, there was an envelope with a name on it—"

Before I could say another word, Meleya pulled the slightly crumpled letter out of her dragon's saddlebag and held it out to me.

"Take it," she said, resigned. "I didn't get the answers I was hoping for about my mom, but maybe you can get yours."

I eagerly took the envelope, but cast Meleya a troubled look. "What happened to your mom?"

Meleya shrugged. "Even if I did believe you about the Rebel Knights, she's the reason I can't leave this place. She needs to be with my dad, now more than ever, but... But I just visited her, and she's trapped inside the Asylum here. I can't leave without her. Although I can do this."

Meleya reached into her dragon's saddlebag once more and pulled out a small stone. She handed it to me, and I saw that the stone had a runemark etched into it. A rune I recognized as one my father often used.

"This is a rift anchor," I said.

"Give it to my father when you get back to the Rebel base," Meleya said. "Tell him I'll find a way to get Mom to him as soon as I can."

With that, Meleya rubbed the area under her tired eyes once more before giving her dragon one last scratch behind the ears. The dragon's tail swished back and forth, causing a small windstorm in the back of the stall. Then she left, heading back toward the main Academy building.

A small bundle of nerves danced around my stomach. Kai, Rhana, and the others would kill me if they discovered I'd brought home a rift anchor belonging to a member of the Black Valkyrie's entourage.

But for whatever reason, I didn't feel like I was doing the wrong thing. I had to make good on my promise to Ivar, right?

Meleya's dragon seemed to agree as he flitted toward me, his four wings moving so fast they were practically humming. He gave me a friendly nudge with his nose, and I formed a ball of starglass in my hand. Catching the energetic dragon's vibe, I rolled the ball across the stable floor and he took off after it like a shot. Then he used his nose to nudge the ball, rolling it around like a happy, oversized puppy.

I chuckled. But my smile faded as I looked down at the envelope in my hands. I read Mom's elegantly written name across its front:

Zerana of Moss Falls

This was it.

Thorn was right there at my side, sending supportive pulses of fire through our bond as I opened the envelope and pulled out the folded page inside.

I frowned as I scanned the page. It looked like some kind of medical record. Across the top, it read:

Mage Hunter Academy Asylum Log: Magi Cure Subject

My heart beat fast. Asylum… I remembered Meleya mentioning that was where her mother was. Had she come to get the alleged magi cure as well? I continued reading.

Name: Zerana of Moss Falls (birthplace possibly not accurate. Suspected birthplace: the Drekai Capital of Zolehiinu)
Age: 35
Sex: Female
Species: Half-born
Magi type: Shadowbinder
Notes: Surgeon hopes that the patient's Drekai blood makes her and her ether well more resilient. Patient's shadowbinding abilities are particularly strong.
Ether well status post soul surgery: Active
Patient status post soul surgery: Deceased
Ether well recipient: The Black Valkyrie

With every word, I grew more and more angry. But that last line put me over the edge as understanding exploded within my chest.

The Black Valkyrie had always been a Psion, but we'd all wondered how she'd been able to become a Shadowbinder as well. Now, it was painfully clear.

The Black Valkyrie was using Mom's ether well.

Vidya had *stolen* my mother's powers and left her for dead.

Tears of rage spilled from my eyes. Now I was the one hiding out in the dragon stables, crying.

Not that I planned to hide out for long.

Asher? Thorn's voice sounded worried as I stood, taking long strides toward the door. My large wyvern positioned himself between me and Swan Spire, spreading his wings as a blockade.

Where are you going? Find Black Valkyrie? he asked. *Too dangerous.*

"No," I replied. "I'm not going to find her."

Where then?

"Hide out here, Thorn," I said. "I'll come for you once I've found the Asylum."

Asher... Thorn thought, his skepticism like wildfire ripping through our bond. *Got the letter. Now back to the safehouse.*

Despite Thorn's plea, I grit my teeth, determined.

"It's too late for my mom, but it's not too late for Meleya's," I said. "I'll go back to the safehouse, but first, I've got to pick up Ivar's wife."

FRAGMENT: POWER

XAN

X an was getting stronger. She could feel it.

Well, she could essentially feel it. Wraiths like her couldn't actually *feel* anything. They weren't among those privileged enough to have a physical form that could feel the soft breeze on their cheeks or taste the savory flavor of fresh scaleberries. They couldn't smell the cindercone pines or even so much as experience the touch of a human hand in theirs. Even the colors of Etheria, so luminous to most, appeared muted to the wraiths. All they could really "feel" was power: the exhilaration of taking it in, and the despondency of losing it.

But for Xan, all of that was about to change.

Xan hissed as a blast of dragonfire ripped straight through her core. The fire ate away at her smoky form, but despite that, Xan forced herself to stay together.

Facing Xan was a silvery, translucent spirit evren—Meleya's *kalavira*, as such protectors were called amongst wraithkind. Xan knew Meleya called hers 'Blink.'

Blink and Xan had been at odds for months, but things had intensified over the past week. They'd been locked in battle all morning as Xan pushed to infiltrate Meleya's mind. Troublesome Blink was a fierce guard, but Xan was cunning and determined.

Back, you pesky dragon! Xan rasped as a long, shadowy blade formed from what humans would call her hand. The weapon was a wraithblade, possessing a fierce, smooth edge along one side while the other boasted a row of jagged, serrated teeth. Since Xan was unbound, the blade was useless against physical beings. But against another spirit in Etheria…

Blink roared as Xan's wraithblade sliced through her wing. It didn't actually cut, only left a glowing, gray mark, but Blink's aura writhed as Xan's blow drained her stamina.

Xan laughed as they continued to fight, Blink's dragonfire and claws tearing at Xan's mists while Xan's blade weakened Blink. The haze that had gathered around the Mage Hunter Academy gave Xan the advantage here. Just a few more blows, and Blink would have no choice but to retreat to an ether oasis to restore her strength.

Sure enough, Xan's next swing left Blink exhausted. Her four wings trembled as she dropped to the ground, barely able to stay afloat. Not wanting to risk having her essence scattered, Blink fled Xan's presence.

Triumphantly, Xan let her wraithblade dissolve into smoke. Blink would be back—She *always* came back. But for now, Xan would be able to influence Meleya uninhibited.

Xan's gray, wispy form raced toward the Academy courtyard. That's where she'd spotted Meleya going upon leaving the dragon stables.

Xan swept down the mountainside, her mind already planning what she would say to Meleya next. Voids, it was good being able to plant thoughts into Meleya's mind, though Meleya was often stubborn about letting Xan's thoughts take root.

It had taken Xan a very long time to gather the strength to speak to a human for the first time. Wraiths fed off of negative human emotion, and Xan had spent long years as a lowly shade, lurking around refugee camps. The people displaced by the skyfalls were the perfect targets—sad, wronged, and alone. Especially those with the shadow wasting, the numbing disease spread by Xan's counterparts who'd infected umbral creatures. Mmm… Xan had no mouth, but she practically salivated just thinking about all the delicious sorrow surrounding so many of those camps.

But now, Xan followed Meleya. She'd chosen Meleya for her power. After all, the greatest wraith of them all was bonded to a Rifter, as well. At least, Agnai, the Wraith King's, chosen vessel *had been* a mere Rifter at the start. Now, with Agnai's help, the great Soul Reaper had become so much more.

Xan chuckled. The vessel Agnai had taken this time around was not so imposing or regal as ones he had chosen in the past, but he was still just as powerful.

Before long, Xan would be even more powerful than they were. All she had to do was defeat enough of her fellow Gray Ones and consume their power. Then she would be on top.

Soon, Xan told herself.

Meleya had just arrived at the courtyard where the other members of the Mage Hunter entourage were sparring. High Prince Mason's combat class had already begun.

It looked like they were practicing their skills with typical Mage Hunter weapons: the silver long seaxe and silver chain whip. Everyone was sparring with a partner, leaving Jax on the sidelines. Meleya took her place at his side as a few of the others cast her curious looks. They must've been wondering where she'd gone when Mason invited her to visit the Asylum.

After a few tense minutes, Jax finally spoke to Meleya.

"I went looking for you after you ran out of class," he said.

"Oh," Meleya said. "I was just... taking care of something personal." Keeping Jax in the dark was now her default mode. Xan couldn't help but take some of the credit for that.

"Sure you were," Jax replied. "I get it, M. It's not worth it to confide in me—drak, I'm probably too stupid to understand what's really going on anyway, right?"

"What?" Meleya sputtered. "Where is all this coming from?"

Xan knew exactly where Jax's negative thoughts were coming from. While Xan lurked behind Meleya, hulking behind Jax was a great, smoky gray being. His legs melded into wispy shadow, but from the waist up, he was broad and masculine. His eyes burned with sapphire voidlight and Xan could make out his bright blue core glowing from within his chest. He was feeding now, his featureless gray form appearing to suck the light out of Jax's tangerine aura.

Calyx.

His face was featureless, but he had marked it with the various names he'd collected over the ages. Titles, as well as the names of his past forms, each from a powerful magi.

Jax was a strong magi. That was why Calyx had chosen him this time. But if anyone could break Jax, it was Calyx.

Oh, how Xan longed to consume the power of an Elder Wraith like Calyx! That would boost her nearly to the top of the Gray Ones' hierarchy. Calyx's might may have even been enough to challenge the Wraith King.

Though every wraith knew Calyx was too loyal to Agnai to ever challenge him.

But Xan... once Xan was strong enough, she wouldn't hold back.

"It's pointless," Jax grit his teeth under Calyx's dark influence. "I try and try, but in the end... drak. Even you won't tell me what's really going on, M."

You cannot tell him, Xan whispered to Meleya. *You have to protect him. If Mason finds out he knows the truth, he will be in danger.*

Xan sensed the turmoil in Meleya's head and heart. Xan was learning, becoming more adept at exploiting Meleya's greatest weakness—her love for others.

"Maybe I *can't* tell you," Meleya said. "Did you ever think of that?"

Her frustration matched Jax's. With so much negativity rising from their argument, Xan too, began to feed.

"You sound just like her," Jax growled. "Right before she left me on the stoop of that tavern without a backward glance."

"You mean your... Jax, this is nothing like that, I swear."

Meleya glanced toward the Black Valkyrie, and Xan followed her gaze. Standing beside the Black Valkyrie, her smoky gray form nearly completely aligned with her host's, was Exusha. Exusha was even stronger than Calyx. Like Calyx, that Elder Wraith wouldn't dare challenge Agnai. Exusha was already bound to her host, having given the Black Valkyrie her voidshard to solidify their bond and giving her greater access to Vidya's physical form.

Still, as Xan watched Exusha and the Black Valkyrie, she noticed that the pair did not align quite so perfectly as they once had. Exusha's wispy, gray movements lagged behind the Black Valkyrie's, and the glow in her once-bright sapphire eyes had dimmed. Evidence that the Black Valkyrie was once again fighting Exusha's control.

Perhaps we could defeat Exusha now... Xan thought. *But no. Even with the Soul Reaper's voidshard at our disposal, I must show patience,* she had to remind herself. If Xan was too hasty, challenging a wraith too far above herself, she risked losing everything and reverting back to a lowly, powerless shade. Or worse, returning to the void and beginning her growth process all over again.

Xan had to be careful. Careful, and cunning.

Xan cast her gaze around the courtyard, looking for a more suitable wraith to challenge. Certainly not Da'Sai, the wraith now bound to High

Prince Mason. Though not yet as powerful as Calyx and Exusha, he was a dear servant to Agnai, and not one Xan would be wise to offend just yet.

That wild young man, Bjorn, had a moderately powerful wraith following him. Xan hadn't bothered to learn the wraith's name, and Xan hated the way he radiated arrogance. Xan was certain she could defeat him fairly easily—especially if she could get Meleya to use Agnai's voidshard again. *That* had helped Xan and Meleya defeat Skapa. Taking Skapa's power had boosted Xan's significantly, making her a real player in this game.

There were a few shades lurking at the feet of some of the other members of the entourage, but they didn't tempt Xan. Sure, Xan would take their power if she could, but they were not truly worth her time. Then, Xan caught sight of Shisya.

Shisya was strong, but not yet an Elder wraith. Xan knew her well—she and Shisya had been shades together for many years. But when Shisya had gone to Ghost Lake sometime last year, she had found Jaira. Jaira was the perfect host. A girl from a small outlander keep, Jaira was driven, ruthless, and hungry for power. Even now, Xan could see her former companion eagerly feeding off of Jaira's energy as together they used their silver whip to taunt and torment Solvai during their spar.

It isn't fair, Xan thought. Shisya had found such a willing host. Meleya, while powerful, was incredibly stubborn, not to mention that annoying spirit dragon constantly trying to ward Xan off, but thankfully Blink was with Sniff for now.

Now if Xan could just defeat Shisya, that might be enough for Xan to join the ranks of the Elder Wraiths.

And with Meleya weakened physically, mentally, and emotionally, perhaps Xan's opportunity would come sooner than later.

In the meantime, Xan continued to suck the dark energy rising from Meleya and Jax's argument into the blue core glowing in her chest.

"Alright then," Jax challenged. "So you *are* gonna swallow your pride and tell me what's going on with you?"

"My *pride*?" Meleya was seething. "You think this is about pride? That I enjoy keeping you in the dark because it somehow boosts my ego?"

"So you admit you're keeping me in the dark. *Why,* M? Give me one drakking reason."

"I... I..." Meleya trailed off.

At that moment, High Prince Mason called out to the group.

"Switch partners! Let's see... Jaira can spar with Solvai, Brigan can pair up with Jax, and let's have, oh, why not Bjorn and Meleya?"

Xan could see the wraith bound to Mason, his void blue eyes glittering with anticipation. It seemed he too, wanted Meleya weakened, and knew that wild Bjorn and his mid-tier wraith just might have the power to push her over the edge.

Xan laughed to herself. Today was the day. Power—but perhaps even more importantly, the ability to really *feel* something—was at long last within her grasp.

Chapter 12: The Spar

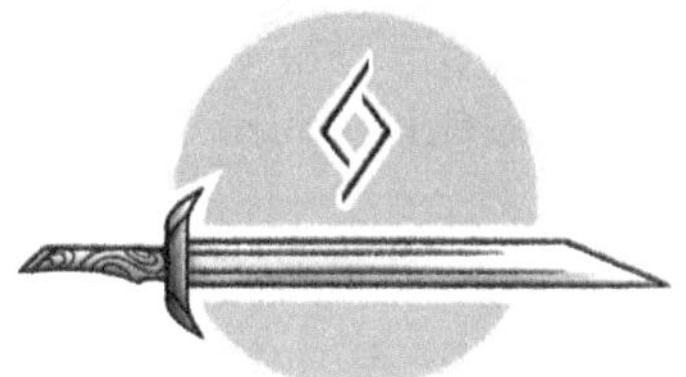

Meleya

Bjorn locked eyes with me from across the courtyard. As ever, they were wild and menacing. Muscles tense, I met him in the middle for the training exercise.

"I want to see some nice, clean sparring," Mason instructed. "We're using real weapons so you can get a feel for the silver, so go easy. That said, all abilities are free for you to use, including magi powers."

Bjorn laughed under his breath, flourishing his long, wicked silver seaxe and assuming a battle stance. "Time to find out, Misthaven. Who belongs on top—humans or magi."

"Magi are as human as anybody else," I said numbly.

"My very existence doesn't put the rest of the realm in mortal danger every day. I don't know how you live with yourself."

Before I could respond, Mason shouted for the sparring to begin.

Bjorn fought like an animal. If it weren't for my rifting, he'd have knocked me out of the ring in under five seconds.

On the opposite scale, my use of my rifting made him fight with even more savage abandon. I yelped as Bjorn's silver blade slashed toward me, missing my side by a mere inch as I leapt backward.

"Keep it civil," Vidya called out. "This is for training purposes only."

"So true," Mason agreed, though I sensed a sinister edge to his tone. His dark side was definitely leading him now.

Bjorn either didn't hear Vidya or simply didn't care. As the fight wore on, I began to feel this match was about more than simple training. I needed to prove I belonged in this drakking world.

I gave a warrior's yell, blocking Bjorn's next strike by catching his blade in a portal-shield. The exit end rushed to the area just above Bjorn's head so that his sword sliced off a bit of his mohawk.

He did *not* appreciate that.

While my yell had been medium-fierce, Bjorn's feral, deafening wail was like something from the void. He came at me without restraint, moving so fast he tackled me to the ground. I lost focus on my runes and my portals dissolved into etherdust.

Bjorn dropped his seaxe in favor of his silver dagger. The edge of his old blade was jagged thanks to the anti-silver substance Asher had used on it back in Swan Spire, and I was certain its dip in the lake from our encounter the other day hadn't improved its condition. But Bjorn had sharpened the voidish dagger all the same.

He managed to land a shallow slash on my thigh as I rolled out of the way. The silver edge sliced through my pants and sent ice cold pain shooting down my leg.

I grunted, but scrambled to my feet, seaxe at the ready.

"Bjorn!" the Black Valkyrie scolded. "This is a practice session only!"

I realized that she and several others were watching us now. In fact, Bjorn's diamondback wolverine-like battle cry seemed to have brought every other sparring match to a halt as our division mates watched the two of us.

"Drak you!" Jax cried, dropping his Mage Hunter's sword and reaching for one of the axes he always kept strapped to his back. He was a split second away from stepping in and ripping Bjorn's head off when I called to him.

"Stop, Jax!" I held up a hand. "I can do this!"

"But M, he's—"

"I need to do this!" I shouted. I could tell Jax didn't like it, and while he lowered his axe, he didn't replace it on his back just yet.

It was hard to explain, but something inside me told me the outcome of this fight would prove something. Not only to Bjorn and the others, but to Mason Drakeslayer as well. I noted the High Prince's smug expression as he watched from the sidelines.

Two new rifts split open between Bjorn and me, their white interiors marking them as entry portals. I used my off-hand to guide the portals into place—right over Bjorn's weapons and hands up to his wrists.

Suddenly, the threatening movements of Bjorn's seaxe and dagger weren't right in my face. Rather, they were jutting uselessly out of the dual exit portals a good ten feet above our heads.

I was grateful I'd managed to scoop his silver weapons straight through the center of the portals before he'd been able to react. I was learning a thing or two about etherarchy here at the Academy too—If he had landed a slash against the outside rim of my rift with his silver blades, my portals would've dissolved immediately. But since the silver only went through the *inside*, my rifts stayed intact.

"Sooty magi," Bjorn snarled, trying to pull his hands back. But my entry portals followed him, pressing even more tightly on his wrists like manacles. He thrashed wildly, and sweat beaded along my forehead as I concentrated on keeping his hands from re-entering the fight.

I could tell a few of our spectators were impressed, but still, I heard Jaira scoff from the sidelines.

"Huh. I guess that's fine if you're too weak to take him."

Her words fueled my anger, but I wasn't stupid. Bjorn was nearly twice my size and he fought dirty. My etherarchy wasn't a sign of weakness, it was part of my strength.

Bjorn darted toward me, kicking with his long legs to try and take me down. When that didn't work, he growled as swings from my seaxe made *him* have to dodge for once.

But I wasn't the only one who'd learned about the limitations of rifting in my Academy classes. Bjorn leaned further through my wrist portals, so that he had more range through the exit ends above our heads. Then he finagled his angle so that his silver blades came down strong on the outer edge of my gold-rimmed exit rifts. His blades cut his own arms, but he didn't seem to care.

My portals instantly dissolved into etherdust. Bjorn, free once more, roared as he swung at me with renewed ire. I expertly blocked, but his sheer force knocked me to the ground.

"Meleya!" Brigan called from the sidelines. "Get out of there already!"

"He's not worth it!" Solvai agreed, her brow creased with worry. "You've done enough—Just throw the fight!"

Beside them, I saw Vidya looking equally distressed. She began runteracing as if planning to intervene, but Mason held up a hand to stop her. She set her jaw in compliance.

"Even your friends don't believe in you, ethercursed." Bjorn swung again, and I rolled across the dirt out of the way just in time. I tried to form a new portal, but precisely when it tore open, Bjorn slashed at it with his seaxe from the outside to dissolve it into the breeze.

"Admit you're not strong enough," Bjorn taunted, his silver destroying my incoming portals faster than I could open them. "Bow before my silver."

You don't have to, you know, my wraith's raspy voice cut through the rage stirring within the walls of my mind. In fact, the Gray One seemed to be feeding off of that energy. *You could easily overcome his silver. You have done so before.*

I yelled with frustration, sweat beading along my forehead as Bjorn stopped my every attempt to create another rift. While he slashed through one portal with his dagger, he suddenly lunged toward me with his seaxe.

I was so focused on trying to rift around his silver that I wasn't paying enough attention to his blades. The sharp edge of his seaxe caught me in the side, sending bitter, cold pain ripping through my ribcage.

I cried out, clutching my side as I ignored the array of protests from the sidelines. Still, I stubbornly raised my sword to block Bjorn's follow-up strike.

If you were immune to silver, he would be powerless against you, the voice rasped.

"That's enough," Vidya said forcefully as she moved toward me.

"Drakking sootfire!" Jax swore as he stepped out of line as well.

"Stay back!" I practically screamed.

"She can do this!" Mason Drakeslayer came to my defense, holding out his arm to block Vidya and Jax from getting any closer. Both looked like they wanted to defy him—especially Jax—but this was the High Prince over all the land. Jax's knuckles turned white as they gripped his axe handle, but his feet stayed rooted to the spot.

Then Mason turned to me.

*"Against the Diamondback's silver ire
Will the Snowstorm find her fire?"*

The High Prince's gaze met mine with an odd, knowing glint. When he called me by the moniker, Snowstorm, it sent a memory flying through my head. Me, back at the Winter Solstice ball, darting in and out of portals freely as I battled the Liberator. My etherarchy had given me me the strength to stand up to the powerful, Wildshaping true dragon and her mighty wraith.

But even that hadn't been enough to defeat her. To do that, I'd needed something even stronger. Something more primal. Like when I was defending Solvai on the field on Mason's first day.

Time seemed to slow as I faced Bjorn. In his burning, manic eyes, I saw even more memories.

I was seven years old, holding my father's hand as he led us away from yet another nomad caravan. They'd seen me use my etherarchy, and forced us out.

Caravan after caravan we'd left behind, all because nobody had the spine to stand up against Evgard's broken system.

In Bjorn's face, I saw the Mage Hunters we'd fled. I saw the cold gaze of Zoren, the Mage Hunter who'd finally captured and imprisoned my parents.

I saw the ferryman who'd taken us to Outcast Outpost, unable to even meet my eye as he led me and my entire squad to the most dangerous station in the realm.

I saw Commander Hildred, our platoon leader back at the Outpost, the day she'd sent Jax and me to our deaths in the Dragon Mists. I heard the voices of her lieutenants singing an old magi hunting song as we fled.

Bjorn's scowl hardened as he stalked toward me, and in him I saw my own mother. The way she'd taught me to hate myself for what I was, both through her words and her example.

I realized I was just as angry with *her* as I was at Evgard.

My eyes closed. All of my anger, resentment, and pure exhaustion condensed into a single, destructive point.

Then I let my wraith in.

Instantly, I felt her cool, gray presence fill my mind. The heat of my rage seemed to flow into her, setting me free. There was a release inside me, and for the first time in months, I felt genuine relief as her power flowed through my every limb. At last, I didn't have to try anymore. I didn't know why I'd been fighting this so much.

I felt compelled to breathe in deeply, the scent of cindercone pines filling my nose. A cool breeze sent chills up my arms. I sensed a giddiness from my wraith.

Hello, Meleya, she thought. *My name is Xan.*

Xan, I thought back.

When my eyes flew open again, I knew they were bright, sapphire blue.

My next portal split the air in front of me with vibrant blue light. It was just taller than I was, and when Bjorn tried to dissolve it with his silver blade, it went right through my portal as if it were smoke.

Unable to stop his momentum, Bjorn stumbled through my portal. With my wraith, Xan, now in control, I thrust my hand upward to form the exit high above us.

Bjorn fell through, hitting the ground with a hard thud. My heart jumped, and my instinct was to apologize and find out if he was okay.

But Xan wasn't finished. She compelled me forward, seaxe at the ready as Bjorn groaned and struggled to his knees. I kicked him in the face and he fell back down, dropping his long, silver seaxe.

Soot! I thought—That wasn't like me.

It felt incredibly strange as Xan controlled my every movement. I grabbed Bjorn's fallen weapon, then held it to his throat.

"Now you know your place," I said under my breath, though my voice wasn't my own. Well, it was in a way, but my voice seemed strangely doubled as Xan's raspy tone used mine. The sound of it sent a pang of fear rippling through me.

There was a light, uncomfortable smattering of applause from the sidelines. I noted Jax, Brigan, and Solvai looking at me with a degree of terror. Even Vidya seemed disturbed.

"Congratulations, Meleya," she said.

"Call me Snowstorm," Xan compelled me to reply, still making me press the tip of my blade dangerously close to Bjorn's throat.

Okay, we proved our point, I thought to my wraith. *Now, let me have my mind and body back.*

Oh, we're not finished yet. Not until we conquer.

We reeled back, ready to swing at Bjorn once more. To my horror, my blade would've plunged right into him if he hadn't raised his jagged silver dagger to block in the nick of time.

"Meleya!" Vidya snapped. "That's enough!"

Xan made me swing again, and Bjorn barely dodged in time.

"I said stop!" Vidya yelled.

"I... I can't!" I replied, my voice coming out weak without Xan's allowance. From the sidelines, I caught a glimpse of Jax and the others standing frozen in confusion.

I continued coming at Bjorn, his blocks getting flimsier with each forthcoming strike. With Xan's strength, I was fast. Xan used me to tear open a new blue portal, which we used to wrench his silver dagger right from his hands. I felt a wicked, involuntary smile form on my lips as we tossed his only remaining weapon to the side.

"H-help!" I cried meekly. "Bjorn, move!"

After his drop through my portal earlier, Bjorn's movements were lethargic. Despite my best efforts, I couldn't fight Xan's hold over my arm as she brought my weapon down toward Bjorn.

To my relief, my seaxe clanged against another blade. Brigan's sword prevented me from striking Bjorn. His strength was enough to stop me.

As I whipped my head up to look Brigan in the eye, my wraith sent another flood of thoughts into my mind. Brigan was a nobleman—part of the class who would see my kind executed.

No, I thought, *Brigan's one of the good ones.*

At that, Xan played a painful memory of Brigan asking me to get the magi cure. That hadn't been all that long ago.

They're all the same, Xan rasped, forcing me to turn my next attack on Brigan.

I screamed as I slashed at my friend. Brigan recoiled, his hand covering the left side of his face. When he pulled back, blood dripped off his fingers and a cut ran from the edge of his eyebrow to his cheek.

"No!" I cried. It looked like I'd missed his eye, but still. I wrestled with Xan inside my head, trying desperately to regain control.

Enough with these weaklings, Xan thought. *Now, to take some real power.*

Xan then forced me to runetrace. It was a symbol I didn't recognize, but apparently it was etherarchy I was capable of because the bright blue rune appeared over my forehead. Blue-tinged violet light seemed to emanate from my seaxe.

Dreamweave etherarchy is not nearly as effective against my kind as Archonic power, Xan thought, *but it will be sufficient today.*

I felt a sharp tug as Xan pushed us toward the sidelines—right to where Jaira stood watching the action.

"Your power is ours, Lightbane," Xan used my voice to say. Despite my efforts to stop myself, my seaxe stabbed toward Jaira's chest.

My hesitance was enough to give Jaira time to block. She held her silver chain whip tightly between her hands to keep my seaxe at bay.

"Get away from me, Jaira!" I stammered. But instead of running, Jaira stood her ground and began to laugh.

Suddenly, her eyes blazed with sapphire energy. Lightning crackled along her whip, which she used to snare my sword and yank it from my grasp.

"You're delusional if you think you can defeat us," Jaira cackled.

For a moment, I sensed panic from Xan. She launched us backward, my finger flying to runetrace once again.

To my horror, this time I recognized the symbol. Xan was opening my rift hold.

"Stop!" I screamed. "Stop it!"

Blue light rimmed a hand-sized portal beside me, and Xan forced me to reach inside. My hand closed around the thin, blue shard and tore it from its ethereal pocket.

"Enjoy the void," Xan forced me to cry as we shot back toward Jaira, the Soul Reaper's voidshard held tightly in my fist.

At the sight of it, Jaira's bright eyes went wide. She scrambled backward, but not quickly enough. I squeezed my eyes shut, but to my surprise, Xan didn't deliver a blow to Jaira's chest.

Instead, she stabbed the voidshard just off to the side, over her shoulder. I saw nothing there, but I felt the strangest, otherworldly resistance, as if I were plunging a dagger into a cloak.

What in the void had just happened?

All at once, I felt a surge of power flow into me. Or rather, into my wraith. Xan's glee made the hairs on my arms stand on end as her laughter resounded inside my head.

Yes! she cried

"No!" Mason Drakeslayer's cry pierced the courtyard. He was pointing to the blue crystal in my hand. "Is that...?"

Oh soot.

"No!" I said, rapidly shoving the shard back into my rift hold. But I knew the damage had been done.

"Liar!" Mason raced toward me, his expression livid. His fierce greataxe glinted as he held it high, fully prepared to do whatever was necessary to take that shard.

Then three shapes stepped between me and Mason—Jax, Brigan, and was that Solvai in falcondrake form?

Meanwhile, someone grabbed me from behind, pinning my arms. Xan made me thrash, trying to escape their grip as I turned my head to see Vidya.

"I'm so sorry, Meleya."

I felt a sharp, welcome dreamblast against the back of my head. Then the world went black.

CHAPTER 13: ESCAPE

ASHER

"Do you have an appointment?"

The lightly accented, feminine voice came from the other end of the dark underground hallway, making me spin around. Instantly, I let my array of starglass keys dissolve into etherdust. Soot, I hoped she hadn't seen me using them to try breaking into this accursed, heavily bolted Asylum door. For that matter, I hoped she hadn't seen me scouring the Academy grounds until I'd found this place in the first place.

The young woman approached, her long red hair swinging behind her as her all-too-familiar face radiated skepticism. My blood froze.

It was Shaya.

Real Shaya.

She stood before me, glanced toward my scale-tipped ears, then folded her arms across her chest.

"Do I know you?" she asked.

"Me? I don't think so," I said hurriedly. Hopefully I hadn't left that much of an impression the day I'd robbed Swan Spire. There were probably lots of dashing, roguish half-borns with turquoise, scale-tipped ears running around, right?

Shaya narrowed her eyes as she repeated her initial question. "Do you have an appointment?"

"Yes," I said, trying to wipe any nervousness from my face. "Yes, of course I do. Didn't they tell you to expect someone from the Evyndara Art

Therapy Association? I'm a painter, here to try out some new recovery methods for those in the Asylum."

Art therapy? Really? Thorn may have been hiding out in the Academy's dragon stables, but his sarcastic thought came loud and clear through our bond.

It's a real thing, Thorn, I stubbornly thought back. Still, yikes. This was definitely not making my list of top ten most believable aliases.

Yet by some miracle, Real Shaya was using a black-lace gloved hand to thoughtfully tap her chin.

"Art therapy," Shaya said. "I'm certain several patients would quite enjoy trying their hand at painting, young mister…"

"Arty," I replied, cringing internally as I said the first name that popped into my head. "It's short for Arthur." I ignored Thorn's uproarious wyvern laughter through our bond.

Shaya, too, gave a chuckle and a tiny snort. "Arty the artist?"

"It was destiny." I shrugged.

"Where are your materials?" Shaya asked. "Canvas, paints, brushes…?"

"That is an excellent question," I said, buying myself time to think. "Exactly the sort of question someone who hasn't studied in the sophisticated field of art therapy would ask. It's only my first day here—It would be ridiculous to think we'd be using real canvas and paint during the first session."

No way this works, Thorn mocked.

You can shut up now, I emoted back.

"Anyway," I said out loud to Shaya. "If you wouldn't mind opening the door for me, I'll just head in, teach my quick class, then be out of your hair. That's all I'm here for."

"That's all?" Shaya asked.

"That's all," I confirmed. Stars, her face was unreadable. I had no idea whether she was buying my story or not.

"What a shame." Shaya shook her head. "Here I was hoping you were that same half-born thief I encountered once before in Swan Spire, here to break the victims of the so-called magi cure out of the Asylum."

My jaw hit the floor.

Shaya shrugged. "My mistake. If only that were the case, I'd have gladly helped you. As one of the healers here, I have access to that door, knowledge of the schedule, not to mention the trust of the patients inside. By Solei's blade—If *only* that was why you were here."

"It is," I nodded vigorously. "That is exactly why I'm here, yes."

Shaya gave a hearty, bubbly laugh with a few more snorts, nothing like the bell-like laugh the Black Valkyrie had adopted while using Shaya's likeness to trick us.

"Well, what are we waiting for, Arthur?" Shaya asked with a wink.

"Asher," I corrected.

"Alright then, Asher," she said with a satisfied grin. "Let's stick it to some high-and-mighty nobles and lead these prisoners to freedom."

Stars. Real Shaya was speaking my language. I don't think I could've grinned wider if I tried.

With a lot of help from Shaya by way of keys, timing, and the gentle coaxing of some of the more reluctant cure victims, we were leading a silent horde westward through the Mirror Forest in no time.

It had been no easy task thus far, but honestly, I was shocked things were going this well. We hadn't run into a single Mage Hunter yet, though I'd overheard something of a commotion back at the main Academy. Thank the goddesses for whatever distraction was allowing for our near-perfect escape.

Other than the sound of hooves on dirt, we were silent as we crept out of sight of the Academy walls. I figured that, with time, the Mage Hunters would forgive us for borrowing a couple dozen kirin from their stables. It seemed a small price to pay for what they'd put these cure victims through.

I rode Thorn near the back of the group, walking along with the others rather than flying. He still thought I was crazy for pulling a stunt like this, but appeared to forgive me when he saw the sleek, reddish-pink female wyvern Shaya rode nearby. It seemed this mysterious, redheaded rebel was also a dragon rider.

I chuckled under my breath as Thorn walked a little straighter in the lady wyvern's presence. Through our bond, I sensed that he was concerned about how polished his antlers looked. I made a mental note to tease him about it later.

I was just leaning over to Shaya to mention how smoothly this was going when the *whoosh* of a crossbow bolt sliced through the air directly between us to land in the knot of a cindercone trunk. Both Shaya and I, as well as our wyverns, yelped and whirled around.

Standing not far behind the group were a half-dozen Mage Hunters in dusky blue cloaks, silver weapons at the ready. At their head, still brandishing her crossbow, was a woman with a thick, white-streaked auburn braid. The cure victims on kirinback stopped in their tracks, looking nervously toward the Hunters. I moved to stand between the two groups.

"That first shot was a warning," the lead Mage Hunter said as she gripped her crossbow. I noted another miniature crossbow holstered at her hip. She had the same smooth, eastern accent as Shaya.

I put up my hands, already wracking my brain for an excuse—and, stars willing, a better one than 'Arty the art therapist' had been.

"Whoa, whoa whoa," I started. "This is all just a big misunder—"

Suddenly, another crossbow bolt came whizzing my way. I didn't have time to react before the bolt clipped my hair loop—and *only* my hair loop, making my warrior's fangknot come undone. My eyes widened as strands of hair fell over my forehead.

"You, put a scale in it," the Hunter said to me. Then she turned to Shaya. "Shaya, what in the stars do you think you are *doing*?"

"Please, Trickshot," Shaya replied as she addressed the lead Mage Hunter.

"Trickshot," I said, cautiously feeling my hair. "That makes sense."

The Mage Hunter, Trickshot, narrowed her eyes at me while she reloaded. I promptly shut up.

Shaya continued. "Don't try to stop us, Trickshot. You know as well as I do that what they've done to these people is wrong. I can't just continue sitting by while they suffer."

"So you've put your life and theirs into the hands of this renegade?"

"Renegade, I like that," I said. Trickshot retrained her freshly loaded crossbow between my eyes. I grimaced and put my hands up.

"He has a good light about him," Shaya replied. "Besides, when I started at the Asylum, I made a promise to do my best to care for these people. That is exactly what I'm doing."

There was a brief standoff as the two—I could only assume they were sisters—stared each other down. That was when I noticed that several of the other Mage Hunters had grown tired of Trickshot's stalling. They prepared to strike.

Likewise, I took a deep breath and readied my ether. I didn't like my chances against all that silver, but I was moments away from summoning my starglass spear.

Before I got the chance, Trickshot whirled on her fellow Hunters, letting her crossbow bolt fly. She pinned one of them to a tree by their cloak, making them drop the silver whip they'd been about to unleash on Shaya and me.

The others seemed stunned, but a few responded quickly to Trickshot's... trick shot. Three long seaxes cut toward her.

Quick as lightning, she dropped her standard crossbow to whip out the miniature one sheathed at her hip. That was enough to pin the next nearest foe, but one of the other Mage Hunters jumped in to defend Trickshot, immobilizing the other two.

I watched, impressed as the second Mage Hunter, an older man with a tan eye patch and a white streak in his hair much like the one Trickshot had, took out several more of his fellow Hunters. I was even more impressed when I realized he was doing so despite missing fingers on both of his hands.

I'd have intervened, since I loved taking down a Mage Hunter or two any chance I got, but Trickshot and her companion quickly wrapped things up; within a minute, the other Mage Hunters lay still on the ground. Not wasting any time, Trickshot unslung her pack and pulled out a couple of mysterious elixirs. She administered a few drops to each of the passed-out Mage Hunters, then faced Shaya and me, alongside the Hunter with the eye patch.

I burst into rigorous applause. "That. Was. *Awesome!*"

Shaya started clapping too, and it was contagious enough that a few cure victims even joined in. The Mage Hunter with the eye patch gave a two-fingered salute.

"Thanks, Mute," Trickshot said, thumping her companion on the shoulder.

"Mute?" I asked. "Why do you call him—oh stars." I was not prepared for such a quick, graphic answer to my question as Mute opened his mouth to reveal that his tongue was missing.

"By Solei's blade!" Shaya put a hand on her chest. "For a second, I really thought you were going to turn us in, Torya." That must've been Trickshot's real name. It was nice, but I liked Trickshot better.

"For a second, so did I," Trickshot admitted. "Then I remembered that you were the reason I joined the Mage Hunters in the first place, you impulsive little scoundrel. Besides, you're right. I, too, vowed to care for these people." Trickshot gestured to the cure victims.

Then she turned to me. "Shaya had just better be right about you."

From the ground, one Mage Hunter groaned. Mute quickly silenced him with a boot to the back of the head.

"We'd better hurry," Trickshot said. "The tonic I gave them should buy us a couple of hours, but it's only a matter of time before High Prince Mason notices the jailbreak and sends reinforcements."

Shaya turned to me, an eager smile on her face and what looked like flecks of almost-glowing gold in her eyes. That was interesting—when the Black Valkyrie had played Shaya, those flecks had been blue.

"Asher, lead the way."

An hour or so into our journey, I found myself bouncing between the head of the group and the rear, ensuring everyone was together and on the right track. Shaya and Trickshot helped keep the group moving as well, while Mute did a surprisingly good job of covering our tracks. I wasn't entirely sure how it happened, but before long, Thorn and I had fallen into step near Shaya once more. I figured it had something to do with Thorn's particular interest in Shaya's dragon bond. I stifled a chuckle as Thorn tossed his majestic stag horns just to get her attention.

Find out her name? Thorn asked me through our bond.

I felt a little strange playing wingman for a wyvern, but called over to Shaya:

"What's your wyvern's name?"

She smiled, giving her dragon's neck a squeeze. "Rose."

Rose the rose-gold wyvern turned toward us and blinked her large eyes. I felt a fiery flutter from Thorn.

Rose—perfect, he emoted through our bond, sounding only slightly sappy about it. Inside, I was rolling with laughter, but I kept it together on the outside for Thorn's sake.

And your name? Shaya's second ascension asked so that Thorn and I could both hear.

Thorn. I'm Thorn. Thorn eagerly responded, and Shaya grinned.

"You know," I continued my conversation with Shaya, "I couldn't help but notice that you seemed pretty eager to turn on the Mage Hunters. If you don't hate magi, why join them in the first place?"

"That's a long-ish story," Shaya replied.

"We've got a long-ish journey ahead of us before we reach the safe-house."

Shaya snort-laughed again, and I gave her my trademark crooked grin. Real-Shaya was similarly bubbly to the Fake-Shaya the Black Valkyrie had played, but still... It was refreshing to interact with this girl. I'd have expected to feel strange and uncomfortable in her presence, especially since I'd sort-of had feelings for Fake-Shaya last summer. None of those feelings resurfaced now, and Real-Shaya seemed like one of those people who instantly puts you at ease. In a way, it felt kind of healing.

As we helped the cure victims on kirinback maneuver around tree roots, mud, and stones, Shaya began her tale.

"All their lives, my family had never given much thought to the High King's laws about magi. To them, executing the people who drew wild dragons near made perfect sense. We had to protect the keeps, right? Then I came along. I manifested shadowbinding powers practically from the moment I was born."

"That's unique," I said. I hadn't shown any signs that I was an Astromancer until I was about eight or nine.

Shaya nodded, and I noticed her subconsciously pulling her sleeves down over her hands. Had she put on a thicker pair of black lace gloves since we'd left the Asylum?

"For whatever reason, I was never very good at hiding my powers," Shaya went on. "Unsure what else to do, my family kept me hidden in the attic for years. It was a small upper room in our already-tiny home above my parents' apothecary shop, filled with crates of extra supplies and only one scuffed-up little window about this big." Shaya used her hands to outline a circle just bigger than her face.

"You weren't allowed to go outside?" I asked, horrified at the thought.

Shaya shook her head, her draketail of red hair swinging to and fro. "I got bored to tears up there."

"No doubt."

"Luckily, I found a couple of knitting needles stored in one of the boxes and convinced Mom to teach me how to knit. That kept me from going completely insane."

She paused her tale to help a cure victim who'd begun to cry. I watched the way she expertly soothed her, reassuring the woman that she'd be alright and was heading somewhere safe. The woman wore a lacy black shawl, had long, smooth hair, and a pair of large brown eyes. I suddenly realized that those eyes—and the woman's features in general—looked an awful lot like Meleya's.

"You're going to be okay, Freya, I promise," Shaya said.

Freya. It was hard to be sure, but I could've sworn Ivar had called his wife Freya that first day we'd trained together on the safehouse roof.

"Freya," I said, urging Thorn to get closer so the woman could hear me. She looked up at me with round, wet eyes, shining in the dappled light of the trees.

"Shaya's right, everything's going to be okay," I said. "We're taking you to your husband, Ivar."

"Ivar?" she asked hopefully.

"Exactly." I smiled. "He'll be so thrilled to see you. We'll be there soon, I promise."

The woman nodded slowly. "Thank you. Thank you, Zoren."

I raised an eyebrow at that. "Umm... My name's Asher."

"But your eyes..." She pointed to my dragonfire green irises. My guess was that she must've known a half-born or Drekai by that name.

Freya blinked hard a few times, clearly confused. This was probably not the time for a joke about how presumptive it was to expect everyone with Drekai blood to be the same person.

Still, learning that we were on the way to Ivar calmed Freya down. Shaya lingered nearby for a few more moments before she and her wyvern returned to walk beside me. Much to Thorn's delight, I knew, as my bond 'accidentally' let his wing brush against Rose's. It was hard to tell with a dragon, especially a dragon with Rose's coloring, but I could've sworn she was doing the wyvern equivalent of blushing.

"So, where was I?" Shaya said, ready to continue her story.

"Knitting in the attic like some kind of hermit granny," I recalled.

Shaya burst into laughter before going on. "That's right. Anyway, this hermit granny was ten years old when I heard there was going to be a special parade coming through our town. A parade featuring the high noble family over all of Evgard."

While Shaya's laughter before had been sincere, the laugh she gave now was short and bitter. "I was thrilled at the chance to see a High King in person. I thought he'd be somehow grander than the rest of us. How wrong I was."

"Nobles do tend to think that way." I shrugged, thinking of the snobby baron over my hometown, Steel Rim.

"Lousy lot of selfish wyvernhogs," Shaya echoed.

"Not all of them. I know at least two and a half nobles who aren't the absolute worst." I nearly shocked myself as the words left my mouth. Me, defending the noble class? But knowing Elle, I couldn't let *all* nobles get slandered like that without saying something.

"My parents forbade me from going to the parade," Shaya went on, "but I was so fed up with the same four walls and tiny window. So I snuck out to catch a glimpse."

Shaya sighed. "At ten, I was as awestruck by High King Magnus as the rest of the crowd. They cheered, reaching out and calling him their 'Great Uniter.' And his true dragon, Noctus... by Solei's blade, he was a sight to see."

"People do seem to love their true dragon riders," I said, once again thinking of Elle. "They've always been held up as heroes."

"No doubt the reason Magnus gained so much support in the first place," Shaya agreed. "Especially with how rare true dragons have become. Anyway, people were tossing coins, flowers, and handkerchiefs at the king's feet. Naturally, I wanted to give tribute as well. I was so caught up in the moment, I didn't think."

Shaya winced at the memory, and I watched as her eyes flashed gold, her hands swirling elegantly as we rode through the forest. Before my eyes, she used shimmering black shadowsilk to form a tiny, delicate rose. She passed me the silk flower and I cupped it in my palm. It was a beautiful use of etherarchy, reminding me of my mother's shadowbinding. Mom didn't specialize in shadowsilk, but I'd seen her use her powers to make things like soft bandages before.

"I made one of these and tossed it before the High King Magnus. Before I knew it, the Mage Hunters had descended. Six of them surrounded me, a completely helpless ten-year-old girl, just for making her High King a flower."

Shaya's bubbly tone turned bitter at that. I could tell the memory was painful to relive.

"They silvermarked me and scheduled my execution for two days from then. Most of my family—my parents and one sister—spent the night in tears outside my jail cell. But my oldest sister, Trickshot, didn't cry. Instead, she rented a winged kirin and flew straight through the night to get to the Ridgeback Mountains."

"Why?" I asked, enthralled by Shaya's tale.

"To get to the Mage Hunter Academy," Trickshot cut in. She and the dappled gray kirin she rode pulled up beside Shaya and me. "I knew I had to hurry if I wanted to get to the Black Valkyrie in time."

"The... the Black Valkyrie?" I said. "Why in the stars would the head of the Mage Hunters be interested in helping some young magi?"

"Shaya wasn't just some young magi," Trickshot explained. "The Black Valkyrie... Well, let's just say my family has been special to her for a long time."

"Since before I was born," Shaya added.

I had a hard time wrapping my head around that, but Trickshot pressed on.

"As the leader of the Hunters, the Black Valkyrie was incredibly busy. But the moment I arrived and told her what had happened, she dropped everything and returned to Dawn Falls with me. We arrived just in time to stop the execution."

"Soot," I said, unsure what to think. "You sure this is the Black Valkyrie you're talking about? As in... the *Black Valkyrie?*"

"Even her position as leader of the Mage Hunters wasn't enough to get Shaya off without a hitch, though," Trickshot continued, ignoring my indignation. "Shaya would be allowed to go back into hiding, but our family had to promise something in return."

"And that was...?"

"Our service," Shaya replied. "Torya became a Mage Hunter first, then our middle sister, Aneya, joined up a couple years later, and is now stationed in the North. A few months ago, it was finally my turn to sell my soul to the High King's broken system."

"Shaya," Trickshot scolded. "You can't say things like that."

"Solei's blade, it's not like I'm picketing the high citadel!" Shaya said. "Besides, *someone* has to say them."

"There it is," I interrupted them, pointing. Through the trees up ahead, I could see the outline of the enormous military safehouse cabin in the woods.

Shaya and Trickshot squinted into the trees.

"I don't see anything," Shaya said.

"You aren't playing us, right?" Trickshot said, fingering her mini crossbow. "Because if you are, I will happily take you out." Near Trickshot, I heard Mute crack his remaining knuckles in agreement.

Of course, I thought. *They can't see the safehouse—their ether signatures aren't in the etherlock yet. Oh stars... It's time to start coming up with a really good story for how all this happened.* Rhana was going to string me up by my toes and throw me in her underground dungeon for sure. And Kai was going to give me the lecture of the century.

Speaking of Kai... Thorn's thought came through our bond as loud and clear as the first spark of a fresh-lit campfire. Then he directed my attention to the tiny mirror gecko who'd just climbed up Thorn to stand atop one antler. The copy of Kai's ethereal familiar, Glint, was staring me down with enormous, narrowed eyes.

"Why, hello there Glint," I said with a nervous chuckle. "Did you miss me? You totally missed me, I can tell."

The mirror gecko rolled her eyes, then scurried along Thorn's neck and into my boot. As soon as she made contact with my skin, I felt the mindlink between Kai and me bloom to life inside my head.

Asher of Steel Rim! Kai raged the second he sensed my mental presence. *Where in the void are you?*

Now that *is a fantastic question, and I'm so glad you asked. First, let's discuss the word 'where'...*

Kai cut me off. *Soot, Asher. Please,* please *tell me you didn't go back to that tower.*

I glanced at the large group of cure victims and three Mage Hunters I was leading straight into the Rebel Knights of the Torch's top secret base.

No, I thought. *In fact, I did not go back to that tower.*

Chapter 14: Sunset

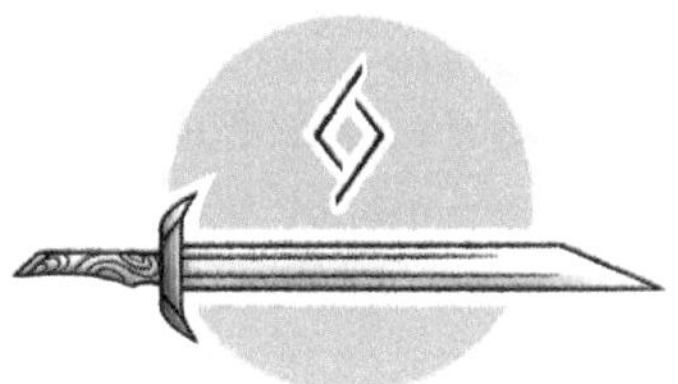

Meleya

For the first time in far too long, my slumber had been dreamless.

Still, I couldn't bring myself to open my eyes. I didn't deserve to wake up.

A lone tear slid from the corner of my eye as I lay there, replaying each awful moment over in my head.

I'd hurt Brigan. I'd nearly killed Bjorn.

I'd shown Mason exactly where he could find the Soul Reaper's void-shard.

I forced my eyes open, fully expecting to see a prison cell where I was awaiting execution.

Instead, I saw the black walls of a smallish room filled with dusty trunks and racks of old, extremely colorful clothing. They looked like... circus costumes? Dusty spydra webs dominated every corner. A single square window about half as tall as I was let in the diffused light of evening. I must've been out for a couple of hours.

I got the feeling I was somewhere in Swan Spire. An attic maybe?

Rubbing my head, I sat up, and the cot I'd been lying on creaked. The sound of a footstep made me whip my head around.

I wasn't alone. A muscular silhouette sat near the window.

Jax stood when he saw that I was awake. Relief and comfort flooded me.

"Thank the goddesses," I said, wrapping my arms around him. I tried to melt into his embrace, but he barely lifted his arms to hug me back. Frowning, I pulled back to get a better look at what he was wearing.

"What's this?" I asked, putting a hand on his shoulder. Or rather, the fabric of the long-sleeved tunic covering his shoulder.

"It's cold out, okay?" Jax subtly pulled away from my touch.

"Okay," I replied. Silence stretched between us for a long moment before I spoke again.

"What happened in the courtyard after I...?" I couldn't finish.

Jax's reply was cryptic. "My mom used shadowbinding to invisibly bring you here. Mason's got the entire Academy searching for you now. Mom's out trying to rally anyone still loyal to her, but things aren't looking good for her side."

"Drak," I cursed.

"Drak," Jax agreed. He still hadn't looked me in the eye once. After what he'd seen me do earlier today, I couldn't blame him.

I swallowed. "Look. In the courtyard... I swear, I didn't mean for any of it to—"

"This isn't working, Meleya," Jax cut me off, and my heart began thudding anxiously. He rarely called me anything but 'M,' and I didn't like the way he said my name now.

"What's not working?" I asked carefully, dreading the answer.

"Us."

It took nearly all my focus to breathe evenly. More tense silence filled the attic as I struggled to form a reply.

"Why? Because of... of what I did? Because Jax, I'm so, *so* sorry. It was my wraith—she took over, and I couldn't stop her. Please believe me."

"I do believe you."

"Then what?" I felt my lower lip beginning to tremble. "Because we've been arguing more lately? I never meant to—"

"It's not that," Jax said, walking past me to stand before the window. The sun was just dipping behind the mountains.

My feet felt rooted to the spot.

"Is it because I didn't tell you about the voidshard?" I asked quietly.

Jax whirled on me, making me jump as he shouted, "Yes! Scorching soot, you've been lying to me since we got here! Even before that! You got that drakking voidshard back in the Dragon Mists, didn't you?"

"Yes," I managed. Technically, it had been a few days after we'd escaped the Mists before Dusty the draccoon had brought me the voidshard, but what did that matter now?

Jax went on, "All that soot about burying Zyri's boomerang—more lies to keep me in the dark?"

"Yes."

"Your so-called evening class with High Prince Mason?"

"He's been forcing me to use the Sight to search for Zyri and the voidshard." I nodded. "He didn't know I had it with me all along."

"Drak, Meleya!" Jax swore. His straight jawline was tense, his eyebrows lowered over storming midnight blue eyes. I'd seen him angry before, but never like this. I couldn't stop the tears from welling up.

Jax continued yelling. "And you didn't trust me enough to tell me about any of this?"

"I was trying to protect you," I cried. "I was trying to protect all of you."

"Well, that worked out great, didn't it?" Jax said. "Your best friend, Duke-man, might have something to say about that."

More guilt hit me like a gust of rushing canyon wind to the face. I wanted nothing more than to disappear through the black floorboards.

"Drakking why?" Jax ran his fingers through his wild, steely hair, and I got the vibe he was half talking to himself. "What did I do wrong this time?"

"Nothing, nothing!" I said desperately. "You didn't do anything wrong. This is all my fault, but we can fix this."

Jax seemed to barely hear me. "I came to this scorching Academy for one reason. *One.* Yet even here, of all places, I'm still stuck in his shadow."

"What do you... Whose shadow?"

"Asher's!" Jax seethed. "It's always Asher. Kari's protective little watch-dog. The Knights of the Torch's new golden boy. Solrac's perfect protégé. And now, on top of it all, your hero."

"What are you talking about?"

"Your mom is safe, M, or at least she will be. The Academy's buzzing with the news that a half-born wearing a turquoise scarf broke into the Asylum and freed the cure recipients. He and his accomplices took out a bunch of Mage Hunters, but Mason's too occupied looking for you to give a flying scale." Jax scoffed. "A half-born wearing a turquoise scarf. Who else could that be, huh? No doubt Asher's taking your mom to safety with the Rebel Knights—and your Dad—as we speak."

Hope and gratitude instantly bloomed inside my chest. Mom and Dad were going to be together again. After all these years, they were finally safe. Safe, thanks to...

"Asher," I said, half under my breath.

Jax's jaw muscles tensed as he watched me say his name. He looked like he wanted to throw something, maybe embed one of his axes into the tower's black walls. I could see the raw pain flashing in his eyes.

"I'm out of here," he muttered, turning on his heel and making a beeline for the exit. "I'll keep Mason's cronies from coming up and finding you."

Panic sent my mind reeling. If Jax walked out that door, I knew things were over between us.

Instead of running to him, I darted to the window. I flung it open, my stomach turning as I looked at the sheer drop down the slanted rooftop to the earth far below. Without thinking, I began to climb.

It was enough to get Jax to turn around. "Soot—What are you doing?"

"You said you don't think I trust you." A fresh wave of tears blurred my vision. "So let me show you that I do."

With that, I threw myself backward out the window.

My feet hadn't even left the sill before I felt a tug from my belt wrenching me to a stop. There was Jax, a telekinetic rune aglow over his forehead as one hand stretched toward me.

He psionically pulled me back to him, holding fast around my waist.

"Half the Mage Hunters here are searching for you," Jax growled, his dark brows furrowed. "That was reckless, not to mention pointless."

My heart raced, partly from the adrenaline rush of nearly falling off a rooftop, but mostly because I could feel Jax's body against mine. He still hadn't relinquished his tight, protective hold around my waist, and I could feel our breathing patterns syncing up.

"It wasn't pointless," I replied, my voice low and soft. Jax's expression softened.

The chilly winds of early spring whistled through the window as he held me, the daylight fading over the mountains.

"I made a mistake by not confiding in you, Jax," I whispered. "I see that clearly now, and I swear I'll never lie to you again. There's no excuse for what I did—I let my wraith influence me long before she took control in the courtyard. I... I think you know what that's like."

Emotions swirled behind Jax's eyes. I wondered if his Gray One was speaking to him even now.

"There's something about this place. The Academy," Jax started, his voice taking on that overwhelmed, rambling tone I'd come to know well. "The Gray is stronger here. Ever since we came, I've been so confused.

So drakking angry. Knights of the Torch are supposed to choose light and drive out darkness, but they're not doing that. *I'm* not. When that thing possessed you in the courtyard, I just stood there like a weak, useless pile of soot. I'm not good enough to be a Knight, not good enough for Solrac, or even my own scorching mother. And I'm certainly not good enough for you, M."

He nearly broke eye contact, but I cupped his face with my hands to stop him. His brows knit, and he looked at me with such raw vulnerability it broke my heart.

"Run away with me," I said, repeating what Jax had said to me the morning he'd taken me to the sunny mountain glade. "You want to see something truly reckless? Jump out this window with me. We'll take our dragons and run before anyone notices we're gone. We could leave everything behind and go, just you and me."

Jax seemed to be considering my plan. My thumb slowly moved along his jawline, easing the tightness.

"But where would we go?" Jax asked. "I won't go back to the Knights—I can't."

"It doesn't matter where we go. We could head north to the Glacier Keepdom, or live with the nomadic caravans in Rengard. Find some corner of the desert and leave all of this behind."

"You'd want that?" His midnight blue eyes were intense, searching.

I answered by sliding my hands around the back of his neck and pulling his face toward mine. I pressed my lips against his in a fiery kiss, desperate to make him stay.

Just when I thought he was going to kiss me back, Jax turned away.

"You don't really want to leave. You could never leave your family—It's not who you are."

"My mom's safe with my father. You said so your—"

"Not just her. Solvai, Brigan, the squad... your instinct to take care of all of them is too strong. When you take the time to think it through, you'll agree."

Numbly, I let Jax step away from me.

"I can't run away from all this and neither can you," Jax said. "But I have to go now. I have some stuff I need to figure out on my own."

"What stuff?" I blubbered. "Whatever it is, we can figure it out together. Just tell me."

I watched helplessly as he headed for the floor hatch that served as the attic's only door.

"I'm sorry," Jax said, his tone empty of emotion as he looked me dead in the eyes and repeated the words I'd told him earlier that very day. "But I can't tell you."

"But—"

"Trust me."

At those two little words, guilt flowed from my toes to my fingertips. Jax began to disappear down the hatch.

Overcome, I cried out, feeling like a complete fool as I tried to get him to stay when he clearly didn't want to.

"Please! You-you're not supposed to give up on someone. Not when you... not when you still love them."

Jax stopped in his tracks, halfway in and halfway out of the exit. He looked down as he spoke.

"You think you love me?"

My voice came out as barely a whisper. "Yes, Jax. I love you."

I held my breath, realizing I'd never said I loved someone out loud like that before. Vulnerability, anxiety, and fear surrounded me instantly. I couldn't have felt more exposed if I were standing naked atop a mountain peak.

Not looking up at me, Jax scoffed.

"Love. Maybe I'm not capable of it."

With that, Jax softly closed the hatch behind him, leaving me alone in the dark room.

Tears still stained my cheeks by the time Vidya snuck into the attic soon after.

"Thank the light you're alright," Vidya whispered, hurrying my way. Only a sliver of moonlight through the window let me see her face, but I could tell she was nervous. Frantic even.

"Vidya," I said, stiffly getting to my feet. I hadn't moved since Jax had left. "Thank you for saving me from—"

"There's no time for all that right now," Vidya rushed. "Mason Drakeslayer has taken over the Academy. They're after you, and me as well. With his father, High King Magnus, *and* the Soul Reaper at Mason's back, none of us stand a chance against him."

Vidya was speaking so quickly I could hardly keep up as she pressed on.

"Those still loyal to me—or at least, those not loyal to Mason—have gathered together in the courtyard. We have to run. At least we have to try. I don't know where to go—nowhere nearby is safe. Not from *him*."

"Him?" I asked.

"The Soul Reaper." Vidya paled as she whispered the name. "He will not take my betrayal lightly. But scorch, I can't stay. We need to go somewhere even he can't reach..."

Vidya continued as my mind went to what I'd seen back in Scryer's Grotto. In the Evyndara crystal, in the very forest where we were now, I'd seen two auras I knew would bring us safety. Earlier today, Asher had promised to bring my rift anchor to my father.

If I was right, Asher had just provided me with a path straight to the Rebel Knights of the Torch's base.

"Vidya," I said, cutting her short. She looked at me, a quizzical expression on her thrice silvermarked face.

"What is it?" she asked.

I squared my shoulders. "I know exactly where we can go."

FRAGMENT: NOTHING

JAX

Jax could still hear the sound of the attic door shutting behind him as he'd walked out on Meleya. It echoed in his ears as he headed down Swan Spire's steps, then continued as he made his way through the crowded, torchlit Academy halls, drowning out all other noise. Everyone all across the Academy, from instructors to cadets, seemed to be going somewhere. Not that Jax cared.

I love you, Meleya had said.

Impossible, the deep, masculine voice of Jax's wraith cut through his mind like a heavy, rusty axe.

Impossible, Jax mentally agreed, picking up his pace. He needed to go... he didn't know. Somewhere. Anywhere before he started crying or something stupid like that. He clutched the quartz crystal clipped onto the side of his belt—one of two Solrac had given him for storing extra ether. The other, Jax had given to Meleya as a gift.

Jax had felt he'd had no choice but to break things off with Meleya. Yes, she'd messed up by putting up her walls and not trusting him, but all that had been an excuse.

Jax had left Meleya so that she couldn't beat him to it.

It was *himself* he couldn't trust. Jax wasn't worthy of Meleya, and these past few weeks had taught him he never would be. His wraith was constantly in his head, and he wasn't sure how much longer he could keep fighting its hold over him. Jax was dangerous, both to Meleya and to the other Rebel Knights.

Jax was heading down the hall leading to the dorm on the Academy's upper floor when he felt a sharp tug on his long-sleeved tunic. It was hard enough to telekinetically yank him off course, dragging him into an alcove overlooking the Academy's central courtyard.

"What in the void," Jax said, looking around and seeing Jaira. "How did you—"

Jax's trailed off as Jaira seemed to shimmer and melt, growing taller, as her hair turned steel gray. It hadn't been Jaira at all, but the Black Valkyrie, wearing an illusion.

"Jax," his mother said. "I've been looking for you everywhere. We're ready to run; I've gathered the rest of your squad and some others, but Mason plans to stop us. Luckily, we have a plan."

"What plan?" Jax asked.

"The Rebel Knights." Vidya gulped. "We have to hope they'll grant us sanctuary."

"You're crazy if you think for a second they'll let you in," Jax said, a bitter edge creeping into his tone. "And even crazier if you think I'll take you there."

"I don't expect you to—"

"They'll kill you on sight," Jax interrupted. "As they should. You betrayed them. You tried to kill the Farseer."

Even in the low torchlight, Jax saw his mother's face grow pale. "Things have changed. *I've* changed."

Jax scoffed. "As if I'd ever believe that."

"It's true. But I understand why you feel that way. I'm no longer worthy of your trust."

"You haven't had my trust since longer than I can remember."

A crash from the nearest open archway got both Jax and his mother to step further into the alcove. They leaned over the balcony railing to get a better look into the Academy's central courtyard, where it looked like someone had just dropped a trunk of belongings. Jax noted a handful of blue-cloaked Mage Hunters gathered together in the far corner, including the other six members of Squad Reckless. Meleya's stark white hair stood out in the moonlight.

"There's no time," Jax's mother said. "We have to get down there. Meleya's going to get us out of here."

"So you're putting M in danger now too just to save your own skin?" Jax bit back. He was too frustrated to think straight. "I know you used her to get me to come to this place. You manipulated her by dangling her mother in front of her like a drakking carrot. Now I'm supposed to believe you have her best interest at heart?"

"Meleya makes her own choices," Vidya replied defensively.

"You saw what happened in the courtyard today!" Jax said, ignoring his mother's attempts to hush him. "*None* of us are in control of any of our choices! What's the point of even trying to pretend otherwise?"

Yes, Jax, his wraith's deep voice added to his mental struggle. *Why try?*

"Oh, Black Valkyrie!" Jaira's disturbingly sing-song voice echoed down the hallway. "Where are you hiding? The High Prince wishes to see you."

"Drak," Vidya swore, pulling Jax back into the alcove once more. Her eyes flashed blue as she activated more shadowbinding power to turn the pair of them invisible.

"And Drakeslayer's not the only one who would like a word," Jaira's eerie taunting continued. "The Soul Surgeon wishes to remind you of the debt you owe him."

Jax's mother began to tremble. "Come with us," she pleaded in a near-silent whisper. "Please."

Jax felt frozen. Torn. He couldn't possibly trust his tyrant mother. That wasn't even an option. But that didn't mean he could stay here at the Academy, either. People were choosing sides—The Black Valkyrie or Mason Drakeslayer. Yes, he wanted to go back to the Knights, but how could he face them?

Jax felt utterly trapped.

You do not have to choose, his wraith whispered. *The Knights of the Torch say to 'choose light', but the Knights have never gotten you anywhere. To them, you are no more than a mindless grunt. A tool to be used and then discarded. They do not deserve you.*

Jax looked to his mother. Her invisibility was flickering, and he could see into her dark blue eyes. Her hand was outstretched toward him.

"Please, JJ," she said.

Suddenly, one of Jax's most vivid memories filled his mind:

"Where are we, Mom?" Jax asked.

Dragonflies filled Jax's stomach as the dusty establishment came into view. Jax and his mom stepped onto the porch, sounds of clinking glass and laughter echoing from the open window. Jax sounded out the tavern name written over the door:

The Naga's Head.

"It's like we talked about," Jax's mom said, giving his hand a squeeze. She knelt on the creaky wooden stoop so that six-year-old Jax was at eye level. Her dark blue eyes were shiny... Was Mom crying? Mom hardly ever cried. What was going on?

"This is your new home," Mom went on.

"You mean our *new home?"*

"Just you, JJ. I've talked to your dad, and he's very excited to spend some time with you."

"My... my dad?"

Jax glanced toward the tavern door as it slowly swung open. Standing in the doorway and looking almost as nervous as Jax felt was a man with medium-length brownish hair and high cheekbones. The stranger shuffled from foot to foot.

"Vidya," he gulped, "you sure 'bout this?"

"It's the only way," Jax's mom replied, getting to her feet. She pulled the man aside and they spoke in hushed tones for several minutes while the knots in Jax's stomach got tighter and tighter.

Finally, Jax's mom returned to give him a hug. "I know this doesn't make sense to you right now," she said, "but there are some things I just can't explain."

She squeezed him so hard Jax began to laugh.

"Can't... breathe," he said melodramatically. His mom pulled back and ruffled his wild gray hair. Then she rummaged through her satchel to pull out a crumpled maroon bandana.

She fingered the cloth longingly before she silently helped Jax tie the bandana around his neck. Then she took Jax by the shoulders and gave him one last long look.

All too soon, Mom was walking back up the road.

Jax froze, unsure what to do. He wanted to run after her, then cry until she agreed to take him with her. But like his mom, Jax hardly ever cried. He was strong. He was tough. That's what Mom had taught him to be.

So instead, Jax just watched her go.

Jax's heart thundered inside his chest. Why isn't she looking back at me? *he thought.*

Mom's back retreated down the road. The backdrop of southern Skygard's dry, dusty Stormshadow Desert sprawled before her while Jax remained behind.

Look back, Mom, *Jax pleaded, battling the hot tears forming at the corners of his eyes.* Look back at me. *His heart beat faster.* Just look.

As if she could sense Jax's plea, Mom turned around.

For a second, Jax thought she was going to run back down the road to the tavern. She would scoop him up into her arms—even though she always said he was getting much too big to be held—and they'd leave this place together. It would be just the two of them, traveling from town to town, lying low and street performing for their dinner like they'd always done.

But Mom didn't come back. She reached out a hand, and Jax mirrored the motion.

Then, she waved. He saw her mouth form the words, "Goodbye, J."

With that, she went around a bend in the road, disappearing amidst the outlander town's buildings, juniper trees, and smokesage bushes.

Jax remained rooted to the spot. He barely registered the strange man he was supposed to call father grunting at him—something about coming inside when he was ready—before the man retreated into the tavern.

Even completely alone on the porch, Jax refused to cry.

Jax jolted back to the present, where his Mom wore the same expression she'd worn the day she'd left. Even her hand was outstretched the exact same way.

"Please," Jax's mom whispered once more. "We have to go."

Jax's expressions hardened. He felt a sort of protective shell forming around his heart.

"You abandoned me once," Jax muttered darkly. "It shouldn't be hard for you to do it again."

Jax then closed his eyes, breathing in deeply as he spoke.

"I choose nothing."

That was enough. Jax felt his wraith seep into his body, from his chest to his limbs to his brain. He'd been fighting the wraith's influence for so long, but now, he wondered why.

His decisions were out of his hands.

Jax had never felt more relieved.

When Meleya's Gray One had taken over, it had pushed her to uncharacteristic violence. But Jax's... as Jax's eyes burned with blue voidlight, he felt completely calm.

Hello, Jax, the wraith spoke within his thoughts. *My name is Calyx.*

"You should go now," Jax muttered, his voice doubled by Calyx's. Jax's mother put a hand to her mouth as she realized what was going on.

"Wraith-bound," she murmured, clearly sickened.

"You should be happy," Jax and Calyx said together. "Is this not what you wanted for your son? At last, he will be safe. Safe from dragons, safe from the Knights... safe from you."

Jax's mother's eyes filled with tears. Deep beneath the numbness, Jax felt a twinge of guilt. But it was nothing compared to the relief.

Jaira was practically upon them now, which meant Jax's mother was out of time.

"Come find us when you're ready," she whispered in his ear, then flinched, as if considering whether to kiss his cheek. Then, swallowing her regret, she reactivated her invisibility and vanished from the alcove.

From his vantage point on the upper balcony, Jax watched the chaos unfold in the courtyard below.

High Prince Mason and his Mage Hunters had discovered the Black Valkyrie's loyalists hiding out there, waiting for their leader. Fighting ensued, but Mason's numbers were far greater.

High Prince Mason swung his greataxe, his prowess on the battlefield unmatched. Since he'd come to the Academy as their new combat instructor, Jax had thought Mason Drakeslayer was a conceited drakpat. But seeing him fight, Jax finally understood why they called him 'drakeslayer.' No one dared to stand against him until Shaw, the Black Valkyrie's loyal Geomancer, stepped up. He was strong and resilient enough to take him on.

Jax watched wordlessly, motionlessly as his squad tried in vain to shift the tide. Brigan crossed blades with two Hunters at once while Edrea stood at his back, her dragonhook spear flying. Erik launched bolts from his crossbow until one from their enemy found his leg, causing him to drop his weapon. Meanwhile, Solvai had become a great, winged falcondrake, keeping as many foes as she could from getting close.

Jax felt another pang as he watched his friend Cam take a gash in the side from a Hunter's silver seaxe. Like Jax, Cam had always felt like an outsider, and had been grateful to finally belong somewhere when Squad Reckless was formed.

You never belonged on that squad, anyway, Calyx's deep voice reverberated through Jax's soul.

And then there was Meleya. Despite all she'd been through today, she fought like a mother dragon protecting her family. Mason's Hunters targeted her, but still, she didn't back down.

Just seeing her like that made Jax want to throw himself into the fight. His instincts told him to jump from the balcony and use telekinesis to get to her side in seconds.

But Jax's feet remained grounded in place. He was no longer in control.

You already made your choice, Calyx whispered. Jax's heart, once calm, began to beat faster.

Below, Jax watched his mother arrive on the scene. She'd been invisible, but now appeared in black-clad glory, a pair of wide, gray swan wings sprouting from her back. In her hands was her long, black dragonhook spear, its blade lined with dark shadowfire.

Unaffected by silver, the Black Valkyrie telekinetically wrenched seaxes and whips straight out of several enemy Hunters' hands. She was a whirlwind on the battlefield as she defended Squad Reckless and the other rebels. After seeing her, a few of Mason's Hunters even switched sides.

In a bid to reassert his dominance, Mason Drakeslayer gave a fierce cry, then used his greataxe to slash the Geomancer, Shaw's, throat. Shaw stumbled backward, collapsing in a lifeless heap, and a few more Hunters rallied around Mason.

The Black Valkyrie tried to shield her team, but she wasn't used to fighting in the defense of others. Ilyan was able to get close using shots of dream energy from his silvery snake to stop his enemies.

Ilyan's silver whip cracked, the bladed end reaching toward Meleya as she did battle with another Hunter. Meleya was Mason's primary target, after all.

Again, Jax tried to move, but found he was still powerless in his own body.

You made your choice, his wraith taunted once more. *And so did she by keeping the great one's voidshard. Meleya's Gray One is clever, but not clever enough. Xan should have used the shard to kill me first.*

The squad's dragons arrived from the stables as Jax's mother launched herself between Meleya and Ilyan. She caught the tip of Ilyan's whip in one hand, ready to yank it away from her former ally.

But Ilyan's whip surged with dream energy, causing Jax's mother to tremble with fatigue. She tried to let go of the whip, but Ilyan's power was too strong. The Black Valkyrie fell to her knees.

It all happened so fast. Meleya moved as quickly as an ashviper as she sent a portal racing across the ground Ilyan's way. Ilyan dropped through it as if it were a trapdoor, releasing his hold over Jax's mother.

Meleya caught the Black Valkyrie under the arms as she slumped. Jax's pulse was flying. Drak! He still couldn't make his feet move.

Then Meleya runetraced, opening a large portal. The first group of rebels was rushing through when a well-placed crossbow bolt shot toward her. Jax's heart froze, but Shaw, somehow alive and well—stars bless that unkillable Geomancer—stepped between Meleya and the oncoming blast. He roared as it took him in the chest before the rest of Vidya's loyalists dragged him through the gold-rimmed portal. Then finally, Meleya and Jax's mother ran through.

Through to the Rebel Knights.

Through to freedom.

No... Jax thought desperately. *Take me with you!*

You made your choice, Calyx reminded him for the final time.

On the outside, Jax was as still as a statue.

On the inside, he was screaming.

ASHER

A literal army had met us at the safehouse border. Soldiers and dragons alike jealously guarded the property line, effectively blocking me and my band of cure victims on kirinback. Thorn faced down one of Rhana's drakes, both dragons giving low growls, ready to strike at a moment's notice.

"I've asked once and I'll ask again," Rhana roared. "Where in the void do you get off bringing this lot of unknowns onto *my* property?"

She stood at the head of the mob holding a crossbow in one hand and a torch bright with green dragonfire in the other. Several more people held torches along with their weapons as well, bathing the darkened forest in an emerald glow.

"We've been gathering new Rebel Knight recruits for months," I called boldly. "I've just brought a few more."

"Along with a trio of drakked Mage Hunters," one older soldier said. I recognized the grumpy bearded man from that day at the Gallant Gopherdrake. He looked even more menacing wielding a greataxe in the torchlight.

The mob murmured, their attention focused on Shaya, Trickshot, and Mute. I felt like an idiot for not advising them to shed their dusky blue cloaks before we got to the safehouse border. Then again, everything they wore screamed Mage Hunter, from their armor to their weapons to their tunics.

The three of them looked just as tense as the mob, their hands on their weapons as well. Meanwhile, the cure victims' expressions ranged from indifferent to confused to utterly terrified. Near the back, I saw Meleya's mother, Freya, silently weeping.

Frustration filled my chest.

"These people have been through enough," I said to the lineup of Knights. "These are the victims of Evgard's so-called magi cure! I promised them safety and freedom."

"A promise you had no right to make, you scorched scale-skin!" Rhana bellowed. Several others muttered in agreement.

"Stars above!" a voice cried from the Rebel Knight throng. Ivar pushed his way through, his bright hair catching the emerald light.

"Be still, soldier!" Rhana called out, but Ivar paid her no heed.

"Freya!" he cried, breaking the tightly formed lines on both sides to envelop his wife in his arms. Freya cried harder as she melted into his embrace.

"Thank you, Asher," Ivar said. "Thank you, thank you."

At that moment, more Rebel Knights came running from the direction of the cabin. I breathed a sigh of relief when I saw Kai, followed closely by Boone, Valla, and Solrac.

"What is the meaning of this?" Solrac asked. "Weapons down, my friends. I'm sure we can resolve this without bloodshed."

"Like the void we can," Rhana thundered. Some Rebel Knights lowered their weapons, but Rhana and the others held strong to their seaxes, crossbows, and dragonhook spears. Rhana's dozen or so dragons didn't back down, either.

"Rhana's right," Valla hissed, hands on the hilts of her dual seaxes. "These silversoots and their not-so-helpless cure victims aren't putting a toe over the property line."

"What are you talking about?" I said. "These people have suffered at Evgard's hand."

"As they should for what they've done!" Valla cried. "Have you stopped for even a second to check who you're trying to bring into our midst?"

Valla drew one blade, then used it to point to one of the cure victims on kirinback. It was some middle-aged woman with wavy brown hair and a face full of freckles. Her pale blue eyes seemed empty, unaffected by Valla's clear threat.

"That's the Liberator," Valla said. "The Wildshaping leader of the Coven of the Gray Ones! I was at the battle of the Winter Solstice—That woman killed King Axel of Rengard and dozens of others!"

At that, nearly all the Rebel Knights bore arms again. Even Boone pulled out one of the starglass daggers he kept holstered at his hips, ready to fire an ether blast at the woman who—to me—looked harmless. Defenseless. Numb.

Trickshot piped up. "I too was at the battle of the Winter Solstice, and I can swear to Lorelai's progress. She no longer possesses the ability to wildshape. That woman is no more a threat to you than a scalefly!"

"*You're* the threat, scorching Mage Hunter!" a Rebel Knight called. Several others cried out in agreement, green torches burning as bright as the fire in their eyes. One man raised a crossbow, training it on Trickshot.

"Don't you touch her!" cried one of the cure victims. The dark-haired man stumbled forward, between Trickshot and the crossbowman. He stood tall and called out more confidently. "We are not your enemies!"

"Cenrik?" Solrac asked, his jaw dropping.

Shaya held up her hands in a show of peace. "It's true, we have come to join you!"

"Drakes alive," Boone cursed. "That ain't... can't be Shaya."

I watched as the others who'd been with us on the heist to steal the true dragon egg last summer took in the sight of her. They were just as shocked as I'd been the first time I saw Real Shaya, and I could tell it only added to their skepticism. Tensions were running sky-high, and I knew things were seconds away from erupting.

"Listen to me!" I called, my eyes glowing gold as I levitated myself so that I was about a head above the others. "These people need our help. As Knights of the Torch, we're sworn to protect magi in need, right? We'll use caution, have Kai read their minds if we have to before we let them in. But it's our duty to do something about the injustice the realm did to them if we can!"

Solrac stepped forward, turning to appeal to his thronged allies. "Asher may be right. The Rebel Knights are, indeed, recruiting, after all. It shouldn't be difficult to vet this group the same way we've been doing with the others."

Solrac gestured toward the throng of soldiers. He let out a chuckle. "This could be the greatest thing that could've possibly happened! Besides, it's not like Asher showed up with the entire Mage Hunter army."

The last word had barely left Solrac's mouth when a massive gold crack split the air directly in front of me. I yelped, and everyone nearby jumped back to give me a wide berth.

Soot, this was the beginning of a Rifter's portal. And it was sprouting from my pocket.

I rapidly pulled out the anchor Meleya had given me for her father and tossed it into the dirt.

Not a moment too soon either. The huge portal burst open, and a veritable army of dusk-blue-cloaked Mage Hunters and even a few dragons spilled into the cindercone thicket along the safehouse border. Silver flashed. Rebel Knights cried out.

My heart froze.

At the rear of the group of Hunters and their dragons, last through the portal before it closed, was a woman in shiny black armor. Gray hair spilled over her shoulders, and she gripped a black, silver-bladed dragonhook spear in one hand.

"The Black Valkyrie," I muttered, automatically burning ether to summon my own starglass dragonhook spear.

Murmurs, shouts, and protests sounded from the Rebel Knights' lineup. Valla dropped her blades as a cloud of golden mist encompassed her. When the mist cleared, Valla had wildshaped into a ferocious polar wolf, poised to attack.

Clearly wanting blood, the Rebel Knights surged toward the Hunters.

"Stop!" Ivar's voice rose above the rest. The front line of Knights suddenly halted in their tracks as Ivar telekinetically yanked them back by their chest plates, cloaks, and tunics. I knew it must've been draining a lot of ether from his already-weakened ether well, but if he was struggling, he didn't show it.

Ivar held back the masses as he charged straight into the group of Mage Hunters.

"That's my daughter!" he cried. He rushed right up to the Black Valkyrie's side, just in time to catch the snowheaded young woman who was falling to her knees beside her. Meleya clutched at her temples, and I realized she was in great pain—probably from having drained most of her ether to get this group through her portal.

Stars, I thought. It dawned on me that most of the Mage Hunters were wounded in some way. Blood stained their pale cloaks, and even the Black Valkyrie was wincing in pain, barely able to stand. One burly man I recognized as the Geomancer from her entourage looked dead—for now, at least.

"Treason!" Rhana shouted, fighting Ivar's telekinetic hold over her. "Dragons, incapacitate Ivar so we can put these Mage Hunters in their place!"

Several of Rhana's guard dragons moved to pin Ivar. Before they got the chance, I hover-leaped into action, taking aim at each dragon in turn as I channeled starglass from the end of my spear. Almost instantly, each dragon had a hefty chunk of heavy starglass weighing down their claws. I knew the starglass wouldn't hold long, especially since most of Rhana's dragons were huge and strong, all on their third ascension.

"Wait!" I cried, hardly believing my own actions as I hover-dashed to put myself between the Rebel Knights and the Mage Hunters. I landed between the groups and cried out, "We can't just rush in like this! Can't you see they're wounded?"

"All I see is a group of silversoots!" the bearded old man shouted. Several others voiced their agreement. Valla in polar wolf form howled. At my back, I saw the Hunters assuming battle stances as well.

Soot.

There was no way I could hold them all off on my own.

And did I even want to?

The Black Valkyrie was here—the woman who'd killed my mother and cruelly stolen her ether well for herself. She was injured. Why not let Valla take her and her followers down?

Out of nowhere, I thought I heard a voice. Mom's voice.

Because it's not right, my laaksi raakai.

Then I heard her clear voice singing the words from the song she'd sung the day she'd given me her scarf:

Sent to tend with wisdom and might...
Share light for ever more...

I shook my head to focus. Now was not the time for one of my weird mom-moments. Mom-ents?

Then suddenly, I wasn't the only one standing between the two unstable groups.

"He's right—This is not the time for conflict!" A young man from the Mage Hunter side stepped out to stand beside me. He was about my age and broad-chested, with dark hair tied into a tidy ridgeknot but for one tight curl that fell over his forehead. A fairly fresh-looking, thin scar cut through his left eyebrow.

I had no idea who he was, but I was just glad I was no longer holding back the dueling tides alone.

The young man continued, confidently addressing the group. "Rebel Knights of the Torch, your apprehension regarding Mage Hunters is completely justified! For too long, our two groups have been at odds, largely because of the mistreatment of magi on the part of the Hunters."

Some Rebel Knights voiced their agreement. A few Hunters shot their companion confused looks.

The young man pressed on. "There will be time enough yet to let your dissension be heard, but for now, I implore you to see reason. It is as my friend here has said..." He put a hand on my shoulder. "We are wounded. We are afraid for our lives. In our hour of need, we have turned to you for refuge and protection. This is a chance to live by your code, Knights of the Torch!"

"The Black Valkyrie was once a Knight of the Torch as well!" spat someone standing near Rhana. "Yet she turned her back on us and brought hundreds of magi to their deaths!"

"We will never let her into our midst!"

"Kill the Black Valkyrie!"

I'd thought this Hunter guy's speech had been off to a great start, but it appeared the mob was too riled up to listen. The Black Valkyrie still looked to be on the brink of passing out as she pointedly dropped her spear and put up her hands, ready to let them take her.

Soot, this wasn't right. But if even my articulate new friend's words hadn't been enough to stop the bloodshed, what could?

My answer came in the form of pearlescent white wings.

The Rebel Knights parted to let Eliana and her true dragon mount land. Even the Hunters took a few steps back in awe, as did the cure victims.

Eliana pulled back on the reins, regally addressing the crowd. Her white ascension armor and matching tiara made her look like a queen.

"Weapons down, all of you," she ordered, her voice carrying throughout the forest. A golden illusion rune floated over Aurora's head, the one that was clearly amplifying Eliana's voice. At their true dragon rider's word, most of the Knights sheathed their blades, as did the remaining Hunters.

"Mage Hunters—" Eliana turned to the Black Valkyrie and the others. "It is plain to see that many of you are badly injured, so I would urge you to speak quickly. Black Valkyrie, what has brought you to our borders tonight?"

The Black Valkyrie's voice came out strained, but her tone was still as silky sweet as I remembered. "Just as you Rebels have experienced a rift with the other Knights of the Torch... so have we. Mason Drakeslayer has taken over the Mage Hunters. He's working with the Soul Reaper and plans to... use the Gray Ones to... overtake Evgard... ahh..."

The Black Valkyrie trailed off as a fresh wave of pain made her grimace. Her face, normally proud and aloof, was ashen.

Murmurs rippled throughout both groups. Gray Ones... Soul Reaper...

Eliana spoke gravely as she held her head high. "One thing is certain: Evgard is in great danger. And I fear the only way it stands a chance is if we come together—Rebel Knights *and* Rebel Hunters."

To emphasize the princess's powerful words, Aurora stretched her neck upward and opened her jaws toward the sky. The pure white true dragon breathed her unique, light-like dragonfire into the sky. Purple and green firelight danced, captivating the rebels on both sides.

It seemed the entire forest stood still as Eliana outlined her plan for moving forward. One-by-one, the Rebel Knights would escort the Rebel Hunters into the safehouse. They'd begin with those whose wounds were most severe, but take care to keep them under heavy lock and key in the cabin's lowest level, the dungeon. From there, at a reasonable pace, Kai would conduct interviews with each newcomer, using his skills as a mind-reader to determine whether they'd be allowed to join the Knights or else remain imprisoned.

It was a good plan, and Eliana spoke with such authority she literally seemed to glow. I wondered if that was yet another of her powers granted through her bond with Aurora.

On the princess's signal, some of the burliest Rebel Knight soldiers surrounded the Black Valkyrie. One even brought out a pair of silver manacles for her, though I knew the Black Valkyrie's blue power was unaffected by silver. Trickshot, a trained medic, persuaded the Knights to let her accompany the first group in order to help heal the most critically wounded as they made their way to the safehouse prison.

As soon as things were underway, Eliana turned to me, a huge smile on her face.

I grinned back, taking a step toward her.

Then she said, "If it isn't my old betrothed, Brigan, Heir Duke of Solhelm!"

My smile evaporated as I realized Eliana wasn't smiling at me.

She slid from Aurora's back, running toward the broad-chested young man who still stood beside me. He met her halfway, wrapping her in a familiar embrace.

I just stood there feeling like a complete third wheel. What was happening?

A trickle of jealousy shot through my chest as Eliana's hug with this tall, athletic stranger went on and on... and *on*.

Clearly, he was no stranger to her.

She'd called him Brigan—her *betrothed*.

Yeah, I'd known Elle had been betrothed. But hadn't his parents called it off months ago when Keep Drakfell joined with the Knights of the Torch?

Part of me felt like I should walk away and give them some space.

The bigger part of me wanted to stay and watch out of morbid curiosity.

"I thought you'd been kidnapped!" Brigan said, finally pulling back.

"And I thought they'd sent you to the border guard at the Dragon Mists!" Elle replied. "Stars, you sure grew up. What happened to that awkward fourteen-year-old I spilled scalemelon cider on at that ball in Keep Rengard?" They laughed at the shared memory.

"Looks like you did some growing up as well," Brigan said, taking in her form-fitting, white armored dress. I narrowed my eyes.

They began chatting up a storm as Eliana introduced Brigan to Aurora. Brigan likewise showed off his regal rusty orange drake, already on her second ascension. Of course, Eliana took a liking to the creature instantly.

I set my jaw, reminding myself that I wasn't supposed to care. Eliana had turned me down, and for good reason. Elle and I together... It didn't make sense.

But Eliana and this Brigan guy...

I had to look away.

As I did, I found Meleya. She was bidding a reluctant goodbye to her father, Ivar, who was carefully escorting her mother, Freya, back toward the safehouse.

Meleya knelt alone on the ground, watching them go. She looked stunned, relieved, and exhausted all at once, and no wonder. She'd had a very long day.

"Hey," I said as I walked up to her. "When you asked me to bring that rift anchor to your dad, you didn't tell me you planned to use it to bring every human, dragon, and ridgerat's uncle to the Rebel safehouse."

"I didn't know where else to go," Meleya said without so much as a smile. "I knew it was a big risk, but…"

She trailed off, watching her parents. Ivar kept a protective arm around his wife's shoulders as she stumbled toward the safehouse.

Stars. In a way, it seemed the cure had robbed both Meleya and me of our mothers. Without thinking, I reached toward her to put a sympathetic hand on her shoulder.

Meleya jumped at my touch and I recoiled as she whipped her head toward me.

"What are you doing?" she asked skeptically.

"Uh," I replied, "just… about to wish you luck as you languish in jail until Kai can give you an evaluation. But you'll be okay. Trust me—prison isn't as bad as it seems, snowhead."

"I've seen my fair share of prisons, but thanks."

"Is that a challenge?" I asked with a sideways smile. "Who's been to prison more times? Because I bet I've got you beat by a mile."

Meleya looked me dead in the eye. "You think you've been to prison more often than once every single week for three years straight?"

I opened my mouth to reply, but no words came so I closed it again. I raised a finger, willing a response to come, but still, I had nothing.

Meleya was completely unamused. Would nothing cheer this girl up?

"Oh, come on," I finally said. "You've got to admit I'm strangely charming."

Meleya's face remained blank.

"Delightfully chuckle-worthy at least?" I suggested. "What about mildly entertaining? I'll even take 'amusingly ridiculous.'"

Still no response from Meleya. Well, none other than the annoyed eyebrow-raise.

I narrowed my eyes at her. She narrowed hers back.

"Immature son of a dragonmutt," she said.

"Stuffy scale-in-the mud," I replied without hesitation.

"Scarf-wearer," she accused.

"Oof!" I put a hand to my chest. "Still hurts just as much the second time."

Meleya's lips remained pressed into a tight line... If she was smiling on the inside, it was buried too deep for me to tell. Without another word, she marched over to her bright yellow evren who was perched nearby.

After she left, I took a good look at the people in the forest around me. Dozens of Rebel Knights stood by, ready to fight the dozens of Rebel Hunters waiting to be escorted to the safehouse. Tensions were still running high.

Just then, I noticed a blue-cloaked Hunter engaged in heated conversation with a nearby Knight. Their interaction was seconds away from turning into a full-blown altercation.

As I hurried over to do what I could to diffuse the tension, I couldn't help but think:

Princess Eliana might've smoothed over the initial explosion.

But the coals from this fire were far from cold.

Memory 2

Solrac's head was spinning. Or was it his heart? These days, it was getting harder and harder to tell the difference.

"It finally makes sense…" Solrac muttered to himself as he hurried up the stairs of the safehouse. "The two symbols, Knight and Mage Hunter… White light brought them together—that must be Princess Eliana, but then…."

Solrac trailed off as golden fire suddenly framed his vision. That was the tough part about being a Seer. Occasionally, extra-powerful omens assaulted one's mind without warning.

In his mind's eye, he saw that same gigantic, shadowy dragon he'd seen first in the Farseer's cove and then again at Veil Falls. Once again, the beast's fierce maw opened wide…

…and clamped shut around Solrac's head.

Solrac shuddered as the vision fled his mind. A horrid, creeping feeling settled over him as a thought occurred to him.

Solrac swallowed. Details varied, but most Farseers of the past had encountered similarly recurring visions.

Visions that predicted their own imminent deaths.

"Surely not," Solrac muttered under his breath, digging deep to find a spark of his usual optimism. "There could be a hundred different inter-pretations for this." But his years of training in omen-reading made it so he couldn't help but wonder: What if his own death *was* the best thing that could happen for Evgard? Maybe it was unavoidable...

Before he could dwell on it any longer, Solrac came face-to-face with a very angry-looking white weasel perched on the wall at the top of the stairs.

"Drak infinity!" Solrac cursed, a hand flying to his chest. "Valla!"

The weasel leaped to the ground at Solrac's feet as a golden cloud of ether swirled around her. When it dissipated, Valla was standing before Solrac in human form, her glare almost fiercer than it had been when she was a frostweasel.

"What in the void do you think you're doing, allowing that woman and her drakking Mage Hunters into our midst?" Valla raged. "We're actually *healing* her now, then inviting her to cheerfully stay as our honored guest at the Rebel Knights' primary safehouse? This is the *Black Valkyrie* we're talking about!"

"Rhana's prison cell will hardly make for a cheerful stay," Solrac retorted, looking past Valla toward the attic door. The same symbol the Farseer wore on his gauntlets, a triangle with a small diamond shape on each of its three points, adorned the door in gold and red.

"I don't care that she's a true dragon rider," Valla went on. "That drakking Princess is a foolish child who's going to get us all killed."

"Eliana is wise beyond her years," Solrac said, "and besides, trusting the wisdom and leadership of true dragon riders has been an Evgardian tradition since the birth of the realm."

"Scorch tradition," Valla seethed, and Solrac sensed a deeper frustration behind her almond-shaped eyes.

"Traditions matter," Solrac said, his thoughts racing. "Despite what we may wish in moments of pain. That said... I believe I must break one today. Valla, I fear I must tell you the truth now—lest someone else does so first. If anyone deserves to hear this from my lips, it is you."

"The truth about what?" Valla frowned. "We've always been honest with one another."

"Oh," Solrac winced. "Guilt can be more ruthless than the fiercest tyrant. Come with me, Valla. As we have done many times before, we must visit the Farseer."

"That's ridiculous," Valla whispered. "You're not the... you can't be the..."

"And yet I am," Solrac said, turning so Valla could get the full effect of the Farseer's rich red robes. The hood was down so she could see his face.

"But all those journeys to consult the Faseer, you and I stood before him together," Valla protested.

"You mean like this?" Solrac's likeness materialized at Valla's side, making her jump. She automatically swiped at him, her blade cutting straight through the illusion. Valla swore.

It took a lot of convincing—showing off the Farseer voice, taking the hood on and off a few times, and even calling upon the Farseer's mysterious ethereal familiar, the mythraven—before Valla finally believed. Solrac sensed deep betrayal behind her eyes.

"Who else knows about this?" Valla asked.

"Only a somewhat random snowheaded young woman named Meleya of Misthaven." Solrac looked down at his feet. "And... Vidya."

Valla shut her eyes to suppress her frustration.

"It is about her that I must consult the omens now," Solrac said. He produced the diamond-shaped wooden hand mirror, placing it on the ground and sitting cross-legged before it. "I have put this off for far too long."

Setting her jaw, Valla sat beside him.

Solrac shifted slightly away from her. "You may not want to be here for this."

Valla didn't move.

Nerves aflutter in his stomach, Solrac set a small handful of runemarked coals in front of them. He traced a rune, and the golden, heatless omenfire flickered to life.

Solrac held his breath. Then he took hold of the mirror's handle and raised it to his face.

The omenfire's golden flames leaped onto the surface of the mirror, setting it ablaze with memory...

Laughter.

Vidya's carefree laugh instantly sent tears spilling down Solrac's cheeks as he watched the beautiful, carefree young woman within the mirror.

Her face was soft, her smile bright as she reached out a hand toward the mirror.

"Come on," she said, and Solrac couldn't stop a trembling hand from touching the mirror's surface, as if he could disappear into the memory. Valla's face was perfectly even as she watched.

"I'm coming, I'm coming!" a voice suddenly called from within the memory. Solrac's own voice, he realized, as he saw a much younger version of himself take Vidya's hand. He still had dark, wavy hair and his left cheek still bore a Psion's silvermark, but Solrac found his own clean-shaven face quite jarring.

With a pang of loss, Solrac suddenly realized where he and young Vidya were. He'd always remember those dingy wooden walls and the faint sound of rushing water. Drak, he could practically smell the musty room as he watched the scene unfold.

They were at the Waterfall Inn. This was where they'd spent their honeymoon after their runaway marriage.

Solrac could hardly see through his tears as young Vidya held up the very mirror through which he now watched the memory.

"It's beautiful," she said, fingering the surface. Young Solrac flipped the mirror over, pointing to the poem he'd carefully etched into its back.

She read aloud, "*Look to each skyfall that flares through the night.*"

"*And know that my love burns even more bright,*" young Solrac finished.

"Brighter every day," young Vidya said.

"And on into forever," young Solrac agreed.

She wrapped her arms around him, and they kissed deeply. Tears flowed freely down present Solrac's face while Valla remained impassive. The memory shifted.

Young Solrac and Vidya were still in that grimy room at the waterfall inn, but young Vidya's smile was gone. She sat at the room's small table, face buried in her hands, shoulders shaking while young Solrac stood in the doorway. He carried a small bag in one arm, and his face was scruffy.

He was about to walk out the door when a small sob from Vidya made him pause.

"I'm sorry," Solrac said, turning back to her. Solrac saw conflict in his younger self's eyes, very similar to the conflict he felt now.

Young Vidya whipped her head up, steely hair flying as she pointed to the doorway. "If you're going to go, just go!"

"Vidya—" young Solrac started.

"Just go!" she cried, getting to her feet. She stormed Solrac's way with fire in her red-tinted eyes. "Go back to your precious Knights of the Torch, and see if I care!"

"You have to understand," Solrac said, his sharp jawline tensing, "I have no choice but to return to the Knights alone."

"So you've said," Vidya seethed. "But that doesn't mean I have to understand a drakking thing. Get out of here, Solrac."

"But Vidya—"

"*Go!*" She shoved against his chest, and young Solrac's face hardened. Without another word, he walked out the door, slamming it shut behind him.

As he watched the memory, Solrac's chest grew tight. He remembered that moment all too well. After a few months with Vidya at the waterfall inn, he'd received word that the previous Farseer had passed away. He'd thought he'd have another ten to fifteen years with Vidya at least; ironically, he hadn't seen this coming. All his years of training had finally come to a head—It was time to stop hiding from his responsibilities and take up the mantle himself.

At the time, Solrac had been terrified. He hadn't felt ready. But above all, it had nearly killed him to leave Vidya behind. Still, he felt he'd had no choice—the previous Farseer had been very clear in their training: nobody, not even those closest to him, could know about his secret calling. It was a centuries-old tradition, and the omens had chosen Solrac to carry it on.

Solrac was so caught up in his own thoughts that he jumped as the memory continued within the mirror.

Crash!

With a cry, young Vidya kicked over the chair she'd been sitting in earlier. She shoved a pile of weathered books off the table and onto the ground, then lit up a psionic rune. Tears burning in her eyes, she telekinetically lifted the large bag of coins Solrac had left for her and dumped them out. The coins clinked as they spilled all over the floor, rolling into corners and through cracks in the floorboards.

In her anger, she raised the wooden hand mirror next, ready to telekinetically smash it to pieces. But just before she slammed it into the wall, she stopped. Young Vidya choked on a sob, then slowly lowered the mirror to her side.

She sunk to the ground, looking at her red, tear-stained face in the mirror's surface. Her voice shook as she spoke to her own reflection.

"I don't need him," she said. "He doesn't deserve me anyway. He doesn't deserve either of us—right, little one?"

As the last words left her mouth, young Vidya placed a hand on her stomach. Solrac's heart nearly stopped as he watched.

"No…" he said. "Impossible."

A million questions he'd never dared to ask himself raced through Solrac's mind. He had no idea how Valla was responding to all this—He was too absorbed in the scene unfolding before his eyes.

Next, the memory in the mirror shifted once more.

Little by little, young Vidya's stomach began to grow rounder as several scenes played in the mirror in quick succession. She stayed in the waterfall inn alone for several months after her husband had left, and Solrac watched as she pored over the same books they'd begun reading together. "I need something that will make me stronger than the Knights," young Vidya murmured as she flipped through the ancient texts. "Something that will make me more powerful than Solrac."

Solrac swallowed. He remembered well those books they'd filched from some of Evgard's oldest libraries. It had begun as innocent research, their arrogant, younger selves believing they could be the ones to help magi and non-magi live in harmony in a land filled with ether-hungry wild dragons.

Solrac knew too well that many of those books held dark secrets, secrets better left unearthed, abandoned to the ravages of time. As a Farseer-in-training, Solrac had stepped away from such dangerous influences. But it appeared that Vidya had only dug deeper.

He watched as she studied from a book called *Legends of the Great Northern Frostdrake*. Flashes of lines she was reading overlaid the vision, and while a few didn't make sense to Solrac, many did:

The frostdrake guards ancient secrets… entrusted by the goddess Streya… the power to sunder the veil for good or ill…
Voidarchy.
…the ability to draw from the power of multiple magi …
…the rebirth of a fallen king in fire…
Voidarchy.

...the power to become like a skymage, or even to restore the ancient legacy of the Guardians...

Voidarchy.

Solrac's mind reeled as young Vidya slammed the book closed, harsh resolve in her eyes.

The vision continued in flashes. Young Vidya's abdomen grew even more, and Solrac's heart ached as he watched her scour the room, fishing fallen coins from the cracks in the floorboards.

When the money ran out, Vidya gathered her few belongings and left the waterfall inn. For a while, she sang on the streets and was able to earn just enough to keep herself fed. Then the memory shifted to portray Vidya living in a secluded cave behind a waterfall with nothing more than a bedroll and a small lantern.

Practically waddling, Vidya stumbled into an apothecary shop. "One vial of scalebark tonic," she said, leaning on the shop's counter for support as a wave of pain rushed through her.

The young girl on the other side of the counter looked concerned. She couldn't have been more than twelve or so, and had thick auburn hair woven into a stout braid over one shoulder.

"Do you need help?" the girl asked, concerned.

"No, just the medicine," Vidya stubbornly replied. Then her eye caught the neatly folded stack of silky drakalope fur blankets for sale on a nearby shelf.

Rubbing her round belly, Vidya asked, "How much for one of those?"

The girl told her the price, and Vidya winced. She quickly scanned the shop until she spotted a display stand holding a row of simple dust scarves.

Vidya pointed. "What about those?"

The young girl hesitated before responding. "Free with the purchase of any herbal remedy." Without another word, the girl pulled a maroon bandana from the stand and offered it to Vidya.

Solrac could tell that Vidya had her doubts about any such sale. But her expression betrayed that a new wave of pain was on its way, so she quickly took the bandana and hurried from the shop. The vision shifted again.

A lump in his throat, Solrac watched young Vidya cringing within her cave as she wrapped her arms around her enormous belly. She cried out, then downed the contents of the little bottle she'd bought from the apothecary shop.

"I can do this," Vidya muttered to herself in the dim, lonely cave. "Thousands of women have done it before, so why not me?"

Solrac felt like his heart might burst. She was about to have a baby—*his* baby—completely alone in a scorching *cave* of all places? Vidya was so young... Did she even know what to do? He should've been there with her. How had the omens not shown him *this*?

Vidya cried out again, then started when she heard a scraping noise near the mouth of her cave. The effort nearly dropped her to the stony cave floor, but she got to her feet, reaching for her dragonhook spear she kept leaning against the far wall.

"W-who's there?" Vidya called into the darkness, prepared to fight off the intruder even in her condition.

The mirror showed a young girl with thick auburn hair step into the light of Vidya's lantern. It was the girl from the shop.

"You need help," the girl spoke quickly.

Vidya glared. "No, I—"

Another agonizing tightening from her abdomen cut Vidya's protest short. Without another word, the young girl rushed to her side.

"What's your name?" the girl asked as she draped Vidya's arm over her shoulders.

"Vidya. And you?"

"Torya," the girl replied. "But everyone calls me Trickshot."

With that, Trickshot painstakingly helped Vidya out of the cave and across the short distance to her family's home on the edge of town. Trickshot's mother was a midwife, and pregnant herself. She was able to get Vidya set up just in time to deliver a healthy baby. Trickshot helped her mother wash the newborn, then handed him to Vidya.

As Vidya cradled the little boy in her arms, she tenderly wrapped him in the thin cloth of the maroon bandana Trickshot had given her.

Finally, the vision showed Solrac the baby boy's face. He squirmed, blinking up at his mother with wide, dark blue eyes. Steely gray hair just like Vidya's stuck up all over his head, and tears pricked Solrac's eyes anew. Solrac was painfully aware of Valla, watching over his shoulder with both shock and trepidation.

"Jax," Solrac whispered. Vidya had lied to everyone about the timing of her tryst with Torsten, but the truth could no longer be denied.

“My son.”

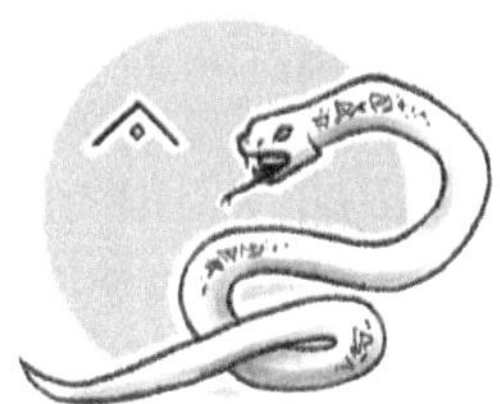

ILYAN

The snake's hiss caused Ilyan to look up from his book. The creature's forked, purple tongue flicked in and out of its mouth as the thick, silvery serpent wove across the floor, in and out of the piles of skystone that filled the Surgeon's observatory.

"Is it time already?" Ilyan absently asked his ethereal familiar. He set his book down on a side table, then adjusted his position in the overstuffed armchair he'd been lounging in. Beside him, a hearth burned with vivid blue flames.

The snake slithered past the Surgeon's telescope to reach the foot of Ilyan's armchair. It then slipped up the side to its usual place draped over Ilyan's shoulders. Ilyan gave the unnamed creature a stroke. Two of Ilyan's own fingers now matched the snake's silver coloring—a result of an injury sustained during the attack on Keep Rengard's Rise the night of the Winter Solstice. Ilyan had lost his pointer and middle fingers that night, but after some trial and error, he'd figured out how to infuse the two silver rings he now wore with the proper runemarks to form his new, chronically-powered illusory fingers.

The wound had been an accident, of course. The southern Coven was a wild, belligerent branch. But they'd never have harmed Ilyan if they'd known who he was and whom he served.

Once Ilyan's ethereal snake had settled, Ilyan began his routine check, reaching out to the small mirror copies of the head snake he had stationed in various places across the realm. Using his familiar this way was a rather ingenious trick Ilyan had picked up from those unsophisticated Knights of the Torch. Their young new Seer—Kai, was it?—had talent, it was true. But that poor outlander was no match for Ilyan, who had trained with the best magi tutors the realm had to offer.

Nor does Kai have an Elder wraith like you do to augment his power, the voice of Ilyan's Gray One resounded in his mind. Ilyan swelled with pride. Not everyone was bound to a wraith in the Wraith King's inner circle.

Lightbane's certainly hadn't been. The evidence of that was clear now that the lowly, would-be usurper wraith that followed Meleya of Misthaven had been able to defeat her so handily.

Scorch, just thinking about young Jaira's two wasted ether wells made Ilyan tsk. From the start, he'd disagreed with the Surgeon's decision to take that uneducated outlander under his wing. Now both of the ether wells tethered to her soul would be dormant. There was a chance Jaira would succeed in drawing another wraith to reactivate them, but wraiths strong enough to form a voidshard were rare in this plane. At least for now.

Yes, few wraiths were as high in rank as Ilyan's. Besides the Wraith King, there was only Calyx. Not even the traitorous Black Valkyrie's wraith, Exusha, could match him. Ilyan's Gray counterpart, Vishai, was one of the ancients, only willing to bond the most intelligent of men. With Ilyan's background, he knew he deserved this.

Ilyan poured himself a goblet of fine Evyndallian wine and took a sip. He could sense that Vishai relished the feeling. Before bonding the wraith, Ilyan hadn't drunk nearly this much. Alcohol typically muddled a Mystic's senses, all the books said so. But Ilyan felt he was an exception, more resilient than lesser magi. Perhaps the wine even *sharpened* his senses.

Now, he was ready to check in on his snakes.

The first snake mirror copy lay hidden in the ornate molding atop the throne of High King Magnus. Ilyan had used his expertise with illusions to ensure that anyone who looked closely at the chair would see only a delicate knot design. High King Magnus was already paranoid enough without knowing he was being observed at all times.

At the moment, the High King was speaking with a squad of soldiers, gesturing with his hands toward a wanted poster in the squad captain's hands. The poster depicted the Rebel Knights' true dragon rider, Eliana of Drakfell.

Ilyan smiled to himself, feeling his wraith's delight as well. The Surgeon had been working on breaking the High King for over a year, gaining his favor and sowing seeds of doubt within him. A kingdom is only as strong as its king, and between worries for his only son's life, war with the Knights of the Torch in Skygard, and the desperation surrounding a rival true dragon rider, Magnus was all but clay in the Surgeon's hands.

"I don't want excuses," Magnus said to his soldiers. "I want the upstart princess and her true dragon apprehended!"

"She seems to have gone underground," the squad captain replied, worried. "We have scouts patrolling everywhere from Evyndara through Rengard, with a squad heading to Behrfell as well."

"What of the western keepdoms?" Magnus asked. "The Princess is Drakfellian—perhaps she's hiding out in her homeland."

"Perhaps, your majesty. But with Drakfell uniting with Skygard, such is enemy territory. We're better off focusing our resources on the war—"

"Surely it is up to me as High King to decide what is best for the realm." Magnus's expression betrayed his deeply seated fear. Beside the throne, Magnus's true dragon, Noctus, gave a low growl of dissatisfaction. But Ilyan was certain the High King was too far gone to heed his dragon's warnings. Their bond had turned cold and distant, likely a result of the host of Gray Ones that lurked at the fringes of the High King's mind, feasting on his distress.

With satisfaction, Ilyan closed the connection between himself and the snake. All was going well in the High Citadel. The Surgeon would be pleased.

The Wraith King will be pleased, Vishai echoed in Ilyan's mind.

On to the next snake.

This tiny familiar was curled in the chandelier of the royal chambers at Keep Rengard's citadel on the Rise. From the perch, it got the perfect view of Ilona, Queen of Rengard, sleeping soundly even as the drums of war beat throughout the Canyonlands.

Ilona was a powerful agent of the Gray, and she was doing brilliantly to fulfill her assignment of sowing chaos and undermining the stability of one of the realm's most prominent keepdoms. This would saturate the land with more desperate and willing hosts once the Gray was finally able to pierce the veil and enter the physical plane.

After the attack on the Rengardian nobility the Coven led on the night of the Winter Solstice, Ilona had turned her efforts to perpetuating the

Canyonlands's war with the Dragon Isles. The more losses on either side, the better it was for the coming Gray. Ilona and the Liberator had moved too quickly, trying to annihilate the Rengardian nobility the night of the ball, but soon, Ilyan's sister would get to see the Canyonlands fall.

Ilyan took another long sip of wine. Few knew that he and Ilona were twins, plucked from obscurity by the king and queen of Kolbohr at a young age. As gifted Seers, particularly in the illusory arts, Ilyan and Ilona had become secret high mages to the Kolbohrian crown. They received the best training, learning everything from illusions to omen reading to mind control. Some Seers refused to practice mind control, claiming it was immoral. But Ilyan felt it was important to be well versed in all aspects of his etherarchy. They'd learned from the realm's most prestigious tutors as the king and queen raised them to be agents of the Coven of the Gray Ones.

Ilona was the beauty, Ilyan the brains. While his sister was sent off to Rengard to seduce King Axel, Ilyan went to work for the Surgeon himself. The Surgeon needed someone talented in Seership, since that was the only power he still lacked—For now. Ilyan had been tasked with helping the Black Valkyrie capture the great Farseer so that the Surgeon, with all nine ether wells, might at last become a Guardian.

And, with the knowledge that prolonged failure would make his own ether well appear more and more enticing to the Surgeon, Ilyan had all the incentive in the world to fulfill his mission.

As he thought of the Farseer, Ilyan switched from checking on snakes to regarding the omenfires. The blue hearth beside him burned as Ilyan traced the proper runes in the air.

At once, the red-robed legend appeared in the flames beside a tall dragonheart palm. Ilyan saw thatched rooftops and a pale green citadel amidst lush seaside foliage. That could only be the Keepdom of Evyndale.

What the Farseer would be doing in Evyndale, Ilyan could not say for certain. Still, logic told him the Farseer would be going there in order to try and recruit the royal family—and, by extension, the entire River Keepdom—to the side of the Rebel Knights. Ilyan chuckled as he took another indulgent sip from his goblet. Ilyan would tell the Surgeon they'd just have to get there first.

Ilyan was perhaps the only one who knew that the Surgeon was just as paranoid as High King Magnus. The only difference was that, whereas Magnus feared Eliana, the Surgeon feared only the Farseer. The Surgeon would do anything to see the Knights' patron silenced. After all, it was the Farseer who'd brought down the Wraith King all those centuries ago.

This time, Vishai thought, *the Wraith King will not make that mistake.*

Momentarily, the image in the omenfire shifted. Ilyan saw the face of a half-born with dark teal scales on the tips of his pointed ears, untidy black hair falling over the young man's dragonfire green eyes. His form was surrounded by hundreds of stars.

Ah, yes, Ilyan thought. *This again.* This wasn't the first time Asher of Steel Rim had appeared in Ilyan's omenfires. The Surgeon thought that this vision was about the hot-headed Knight, Asher, himself. The Surgeon even hoped to recruit Asher to their cause. But Ilyan was too intellectual to be fooled by that. This vision was about Evgard and the Dragon Isles, represented by a half-born. It could only be showing Ilyan that on the night of the convergence, both halves of this land would fall to the Gray.

Sure enough, the vision showed the half-born trapped by gray bonds. He struggled uselessly against them as a figure suddenly loomed over him, a seaxe held over his chest.

The figure came into focus and Ilyan saw Meleya of Misthaven. Voids, this girl was clever, a true master of deception. She'd fooled them all, even Ilyan, into thinking she was searching for the Surgeon's voidshard during her time in Scryer's Grotto under High Prince Mason's watchful eye. But all the while, Meleya had kept the shard concealed within her rift hold.

Yes, this girl was throwing a cracked scale into their plans. The Surgeon had been livid with Mason, striking the fear of the void into his heart and leaving him scarred. But the Surgeon had good reason to be angry. They needed that voidshard before the convergence, or all would be lost for centuries more.

Ilyan had warned against hiding the shard in the Dragon Mists, but the Surgeon had insisted. The Mists swirled with wild magic, making it nearly impossible for any Seer to get a clear reading on the future of anything that lay inside. That was the point—The Surgeon was desperate to keep the Farseer in the dark regarding their plans. He'd planned to retrieve the voidshard at the last possible moment before the convergence, then use its power to bring about the Gray Age once and for all.

Speaking of which, Ilyan still had once last snake to check in on.

Turning away from the omenfire, Ilyan connected with the final mirror copy of his ethereal familiar. This one was just up the stairs from the observatory where Ilyan now sat, hidden amongst the jars of stolen ether wells in the Surgeon's lab.

The Surgeon was there, sitting in meditation. Though his wraith-bound ether wells made that difficult, each day, he worked diligently to attune it, the greatest weapon Evgard had ever known:

The Veilblade.

The unnaturally long, silvery sword hovered in the air before the Surgeon, its sharp end pointing skyward. Violet dream energy swirled all around it, coalescing in a nebulous core set at the base of the blade. A row of delicate serrations ran up the backside of the blade while runes adorned its length. The gleaming crossguard swept out like the points of a star.

Ilyan knew everything there was to know about the Veilblade. It was one of three artifacts fabled to have once belonged to the sky goddesses before the world existed, and the only such artifact thought to still be in Evgard. For centuries, the legacy of northern frostdrakes had protected the blade of Streya.

At least, until one of the Wraith King's servants bonded the great warrior, Mason Drakeslayer. The High Prince had nearly died completing his task, but it had all worked out for the best. When the Surgeon brought Mason back from the brink, it had put the High King in his debt. Soon, Evgard would be synonymous with the Gray. The Capital was theirs, as was Ilyan's native Kolbohr, with more Keepdoms soon to follow. They wouldn't be hard to convince, either, especially once they saw how the Gray would protect them from wild dragons. Etherarchy drew them in, but voidarchy was pure.

That is correct, Vishai whispered, urging Ilyan to take another sip of wine.

Ilyan finished the wine, then leaned back in his comfortable chair. The snake hissed as it slithered from his shoulders, returning to its place at Ilyan's feet. The Wraith King had many followers, but Ilyan knew it was he who stood above the rest, both in prestige and intellect. That was why he was the Overseer.

Chapter 16: Interrogation

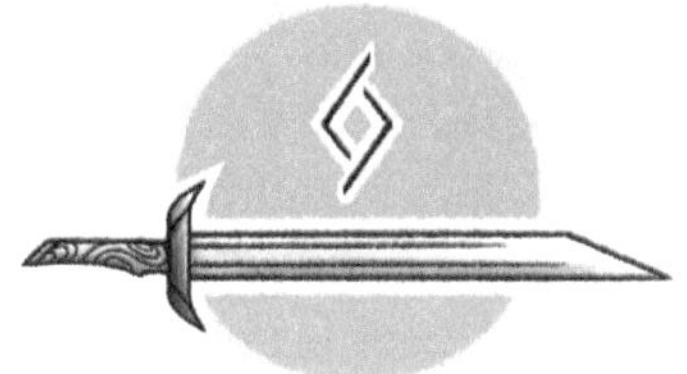

MELEYA

In a lot of ways, being in prison with Mom and Dad felt all too familiar.

Of course, this was the first time I was *inside* the cell with them.

Each of the dozen or so cells beneath the Rebel Knights' safehouse was packed wall-to-wall with either Mage Hunters or cure victims as we waited our turn for Kai's interrogation. It was an arduous process, and I only saw Kai emerge to collect the next prisoner every twenty minutes or so.

Meanwhile, Mom, Dad, and I sat together in a far corner. Dad didn't need to be here, since he'd already joined the Knights with the others Boone had brought, but he insisted on staying with us. Dusty, my father's ethereal pet draccoon, perched on Dad's shoulder, looking almost as uncomfortable as I felt.

Mom had her hands in her lap, her newly unblemished face staring nervously at Dad's hand on her knee. She hadn't spoken a word since they'd locked us in here, despite Dad's tireless efforts to put her at ease.

"Ain't this great, Freya?" Dad asked as cheerfully as he could. "Before long, Kai'll clear the two of y'all and we'll finally be both free *and* together all at the same time. That ain't been the case for what, four, five years now? Everythin's gonna be normal now."

Mom didn't reply. Dad turned to me, an earnest expression on his scruffy face.

I swallowed hard, knowing right away what he was asking of me. He wanted us to settle into our usual routine, where Dad and I babied Mom into being alright. Where we did everything in our power to keep her from tottering over the edge. We'd been at this for years, even before the Mage Hunter, Zoren, put my parents in prison. Everything we did was to protect Mom, to keep her from having to face reality.

I ground my teeth together, resentment bubbling up inside me. This time, I didn't want to go along with Dad's charade. Maybe it was because of the emotional wild-dragon-ride I'd been on over the past twenty-four hours, but I was tired of this game. I couldn't keep playing.

"But everything's not normal," I said quietly.

At that, Dad closed his eyes. Dusty let out a nervous little squeak, and Mom looked up, dark brown eyes staring vacantly at the Mage Hunter pauldron on my shoulder rather than looking me in the eye.

I continued, "Things are never going to be normal. Not when I have to keep pretending to hate myself for being a magi."

"Don't be silly, Meli," Mom said with a weak laugh. "You're no magi. You're too young to have manifested powers anyway—"

"Mom!" I said. "I'm going to be *eighteen* years old this fall. I'm a trained soldier, and I've been to the Dragon Mists and back. I attended the Mage Hunter Academy under the Black Valkyrie. And Mom… Mom, I'm a magi. A Rifter, like you. And I'm proud of that."

My voice broke on that last part. A few people sharing our cell were staring at my display, and Dad shot me another look.

"Mels…" he started.

But I didn't care who was watching. I felt like a campfire that had been reduced to embers, struggling to persist over the howling winds. My own mother felt like a stranger to me. I'd lost Jax. I'd hurt my best friends. Guilt flowed through my veins with every beat of my heart. I was far beyond caring about appearances.

Mom's lower lip trembled as she looked at the ground.

"You always taught me to hide my powers," I continued. "To be ashamed of them. But I love my powers, Mom. Mom…" I bent lower, trying to get her to look me in the eye. She turned away, squeezing her eyes shut as if the very sight of me brought her pain.

All at once, I realized that it *did*.

"Look at me, Mom." I tried to speak firmly, but my voice was shaking. "Just look at my face."

I sat up straighter, pushing back any flyaway white hairs that had come loose from my braid. Mom turned to face me, though her eyes were still closed.

"Please," I whispered.

Slowly, she opened her eyes.

"What do you see?" I asked. Despite how uncomfortable I felt, I forced myself to maintain eye contact with her.

"I... I..." Mom started, and I could tell it was just as hard for her. "I see the brand they left on my baby. I didn't protect you well enough, and that silvermark is a mark of my shame."

"A mark of shame," I repeated. Tears welled in my eyes. "That's all you'll ever see, isn't it?"

Mom's face screwed up, and more guilt made my stomach twist. The entire cell had gone silent, though most pretended to be busy looking through the bars or twiddling their thumbs.

There was a sudden clanging noise as the prison door swung open.

Kai's voice filled the room. "Meleya of Misthaven?"

"Here," I replied, trying to keep my voice even. Kai made his way toward my cell, then used a key to unlock it. Two bulky Rebel Knights stood guard to his left and right.

Kai held the door open, his expression serious as he nodded my way. "You're next."

I'd spoken with Kai twice before—once behind the command center in Keep Rengard, and once over his gecko mindlink. Both times, I'd thought of him as an introverted bookwyrm type.

But as I sat at the wooden table before him in the stone, windowless room, I realized that was *not* always the case.

"State your name, Meleya of Misthaven," Kai barked. He leaned across the table, the light from the iron chandelier overhead making his intense expression all the more fierce. A complex Mystic rune glowed from his forehead, and he wore the same over-the-top amount of plate armor I'd seen him wearing the first time we'd met.

"But you just said my—"

Kai slammed his hand against the table. "State your name, Mage Hunter."

My eyes widened. "Meleya of Misthaven."

Kai whipped his gaze down toward the table where a tiny silver gecko perched regally atop the back of my hand. Glint, the mirror gecko, was acting as some kind of mindreading link so that Kai could determine whether or not I was telling the truth.

Kai's ethereal pet lizard gave two deliberate blinks of her enormous, shiny eyes, which Kai seemed to take as a 'yes.'

"Your age?" Kai barked again.

"Seventeen," I gulped, and Glint blinked twice again.

"What type of magi are you? And what class?"

"Mystic," I replied. "Rifter." Two blinks.

"Now, say you're a two-ton wyvernhog who likes to sit around and drink golden boltbrew all day."

It was my turn to blink up at Kai. "I'm sorry?"

"Just say it."

"Okay..." Feeling like an idiot, I looked Kai in the eye and said, "I'm a two-ton wyvernhog and I like sitting around all day drinking golden boltbrew."

Kai glanced at Glint, who gave her creator a calculated single blink. Kai seemed satisfied. One blink must've meant I was lying.

"Just so you know," I said, "the gecko really isn't necessary. I've sworn off lying ever again. Not that I was ever any good at it to begin with." At that last part, Glint double-blinked in agreement.

"Glint stays right where she is until I say she's done," Kai said, his voice hard. Glint gave me what I could only interpret as an apologetic cock of the head. At least one of my interrogators was nice. I wondered what Kai's problem was.

"You've spent the past few months training with the Mage Hunters, correct?" Kai went on.

"Uh, yeah." I felt the weight of the dusky blue cloak heavy on my shoulders.

"And during that time, what was your opinion of the Knights of the Torch?"

I furrowed my brow as I contemplated how to answer his question. "Mixed. For a long time, I wasn't sure what to think. I learned about the attacks the Knights had led on several cities in the capital keepdom, and that made me skeptical. But... I was pretty close to a certain Knight who insisted that Solrac and those who followed him would never be a part of something like that."

Kai narrowed his eyes at Glint, who blinked twice again.

Kai whipped out a black leather notebook and hastily scrawled a few notes before continuing his intimidating interview.

"I'm assuming this Knight was one Jax of Blackfjord, is that correct?"

"Yes," I replied, my voice suddenly quiet. Two blinks from Glint.

"And what was the nature of your relationship with Jax?"

For a long moment, I didn't answer.

Kai put both hands on the table and leaned closer. "Did he hire you to help him? Were you working with the Mage Hunters to try and win him over to your side? What was the nature of your relationship with Jax of Blackfjord?"

I swallowed the lump rapidly forming in my throat. "Jax and I are—that is, we *were* romantically involved."

I nearly choked on the words. Kai's expression almost shifted for a second, and I could've sworn his cheeks deepened in color, as if he regretted asking. I heard a tiny croak from my hand as Glint gave me a sympathetic pat along with her usual double blink.

"Scorch, Jax," Kai muttered under his breath. "How do you do it?"

"Things are over between us now, though," I clarified. "Jax refused to flee the Academy with the rest of us, and I don't actually know if he plans to keep spying for the Knights or if he has other ideas. I... I'm worried about him."

Soot. I held back tears I didn't know I was hydrated enough to cry while Glint gave Kai another double blink.

Kai took more notes in his journal, then turned to me once more.

"And what is your current opinion of the Knights of the Torch?" he asked. "The Rebel ones, I mean."

"Well, for starters, you're giving me and my Mage Hunter friends a chance despite having every reason not to trust us. If you'd turned us away, some of them might be dead right now. So at the very least, I would never betray that kindness," I answered honestly. "And if your mission really is to make things better for magi without harming innocents, then I'm all for it. As much as it would pain me to admit that that thieving Astromancer friend of yours might've been on the right side all along." I tried to smile at him, but still couldn't pierce his hard exterior.

He coughed into his fist. "Speaking of Asher… When did the two of you first meet?" "At the Rise in Keep Rengard," I replied, wondering where he was going with this.

"Why did you attempt to engage him in a fight?"

"I'd just joined the guard, and he was robbing the command center." Glint was double-blinking up a storm.

"You drew your weapon on him again in Swan Spire," Kai went on, more menacing with every word. "Why?"

"I… I guess because I'd just joined the Mage Hunters and he was stealing from the Black Valkyrie."

"Do you plan to continue your habit of drawing your seaxe on Asher at any given moment?"

My cheeks were growing hot. "Does Asher plan to continue running around robbing people and being a general menace?"

"Asher doesn't plan."

"Another reason to find him irritating," I grumbled.

"And if he were to do something you find irritating again, say, tomorrow?" Kai asked, leaning over the table again. "Would you threaten his life once more?"

I got to my feet so that we were on the same level and leaned over the table toward him as well. "Drak, Kai, if you have a problem with me, just say it!"

Kai paused, and for a long minute, we stared each other down. I could feel Glint squirming uncomfortably on the back of my hand.

Finally, Kai sighed.

"Alright then," he said, lifting a finger to trace gold lines through the air. Another rune joined the first over his forehead. A tiny version of the same rune lit up along Glint's back.

"Are you familiar with Seer powers?" Kai asked.

I frowned. "We studied all nine magi types at the Academy. Seers are mind readers."

"Correct. We also have the ability to see omens of the future. 'Reading the mind of fate,' if you will. Of course, the future is always uncertain, and there's a ninety-to-ninety-six percent chance I'm the least-gifted omen-reader in Seer history—I once predicted the demise of a toy city." Kai winced at the memory. His intimidating demeanor vanished as genuine worry appeared on his face, and my heart softened instantly.

"But…" Kai went on. "Well, there's one omen I've been seeing regularly. If you don't mind, I'd like to show you. Maybe by showing you, it'll stop appearing in my omenfires. Bear in mind, omens are very symbolic and confusing even at the best of times."

No sooner had I nodded my approval than a vision opened up inside my mind.

Gold flames rimmed a scene showing a night sky filled with stars. Stars in my least-favorite color: void blue. The stars lit up a single long table in the room's center.

Atop the table, I saw Asher. He struggled against bonds that held his legs and wrists in place as the stars danced all around him, almost as if they were mocking him.

Suddenly, I saw myself appear from the shadows. I seemed to step out of a wall of lightning-blue fire, its azure light burning in my eyes. Or were my eyes casting the blue light themselves? I couldn't tell.

Soon I reached the table where Asher lay trapped. The strange blue stars fled in fear. Finally, Asher screamed as I leveled my blade at his chest.

Then the vision vanished. The hand that wasn't holding Glint flew to my face.

Across the table in the stone room, Kai was looking at me. His expression was grim.

Kai spoke slowly. "I have nothing against you, Meleya. In fact, I think you're a good person, and I want you to join the other free Rebel Hunters upstairs."

I swallowed, still reeling from the vision as I prepared to leave the interrogation room.

"But before you go, I have just one more question to ask you," Kai said. I paused as Glint stared up at me from the back of my hand.

Kai went on. "Asher is my best friend. Can you promise to never do anything to harm him?"

My heart thudded in my chest. I wanted to reassure Kai that I wasn't capable of anything as awful as what I'd seen in the omen. I thought of my best friends, Solvai and Brigan, and how I would do anything to keep them safe.

But all I could think about was what I'd done to Brigan in the Academy courtyard while under the influence of my wraith. *Could* I honestly tell Kai I wouldn't hurt Asher?

"I promise," I whispered, my pulse still racing.

With that, I set Glint carefully down on the table before hurrying toward the door. Before I left, I turned back just in time to see Glint look up at Kai.

My heart sank when she only blinked once.

Life at the safehouse took a lot of adjusting to. While Kai and Glint had only let those they'd deemed friendly join the others, there was still a clear tension between Rebel Knights and Rebel Hunters. Both sides had hurled more than a few insults and punches. Trickshot and her healer apprentice, Brigan, had their hands full tending to each new black eye.

Meanwhile, Shaya did her best to calm the main aggressors down before things got worse. Still, there was a looming black cloud hovering over the entire safehouse:

What were the leaders going to do with the Black Valkyrie?

Many of the Rebel Hunters, myself included, didn't want any harm to come to her. I truly believed she'd changed. But the hate ran deep in the Rebel Knights' blood. Princess Eliana had done her best to listen to both sides, but last I'd heard, the Knights were winning her over—and that wasn't good for Vidya. Not that an ex-Hunter like me was privy to any real information on the matter.

Besides the drama, I found the safehouse to be a truly fantastic place. The number of rooms in the log cabin seemed endless, from the three-levels-deep basement to the second-story attic. The sleeping quarters reminded me of the barracks, so I felt right at home sharing with Solvai and my other female squadmate, Edrea, as well as Trickshot and Shaya. At first, they'd put us in the same room as some female Knights, but after one of them got into a shouting match with Edrea the first night, they'd split us up.

Mom and Dad got their own room, though I hadn't been to visit them since our conversation in the prison. I felt bad for the way I'd lashed out at Mom, but I was still angry with her. I needed more time.

But it wasn't the sheer size of the cabin that impressed me most. It was the use of etherarchy. Ether-powered objects were everywhere, from the Lightwielder's torches brightening the halls to the Woodweaving-infused crates that held and preserved Rhana's endless pantry. Her defense system was the most elaborate I'd ever seen.

And the most personally relieving. Since coming to the cabin, I hadn't felt the influence of my wraith even once. It turned out that Rhana was concerned with more than just physical threats, and had incorporated some kind of wraith-repelling barrier into her property line using ancient Guardian-era technology called 'etherlocks.' Even the nightmares about the Soul Reaper didn't haunt me here. I still had the shard in my rift hold, but it now felt dormant.

Despite that, I felt a sort of emptiness inside as I sat with my knees tucked against my chest in the window seat of my shared room. Looking out, I saw the cindercone trees that matched the reddish-brown logs that made up the safehouse cabin. Off to the side was the clear blue lake just off the cabin's west wall, and I could see the lush little island in the center. Nearly obscured by the island's trees was a beautiful little chapel dedicated to the three goddesses. This safehouse had everything and then some.

I wasn't sure how long I'd been staring out the window before Solvai joined me in the wide, cushioned seat. First, she wordlessly wrapped a soft aldraka-wool blanket around my shoulders, then sat across from me.

Solvai gave a small smile. "Did you know there are great sapphire herons in the lake here?"

I squinted down at the water where I saw a couple of long-legged, long-billed birds with blue-tipped feathers.

Solvai went on excitedly. "There are even a couple of nests down there in the trees, and this morning, I saw the eggs hatching. The mommy and daddy herons have been bringing them food, and Meleya, they're so interesting! The babies are so soft and fuzzy, and one is totally blue. I'm sure the coloring will tame to normal by the time he grows up, but scorch if he isn't cute now."

Solvai laughed, and I cocked my head. "Did you say you've been watching the nest all day?" I asked.

My friend nodded, then reached under her collar to pull out a tiny brown feather tied beside the carved falcondrake charm she always wore around her neck. The feather had a little wooden bead at the base, and I noticed intricate markings cut into it.

"Been practicing with my newest Wildshaper's totem," Solvai said. "This one lets me transform into a ridgebacked wren—one of the tiniest, quietest birds in the Ridgeback Mountains. But the best part is, transforming into one lets me get the perfect view of the new baby herons in their nest!"

"Bird nerd," I teased.

Solvai shrugged. "Birds make me happy." At that, she gave me a pointed look. "Speaking of which, I don't believe I've seen you smile once since we got here. Meleya..."

Solvai trailed off, and I knew exactly what she wanted to say but felt she couldn't. Not after our argument back at the Academy.

One look at her worried, pleading face sent tears springing to my eyes. My shoulders shook as I pulled the blanket more tightly around me.

"Solvai," I said between sobs, "I'm the worst friend in the eight keepdoms. I'm so sorry for everything."

Solvai's eyes were shiny too. I lost any resistance as she pulled me closer so that I was lying on the window seat, my head in her lap. Then she began smoothing my messy hair, gently moving the flyaway white strands out of my face and back over my ear.

"Talk to me," she said, and the floodgates opened in full force.

I blubbered to her about my wraith, and about how afraid I'd been of her growing influence over me. About what a relief it was to be here where Xan couldn't get to me.

I went on, and Solvai listened to my every word as I spilled my guts about my seemingly impossible relationship with my mom.

Then, most of all, I cried over Jax.

I missed Jax with every fiber of my being. I'd never felt this way about anyone before, and I didn't think I ever could again. Solvai cried with me as I shared the story of our messy breakup in Swan Spire. I felt a burning hollowness in my chest when I thought about him still battling a wraith of his own.

As I spoke, I clutched a small, white crystal in my hands. It was the quartz Jax had given me back at Outcast Outpost. Since getting to the safehouse, I hadn't been able to bring myself to refill the crystal with spare ether. I still kept it on my belt, but now it hung cold and empty.

Kind of like my heart.

At some point during our conversation, Solvai pulled out a little block of wood and her whittling knife. She began carving away at the wood and, before long, I began to see a great sapphire heron taking shape in her hands.

After what must've been over an hour, I gave a long sniffle and turned to Solvai.

"What about you?" I asked. "Sapphire herons and teary best friends aside, how are you adjusting to life at the cabin?"

"Well…" Solvai started, making a long, confident stroke with her knife along the wood. "Funny you should ask. I actually had something I wanted to talk to you about. I need some advice."

I looked at her, questioning.

Solvai spoke more quietly, as if she was worried about being overheard. "You remember Captain Cenrik, right?"

"Of course," I replied. Cenrik had been the Captain over Keep Rengard's army while Solvai, Brigan, and I were in basic training. We'd watched Mage Hunters arrest him the day we became real soldiers.

Solvai's eyes were glued to her carving as she spoke. "Growing up with my mother as the army's head dragon keeper, I saw Cenrik a lot. This might sound silly, but in a lot of ways he was like a father to me. After all, until recently, I thought my father was this strong, capable, military leader. Obviously, my opinion of my real dad has changed."

Solvai grimaced, and I understood why. I'd have mixed feelings too if I'd learned I was related to Torsten, the town drunk who'd been secretly working with the Coven of the Gray Ones. Still, he'd been a good mentor to me, and he was Jax's father too. Though I could never quite see Jax and Solvai as half-siblings.

"Anyway," Solvai continued, "Cenrik is responsible for making me Captain of Squad Reckless—Apparently, he's always seen leadership potential in me, even when I couldn't see it myself."

"He was right," I nodded. Solvai had struggled at the start, but she was responsible for leading our squad out of trouble countless times.

"Yeah, well now…" Solvai stopped carving to look me in the eye. "Now he wants to offer me a seat on the Rebel Knight council."

"What?" I could hardly believe what I was hearing. Not because I didn't believe in Solvai, but because… well, lots of reasons. She was young, not to mention an ex-Mage Hunter. People were bound to protest that. But then again, maybe Cenrik saw it as a way to confront and heal the rift between our groups.

Solvai pressed on, speaking fast. "It wouldn't be official unless I chose to become a Knight first. See, the Knights of the Torch have always been led by a council of three: a Mystic, an Archon, and a Sentinel. The schism tore the council—they call it the 'Triarchy'—apart, but they're starting it anew here among the Rebels. As a Psion, Solrac will represent the Mystics, and despite him losing his Lightwielder's ether well, they've chosen Cenrik to represent the Archons."

"Which leaves you, a Wildshaper, to be the Sentinel," I finished.

"Indeed." Solvai put down her carving tools, and I noticed her hands were slightly trembling. "They wanted someone more established with the Knights, like the other Wildshaper, Valla. But with her gone, there aren't all that many Sentinels floating around. Most are about as green as me anyway. So, Cenrik put my name forward. Solrac thinks—and I quote— 'This is the greatest thing that could've possibly happened to the Rebel Knights.' But I'm not so sure he's right."

Solvai looked down at her lap. It suddenly made sense why she'd spent the day observing waterfowl. She'd needed to clear her head.

I scooted closer to my friend and wrapped half the blanket around her shoulders so we were sharing it. She sighed.

"I don't know why all these high-ranking positions keep falling into my lap," she said. "I'm so quiet and awkward. Why would anyone listen to me?"

"Squad Reckless listens to you," I said.

"That's because they *know* me. Besides, it took a long time before you all took me seriously. I'm just not a natural-born leader."

I watched as Solvai rubbed at the falcondrake charm around her neck. Then I gave her a light nudge with my shoulder.

"So you're not a natural-born leader," I said. "But you've already proved you can *become* one. Doesn't mean your shyness will magically go away—in fact, it may never leave. That doesn't mean you should hide your light when there's a difference only you can make."

That was something I'd learned firsthand over the course of the past year. I'd gone from fearing my powers to embracing them and using them for the good of others. Solvai had gone through a very similar process.

"I think you should accept the position," I said. "To the void with what anyone says."

"Really?" Solvai asked.

I responded with the Guard's Salute, bringing my right fist to my left shoulder. Gratitude in her eyes, Solvai saluted back.

CHAPTER 17: EXECUTION

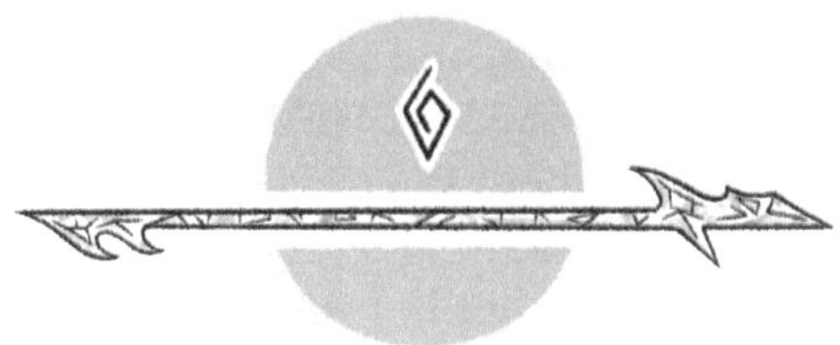

ASHER

"**A**bsolutely not!" Solrac's voice carried across the field. He, His Majesty, and Boone stood at the edge of the safehouse's northern boundary. Between them, Valla crouched on the ground as she looked through her travel pack.

"You gotta admit, the whole idea's more crazy'na wyvernskunk drunk off his scales," Boone added. His Majesty barked in agreement.

Kai and I hurried to join the group. "Wait—Where's Valla going?" I asked.

"Nowhere, if I have a say in it," Solrac said.

"Well, you don't," Valla said. She busily tucked a third extra knife into a sheath clipped to her boot. Satisfied with her extensive arsenal of weapons, Valla closed the travel pack and slung it over her shoulder, then rose and gave a whimpering His Majesty a farewell pat on his giant bloodhusky head.

Valla looked at Kai and me. "I'm going after the Everflame," she said.

"The Everflame?" Kai repeated, eyes widening. He and I exchanged glances.

Boone spit at the ground. "Drakked thing don't exist. If it did..." Boone shot Kai a sidelong look. "...Kaidan and Kalari done would'a found it."

Kai's mouth fell open. He gripped his black notebook tightly.

"My... my parents?" Kai's voice was no more than a whisper.

"Kaidan and Kalari aren't the first Knights we've lost to the search," Solrac plowed ahead. "But soot if they won't be the last. Boone is right, this is a suicide mission. I forbid you from going."

"Like I said before—" Valla narrowed her eyes, "that's not your call. It's worth the risk."

"Valla's right," a new voice said. "The path to the Everflame is dangerous, but worth the risk."

Joining us was a man in his early thirties with dark hair—the same man who'd stepped between Trickshot and the aggressive Rebel Knights that first day the Rebel Hunters joined us. He'd been the one who compiled that case full of information about the Coven of the Gray Ones.

"Thank you, Cenrik," Valla said.

Cenrik no longer wore the simple tunic he'd worn as a cure victim; rather, he donned a set of plate armor from the safehouse armory. Not ascension armor, I noticed, though as a former captain of the guard, I was willing to bet Cenrik had once been a dragon rider. I wondered what might've become of his dragon bond.

"While I am no longer tormented by the Gray Ones," Cenrik began, "I have no doubt that these dark spirits plot against us. They wish to overtake our world. If we could at last succeed in restoring the Everflame, we might stand a chance."

"But what does this Everflame actually do?" I asked.

Cenrik got a reverent look in his eye. "Followers of the light believe the flame of the first true dragon holds the power to purify all who gaze upon it of any darkness. In short, the power to purge voidarchy and restore light."

"Religious soot and nonsense if you ask me," Boone grumbled.

"Agreed," Solrac said. "The Farseer has not been able to confirm that this Everflame still burns. That power was lost long ago..."

Valla stuck out her chin. "Well, if I don't come back, you'll finally know for sure." With that, she turned on her heel and began to stalk away.

Solrac reached out, clasping a hand onto her shoulder. Valla froze, then turned to him soberly. He didn't say anything, but I could sense tension between them thicker than dragonhide. His Majesty let out a low whine and his pointed ears drooped.

"I can't stay here," Valla said with resolve. "Goodbye, Solrac."

That was perhaps the most weighty 'goodbye' I'd ever witnessed. No one spoke as Solrac slowly relinquished his hold on her shoulder.

"Goodbye," Solrac quietly answered.

Then, without another word, Valla's skin began to glow with Sentinel patterns. A cloud of golden mist encompassed her, and the next thing we knew, we were watching a huge, pure white polar wolf disappearing into the thick cindercone pines. A mournful howl pierced the air, and I felt a pang as His Majesty answered it. Valla and I may not have always seen eye to eye—frankly, I think she struggled to get past my *ears*—but I couldn't help but pray to any goddesses out there that she came back safely.

This might've been the first time I'd gone to prison by choice.

But this time, it wasn't me who was locked up and surrounded with silver. It was her. The bane of my existence. My greatest foe. The woman who'd caused my mother's death after first cruelly stripping her of her power.

The Black Valkyrie.

And today at dawn, the Rebel Knights planned to execute her.

Valla must've been *really* eager to leave the other day, since she hadn't even stuck around to see it.

I wasn't entirely sure what sense of poetic justice drove me to descend the steps before sunrise this morning. All I knew was that I needed to see the Black Valkyrie one last time. I needed to speak with the cold, heartless woman who was probably the last one to see my mother alive.

Thorn had offered to go with me, but I assured him I could handle this on my own. Besides, now that he was on his second ascension, there was absolutely no way he'd ever fit down the safehouse staircase that led to Rhana's dungeon.

The Rebel soldier guarding the jail was half asleep, so it wasn't hard to convince him to let me take over. Once I heard his last footstep fade, I descended the final few steps and entered the jail.

There were six or seven cells lining each wall, with a wide corridor running between them. While the cells had been overflowing when the Rebel Mage Hunters had first arrived, now, only a few occupants still remained.

Most, including the freckled, brown-haired woman who Valla and the others had called 'the Liberator,' slept soundly on their cots. I spotted Shaw, the indestructible Geomancer Hunter, sleeping in one of the silver cells designed to hold magi.

But the dark silhouette in the furthest cell sat silent and awake. She wasn't in a silver cell—her etherarchy was immune to silver anyway. Rather, her cell was specially designed to chronically drain the ether of any magi locked inside it. Crystals set at intervals inside the cell emitted a whitish mist as they constantly sucked ether from Vidya's wells, keeping them too drained for her to access her powers. Stars, Rhana really was prepared for anything.

For a moment, I thought about turning back. But then the Black Valkyrie looked my way, her midnight eyes catching the dusky gold light of the single Lightwielder's torch on the wall.

"Hello, Asher," she said, her usually silky-sweet tone sounding monotonous. "Come to say goodbye?"

I didn't respond right away. I was too caught off-guard by her appearance—gone was her menacing black armor and swan-feathered cloak. Instead, she wore a simple light brown tunic, her steely hair pulled into a low draketail. She had no weapon, and heavy chains kept her ankles bound to the floor.

"You came to visit me when I was in prison at Keep Drakfell," I finally said. "You offered me the chance to join you in exchange for my life."

"And you didn't take it," Vidya replied.

"No."

Vidya sighed, turning away from me to stare blankly at the bare stone wall. "Tell me, then. Why have you come here, sweet Asher?"

I set my jaw, speaking quickly so that I didn't lose my nerve. "You have something I care about. At least, you have a piece of her."

Vidya pursed her lips. "So you know the truth."

In a sudden rush of anger, I gripped the bars of her cell until my knuckles went white.

"The fact that you ripped my mother's ether well from her soul and left her for dead? Yeah, I know."

"It wasn't like that," Vidya said calmly.

"Oh really? Please, enlighten me."

Vidya bit her lip, but held her head high as she continued staring at the wall. With her every word, I felt increasingly sick to my stomach.

"The soul surgery process was far more experimental in those days," she said. "Nobody survived it—neither the patients *nor* their ether wells. But the Surgeon, that is, the Soul Reaper... he was interested to see if those with Drekai blood would be more resilient."

Hot tears threatened to spill over at any moment. "Why her?"

"The Soul Reaper asked me if I knew of any powerful Drekai or half-born magi," Vidya explained. "Zerana was the most powerful I'd ever seen."

I slammed my hand into the bars, sending a dull, ringing echo throughout the prison. A few prisoners stirred, but I didn't care. "And that's a good enough reason to lead someone to her death? My *mother* dies, and you move on without a second thought?"

In my rage, my irises flashed with golden etherlight. Within moments, I was holding my starglass dragonhook spear, shoving the tip through the bars to stop a mere inch from Vidya's throat.

She didn't flinch. She didn't even look my way. It was as if she hoped I would kill her. As if she wanted *me* to be her executioner now rather than wait for the ceremony at dawn.

Bitterness filled my chest, and I suddenly couldn't stand to look at the Black Valkyrie for a second longer. I pulled back my spear, then turned on my heel and began storming back toward the exit.

I'd only gotten about halfway down the corridor when a sound I never thought I'd hear stopped me in my tracks:

The Black Valkyrie was crying.

I turned back. Sure enough, she was hunched over in her cell, weeping openly.

For several long minutes, I just stood there, unsure what to do.

Eventually, Vidya spoke through her tears. "Of all the unspeakable things I've done, the one I regret most is robbing an innocent boy of his mother."

My gut twisted at her words. She seemed genuine—but that's what I'd thought about fake-Shaya all last summer.

"Stop this," I said. "Stop trying to manipulate me."

Soot, why had I come here? What had I hoped to gain? Some kind of closure? An apology? None of that would've made a difference. This was still the same old Black Valkyrie, up to her same old twisted deception—

Raakua, min zaaki, came a voice to my heart.

Every prior thought fled my mind. All the hate and anger gave way to hope.

Those were Drekai words: *Peace, my son.*

It had to be Mom. Who else could it be?

I listened, but heard nothing more. Still, my mind was racing with thoughts of my mother and what she would say if she really were here.

I swallowed the lump in my throat along with my pride as I walked back down the corridor to stand before the Black Valkyrie's cell.

But... the woman I saw in that cell was no longer the Black Valkyrie. I couldn't quite explain it, but it was more than just her black armor that was gone.

"What is it you want, Vidya?" I asked.

Through her tears, she replied, "A chance to make things right." She squeezed her eyes shut. "But I don't deserve it."

The sound of a door slamming made me jump. Several pairs of footsteps began descending the stairs.

Vidya hurried to her feet and squared her shoulders. Within moments, I couldn't even tell she'd been crying at all. Her expression was as cold as ever as three of the Rebels' burliest soldiers entered the prison.

They gave me nods as they wordlessly filed down the corridor and opened Vidya's cell. Two took her by the arms and the third lagged behind, prepared to intervene should Vidya try anything.

Somehow, I knew she wouldn't.

A chance to make things right, Vidya had said.

Dawn had come more quickly than I'd expected. The Black Valkyrie was on her way to the gallows. In less than an hour, it would all be over. I'd have what I'd always wanted—revenge on the Black Valkyrie.

All I had to do was... nothing.

Soot.

I'd never been very good at that.

Before I could reason myself out of it, I took off following them up the stairs.

"You're out of your mind," Cenrik said.

"Those scales on your ears obstructing your judgment?" Rhana added.

"Who are ya, boy," Boone asked, "and what've ya done with Asher of Steel Rim?"

"We've been over this already," Princess Eliana said. "The Rebel Knights' leadership council has already agreed on the Black Valkyrie's execution. The decision was unanimous. Well, almost." Her gaze briefly flickered to Solrac, who stood on the fringes of the circle.

Sunlight was just streaming over the mountains as we gathered outside the dragon stables. Vidya and her burly handlers stood only a short distance away, the noose silhouetted in the early morning light.

I'd arrived just in time, pulling the group of Rebel Knight leaders aside before they'd had the chance to move forward with the execution.

I gritted my teeth, speaking passionately. "If we kill her, then we're no better than she is. No better than this sky-forsaken realm that kills magi like us for merely existing."

"But Asher," Kai said, "she isn't merely existing. She's a threat to everything the Knights stand for. A dark magi, a charlatan, and a murderer."

"And if she really has changed? She willingly came here," I pressed. "Something just doesn't feel right about this."

"Something doesn't *feel* right?" Rhana's gaze couldn't have been sharper if her irises were actual daggers. "This is why you're not on the leadership council. Your drakked feelings would bring down the realm. You weren't hired to have opinions—you were brought on as the distraction. Stick to what you're good at, scaleskin."

Rhana's words were harsh, and I doubted she completely meant them. Still, I felt my resolve weakening.

"Now, Rhana," Ivar chimed in. "Lesson number three in life: Disregardin' feelings is just as foolish as disregardin' logic. You need both to operate. Maybe Asher's got a point. And another thing..." Ivar crossed his arms, drawing himself to his full height as he looked Rhana dead in the eye. "If you don't quit takin' shots at Asher for his half-born heritage, Dusty and I are gonna have to give you a haircut you don't much like."

Dusty gave a vaguely threatening chitter. Rhana seemed thrown off by someone finally challenging her, and backed off. I cast Ivar a grateful glance, and he nodded as if to say he was sorry for letting her get away with it for so long.

"What I don't understand," Kai said, "is what's gotten into you, Asher. You hate the Black Valkyrie more than anyone."

"I believe the Black Valkyrie is already dead," I said, trying to sound sure of myself. "All I'm asking is that we give *Vidya* a chance."

I was sweating under the pressure of everyone's gaze. While everyone else had been very vocal about their opinions on the matter, Solrac, for once, was still standing silently at the back, his arms folded.

"Call upon the Farseer," I suggested. "He can read her mind—let us know if she's changed or not. If she hasn't, I'll happily pull the lever on the gallows myself."

Rhana narrowed her eyes. "The Farseer doesn't just appear whenever some half-born comes calling—"

Thick, white smoke suddenly spilled across the ground around our feet. When we looked up, a tall, hooded figure in red emerged from the source of the cloud.

Everyone, including me, took a step backward, inclining our heads before the Farseer. Scorch, had he planned on making the realm's most perfectly timed dramatic entrance?

"The half-born is correct," the Farseer said, his voice echoing mysteriously as his shiny, white eyes glowed within the darkness of his hood. "I will speak with the Black Valkyrie to discern where her loyalties now lie."

Not even Rhana dared question the Farseer. He raised a red-scaled, gauntleted hand toward the gallows where Vidya stood.

"Vidya," he said, "come with me."

FRAGMENT: CONFRONTATION

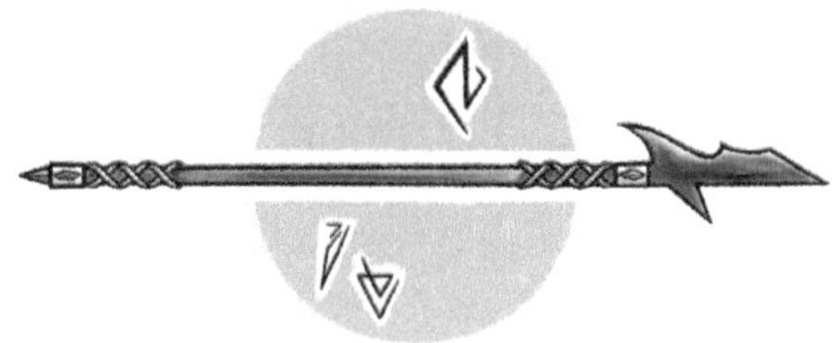

VIDYA

Vidya heard the click of a lock on the other side of the attic door. The Rebel Knights were locking her in. How sweet. As if a lock could stop her from escaping if she truly wanted to.

For that matter, these manacles binding her wrists and ankles were largely useless as well. Yes, there was silver in the alloy. These bonds were meant to trap magi.

But Vidya was so much more than just a magi. She was a skymage.

No, she thought. *Call it what it is.*

Voidmage. Vidya was a voidmage. Her power came not from the goddesses and the ethereal plane, but from the void itself. The Gray Ones.

Even now, the token of her power lay inside the gold locket around her neck. Her voidshard, the token of her bond with her wraith. Vidya's own name was carved onto one side, while the other bore the name of her Gray companion, Exusha.

For now, the bond felt cold. Exusha couldn't cross the safehouse border—not with the ancient etherlocks in place. Vidya was alone in her head for the first time in many years.

More *herself* than she had been in many years.

Standing across from Vidya in the narrow, dusty attic was her old rival. The man she'd spent years despising, longing for the opportunity to destroy him and all he stood for. His red-gauntleted hands moved smoothly as he placed an illusion of silence over the room. When Vidya looked closely, she could just make out the shimmering violet dream energy lining the log walls. Then, he stared her way, his eyes glowing from within his hood.

The Farseer. Or, more accurately...

"Solrac," Vidya spoke with silky sweetness.

The Farseer stood proud and still, antlered staff in hand, for several long seconds before slowly moving one hand toward his face.

In a swift motion, the Farseer pulled back his hood. The once mysterious, shadowy enigma truly was just Solrac. His Psion's silvermark shone from his left cheek, his dark hair styled to tousled perfection. His goatee was as well-manicured as ever, and his eyes... those dark, earnest eyes stared into Vidya's.

A hundred emotions surged through Vidya: Loathing. Fear. Regret.

"I believe there's no point in keeping up the illusion here," Solrac said, passing the Farseer's runemarked staff from one hand to the other. "Not when it's just us. Not anymore."

"No, I suppose not," Vidya said, sticking out her chin.

For another long moment, neither of them spoke. Then Solrac took a deep inhale.

"To business. You are only still alive because Asher—of all people—thought you deserved a chance. A chance to prove you've changed, and that the information you possess could be of value to the Rebel Knights."

"My information will be what saves you."

"I shall be the judge of that."

A psionic rune suddenly came aglow over Solrac's forehead as he telekinetically propelled himself forward by his robes. Within a split second, he was standing directly in front of Vidya.

Vidya didn't flinch. "If there really are no more secrets, then tell me. Are you a Psion, as you've always said? Perhaps a Rifter—I've seen you use portals before. Are you a Seer to match your grand, precious alter ego? Or, pray tell, are you all three? A true skymage for a new era."

"I am a Seer," Solrac said. "A Seer and nothing more." He spoke quietly, and Vidya noted a slight shake to his voice. It triggered something in Vidya, an emotion she'd buried long ago. Sympathy.

For a second, that made her resentful. The old hate began to resurface as she looked into the face of the man who had abandoned her, pregnant and alone, in an unfamiliar keep.

She was seconds away from digging deep to access her Archonic powers. She could take down the vulnerable Solrac easily.

At the thought, Vidya felt a gentle tug in her heart.

The impression gave her pause. What would be the point of fighting Solrac? Vidya didn't want to, not really. Not anymore.

Stars, things were different without Exusha pressing in on her consciousness. Her perspective seemed to have expanded. The consequences of her choices had never felt so clear. So real.

Again, Vidya felt a light, comforting warmth, as if some unseen being was glad that Vidya had resisted her habitual urge toward violence and hate. This wasn't the first time she'd felt an odd sort of connection through the ether well she'd taken from Zerana.

Solrac continued. "Well, I'm both a Seer, and an incredibly skilled fraud. Various relics allow me to channel psionics and rifting. But this… this is all my own power." He set the antlered staff on the ground before tracing a rune. A Seer rune Vidya recognized as one meant for mind reading.

Right. She was here to be interrogated.

"May I?" Solrac asked, holding out a hand.

Vidya arched an eyebrow, her tone sarcastic. "Do I have a choice?"

"Yes."

Drak Solrac's sincerity. Looking proudly down the bridge of her nose, Vidya placed her hand in Solrac's. Even after all this time, his touch sent warmth like lightning racing through her veins.

The mental connection solidified, and Vidya could feel Solrac probing her consciousness. If she lied now, he'd know it.

"Tell me what you know," Solrac said. "Upon arriving at the safehouse border, you said Mason Drakeslayer is working with one you called the Soul Reaper. That they plan to use the Gray to overtake the realm."

"Yes," Vidya explained. "The Soul Reaper. The Surgeon to those who follow him. He's the one who performs the soul surgeries, after all."

"Surgeries," Solrac repeated with a grimace. "Ether well transplants… the strange voices… of course. The Soul Reaper is collaborating with High King Magnus to find a cure for etherarchy. I had a vision of him last summer."

"That's right," Vidya explained. "But the cure is just a front. A ploy to get more ether wells for the Soul Reaper and his followers. Skymages, he calls us. After the ancient order of multi-powered magi who served the all-powerful Guardians. But we're not skymages. Our power comes not from the light, but from the void."

Vidya turned so that Solrac could fully see the three silvermarks running from her left cheek up to her temple: Psion, Shadowbinder, and Wildshaper.

Vidya went on. "Two of the ether wells I possess once belonged to others. Great magi whose power is now mine to wield through the Gray arts."

"Zerana," Solrac said with sudden understanding. "And Lorelai?"

Vidya nodded. "The Soul Reaper has convinced High King Magnus that these ether well surgeries are the answer to his woes regarding magi. By removing their ether wells, he will go down in history as the monarch who stopped the dragons from ravaging the keeps in search of ether. Magnus allows the Surgeon to do as he pleases with the discarded ether wells. When they don't break during the operations, the Surgeon bestows the corrupted ether wells—no longer a draw for wild dragonkind—upon his most loyal followers. Those bound to Etheria's most powerful wraiths. He calls us skymages."

"Skymages," Solrac repeated. "Anciently, they were multi-powered magi."

"So you do remember the legends we used to read together," Vidya said. "Do you also remember where the skymages got their power?"

"It was bestowed upon them by Guardians." Solrac's eyes widened. "So, if the Soul Reaper is bestowing powers to his servants... drak."

"Yes." Vidya nodded. "He plans to become the first Guardian in a thousand years."

"That is not how it worked," Solrac protested. "Guardians served the light. They didn't steal their power from others."

Vidya pursed her lips. Solrac's eyebrows knit with concern.

"Tell me everything you know," he said.

With Solrac's mind-reading rune in place, Vidya knew she couldn't lie to him. Lying to him was pointless now, anyway. All too aware of his hand in hers, Vidya disclosed all she knew regarding the Soul Reaper and his plot to flood Evgard with the Gray. How he obsessively charted stars, determining that he would make his move on the night of the convergence of mythic stars.

Solrac knew no less than Vidya about the looming convergence of the Dragon, the Phoenix, and the Dire Wolf constellations. The last time the three great star networks aligned was a thousand years ago, when the first Evgardians came to this land on skyboats. The Drekai had appeared shortly thereafter, and many wars had taken place, ended by the Guardians.

"The Soul Reaper plans to assemble an army," Vidya went on. "He already controls the High King, and Keep Kolbohr is in his pocket as well. He still has agents in Rengard, I'm certain of it, and it's only a matter of time before he makes a play for the rest of the realm."

"This is why the omens have been telling us to recruit," Solrac muttered. "We must match his forces."

Vidya scoffed at that before continuing. "There's more. I believe the Soul Reaper plans to corrupt the Veilblade."

"The Veilblade? Surely not—I saw nothing regarding this in the omen-fires. Unless... stars. The frostdrake?"

"The old legends were correct. It *was* guarding something."

"Of course. It all makes sense—Mason Drakeslayer is a pawn of the Soul Reaper," Solrac murmured.

"One of his Gray servants is bound to the High Prince," Vidya confirmed.

"That's why he wants to become a Guardian," Solrac said, putting the pieces together. "The legends say that only a Guardian can properly wield artifacts of the goddesses."

"He's only missing one ether well," Vidya said. "And he's determined that he complete his Guardian powerset with a very specific one."

"That of the Farseer," Solrac filled in.

"That's why we pursued him—you—so relentlessly. The Surgeon let Magnus believe it was to help his son, but that was only to procure every resource possible. He will not rest until he has what he wants."

Solrac looked down. "The omen... the gray dragon consuming me... it's the Soul Reaper."

"He plans to wipe out everyone who stands in his way," Vidya said, keeping her voice aloof. "That includes the Knights of the Torch. *Especially* the Knights. That's why he put so much work into molding me. I'm his warrior, the weapon meant to bring the Knights to their knees."

Solrac's sharp jawline tensed. This was the moment of truth. "And now? Is that still what you want?"

Vidya pressed her lips together. For so long, she'd wanted nothing more than to take down the Knights. To hurt them where it mattered most. To make Solrac pay.

"Yes," she replied automatically.

Solrac's grip on her fingers tightened, his eye twitching ever so subtly as he sensed the lie. Was it a lie? Scorch. Vidya could hardly believe it.

"Vidya," Solrac said, raising an eyebrow. There was a long, heavy silence.

"Vidya," Vidya finally said, briefly adopting Solrac's accent as she echoed her own name. Then she laughed. "Throughout all these years, no matter what I did, no matter what horrific things you saw me do, you've always seen me as that lanky teenage girl who ran away from her responsibilities to become a drakking circus performer."

"That is true," Solrac replied. "Though 'lanky' is not the word I would have chosen."

Vidya raised an eyebrow, still fully aware of her hand in Solrac's. "And what word would you choose?"

Solrac let out a soft exhale. "It is impossible to choose just one word to describe you. But 'enchanting,' 'radiant,' and 'fascinating' are as near as the limitations of words permit."

Vidya scoffed. "Drak your theatrics. Who are you trying to impress here?"

"My wife."

Vidya scowled, yanking her hand away. Their mental connection severed instantly. The chains connecting her manacles clinked.

"I wasn't your wife for more than a few weeks. Our marriage was an impulsive sham and you know it."

"Impulsive perhaps," Solrac replied fiercely, "but certainly no sham. I made a vow to stand by your side from that moment and into—"

"—'and into forever. In this world, the afterlife, and what lies beyond. I am yours, body, mind, and soul.' Don't quote our vows to me, Solrac. Not after what you did."

In her frustration, Vidya's eyes flashed as she activated her archonic ether well. Her forearms became pure shadow, and with a clang, the useless silver manacles fell to the attic floor. Solrac took an automatic leap backward.

Vidya pressed on. "Pretend all you want that your fancy words and promises mean something. You may have everyone else fooled into thinking you're worthy of their trust as the noble head of the Rebel Knights of the Torch, but not me. I know the real you."

Vidya roared, launching toward Solrac with her hand outstretched. She didn't have a weapon, but she didn't need one. Her finger runetraced fast as she psionically held Solrac in place by the scruff of his Farseer robes.

Likewise, Solrac sprang into action. He reached toward the gnarled staff lying on the floor and used some telekinesis of his own to pull it towards him. The staff glowed with runic power as Solrac held it against Vidya's neck.

Both of them froze, waiting for the other to make their move. Would they go back to their old dance? Eternally entangled in a battle neither of them really wanted to win but were too stubborn to end?

They held their ground for what felt like hours. At any moment, one could end the other.

Solrac finally broke their silence.

"Leaving you was the greatest mistake of my life…"

Vidya clenched her teeth, preparing another biting response.

Before she got the chance, Solrac finished his thought.

"Leaving the two of you."

At that, Vidya gasped. Her runes dissolved and she stumbled backward so far she bumped the attic wall. Solrac stood firm, gentleness in his gaze.

"You…" she rushed. "I don't know what you mean."

"My wife and son deserved better." Solrac's voice was tender.

Vidya's was harsh. "*My* son."

"I know Torsten is not Jax's father," Solrac said. "It seems I wasn't the only one with a secret back at the waterfall inn."

Solrac's expression betrayed his pain. "You knew you were expecting when I left. Why didn't you tell me the truth?"

"How could I?" Vidya snapped. "It wouldn't have mattered any-way—You'd made your choice. You chose your precious Knights of the Torch."

"It was more than that!" Solrac cried. "My time had come to take up the mantle of the Farseer. It was something I'd prepared for my entire life. I felt trapped. I thought I would have more time to figure things out, to make things right. But not a day goes by that I haven't regretted leaving you as I did. I can't believe I was so blind. And now that I know the truth about Jax—"

"Don't you dare talk about Jax!" Vidya said. "You are not his father! Not in any of the ways that matter!"

"That boy deserves to know the truth!"

"That *boy* is no longer a boy!" Tears sprang to Vidya's eyes. "You threw away your chance to parent him the same as me!"

Drak. Vidya hadn't meant to include herself in that last part.

But scorch, it was true. For years, she'd planned on winning Jax over. There'd be time to get her son back—not yet, but soon. That's what she'd always told herself.

Vidya recalled her last conversation with Jax back at the Academy. When she'd tried and failed to convince him to return to the Knights with her and the others.

I've changed, she'd told him.

As if I'd ever believe that, Jax had replied.

Overcome, Vidya dropped to her knees and wept.

Solrac let the Farseer staff fall to the ground with a clatter, then practically flew to her side. In her weakness, Vidya didn't even recoil when he wrapped his arms around her. For one small moment, it was as if no time had passed since the days when they truly loved each other.

"Jax manifested his powers young." Vidya stared at the ground, unable to look her husband in the eye. "I thought I'd trained him to be careful, but it wasn't long before a Mage Hunter caught him with a runemark over his forehead. I pleaded with him not to report Jax, and the Mage Hunter offered me a chance to save my son. It seemed the Hunters needed more cadets—particularly ones with etherarchy like me. Even back then, the Soul Reaper was beginning preliminary experiments regarding soul surgery and the alleged magi cure."

"So you struck a deal," Solrac finished for her. "You'd join the Mage Hunters in exchange for Jax's freedom."

Vidya nodded and wiped her nose. "Leaving him with Torsten was the only solution I could think of. At the time, he was living in Rengard, but once I told him—*lied* to him about our son, he returned to his business, the Naga's Head, in southern Skygard to raise him there. I thought—" Her voice faltered and she began to hyperventilate.

"Oh Vidya…" Solrac stroked her hair. "We were both so caught up in ourselves that we let what mattered most slip through the cracks."

"I thought I could protect him," Vidya spoke through her tears, her fingers closing around the fabric of Solrac's robe. "I was willing to let them test voidarchy on me in hopes that, one day, Jax would choose it too. Then he'd be immune to silver, and the crown wouldn't view him as a threat to the realm. His ether well would no longer attract dragonkind. Power protects. But the Gray... the wraiths. I thought I could harness the wraiths to serve me. But I was wrong. There's no controlling the darkness."

Vidya bit her lip. Her deepest, innermost thoughts spilled out of her before she could reign them in. "I no longer wish to see the Knights ruined. Nor you, Solrac. That fire is gone. It perished the moment I realized my quest for power lost me my son."

"He's not lost," Solrac said. "He's still infiltrating the Academy."

"No." Vidya shook her head. "His wraith is strong, I can sense it. The Soul Reaper knows it too, and he won't let Jax go without a fight." Ice gone, Vidya melted into Solrac's embrace.

"Then neither will we," Solrac said, drawing Vidya close. "Neither will we."

MELEYA

The nightmares were gone, but the fear remained.

I could hear my roommates' slow, even breathing as they lay peacefully in their bunks. Meanwhile, every time I closed my eyes, I was terrified I'd see gray mists, bright blue lightning, or the Soul Reaper's cold, eerie gaze sending dragonbumps down my arms.

Worse still, when I did drift off, I heard the dripping of water and felt the chilly, still air of Scryer's Grotto all around me. Mason's voice echoed in my ears, telling me I needed to stay for another hour, then another and another.

I woke with my heart thudding in terror.

It was irrational, and I knew it. If either the Soul Reaper or Mason was able to find me through the Rebel Knight's safeguards here at the cabin, they would have done so by now. They couldn't reach me here.

So why couldn't I retrain myself to sleep normally?

I stared at the ceiling, the dim moonlight filtering through the window highlighting the sloping patterns in the wood grain that I'd subconsciously memorized. The longer I looked, the more every pattern seemed to look like a dragon—winged dragons, wyrm dragons, plump dragons...

Ugh. No matter how dull my thoughts, sleep still evaded me.

My racing thoughts drifted to the big, beautiful kitchen downstairs. Rhana had given everyone permission to use it, along with her vast food supply, anytime they wanted, as long as they left things as spotless as they found them. I'd spent an embarrassing amount of time wandering through her shelves of ingredients and overlooking her kitchen's fine cookstove, oven, and countertops.

But I still hadn't been able to bring myself to actually cook anything. For whatever reason, doing so felt wrong. As if, after all that had happened over the past few months, I was no longer worthy of doing something so normal. Something so... *me.*

For a while, I thought about Vidya. Some people were surprised that the Farseer had cleared her to stay at the safehouse freely and without restriction. After all, this was the Black Valkyrie, the Farseer's bitter enemy. But I had no trouble believing that Solrac wanted to give the woman he once loved another chance. Still, she stuck mostly to herself to avoid retaliation from those who wished her dead.

After several more long minutes of trying to decide whether the pattern surrounding a knot of wood in the ceiling looked more like a wrinkled, bearded drake or a baby wyvern hatching from its egg, I gave up on sleep entirely. Silently, I got dressed, then slipped from the room and into the hallway.

I had a vague plan to find a nice, quiet place to wait while I got tired enough to sleep. I knew the safehouse library had some chairs and tables—Maybe studying from my old Mystic runebook would help.

But as I crept closer to the library door, I noticed golden light spilling from inside from one of the Lightwielder's torches. Either someone had forgotten to douse it before going to bed last night, or someone else in the safehouse was just as restless as I was.

"Brigan?" I said when I peeked around the doorframe. Amidst the shelves, I saw my friend sitting at one of the wide tables. He had a thin, well-worn book with a dark red cover open before him. Like me, he was fully dressed, but also like me, his hair was a bit of a mess.

I couldn't help but break into a smile. Brigan's hair was normally pulled back into a perfectly neat ridgeknot, other than the one corkscrew curl he liked to style over one side of his forehead. Now, hundreds of curls sprang every which way, as if he too had spent the last few hours tossing and turning.

"Meleya," Brigan said, his hand flying to his wild hair. For a second, he looked like he was going to try fixing it, but quickly realized the damage had been done and pulled his hand away. "Shouldn't you be asleep?"

"Shouldn't you?" I countered, inviting myself into the library with him. He automatically scooted over so I could take the chair beside him.

"I couldn't," Brigan admitted. "Came here to read—might as well be productive."

The way he said it made me feel like this was a common occurrence. I realized this wasn't the first time I'd found him outside his room reading in the dead of night.

I took a seat beside Brigan. He smiled at me, revealing dimples on either side of his mouth.

I nearly smiled back, but stopped at the sight of a long, pale scar running through his left eyebrow and onto his cheekbone. His eye was untouched, and the cut no longer looked painful, but I couldn't stop the fresh wave of guilt that pulsed through me.

Noticing my gaze, Brigan gently touched the scar with his fingertips. "I healed it as best I could right after it happened," he explained apologetically, "but Trickshot wasn't around for obvious reasons, nor am I anywhere near as skilled as she is yet. Plus, Bjorn's injuries were more pressing at the time, and I used up most of my supply of liquid light healing him. Not that something ether-based like liquid light could do much to stop the scarring from a silver weapon anyway."

"Oh Brigan," I swallowed.

"Trickshot's been teaching me a lot more since we've been here at the safehouse," Brigan rushed on. "I may not be able to heal this scar, but gauntlet down: At least it makes me look like some kind of war hero."

He flashed me another brilliant smile that made tears well up in my eyes. I looked down at my hands—the hands that had wielded the seaxe that had scarred one of my best friends for life.

Brrring! I suddenly felt Sniff communicating with me. I could tell he was trying to tell me he didn't think it was my fault.

"It's completely my fault," I said aloud, speaking both to Sniff and Brigan. Part of me wanted to shut down and slink back to my room, but Sniff played an encouraging melody in my heart. I remembered how liberating it had felt to open up to Solvai, and knew that Brigan deserved better.

"I'm so sorry, Brigan," I said, squeezing my eyes shut. "I'm sorry for what I did to you and the others in the courtyard at the Academy. And I'm sorry for letting myself get to that point by shutting down. I thought I could handle it all on my own, but I realize now how wrong I was. I know it doesn't change anything, but I swear, I'll never let something like that happen ever again."

"Hey, hey," Brigan spoke soothingly. "Look at me."

Cautiously, I forced my eyes open. Beyond the scar I'd given him, I found Brigan's warm, brown-eyed gaze, and felt that old familiarity that always calmed my racing pulse.

"Gauntlet down," Brigan started, his voice grounded and confident. "You've been through enough without beating yourself up about this for a second longer."

Brigan didn't have to recite his specific points for me to know he was talking about the wraith, my breakup with Jax, and the subsequent flight to the safehouse for refuge.

"But what I did was unforgivable," I muttered.

"False." Brigan snapped his fingers. "I just forgave you. It's done."

"But Brigan—"

"It's done," he repeated. "It's time to give yourself permission to move forward."

I chewed my lip as I mulled that over. There was a moment of silence, which came to an abrupt end when a low, loud rumbling sound came from Brigan's stomach.

I snorted, and he gave an embarrassed grin.

"Sorry," he said. "I might've been busy and missed dinner last night."

"Brigan!" I scolded. "That's just plain unacceptable."

I scooted my chair backward but froze before standing. I'd been about to drag Brigan to the kitchen where I planned to whip up a midnight snack. But I still hadn't cooked since getting here and, for whatever reason, doing so felt like a big step. Was I ready to, as Brigan put it, give myself permission to move forward?

A second, even louder growl from Brigan's stomach answered my question.

"Come on," I said, getting up. "I speak fluent tummy-rumble, and yours is begging for a piece of honey fry bread."

Within the next half hour, I was finally home again.

Mixing bowls, sacks of flour, and frying pans surrounded me. The satisfying crackle of frying dough filled my ears, and the scents of bread and honey butter danced throughout the kitchen. My soul felt a million times lighter as I placed a plate bearing a perfectly crisp disk of honey fry bread in front of Brigan.

He took a bite, and his eyes rolled back in his head with contentment. I bit into the test bread—the first attempt that had turned out a little misshapen and too dark on one side. The crispy dough's warm savoriness merged harmoniously with the sweet creaminess from the honey butter.

"Gauntlet down," Brigan said between bites. "I don't care what grand feasts they serve in Etheria in the afterlife. Nothing beats a piece of Meleya's bunker-famous honey fry bread."

I smiled wider than I had in weeks as I prepared to fry up the next ball of waiting dough. I'd prepared a bigger batch than I'd ever attempted before—hopefully enough to feed at least some of the small army that resided here at the safehouse when they all woke up.

After he'd finished the last crumb from his plate, Brigan joined me near the stovetop. I continued cooking while he leaned back against the counter with his arms folded across his broad chest.

"So," I began, "what exactly were you busy with last night that made you miss dinner?"

"Just some meetings," Brigan said.

"Oh?" I raised an eyebrow. "Meetings with Princess Eliana?" I did nothing to hide my curiosity surrounding the nature of Brigan's relationship with his ex-fiance.

Brigan's cheeks deepened in color. "Eliana's begun to think of me as a sort of... advisor."

"Advisor," I repeated skeptically. I smiled and nudged Brigan—Everyone had seen the way he and Eliana had looked at each other when they'd first united the Rebel Knights and the Rebel Hunters in the forest outside the safehouse.

"We work well together is all I'm saying," Brigan said defensively. "She's smart, articulate, a natural leader, and..." he trailed off.

"...the most beautiful woman you've ever laid eyes on?" I supplied with a chuckle, dropping the next ball of dough into the bubbling oil.

Brigan's voice came out gentler than I'd expected. "One of them, perhaps."

I turned toward him and was surprised to see him looking back at me, his gaze soft as he studied my face. I was instantly embarrassed about my looks—no doubt I was sweating before the hot stove, and there were probably flour smudges everywhere, not to mention the dark circles under my eyes from lack of sleep.

Cheeks warm, I looked away. Soot, I'd been teasing Brigan about another girl, fully assuming he'd forgotten all about the feelings he'd once had for me. It had been so long since that night he'd invited me to join him at the Winter Solstice Ball and I'd had to turn him down. Between the months spent at the Academy and our time here at the safehouse, I'd figured that door had closed.

But the look in my friend's eyes told me he didn't quite see things the same way.

Subconsciously, my hand closed around the empty quartz crystal hanging from my belt. I definitely wasn't ready for anything like that. I still felt like I never would be.

"Anyway," Brigan said, catching on to my awkwardness and doing his best to sidestep it. "I heard that they're planning an initiation into the Knights of the Torch for any new members who are ready to join. Probably within the next few weeks."

"Really? Are you planning to join?"

"Without a doubt."

Brigan sounded so sure of himself. But as for me… I felt a sense of dread. I'd clearly been wrong about the Knights—at least the Rebel Knights—being a group as destructive as the Coven of the Gray Ones. I owed them my life, as well as those of my family and friends. Still, joining them reminded me of the moment I'd shed my orange guard's cloak and donned the dusky blue Mage Hunter's cloak for the first time. If I jumped headfirst into the Knights of the Torch, would things end badly for me all over again?

"Brigan?" I asked, adding another fry bread to the ever-growing heap. "I wonder—could I request a 'gauntlet down' from you?"

Brigan's eyes lit up. "Nothing would make me happier. What are you looking to debate?"

"The Knights of the Torch. Is their cause just, or are they just another group of magi anarchists?"

Brigan laughed heartily, and I had to shush him so that he wouldn't wake anyone sleeping in the adjacent rooms. He apologized, then dashed back to the library. Apparently, debating my topic of choice required a literary citation.

When he returned, he held the same thin, old-looking red tome that he'd been reading when I'd found him in the library earlier. A closer look allowed me to see the title, *The Knight's Code*, written in gold lettering.

"King Axel gave me this the night of the Winter Solstice ball," Brigan explained, his voice full of reverence for the slain king. "It answers every question about what the Knights of the Torch stand for—at least, what the Rebel Knights stand for. It's why Solrac and the others turned their backs on the so-called Knights in Orothion: Vesta and the others stopped living by the code."

"What code?" I asked. I vaguely remembered Jax mentioning something about a code back at Outcast Outpost.

Brigan went on, "The Knights of the Torch swear to uphold four basic pillars, like principles. The first is to always 'choose light.'"

"Choose light," I repeated. "What does that mean?"

Brigan gestured with his hands as he spoke. "Light just means goodness or positivity. It's representative of a standard by which to determine one's choices. When you find yourself at a crossroads, step back and evaluate. Which choice puts more goodness into the world? That choice is considered 'light.'"

Brigan smiled as he continued. "That's another reason I've been so eager to learn about becoming a medic from Trickshot. Not only does liquid light fascinate me, but healing is something I see as putting more light into the world. Trickshot even says I have a knack for it. So when we were asked to choose a specialty at the Academy, the choice was easy."

I could tell by the way my friend spoke that he was passionate about what he'd been reading. Not only was his enthusiasm contagious, but I felt compelled by the things he was saying.

Over the past few months, I'd faced dozens of difficult choices. Looking back, it was clear that I'd chosen wrong too many times to count. I liked the idea of having a guide for making future decisions easier, something solid I could turn to when I myself felt anything but.

"Meleya? Brigan?" Solvai appeared in the hallway, rubbing sleep from her eyes. But when she caught sight of the massive pile of honey fry bread, she was suddenly wide awake.

"Meleya!" she cried. "You didn't."

"Oh, she did." Brigan grinned as I prepared Solvai a plate. She eagerly sat down at the counter and dug in.

Solvai sighed happily, then spoke with her mouth full. "Just like back in the bunker on the Rise."

"That's what I said!" Brigan grinned. The three of us shared a moment as we remembered the little overgrown adobe shelter we'd found during basic training. We'd turned it into our secret sanctuary. I wondered if we'd ever see it again.

For a while, it was just the three of us, the same way it used to be back on the Rise. So much had changed—Both of my friends now had prominent leadership positions in the Rebel Knights, and our encounters with voidarchy had left all of us scarred in different ways. But the way we felt about each other hadn't changed one bit.

The sound of footsteps came from the hall. They must've recognized the smell, because before long, I recognized Edrea's voice.

"Did I hear the snowhead made breakfast?" she asked, the other two members of Squad Reckless, Cam and Erik, following close behind. Erik was limping slightly after having taken a crossbow bolt to the leg during our escape from the Mage Hunter Academy, but I was glad to see that he was doing alright. We were all together now—almost.

"This day just got ten times better," Cam said, rubbing his hands together as he looked over the food.

It was nearly sunrise now. As my squadmates ate, I noticed Brigan hurriedly tying his hair back into a ridgeknot, though it wasn't quite as neat as usual.

"So," Solvai began, pointing to Brigan and me, "what were you two talking about before we so rudely interrupted?"

Brigan and I exchanged glances, and Edrea looked up from her fry bread so fast her dark hair whipped Cam in the face.

Brigan held up *The Knight's Code* as he smoothly replied, "Discussing religion and philosophy."

I shot him a look. "No we weren't. We were just going over the Knights of the Torch's code and stuff."

"As I said." There was a twinkle in Brigan's eye.

"The Knights have a code?" Erik chimed in, barely glancing up from the drawing he was working on between bites of fry bread.

Brigan opened his book, holding up a finger each time he recited a principle. "Choose light. Burn bright. Drive out darkness. Light the way."

"What does it mean?" Edrea asked.

From there, Brigan launched the entire squad into a conversation about each of the Knights' pillars. He went over what he'd said earlier to me about choosing light, then explained how 'burning bright' meant to develop your gifts, whatever they may be, for the benefit of others.

"Sounds like it's Meleya's duty to keep cooking!" said Cam. "Drive out the darkness from unlit kitchens!" The group laughed, and I passed Cam another piece of fry bread.

"There's that, yes," said Brigan. "But driving out darkness has more specific connotations, too. Since the beginning, one of the Knights' primary objectives has been to track down and destroy dark objects."

"Like weapons?" asked Edrea.

"Could be." Brigan nodded. "But really it could be anything infused with tainted etherarchy. Items, creatures... even the darkness within ourselves."

I instantly thought of voidshards, voidarchy, and wraiths. I'd asked the Triarchy what they thought I should do with the Soul Reaper's voidshard that was still in my rift hold. They'd discussed many options, but in the end they'd decided that, if I was willing, the safest place for it was right where it was.

"What about the last one?" asked Erik, putting his drawing to the side. "How do you 'light the way'?"

Brigan smiled. "By sticking to the first three pillars, of course. When you choose goodness, develop your gifts, and rid the world of evil, you light the way for others to do the same."

It wasn't until he'd finished speaking that I realized I'd been clutching my once-empty crystal, subconsciously filling it with the spare ether coursing down my fingers.

Gauntlet down: I might make a better Knight of the Torch than I'd thought.

FRAGMENT: LIGHT

BOLT

Once the human soldiers vacated the training field, Bolt assembled the dragons.

Bolt felt the need to do her part as keenly as anyone at the Rebel Knight safehouse. While her rider, Brigan, had become devoted to the Knights' Code, so too had his drake. For Bolt, following that code meant sharing her gifts with those in need.

And right now, that meant helping train the young true dragon, Aurora.

Bolt had gotten a few of the other mythic dragons involved in Aurora's training as well. Today, Thorn and Sniff joined them on the training field.

Well, Thorn joined them on the field. Sniff was busily zooming across the field, around the field, and over the field.

Bolt occasionally managed to slow Sniff down enough that he could show Aurora how to access astromancy. Sniff sneezed bouts of ether bolts straight up into the air, and with a few pointers, Aurora was able to dip into her astromancy as well. Though—bless Sniff's scales—Aurora's method was significantly more... sophisticated. Her ether blasts manifested alongside her light-like dragonfire, imbuing it with more power and extra reach.

Brrring! Sniff trilled as Aurora's ether-enhanced dragonfire spiraled into the sky above the training field. Sniff flew a few loops around the green, purple, and white jet.

Brilliant, Aurora, Bolt gave the white true dragon an approving nod. Aurora's eyes shone shyly.

Thorn's turn came next. Bolt supervised while Thorn helped Aurora learn to activate her woodweaving powers. A cracking sound rippled across the field as Thorn's scales thickened, becoming as impenetrable as the bark of a diamondoak tree. He launched his tailblade into a nearby tree, and Aurora's eyes gleamed with excitement.

Aurora gave it a try, woodweaving wildmarks glowing along her tail as she swung it forward like Thorn had, but instead of a thorny tailblade launching forward, Aurora's tail sprouted... wildflowers.

Lovely little white yarrow flowers sprinkled onto the ground. A few landed on Thorn's head and antlers, too. Thorn shook his head to scatter them, which made Aurora chuckle.

Well, Bolt thought with amusement, *It wasn't as though* every *power Aurora learned would be immediately useful.*

As Aurora practiced, Bolt noticed that Thorn was no longer engaged in teaching. Rather, his dragonfire green eyes were on something near the dragon stables.

Bolt followed Thorn's gaze to find a pale reddish gold-colored wyvern stretching her wings. It was Rose, the wyvern of the former Mage Hunter, Shaya. She must've been preparing to go on a hunt.

Thorn gave a draconic sigh. Bolt chuckled.

The sound broke Thorn from his reverie. *Huh?* he thought.

Oh, nothing, Bolt thought back, taking a few steps closer to Aurora and Thorn. *Just... you seem hungry.*

Hungry?

Very, Bolt assured him. *Why don't you join Rose over there for her hunt? I'll take over with Aurora.*

The idea got Thorn's wings to perk right up. Nervously, Thorn made his way toward the stables. Halfway there, he hesitated. It took encouraging looks from Bolt, Sniff, and Aurora to get Thorn to pluck up the courage to approach Rose.

Thorn's tail was practically trembling with excitement as he and Rose took to the skies. Together, they soared over the safehouse's western forest.

Bolt nodded with approval while Aurora gave a pleased little roar. Sniff let out a series of musical trills as he flew a loop. Doing so made him catch sight of his own tail, which he promptly began to chase.

Aurora was young, and looked like she might've been interested in joining in Sniff's antics, but Bolt sent her feelings like ocean waves to calm her soul. She still had training to do.

Come along, Aurora, Bolt thought.

She led Aurora away from Sniff where she wouldn't get distracted. Then, Bolt guided Aurora through their usual exercises. As a Lightwielder drake, Bolt hoped to share what she knew with the true dragon.

Light takes many forms, Bolt said. *It shines, it warms, and it strikes. It cuts, protects, and restores. It reveals what was once hidden. Connect with your inner light, Aurora.*

Within a second, Aurora's claws began to glow softly gold. She gave a nearby stone a slash, and the light edge sliced the stone cleanly into pieces as if it were clay.

Bolt beamed. Aurora had always had a knack for lightwielding. With Bolt's assistance, her skill with it had only grown.

Yes, Aurora was doing well with many of the Archonic and Sentinel disciplines. But for whatever reason, she still struggled with the Mystic arts. Perhaps it was, in part, because here at the safehouse, there weren't many Mystic dragons to train with.

Despite that, Bolt wanted to help out in any way she could.

She encouraged Aurora to give it a try. Dragons didn't need to runetrace the same way human magi did, but Mystic etherarchy still drew from the mind.

Like the churning ocean feeds into a river, focus your mental energy, Bolt thought.

There were a few seconds of silence as Aurora closed her eyes. Then she reared back her head, opening her jaws and sending a stream of lime-and-violet dragonfire rippling upward.

But there was something different about Aurora's flame this time. Firstly, it emitted a halo of golden light, left over from their previous training exercises in lightwielding.

Secondly, as the dragonfire cast its light over the training field, Bolt caught glimpses of other colors. Misty clouds of emerald and brown clinging to the trees. Soft orange streaks trailing from the dragonflies passing over the grasses. And a jovial, dancing mist surrounding Sniff. Even he stopped chasing his tail, captivated by the etherarchy Aurora was performing.

Bolt caught sight of a faintly glowing rune over Aurora's forehead. It was a rune Bolt recognized from the times she'd seen Brigan's friend, Meleya, use it. A rune for the Sight.

Aurora's eyes darted back and forth, bright as she took in the auras. As the fire and auras faded, so too did the rune. Still, it was clear—Aurora had finally been able to tap into an aspect of her mystic power. Rifting.

Well done, Aurora, Bolt said. *Well done.*

Chapter 19: Sanctuary

It felt odd being summoned by the newly-expanded leadership board of the Rebel Knights of the Torch.

Especially since my best friend, Kai, was part of the board. He looked so serious as he sat there, solemnly awaiting my arrival. The safehouse's secret war-council chamber was as epic as one might expect, though with a certain Rhana-esque flair.

High-backed chairs surrounded the long, firemaple wood table, and every wall was adorned with intimidating animals. A stuffed cougardrake prowled on a wall-mounted log to one side while a family of stuffed tusked squirrels lurked on the other. Just behind the head seat was the fierce mounted head of a majestic dragonelk, antlers wide, staring at me as if he could read my soul. I immediately named him Old Buck in my mind.

Several other familiar faces had places at the table in the safehouse's secret council chamber along with Kai. Rhana was here, as were Boone, Ivar, and Trickshot. At the head of the table were three seats of honor reserved for the Rebel Knight Triarchy, the elite council of leaders representing the three branches of etherarchy.

Solrac, of course, was there as the Mystic representative, His Majesty the bloodhusky at his side. In the next head chair was Cenrik, the Knight who'd been among the cure victims Shaya and I had rescued from the Asylum. As a former Lightwielder and seasoned Knight, he represented the Archons.

The third and final chair was occupied by a young woman no older than me. She had wavy brown hair, lots of freckles, and a Wildshaper's silver-mark on her cheek. I recognized her from the day the Black Valkyrie's entourage had chased me out of Swan Spire. She looked nervous, and I noticed Kai of all people giving her an encouraging nod. They must've been spending time together as members of the board.

Along the side of the table I saw Brigan sitting beside Elle. Or rather, based on the tiara she wore with her armored white dress, she was Eliana today. Soot, why'd they have to look so good together? I tried not to let that bother me as I took a seat at the far end of the table opposite the Triarchy.

"Thank you for coming, Asher of Steel Rim," Solrac said with only a slightly indulgent amount of grandeur.

"'Twas an honor to be summoned," I replied with equal ceremony. Solrac and I shared a silent chuckle.

"We have much to discuss," Cenrik took over. "The other Rebel Knight leaders and I have spoken at length regarding your proposal to send a quest team to Orothion."

"To Orothion?" I said, leaning forward. "You mean..."

"Yes." Cenrik nodded. "On a quest to rescue your father, Akayto, as well as Kari of Steel Rim."

"Yes!" I literally hover-jumped out of my seat. Elle snickered, and Cenrik shot her a questioning look.

Solrac picked up where Cenrik had left off. "The quest will not be easy. We plan to send a team of mostly magi, which means you'll be likely to attract wild dragons. Additionally, the objectives of the quest will be twofold. The primary mission will be to quickly and quietly retrieve Kari and Akayto, of course. You see, if we can just get them out of Orothion, Vesta loses her edge in her war with Magnus. No more rifting her armies around, and no more special weapons from Kari. Eventually, we hope the other members of the Triarchy, Zel and... Drak, what was the name of the fellow they've replaced me with?"

"Signus," Rhana said. "An old friend of that scale-skin, Zel."

"That's it." Solrac snapped his fingers. "We can only hope the two of them can make Vesta see sense. The Orothion Knights aren't as stable as they'd like their followers to think. They're desperate to secure the support of the ruling nobles across Skygard and Drakfell."

"Including my parents," Elle said. "So far, they've done their best to remain neutral, but I don't know how long they can hold out before Vesta forces them to choose a side."

"But if we can end this schism," Cenrik said, "it'll earn us Behrfell's support, too. Without that, we don't stand a chance against the Gray a year from now. Thanks to the Farseer's interrogation of the Black Valkyrie, we are certain that that is when the Gray will make their move."

"The convergence of mythic stars," I said, making eye contact with Kai. He and a few others around the table nodded.

"We must be prepared to defend the realm on that day," Solrac said. "It all starts with this quest."

I nodded, then asked, "And the secondary mission? You said there were two."

The room fell silent, and I saw more than a few grimaces. Apparently, this council wasn't entirely united regarding the secondary mission.

"Aurora and I will be part of the quest team," Eliana finally said, her expression determined. "I plan to use this opportunity to draw more recruits to our cause."

Now it was my turn to grimace. "But... isn't there a bounty out on you and your true dragon's heads? From High King Magnus himself?"

"It is... less than ideal, I'll admit," Solrac said. "But the young princess insists she's willing to take the risk. Things in Evgard are shifting much more quickly than any of us expected, for better or worse."

"For better if I can help it," Eliana said.

"That's right," Brigan chimed in. "The people of Evgard deserve to know they have options. We must put to rest the antiquated notion that magi aren't worthy to grace our keeps. I can think of no better way to do that than to unite them under the banner of Eliana, true dragon rider for the people."

Eliana held her head high. "Light the way!" she said. Brigan and the others echoed her rallying cry.

"That said," Cenrik went on, "While Eliana's role is pivotal, the one actually leading the quest will be Solvai. As an experienced squad captain and sitting member of the Triarchy, she will lead while Eliana serves as more of a figurehead."

"Figurehead?" Elle balked at the word. I got the feeling this was the first she was hearing of this.

"Yes," Cenrik continued calmly. "I've been informed of the way you've behaved in the past while on recruitment missions. Given your history of disregarding instruction, we as a council have determined that Solvai will monitor your actions while on the quest."

Elle was indignant. "Disregarding instruction... What are you talking about?"

"Did Boone not ask you to lie low during your recruitment near Aura Ridge?"

"Yes, I suppose he did, but—"

"Were you not aware that your actions were what alerted the Capital soldiers who later ransacked the Gallant Gopherdrake safehouse?"

Elle's cheeks flushed. "You mean our light show with Aurora's dragon-fire? But I was just trying to catch the attention of potential recruits."

"Yes, and in the process, you jeopardized the safety and resources of the Rebel Knights of the Torch." Cenrik's tone was sharp. "The realm is not in a position where we can afford to take risks on those unwilling to conform. By the light, the true dragon chose you for this position, Princess Eliana. I believe you will grow into it."

Elle's mouth was open, and for a second I thought she was going to protest. Instead, she slowly closed it, straightened her posture, and politely folded her hands atop the table. It made my chest feel hollow just watching. I remembered our conversation back in the dragon stables, and wondered if this is what Eliana had meant about properly fulfilling her duty.

"The Farseer has pondered this quest," Solrac said, "and sees pathways for both success and failure. It is vital that we select the right team to accomplish this mission, both to unite the realm for light and to rescue Kari and Akayto so that Vesta cannot continue to use them to sow violence against the crown. Additionally, the Farseer has foreseen that this quest—if successful—will not only lead to the rescue of our friends, but many others as well."

"Solvai will lead the quest," Cenrik said. "And the Farseer has chosen Kai to go as well, Many things will require his skills as a Seer and planner if this quest is to succeed. Additionally, Brigan of Solhelm has agreed to come, both as a protector and healer."

Brigan and Eliana exchanged glances.

Great, I thought as Cenrik continued outlining the details of the quest. *Elle and her uppity-nobleman former betrothed out on a quest to save the realm.* I made eye contact with Old Buck, the mounted dragonelk head, looking for some sympathy in those great beady eyes.

Poor Asher finally has some competition, wah.

I jumped at the dragonelk's mental reply—or rather, the reply of Thorn channeling an idiotic, lilting elk voice through our bond.

I played along. *Well, Sir Old Buck, that wasn't very nice.*

Says the guy who was flirting with two girls at once just last summer, Thorn-slash-Old Buck thought back.

Whoa! I protested though our bond. *One of those girls was Fake-Shaya, and was actually a forty-something-year-old killer in disguise.*

That makes it way worse.

Excuse my bluntness, Old Buck, but what would a dragonelk know about things like that?

Old Buck knows matters of the heart... Thorn thought back, adding a sappy air to his elk voice.

I snorted aloud.

Everyone looked at me. Some were confused, while others, like Kai, just rolled their eyes.

I coughed. "So, um. Anything else we should know about this quest?"

"Sure thing," Ivar said. "Eliana's been talkin' to us about turnin' this honor duel you've got comin' up into an opportunity to get some answers about the Gray from the Drekai."

Ivar looked at Elle. She glanced toward Cenrik, who nodded for her to speak.

"Upon reflection," Eliana said, "the Triarchy has decided to send word to the Drekai empress and her generals. We plan to propose a bid for information—If our champion wins, they share what they know about voidarchy. Given the things the Black Valkyrie has told us regarding the Gray threat, such an alliance could turn the tides in our favor."

Boone nodded. "Don't relish the idea of try'na work with them folks from the Dragon Isles, but if there's one thing the Dragon Wars taught me, it's that them drakkin' Gray ghosts're a hundred times more dangerous'na half-starved scaleshrew is to a lone sootworm."

Those used to Boone nodded along, while others shot him quizzical looks. Brigan tried to cover a guffaw with a cough.

I, however, didn't see much humor in the situation. "And what happens if the Drekai champion wins?" I asked.

Elle pressed her lips together before solemnly replying, "I give them what they wanted in the first place. I give the Drekai the true dragon my father stole from them as an egg, along with the service of her rider."

My mouth fell open. I wanted to protest, but the weight of the pressure was too great for me to even speak. Everyone else just sat silently by. They'd clearly known this was coming.

Eliana continued. "Should all go well with the quest to Orothion, the others will return to the safehouse while you and I continue west. Should the Drekai agree to this, the duel between you and Kheradok will take place this fall in the Dragon Isles' capital city of Zolehiinu."

"Stars," I whispered, still hardly believing my ears.

The council continued talking about the quest and the intricacies of the politics involved in the mission, but I couldn't focus on any of it. In a haze, I got to my feet and began heading for the door.

"Wait, Asher," Solrac stood. I turned to see his concerned goateed face. I bit the inside of my cheek to distract myself—not that I was going to cry, but... well, just in case.

"The choice is entirely yours," Solrac said. "Whether you accept this plan or not will not reflect badly on you in any way."

The room was clearly waiting for my answer. I looked into each of their faces, from Rhana's harsh stare, to Kai's solemn one, to Elle's distant, noble gaze.

I sighed.

"When do we leave?" I asked.

"One week from today," Kai said, glancing down at his black leather notebook.

I gave a short nod, followed by an unceremonious, "Okay."

Then, with one last woeful nod to Old Buck the dragonelk, I closed the door behind me.

I stood inside the chapel feeling like a moron.

I wasn't entirely sure what drove me to the sanctuary of the three goddesses that was hidden among the trees on the safehouse's lake island. But after that meeting, I wasn't sure where else to go. I could've gone flying with Thorn, but when I'd passed the stables I'd seen him sharing a drakalope with Rose, Shaya's sleek reddish-gold wyvern. The least I could do was not interrupt their moment.

That had led me to hover-jump across the lake. Part of me had just wanted to see if I could do it in one gargantuan jump. It turned out I *almost* could. I'd left my wet boots to dry outside as I entered the small, island-bound chapel.

I usually wasn't one to notice architecture, but the chapel's design was undeniably beautiful. Dark brown wooden beams carved with detailed suns, moons, and stars framed clear glass walls and ceiling panels. Through the panels, I saw lush green trees and bushes surrounding the small building. The morning sun streamed through the roof and onto several pews inside the chapel, and the ornate double doors took up most of one wall, while a larger-than-life statue of each goddess—Streya, Solei, and Selene—stood at the center of each of the other walls.

I shuffled my feet before the wooden statue of Solei, the spirit goddess, on the east wall. She was supposedly the patron of all Archons, if one believed that kind of thing.

Which I definitely didn't.

Probably.

"I have no idea what I'm doing here," I muttered aloud. But even as I said the words, I knew they weren't true. I'd come here with a crazy, embarrassing, stupid prayer.

"Hello there, Lady Spirit Goddess," I began, staring at Solei's enormous, sandaled feet. "I wonder if you could do me a favor and uh... hear my humble petition. See, I've been wondering something lately—Two things, actually. The first is if I'm going completely insane."

As I looked up into the statue's smiling face, I couldn't help but feel like she was laughing at me. Of course I was going insane. I was talking to a giant block of wood.

But I'd come this far.

"The second is... well, I was wondering if you know my mom. If she's... well, *around* in the spirit plane, trying to communicate with me. I've been hearing things, and I'm not certain it's not all in my head. But..." I swallowed the massive lump forming in my throat. "But Solei, Mom left me too soon. Maybe I just *wish* I were hearing her voice because there are still so many things I desperately wish I could say. So much I never got to ask her."

A tear sprang to my eye as the words left my mouth. What exactly *did* I want to ask Mom? What would I even say if she were here?

For too long, I'd felt that my life had one purpose: To kill the Black Valkyrie. But I'd just had the chance to watch that woman die for her crimes, and I'd stopped it. Me. I'd personally stood in the way of the Black Valkyrie and execution.

And now, with the pending quest and the upcoming honor duel and all that was at stake... It seemed everyone had an idea of what they wanted from my life.

Everyone but me.

The tear cut across my cheek as I realized what I wanted to ask my mother.

"Why am I here, Mom?" I whispered.

Almost right away, I felt a soft, cool breeze against my back, and I wondered if Mom—somehow—really was listening. My ears pricked as I waited to hear her voice.

"Asher?"

My heart leaped as I whirled around.

But of course, it wasn't Mom standing in the chapel doors.

It was Meleya.

"Oh, hi, snowhead," I said, forcing my voice not to crack. "What're you doing here? I didn't know you were the religious type."

"I'm not. Not really," she said. "Sniff and I were fishing in the lake when I noticed some of the plants here on the island were bearing fruit. Perfect for a pie. I was picking blazeberries outside the chapel when I saw the door ajar."

Meleya put down a little basket full of the sweet, red-and-orange-streaked fruit as she took a baby step closer.

"Were you crying?" she asked, cocking her head.

"No," I rushed to answer, quickly wiping my face with the back of my thumb. "And if I was, it was because I was admiring the craftsmanship of such a fine statue. Art, am I right?"

Meleya's skeptical gaze softened as she walked across the room to stand beside me. I didn't dare look her in the eye, not yet.

"You had a really good relationship with your mom, didn't you?" Meleya asked gently. Soot. She must've heard what I'd said just before she walked in. Then again, she was the one who'd held on to the envelope with Mom's name on it for months while she was at the Mage Hunter Academy. It might've been easy to guess. Whether I liked it or not, Meleya and I shared a weird, unique connection.

"You're a Rifter," I said suddenly, turning her way.

"You're a genius," she replied sarcastically, pointing to the mark on her cheek.

I plowed ahead before I could lose my nerve. "Is Etheria real? The spirit plane—is it literally all around us, or is it just some Mystic-y mind trick to help you interpret abstract concepts or something?"

I shuddered at my use of the phrase 'interpret abstract concepts.' Yeesh. I was spending too much time around Kai.

My question seemed to catch Meleya off guard. "Maybe that's all it is," she replied. "But I know Etheria is real—For good or for bad, for light or for dark."

She got a faraway look in her eyes, and I could tell she'd seen some dark, ethereal things that still haunted her. I almost put a hand on her shoulder, but the last time I'd tried that, we'd ended up arguing.

"It's okay if this is too much to ask," I began, holding my breath, "but I wonder if you could tell me what you see in Etheria."

"Right now?" Meleya's brows knit.

"Yeah."

I met her gaze, and something in my expression made her large, round eyes grow even more. She nodded, then traced a Rifter's rune I knew well. Since going blind, it was the one Dad traced all the time. Gold light followed her finger as the Sight rune shone over her forehead and cast little sparkles onto her face and into her irises.

Her pupils shrank. She looked around the chapel, her whole demeanor lightening.

"The general aura here is like celestial lights. Sunlight, moonlights, and starlight all at once." Meleya's voice was animated. "Each wall emits a distinct color, probably because of the goddess it represents. There's a bright, intelligent blue cloud surrounding Streya..."

Meleya gestured toward the mind goddess statue near the north wall, and sure enough, I could feel a sort of cerebral vibe from that direction. She gestured toward the west wall next.

"Selene's aura is a rich, mysterious red. Like the lifeblood of humanity, animalkind... even the earth itself."

"Yeah," I said aloud, catching the same feeling.

"And Solei..." Meleya looked up at the eastern wall where we now stood.

"Yellow," I replied without thinking. "Like the first rays of sunlight breaking over a mountain peak."

I instantly felt like an idiot. I couldn't *feel* colors. Meleya was gonna think I was crazy—

"Exactly!" She beamed at me. "How did you know that?"

"Vibes? Or maybe I'm sensing it through you somehow—Archons are spirit-based magi, so we operate on feelings." Her smile was bright and contagious.

It was also sort of pretty. I suddenly realized I'd never seen Meleya smile before. Not really.

"Your aura is like rays of light too," Meleya went on, absently reaching for the air around my shoulders. "But instead of golden yellow, it's the most brilliant shade of turquoise. Clouds of fast-moving energy all around you, but especially near your heart where your ether well is."

"Yeah?" I asked, leaning forward.

Meleya laughed. "It's a pretty hyperactive aura, I've gotta admit. Hundreds of little lights darting this way and that."

"That sounds about right," I chuckled.

Then Meleya's expression turned more serious. "But it's also strong and regal. Noble, powerful clouds that demand respect. You're someone people can look up to—a leader—or at least, you could be."

All at once, my enthusiasm died. I didn't feel like a regal, powerful leader. Leadership was for people like Elle, Brigan, Rhana, Solrac... Soot, I could barely handle following Kai's simple plans. I was no leader.

I was the distraction.

Not the hero. Certainly not the Rebel Knight champion.

I was a simple half-born thief from Steel Rim. That was all I was ever going to be. That was all I ever *wanted* to be.

"Sure," I said with a dismissive snort. "So you're an aura interpreter too, I guess?"

Meleya's face fell, and I instantly regretted my words. I was feeling bad about myself, but I certainly hadn't meant to take it out on her.

Before I had the chance to take it back, Meleya dismissed her Sight rune and set her jaw.

"Sorry for interrupting," she said, hurrying back toward the chapel doors. In her haste, she accidentally knocked over her basket of blaze-berries.

"Drak," she cursed, already scooping them back up. I moved to help her, but she put up a hand.

"I've got it."

"Compulsive tidying really is your thing, huh?" I said unhelpfully.

Meleya shot me a glare as she got to her feet, holding tightly to her basket.

"I hope the floor berries in my pie make you sick," she said. "Just you, though."

"Oh really?" I tapped my chin. "Your insults are getting better, I'll say that. But be careful what you wish for—the floor berries may somehow exclusively make me sick, but you'll be the one who will be far sicker. Sick with guilt at my bedside as I lay dying."

Meleya tried desperately to think of a comeback for a few seconds. When nothing came, she made a frustrated little grunt before turning on her heel and storming through the chapel doors.

As I watched her go, I suddenly felt the hairs on my arms standing on end. A chastising but loving voice, as clear as day, sounded in my heart.

Asher...

Mom.

Feeling both thrilled and guilty all at once, I turned back toward the Solei statue and gave the goddess my best salute.

CHAPTER 20: THROUGH FIRE

MELEYA

I was fairly certain that whoever thought up the ancient Knights of the Torch initiation ceremony had been a psychotic pyromaniac.

I stood before the wall of golden fire, knees shaking. The mystical flames may not've actually been giving off heat, but I was sweating nonetheless. They seriously expected me to walk through this fire?

Brigan had already gone through, coming out on the other side just fine. Happy, even. Solvai, Edrea, and the rest of my squad had gone through as well, as had several of the cure victims and former Mage Hunters. All had survived.

Now it was my turn.

For some reason, I held my breath. Then I stepped into the flames.

I instantly felt a sense of calm. My nerves washed away in the cool fire, which appeared white rather than gold now that I was in its midst.

Against the white, I could see my own indigo aura as clearly as if I'd been using the Sight. In fact, everything in here reminded me of seeing into the spirit plane, though on a less detailed level.

It felt like I'd stepped into another world. Time seemed to slow, or maybe it didn't matter altogether. This had to be Etheria, because I saw Blink flying toward me, her silvery wings trailing wisps of fine, gossamer mist with every flap. I smiled as her familiar drumbeats filled my heart.

Then before I knew it, I'd stepped back into reality once more.

The wall of cool golden fire was at my back now. The fresh scent of cindercones filled the air around the safehouse as the dying light of day shone in orange beams over the peaks to the west. The sound of people chatting and milling about rang in my ears.

"Mels!" Dad's strong arms wrapped around me. Several others, including Brigan and Solvai, smiled at me from their places surrounding an outdoor table laden with drinks as they chatted amongst themselves.

I'd made it through the initiation fire. I was a Knight of the Torch now.

Dad's eyes lit up. "Solrac asked me to give you this," he said, pulling back and sticking a hand in his pocket. He frowned, then began frantically patting his clothing.

A familiar chitter sounded from behind Dad, and the pair of us whirled on Dusty the draccoon. Dad's ethereal familiar grinned wickedly as he clutched something small and shiny in his tiny hands.

"You give that back, you ring-tailed scoundrel," Dad ordered, and Dusty crawled up Dad's back to drop the object into his hands before perching on his shoulder.

Dad rolled his eyes and I chuckled at the little creature's antics. It was good to see them back together after Dad's three-year stint in a silver-laden prison cell.

Dad then passed the shiny thing to me. It was a gold coin, which felt heavy and cool in my palm. On one side was a torch, the symbol of the Knights, while the other bore an ornate triangular symbol and some tiny lettering in a circle. I quickly realized it spelled out the four pillars of the Knights—'choose light, burn bright, drive out darkness, light the way.'

"Every new Knight gets one of these," Dad said. "Rebel or not. Been this way since ancient times, they say. It can help rally support or get you into safehouses should the need arise. Plus, it's a pretty little thing."

I pocketed the coin. It reminded me of the silver Mage Hunter's coins they gave out to new Hunters after they graduated from the Academy. It seemed the Knights preferred to give their initiates a token at the start of their journey instead. I liked that.

As I hugged my father once more, I glanced back toward the cabin in which Mom had hidden herself away. She and I hadn't spoken since our first day at the safehouse. I still wasn't sure what to say.

Dad seemed to catch onto my thoughts. He opened his mouth, but I cut him off.

"You've taken this whole 'joining the Knights of the Torch thing' in stride," I said.

Dad grinned. "Boone told me all about the Knights on our journey from Rengard," he said. "Can't think of nothin' I'd like more outta my life than to fight for somethin' good. 'Specially after my uh... somewhat questionable past occupations."

Dusty gave a fond squeal. He knew as well as I did that Dad was referring to his days as a highwayman in the north. He'd robbed more than a few passing noble carriages blind. It was how he'd gotten my dagger—the fancy, antler-handled one I kept in my boot as a backup weapon. For a time, I'd lent the dagger to my squadmate, Erik, but he'd returned it back at the Academy.

I smiled at Dad. "I heard you're getting promoted to Commander over the Rebel army here."

"Sure am!" Dad stood a little taller. "Your old Captain, Cenrik, will be takin' charge over the masses, but he's trainin' me and a few others up to help oversee some things as well. Speakin' of, I was supposed to find him tonight at this li'l get-together. Got a couple'a things I wanted to ask him."

Dad cast his eyes over the gathering of Knights here to celebrate the initiations. He found Captian Cenrik chatting with Rhana and some others, and I nodded for him to go ahead.

I was about to grab a drink and join Brigan and Solvai when I noticed Asher was with them. He was putting on quite the show, trying to balance a mug of golden boltbrew on his head. Several people watched and laughed, including my friends.

I, on the other hand, rolled my eyes. This could only end in disaster.

"Three... two..." I counted down.

Sure enough, just as I reached 'one,' Asher's mug slipped. He got a faceful of bubbly drink and his fans got a good laugh. Based on Asher's silly grin, he wasn't the least bit upset about getting messy.

Meanwhile, all I could think about was how he now needed to wash his face, hair, and probably his jacket too. Not to mention the mug that was now lying in the dirt—that'd need washing as well.

Fighting the urge to clean up after him, I turned toward the treeline and saw the telltale glint of metal catching sunlight.

Of course, I thought as I approached the metal device. It was one of the three etherlocks surrounding the cabin—old guardian-era devices designed to keep the safehouse... well, safe. The etherlock was about as long as my forearm and was shaped like a triangle with a diamond coming off of each point. A white crystal filled the center.

With a start, I realized that the shape matched the symbol on the Knights of the Torch's gold coin I'd just gotten. I wondered about its meaning, but when I'd asked about the etherlocks upon arrival, they'd just told me they were taken from Orothion long ago, made using old technology we no longer possessed. Secrets that had died with the Guardians.

All I knew was that this mechanism was what kept the wraiths out. What kept Xan from being able to influence me. As long as I was within the boundaries here, I was safe.

But out there...

I looked into the darkening Mirror Forest and shivered. Despite the warm night, I pulled my simple brown cloak more tightly around my shoulders.

The sound of a scuffle pulled my attention, and I realized I wasn't alone on the edge of the base.

Three soldiers, including a gruff-looking older man with a long beard, were half-dragging someone wearing a hooded cloak. One of them gave the person—clearly a female—a shove toward the treeline.

"Go back to that drakked Academy where you belong, silversoot," one person said.

"Or better yet, go get yourself killed by umbrals in the Mirror Forest," the bearded man added. "You're practically one of them, anyway."

"Hey!" I yelled, already runetracing. A gold-rimmed portal tore open before the bullies' cloaked victim and she stepped through to stand behind me.

"That's right, little Mage Hunter," the bearded man called out. "Defend your dark queen. The Farseer may've deemed her worthy of staying among us, but I miss the days when the Knights of the Torch were pure, unsullied by silversoot filth like the two of you."

I realized the woman they'd been harassing was Vidya. She stepped up beside me, her expression as lofty as ever from within her hood.

"Lucky for you three, I don't give a scorching scale about your approval—or anyone else's for that matter."

The altercation might've gone on longer, but just then Captain Cenrik called to the bearded man. He and his companions shot both Vidya and me one last dirty look before returning to the party.

"Did they hurt you?" I asked Vidya once we were alone.

There was a dark glint in Vidya's eye. "They're alive, aren't they?" She quickly shook her head as if to clear it, then sighed. "I'm sorry—I don't mean that. It's hard getting used to not feeling vindictive all the time."

"What do you mean?" I asked.

"Here within the boundary—" Vidya spread her hands. "I'm sure you've noticed that our wraiths can't influence us."

I nodded.

Vidya wandered closer to the etherlock at the edge of the property line. Just a few steps further would put her beyond its protection.

"She's close by, I'm certain of it," Vidya said. "Yours too?"

I swallowed, recalling the chill I'd felt earlier. I runetraced, and soon the Sight bloomed before my eyes.

In the trees only a short distance away, I saw her. Xan's shadowy form, lurking, and beside her, another, more substantial feminine wraith that must've been Vidya's. I got the feeling they couldn't see us, or even the safehouse at all—just more trees. But they seemed to somehow sense that we were near, and were looking for a way in.

I described what I saw to Vidya, and she nodded, unsurprised.

"All wraiths crave power," Vidya said. "Some, like mine, are subservient to it. They are loyal followers of the highest wraith—that of the Soul Reaper. Others will do anything for a place at the top, constantly fighting their own for more power. I don't believe your wraith will ever leave you as long as you have the Soul Reaper's voidshard."

"Isn't there any way to destroy it?" I asked.

"The only way to destroy a shard is to kill its wraith," Vidya replied. "And the only way to kill a bonded wraith is by the might of an even more powerful one. No wraith is stronger than that of the Soul Reaper."

Vidya hesitated, taking a step closer to the boundary. Through the Sight, I saw that she was moving toward her wraith. I tensed.

She then reached under her collar to pull out a locket emblazoned with the sun symbol of the goddess Solei. She popped open the locket and held a thin, blue shard in her hand.

She passed it to me, and I read the two names. The first was Vidya. The second...

"Exusha," I read, a little chill settling over my shoulders.

"The name of my wraith." Vidya nodded. "A wraith with a purpose: An ancient warrior determined to fight on behalf of the Wraith King."

For a moment, I worried Vidya would step across the boundary and become one with her wraith again.

Then she took a step backward, taking the voidshard from my hand and returning it to the locket.

Vidya swallowed. "I'll admit, I've considered asking you to use the Wraith King's shard to destroy my wraith. It certainly has the power. But that would only grant the Soul Reaper *more* power. A fruitless, destructive cycle."

She sighed, turning my way. "The Soul Reaper will not rest until his voidshard has been recovered. I think the Triarchy is wise to leave it in your care for now. I trust you."

"That makes one of us," I muttered under my breath.

Vidya pursed her lips. I glanced away.

She then stepped up to me and took my chin in her hands, tilting it upward to better examine my face. She ran her thumb over my silvermark.

"I've done some unforgivable things in my time," she said. "Far worse than you, skies know. Do I regret those things? With every bone in my body. But I refuse to let my past immobilize me. Wear your scars with pride, Meleya. Our broken pasts are what will make us strong enough to face the future."

She pointedly pulled back the hood of her cloak, then undid the latch, letting the fabric fall to the earth below. She gave her iconic steely gray hair a toss. It was a somewhat dramatic gesture, but the message was clear. She wasn't going to hide from anyone.

I watched as Vidya returned to the safehouse. With the Sight still activated, I could see the proud lavender clouds of her aura, along with the more fragmented splashes of teal and black from the auras of those whose ether wells she'd taken. She got several disapproving looks from strangers along the way, but she didn't flinch.

I let the Sight rune go out. Something in what she'd said compelled me to unlatch my own simple brown cloak. When I'd put it on before this evening's ceremony, it hadn't been because of the cold, but out of habit. For years, I'd worn a cloak, whether it was the cloak of the guard, or that of the Mage Hunters. It would be hard getting used to life without one. But I was tired of wearing a uniform someone else had chosen for me.

I was just gathering up both my cloak and the one Vidya had left on the ground when I heard someone whisper-yelling my name. Brigan was still standing near the drink table, gesturing for me to join him.

I jogged over and my friend pulled me close enough to whisper in my ear.

"Don't look now, but I think Solvai is on a date," Brigan said.

My eyes widened and I immediately began scanning the area.

"Shh," Brigan said with a dimpled grin. "I said *don't* look now. Here."

Brigan moved so that when we faced each other, I got the perfect view of the lake over his shoulder. Silhouetted in the sunset by the shore was Solvai pointing out the sapphire herons. At her side was a young man wearing a completely unnecessary set of too-heavy plate armor. Kai was clinging to her every word, animatedly sharing his own thoughts on the majestic dragon-birds.

"It's true," I said, clapping one hand over my mouth as I shoved Brigan with the other. "How did this happen?"

Brigan shrugged. "One minute she's sipping golden boltbrew, the next Kai's over here asking if she had any 'wildshaping insight' regarding the animal life around the lake. I swear Kai's seen her carving the herons out there before—He knew exactly what he was doing."

"Kai playing it smooth," I mused. "I wouldn't have guessed."

"Smooth is one word for it," Brigan replied. "Although at one point he *did* mention how intrigued he was by the properties of the waterfowl's feces as fertilizer."

I snorted. Then I jokingly folded my arms and in my best Kai voice said, "Hey there Solvai, you wanna check out some bird droppings with me?"

Brigan caught on, slipping into a high-pitched impression of Solvai. "Why Kai, you sure know how to make a girl's heart flutter."

We both burst into laughter.

The sound of it drew Asher toward us. He'd hover-dashed to our sides within a second.

"Are we talking about Kai?" he asked eagerly. "Because I just want it out there that I begged him not to wear that armor tonight. I pleaded with him on hands and knees."

Brigan slapped Asher on the back. "You did your part, Asher. Nobody blames you."

At once, I recalled the interaction between Asher and me the other day in the safehouse's island sanctuary. We'd been talking about auras when suddenly, he'd turned the entire conversation into a joke. My cheeks grew hot at the memory. Everything was always a joke with Asher.

"Then again," I said, "Kai's not the one with dripping wet hair from dumping a mug of boltbrew over his own head."

I tried to sound lighthearted and teasing, but when I spotted the afore-mentioned mug still lying on the ground, I couldn't help but pick it up and set it on the table.

"Whoa," Asher said, running his fingers through his longish, messy bangs. "Don't tell me you didn't know golden boltbrew was the latest trend in hair styling products."

Brigan laughed, but I raised an unimpressed eyebrow.

"Ha," I said with less than no emotion.

"Come on, Mel." Asher wouldn't quit giving his crooked grin as he grabbed a fresh mugful of the fizzy drink. "If you think I look good, you should see what the bubbles do for snowheads."

"Don't you dare waste a perfectly good drink," I warned.

"Only if *you* don't dare waste a perfectly good opportunity to get a free styling job from the Badlands' best barber," Asher countered.

My cheeks flushed with annoyance. Brigan was just standing there laughing. Asher approached, and I wasn't about to find out whether or not he was joking about using the beverage as a hair care product. I assumed a battle stance and prepared to runetrace.

"Asher, if I may offer some advice, women do *not* like being doused in boltbrew." Solrac appeared, a twinkle in his eye. "Believe me."

To my relief, Asher stopped his advance. We narrowed our eyes at each other, then he pointedly chugged the entire mug in one swig. I made a face and he crossed his eyes in response.

I was trying to think of a good way to tell Asher just how juvenile I found him when Solrac cut my thoughts short.

"Meleya of Misthaven," Solrac said, clapping his hands together. "Might I have a word?"

Asher jumped in. "Only if she can handle setting down her neatly folded laundry."

He pointed to the cloaks I was still carrying. I pressed my lips together and made a few halting, frustrated sounds, all of which were entirely incoherent.

"Don't hurt yourself," Asher advised.

"I'm not the one in danger," I seethed.

Brigan could tell I was at my breaking point, because he put a hand on my shoulder and wordlessly took the cloaks. He nodded for me to join Solrac, and rather than spend another second in Asher's presence, I obliged.

Solrac waved me over to a dense, old diamond-oak tree with thick, buttress roots. Solrac handily sat on one as if it were a bench, then patted the seat beside him.

I went to join him, but then jumped when a great, hulking bloodhusky emerged from the shadows. I'd nearly drawn my seaxe when I remembered I'd seen this big red wolf-dog before. He'd accompanied Valla and Boone when they'd come to help in the battle on the Rise back in Rengard. He'd shared a special connection with Jax as well—What had Jax called him again?

"Good evening, His Majesty," I said, giving the bloodhusky a hesitant pat on the head.

He woofed with satisfaction at the sound of his name, then gently nudged at my belt.

I cocked my head. "Are you looking for food or something?"

"No," Solrac cut in, stroking His Majesty's neck. "No, I'm afraid he's looking for something much more valuable. It seems he recognizes your crystal."

"Oh," I said, reaching for the quartz tied to my belt. The quartz Jax had given me.

His Majesty barked and panted, looking around as if Jax might walk up at any moment.

Solrac sighed, sounding genuinely sad. "Sorry, my friend. Jax will not be joining us this evening." The bloodhusky whined, but seemed to understand as he curled up on the ground at Solrac's feet.

"Will he ever?" I found myself asking. "I mean, will Jax rejoin the Rebel Knights?"

Solrac turned to me. For a second, he paused, and I noticed his sharp jaw twitch. "Are you asking for my opinion as Solrac, or are you asking someone a little more... profound?"

I knew instantly what he meant. There was a hint of challenge in his tone—He hadn't forgotten the day I'd accompanied the Black Valkyrie up to the High Ridgebacks in search of the Farseer. The battle between the two legends was one I'd never forget.

"I haven't told anyone your secret," I whispered. "And I don't plan to, either."

Solrac seemed to let out a breath. "For that, I cannot thank you enough."

I nodded. "You saved my life in the Dragon Mists. Your omens ultimately got both my parents here. It's only right I keep your identity to myself."

"Not many would have the will—or ability—not to spill the scales."

"I just have one question," I said, glancing from left to right even though I was already certain we were alone. "Are you... immortal?"

Solrac broke into a wide grin. "That is the mystery, isn't it?"

I waited, but it seemed Solrac had nothing more to say on the matter. He moved on, effectively distracting me with his next statement:

"I've been seeing your face in my omenfires for a long time, Meleya of Misthaven," Solrac said. "You are far more kindhearted than I would've expected."

"What?" I said. "You saw me before we met?"

"Indeed. Many times the Farseer has seen a vision of you, surrounded by stars, wielding a seaxe."

"Asher's there too, isn't he?" I asked.

"Why, yes." Solrac frowned. "How do you know this?"

I inclined my head toward the lakefront. "Kai showed me the same vision when I first got to the safehouse. It was almost enough for him to not let me in."

"Kai's already seeing visions regarding the convergence?" Solrac murmured to himself. "Stars, he's further along than I thought."

"What do you mean?" I asked.

"Nothing to concern yourself with," Solrac rushed. "But that does explain Kai's hesitance regarding what I'm about to ask you."

I stiffened. "What's that?"

Solrac grinned and his voice slipped into a grand, storyteller-like tone. "A quest is underfoot. A daring mission to rescue two of our own, trapped at the hand of the tyrant, Vesta, in the wrongfully-taken castle of Orothion. For the Rebels to survive what is to come, a team of travelers must brave the land between here and Skygard in order to save these noble Knights."

He spoke so eloquently, it was hard to imagine he wasn't spinning an epic tale of great legendary heroes from the past.

"You, Meleya of Misthaven," Solrac continued, "are hereby called to join this grand quest. Without you, the omens predict great peril—and, according to a reluctant Kai, a far lower likelihood of success, approximately seventy-one percent or something."

"Wha—me?" I stammered. "Why?"

"The choice is yours, of course," Solrac said, his voice returning to its more natural, grounded tone. "But I'm sure you're aware of the dearth of Rifters—not only among the Rebel Knights, but throughout the land of Evgard after the late high queen's purge."

That was true. Out of all the magi here at the safehouse, I was the only Rifter. Not even my mother could use teleportation anymore.

"Your skill would be invaluable in the role of travel specialist," Solrac said.

"Travel…" I muttered. "But… that would mean leaving the safehouse."

"True," Solrac said.

I glanced behind me toward the treeline that marked the safehouse boundary. Out there, I'd be vulnerable to the mental attacks of Xan once again. No wonder Kai worried about me being near Asher—*Everyone* on the quest with me would be in danger.

The word 'no' was on the tip of my tongue when I felt a sudden thrumming through my bond with Blink.

Ba-doom. My spirit dragon was reminding me I wasn't alone.

Trrring! Sniff echoed the sentiment. Just feeling my connection to my twin evren filled me with confidence.

But something else nagged at the back of my mind. Flashes of being in Scryer's Grotto raced through my head. The fear. The loneliness. The cold. The agony I felt each time I pictured High Prince Mason's face.

He'd wanted to use me for my Rifting abilities as well.

This is different, I told myself. But was it really?

"Do I have a choice?" I asked quietly.

Solrac seemed to sense the reluctance in my expression. Likewise, His Majesty gave me a tender nudge on the knee with his snout.

"Absolutely," Solrac replied. "Though the stars burn certain trails through the heavens, your path is not yet written in them. That pen is one only you can wield."

I wrung my hands as I contemplated what *I* wanted to do. I recalled that night in the kitchen when Brigan and I had discussed the four pillars of the Knights of the Torch. To 'choose light' was meant to help make difficult decisions easier.

The question was, what choice would put more good into the world now? Me staying at home to ensure I didn't hurt anybody?

Or leaving home to do what I could to help?

I felt a familiar pang at the very idea. All my life, I'd traveled from place to place. Would I ever get to put down real roots?

In the back of my mind, I couldn't help but think of the Soul Reaper's voidshard. Was it safe for me to leave the cabin while I still had it? I was certain Solrac had considered that, since he was one of the ones who'd told me it was safest in my hold.

"By the way," Solrac interjected, "I never answered your earlier question. The one about whether or not Jax will rejoin the Rebel Knights."

I looked up into Solrac's watery eyes as he went on.

"He, too, must forge his own path ahead. Not even the Farseer can predict what is to come for him when Jax himself has not yet decided who he wants to be. But as Solrac..." Solrac got a faraway look in his eye. "As Solrac, I can only pray we have not seen the last of Jax. He is more precious to me than all the omenfires, staffs, mythravens, or power in the world."

I nodded. I had no idea Solrac cared so deeply for Jax, but it made me happy. I knew how much Jax looked up to Solrac.

I could see why. There was something sage about Solrac—something even deeper than his role as the Farseer. He was a true Knight of the Torch, doing his best to choose light and drive out darkness.

That's what I wanted for myself.

"I'll go on the quest," I said. As the words left my mouth, I felt a sense of peace.

Solrac beamed. "I cannot thank you enough, Meleya of Misthaven."

I smiled back. His Majesty barked with glee, and I felt both my dragons playing music through our bond. They were excited about our next adventure.

So was I.

Solrac clapped his hands together. "This is the greatest thing that could've possibly happened! The other members of the team will greatly benefit from your expertise."

I put a hand to my chin. I hadn't even thought about who might be joining me.

"Who else is coming on the quest?"

Solrac grinned. "You'll be pleased to hear that your two best friends have already accepted positions on the team. Brigan will be going as a medic, while Solvai will represent the Triarchy as she leads the quest."

"Really?" My eyes lit up.

"Indeed! Princess Eliana will join you as well, and Kai will go as a planner."

I nodded. While I got the vibe Princess Eliana wasn't entirely sure what to think of me, I knew it was a strong team.

"Oh," Solrac said with a twinkle in his eye. "And one more person will complete the group. Every good quest needs a bit of a wild card, after all."

My heart froze. What was that supposed to mean?

"Who's the final team member?" I almost didn't dare ask.

With a laugh, Solrac replied.

"Why, none other than Asher of Steel Rim, of course."

Every fiber of my being instantly cried out, begging me to change my mind about going on the quest.

Asher. Why did it have to be Asher?

Sensing my distress, Solrac gave me a pat on the back. "As a consolation, I have something for you."

Then he dropped a chunk of crystal into my hand. Not just any crystal—a gleaming, shimmering skystone, brimming with ether.

I looked up at him, surprise written on my face. I'd never been given such a costly gift before. "What's this for?"

Solrac laughed. "Bring it to your dragon. He'll know what to do."

Sniff was so eager to swallow the huge chunk of skystone, he nearly took off my hand.

After Solrac had given me the stone, I'd just stared at it in awe for a while. I'd never held something so valuable. It must've cost a fortune.

Moments after consuming the skystone, Sniff's eyes shot open. Mine did too—His dragonfire green irises burned with gold archonic light, and a whole row of mystic runes shone over his forehead. Gold Sentinel patterns flowed along his hide.

That didn't make any sense. Sniff was an Archon, not a Mystic or Sentinel.

But he wasn't finished. A cloud of golden ether like the one that surrounded Solvai when she wildshaped encompassed Sniff, lifting him a few feet off the ground.

"Sniff?" I asked. I took a step closer, but jumped back again when brilliant, yellow scales began to rain down from the cloud in chunks like shattering crystals. As the scales hit the ground, their bright, lemon-yellow color mellowed into a gleaming gold.

My jaw dropped as the cloud dissipated to reveal Sniff hovering proudly in the air. His four wings were wider and stronger. His hide was thicker now as well, with extra ridges along his neck and the end of his tail. His horns were longer, and his coloring, once a bright, beacon-like yellow, had darkened into a rich yellow-gold, just like the shed scales now scattered in the grass.

Sniff reared back and gave a mighty roar. His eyes were still round, his fox-like ears still erect, but his features had lost some of their young, puppy-like qualities. I blinked in amazement as I took in the sight of my newly ascended dragon bond.

I threw my arms around Sniff's nose. It was larger now, and I had to spread my arms a little further as he nuzzled me back as energetically as ever.

A joyous, flute-like melody played in my heart, and along with the melody, for the first time, words:

Hi there!

"Hi there yourself, Sniff!" I said back, scratching him behind the ears.

I carefully gathered up each shed scale. Solrac had warned me that there wouldn't be enough time for anyone to forge my new ascension armor before leaving on the quest, but that was alright with me. For whatever reason, I didn't feel like I *should* be wearing ascension armor. That was an honor reserved for leaders and mighty warriors. After what I'd done during my time at the Academy, I'd feel strange donning dragon scales.

Ready for quest! Sniff told me.

I smiled. "Almost. First, we need to pack up our supplies—water, food, cooking implements, clothing, bedding, etcetera. Then we need to make sure everyone else has their respective items. Oh, there's also ensuring we all have our primary weapons and backup weapons, *and* that they're all sharpened. We'll need maps, too, and I'll need to start on a meal plan right away."

Throughout my speech, Sniff's tail-wagging had gone from vigorous to medium-paced to a complete stop while he waited to see if I was finished.

Laughing, I gave him a little rub on the head. "*Then* we'll be ready for the quest."

LOTHAR

Lothar's eyes were closed as he focused on opening his senses, feeling the world around him. The chirping of early-rising birds floated on the mountain breeze. The summer air was warm as it rustled the cindercones. The stone grounded Lothar to the earth as he sat outside the Academy dragonstables.

Next, he focused on his mind, allowing his imagination to wander. He envisioned where he wanted to be at the end of the day and what he wanted to accomplish.

Finally, Lothar centered himself, trying to connect with his inner self. When he went to sleep tonight, he hoped to be a better person than he'd been when he woke up this morning.

Lothar quickly jotted down some notes regarding his goals for the day. When he finished, he carefully replaced his quill pen in the pocket of his tunic. The quill was light but sturdy, with a black-and-white speckled feather. It was one of Lothar's most valued possessions.

Lothar had been meditating this way for almost a full year now. He felt like a new man compared to what he'd been so long ago when Asher of Steel Rim had first given him instructions on how to properly meditate. For months now, Jaira and the others had been attempting to convince him that Asher was no great skymage, but Lothar remained quietly skeptical.

To the contrary, Lothar had reason to believe that Asher was far wiser than anyone gave him credit for. After all, the meditations had opened

Lothar's eyes to something that should've been obvious to him from the start:

Jaira was literally crazy.

Not just Jaira, but all of the Mage Hunters who claimed to be 'sky-mages.' Lothar had always loved books, and he'd read more than his fair share of legends about the great Guardians and the extra-powerful magi who worked with them as harbingers of light. But Jaira and the others... Now that he'd worked with them long enough, Lothar understood that they did the opposite. Lothar hadn't been to the lair of the great Surgeon as Jaira had. Stars, Lothar hadn't even met the Surgeon they all esteemed so highly, the man they claimed would save Evgard by enacting the cure for the masses and purifying the ether wells of those deemed worthy. Jaira said that if Lothar played his scales right, it was only a matter of time before he'd be welcomed into the inner circle too.

Once, he would've seen that as an honor. Now, the very thought of it filled Lothar with dread. The Black Valkyrie and Snowstorm had been right to leave when they did.

If only Lothar had gone with them. But loyalty to the nobleman he served had demanded he stay behind.

"What do you think about Mason?" Lothar asked, turning to the vibrant green, second ascension evren perched beside him.

Jade thoughtfully cocked her head. When Jade and her rider, Jax, had arrived at the Academy last winter, Lothar had been glad. He'd been hoping for the chance to apologize to the dragon whose heartscale he'd once possessed. Lothar's old dragon bond.

Forced dragon bond.

Back then, Lothar hadn't realized what it meant to bond a dragon. Forced bonds were the norm in the capital, and when they'd pried Jade's heartscale from her as a hatchling to give to the High Prince's personal servant, nobody—Lothar included—had thought twice. Lothar had even felt wronged when Jade chose Jax instead.

But since coming here, Jade had forgiven Lothar. He hadn't meant to abuse the privilege of being a dragon rider. Now, she often joined him during his daily meditation.

Jade spoke to Lothar's mind. *I find High Prince Mason cruel and frankly unamusing.*

"He's not, though," Lothar said. "He's always been a bit of an arrogant show-off. He cares too much about gaining the approval of others, especially his father. But never once was he cruel to me or any of the other servants in the castle."

Jade made a deep rumbling sound.

Lothar sighed. "He was like a brother to me. Everything changed when he went north to slay that scorched frostdrake. As if the old Mason never truly reawakened after his odd shadow wasting sleep."

I am sorry, Jade thought. *I understand how difficult it is when someone you care for becomes distant.*

Jade seemed to sigh, resting her scaled head on her folded-up forewings.

Like bonds, Jade continued, *outcomes cannot be forced. Sometimes we can only wait patiently while those we love work things through for themselves.*

Lothar frowned. "Perhaps you're right."

As for me, I choose to stay by Jax's side. But you, Lothar... What will you choose?

Lothar set his jaw. "If Mason comes to his senses, good. If not... well, I can't keep biding my time taking part in something I know to be wrong. I'm going to leave the Hunters."

You've said this before.

"I mean it this time. Next time I see Mason, I'm going to tell him I'm out."

Jade growled in approval. Lothar smiled, reaching out to stroke the short horn on Jade's snout.

"You! Get the void away from my dragon!"

Jax suddenly appeared on the cliffside, his expression intense. Lothar jumped away from Jade.

"She's not yours anymore," Jax said, clasping the green heartscale around his neck as he stepped protectively to his evren's side.

"I know that." Lothar put up his hands as he shrank back. Jax never came to the stables this early.

Jade sniffed, locking eyes with Jax. Lothar figured she was speaking to him through their bond. Whatever she said was enough to get the perpetually frowning young man to at least stop glaring Lothar's way.

Jax sighed. "Sorry." Then he turned to Jade. "Come on, let's get you saddled up."

"Where are you going?" Lothar asked.

"Evyndale," Jax replied. "Drakeslayer just doled out our next assignments."

"What assignments?"

"He can explain it himself." Jax nodded down the path leading toward the Academy. Lothar's gut began to twist when he saw Mason, Jaira, and Bjorn headed their way.

This was it. He had to tell Mason he was leaving. Scorch, Lothar hadn't expected the moment to come so soon.

"There you are, Lothar!" Mason called. He and the others hurried to where Lothar, Jade, and Jax stood outside the stables.

"What's going on?" Lothar cocked his head. Jaira rolled her eyes as if Lothar had just asked the dumbest question in the eight keepdoms.

Mason grinned.

"Two tasks await us, don't you know?
First, Bjorn, myself, and Jax will go
To the River Keepdom in the east.
By our clever words we'll gain at least
A few more allies to our cause
Before that wretched Farseer does.
And should we catch him on our way
The Surgeon soon shall sing our praise."

Mason briefly paused, looking around for a reaction to his poem. Jaira and Bjorn nodded approvingly while Jax showed no reaction at all. Out of habit, Lothar gave Mason a few claps.

"Well put," Lothar said. "But actually, Mason—

"Drakeslayer," Mason corrected.

Lothar furrowed his brow. Before his coma, Mason hadn't minded when Lothar called him Mason. He'd preferred it, even.

"Right," Lothar started.

Mason cut him off. "My father wants us visiting some of the highest ranking nobility in the realm. With the Rebel Knights flaunting their dragon rider, it's up to me to secure their allegiance to the Great Uniter. Jax and Bjorn will serve as my bodyguards."

Bjorn gave a wild-eyed nod. Once again, Jax showed no emotion as he cinched Jade's saddle. Jaira had disappeared into the stables, her step determined.

Lothar pressed on. "Drakeslayer, I was hoping to speak with you in private about—"

"Quite right," the High Prince interrupted again. "Don't worry, We've got a special task in store for you and Jaira."

Before Lothar could say another word, Mason ushered Lothar off to the side where the others wouldn't overhear. Then he continued his poem in hushed tones.

"As for you and Jaira, ginger friend,
I'm sending you both to apprehend
A prize without which I'm undone.
For this, don't hesitate to run
for a gem, the veilblade to adorn:
The Surgeon's voidshard from Snowstorm."

"Snowstorm?" Lothar instantly understood why Mason wanted to keep Jax in the dark about this particular assignment. "You want Jaira and me to retrieve the blue crystal Meleya wielded in the courtyard the day the Rebels fled."

"I'd go myself," Mason said, "were it not for my political sway being so vital on the diplomacy end of things. Still, I know I can trust you, Lothar."

Guilt filled Lothar's chest. "Actually—"

"You won't let me down," Mason continued. "You've always been someone I can trust."

Oh, scorch.

"Uh," Lothar mumbled. The confidence he'd felt during his morning meditation was waning fast. Still, he'd made up his mind. "Actually, Mason, I've been wanting to speak with you about something. A... reassignment of sorts. See, I'm not sure I want to be a Mage Hunter anymore."

Mason frowned. Behind him near the stable wall, Lothar saw Jade give an encouraging draconic nod.

"I need you to get that voidshard," Mason said, and Lothar sensed the genuine urgency in his tone. "My father trusts the Surgeon, and he must be appeased. Doing so will help me win my father's favor. Please, Lothar—you know what that means to me."

Lothar did. After the loss of Mason's mother, the High King had grown, in Lothar's opinion, quite paranoid. Terrified of death. It had taken a toll on Mason as well, and Lothar suspected it was part of why he'd gone north after the frostdrake in the first place. Perhaps Mason thought that by slaying the mighty creature, he would at last win his father's approval. Still, Lothar wasn't sure. Mason was very tight-lipped regarding his mysterious journey, even before the strange shadow wasting.

"What would *she* say," Lothar asked slowly, "if she were still here? Your mother?"

That question jarred Mason. For a second, it was as if a haze over his eyes cleared.

"Even she made mistakes," Mason said quietly. He shut his eyes, as if warring with himself inside his own mind. " We're in too deep, Lothar. We have to see this through. But after all this, maybe things can finally go back to the way they were."

Mason's voice quavered on that last part. When his pale eyes met Lothar's, they were desperate.

"Will you help me?" Mason asked.

Lothar's resolve crumbled. He couldn't abandon his friend. "Of course," he heard himself saying.

Mason's grin ran from ear to ear. He called for Jaira to join them, then reached into his crisp, ornate satchel. He pulled out a small pouch, spilling its contents into his hand. Three rough gemstones shone with an odd gray light. The very sight of them made Lothar feel uneasy.

"These will help the pair of you," Mason said. "The Surgeon gave them to me—shadestones, he called them. Each one contains a... helper of sorts. A creature that will aid you in the capture of Meleya and retrieval of the voidshard she keeps in her rift hold."

With that, Mason slid the sinister stones back into their pouch and shoved it Lothar's way. When Lothar didn't move to take it, Jaira did.

Mason continued. "Ilyan's omens say Meleya will soon leave obscurity, heading west. Best set traps all along the Mirror Forest's western boundary just to be safe."

Jaira nodded eagerly before hurrying back over to the stables. Meanwhile, Lothar grumbled something, which Mason took as approval.

"I really appreciate this, Lothar. You truly are my oldest friend." For just a moment, it seemed the old Mason, the *real* Mason, was back.

Then just as quickly, he snapped back, sincerity exchanged for disconnected ambition.

The High Prince clapped twice. "Now, make haste! Our journeys begin."

With that, Mason hurried toward where Jax and Bjorn stood. Mason's navy drake, Cosmos, awaited him, while Bjorn sat atop a third ascension drake of his own. No doubt it had been borrowed from the capital, the creature's heartscale forcibly taken.

Meanwhile, as Jax took his place in Jade's saddle, the mighty green evren was looking at Lothar with deep disappointment in her dragonfire eyes. Disappointment, but not surprise.

"I had no choice," Lothar mouthed to her.

Jade responded with thunder to his mind. *Wrong. I know what it's like to truly have no choice.*

Lothar felt sick to his stomach as Jade and her party took to the skies, heading east toward Evyndale.

Meanwhile, Jaira had emerged from the dragon stables once more. Lothar started—She wasn't alone. Two mighty third ascension dragons flanked her, and Jaira held two heartscales on leather cords in her hand.

"This one's mine," Jaira said, tying a sage green scale around her neck. The wyvern to her right growled in his throat, crouching low as Jaira forced him to kneel. She gave a cold smile as she mounted the dragon.

"It's only right I get Cenrik's old dragon too," Jaira chuckled. "Plus, Luster is a Lightwielder, like me. As for you, Lothar..."

Jaira held out the other heartscale. This one was a rich shade of brown to match the other wyvern, a majestic creature with deep pain in her dragonfire green eyes.

"You should count yourself lucky," Jaira said, still holding the heartscale necklace out to Lothar. "She once belonged to a King—the late King Axel of Rengard. She won't speak to anyone, but Lantha's her name, I think."

Lothar thought he'd recognized the sad, beautiful wyvern. Guilt coursed through him, but he was in too deep to turn back now.

Sorrow in his heart, Lothar took Lantha's heartscale and tied it around his neck.

FRAGMENT: CHAINED

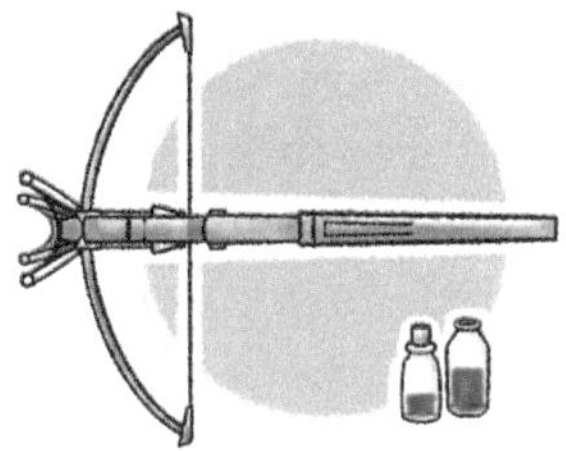

KARI

Kari had always been chained to her workbench... just never quite like this.

The heavy, silvery-gray iron cuff held snug around her ankle as she swung her hammer in a rhythmic beat, pounding a bar of glowing hot metal on the anvil before her. She needed to be precise with her timing in order to get the shape exactly right.

Suddenly, an earsplitting yell shattered Kari's focus.

"Dragonfire in the hole!"

Boom!

The workshop instantly filled with goldish-white smoke so thick Kari couldn't see her own hand in front of her face. She coughed, waving an arm around to try and get it to disperse. In the process, she had to abandon the beautiful strip of metal she'd been working on.

"Enya," Kari scolded. "Maybe give a little warning next time before blowing up the workshop?"

Enya's voice rose through the fog. "Why you think I done hollered 'dragonfire in the hole' before I lit 'er up?"

Kari sighed and shook her head. When the Farseer had sent her little brother Kai and his best friend, Asher, away on a mission, Kari had been excited to not have to play babysitter for once. But it turned out that working with Enya in the ancient skyforge of Orothion came with a whole new set of challenges. Squinting through the smoke, Kari went to her chalkboard tracker labeled 'days without explosion' and reset it to zero.

"So much for explosive crossbows," Kari said, grabbing her checklist and crossing that idea off. "Maybe the cannonbolt will be more successful—Be right back, Enya. Clean this up, will you?"

"Yes, boss!" Kari's apprentice said, tossing the ringed tail of her trademark draccoon-skin cap over her shoulder. There was a clinking sound as Enya's chain dragged across the floor. She, too, was a prisoner. A known 'Rebel' Knight being forced to serve those here in Skygard.

With smoke-smudged cheeks, Enya grabbed a bellows to try and clear the smoke. It was inefficient and slow-going, but Kari had bigger things to worry about. Lady Vesta herself was coming to inspect Kari's work any moment now, and if she didn't have any working prototypes ready this time, Kari knew there'd be trouble.

It wasn't like Kari was *purposefully* delaying the completion of her projects for Lady Vesta.

She was just...

Okay, she was *absolutely* delaying. The longer Kari put off finishing the lineup of deadly weapons designs, the less likely those weapons were to be... well, deadly. Kari normally loved coming up with new and interesting designs, especially for crossbows. But she hated the idea that her work would be mass produced and used to end hundreds of lives in the Knights of the Torch's war with the Evgardian Capital. So she'd focused the majority of her time on making the less-lethal designs actually function. They were tricky, but hopefully those would tempt Lady Vesta enough to grant her more time.

It hadn't been easy remaining behind when Solrac and the other Rebels had been forced to flee Orothion. A big part of why Kari volunteered was because the thought of leaving her tools and works-in-progress had been too much to bear. For a while, Kari had played her part well, feeding the Rebels information from the inside. But when the Triarchy had discovered Kari's mirror copy of Glint the mindlink gecko, they'd wasted no time using silver to squash the poor ethereal familiar. They'd chained Kari up after that.

Kari and Enya weren't the only Rebels still here, either. More than once, Vesta had threatened to hurt Akayto if Kari didn't meet her demands. Kari hadn't seen the man who was like her second father in weeks, and she could only hope he was alright.

Hope, and work.

Chain dragging behind her, Kari left the workshop and headed into the grand, central skyforge. All the smiths here at Orothion shared the spacious forge, as well as the glorious, triangular, dragonfire furnace inside.

The skyforge was everything Kari could've hoped for and more. Built during the Guardian era, an intricate metal framework formed a massive dome overhead. The dome was made from what Kari suspected was some sort of starglass alloy that darkened during the day to keep the light even throughout the forge, but became clear at night so you could perfectly see the stars. Skystone infusion powered it, and if Kari hadn't been so busy, she could've spent weeks studying it.

"How are those blackfire bolts coming, Daro?" Kari asked, joining her smithing partner at the furnace. He saw her coming and pulled a piece of glowing metal from the emerald flames.

"Really well," Daro replied, hitting the cylinder of metal with a few precise blows of his hammer. He set it down to cool then removed his protective mask, revealing thick black hair falling over his eye. As usual, Daro's muscular build and good looks distracted Kari from the work, at least for a second.

Likewise, Daro took a moment to give Kari an approving glance. They'd been drawn to each other ever since the Knights had assigned them to work together in the skyforge. With both of them so invested in their work, the on-again-off-again relationship suited them both nicely.

Still, Daro wasn't chained the way Kari and Enya were. He, like so many others here, hadn't fought back when Vesta had sent Solrac and the Rebels running for their lives.

"I figured out how to get the capsules to only burst on impact, releasing the shadowfire onto the target," Daro explained, gesturing to the crossbow bolt shaft he'd been working on. "You were right—the key was adjusting the placement of the liquid shadow capsule to the front of the bolt shaft, and letting the bolt's head recoil on impact to crush the capsule inside."

"Brilliant," Kari said, picking up one of the hollowed pieces of thin crystal they had sitting on a workbench near Daro's workstation. "If we strengthen the back end of the capsule and make it conical on the inside, that'll minimize the chances that it bursts prematurely, and maximize the chance it explodes toward the enemy."

"Great idea," Daro agreed.

Kari was torn, part of her thrilled to see the progress, but dismayed to see it in one of her more lethal projects.

They finished making the tweaks to their prototype crossbow bolts just as Vesta and Zel, two of the current Triarchy's sitting members, made their way to the duo's place in the skyforge. Lady Vesta's expression was as hard as ever as she narrowed her eyes over her Geomancer's silvermark. She looked as if she'd rather be anywhere but here.

"What's with all the smoke?" she asked, nodding toward the open door of Kari's workshop. She wrinkled her nose. "Is this a forge or a cheap sauna for anvils?"

In contrast, Zel was beaming, his bright smile adding hundreds more wrinkles to his aged face. He wore a Shadowbinder's silvermark, and waved eagerly at them. Kari couldn't help but wave back. She wondered what kind of blackmail Vesta must've had on Zel to get him to go along with her plans. Then again, maybe the kindly old half-born was just starting to go senile.

"Hello there, bright young inventors! We are so excited to see what you've come up with today!" Zel said, his dragonfire green eyes bright.

Vesta rolled her eyes. "Let's get on with it already. We just shipped out another squadron of soldiers this morning. By the time we send out the next one, I'd like to see them armed with weapons that'll make those drakked Capital Riders look like a pack of witless drakalope."

"Right." Kari cleared her throat as she began to explain the mechanics of her and Daro's shadowfire crossbow bolt, but Vesta cut her off.

"Blah blah blah. I don't need a tour of your obsessive compulsive mind, inventor. Does it work or not?"

"Yes," Kari replied shortly.

"We *must* have a demonstration," Zel said, clapping his hands. "Best way to win folks over is by way of a good demonstration. Vesta?"

Vesta's jaw tightened. She knew what Zel was asking as well as Kari did.

"Alright then," Vesta grumbled as Zel gestured for a group of soldiers standing guard outside the forge to join them. One soldier bent down, carefully unlocking Kari's chain. Another did the same for Enya as she emerged from the forge.

But the freedom from the chains wasn't real freedom at all. Not when the soldiers stood at Kari's and Enya's backs, ready to step in the second they tried anything. Not that either of the young women would dare. They were innovators, not fighters.

Vesta led the whole group up a set of stairs coiling around the forge's outer wall, then through a door that led to the terrace. From here, Kari could hear the sea raging far below, off the edge of the cliff.

The terrace above the skyforge was magnificent. The enormous gold-and-starglass dome's exterior stood proudly in the terrace's center, glinting in the noonday sun. The terrace was set on Orothion's tallest tower, and had stairs leading up to the rampart that was the castle's southern point. That was where the lighthouse stood. It was a marvelous contraption, lighting the way for ships by way of a pyre and adjacent modular reflector—a large, round disk of reflective metal. Kari cast it a wistful glance. Yet another mechanical triumph she wished she could study rather than pour her skills into weapon-making.

A feral snarl sounded across the terrace. There at the base of the rampart stood an iron cage. Inside, their test subject.

The drekling's hunched, bipedal form was thin and weak, its body riddled with bruises and scrapes. Its scaled, draconic nostrils were flared with rage as it scurried back at the sight of Kari and the others. The beast's eyes were bloodshot, accentuating the dragonfire green of its diamond-shaped irises. Thick, shimmering, black ropes infused with Zel's shadowbinding wound around the creature's wrists at the ends of its too-long arms.

Beside the cage was a man with posture nearly as hunched as the drekling's. He had a twitching eye and a Psion's silvermark on his left cheek.

"Ah, there you are, my esteemed colleagues," the man said, wringing his hands together.

"Afternoon to you too, Signus, my old friend!" Zel gave a jolly wave.

Vesta was less enthusiastic as she greeted the third member of the Triarchy—the Mystic who they had appointed to replace Solrac. "Up here harassing the drakked drekling again?"

Signus shrugged. "I didn't want to miss today's demonstration."

There was a pause, and Zel gave Vesta a little nod. She cleared her throat.

"Let's get on with it then," Vesta said. Then she nodded to Kari.

Kari's palms began to sweat as she held the blackfire bolt crossbow. She and Daro exchanged glances, and she passed it to him.

Daro took aim and pulled the trigger. Just as they'd hoped, the thin crystal capsule in the dart exploded onto the drekling on impact. Black shadowfire tore across its scales, and the creature roared with rage.

But before the shadowfire could eat too deeply into its flesh, the shimmering shadow ropes activated. The drekling's body phase-shifted, becoming as shadow while the weapon's fire dissipated, leaving the beast scarred but alive.

Kari winced as she spoke. "These blackfire bolts can be launched from roughly the same distance as a regular crossbow bolt. The shadowfire should work well at disintegrating the scales of the Capital Riders' mounts without requiring much retraining on the part of your soldiers, if any at all."

"Impressive," Vesta said. "What else have you got, inventor?"

Enya looked into the large, weapons-filled crate Daro had brought up from Kari's workshop. "We ain't got explosive crossbows, I can tell y'all that," she said, pointing to the smoke smudges streaked across her cheeks.

"Another so-called 'failure'?" Vesta folded her arms, narrowing her eyes Kari's way. "You're not stalling again, right, Rebel wannabe?"

Thinking of Akayto, Kari rushed to reassure her. "No, I swear I'm working as efficiently as is reasonable. The explosive crossbow is obviously still a work in progress, but we have several functional prototypes for other crossbow upgrades."

"Of course you do!" Zel chimed in cheerfully. "You are doing wonderfully, my dear. Vesta's just upset they ran out of draquila in the kitchens today. She does love her afternoon drink, don't you, Vesta?"

Zel gave a wide, cheesy grin. Vesta was practically seething as she mumbled something borderline unintelligible about Zel's red scale-tipped ears from the corner of her mouth.

"Right then," she finally managed. "What's next?"

The demonstrations continued. The drekling hated being ensnared in the net launcher, but far worse was the Dreambolter. The heavy head of its multi-component bolt first hit a sheet of silver—melted down from an old Mage Hunter's pauldron to be used in exhibitions like this one. The physical bolt got lodged in the silver, but pierced it deeply enough that it allowed the ethereal component to activate past the silver.

A conical, violet blast of stored dream energy burst from a chamber within the bolt's head to hit the drekling in the leg. That dropped it onto its back, twitching and unconscious.

"Scorch," Daro cursed. "It wasn't supposed to be potent enough to knock it out—especially while it's wearing the phase-shifting ropes."

"Exactly," Kari agreed with a frown. "I'll have to decrease the amount of liquid ether in the amplification chamber. I hate to think what it might've done if the blast had hit the drekling in the head or heart."

"No need to worry about that now, poor dear," Zel said, trying to raise Kari's spirits. "What's next?"

"Just one more," Kari said. "The Dreamdart Repeater. While the Dreambolter fires a single, concentrated dreamweave blast, this one can fire a sequence of dreamdarts that pass through any non-silver enemy armor and drain them of energy, no physical crossbow bolts required."

"Demonstrate," Vesta said. The dazed drekling had just gotten up, its eyes unfocused. It was miserable.

Reluctantly, Kari handed the invention to Daro. It was a sleek, full metal crossbow, with runemarked crystals at each end of its bow, and a larger one on the stock above the trigger where a bolt would normally go. It had no bowstring, but as Daro charged it, the two runemarked crystals at the end of the bow sent jets of dream energy into the central crystal. The violet energy coalesced there, ready to be fired off as dreamdarts.

Daro rapidly unloaded five dreamdarts into the wretched creature. Though this was Kari's least lethal design—dreamweave energy couldn't kill, it only drained an opponent's energy—the beast was already so worn down that Kari could see the will to live leaving its eyes with each successive hit. The awful Signus laughed, but Kari wilted at the sight of it.

"Enough," Vesta called over the drekling's tired, anguished roar. "It's drakking perfect. Make enough for the whole scorched army." Then she turned away, toward the door that led back to the skyforge.

Zel lingered, placing a frail, wrinkled hand on Kari's shoulder. "Don't worry, dear. Vesta is harsh, but you have done well. Your blind friend, Akayto, will be safe, I promise you."

Kari bit her lip. "Why don't you stand up to Vesta, Zel? You must know this is wrong."

Zel gave a sigh, his permanent smile faltering for only a moment. "Sometimes we must suffer a little now to get to what is right down the line. I'm sorry, my dear, but my hands are tied."

With that, Zel headed back into the skyforge, Signus and Daro close behind.

When Kari and Enya didn't move to follow right away, the soldiers at their backs tensed, ready to make them move.

"I'm a comin'," Enya complained. "Don't get your scales in a twist."

As half the soldiers escorted Enya back to the workshop and her chains, Kari wondered: How much longer could they do this? Kari hated being an instrument for darkness, but she couldn't let them harm Akayto. Likewise, Kari couldn't help but wonder what awful tasks Vesta was forcing Akayto to perform with his rifting, likely using threats to *Kari's* life. It was all such a mess. Knights of the Torch were supposed to be brave servants of light, protectors of the realm. Not perpetuators of bloodshed.

Twang!

The noise pulled Kari's attention back to the drekling's cage. It turned out Vesta hadn't left after all, and now, thanks to her, a smoking blackfire bolt jutted out of the remains of the beast inside.

She'd removed the phase-shifting ropes. The drekling lay perfectly still, finally at rest.

From across the terrace, Kari and Vesta locked eyes. Then Vesta left without another word.

GLINT

T here was much to keep track of.

Glint didn't mind this. Gathering data was what Glint was created for.

That was why today's daily Glint check-in was extra important—Today, Kai and the others would be departing on their quest.

Glint Prime, Kai's original mirror gecko familiar, sat perched atop Kai's extra-large shoulder pauldron. Kai was in his room at the safehouse, going through his packing list for perhaps the eighth time that day.

Kai was busy. This was fine. Glint could run the check-in all on her own.

First was Glint One. Color: Red. Assignment: Solrac, Duke of Glacia (Male, forties, Psion. Notes: Secretive and dangerously optimistic).

Calling Glint One, the original Glint sent a pulse through her network of mirror copies.

Here, Glint One pulsed back, and Glint felt a tiny tingle in her webbed feet.

Data report, Glint ordered.

Solrac is in a meeting with the other members of the Rebel Triarchy, Glint One answered rigidly. *They discuss the significance of the upcoming quest. Would you like a full report on my observations so far, or a summary?*

Summary. Definitely summary. Glint thought back. Glint One tended to get long-winded.

They have discussed the need to rally the support of other Keepdoms, Glint One began. *They already know that the Queen of Behrfell will not break her neutrality unless they successfully end Vesta's war with Evgard and reunite the Knights of the Torch. Meanwhile, the Farseer plans to visit the King and Queen of Evyndale to see where they stand while Solrac visits with Ilona, the Queen of Rengard.*

Glint nodded along as she organized the data in her mind. She would share the simplified information with Kai so that he would not become overwhelmed.

Additionally, Glint One went on, *the Triarchy council discussed something possessed by one of the team members questing to Orothion and whether or not this item would pose a threat.*

What is this item? Glint asked.

It is called a voidshard. A voidshard belonging to the Soul Reaper, safeguarded within the rift hold of the team's travel specialist. Evidence suggests that objects kept in an ethereal space are more difficult to track down or foresee via omen-fires. The best chance of keeping the voidshard from falling into the hands of the Soul Reaper is to let it remain exactly where it is. Currently, Meleya is the only Rifter among the Rebel Knights, so is the only one capable of producing a rift hold. It will be safest with her. The Triarchy plans to inform Kai of all this before departing on the quest.

Very good. Requesting visual for our records.

Sending visual.

Immediately, Glint One's perspective played out across Glint's mind. She was perched beside a stuffed squirrel on a shelf behind where Solrac sat in the cabin's secret war council chamber. Beside Solrac were two others. The first was Cenrik (Male, thirties, former Lightwielder. Notes: Competent and religious).

And the second...

Glint zeroed in on the young woman with wavy brown hair and a freckled face. At the sight of her, Glint could not resist a knowing chuckle.

It was Solvai of Keep Rengard (Female, eighteen, Wildshaper. Notes: Kai thinks about Solvai at least one-hundred-twenty-six percent more than any other person. Said thoughts are largely recreational rather than practical. Kai finds Solvai both compelling and observant, wholly deserving of her seat on the Triarchy. Also, he finds her rather attractive).

This pleased Glint. Kai had a tendency to overthink. But with Solvai, his thoughts took a backseat to his emotions. This was good for Kai.

Since her arrival at the safehouse, Glint had spent a fair bit of time casually observing Solvai's thoughts. Only surface thoughts; Glint would never pry unless it was necessary, at Kai's order on behalf of the Knights. But she'd gleaned enough to know that Solvai enjoyed Kai's company as well. Solvai had long felt overlooked beside her dynamic friends, but Kai truly *saw* her.

Glint found it all tremendously adorable.

Glint stored the image of the Triarchy council's meeting in her mental databases. Before moving on with the daily Glint check-in, Glint asked, *I assume Solrac's mental blocks are still in place?*

As expected, Glint One answered in the affirmative. Solrac had some of the most impressive mental wards Glint had ever encountered. Likely from some kind of Seer relic. Glint had searched for said relic, but had never found one, so Glint was not sure exactly how he managed it. What she did know was that there was no way she or any of her fellow Glints was getting into Solrac's thoughts unnoticed.

This was a pity. Glint was ninety-seven percent certain that Solrac's innermost thoughts would be utterly fascinating. Particularly since the unexpected arrival of the Black Valkyrie, or rather, Solrac's former lover, Vidya (Female, forties, Psion-slash-Shadowbinder-slash-Wildshaper. Notes: Dangerous).

Glint had noted much concerning the romantic tension between Solrac and the two ladies in his life, Vidya and Valla (Female, thirties, Wildshaper. Notes: Loyal, skilled, and also dangerous). Glint would not dream of sharing notes of this nature with her creator, Kai. Kai did not care for tales of excessively entangled romance and epic drama, anyway. These notes were solely for Glint's personal enjoyment.

Glint *lived* for the intrigue.

Valla's recent departure left Glint feeling terribly curious. What had happened between her and Solrac to make her leave after all these years? Glint Seven was assigned to Valla and might have insight. Glint nearly broke protocol to request Glint Seven's report early.

But of course, she stopped herself. Break protocol? Glint was not a barbarian.

Glint watched through Glint One's eyes as someone else joined the Triarchy at their meeting.

"Ah, come in, Princess Eliana," Cenrik beckoned for the newcomer to join them.

Glint's ears pricked at the sight of Eliana, Princess of Drakfell (Female, eighteen, non-magi. Notes: Has the least smelly boots among all of the Glints' assigned humans).

Eliana appeared surprised when the first thing Cenrik did was offer an apology.

"I'm sorry for hurting your feelings at the council meeting regarding the quest," Cenrik said.

Glint watched with interest as Elle spoke boldly. "You mean when you called me a figurehead?"

"Yes. I did not mean to cause offense. I was—I *am*—only trying to respect the wishes of a King—and a father."

Elle raised an eyebrow.

Solrac chimed in. "Your father, King Rodan of Drakfell, has written to the Triarchy. His situation is a precarious one. He writes that while his true loyalties lie with the Farseer and those of us deemed Rebels, he must play his part to keep the peace with Lady Vesta and the Knights at Orothion. The last thing he wants is war with Skygard on top of his betrayal of the High Throne."

Elle nodded. Glint noted.

"King Rodan also brings up a few concerns about you," Cenrik continued. "Concerns I share. He asks that we take every precaution to ensure your safety, since, while he does not doubt your skill in a fight, he reminds us that your practical experience has been limited."

Glint sensed Elle squirm at that. While Glint did not relish breaking protocol, she *did* value gathering complete data. Glints Two through Seven would have to wait their turn.

Calling Glint Eight, Glint Prime sent out a pulse to her counterpart assigned to Elle.

Here! Glint Eight replied right away.

Requesting insight regarding Eliana's opinions surrounding the current interaction with the Rebel Triarchy.

Connecting with Eliana now.

Glint Eight subtly tapped Eliana's consciousness and flooded the network with Elle's thoughts. The princess felt that if she was inexperienced, it was her father's fault. There was a reason she'd had to disguise herself as a dragon keeper's assistant just to escape the court every once in a while. Her Uncle Aradan, on the opposite scale, had always encouraged her.

When Elle thought of her Uncle Aradan, Glint noted the worry surrounding her thoughts. When Glint asked Glint Eight for possible reasons for this worry, she responded with efficiency:

In Elle's most recent letter from her mother, she learned that her Uncle Aradan has gone missing. Not even his wife and children know where he is. Elle wonders if her father's anxiety regarding his brother's disappearance is the reason he writes to the Rebel Triarchy now.

Noted, Glint thought with concern.

Solrac continued speaking, seeming more aware of Elle's feelings than Cenrik was. "King Rodan assumes the blame for your situation, in part. After all, he was the one to take the true dragon egg from the Drekai in the first place."

"But what's done is done—you *are* the true dragon rider," Cenrik said, and Glint sensed a note of regret in his tone. "It is up to you to lead the realm out of darkness."

Elle swallowed. "I intend to."

Cenrik went on. "Your involvement in the quest is our attempt to both increase the Rebel Knights' support *and* keep you safe. Surrounded by a capable team, you'll still be visible to the realm, but no longer so near the Mage Hunter's base. That said, I would ask you to watch yourself. I see my younger self in you—impulsive, a taker of risks. But such a disposition cost me much in the end."

Cenrik absently reached toward his chest, and Elle wasn't sure if he was talking about the loss of his ether well or his dragon's heartscale. Probably both.

Cenrik sighed. "All I'm asking is that you stay focused on the task at hand. Recruit, stick to Kai's schedule, and default to Solvai's command." Cenrik paused, looking to Solvai, who nodded solemnly to Elle.

"Become the icon the realm needs," Cenrik finished. "Be Eliana, true dragon rider for the people."

The Triarchy dismissed Elle, and Glint took a moment to store this new data in her mind. She would synthesize that which would matter to Kai and keep the rest to herself.

Now, back to protocol.

Next on the list was Glint Two. Color: Orange. Assignment: Kari of Steel Rim (Female, nineteen, non-magi. Notes: Kai's sister and expert inventor).

Glint already knew she was unlikely to get a response from Glint Two, seeing as Glint Two was currently... well, dead. In stasis? Un-summoned?

What *was* the ethereal familiar equivalent of death, after all?

Glint paused, staring into oblivion for a moment as she contemplated her own existence.

Moving on.

Glint then focused on Glint Three. Color: Yellow. Assignment: Jax of Blackfjord (Male, nineteen, Psion. Notes: Muscles, bandana, arrogant).

Those were Kai's notes. But Glint had observed a different side of Jax.

In particular, Glint *Three* saw a different side of Jax.

No irregular activity to report, Glint Three responded to the call with notes of sadness. *I remain at my post in the terrarium in Jax's room at the Mage Hunter Academy, though Jax is no longer here. I worry. Still, before his departure he placed my habitat in a very well-lit area and left me with a very large supply of spiny crickets.*

Delicious, Glint thought back. *Hang in there, Glint Three.*

Glint Three let out a tiny croak before she began munching on a spiny cricket.

Next was Glint Four. Color: Green. Assignment: Asher of Steel Rim (Male, eighteen, Astromancer. Notes: Kai's best friend and resident loose cannon).

As usual, Glint Four seemed jumpy and on-edge. Glint could not blame her. Being assigned to Asher was quite the task. Currently, she was scuttling across the yard in search of her assignment so she could take her usual place inside his boot. He'd run off before Glint Four had been able to situate herself this morning.

Report pending! Glint Four huffed.

Noted, Glint replied. Glint Four deserved a vacation.

Glints Five and Six, colored blue and indigo, were assigned to Boone of the Bramblewilds (Male, sixties?, Astromancer. Notes: Superstitious, exceedingly difficult to interpret), and Ivar of Stonekeep (Male, forties, Psion. Notes: Has a kleptomaniacal draccoon familiar).

Both Glints reported that the Rebel army's daily training was going well. Despite the High King's proclamation that the Knights' true dragon rider was the realm's most wanted outlaw, every day it seemed more recruits wanted to join her forces.

Next was Glint Seven. Color: Violet. Assignment: Valla of White Cliff (Further notes: Harbinger of weapons, grumpiness, and unrequited love).

That last part was Glint's personal note, not Kai's.

Glint Seven was in that strange space-between-spaces where ethereal familiars went when they were in a Wildshaper's pocket during a shift. Valla was in polar wolf form, but Glint was still connected to her consciousness. Kai had once spent an entire day and a half trying to comprehend the intricacies of that particular phenomenon, but since such a case was so specific, there were no texts with much to say on the matter. Perhaps one day Kai would write such a tome himself.

Valla raced across the snowy wastes of northern Behrfell, the icy winds cutting over her thick white fur. She moved so quickly she barely left tracks, a lone wolf on a mission.

Following both leads from other Rebel Knights and her own senses, Valla's search for the fabled Everflame was taking her far from civilization. She hadn't spent the night in a real town for a week now.

Calling Glint Seven, Glint channeled through the network. *Requesting status report.*

Glint Seven's reply came in muddled. *Valla continues... on her journey toward... Should reach the northernmost... in a matter of days...*

The hazy connection interested Glint. Perhaps the Glints had at last discovered the limit to their range? Or was something else affecting their communications?

Noted. She would alert Kai of this at some point. Not yet, as he was quite busy with his preparations for the quest. This was only a 'two' on the urgency scale, after all. Besides, Glint worried that Kai would become overly concerned regarding this finding since Valla was on the same mission his parents had been on when they went missing.

Across the Glint network, the Glints shared a moment of silence for their creator's parents.

The moment of silence was brief, of course. Glint was in the middle of the daily Glint check-in. And she was not a barbarian.

Report ready now! came Glint Four's sudden thought. *Asher located!*

Proceed, Glint Four.

Asher is joining the rest of the quest team in the dragon stables. It is not yet time for departure, but it is close.

Excellent, Glint replied. *Requesting visual.* Kai would want Glint to ensure that each member of the team was appropriately prepared.

Glint Four's perspective bloomed over the Glint network.

Four young adults stood in the stables. Glint observed Asher as he flashed the group the expected asymmetrical smile.

"I know Kai'll be going over his supplies right up until the last minute," Asher teased, "but don't tell me you three are still packing too."

The first to respond to Asher's quip was Meleya of Misthaven (Female, seventeen, Rifter. Notes: Possibly Asher's bane, makes delicious fry bread).

"Don't tell me you haven't even started packing," Meleya said, looking Asher over. He carried no pack, no satchel, nothing.

"The land has everything I need," Asher said, though Glint knew his satchel was already stowed in Thorn's saddlebags. Packed *light*, but still packed.

"Classic Asher," said Elle, arriving on the scene.

Glint Eight, Glint called for the final white gecko's report. *Any updates?*

None since Elle left the Triarchy, Glint Eight replied. Then she slyly added, *Although, I can confirm that she is experiencing above average levels of emotion while observing Asher.*

Aww, various Glints chorused. The Glints had rather enjoyed observing Asher and Eliana's relationship unfold. Glint had been both heartbroken and intrigued when Eliana had rejected Asher after waiting so long for him to be ready for a relationship. A slightly deeper—and confidential, of course—dig into Eliana's consciousness had made Glint aware of a certain secret encounter between the princess and the General of the Drekai army. Glint's toes tingled just thinking about the drama surrounding poor Eliana, and that didn't even include—

"Gauntlet down: We should all be better about living off the land more."

—Brigan, Heir Duke of Solhelm (Male, eighteen, non-magi. Notes: Heir to the fourth house of the Canyonlands. Intellectual, talks a lot). Otherwise known as Eliana's former betrothed.

Glint let out the gecko equivalent of a giggle. This journey was bound to be interesting.

Meleya confronted Asher. "You're saying the *land* is going to provide you with a clean change of socks?"

"Sure." Asher shrugged. "The land and I go way back."

"So far back it knits for you?"

"It probably could. But typically it sticks to simpler things like rivers for washing this pair of socks out." Asher stuck out a foot toward Meleya.

"I know you're a nomadic desert scrub, but surely you've heard of a river, right Mel?"

Meleya narrowed her eyes. "If you don't have a backup pair, what're you planning to wear while those socks dry out?"

"I guess I'd have no choice but to..." Asher mockingly gasped, "go barefoot! Ever seen a half-born's toes? They look just like a human's toes—"

Everyone looked to Asher, clearly expecting him to say 'but' and continue speaking. It quickly became apparent that his sentence was over.

Brigan burst into laughter. Meleya's glare intensified.

"Immature son of a dragonmutt," Meleya said.

"Stuffy scale-in-the mud," Asher countered without hesitation.

"Scarfity scarf-wearer person," Meleya responded.

"That's *still* the best you've got?"

Frustrated, both Asher and Meleya turned away from each other. Still, Glint caught a hint of a smile playing at each of their lips.

Possible inside joke detected, Glint noted.

Meanwhile, Eliana watched the interaction with... confusion? Discontent? Perhaps a hint of... suspicion?

Defeatism, Glint Eight added, subtly tapping into the princess's thoughts. *Longing. Eliana remains mellow after the warning from the Triarchy council to keep her instincts in check. She must maintain a noble gait and behave with extra propriety on this quest, and wishes she were more free—like Asher and Meleya.*

Noted, Glint noted.

Eliana also recognizes the objective truth that Asher's black hair contrasts nicely with Meleya's white.

Very much noted, Glint further noted. *She is correct about this.*

Glint was so engrossed in the scene that she barely noticed that Kai was on the move. Before long, she'd joined Glint Four, Glint Eight, and the others in the dragon stables. Solvai, too, arrived, and Glint noted the exchange of secret smiles with giddiness.

"We should get going," Kai said to the group, eyes glued to the miniscule notes he'd scribbled in his black leather notebook, "if we're going to make it to Ashfalcon Point by this evening."

"Wait—" Meleya stepped up. "First, does everyone have their personal belongings? I'm talking clothing, hygiene items, bedrolls, cloaks, and heartscales."

Without hesitation, Solvai and Brigan replied with a resounding, "Yes, Meleya." The others tapped their chins, trying to decide if they were missing anything.

Meleya went on, "Do you have your primary weapons? Spears, seaxes, sabers, etcetera?"

"Yes, Meleya," Solvai and Brigan answered first, but Eliana caught on as well. Asher looked on, clearly amused, while Kai scanned his notebook, a troubled look on his face. Glint could sense that he was used to being the only preparer in the group, and he was not sure if he liked being upstaged.

"How about your backup weapons?" Meleya asked.

"Yes, Meleya," the group replied together. All except Asher, who answered with a mocking, "Yes, Mother." Meleya ignored this.

After Meleya had distributed labeled sacks of snacks, gotten Brigan and Asher to refill their canteens, and sent Eliana, Solvai, and Kai to relieve themselves, the group was finally ready for departure.

Still, as they left the dragon stables, Glint noted that Asher could not help but launch a small starglass sphere at the back of Meleya's head. When she whirled on him, he feigned innocence. She narrowed her eyes, but Glint sensed a strange sort of magnetism between them.

Glint wondered...

As Glint watched Asher and Meleya go, she could not help but give a little gecko grin.

Yes, she thought. *This journey is going to be very interesting indeed.*

The other Glints replied to the observation in unison:

Noted.

CHAPTER 21: LEIF

ASHER

The wind cut across my face, pulling my hair free from its knot as Thorn and I soared over the Mirror Forest. The open air was as cool and refreshing as ever, the scent of sap and smoke rising off of the cindercone pines below. Higher we flew, giving me the perfect view of the series of lakes below reflecting the blue sky.

Interrupting the majesty of it all was a constant stream of frustrated mutterings as Kai held onto my waist. When Solrac had shown up at the dragon stables to wish us well on our quest, he'd informed Kai that our mode of transportation would require traveling as light as possible. That included Kai shedding his excessive plate armor.

"But Brigan's bringing his armor," Kai had complained.

"Brigan's armor is not superfluous," Solrac had said with a grin.

"Superfluous?"

"A wholly unnecessary, unfashionable waste of time, yes." Solrac had nodded eagerly. "You are incredibly useful in a fight, Kai, what with your vast knowledge and skill with illusions, but let us be honest. If you got close enough to an opponent that your plate armor would come in handy, you would not stand a chance against such a foe anyway. That said…"

With characteristic ceremony, Solrac produced a parcel wrapped in brown paper and handed it to Kai.

"What's this?" Kai had asked.

"A little gift for a budding young Seer." Solrac's eyes had twinkled.

Kai had unwrapped the package to find a set of tailored robes in a dusty shade of red. The tunic came to just below his knees and featured several hidden pockets filled with runemarked quartz crystals for storing extra ether.

It was *by far* the most stylish thing Kai had ever owned. Grumbling all the while, he'd removed his plate armor in favor of the robe. I could tell he secretly liked the way he looked in it, though he'd continued to have a bad attitude as we prepared to leave. As it turned out, we also needed to limit the number of dragons joining us on our journey. That meant Kai had been forced to say goodbye to his dragon, Flint, in order to ride behind me.

Meanwhile, Brigan had bid his dragon, Bolt, farewell too. Bolt was a wingless drake, and while those were great to have around for a fight, this journey was definitely one for flyers. Brigan sat in the saddle behind Meleya as Sniff zigzagged through the air below us just for fun. Second ascension sure looked good on Sniff.

I could just make out a tiny, brown bird clinging to Sniff's saddle in front of Meleya. That was Solvai in ridgebacked wren form, hiding from the wind and doing more than any of the rest of us to lighten the load.

At the head of the group was Eliana, her dark hair streaming out behind her and contrasting against her bright white armored dress and Aurora's white scales. At least, that's what I saw. In addition to muttering complaints, Kai was running a complicated illusion to keep our party all-but-invisible to anyone below. It was the same etherarchy he'd performed the day we'd robbed Swan Spire, masking our dragons' underbellies to look like the bright blue sky.

Orothion was hundreds of miles away from Rhana's cabin in Evyndara. Normally, it would take a long time to travel there, even on dragonback.

But normally, people didn't travel with a Rifter.

"Ready, Meleya?" Eliana's voice floated on the wind.

I saw Meleya squint into the distance. "A little higher!" she called back. The three dragons obliged.

Once Meleya was satisfied, she focused on a far point in the west. Then she runetraced, a large portal opening up before us. I could see the other end as a smallish, gold-rimmed speck with a black interior.

"Go ahead!" she called.

The others hesitated, but not me. At my encouragement, Thorn shot through the rift.

I whooped as we emerged about a hundred feet away. Elle and Aurora weren't far behind, followed by Sniff's group.

"Keep going!" Meleya yelled. I could see the concentration on her face as she activated the next set of portals.

Without wasting time, we shot through the next rift and the next. With each jump, my excitement grew. I'd seen skyskipper dragon migrations before, and had always been fascinated watching them rift across the sky, crossing vast spaces in relatively short amounts of time.

"Rifting is awesome!" I cried, throwing both hands up into the air. Kai wasn't happy about nearly getting jostled out of the saddle, but even he seemed impressed by Meleya's etherarchy.

Sniff was so excited about it he was flying loops. Meleya tried to calm him down as she did her best to shield little bird Solvai from getting launched into empty space. Meanwhile, Brigan clung on for dear life.

I grinned at the show. Through our bond, I teased Thorn, *Maybe Sniff and I should've bonded!*

Thorn's scaly shoulders shook with laughter. *As if the two of you together would survive one day. Pure chaos.*

Our party had just swept through our next set of portals when I caught sight of them: a series of tiny, floating spheres, littered high and low throughout the sky. At first, I figured they were nothing more than a trick of the light, but a second look let me see that each one was only about as big as my fist, and crackling with gold, lightning-like light.

"Are you guys seeing this?" I said, pointing to the spheres. They covered a pretty wide area, and we were right in the middle of it. "Kai?"

Before Kai could reply, Brigan shouted, "They look like revealing flares! We studied them at the Academy. They're similar to Lightwielder's torches—they're supposed to reveal illusions."

As Brigan explained it, the nearest revealing flare flashed, exploding in a blinding blaze. A wave of light rippled through our illusion, dissolving it on contact.

Kai cursed as he felt his etherarchy fail. "Soot! We're completely exposed!"

I gulped. "And it looks like we have company…"

I pointed northward, where a pair of dragon riders were winging their way toward us at high speeds. They wore dusky blue Mage Hunters' cloaks, and even at so great a distance, I thought I recognized the red hair on one and the thick eyebrows on the other.

Lothar and Jaira.

"We can lose them!" Eliana said, taking charge. "Meleya, get us out of here!"

Meleya rushed to trace another rune and another rift appeared. While most of her portals thus far had only taken us a hundred or so feet, I couldn't even see the other end of this one. I thought I saw a tiny pinprick of gold near the distant mountainside... Could that be the exit rift? I wasn't a Rifter myself, but I was certain I'd never seen even my dad make a jump that far. And *definitely* not for this many people.

Jaira and Lothar were nearly upon us, and I could see Jaira had some kind of open pouch in her hands. Who knew what other tricks they had up their sleeves?

"Go!" Meleya ordered.

Aurora led the way through the portal with Thorn hot on her wings. Just before we passed through, I extended my hand toward the Mage Hunters, digging deep to access my ether, and launched a double ether blast that solidified into starglass on contact with each of their wyvern's wings. Not enough to down them, but enough to sabotage their flight pattern. No way they'd be able to slip through Meleya's portal after us.

Still, as Jaira's wyvern veered off course, I thought I saw Jaira chuck something at the rift. It was hard to be sure, but it looked like a small, glowing gray stone. Thorn and I vanished through the portal before I could get a better look, Sniff tumbling through directly behind us.

This was by far the farthest jump yet. Sure enough, we emerged in the air above that mountain I'd seen, so far from Jaira and Lothar that I couldn't even see them through the clouds.

At first, I was thrilled. We'd done it!

Then, I gasped—Meleya was slumped over in Sniff's saddle. She dropped from the saddle so fast Brigan didn't have time to react.

I didn't think. Leaving Kai to fend for himself, I launched myself from Thorn's back, my eyes burning with golden etherlight. Hover-dashing in full force, I shot through the air like a comet to catch up to Meleya.

I caught her around the waist just before she hit the trees. The second she was securely in my arms, I reversed my levitation to slow our descent through the vibrant red-and-orange canopy of firemaple trees.

Despite my best efforts, several branches hit us on the way down. A few clumps of the crackling firemaple leaves caught fire as they rubbed together. Some singed us, but luckily most only smoldered, burning up before they hit the ground so that they didn't start forest fires.

When we touched down on the forest floor, I quickly laid Meleya on the ground to check that she was okay. Like me, she had a few minor burns and scratches from our less-than-smooth landing. Her thick black lashes fluttered madly as her eyelids struggled to open, as if she was battling unconsciousness. That jump must've drained her entire ether well.

My heart began to beat faster. "Mel?" She didn't respond. For a moment, I thought about shedding my ascension bracers and putting them on her. But regeneration powers couldn't heal an ether overuse headache.

From above, more firemaple leaves burned up as they fell, signaling the arrival of the rest of our team. They landed beside a particularly large, rounded pile of firemaple leaves, which shuddered as they disturbed it.

Eliana's hand flew to her heart as she looked at Meleya. "Is she alright?"

A gold cloud was just dissipating from around Solvai as she wildshaped back into human form. "Can you hear us, Meleya?"

"Mm..." Meleya tried to answer.

I learned that Sniff had *very* little sense of personal space as his huge draconic head appeared an inch from mine so that he could get a look at his rider. Brigan was right behind him, pushing me out of the way as he knelt on the ground beside Meleya. Gently, he helped her sit up, cradling her with one arm while using the other to rifle through his medical bag.

"Someone bring her canteen," Brigan said. "Best thing for quelling a Mystic's ether overuse headache is water. Let's see... I know I have a yarrow and scalebark compress in here somewhere."

I found the canteen in Sniff's saddlebag and passed it to Brigan. He was just helping Meleya drink when Kai gave an exasperated sigh.

"Those scorched Mage Hunters," Kai cursed. "How did they find us?"

"What do they want?" Eliana asked.

"M-me," Meleya managed, clutching her temples. "Shard."

"Don't try to talk," Brigan said.

"She means they're here for her," Solvai said. "They know she has the Soul Reaper's voidshard in her rift hold—Mason must've sent them to get it back."

"Voidshard?" I asked. I knew as much as the next Knight about the Soul Reaper at this point, and had even learned about the voidshards that magi with blue etherarchy used to make themselves more powerful. Stories about a Gray One overtaking Meleya had reached me too, but I didn't think she'd gone so far as to have a voidshard herself. Then again, it sounded like it wasn't hers.

"The Farseer said the voidshard wasn't going to be a problem," Kai said. "As long as we kept it locked up in Meleya's rift hold."

"He said it *probably* wasn't *likely* to *stop* us from reaching Orothion," Eliana corrected.

Kai pressed his lips together. "Ugh! Drakking omens." He glanced at his black notebook, then swore again. "With Meleya's ether well drained, we'll never reach Ashfalcon Point by nightfall."

Eliana tensed. "You mean we've lost the whole rest of the day?"

"Well, there's a chance we could make it if we pushed through on dragonback from here—"

I cut Kai off. "Are you kidding? We can't push through with Mel like this."

Meleya scowled as she continued drinking from the canteen. Brigan was pressing a cloth-wrapped compress to her head, and she was at least sort-of sitting up on her own now, but she was still very pale.

Eliana piped up, her tone flat and authoritative. "Of course we must consider both the urgency of our quest and the well-being of the members of our team. Surely we can strike a balance between the two."

"Surely we can..." I repeated, my exasperation growing. Elle was playing the diplomatic but distant noblewoman again. "I'm sorry, but your adoring fans at the Devilish Dragonmoose or whatever are gonna have to wait to have their babies kissed until our travel specialist can put two words together."

"Calm down, Asher," Eliana said, only *barely* not in need of her own advice.

"We'll have to rework the entire schedule now," Kai said. "Not to mention the fact that we now have to account for Mage Hunters on our tail."

"You don't think they could still be tracking us after a jump that big, right?" Eliana asked. She and Kai started talking through the ramifications of Jaira and Lothar's trap.

Meanwhile, Solvai was speaking to Brigan.

"Did you recognize the brown wyvern too?" Solvai's forehead was creased.

"Lantha." Brigan nodded. "And if I'm not mistaken, the one Jaira rode was Luster, Captain Cenrik's bond."

Solvai's gaze darkened at that.

As they spoke, I noticed Meleya wincing. "We c-can't stop on my account," she said stubbornly, pushing Brigan's compress away from her head. "I'm fine."

"You're clearly not," I replied.

Meleya stuck out her lip. "I'll be the judge of that."

Purely to prove me wrong, Meleya struggled to her feet. Brigan was distracted by his conversation with Solvai and allowed it.

The second she was standing, Meleya's hands flew to her temples and her eyes partially rolled back in her head. I instinctively reached out to catch her before she fell.

"Well there you have it, folks," I said with mock drama. "You saw it here first—Mel is perfectly fine. Let's absolutely get her back in the saddle."

Sniff's growl turned from approving to protective as he narrowed his eyes my way. Apparently, he wasn't great at detecting sarcasm.

"Let go of me," Meleya said.

"Let go of your pride," I countered. For whatever reason, that made her recoil.

"What's going on?" Eliana was suddenly very aware of Meleya and me. For some reason, Elle's mirror copy of Glint popped her head out of Elle's boot as if to get a better look at what was going on. Stars, this was getting chaotic.

"Meleya, you need to sit down," Brigan said.

Meleya tried to say something, but her headache nearly made her throw up.

"We're less than an hour into the quest and we're already at a drakking standstill..." Kai was saying.

"We can afford to miss one recruitment!" I said.

"If the omens are right about what the Rebels face, then no, we can't!" Kai insisted.

"Please relax, everyone," Solvai said, her voice small as she tried in vain to diffuse the tension.

Everybody was practically shouting at one another when there came a sudden, sharp rustling sound. We all looked for the cause of the disturbance, but couldn't see anything. Then something growled, bringing all our petty arguing to a halt.

Very slowly, what we'd taken to be a large pile of leaves began to rise. Taller it grew, red and orange maple leaves shedding onto the forest floor before they burned away into nothing. A short snout emerged, along with rows of razor-sharp teeth and a pair of enormous padded paws with five claws, each as long as my hand.

"Ursadon," Brigan muttered.

"Woodweaver," Kai squeaked.

"Umbral." Solvai pointed to the enormous dragon-bear's glowing blue eyes. Sure enough, as the firemaple-leaf camouflage faded, I saw the telltale gray coloring spreading across its hide.

Something about it was off, though. The beast's form wasn't wispy and curling with smoke like most umbrals. In fact, it seemed as if it was actively *turning* umbral as it rose to its feet. But how?

Then I spotted it, there at the ursadon's feet. The small, gray stone Jaira had chucked through the portal. It must've fallen to this spot the same way Meleya had. It no longer swirled with gray inner light as I witnessed the last of its dark power flowing into the huge dragon-grizzly.

Oh soot.

Before any of us had time to react, the ursadon gave a fierce, hair-raising roar. Lightning-blue wildmarks flowed along its arms and onto the ground, and at the beast's command, the roots of the nearby firemaple trees sprang upward, reaching toward us.

Several members of our group screamed as the bear used its wood-weaving power to snare them snugly in the cage-like roots. Everyone was trapped instantly.

That is, everyone but Sniff and me. Sometimes it paid to be a hover-dashing harbinger of... how had Thorn put it?

Pure chaos.

Sniff began to sneeze violently, sending blasts of ether at the wood-weaving ursadon. The dragon-bear's thick hide was somewhere between scales, fur, and firemaple leaves growing in thick, spiky clumps like protective, layered red-orange armor, accented by that odd splash of umbral gray.

Sniff's ether darts certainly annoyed it, though. The ursadon roared, raking his flaming claws at Sniff.

Sniff's distraction had given me time to summon my dragonhook spear. Hover-dashing into the fray, I slashed my starglass blade against the gigantic, fiery grizzly claw just in time to give the 'astro-nova' move I'd been practicing with Ivar another try. My eyes blazed gold.

I'd been going for a massive ether burst, but ended up with more of a wild ether torrent. It went straight into the bear's arm, leaving jagged white lines across its hide.

The beast turned his ire on me, eyes boring into me like glittering, beady sapphires. Soot, he wasn't even fazed. His lips curled back hungrily. It was time for a show—hopefully one that could distract this beast from my friends who remained tangled up in the roots.

"Nice moves, demon leaf-bear," I said, grunting. "You are a foe truly worthy of a distinguished name."

I yanked back on my weapon, then rammed it blade-first into the creature's chest. His thick natural armor was enough to crack my starglass spear.

Impressive.

I jumped, levitating so I could meet the ursadon's eye.

Ceremoniously, I said, "I think I'll call you Leif."

Unceremoniously, the bear swiftly backhanded me with its paw, sending me flying. Slamming into the tree hurt *bad*, but I felt my regenerative ascension bracers already working to heal me. Fortunately, spending years cragchasing, taking down wild dragon goats and ridgerunners in the cliffs near Steel Rim, really taught me how to take a hit.

I summoned more starglass to reform my spear, then even more starglass to create armor over my chest and back. All around me, firemaple leaves burned in a cascading flurry as they fell to the earth.

Meanwhile, Leif was thinking about going for my trapped friends. Not about to let that happen, Sniff hover-flew straight toward our foe's gigantic head.

Leif roared as Sniff's impact knocked him backward. But he was back on his feet in an instant to get revenge on the golden-yellow evren. Another power-packed swipe from Leif sent Sniff crashing into the grove, burying him in a deep pile of firemaple leaves. Sniff growled as the leaves burned him—He didn't have regenerative bracers like me.

Seeing that Sniff was injured, Leif moved toward him, aggression burning in his umbral blue eyes. More roots rose up to pin Sniff in place. My hover-dashing put me between Leif and Sniff just in time.

Leif was just rearing back, enormous jaws wide open as he prepared to breathe a blast of firemaple flame at us. Eyes burning, I formed a circular starglass shield that deflected the white-hot spray. My shield held up until I let it dissipate with Leif's fire.

"Wow, Leif," I grunted. "Your breath actually doesn't smell half-bad. Sort of sweet and campfire-y."

Leif responded to my compliment by rising to his full height and preparing to maul me.

Before he got the chance, something zoomed past the ursadon's nose, drawing its attention. Looking over, I was surprised to see…

Me.

At least, an *illusion* of me, standing epically and windmilling my spear, taunting the ursadon to come at me.

Oh, yes! I thought as I felt Kai's mindlink activate. *Double trouble?*

The ever-present backup plan, Kai confirmed. He was still trapped in the roots, but I got the feeling my best friend actually preferred a little separation from the action.

While Leif struggled to decide between attacking real me or fake me, I noticed that Solvai had escaped her root-prison by shifting into ridge-backed wren form. Rather than jump right into the fight herself as I might've done, she was now working to cut away the roots that held Thorn captive. As a second ascension wyvern, Thorn would be the most useful in bringing Leif down. Smart.

Kai made illusory me turn a backflip, and that was enough for Leif. The beast lumbered toward the illusion, which gave the newly freed Thorn the perfect opportunity.

Angular golden markings glowed from his scales as my dragon bond activated his diamondoak scales, making bark-like armor even tougher than Leif's hide. Thorn inclined his head, barreling into Leif and using his antlers to throw the behemoth bear into the grove. Leif thumped hard against a tree, then dropped onto the ground. Another cascade of firemaple leaves smoldered.

Roaring, Leif got on all fours just in time to go antler-to-claw with Thorn in an epic wrestling match. I prepared to assist my bond, and I wasn't the only one.

As soon as Solvai had freed Brigan, the pair of them entered the fray. I was a good fighter as I hover-dashed and levitated around Leif, trying to land a hit, but Brigan and Solvai left me impressed as they showed me how a trained squad did it.

In falcondrake form, Solvai raked her talons across Leif's side. That allowed Brigan to come in from the other side with a hack to the neck from his seaxe. Blow after blow, the pair of them circled the bear, literally whittling away at Leif's defenses. My old squad captain, Sven, would have been proud.

Taking a cue from Brigan and his sturdier weapon, I dismissed my starglass spear in favor of a heavier starglass warsword. I felt a rush of satisfaction when my next strike chipped away a cluster of Leif's spiky natural armor and left a cut on his part-umbral arm.

That was when Aurora and Elle joined in. A quick glance back toward their root cages let me see the scorchmarks Aurora's dragonfire had left when they'd freed themselves.

Fiery maple leaves surrounded them like a halo as more of Aurora's flames ripped across the air to blast Leif from behind, causing him to growl in frustration. We had him surrounded. It was only a matter of time before—

Whoosh!

Leif set himself ablaze with a torrent of flame and foliage. The tendrils of fire were gray at the tips, a sign that the voidarchy within him was growing stronger. The fireblast launched us all backward.

True to his name, Leif had left the grove incredibly... leafy. Not to mention smoky. I heard shouting and roars, and the next thing I knew, Elle was screaming.

I raced toward the sound, and found Leif looming above her, standing at his full height. He'd already landed a gash on her arm, and was preparing for another strike.

Not likely, Leif, I thought.

Hover-dashing instantly put me between Elle and the bear, levitating at eye-level. My starglass warsword was ready to redirect Leif's claw.

The only trouble was, Leif didn't come at me with just his claw.

Pain ripped through my leg as the ursadon's jaws clamped down hard. My bracers worked overtime to keep me from going into shock as the red of my blood got lost in the red of the leaves. Soot—was Leif umbral enough to give me the shadow wasting?

There wasn't time to worry about that now. Biting back the pain, I had to drop my starglass warsword to stop Leif from thrashing and killing me. Surging my torso forward, I grabbed hold of the scale-like fur on Leif's enormous head. Then I channeled more starglass to form a haphazard sort of muzzle onto him that extended to his shoulders to keep him from shaking his head back and forth and breaking me. The crystalline muzzle also doubled as a handhold for me, and with it, I could sort-of control

Leif's movement. Leif roared with rage. At least, he tried to. Poor Leif—It must not have been easy to get a good roar out with his mouth full of *my leg*.

"Let me go and you can roar all you want!" I grunted, holding on for dear life. Leif glared at me with burning umbral blue eyes.

As the smoke cleared, I saw Brigan, wielding my starglass warsword. Using the last of my strength, I wrenched free from Leif's jaws. Levitating, I grabbed hold of the starglass muzzle. Then I yanked back on Leif's head, leaving his giant bear belly unprotected.

Brigan didn't hesitate. He stood directly in front of the ursadon, his back practically against him. Then, using a reverse-grip thrust, Brigan plunged the extra-long starglass blade up under the beast's ribs and straight into his heart.

The sapphire light faded from Leif's eyes as his enormous body slumped to the side. In fact, all of the grayness seemed to retreat from his form as whatever voidarchy Lothar and Jaira had infected him with disappeared. It seemed their creepy wraith rock was a one-time-use deal.

I dismissed the starglass muzzle as Leif's jaw went slack, then I dropped to the forest floor and clutched my leg. It looked bad, but my bracers were already sealing up the worst parts of it. In fact, they may have been the only thing that had kept my leg from breaking. Unfortunately, I could sense that the regeneration was slowing down as the inherent ether within Thorn's shed scales ran out.

Once Thorn had finished freeing Kai and still-ether-drained Meleya from the roots, the group gathered around, checking on one another to make sure we were all in one piece. Sniff and I had evidently gotten the worst of it, but we'd pull through. Meanwhile, Brigan was already pulling out the crystal vial of liquid light he'd made while studying the healing arts with Trickshot. Trickshot had a unique vial that was enchanted to refill with sunlight, but Brigan's was made using the shed scales from his lightwielding dragon, Bolt. It, too, refilled automatically over time, even without the sun.

Brigan applied a few drops to my leg, checking for signs of the shadow wasting. Luckily, it seemed that any umbral poison that might've infected my wounds had vanished along with the ghostly spirit that had possessed the ursadon.

"Let's make a deal," I said to the group. "No more encounters with Mage Hunters and their creepy voidish possession rocks, alright?"

Everyone agreed.

After our encounter with Leif the ursadon, any thoughts of continuing our travels today swiftly faded to a distant memory. The true dragon fans at Ashfalcon Point would just have to wait.

Despite having literally passed out in the air earlier, Meleya insisted on being the one to make supper. To be fair, the act of cooking seemed to genuinely reinvigorate her, not to mention her slow-cooked Leif stew was absolutely delicious.

That evening, our group sat in a quiet circle around the fire. Things were still a little tense after our earlier argument, but the fight with Leif seemed to have bonded us in a way. We made a good team.

Kai was rewriting his plans in his notebook and Solvai sat beside him. She'd whipped out a knife and was whittling away at a chunk of firemaple wood. Meleya was already asleep on her bedroll, Sniff hanging from a tree above her like a bat.

Brigan and Elle sat together on a log in the firelight. They sat close, though I guessed that was because Brigan was still working on healing her arm. Leif's claws had left a deep gash, though Elle had pointedly kept quiet about it until Brigan had finished tending to Sniff.

Brigan had his fine, fancy medical bag open near his feet. He really seemed to know what he was doing as he pulled out various salves and bottles, applying them to Elle's upper arm. They spoke in low tones, and they both kept smiling. I was glad she was going to be okay, but still… she could smile less about it, right? Watching the way Brigan carefully bandaged her up almost hurt more than the near-mauling I'd suffered from Leif.

Your turn next? Thorn's thought came through our bond as my wyvern nudged me from behind. Thorn was probably right—Though Brigan had already used liquid light to heal the worst of it, my leg was starting to sting pretty badly again. With my ascension bracers' power momentarily depleted, it would've been nice to get some of Brigan's mystery herbs to relieve some of the pain.

But I found myself shaking my head at Thorn. I was fine.

Totally fine.

Brigan was on watch when the pain in my leg roused me. He looked my way as I stirred.

"Morning, your royal dukeness," I whispered, sitting up.

Brigan gave a low chuckle. "Morning? Try midnight."

I looked skyward, and sure enough, hundreds of stars blinked back at me.

I grimaced, glancing down at my remaining scratches, red and angry on my shin.

"Got any more of that herb-y healing salve by chance?" I asked.

Brigan's eyes narrowed at my wound. "Why didn't you say anything earlier?" He was already going for his medical bag.

Creeping silently so that I wouldn't wake anyone, I joined Brigan on the log near the fire pit. The flames had died down, but warm, red-orange embers matched the grove's leaves.

First, Brigan used some water from a canteen and a clean cloth to wash my wound. I bit the inside of my cheek and glanced away, looking for something to keep my mind off the pain.

I quickly found just that.

Elle slept soundly across the way. Her hair lay strewn around her head in a whimsical, tangled halo, and I couldn't help but smile. She'd changed out of her white dress into a more comfortable tan one for sleeping, and it reminded me of the old days when we'd muck out stables together. I wondered if those days really were gone for good.

"So," I began, trying to sound casual as I struck up a hushed conversation with Brigan, "you and Elle were engaged for a while."

"Only our whole lives," Brigan said as he worked. "Our parents had it in their sights the moment we were born, but I guess it only became official when we were eleven."

"If I can ask, why'd the King and Queen of Drakfell pick you?"

Brigan shrugged. "Marks, to be honest. Solhelm may only be the fourth house of Rengard, but it's one of the wealthiest keeps in the Canyonlands.

We're right on the Scarlet Strait's southern shore and at the head of one branch of the Ridgeback River—the perfect trade port."

Brigan finished mixing up his healing salve, then began applying it to my wound. Instantly, I felt cool relief.

"An alliance between my house and King Rodan's was a smart move," Brigan went on. "It meant increased wealth and protection for Drakfell and… well, status for me. I'd have eventually become the King of an entire keepdom."

"And that's something you'd actually want?" I asked. "No offense, but you seem like a decent guy. Not some power-hungry noble."

"I'll take that as a compliment." Brigan gave a wide, dimpled grin. "I don't crave power for its own sake, but I do long for the opportunity to make the world better."

I raised an eyebrow. "And what do the real power-hungry ones tell themselves?"

"Probably the same thing." Brigan and I chuckled. He cleaned the salve from my leg, then began rummaging through his kit once more.

"Still, I can't help wanting to do something about the magi plight," Brigan said, lost in thought. "I want a more just world for those born with etherarchy, but it's not as simple as treating them the same as anyone else."

"Sure it is," I countered. "Magi are exactly the same as anyone else; they just have different gifts."

"Potentially destructive gifts," Brigan said somberly. "I can see why they formed the Mage Hunters in the first place."

"There are a lot more good magi than bad ones," I felt myself growing defensive. "I can name at least a dozen honorable magi, all oppressed because of something they can't help."

"As can I. But I've also fought an entire army of dangerous, corrupt magi. I lost countless fellow soldiers to them and nearly lost my family. Just because you're oppressed doesn't mean you're a good person."

"That's easy for a noble to say," I instinctively shot back. But then I bit my tongue, mulling Brigan's words over.

"That's another reason I'm grateful to have found the Knights of the Torch," he continued. "Gauntlet down: Their code isn't only an excellent guide for your general Evgardian looking to live a more meaningful life. It's also a guide for leadership."

"How so?" I asked.

"Think about it, it all points toward the right way to serve others, which is what leadership *should* be," Brigan said, growing more animated while still trying to remain quiet. "Choose light. That's a somewhat literal part of why I wanted to become a healer—I've always been interested in liquid light and its healing properties."

On cue, Brigan pulled out a tiny crystal vial filled with the glowing golden substance. He poured a single, tiny drop of liquid light onto my wound, and the scrape instantly shrank back to almost nothing.

"If physical light can do this," Brigan said, "just think of what other forms of light could do to heal our broken nation. The rift between magi and non magi."

"Or," I added, surprised at my own burgeoning enthusiasm, "the generations-old hate between humans and Drekai."

"Yes!" Brigan agreed. "To me, being a ruler isn't about amassing power. It's about—"

"Taking on extra responsibility," I finished.

"Exactly. The responsibility to choose light."

"And helping it grow. Burn bright," I said, recalling the second pillar of the Knights' code.

"Drive out darkness..." Brigan continued.

"Light the way," we finished in unison. We both gave amused snorts, but a moment of understanding passed between us.

Soot. Of all possible noblemen to befriend, I just had to pick the one who had a very good shot at wooing the girl I cared for. He really was the perfect match for Elle—at least, *Eliana*. And Brigan wasn't even acting. This was just who he was.

Once Brigan had finished with my leg, I offered to take over watch duty for a while. Brigan grabbed his bedroll from one of the saddlebags and laid it out near the fire. Before settling down, I saw him tiptoe over to where Meleya slept.

Her face was tense, as if she were having a bad dream. She'd been shifting in her sleep and her aldraka wool blanket had slipped off. Brigan moved more slowly than a scalesnail as he gently replaced it over her shoulders.

As Brigan turned in, I couldn't help but wonder about Brigan and Meleya. I knew they'd been close friends for forever, but was that all?

I was too distracted to dwell on it as I looked up at the starry night sky. Far in the distance to the south, I saw a trio of bright green comets.

Skyfalls. Those skyfalls would bring both skystone and wild dragonkind to the fortunate—and unfortunate—keeps nearby.

Despite the peril the skyfalls brought, their beauty was undeniable. They burned the same color as my Drekai legacy eyes.

And Mom's.

So softly I almost couldn't hear my own voice, I began to sing.

You are a link in a legacy of light
A chain that spans the ages
Sent to tend with wisdom and might
Through bright or darkened stages

We will guide you
Ever beside you
We who've come before
Do not fear
Your time draws near
Share light forevermore

As I finished my mother's song, I felt a distinct warmth bloom along my back and shoulders. Part of me wanted to turn around, but instead, I just closed my eyes, whispering.

"I love you too, Mom."

CHAPTER 22: VOIDGATE RIVER

MELEYA

The morning after the 'Leif Incident', I told Princess Eliana and the others that my ether well was replenished and good to go.

It was true—The night's sleep had almost filled my well up to the top again, and my ether overuse headache had mostly subsided. I was still tired, but that wasn't what really worried me.

Last night, I'd had another nightmare.

I'd been somewhat prepared for that. After all, I still had the Soul Reaper's voidshard in my rift hold, and without the protection from the cabin's ancient etherlocks, I was vulnerable again. My skin still crawled from the bleak dream featuring the man in the tattered robes. The Soul Reaper.

We are coming for you, Snowstorm, he'd promised.

I shuddered at the very memory. There was no hiding behind Zyri anymore. The Soul Reaper knew exactly who I was, and he'd already sent Jaira and Lothar to find me. Their attack with the umbral ursadon hadn't gotten anyone killed this time, but who knew what else the voidmages had up their sleeves?

For the umpteenth time since yesterday morning, I wondered if leaving the safehouse had been the right decision.

I remembered the final moments before we'd left the safehouse boundary. Dad had come to wish me well, but Mom had chosen to remain behind. According to Dad, she was improving, and no longer thought I was a seven-year-old non-magi. But ever since that first day in the

368

safehouse jail cell, she couldn't regard my silvermark without bursting into tears.

Dad asked if I'd be willing to go to her, but I'd said no. Part of it was down to stubbornness, and the other part was nerves. I was so worried about Xan returning that I didn't stop to think about how my not saying goodbye would make Mom feel. My choice already left me with a pit of regret in my stomach.

Momentarily, our traveling party was ready for another day of skyskipping. Various doubts swirled inside my mind as we rose high above the firemaple grove, flying west to gain both altitude and momentum for the first round of jumps. I found myself scanning the skies for dusky blue cloaks.

Imagine having no reason to fear the voidmages, Xan's voice rasped in my head. *We are stronger than ever. If you would only grant me control, we could become great enough to challenge even the Soul Reaper himself.*

I set my jaw. Along with the nightmares, it appeared Xan was back, too. But this time, I refused to let her weaken me through isolation.

Solvai, in ridgebacked wren form, huddled in front of me in the saddle, keeping out of the strong winds so she wouldn't blow away. She looked up at me, her hazel eyes bright with concern even in this form. At my back was Brigan, strong and secure.

"Umm," I began, feeling silly. But I forced myself to keep talking. "So, my wraith is back."

I bit my tongue. How would they respond? The thoughts Xan put into my head were so... dark. I worried that my friends would think less of me.

But the little bird foot gently taking hold of my finger as I gripped the saddlehorn sent that thought back to the void where it belonged. Behind me, Brigan's voice was gentle but firm.

"Thank you for telling us. Do you want to talk about it?"

I swallowed. Then I told my friends about the nightmare and the whisperings I heard from Xan. The details didn't seem to matter so much as the mere fact of articulating what I was seeing, hearing, and feeling. Brigan and Solvai, as well as my twin evren bonds, listened intently.

When I finished, Solvai brushed her wing along my hand while Brigan gave me a light squeeze around my waist.

"I wish I could take the voidshard for you," Brigan said. But he knew what the Farseer had said—The safest place for the shard was right where it was, in the spirit plane where the Soul Reaper couldn't sense it well.

Brigan went on. "We're going to get through this—find a way to get rid of that Gray One once and for all. This isn't forever, Meleya. And even if it is, we're here for you. Same way you've always been there for us."

Solvai couldn't speak in this form, but she nodded her feathered head vigorously. Through my bond with my dragons, I felt a chorus of flute and drums.

I nearly started crying with gratitude. Xan's cold presence was nowhere to be found. It was as if my friends' care had driven her away.

We were nearly high enough to start sky-skipping, and I could tell that Asher, Kai, and Eliana were looking to me for a signal. Brigan must've been able to tell it was time too, because at once I felt his grip tighten around my waist, his fingers grasping at the fabric of my tunic.

"You okay?" I turned toward him over my shoulder.

"Sorry." Brigan's grip loosened, but I could still feel the tension in his muscles. I glanced backward to see Brigan's eyes were shut tight.

Realization dawned on me as we cut through the brisk morning air. "You're afraid of heights."

Brigan let out a breath. "Let's just say I'm glad to have bonded a drake rather than a flying dragon."

A patch of rough air jostled us. Solvai the wren was fine, her tiny feet clinging tightly to the lip of the saddle. But Brigan's arms and legs stiffened, and I felt his fingers clutch my tunic even more tightly.

I put my hand on his to let him know he was secure. "Hold on as tightly as you want," I said as a string of encouraging musical notes played in my heart. "And know that Sniff would never let you fall."

Sniff sent his thought to both Brigan and me: *Brigan is among Sniff's favorite humans! Easy!*

Brigan gave a nervous laugh. "I appreciate that, Sniff. And Meleya."

I felt Brigan relax somewhat as his arms wrapped more securely around me.

For one brief, painful moment, I remembered flying with Jax. I'd held fast to his waist, my head resting on his back. His inner heat had warmed me to my core.

My sunlight, I remembered.

I reached for the quartz crystal at my belt, trying to ignore the hole in my heart. I wished Jax was here questing to Orothion alongside us. He'd have been amazing in the fight against Leif the ursadon, and he would have loved a bite of the stew I'd made last night. And, if only he were here, I'd have confided in him about Xan and the nightmare in a heartbeat.

But that was no longer in the stars. My pride had lost me Jax, and I needed to get used to it.

All at once, I realized the others were looking my way. Soot. They were waiting for me. I quickly traced the rifting rune in the air and the skyskipping began.

The day went by quickly. I rifted us westward, in and out of portals throughout the morning. Then I took a break during the afternoon, letting the dragons do the heavy lifting while my ether supply replenished. We stopped off at the tavern in Ashfalcon Point, where Princess Eliana met with a group of Rebel Knight supporters.

After that, Kai informed us that we were 'seventy-one percent closer to being back on schedule.' When he asked if I was feeling up to closing that gap, I squared my shoulders and prepared for yet another round of skyskipping.

We traveled that way for days, stopping at taverns, saloons, and town squares so that Princess Eliana could make an appearance. We had to be careful, using Kai's mind-reading geckos to predetermine whether the people would be receptive to Eliana and the Rebels or if they'd prefer to turn her in to High King Magnus for the reward. We'd skipped over several towns, and more than once we'd ended up using my rift anchors to make a hasty exit before too many guards showed up.

Kai and Solvai spent hours poring over our weathered map of Evgard, determining the most efficient route that would still allow us to visit as many towns as possible. Ultimately, they decided it would be best for us to dip pretty deeply southward so that Eliana could put in an appearance at a few prominent keeps in northern Rengard.

"As long as we steer clear of Kuakiina Canyon," Brigan said, looking over Solvai and Kai's shoulders.

"What's wrong with that area?" Kai asked.

"For starters," Asher chimed in, "*Kuakiina* mean's 'death' in Drekai."

"Crime is high around there," Brigan added. "My home keep, Solhelm, is near enough for me to know. We always tell travelers to avoid those towns—Shadow Flats, Drakesthorpe, and Scorpio's Shadow. The amount of wild scorpios there give thugs too much free reign."

"I've heard of Scorpio's Shadow," I said with a frown. "A woman we used to travel with from the Copperhead Caravan once told us a scary story about a monster in the mountains who uses scorpio venom to kidnap young women who wander off on their own. She was probably just making it up to keep us in line, but still... she swore it was true." I shuddered at the memory of her solemn face lit by the campfire's flames.

"We'll have to get close when we pass by Streya's Oasis." Solvai pointed to the map. "But avoiding those places shouldn't be a problem."

I saw Eliana watching the conversation with a frown on her face. I could tell she didn't like the idea of skipping those towns, but for now, she kept her mouth shut.

As we carried on, people took to Princess Eliana instantly. And how could they not? She was the epitome of nobility, with her white armor, gleaming tiara, and true dragon. Her perfect demeanor was exactly what I'd expect from a princess, and the crowds cheered each time she called out, 'Light the way!'

Every so often a wild dragon would swoop toward our camp at night, drawn by the ether in our magi. Luckily, the attacks rarely involved more than one wild dragon, and with such an experienced group of fighters, not to mention Sniff, Thorn, and Aurora, we were able to drive them away in no time.

As for Jaira and Lothar, we still hadn't seen them since that first day. The others figured they were gone for good, but I had my doubts. I knew that Mason would stop at nothing to capture me and return that voidshard to his master. The nightmares still assaulted me at night, but talking things through with Solvai and Brigan just before bed kept them from being overwhelming. Xan hadn't spoken to me in days either.

Toward the end of the week, heavy clouds rolled across the sky. Kai had instructed us to keep the long, winding Voidgate River in our sights as we flew due west, but with so much fog, I couldn't see it anymore. I could hardly see into the distance at all, which made skyskipping extremely difficult. My jumps were extra short, but I knew we had to press on if we wanted to keep to the schedule.

I'd gotten good at rationing my ether supply so that I ran out near the end of each day. But today, my temples were throbbing by midday. By late afternoon, my headache was bad enough that shards of light were refracting at the edges of my vision.

Still, I refused to ask for a break. We had a schedule to keep, and everyone was counting on me. I could do this.

After a couple more particularly short jumps, Princess Eliana glanced my way. She took one look at me and declared that we'd be stopping for the evening. Kai wasn't happy about it, but through my bond with my dragon, I sensed flute-like notes of relief. Sniff must've been picking up on my fatigue, too.

We landed in an area just south of the Voidgate River near a thick grouping of mountain junipers and diamondoak trees. I stumbled slightly as I dismounted, but I was certain I'd be okay after a few minutes of rest.

I tried to take a quick nap, but my mind just couldn't seem to relax. We'd flown right through lunchtime, which meant the group was going to be extra hungry when dinner rolled around. If I got started making that now, maybe I could take a real rest afterward. My ether well was low, but I figured I had just enough to briefly access my rift hold.

Back at the Academy, I'd kept the Soul Reaper's voidshard smack in the middle of my rift hold where it cast a dismal glow on all my favorite spices. But before leaving the safehouse, I'd made some adjustments.

After studying from the runebook my old mentor, Torsten, had given me, I'd figured out how to significantly expand my rift hold. What had once been a mere spice cabinet was now a tasteful, moderately sized, ethereal walk-in pantry. Dad had helped me put in a shelf on each side and another along the back. There were stacks of pots, pans, and other cooking equipment, as well as rows and rows of ingredients. Ears of corn, a few summer squash, and bags of dried beans sat neatly in their places. Canisters of sugar and flour lined one shelf while onions in a mesh net hung from another. All my go-to spices had a place of honor right near the front.

The voidshard was hidden away in the furthest corner. I'd first wrapped it in cloth, then stuck that cloth in a fancy pouch Solrac had given me. It was monogrammed with a golden 'S' and it was posh enough that there was actually real gold in the thread. Finally, I'd stuffed that pouch into a sack of rice and shoved it under the back shelf behind several other bags of rice.

I wasn't sure if any of that really made a difference, but the nightmares *were* milder than before, *and* the shard hadn't once escaped my rift hold.

Either way, keeping it out of sight really helped to keep it out of mind, too.

Before my ether well drained entirely, I quickly grabbed a sack of potatoes, a cutting board, and a sharp knife. I set up the dinner prep, kneeling beside a semi-flat stone as a countertop, though it seemed to be tilting at a steeper incline every second... Or was that just my headache messing with my vision? Stars... I was still seeing a lot of stars, too.

I was about halfway through chopping the first potato when my knife slipped. I grimaced, hurriedly pulling my freshly nicked finger away from the food.

"Soot," I muttered. It wasn't like me to cut myself while cooking.

I hated to stop my momentum, but I got to my feet, hoping to ask Brigan for a bandage so I could finish up.

I nearly ran right into Eliana, who was standing directly behind me.

"Whoa," I said. "How long have you been standing there?"

Ignoring my question, she said, "You don't have to be such a martyr, you know."

Cradling my finger, I raised an eyebrow in surprise. "What does that mean?"

The princess sighed, her voice as formal as ever.

"Meleya of Misthaven, I am responsible for the well-being of each member of this team. I'd much rather cover a hundred miles less each day and extend our trip than watch you abuse yourself like this. Additionally..." She gestured to the ingredients I'd laid out for tonight's dinner. "...you're doing too much between skyskipping sessions. Out of all of us, you're the one who needs the most rest. As of right now, I'm taking you off of cooking duty."

"What?" I said indignantly. "But cooking helps me relax, I swear."

Eliana glanced skeptically toward my finger where a tiny bead of blood had formed. I thought about arguing further, but then I remembered what Asher had said to me on the first day of our journey:

Let go of your pride.

I gave a very, very long exhale before reluctantly saying, "Okay."

Eliana nodded. "Very good."

"But I just have one question," I said.

"What's that?"

"Who's gonna make dinner then?"

Eliana hesitated, glancing briefly toward each member of our group. Brigan was good at a lot of things, but he had once tried to chop an onion with the skin still on. Having grown up around the army mess hall, Solvai wasn't much use in the kitchen either. Eliana visibly winced when she looked at Kai. I got the feeling she'd tried his cooking before and didn't dare do so again. Asher was nowhere in sight, nor would anyone with half a brain trust that menace anywhere near kitchen knives and hot cooking fires.

When Eliana turned back my way, she gave a resigned sigh.

"Until further notice, I will be taking over the cooking."

My eyes popped. "You? But you're a... a..."

"A princess?" Eliana finished. "That may be so, but that doesn't mean I'm helpless in practical matters."

Eliana and I glanced toward my half-chopped potato and the waiting pile of other ingredients I'd been planning to turn into a crispy fish and potato skillet. Regretfully, I began to walk away.

"Before you go—" Eliana put a hand on my arm, "perhaps you might leave me with one or two pointers?"

I couldn't help but chuckle. "Of course."

Eliana broke into a bright smile. I smiled back—This was the first time I'd seen a crack in her dignified mask.

I did my best to explain how to make the simple dish. Eliana listened intently, nodding along.

"Don't go overboard on the scaled poblano," I said in final warning. "Get too many pepper seeds in there and it'll be too spicy for Solvai and Asher."

"Right," she nodded, looking only slightly lost.

I gave her a light shove. "Don't overthink it."

It nearly killed me to leave the meal unfinished, but I forced myself to walk away.

Meanwhile, my finger had stopped bleeding, and upon second look it didn't seem like a big enough deal to get Brigan to whip out his medical supplies. Instead, I headed to a secluded spot along the river where I could refill my canteen. Maybe some water would ease my headache.

I knelt at the stream beneath a hanging diamondoak branch. I took in a few deep breaths, trying to focus on relaxing.

Unfortunately, the more I focused, the more impossible it seemed. How was I supposed to relax, especially if I wasn't allowed to cook?

My head pounded. I could feel my wraith lurking at the fringes of my consciousness, threatening to fill my mind with insecurity. Loneliness. Even guilt for not being able to manage everything without help.

Before the dark thoughts could take root, something caught my eye. There, caught in the river's swirling current near the bank, lay a crystalline object. I frowned as I plucked it from the water.

It was a piece of starglass formed into the shape of a tiny longboat. I tilted the boat to pour out the water that had filled it while stuck in the current.

"You caught it!" Asher's voice made me jump. Whipping my head around, I saw him crouching beside the river only a few yards away.

"What are you doing here?" I demanded.

Asher chuckled, holding up his canteen. "It's a free river. Anyone can refill their water here anytime they want; even obnoxious, scarf-wearing, bedhead-having half-borns."

"Not everything I say to you is an insult, scalebrain," I replied.

"You're right. They're *bad* insults." Asher winked.

I narrowed my eyes. "Anyway, you don't have bedhead. Your hair's just... windswept. Messy, but not in a bad way."

"Whoa. Was that almost a compliment?"

"No," I insisted. "It was a fact. Learn the difference."

"Yes, Instructor Snowhead." Asher mock-saluted as he strode over to me and swiped the little starglass longboat out of my hand.

Asher examined his creation. "I'm having trouble getting it past the current there. Maybe if I give it a wider base..."

With that, Asher's eyes glowed gold as he modified his boat. I watched his precision with fascination.

Asher spoke as he worked. "Kai, Kari, and I used to do this all the time as kids. Make fleets out of starglass and whatever else we could find—twigs, leaves, walnut shells..." Asher chuckled, caught up in memory.

"What was the point?" I asked.

Asher pointed to various parts of the river. "To see if we could get the whole fleet past obstacles like rough currents, fallen logs, and jutting rocks like those."

"Just... because?"

"Because it was fun! Don't tell me you never did stuff like that with your friends growing up."

I shook my head. I hadn't done stuff like that with friends growing up because, until meeting Brigan and Solvai at basic training, I hadn't *had* any friends. Unless I counted my dad's thieving ethereal pet draccoon, Dusty.

"Oh, *now* it makes sense! That's why you're so stuffy and dull," Asher teased, melodramatically bonking himself on the forehead. He shoved his starglass boat back into my hands and instantly started forming two more in his palm.

"Why're you still just standing there?" Asher asked. "We've got to get these ships in shape in time for their launch!"

"Um…" I said, still unsure whether or not to play along. "What do I do?"

"For starters, we need a sail—maybe that'll help it balance better in that current. See anything that could work?" Asher spoke animatedly as he set down the other two boats and began combing the forest floor.

Without thinking, I scanned the ground and spotted a nice big diamondoak leaf. I picked it up and held it out to Asher.

"That's perfect!" he exclaimed. "Wanna grab a couple more for the rest of the fleet?" Asher scooped up a handful of fallen juniper berries, which he began loading into the boats' interiors.

"What're those for?" I asked. The berries couldn't possibly be useful in keeping the boats afloat.

Asher grinned. "Cargo."

I snorted, and didn't fight my half-smile as I began searching for the largest, prettiest diamondoak leaves the forest had to offer.

I had no idea how much time passed as Asher and I bedecked our tiny fleet of starglass longboats. We secured the juniper berries using long blades of grass, then wove my diamondoak leaf sails through sharp twigs and stuck them in the center. I even tied a scaly, needlelike juniper sprig to the front end of our lead ship. Asher laughed at me, but I swore the sprig was dragon-shaped and made the perfect figurehead.

Finally, the fleet was ready for launch. With disappointed groans, we watched our boats capsize almost immediately in the swirling river current.

Asher didn't let our failure get him down. Eagerly, he levitated himself over the stream to fish out each longboat while I gathered new juniper berry 'cargo.'

We made a few adjustments to the design by crudely whittling down twigs to use as outrigger-style support floats. This time, the fleet made it past the whirl in the current, but got stuck at the fallen log.

Lamenting, we inched along the log to retrieve the boats. I slipped and nearly fell into the water, barely catching myself in time.

But my stumble jostled the log, freeing the boats from the trap. The river pushed them outward and around the log, heading downriver.

"They're floating toward the rocks!" I cried.

"Follow them!" Asher said.

We scurried off the log, running along the river's edge to follow the boats. We yelled with glee every time the fleet made it past a new obstacle.

"They're almost to the finish line!" Asher called, pointing to a winding spineweed vine draped between two diamondoak trees on either side of the stream.

I squealed with delight as all three of our starglass creations sailed safely under the vine. Asher whooped, and the two of us instinctively threw our arms around each other, jumping up and down.

My foot slipped on the muddy riverbank, and I yelped as the two of us slid toward the river. Both Asher and I splashed in the water up to our knees.

Asher laughed, clutching me tighter in case I fell again. Instinctively, my arms wrapped over his shoulders around his neck.

As we stabilized each other, I found myself looking up into his bright dragonfire green eyes. Through Asher's shirt, I could feel his heart pounding from our run along the river. With a start, I realized that my heart was thundering too—and not just from the running.

I breathed in, Asher's scent reminding me of fresh air and earth after a rainstorm. I wondered if it was a result of him being so near the river, or if he always smelled like that.

Not that I planned to find out.

At the same time, Asher and I seemed to realize we were still hugging. Faster than a skyskipping evren, Asher and I dropped our hands to our sides.

"Umm…" he said. "Congratulations on the successful launch of Starglass Fleet Number Forty-two."

"Likewise," I replied, formally holding out a hand. Asher grasped my forearm, mimicking the stiffness of a ship's captain.

"And perhaps even more important," Asher went on, "congratulations on your advancement from stuffy scale-in-the-mud to almost-a-normal-human-being... in the mud."

He nodded toward my boots as they sank deeper into the river's silt. I snorted, then began to laugh.

I kept laughing, far longer than such a ridiculous joke deserved. As I did, I felt something release. My wraith was so far away I couldn't even feel her, and my headache, while still there, had eased considerably.

Not wanting the others to get any weird ideas, Asher and I hurried back to camp. The sun was low in the cloudy sky, and Eliana had just finished making dinner as the group gathered around the campfire. Her normally long, flowing hair was piled into a messy bun atop her head, and I even noticed a few beads of sweat along her forehead.

She hesitantly passed us each a plate, apologizing in advance for the fish's level of crispiness, how overdone the potatoes were, and the over-salting of the whole dish. But despite Eliana's dozen self-proclaimed failures, the meal wasn't half-bad. Kai's compliment that 'it didn't even need the illusion for improved taste' he'd been preparing said it all. Elle laughed. I'd never seen her less guarded, and I'd never liked her more.

After dinner, the group stayed by the fire, listening to Solvai play a lonely tune on a carved wooden whistle. The sound carried on the wind where the dark twilight sky swallowed it up.

As I leaned against a log, I found myself sinking deeper into relaxation. Such a long break from skyskipping, not to mention the distraction down by the river, had left me feeling better than I had in a long, long time.

I'd nearly fallen asleep three or four times already when I finally relented and grabbed my bedroll from Sniff's pack. Snuggling down into the warmth of my travel blanket, I felt something small jab against my hip.

I'd been so tired I'd forgotten to even take off my belt. There was my quartz crystal, hanging in its usual spot.

After untying the belt, I held the quartz in my hands, feeling the smooth planes with my fingertips.

The sound of laughter pulled my attention. Across the campfire, Asher was sitting beside Eliana, his crooked grin working its magic in full force. Eliana was still as relaxed as she'd been during dinner, making goofy faces with Asher in the low firelight.

They seemed deep in happy conversation, something I hadn't seen from them before. I felt a sudden, completely irrational tug in my gut. I knew Eliana and Brigan had history, but what exactly was the princess's relationship with Asher?

And why in the void did I care?

Asher saw me watching them from my bedroll and gave a little salute. "'Night, Mel," he said.

"Goodnight," I replied as I carefully set the quartz crystal down beside me.

FRAGMENT: ARMORED

JAX

Jax carefully picked up the quartz crystal from the table beside his bed at the inn. The quartz was empty—He hadn't had the energy to refill it with extra ether in weeks.

Jax held the white crystal in his hand for a long moment as a feeling of longing washed over him. Drak. Even after all this time, Jax couldn't get through a single day without thinking of her.

What was she doing right now, he wondered. Probably cooking.

Was she happy? Jax hoped so.

Was she thinking of him, too?

Of course not, came the wraith's deep, pervasive reply. *You are nothing to her. Nothing to anyone.*

"Nothing," Jax mumbled, letting Calyx's presence numb him. After all, wasn't numbness preferable to pain?

If you believe that, Calyx said, *then give in completely. Accept my voidshard.*

Before Jax's eyes, a thin, blue crystal gradually materialized atop the bedside table. The crystal glowed with otherworldly power, and Jax could see Calyx's name scratched in white along one plane. The other side was blank.

One drop of blood will etch your name upon the shard, binding us, Calyx said. *Think of it—You will feel nothing. No more anger, no more heartache. Decisions out of your hands. Does that thought not bring you relief?*

Jax set his jaw. It was one thing to escape the pain by allowing Calyx to take over every once in a while, another thing entirely to bind him to it permanently. But each time the wraith slipped into Jax's mind, it got a little harder to resist the shard.

You are serving the Gray already. The Knights would not accept you now.

Jax knew Calyx was right. At this point, why resist?

But Jax clutched the pure, white quartz in his hand.

"No," he replied to the wraith out loud. The voidshard faded from the bedside table.

Momentarily, there was a sharp rapping at Jax's door, followed by Bjorn's voice.

"You in there, ex-Knight? Drakeslayer says it's time to go."

"Coming," Jax replied, already reaching for the long-sleeved tunic hanging over the edge of his bed. He pulled it on, then layered on his Mage Hunter's pauldron, chest plate, and tassets. Jax had never been much for heavy armor before, but things were different now. He sheathed the standard Mage Hunters' silver seaxe at his hip, being careful not to touch the silvered blade. He was immune to silver while the wraith was controlling him, but without the permanent bond through Calyx's voidshard, silver still burned like ice.

Finally, Jax secured the empty quartz crystal to his belt before heading out the door.

"And now you see, dear Queen so fair, and proudly stalwart King,
Why we do hope that you accept these noble gifts we bring.
In exchange for fealty to the High throne and the Gray,
We promise safety, wealth, and wild dragons kept away.
While that roguish demon Farseer sows his songs of fear and lies,
Pledge your troops to Magnus, then watch the Knights' demise."

Jax was honestly astonished how effective Mason Drakeslayer was at winning over uppity nobles. The High Prince gave a deep bow as his poem left the king and queen of Evyndale literally applauding.

"It's true what they say about you, Mason Drakeslayer," the plump, big-nosed king chuckled. "Your wit is as sharp as your blade."

"As are his looks," his equally plump wife agreed.

Mason gave a charming, show-offy laugh. "I'll drink to that."

He raised a glass of wine, as did the king and queen. The few others at the lavish banquet table did the same, drinking deeply. Chatter started up, Mason Drakeslayer laughing with the king and queen as they discussed the specifics of their newly struck alliance.

The Surgeon will be pleased, Calyx's voice echoed within the walls of Jax's mind. *Drakeslayer and his Gray One play their part well. As we soon will ours.*

What are you talking about? Jax asked.

All in its time, Calyx answered vaguely.

Servants stood at the ready, pouring more wine as the goblets ran out. At his place beside Jax, Bjorn was already on his third cup.

"Are you sure you won't have any, sir?"

Jax turned to see a serving girl offering him a drink. She batted long, thick eyelashes at him.

"For the third time, no," Jax grumbled, turning away. The serving girl reluctantly moved on.

"Why won't you drink?" Bjorn asked, grabbing a handful of wyvern-shrimp and somewhat barbarically stuffing his face. A few of the Evyndalian nobility cast him unimpressed looks, but said nothing. Bjorn and Jax were the High Prince's personal bodyguards, after all.

When Jax didn't answer Bjorn's question, he repeated it:

"Come on, ex-Knight. Why don't you ever drink? In every tavern we've been to, you refuse."

Jax flexed his jaw. Bjorn got bored of waiting and changed the subject.

"When do you think the Farseer will show?" Bjorn asked, quietly enough so the nobles wouldn't hear.

"He won't," Jax muttered. "He's the drakking Farseer. He knows we're here, and probably that the Evyndalians are inevitably going to side with the Gray. He wouldn't touch this place with a ten-foot wingspan if he knows what's good for him."

"Then why do Snake Eyes' omenfires say he will?"

"He won't," Jax insisted. Then he stubbornly drank his glass of water.

As he did, he narrowed his eyes at Bjorn. "What's your game anyway, mohawk? You claim to despise magi, yet you obey Drakeslayer, Snake Eyes, and the rest without question."

Bjorn took a long, indulgent swig from his goblet, then wiped his mouth with the back of his hand. "What better way to get at the ethercursed than to give them a taste of their own poison?"

Jax made a face, sorry he asked.

Bjorn continued, "Besides, the blue power Mason and the others use is something greater than etherarchy. Voidarchy doesn't draw the dragons. It's power in its purest form."

The way he said it seemed almost hungry. But the idea of Bjorn becoming a magi left Jax without an appetite.

Just before sundown, the streets of Evyndale were loud. The shouts of vendors trying for final sales rang throughout the marketplace, and the cries of wyverngulls rose up from the nearby beaches. The air was thick and humid, condensing into beads of water that slid down the thatched rooftops.

The hot, muggy air made Jax sweat under his armor. Maybe he'd head back to the inn and change, then... what? Go to bed early? Drak, Jax missed his friends. Both the Knights and his squad. At this point, even that scorched half-born Asher would've been a welcome sight.

The grand palace Jax had left behind stood proudly on the hillside, surrounded by tall dragonheart palms. Mason and the others were still there celebrating the alliance, but Jax had left once he saw the unfocused look in their eyes that definitely meant they were drunk.

As Jax walked, he let himself slip into memory:

The hazel-eyed stranger showed six-year-old Jax to a cramped, chilly wine cellar with a straw mattress in one corner. This would be Jax's new room. The man—Torsten—promised that there would be breakfast before the tavern opened in the morning, and that he'd send down some dinner each evening, but that it would probably be best to avoid going upstairs after dark. That was when the Naga's Head tended to get a little rough.

"Goodnight," young Jax called out, "Father."

That made Torsten pause. He grumbled something under his breath, then didn't look back as he retreated up the stairs.

That was the first and last time Jax had called him father.

Life passed slowly at the tavern. At first, Torsten seemed to do his best to make Jax feel comfortable, but it quickly became apparent that the man resented him. Over time, Jax learned that until his mother had asked Torsten to return to

Skygard to take care of him, the man had been trying to start a new life in Keep Rengard.

But the past had dragged him back here. Jax had dragged him back here.

By and by, Torsten became less hesitant about letting Jax know it, too.

Torsten started drinking more frequently after the bar closed late each night. Before long, he stopped waiting until closing time.

Even at such a young age, Jax could see what the alcohol was doing to Torsten. He drank to escape his pain, but in doing so, lost himself.

Torsten got annoyed when he'd find Jax hiding under the bar during the day. But Jax hated being trapped in that dark, smelly basement. He felt like a prisoner.

Not that being upstairs was much better—at least, not when Torsten was in one of his moods. Jax would entertain himself by playing with the empty drink bottles. They were perfect for practicing psionics.

Once during the evening rush, Jax was sitting under the bar in his usual hiding place when he heard an angry patron asking for another bottle of draquila. Torsten was busy with another customer and, without thinking, Jax lit up a psionic rune. Remaining out of sight, he telekinetically pushed the bottle across the counter toward the yelling man.

The man hadn't seen Jax, but cursed at the use of etherarchy. Torsten dashed across the bar to grab the bottle before anyone else saw anything, and Torsten, as drunk as the patron himself, argued about what had just happened. Meanwhile, Torsten cast sidelong glares at Jax cowering beneath the bar.

That night after everyone had left, Torsten yelled at Jax. He called him careless, foolish, and accused him of being the root of all his misery. Jax knew it was mostly the alcohol talking, but each word cut like an axe.

Things only got worse from there. Torsten stopped trying, both as a father and as a man. His waistline grew, his hair became stringy and unkempt, and his eyes seemed to have a permanent glaze over them. A canteen of draquila became his constant companion.

The bar fell into disrepair. As Jax grew older, he did his best to fix up the shabby tables whenever brawling patrons destroyed them. He repainted the fading sign on the door and restocked the bottles. By the time he was eleven, he'd learned to mix dozens of different drinks in rapid succession during the evening rush. Still, there was nothing he could do to keep more damage from occurring each night when the rough crowd began to brawl.

Torsten barely seemed to notice everything Jax was doing. Jax watched his so-called father with growing resentment, determined to never become anything like him.

While Torsten over-ate and rarely left his old, rickety rocking chair, Jax got stronger. He no longer bothered using telekinesis when it was time to bring in a new shipment of mead or whiskey—He lifted the barrels himself. After hours, he trained in his wine cellar bedroom, doing push-ups on the cold stone floor or chin-ups using Torsten's old, broken spear shaft balanced between stacked wine crates. Jax was determined to become capable of putting a stop to the near-nightly bar fights.

If Jax was going to be stuck in this prison, he was at least going to control the only thing he could:

Himself.

For years, the only thing that kept Jax sane were Solrac's visits. Solrac was an old friend of Jax's mother and, as a Psion himself, he'd taken on the task of secretly mentoring young Jax in etherarchy. Once a week, Solrac and his fun-loving bloodhusky, His Majesty, would take Jax away from the tavern and down to the beach or the flats or the mountains. There, they'd spend hours training. Solrac even said Jax had natural talent, and it wasn't long before his skill as a Psion had surpassed Solrac's.

But every time, Jax still had to go back to the Naga's Head—and Torsten.

Solrac said Jax was too young to leave, and Jax knew he was right. Still, Solrac promised that someday, if Jax wanted to, he'd take him away from this place and let him become a Knight of the Torch. Solrac's lifestyle was dangerous, but Jax found every story thrilling. He longed to be a part of them.

Meanwhile, Torsten continued to grow more careless. Jax wasn't the only secret magi at the Naga's Head, and more than once an intoxicated Torsten had runetraced while the bar was still open. Usually, he was using his teleportation abilities to grab a bottle or spool of thick thread for weaving without having to leave his chair. Jax had needed to pay off more than one patron for their silence.

Jax was fourteen when he stopped his first barfight. The men were far older than him, and clearly surprised that someone so young could pack such a hard punch. The fact that they were drunk out of their minds certainly helped. Torsten had been pleased, almost smiling at Jax that night as he sat drunkenly weaving an intricately patterned blanket in the corner.

That night, Jax tore off the sleeves of all his tunics. He was young, but he looked strong. This way, maybe patrons would think twice before starting fights.

Of course, Torsten's favor didn't last. One night when Jax was sixteen, Torsten came out of his room, his gaze even darker than usual. He had an empty bottle tucked under one arm as he rubbed at the black woven band around his wrist. Jax had asked about the marriage bracelet a few times before, only to have Torsten snap at him to "drakkin' mind yer own business, boy."

The bar was dark that night as Jax finished closing. Only the dim orange lamplight let Jax see Torsten approaching.

For a while, Torsten had just stood there, silently watching Jax restock the bottles on their shelves along the back wall. Then suddenly, Torsten spoke.

"Ain't it convenient you got your mother's colorin.'"

His voice startled Jax, making him drop a full bottle of imported Evyndallian rum. The bottle shattered on the floor, the dark liquid draining through the cracks in the floorboards and undoubtedly staining the boards.

"Drak," Jax swore.

"Drak is right," Torsten echoed, raising his voice. "You got any idea how much one of them bottles costs? How're you gonna pay for it, boy? How?"

Jax set his jaw. He'd seen Torsten drunk and angry many times before. Arguing with him never helped. The only thing to do was endure it until he tired himself out.

But tonight, there was something extra sinister in Torsten's watery hazel eyes. Jax's gaze flickered to the black marriage bracelet on his wrist and he wondered if today was some kind of painful anniversary.

"Answer me when I'm speakin' to you!" Torsten suddenly raged, rushing up to Jax and grabbing him by the maroon bandana he wore around his neck. "This is all your drakkin' fault. I should be back in Keep Rengard now 'stead of saddled with you."

Torsten called into the oblivion, "Scorch you, Vidya—I don't even remember that night! My entire life, upended on nothin' more that your sooty word! Stars know you might have used memory-alterin' charms on me, you sky-forsaken sootfire!"

Jax wasn't sure what Torsten was talking about. But with every syllable, Torsten's grip grew tighter on the bandana around Jax's neck. Jax tried to wrench free, but Torsten, while badly out of shape, was still a large, full-grown ex-soldier. But at sixteen, Jax was stronger than ever.

"Let... go..." Jax said, squirming. When Torsten didn't, Jax kneed Torsten in the gut then shoved hard against his chest. When Torsten lost his grip, Jax ducked into his old place underneath the bar.

Torsten's expression was livid. "How dare you lay a hand on me, boy!" In his anger, he violently shattered his empty bottle against the edge of the bar.

Fragments of glass exploded in every direction. Jax used his hands to shield himself, but a few pieces made it through—including one jagged shard that cut across his lower lip.

Torsten was yelling again, more soot and scales about how his life had been ruined. He grabbed a few more bottles off the shelf, recklessly smashing them against walls or the floor. No doubt he'd blame Jax in the morning.

A few days later, Solrac returned to the bar. He'd taken one look at the fresh scar on Jax's lip before half-dragging Torsten into the back room. They'd exchanged heated words, then Solrac had stormed out of the room and told Jax to pack his things.

"What things?" Jax asked, already on his feet. He could see Torsten's silhouetted profile through the door, not moving. Jax knew better than to expect a goodbye.

Jax left the Naga's Head tavern behind without so much as a second glance back down the dusty road toward his father.

A sudden movement from behind a building pulled Jax from the memory. There, near a fishmonger's shop, Jax caught the flash of glossy black feathers. A large bird landed on the thatched palm roof, staring at Jax with shining eyes.

Jax's heart skipped as he recognized the mythraven. The runemarks on its feathers were unmistakable.

"The Farseer," Jax whispered, scanning the street. There—red robes disappearing behind the next row of buildings.

Without thinking, Jax took off after him.

A throng of chattering townspeople and merchants almost immediately blocked his path. Jax pushed his way through toward the retreating back of the man in red robes. When people saw Jax's dusky blue cloak, some stepped aside.

"Mage Hunter," one muttered.

"Chasing a magi?" another questioned.

"Out of his way!"

Soon, Jax had cleared the main streets, continuing his pursuit down darker, less populated alleys. The Farseer seemed to be luring him to the outskirts of the city, away from prying eyes.

Finally, they reached a large grist mill with an enormous waterwheel. The mill was closed for the night, with several carts filled with sacks of grain parked outside. Crates filled with tools sat in neat rows along one wall.

There on the riverbank, as still as a statue, was the Farseer. His eyes glowed from within the darkness of his hood as the mythraven swooped in to land atop the antlers mounted on his gnarled, runemarked staff.

Jax hesitated before jogging up to meet him. Could this be a trap? Did Jax care even if it was?

"Great Farseer," Jax said as he joined the legendary figure in the shadows by the river. "You shouldn't be here. The other Mage Hunters, they want to capture—"

The Farseer removed his hood.

Jax literally stumbled backward. "Solrac?" he gasped.

"My boy." Solrac didn't wait another second before throwing his arms around Jax. Jax was too confused to return the embrace. Why was Solrac dressed as the Farseer? And he'd certainly never called Jax 'my boy' before. What was going on?

"There is so much to say," Solrac said. He was smiling wide.

"So say it," Jax replied, brows furrowed.

Jax could hardly believe his ears as Solrac revealed that all along, he'd been the Farseer. The whole time Solrac was explaining, Jax felt a growing sense of dread.

"If all this is true..." Jax glanced over his shoulder, "then why in the stars are you here? You've gotta know the Mage Hunters are still after you."

"Of course I know that," Solrac said. "The omenfires told me all about Mason Drakeslayer's little plan to ensnare me for the Soul Reaper. But I had to come."

"Why?"

"I came for you, of course."

Jax felt a lump growing in his throat. "Really?"

"Of course," Solrac replied. "I'm here to bring you home."

"Home," Jax repeated.

Solrac's eyes were shining. Were those tears?

"At last," he said, "the three of us will be together."

Jax frowned. "What do you mean?"

"Your mother didn't want me to come. She still thinks you're not ready to know the truth. But I believe you deserve to know. Drak, I wish *I* had known sooner."

A pit appeared in Jax's stomach. What was Solrac saying?

I think you know, came Calyx's cold, taunting voice. A churning storm began brewing in Jax's chest.

"The truth about what?" Jax asked.

"How can I say this?" Solrac mused as he looked Jax over. Why was he looking at him like that? Sorlac clapped his hands together, whatever great news he was about to share thrilling him to the core. The storm inside Jax swirled. He suddenly felt sick.

"Just say it," Jax said.

"Jax," Solrac said, "Torsten isn't your father."

Jax bit down so hard on his cheek he tasted blood.

Solrac then spoke two realm-shattering words that made the revelation about him being the Farseer seem like nothing at all:

"I am."

Jax felt like someone had just doused him with a full bucket of ice-cold water.

Solrac... his father?

A hundred emotions raced through Jax like a skyfall slicing through the night.

First, relief.

That meant Jax bore no relation to Torsten. Instead, he was the son of Solrac, the man Jax had looked up to his entire life.

Next, confusion.

Why had his mother lied to him? How was it fair that he'd had to go nineteen years without knowing the truth?

Then, anger.

"You mean... you mean to tell me—to tell me that... that..." Jax sputtered, so flustered he could hardly speak, "that I missed out on the chance to be with you? Instead—instead she made me grow up with Torsten?"

The storm inside Jax came to a head. He could feel Calyx's gray presence, swallowing up every other emotion with tumultuous clouds of bitter resentment. Feeding on it. Stoking it.

"Don't you see? This is the greatest thing that could have possibly happened!" Solrac was still oblivious to Jax's emotions. "We are *family*.

And on top of it all, as the child of the Duke of Glacia, you will inherit all I possess."

Jax scoffed.

Solrac frowned. "I know this is a lot to take in—"

"You think?" Jax interrupted. "My mother abandons me on the steps of a bar and you expect me to give a scale about some drakking title?"

"I'm certain Vidya was just trying to do what was best for you—"

"Best for me?" Jax spat. "She lied to me! What kind of mother does that to her own child? In what voidish reality was Torsten *best for me?*"

Solrac's expression crumbled. "I hoped you would be happy, my son."

"Don't you call me that!" Jax cried, taking a step backward. His blood was boiling, his eyes hot with tears as he pointed an accusing finger at Solrac.

"You... you left her. You left *us.*"

"I truly believed I was making the right decision at the time, and that I'd even be able to return someday," Solrac said. "But if I had known about you... well, that would've changed everything."

"Would it have? Really?"

"I..." Solrac hesitated. "I hope so. Jax..."

Solrac reached toward Jax, arms outstretched as if he was going for another hug. But Jax turned away to avoid it.

As he did, the blade of Jax's long seaxe turned in such a way that the sword brushed against Solrac's leg. Such a light brush should've been inconsequential, but the nearness of the silver blade made Solrac's entire form flicker.

Jax gritted his teeth as understanding washed over him. Illusion. Solrac wasn't actually here—He was just projecting himself using the mythraven. Just as he must've done a thousand times before as the Farseer.

Jax had to shut his eyes just to stop seeing red. "How am I supposed to believe you would have been there for us then if you aren't even really here for me now?"

"Jax—"

Before Solrac could say anything more, Jax drew his silver seaxe. With one solid slash, he sent Solrac's illusory form dissolving into etherdust. The mythraven cawed, a few feathers fluttering to the ground as it flew into the darkened sky.

But Jax didn't stop there. His finger flew to trace a psionic rune, and with a cry, Jax telekinetically hefted three of the crates along the mill's wall. Tools went flying as he tossed them through the air.

Jax could feel his wraith feeding off of his rage, egging him on. The extra push was enough to take him over the edge. Crate after crate crashed to the ground.

Next, Jax focused on the enormous water wheel connected to the side of the mill. He grunted, muscles bulging as he ripped the wheel from the building and tossed it into the stream. Water splashed onto Jax, but he didn't care.

That was when Jax heard a second thud. He whirled, wondering if he'd find Solrac again. But instead, he saw Bjorn, standing beside the nearest cart from the mill. The cart was on its side, the sacks of grain stored within it spilling everywhere. A few caught on some of the tools Jax had scattered across the ground, wasting the flour inside.

"Bjorn?" Jax called out, suddenly nervous. Bjorn must've followed him here. How much had he seen and heard?

"Hey there, ex-Knight," Bjorn said. His eyes were wild as he flipped another cart, spilling more grain sacks into the dirt. "Looks like we were both right. The Farseer *did* show up; he just wasn't man enough to show up in person. Gotta say, I'm impressed. I thought you were secretly still loyal to those Knights of the Torch, but the way you tore that illusion apart..."

Bjorn paused, locking eyes with Jax. The, lips curling into a sadistic grin, Bjorn went on:

"But at least it was all worth it to uncover the truth. Next time, that ethercursed Duke of Glacia won't stand a chance."

Jax's heart sank. What had he done?

Bjorn laughed wickedly. "Come on. Drakeslayer's gonna love hearing this."

Bjorn turned to leave, and Jax felt a dark urge from deep within him. Bjorn was the only one who knew Solrac's secret. With the element of surprise on his side, Jax was willing to bet he could ensure Bjorn never reached Mason. He could make it look like they'd lost a fight with the Farseer...

He took a step toward Bjorn's back.

But the sadistic nature of the thought was enough to stop Jax in his tracks. He hadn't realized he was capable of even thinking something like that.

You are capable of more than you realize, Calyx spoke to Jax's mind.

Not that, Jax grit his teeth.

Then Bjorn turned around, and the opportunity was gone. "You coming, ex-Knight?"

Jax flexed his jaw. Just because he wasn't willing to kill Bjorn didn't mean he couldn't incapacitate him or something.

Then again, Calyx thought, *doesn't Solrac deserve to be exposed for what he did?*

Just like that, Jax's anger resurfaced. As he followed Bjorn back into town, he once again chose to do nothing.

FRAGMENT: SCORPIO'S SHADOW

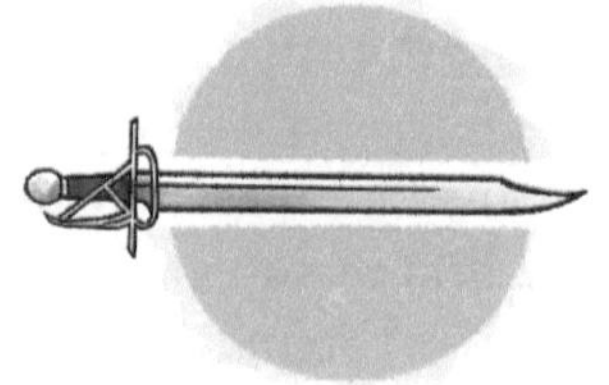

ELLE

S *corpio's Shadow: One Mile. Magi and Drekai not welcome.*

"Well, that's a double no-no for me then," Asher quipped. He circled the dilapidated wooden road sign and ripped off a sheet of paper that had been nailed to the other side.

"And a *big* no-no for you, Ell...iana," Asher said, holding up yet another wanted poster featuring Elle and Aurora's likeness. "One-hundred gold marks... Who votes we turn the princess in for the reward money and then break her out?"

Thorn gave a low wyvern chuckle, but everyone else was a little too weary from the journey for Asher's jokes right now.

"It's like I said before," Brigan said, pointing to the map Kai was busily examining. "This area is bad news."

"We'll definitely be skipping this town." Solvai nodded. "No recruiting here. We'll go around, find a place to camp for the night further west. From there, we won't stop until we reach Orothion."

Elle pressed her lips together. Glancing down the long, dusty road, she could see the town of Scorpio's Shadow at the base of a lone, low mountain. The faint adobe buildings had reddish rooftops made from overlapping tiles like dragon scales, while the mountain itself was a barren wasteland. From here, Elle couldn't see any life on its grayish-brown, stony surface.

Except...

Elle took a few steps closer to get a better look. Tiny winged shapes were swarming the peak.

"What are those?" Meleya asked, squinting.

The skies seemed to take her question as a cue. Within moments, one of the shapes broke free from the others and began winging its way toward the group. Before long, Elle could make out a dark, sinister creature with a scaled body, a serpentine face, and a segmented, curved tail ending in a horrid bulb and stinger.

Elle suddenly understood the town's name.

"Scorpio!" Kai shouted, already dashing to hide behind the dragons. The rest of the group drew their weapons, but Sniff beat everyone to the kill. Four wings moving fast as a hummingbird's, Meleya's evren swept toward the scorpio, jaws snapping, and caught the beast around its neck. The scorpio hissed but, despite Sniff's thrashing, it managed to curve its stinger toward him. The stinger struck true.

"Sniff!" Meleya cried as the creature's venom shot into Sniff's flank. The evren's already-huge eyes grew even larger as his pupils shrank to pinpricks. For a brief moment, Sniff's whole golden-yellow body seemed to tremble with sheer energy.

Then, in a tangle of gold and reddish-black, they dropped.

Sniff and the scorpio hadn't been all that high in the air, so they didn't fall far. Dust puffed up around Sniff as he collided with the ground. Meleya rushed to his side.

Meanwhile, Elle was already on Aurora's back. The pair of them were at the scorpio's side in an instant, Elle's saber slashing while Aurora's front claws raked its armored exterior. The wyvern-scorpion was only about the size of a coyote, and no match for Elle and Aurora.

Vivid green blood sprayed as the scorpio gave its final hiss. A few drops landed on the hem of Elle's travel dress, which she found rather annoying. That was bound to stain.

Of course, her personal cleanliness wasn't really a priority right now.

"Is Sniff okay?" Elle asked, landing near where Meleya knelt beside her dragon.

"Wake up, Sniff!" she was pleading, brown eyes frantic. "Come on, boy."

Sniff grumbled, but didn't open his eyes.

"He's going to be fine," Kai said, emerging from his hiding place behind Thorn. "Based on its translucent, reddish-black coloring, that was a common scorpio. Their venom gives its victim a jolt of adrenaline in order to fill their blood with energy right before it feeds."

"Gross," Asher said.

"Gross, yes, but it means Sniff'll be alright," Solvai said.

With a second witness to Sniff's safety, everyone relaxed as they gathered around him and Meleya. Brigan even knelt beside the fallen scorpio, using his blade to cut off the tip of its stinger and wrapping it in thick cloth to save for later, probably to extract its venom for medicinal purposes.

"I once rescued an evren-dove who'd been stung by a common scorpio," Solvai continued, "She was fine after about twelve hours."

"It would've been better if it had been an emperor scorpio," Kai went on. "Their scales are pure black, but its venom is—"

"—mostly harmless," Solvai finished. "It might make you dizzy for an hour or two, but nothing more. But if Sniff had been stung by a—"

"—fire scorpio, that would've been a different story," Kai said. He and Solvai had locked eyes, slowly walking toward each other. They'd clearly forgotten anyone else was here.

"Fire scorpios are recognizable by their vivid red coloring," Solvai said. "The most feared of every known scorpio variety in Evgard's southern keepdoms. One sting from a fire scorpio..."

"...is absolutely..."

"...deadly," both Kai and Solvai finished in unison. They were standing face to face by now, and each gave a fond sigh as they connected over murderous draconic arachnids.

A chuckle on her lips, Elle turned to the others to see if they'd noticed. She found Asher and Brigan already exchanging amused glances with each other.

"Well—" Asher leaned over to Brigan and Meleya, "I guess this tops their waterfowl feces-inspired date."

"What?" Elle cocked her head.

"Just something from the other day at the initiation ceremony," Asher chuckled.

"You had to be there," Brigan added.

Elle bit her lower lip. She had been at the initiation ceremony, just not laughing around the drink table with the others. She'd been with Rhana and Aurora, ensuring the new members of the Rebel Knights could look to her as a symbol of dignity, just like Rhana and Cenrik had instructed.

It was her duty.

But scorch if Elle didn't miss the freedom.

Before embarking on the quest, the Rebel Knight Triarchy had reminded her just how important that duty was. It was up to Elle to unite the realm. According to the Farseer, the Knights would ultimately be the last holdout against the Soul Reaper and the Gray. If the realm was to stand a chance, they needed all the aid they could get.

Be Eliana, Elle mentally repeated the words Cenrik had said, feeling the pressure like heavy bricks on her shoulders. Rhana had warned against distractions as well. That had been High King Magnus's downfall—He'd let ambition cloud his judgment, sacrificing his moral code on the altar of uniting the keepdoms. Cenrik had warned her against the same. She had to put her duty above all else. She had to prove to Cenrik, her father, Rhana, Kheradok... Scorch, she had to prove to the entire *realm* that Aurora had made the right choice in choosing Eliana.

Besides that, she had to prove it to herself.

And right now, that meant ducking her head and sticking to the schedule.

Yet, the words that came out of Elle's mouth didn't exactly reflect that.

"We need to recruit in this town," Elle declared.

"I'm sorry, what?" Asher said.

"Here?" Brigan asked in disbelief.

Solvai tore her eyes from Kai to shake her head vigorously. "Absolutely not. Scorpio swarms and high crime rates aside, this place is clearly not friendly to Rebel Knights."

Elle marched over to the wooden sign that marked one mile to Scorpio's Shadow. Beside the space where the wanted poster offering a huge reward for her capture had hung, there was another yellowed sheet. Elle tore it from its nail and held it up so the group could see it.

"Today is the first day of their three-day Topaz Festival," Elle said, pointing to the sheet. "We couldn't ask for a better opportunity to recruit. The whole town will be gathered in the square tonight."

"The whole *unreceptive* town, yes," Solvai said.

"We won't know they're unreceptive until we try them," Elle answered. "They deserve a chance, same as any other town. This is why I'm part of this quest team, isn't it? To give the people of this realm the opportunity to choose light rather than get absorbed into the Gray. I just want to do my job."

"Not when it might jeopardize the rest of the quest." Solvai folded her arms. "Getting to Orothion to save Kari and Akayto and stop Vesta's war—*That* will gain us the most support in the long run. You don't have to visit every small town."

"Even the small towns matter. And if something goes wrong, we'll just—"

"Eliana, I'm sorry, but as the leader of this quest, I'm making this call. We're skipping Scorpio's Shadow."

It was plain to see that Solvai hated every second of this confrontation. The others were uncomfortable too, as they stared at the two young women, the beating summer heat only adding to the tension.

"Team!" Solvai gave a barking command. "Move out!"

Elle silently joined the group as they headed toward some ravines south of Scorpio's Shadow, far enough away that the scorpios wouldn't be an issue. All the while, she kept glancing back at the lonely little town at the base of the mountain.

Didn't they deserve the chance to choose light too?

That evening, from their hideout in the ravines, Elle could just see the torchlight of the festival burning like coals at the foot of the mountain. When she strained, she thought she could hear the faintest music. That might've been down to her enhanced senses through Aurora's abilities as a Sentinel. Now that night had fallen, the scorpios seemed to have quieted down, though Elle could still see a few shadows circling the peak.

Asher and Thorn were out hunting drakalope to replenish the group's waning meat supply. Elle could see Solvai and Kai sitting together in the distance to the east, silhouetted against the starry sky as they discussed the best routes for the remainder of the journey. Meanwhile, Meleya was asleep, tired after another long day of skyskipping as she lay beside Sniff. He still hadn't roused since the scorpio sting, but at least he seemed fairly normal aside from the occasional twitch as the venom worked its way out of his system.

Beside Elle, Aurora kept looking toward the town as well. At least she was on her side. Through their bond, Aurora spoke:

Can we go?

No, Elle bit her lip. *We have to do the right thing.*

But *was* standing by the right thing? Once again, Elle reflected on her conversation with Cenrik. He, Solrac, and Solvai made up the Rebel Knights' Triarchy, the leadership council that was meant to bring balance to body, mind, and spirit. As a Mystic, Solrac had always done his part to bring logic and clever problem solving to the table. Meanwhile, Solvai was doing her part as a Sentinel, thinking through the practical ramifications of their decisions.

But as for Cenrik, a former Archon, Elle couldn't help but wonder if the loss of his ether well had left him without hope. For him, the Rebel Knights were only recruiting for the war to raise their numbers and give them a better chance of stopping the Gray army.

But for Elle and Aurora, it was about the people. Each new person that found purpose in the Knights was just as much of a victory as recruiting the whole of Behrfell.

What if this is *the right thing?* Aurora asked.

Elle met her dragon's emerald eyes. Through their bond, Elle felt light like a beacon lighting her way forward.

Quickly, Elle changed into her white armored dress and shining tiara. She scribbled a note to say they'd gone out hunting as well. Then, silently, the two of them took off toward Scorpio's Shadow.

Castanets clapped and lutes strummed. Wide, colorful skirts swirled as the townspeople danced in the square. The first day of Scorpio's Shadow's annual summer Topaz Festival was in full swing.

With Elle and Aurora right at the center of it.

At first, she and Aurora had stuck to the background, speaking with one person at a time as they got a feel for whether or not the place would be safe. But slowly, they'd made their way out of the shadows. Before long, a crowd had gathered.

"Can I touch her scales?" a young girl asked, pointing to Aurora with awe in her eyes.

"Of course." Elle smiled. The girl giggled, then reached out a hand. A gray hand, Elle noticed as the girl's sleeve fell away.

"Shadow wasting," Elle muttered quietly.

"Yes, sorry," a woman said, a man at her side. The pair could only be the girl's parents. They approached Elle and her mount with reverence.

The girl's mother said, "She took a bite from an umbral rat when she was very young. It's taken all our life savings just to keep her supplied with enough liquid light to keep her from becoming hollow. She wouldn't be the youngest person the Capital soldiers have sent on to Kolbohr. But with you here, perhaps..."

A man jumped in, "Are the legends true? Do true dragons have the power to heal the shadow wasting with their flame?"

"Oh," Elle said, taken aback. Aurora had the capacity to access all nine types of etherarchy, just like the Guardians once could. But while Elle, too, had heard the stories about Guardians being able to perform miraculous healings, she and Aurora couldn't do anything like that. Not yet. And they certainly couldn't heal the incurable shadow wasting.

Elle was about to offer a heartfelt apology, but Aurora seemed to have ideas of her own. She looked into the sweet little girl's eyes, and through her bond with Aurora, Elle could feel her dragon connecting with the girl. Aurora deeply felt her pain.

A symbol began to glow over Aurora's forehead that Elle had never seen before. Intricate patterns lit up along her scales and her eyes shone with gold light as she leaned toward the child. Then, she let out the softest breath of fire toward the girl's hand.

For a moment, Elle worried that Aurora would burn the girl, but something was different. Aurora's fire was still light-like in nature, but instead of its usual green and violet, the rippling light was pure white.

As the white flame kissed the girl's skin, all the grayness instantly retreated, fleeing before Aurora's light.

Stars. Elle was certain of it—The girl was fully healed.

Elle watched, just as awestruck as the cheering crowd. The girl's parents had tears in their eyes as they thanked Elle profusely.

Meanwhile, Aurora sank to the ground, resting her head on her foreclaws. Through their bond, Elle could sense that whatever etherarchy Aurora had just used had drained her completely. Almost dangerously so. This wasn't something she could do again and again.

"Rest, girl," Elle whispered, stroking Aurora's neck. "You did well."

Aurora could barely manage a low growl of gratitude for Elle's praise.

Meanwhile, the healed girl's father addressed the throng. "The High King is wrong! Princess Eliana is no usurper. She and Aurora are the realm's salvation!"

"She is this *town's* salvation," said another. He was a pompous man with a round, shiny nose, who pushed his way to the front. "Ain't any of you seen what High King Magnus is offerin' for her capture? Enough to buy the guard-power to rid our town of them drakkin' scorpios once and for all."

Elle tensed. With Aurora drained of energy, she couldn't take to the skies at a moment's notice like she'd planned.

Luckily, it seemed the majority of people were on her side.

"Scorch the High King!" proclaimed the little girl's father. "And scorch anyone who speaks against Eliana, our true dragon rider!"

The crowd hurrahed the shiny-nosed man into silence. Elle took the opportunity to rally the townspeople.

"Light the way!" she cried, raising her hand as if she were holding a torch.

"Light the way!" the people responded, copying the gesture. Elle was beaming. Cenrik and others may see this as an inconsequential victory, but Elle disagreed. It wasn't inconsequential to the people here.

Then, in the back of the crowd, a head of bright white hair stood out. She was wearing a bandana over her face to hide her silvermark, but even still, Meleya was unmistakable.

As Meleya made her way across the town square, Elle greeted as many new people as she could. When Meleya reached Elle's side, she was indignant.

"What in the stars are you doing?" Meleya asked.

"My duty," Elle replied, helping another child stroke Aurora's flank.

"Solvai and the others are going to kill you if they find out," Meleya said.

"You mean you haven't already told them?"

"Not yet. I wanted to give you a chance to come back first. The last thing this group needs is more conflict."

Elle took in Meleya's tapping foot, her folded arms, and the worry in her expression. She was no doubt wanting to get back to Sniff, and needed to get to sleep herself if she was going to have the energy to skyskip the next day.

Reluctantly, Elle bid the people of Scorpio's Shadow a final goodnight, then she and Meleya headed out of the square, a very sleepy Aurora walking alongside them. Aurora wouldn't be able to fly, but if they could find a suitable place for Meleya to rift them toward camp, they'd be back in no time. But first, they had to ensure nobody was following them.

They headed down a few side streets, weaving through the adobe buildings until they found a secluded alleyway.

"Alright," Elle said. "Now, why don't we just—"

A strange thud cut Elle short. She turned around to find Meleya on the cobblestone street, out cold. Aurora's eyes were just rolling back in her head as well.

Scorch.

Elle reached for her saber, but no sooner had her hand closed around the hilt than she felt the hot and fiery sting. Her heart started racing, and within a second she was lying flat on her back, looking up into the snake-like face of a reddish-black scorpio.

But wait... the scorpio was changing. This one was different... not just an animal. In a puff of vivid gold mist, the scorpio shifted into a tall man with salt-and-pepper hair and cold, pale eyes. A Wildshaper. He was holding a crinkled yellow page in his hands—a wanted poster. With darkness in his expression, he compared Elle with the drawing on the paper. Suddenly, he broke into an awful, hair-raising smile.

"The High King will pay handsomely for you," he said, his voice like a hiss. "But this says nothing about the condition in which he wants his new rival brought in now, does it?"

Oh no.

That was the last thought Elle had before she succumbed to the scorpio's venom.

Elle wasn't sure how long she'd been out. Hours? A few minutes? Surely not days.

"Eliana." Meleya's whispered voice sounded distant. "Eliana, are you awake?"

"Hmm..." Elle mumbled, forcing her eyes open as she remembered the tall, pale-eyed Wildshaper. Stars, where had he taken them?

Rich red-violet curtains draped across windowless stone walls. She and Meleya sat on a lush rug adorned with intricate bronze patterns, and there were jewels and gemstones everywhere, from the doorframes to the room's support beams to the hearth. A roaring fire warmed the room, so why was Meleya shivering?

That's when she noticed that Meleya's wrists were bound in silver manacles, a short length of delicate silver links connecting them. But it wasn't Meleya's chains that made Elle's jaw drop.

It was her clothes.

Gone were her nomad-style leather armor and simple tunic. Instead, she wore a red-violet dress that showed off a surprising amount of her leg through the slits on either side. A tight bodice laced up her torso, and she had no sleeves other than wispy scraps of fabric hanging off the sides of her shoulders. She wore a heavy-looking ruby necklace, and... scorch. Had someone pierced her ears?

Elle was dressed similarly. Her heart sank as she realized what was going on. It seemed Meleya's shaking was about more than just the silver.

"The man who took us calls himself Lord Scorpio." Meleya's voice was small. "We're in his palace beneath the mountain, Scorpio's Peak. He said he's already sent word to the Mage Hunters that he has you and the true dragon. They'll be here by morning."

Elle's hand flew to her collarbone. Aurora's heartscale was missing.

"Where's Aurora?" she asked, panic rising in her chest.

"With Lord Scorpio in the throne room," Meleya said. "He tied her up there before bringing us here. A couple of maids came by next to give us these—" Meleya held up the silky skirts of her dress, "then said to... to wait for Lord Scorpio."

She could barely finish the sentence. Her knuckles turned white as she gripped her skirt, and her breathing became rapid and shallow.

"The door's bolted shut, I've already tried," Meleya squeaked. "No windows. Even the fireplace is too small to get out of. The only way out is through the secret door at the top of the mountain, and according to the maids, the scorpios out there are under their wildshaping Lord's command and would kill us in seconds."

Elle swallowed, the gravity of the situation weighing more heavily with each word. "How long do we have before he comes back?"

Meleya tried to reply, but could only shake her head and shrug her bare shoulders. She squeezed her eyes shut as she sputtered, "I... I was going to make drakalope steaks and eggs for breakfast tomorrow. And I brought some cinnamon along—I was going to try out a new sugared bread for a pick-me-up after lunch."

"Don't worry about that right now," Elle said.

Tears flowed down Meleya's cheeks. "But who's going to cook for everyone? They'll... they'll be hungry."

"Shh..." Elle said, scooting closer to Meleya. She put an arm around her and pulled her close. Elle was terrified too, but she knew the army had very strict codes of conduct when it came to treatment of female soldiers. Meanwhile, a life in court had better prepared Elle for how to deal with unwelcome male attention. Of course, she'd never experienced anything like this.

"Eliana," Meleya said. "What do we do?"

Elle paused for a long moment before replying. "You can call me Elle, if you want."

"Elle?" Meleya repeated.

"I like Elle better than Eliana if I'm being honest. But it's always felt too casual for when I'm acting as the princess."

"I think I've heard Asher call you Elle a few times," Meleya said.

"Probably. When Asher and I met, I was pretending to be an assistant dragon keeper."

"Really?"

Elle laughed, then, just to have something to distract them, she launched into the story of how she'd met Asher and worked with him in the stables in Keep Drakfell. They'd both been keeping a secret about their true identities, and had spent many pleasant hours together mucking out stalls.

"So," Meleya began, somewhat hesitant, "is Asher the only guy you've ever had feelings for?"

Meleya's question surprised Elle. Meleya clearly wanted to keep the conversation going so as to not think about their current situation, but Elle sensed there was more behind Meleya's curiosity.

Elle gave Meleya a sidelong glance. "You know, a proper princess would deny having any such feelings outright."

Meleya raised an eyebrow. "So this is your test then. Are you a proper princess?"

Elle tilted her head back and forth as if she were trying to decide. Then, despite everything, she laughed. "Okay, so I like Asher. But I can't exactly say he's the only guy I've had feelings for."

"Brigan?" Meleya asked.

Elle bit her lip. "Brigan's sort of perfect—exactly the kind of guy I *should* like."

Meleya nodded along as if she could relate. "But…?" she prompted.

Elle hesitated. Then she realized she would love nothing more than to share her feelings with someone.

Meleya listened intently as Elle told her all about her encounter with General Kheradok in the woods outside the safehouse. It was silly and girly, but Elle told her all about the way her heart had pounded when he'd kissed her.

"Soot, you're in trouble," Meleya teased.

"I know," Elle replied.

"So what happens when General Kheradok and Asher duel at the end of the summer?"

Elle put her hands to her head. "I don't know."

Meleya raised an eyebrow, holding up two hands. "So: If you had to pick, who would it be? Asher or Kheradok?"

Elle sensed the tension in the question and got the feeling she knew which answer Meleya was hoping to hear. Still, Elle wasn't much for hiding the truth. She let months worth of pent-up feelings spill out.

"As 'Elle,' I would want nothing more than to be with Asher," Elle said. "But as 'Eliana,' I know such choices are out of my hands. Now that I'm the true dragon rider, all eyes are on me, and there are certain expectations that come with that. I have to show everyone that Aurora didn't make a mistake, which means my liberated days of pretending I'm a stablehand are over."

Meleya leaned closer, just listening.

Elle sighed, brows knit. "Can you imagine poor Asher having to wear stuffy suits and attend council meetings all day?"

The very idea made Meleya chuckle. "He'd rather stick scales in his eyes."

"Exactly." Elle's smile was sad. "I could never ask that of him." Then she locked eyes with Meleya. "But the two of you, on the other hand…"

Elle stifled a giggle as Meleya suddenly sat up straight. She stammered incoherently, some soot about not knowing what Elle was talking about.

"Relax," Elle said. "All I'm saying is that Asher and I can't have a future, so don't hold back on my account. A Seer dragon friend of mine once said not to trust Asher with my heart unless I wished for a fight. Well... consider this me avoiding a fight."

Elle looked down, suddenly remembering the dress and jewelry she'd been forced into. The first tear escaped her eye.

"Then again," she said, "maybe I won't have to worry about any of that anymore."

Now it was Meleya's turn to put her arms around Elle. At least, the best she could while cuffed in silver. When Meleya spoke, her voice was calm and even.

"Have you ever wondered what it looks like in the spirit plane when a dragon bonds you?"

Elle cocked her head.

Meleya went on. "I was using the Sight when Sniff bonded me, so I saw what happened to our souls. A piece of his bound itself to me, even more strongly than these cuffs. Likewise, some of my aura—my crazy, reckless, indigo aura—now glows in the void left by his heartscale."

"Interesting," Elle said, trying to follow. "But what exactly are you implying?"

"I'm saying, what if your true dragon didn't choose you *in spite* of your personality, but *because* of it? I've seen you charm the scales off of strangers when you're recruiting for the Rebels—You're at your best when you're being yourself. Drak the mold of what you think a leader of Evgard is supposed to be like. That hasn't gotten us anything but more magi executions and more war with the Dragon Isles. That, and a High King who's so worried about losing his power that he put a realm-wide, hundred-mark bounty on the head of an eighteen-year-old girl. Lead the way your heart tells you to."

For a few minutes, Elle and Meleya sat quietly, the only sound coming from Meleya's teeth occasionally chattering from the silver.

Finally, Elle said, "Stars, Meleya. You'd make an excellent politician."

Meleya smiled. "Thanks, but I want to live out my days in a quiet little corner of the realm with nothing more than the people I love, my dragon, and a vegetable garden."

Elle sighed. "The best candidates usually do."

The pair of them jumped when the door suddenly burst open. Meleya clung to Elle's arm as the pair got to their feet.

But it wasn't Lord Scorpio in the doorway—It was one of the maids.

"The Mage Hunters are in the throne room," she said. "You're lucky—They're here early. Follow me."

Elle was shocked to find Lord Scorpio locked in a heated conversation with none other than Jaira and Lothar. Elle knew their group had stopped a lot in towns along the way, but still, in order to keep up with Meleya's skyskipping, the Mage Hunters must've run their dragons ragged. The thought made Elle's blood begin to boil.

The maid led Elle and Meleya to the door, while her lord and the Hunters negotiated near the throne across the grand room. In the far corner, Elle saw Aurora, cowering as three scorpios guarded her. She seemed sedated somehow.

Elle wanted to run to her dragon, but one of the maids grabbed hold of her arm. She shook her head, pleading in her eyes. A few more maids had joined them in the doorway. Elle sensed all of their deep-seated fear and refrained from running across the room.

"...that many marks for the snowhead would be completely ridiculous," Jaira was saying, her thick brows lowered, her arms folded.

"If the magi is as valuable as you say, the extra marks shouldn't be an issue," Lord Scorpio replied, his voice like a cold hiss. He was taller than both Jaira and Lothar, his presence sinister and commanding.

Beside Elle, Meleya tensed. They had to be talking about her. A few more maids joined them in the doorway.

"We'll do twenty gold and not a copper more," Jaira said. She was clearly doing her best to come across as authoritative, but even she squirmed under Lord Scorpio's gaze.

"Fifty gold marks," said Lord Scorpio. "If you want her for twenty, you can come back next week and perhaps I'll reconsider."

"Now, see here, Sir—" Lothar tried, looking disgusted.

The bone-chilling hissing of a pair of scorpios cut Lothar short. He jumped back to avoid the creatures as they crept nearer.

"You've already got your hundred gold for the princess and her true dragon." Jaira swallowed. "Take the twenty for the Rifter and be grateful I don't report you as an unregistered magi."

Lord Scorpio's eyes darkened as he advanced toward the Mage Hunters right along with the hissing scorpios. Elle got the feeling this wasn't going to end well. The ever-growing cluster of young women around her trembled.

"Perhaps I'll accept a reduced price," Lord Scorpio said, his skin beginning to glow with golden wildmarks, "and you can stay a night or two yourself."

Lothar had no sooner drawn his seaxe than the pair of scorpios's stingers whipped forward, fast as lightning. Both Lothar and Jaira dropped to the floor. Jaira cried out as she fell, letting something slip from her hand in a last-ditch effort to fight back.

It was a small stone swirling with gray. Elle and Meleya exchanged looks as they watched the shadowy umbral spirit spiral out of the stone. It was the same sort of dark relic the Mage Hunters had used on Leif the ursadon, only now instead of possessing a dragon-bear, the umbralizing wraith servant went straight into...

Lord Scorpio.

Inhaling through his nostrils, the demonic lord turned to the group of his victims gathered in the throne room doorway. The young women huddled together as his pale irises went a vivid umbral blue that filled his entire eye. His face went eerily gray as whatever wraith spirit Jaira had thrown at him enhanced his power.

The wildmarks on his skin changed from gold to a burning void blue, pulsing as he compelled more scorpio servants to suddenly slam the throne room door, causing the shrieking group of girls to shrink deeper into the room.

But even as the other young women cried out in terror, searching for an escape, Elle caught a glimpse of white around Lord Scorpio's neck—Aurora's heartscale. She could only hope the wraith wouldn't realize what he had. She'd do what she had to to make sure of it.

Elle turned to the gathered group of maids. There were at least nine of them now, including herself and Meleya. Meleya looked terrified, but gave Elle a nod. It was now or never.

Shoving down her fear, Elle shouted, "Light the way!"

Then, they charged.

CHAPTER 23: FIRE

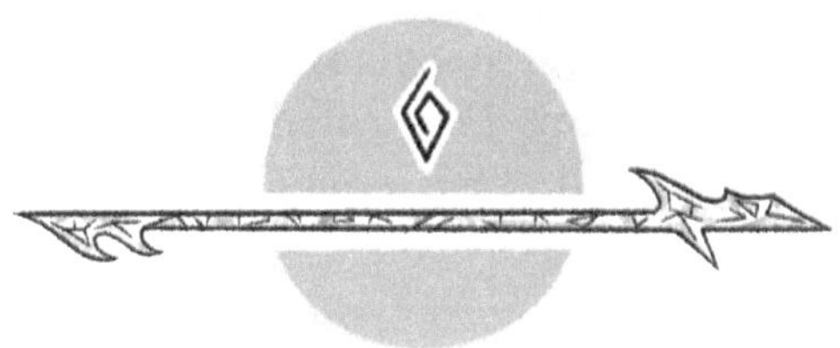

ASHER

It turned out hundreds of venomous wyvern-scorpions were nothing when you were as motivated as I was.

Okay, not nothing. Brigan, Kai, Solvai, and I were fighting for our lives here, racing up the mountainside on dragonback. Brigan fought fiercely from Sniff's back while a somewhat fearful Kai took out scorpios with both crossbow bolts and purple darts of dreamweave energy.

Solvai had shifted into falcondrake form and did battle alongside them. With her mighty brown wings and four menacing claws, she was lethal as she slashed monster after monster. She caught one mid-air with her powerful beak, then tossed its lifeless body against the stony mountain.

The light of dawn was just breaking over the peak, glinting off of the tiny topaz gems that dotted the mountainside. It had been one void of a night. When Thorn and I had returned from our hunt to find Elle, Aurora, and Meleya gone, my heart had dropped into my feet. I hadn't bought Elle's note about going hunting for a second, and when Sniff had woken from his scorpio venom coma panicking, that had confirmed it.

From there, Sniff had surprised us all with his spot-on tracking ability. It was more than the connection a heartscale could provide. Rather, it was as if he had some kind of supernatural force guiding him straight up the side of the mountain to where his rider was trapped inside. Sniff couldn't articulate all the details, but he warned us about Meleya's fear, her desperation, and just how much we needed to hurry.

And based on Sniff's roars, her fear had just spiked. Something sinister was happening inside that mountain.

Thorn and I moved as one, his dragonfire torching a half-dozen hissing scorpios at once while I decapitated a whole row of the flying, venomous beasts with my starglass spear. We dodged the sting of one reddish-black scorpio, then Thorn sliced it in two with his tail spike.

Several more stings thudded uselessly into Thorn's diamondoak armor, and another glanced off of the starglass armor that covered my chest and back. At Solvai's suggestion, I'd formed starglass armor for the other members of our team as well. The scorpios weren't used to prey that fought back.

Despite our best efforts, these scorpios wouldn't let up, and what's more, they were clearly drawn to the ether wells of me, Kai, and Solvai. Each time we used our powers, we drew them like starmoths to flame.

"It's not enough!" Brigan called, expertly using his shield to block a pair of scorpios as they flew toward him and Sniff. He quickly took out another with a hard blow from his seaxe, but he had to block two more stingers with his shield.

"We've destroyed so many scorpios already," Kai called over the hissing and slashing of battle. "But there are still at least six times as many between us and the summit!"

Kai was right. We needed something big.

"Time for a show," I muttered with determination. My eyes burned with golden etherlight.

I placed a hand on Thorn's flank, channeling some of my levitation abilities into him. White ethermist began to billow around us, ready to amplify what I was about to do. It was a power I'd sort of managed before, but never with this much precision.

Then again, I'd never had a better reason to make it work.

In what definitely felt like a breakthrough in my powers, Thorn and I hover-shot through the cloud of scorpios ahead of us like a golden, ether-tailed comet. We stopped only a short distance from the summit, still practically glowing with brilliant white light.

"You want ether, sting-beasts?" I called, cupping my hands around my mouth. "Well, come and get it!"

When the tidal wave of hungry wyvern-scorpions swarmed me, I was ready.

I tucked into a ball, drawing as much ether from my well as I could spare. As I did, I felt the breakthrough I'd been aiming for in my combination of training from Boone and Ivar.

My eyes blazed gold, then I exploded, throwing my arms out to either side. I yelled at the top of my lungs as a crackling white pulse of pure ether rippled off of me and Thorn from every side. Thorn roared with power.

My crazy 'astro-nova' was so strong, every remaining scorpio on that peak hissed as jagged, white ether scarring ripped across their scaled bodies. I briefly panicked when I realized my ether pulse was going to hit my friends further down the mountainside, but I was able to apply the same precision I used when forming starglass to keep the blast from touching any of them.

The scorpios seemed to freeze, briefly hovering stiffly in the air. Then all at once, they went limp, thudding to the earth like a hailstorm all around me.

Without the hissing and flapping of scorpios, the mountain seemed eerily quiet. Before long, Sniff had hover-flown to catch up, Brigan clinging to his neck for dear life. Solvai and Kai were close behind.

There! Sniff's voice sounded inside my head as he zipped toward an ornate metal door in the cliffside.

The door was bolted shut, but such locks had never been tested against body slams by second ascension dragons.

Our small army burst into the underground palace. We immediately met a pair of pitch black scorpios who guarded the door from the inside. Brigan took one out with one slash from his seaxe while falcondrake Solvai crushed the other with her talons, blocking its sting with the starglass armor I'd made for her falcondrake form. A handful of other scorpios headed our way, but Sniff took them on.

Meanwhile, the rest of us surveyed the vast throne room, looking for blood.

And soot, did we find it.

Six or seven girls were either clutching stings or laying still from one. Among them I spotted two forms in dusky blue cloaks, struggling to get up... Was that Jaira and Lothar?

I forgot all about the Mage Hunters when I saw Elle lying in the middle of the floor. Her eyes were fluttering and there was a scorpio stinger puncture on her leg, blood from her wound dripping onto the cold stone floor. She wore a deep red dress unlike any I'd ever seen her wear before.

I was a split second away from hover-dashing to her side when a scream snapped my gaze to the far end of the ballroom.

Meleya struggled against the harsh grip of a tall, broad man with oddly gray skin. She wore a tight-fitting dress with one of its wispy sleeves torn, most likely at the hands of the man who held her against a wide, gem-covered throne. He had both her arms pinned above her head, and I could tell from here that Meleya was shackled with silver. And her face... her face betrayed sheer terror.

Flames tore through my body, boiling my blood as I charged toward the man with my starglass spear poised to strike him down. He turned to me with pale, unfeeling eyes—umbral blue eyes—then roughly tossed Meleya off to the side to face me. She landed hard on the ground, crying out as her manacled hands stopped her from being able to properly catch herself. I nearly changed course to run toward her and make sure she was okay, but out of the corner of my eye I saw Brigan doing just that.

Good.

That left me room to take care of this monster.

I was about to stab my spear into the tall man's heart when a cloud of blue mist suddenly enveloped him. Momentarily, the cloud burst as he morphed into an unnaturally massive scorpio and thrust his head toward me, snakelike jaws wide and stinger dripping with emerald green venom.

While splotches of gray and unnaturally blue eyes indicated that some kind of voidarchy was at work, the majority of his carapace exterior was bright red.

He'd become a gargantuan fire scorpio—the kind Solvai and Kai had said was lethal.

My hover-dashing instincts kicked in in the nick of time. I rolled out of the way, sending out a pulse of ether that struck the fire scorpio's side and got him hissing in rage.

As he hissed, other scorpios flew our way, like they were responding to his commands. They advanced on me, and between my starglass armor and spear I could barely keep their stings at bay.

But then Thorn joined me, launching a tail spike that pegged the great red scorpio in the neck. That got half of his scorpio army going after Thorn, but my wyvern's diamondoak armor held strong.

Kai and Solvai came next, Solvai's falcondrake claws raking against the monster's flank as Kai shot a massive dart of purple dream energy right at its head. Our wildshaping enemy went crosseyed with dizziness.

My friends had bought me some time, and I didn't intend to waste it. I hover-dashed through the remaining scorpios and behind our real foe's head. I hovered directly beside the stinger, which was twitching madly as it whipped around to get a clean shot, so fast it was practically blurry. But I was faster.

Starglass spear in hand, I flared my levitation etherarchy to strike like a skyfall, driving my blade directly into the bulb of the stinger. The monster hissed, arching its blood-red back in a way that made the hairs on my arms stand on end.

Then, using my spear, I twisted the deadly stinger and drove it straight into the scorpio's own back.

The beast hissed and twitched in agony. Blue clouds sputtered all around the giant fire scorpio as he reverted back to his human form, red blood and emerald poison mixing on the floor.

Gray mist swirled out of him, dissipating the same way it had Leif the ursadon. The scorpio man's bright blue eyes paled, staring vacantly ahead as he drew his last, ragged breath. Above him, his recently departed wraith glared at me with glowing blue eyes before folding in on itself and imploding in a burst of gray. The rest of the scorpios fled.

The throne room was silent but for the whimpering of the young women. Kai and Solvai were rounding them up, looking them over to make sure they were alright. They seemed scared witless, and who could blame them?

As for Jaira and Lothar, they were nowhere to be seen. They must've slipped out the door, too weakened by the scorpio venom to take us on for now.

Meleya's crying reached my ears. I turned around to see that she'd collapsed into Brigan's arms, her face buried into his chest. He held her tightly, one hand protectively around her while the other soothingly caressed her long, white hair. Sniff stood by as well, pointed ears erect with worry.

Elle, I suddenly thought.

Relief flooded me when I found her sitting up, rubbing her head. She must've only been stung by one of the black emperor scorpios who'd guarded the door. Still, I wanted to tell Brigan to get over to her and get some liquid light on her wound right away. But by the looks of things, Meleya needed Brigan as much or more than Elle did right now.

Wordlessly, I shed the bracers on my forearms—the ones forged with the regenerative powers of Thorn's scales. Trying not to tremble, I tied the black-and-copper bracers onto Elle's arms.

I forced myself to wait, holding her hand as the power took effect. First, gold patterns lit up the bracers. Then, before my eyes, I watched her bruises and cuts heal, all the way down to the inflamed scorpio sting on her leg.

"Thanks for that," Elle said, breaking our silence.

"Did that snake of a man…" I trailed off, looking into Elle's bright amber eyes.

"No," she replied. "He tried, but Meleya chucked a ruby necklace at his head. He tried to keep us from running, but I'd managed to get Aurora's heartscale back. He didn't expect me to be as strong as I am with Aurora lending me her power."

Elle's hand was still in mine, and I suddenly realized she was shaking.

"Thanks for skewering that creep," she said, trying to joke away her lingering fear.

"Anytime," I replied, eyeing her bare shoulders. "Are you cold?"

"I'm fine, but that reminds me. Do you have our supply of silverbane?"

"Yeah," I nodded.

Elle used her head to gesture toward Meleya. "She could use it."

I followed her gaze and saw that Meleya's wrists were bound in silver. My gut wrenched as I realized that on top of everything else, Meleya had been enduring freezing cold pain and no access to her ether. No wonder she'd had to resort to chucking jewelry.

I gave Elle's hand one last squeeze then made my way across the room to Meleya. Brigan was still holding Meleya tightly, and I noted a patch of water from her tears on the front of his tunic.

"You're alright, you're alright," Brigan spoke in a soothing tone. "You're safe now."

Brigan's eyes were closed, and neither of them had noticed my approach. With a pang, I suddenly became worried I was interrupting something.

Part of me wanted to get their attention. Get Brigan to go make sure my bracers had done a good enough job with Elle's wound. That way, I could personally check in with Meleya and help her remove the silver manacles myself.

Instead, I subtly tapped Brigan on the shoulder. He looked up, and I silently passed him the silverbane. He recognized the little starglass vial and gave me a grateful nod before I turned around and returned to Elle and Aurora.

For such an isolated frontier town, the folks of Scorpio's Shadow sure knew how to put together a party.

It was the last day of the town's annual summer festival. The town was so grateful for what we'd done to rid the mountain of the scorpios and free those young women from Lord Scorpio that they hailed us as heroes. Additionally, they announced that they were officially renaming the town 'Topaz Sierra.' The baron even made a big show of tearing down that awful 'magi and Drekai not welcome' sign outside town, and they ceremoniously burned every one of Eliana's wanted posters in a great bonfire.

The sun was low in the sky as bright torches lit the town square. Delicious smells filled the air, as did the sound of laughter and music. A small group of musicians with lutes, castanets, tambourines, and drums played together around the fountain in the center of the square.

Eliana seemed different after her experience with Meleya under the mountain. Tonight she wore her white armored dress, but she'd added an elegant dark purple sash and a few purple flowers to her hair. Aurora put on a little show with her unique, lightlike dragonfire, making children squeal with joy and adults watch in wonder. Elle laughed, joked, and spent way too many marks on the various street vendors.

She was so... Elle. Not the stiff, regal princess I'd come to expect. Just Elle. I couldn't help but smile, my pulse picking up as I watched her from across the square.

Meanwhile, I was having about as much fun as Elle was. The children here flocked to Thorn, and before long I found myself giving free dragon rides above the square. At first Kai had complained about the festival delaying our plans, but he didn't seem too broken up about it as he explored the torchlit square with Solvai. Once, I even caught them holding hands.

Meleya had barely left Brigan's side since we'd found her and Elle in the throne room under the mountain. I could hardly blame her. He was her best friend, her familiar protector. Her safe space.

Only now, she seemed to be the only one not particularly enjoying the party. Currently, Meleya was standing awkwardly off to the side while Brigan spoke animatedly with a member of the local baron's court. She nodded every once in a while, but I could tell she wasn't really paying attention. I thought I noticed her eyeing a few of the nearby food carts, probably looking for inspiration.

After letting a set of twelve-year-old twins take Thorn for a very low-flying, closely supervised spin, I asked my dragon if he'd be alright on his own for a moment.

My wyvern barely heard me. He was too busy showing off his wood-weaving armor trick, gold patterns lighting up along his body as his scales grew suddenly thicker and harder.

I left the kids oohing and aahing over my dragon bond while I made my way toward Meleya. Brigan gave me a friendly nod as I joined them, though his mouth didn't stop for one second as he and the courtier debated whether or not it was more economical to centralize crop production into the keepdoms with more fertile farmland.

No wonder poor Meleya was all but asleep on her feet.

"Those new?" I asked her, pointing to her hand as it absently rubbed at her earlobes. She wore a pair of tiny, black, spherical stud earrings.

"Huh? Oh, yeah," she replied, tucking her hair behind one ear so I could get a better look. "They uh... pierced my ears while I was under the mountain and the ones Lord Scorpio's servants put in were heavy. Elle gave me these instead."

A wave of emotion rushed through me, but the look in Meleya's eyes told me the last thing she wanted to talk about right now was what had happened under the mountain. What she needed right now was a good distraction, and a rousing discussion about crop production wasn't going to cut it.

"You hungry?" I asked, gesturing to the nearest food cart.

Meleya cast Brigan a quick glance, realized he wasn't even close to wrapping up his conversation, then shrugged as she fell into step beside me.

"So, where would you like to—" I started, but Meleya was already making a beeline toward a cart serving some kind of stuffed fried pepper wrapped in little strips of wyvernhog bacon with corn salad and squares of flatbread on the side.

"How much for these?" Meleya asked the vendor, pointing to the bacon-wrapped peppers.

"Four copper per meal," she replied, holding her serving spoon over the corn.

I was about to fork over eight copper marks when Meleya cut in again.
"How much for just the bacon-wrapped peppers?"

The vendor eyed Meleya. "One copper each."

"We'll take two," Meleya replied, handing over the marks. As we took our food and left the cart, it was my turn to eye Meleya.

"You nomads eat like scaleshrews," I said, holding up the little pepper. "You think this is enough to fill us up?"

"No," Meleya said, "but look at all the different food carts here. You want to fill up on mediocre corn salad and dry bread? Or would you rather save some marks and just get the good stuff?"

My crooked grin came out strong. "You just might be the cleverest scale-in-the-mud I've ever met."

Meleya smiled back, holding up her fried pepper. "On three?"

Nodding, I started the countdown. "One... two..."

"Three," we said together.

The succulent taste of crispy wyvernhog bacon hit my tongue, followed by the pepper, then the creamy, savory cheese inside. My eyes rolled back in my head and I melodramatically pretended to faint.

Meleya looked satisfied with the taste as well, and I could practically see her mind whirling as she examined her half-eaten entrée.

"I wonder what kind of cheese she used," she muttered. "I'll have to ask. Might be good to add a little bit of minced garlic. And the spice level..."

Suddenly I exhaled through o-shaped lips. The heat of the pepper was just hitting me, and while it was good, I didn't like the way my nose started tickling. I made a face.

Meleya passed me a canteen of water as if she'd been anticipating this.

"...just a little too much for Asher," she finished, talking to herself. "I bet we could make these with poblanos just as well, though."

I took a swig, which helped to douse the small fire in my mouth. "Thanks. Where to next?"

"There," Meleya replied, hurrying toward the next cart. It looked like the man running it was serving some kind of spiced apple tart.

We spent the next half hour going from vendor to vendor, haggling over marks and sampling the best they had to offer. Many foods were delicious, a few were wildly disappointing, but it was some of the most fun I'd ever had while eating. By the time we were finished, we had very full bellies and Meleya had meal plans for the next month.

She'd also collected more than a few ingredients she stowed in her pantry rift hold. I told her she was the strangest Rifter I'd ever met as she giddily organized spiny tomatillos, dragonberry honey, and a whole arsenal of peppers she went back and bought off of the vendor from the first cart. She arranged them in order of spiciness, ending with something called a ghost pepper.

"Ghost pepper?" I asked. "Is it really that spicy?"

"You'd hate it," Meleya assured me. I reached for it, but she caught my hand, warning me that it was so hot it could even burn my fingertips. I thought about calling her bluff and grabbing her crazy spice-aholic ghost pepper anyway, but didn't dare. Meleya wouldn't joke about ingredients.

Then the sound of the musicians striking up a new song caught my attention. While the festival music thus far had been laid back, this tune was more far more upbeat. I noticed people were clearing the town square to make room for dancing. Already several couples spun in time with the music.

Just across the square, I saw Brigan leading Elle onto the impromptu dance floor. Elle's long skirts swirled elegantly, and it was clear that the two of them had been dancing at noble galas their entire lives. Couples cleared the way to let them through, and I couldn't help but think how good they looked together. How natural.

How heartbreaking.

But Elle had made herself clear those months ago at the safehouse stables: She didn't want me anymore. She'd moved on. I wanted to forget my feelings for her too, but soot. Now *I* needed a distraction.

Turning to Meleya, I suddenly exclaimed, "You wanna dance?"

"No," Meleya replied, shrinking away from the square. "I don't know how to dance."

"That's fine—I do."

With that, I stepped out onto the square alone and began doing a ridiculous jig involving a lot of melodramatic arm movements and some absurd kicking in time with the music. It was bad enough that the bystanders gave me a wide berth, and I even heard one offer a deeply concerned, "Oh dear."

Meleya snorted, then spent the rest of the song trying to get me to stop. Obviously, that only made me dance harder, adding a few somewhat-violent head flips, one of which sent my hair loop flying across the square.

"I don't know him," Meleya told a disturbed passerby.

The song ended, and I gave a deep, over-the-top bow, my hair falling over my eyes. When I looked up, Meleya was giggling uncontrollably and shaking her head.

"That was the single most terrible dance I've ever seen," she said. "I hope it was worth your reputation."

"It absolutely was."

"Oh?"

"It got you to smile."

Meleya's cheeks flushed red, and she took a step closer to me. I did the same, and the backs of our hands swung forward to brush against each other's. We left them that way.

Stars. It was just the dancing that had my heart pounding, right? Looking at Meleya, I realized the contrast between her dark brown irises and her bright white hair was kind of stunning.

Then, all at once, Meleya blinked as if to snap herself out of the moment. She quickly swung her hand back.

"Uh," she started. Then she blurted, "It's a warm evening, isn't it? I guess it makes sense—summer and all that. Huh."

I was certain Meleya didn't give a flying scale about the weather, but I couldn't help but chuckle as she shed her light cloak. Beneath the cloak, there was a small tear along the sleeve of her tunic.

"Uh oh." I pointed to the seam. "Watch out, or your sleeves'll fall off and you'll look like Jax."

Meleya's whole body tensed. "Wh-what?"

"Jax?" I shrugged. "You remember Jax, right? He was with the Knights before, working undercover at the Academy at the same time you were there. You know, gray hair, muscley guy, always rips the sleeves off his tunics for no reason—"

Meleya swallowed. "Didn't you... I thought Kai would've told you..."

"Told me what?" I cocked my head. "You and Jax *do* know each other, right?"

"Yes," she said quietly, looking down as she clasped the quartz crystal on her belt. "I know Jax. He and I..." She dropped her voice so low I could scarcely hear. "Jax was my boyfriend."

My mouth fell open.

I didn't often find myself speechless, but it was almost too much. I tried to picture it:

Meleya had gone out with *Jax*—the jerk who'd punched me in the jaw and gotten me drafted into Keep Drakfell's guard. The one who'd bragged about kissing seventy different girls without even bothering to learn their names. The guy who'd dated Kai's sister, Kari, accidentally come on to his *own mother*, and even after I'd thought we were *almost* starting to become friends, had completely snubbed me before we'd parted ways in Orothion.

And now... last I heard, he was still with the Mage Hunters. I assumed he was doing some top secret undercover work, of course. Then again, just before we'd left on the quest, I'd heard some of the rebel Mage Hunters talking about how Jax had *chosen* to stay behind. I wanted to believe he didn't have it in him to turn his back on the Knights, but I wasn't sure I could.

"I assumed everyone knew about that by now," Meleya said, still looking down. She seemed genuinely saddened by the mere mention of Jax's name. It just didn't make sense. Meleya didn't seem like the type who would've gone for a guy with a bad attitude and an obsession with bicep curls. It baffled me, and for whatever reason, made me feel just the tiniest bit hurt to think of her as number seventy-one.

Meleya no longer seemed to be in the mood for a party. She thanked me for the evening, then said she was going to go find Sniff.

"You sure you won't stay?" I asked.

"I'm not much for crowds." Meleya shrugged. "She, on the other hand..."

Meleya nodded toward the center of the square. Elle was no longer dancing with Brigan, but on her own, twirling and clapping her hands for an adoring group of townspeople. I couldn't fight my smile as I watched.

When I turned back toward Meleya, she was already gone.

Elle had spotted me. She gave a little wave, incorporating it into her next spin.

Matching her energy, I spun too, ending with a salute. A few spectators chuckled.

Not about to be one-upped, Elle grabbed her skirt and gave it a flourish, showing off her fancy footwork. Those watching loved that. But not as much as they loved my next move—a little something I decided to call the 'hover-chata.'

The moment I incorporated my levitation, Elle stopped messing around. She gave me that mischievous grin, and then, it was on.

I heard one townsperson call out a warning that my dancing was a little on the wild side, but that didn't stop the rest of them from going wild as Elle twirled, clapped, and swung her way over to me. I met her in the middle, and before I knew it she'd grabbed my hand, placed it on her hip, and we were dancing.

Intense, spicy music filled the square as the musicians caught onto our little contest. Instinct took over, our feet moving in synchronization as we spun across the square.

Elle was amazing, her skirts twirling and her long hair flying. Thorn must've been among the onlookers, because I felt his fiery encouragement through our bond.

The music compelled me, and though I wasn't formally trained like Elle, it was as if we could anticipate each other's next movement. I could tell the entire crowd had their eyes on us, but all I could see was Elle.

"You ready?" I asked.

"So ready," she replied.

I dug deep, burning ether. I pulled Elle close and my eyes glowed gold as I levitated us right off of the ground of the square. The crowd ahhed.

Still, we didn't stop. I channeled some of my levitation into Elle, and then we were dancing on air. She laughed, taking the change in stride.

"You get at least six points for that!" she cried.

The music swelled, and I wrapped both hands around her waist. She flung out her arms, completely trusting me as I spun her in a circle.

White ether trailed from her body as I levitated her into the air. Her feet swung upward above her head, skirts sailing while I tethered her to me by holding her hand.

More gasps echoed through the square. Time seemed to slow, Elle's face betraying pure thrill as she smiled down at me. My heartbeat thudded in my chest.

I caught her on the way down, spinning her into a mid-air dip and slowly levitating us to the ground just as the music ended. For one last moment, it was just her and me in the lull.

"And you get at least twelve points for that," I said. Elle flashed her brilliant, mischievous smile, and my heartbeat somehow raced even faster than it was already.

Then the crowd erupted with applause and whistles. This was probably the first time they'd seen an archonic hover-dance, and it wasn't one they would forget anytime soon.

And, looking into Elle's bright amber eyes, neither would I.

Elle and I stayed to the very end of the party, long after the rest of our team had gone to bed. The baron of Topaz Sierra had insisted we all stay the night at his estate. Even our dragons got luxury accommodations in his fine stables.

The two of us were walking through the baron's covered walkway on our way in for the night. Elle carried her shoes, her feet tired out from all the dancing.

"So, it looks like Elle is back?" I asked.

"Yes," Elle replied. "Scorch the expectations. This realm doesn't just need *a* light. It needs mine."

That made me smile. "I couldn't agree more." Then, without thinking, I kept talking. "Does this change anything about... us?"

The second the words left my mouth, I regretted them. We'd just had a great evening. Things were going well, and I might've just crossed a line neither of us was ready to cross. Things were more complicated on my end now, too. I wasn't entirely sure why, but they just were. I suddenly recalled the taste of spicy peppers. The image of big, brown eyes.

As I feared, Elle's smile immediately disappeared.

"You know it can't, Asher," she said. "I wouldn't want you to..." She trailed off, as if unsure how to articulate her thoughts.

"Me to what?" I asked. The sinking feeling in my stomach grew worse with every passing second.

"There are just too many factors to consider," Elle said. "For example, General Kheradok."

I squinted. "What about General Kheradok?"

Elle's cheeks reddened. "Just that... you and he are going to be fighting in an honor duel that may or may not secure an agreement between the Isles and the Rebel Knights. And in case you forgot, Aurora's and my entire future depends on the outcome of that duel."

"Of course I didn't forget."

"All I'm saying is that it might not look good if I show up to the Dragon Isles on your arm. The Drekai may see that as a threat, and I wouldn't want Kheradok getting any ideas—"

"Why, though?" I asked. I couldn't help but notice the way Elle's cheeks flushed every time she said the general's name. What was she not telling me? And why was she embarrassed about it?

"Why would we want to hide anything between us from *Kheradok*?" I asked.

Elle swallowed. "I suppose I should've told you sooner."

That pit in my stomach became as deep as the impact crater after a skyfall as Elle hesitantly told me about her encounter with Kheradok just outside the safehouse boundary. He'd threatened to take her dragon, nearly assassinated her, then... then...

"He *kissed* you?" I said, dumbfounded.

"It's like I always say," Elle said defensively. "A kiss isn't a proposal. Besides, I didn't kiss him back. I couldn't."

For months, the prospect of dueling the Drekai General had made me want to crawl under a rock and hide. But now... now I wanted nothing more than to drive my starglass spear straight through him.

I kicked some loose gravel underfoot. "See, this is why I can't stand nobles," I muttered angrily. "It's always politics and appearances over real humanity."

"Do you really feel that way? Still?" Elle asked, raising her eyebrow in challenge.

"Do I have reason to feel otherwise?"

I crossed my arms, awaiting her response.

Before she could give one, we heard a commotion coming from the door to the baron's estate. Within a moment, the baron himself appeared, along with a few members of his high guard and the rest of our quest team.

"There you two are," the baron said as the whole group hurried our way.

Worry immediately displaced my frustration. "What's happening?"

"That's what we all want to know," Kai said.

"I wanted to show all of you together," the baron said. "A messenger just arrived with another wanted poster, straight from the Capital Keepdom."

"We already know the High King is after Eliana," Brigan said, rubbing his tired eyes.

"The poster is not for the true dragon rider." The baron grimaced as he produced a large, folded sheet. "It's for the Farseer."

The baron unfolded the poster to reveal a well-dressed man with tousled hair, a Psion's silvermark, and a highly recognizable goatee.

My eyes popped as protests erupted from our group.

"The *Farseer*?" Brigan was wide awake now. "But this is Solrac!"

"There must be some mistake." I shook my head in disbelief.

Solvai looked completely dumbfounded, while Elle had seized the poster to read the fine print for herself.

Kai was sputtering, "But... but Solrac can't be the Farseer. As a Psion, he was never even on my list! There was a zero-percent chance. Well, as close to zero as can be reasonably predicted; technically, I suppose it was more like a zero-point-two-four-percent chance, but that would've been true of literally anyone..."

Was it just me, or did Kai seem extra disappointed to learn that Solrac was the Farseer? More than disappointed—He seemed crushed.

"How did this happen?" Brigan asked for all of us.

The baron replied solemnly, "Word is that a pair of Mage Hunters unmasked him in Evyndale. The Duke of Glacia has been forced to go underground."

As the others continued to express their shock, I noticed Meleya was keeping quiet.

I caught her eye. "You knew," I said.

Everyone fell silent as they turned to Meleya. She bit her lip before nodding. "It's true. Solrac is the Farseer. Vidya and I learned the truth back when we were at the Academy."

"Soot and scales!" Brigan swore. "Is he a Psion or a Seer?"

"How did he keep it a secret for so long?" Solvai threw in.

"Is he immortal?" I asked at the same time.

"I..." Meleya paused. "I'm not sure about any of that."

"Look at this—" Elle held up the poster. "The High Throne's offering one thousand gold marks for his capture."

"One *thousand?*" Kai's eyes grew to the size of dragon eggs. That many marks could buy the lowliest pauper an entire estate and a title in the keepdom of their choice. They'd never have to work again.

"Soot," I said. "Jealous the High King only values you at one hundred, Elle?"

Elle narrowed her eyes, but didn't respond to me directly. I felt a quick tightening in my chest.

As we continued to marvel at the poster, comprehending the impossible truth evident before our eyes, that sinking feeling within me grew. With the Farseer exposed, what did that mean for the Rebel Knights?

More than that, what did it mean for the realm?

CHAPTER 24: THE CAMP

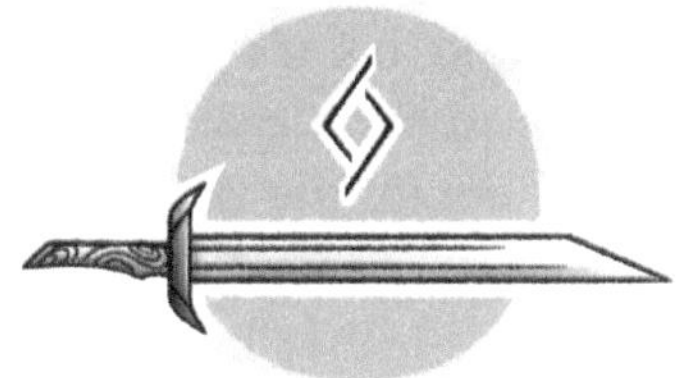

MELEYA

I couldn't take my eyes off of the endless water below as we soared over the Scarlet Straight toward Skygard. I'd never been to the ocean before, and I found the roiling, deep blue expanse both gorgeous and intimidating. I clung to Sniff's saddle a little more tightly than usual.

With my ether well pretty low from a long morning of skyskipping, I rested while the dragons did the heavy-lifting for our final stretch of travel. From his place on Thorn behind Asher, I could see the glow of a gold rune over Kai's forehead. Our group had to stay close to him so that his sky illusion on the underside of our dragons would stay intact, keeping any patrols from seeing us fly in.

Nevertheless, we kept a wary eye out for both soldiers from the Capital and scouts from Orothion. And, as always, we kept our eyes peeled for the dusky blue cloaks of Mage Hunters. We hadn't seen a sign of Jaira and Lothar since they'd fled Scorpio's Shadow, but with the Soul Reaper's etherarchy on their side, we never wanted to rest too easy.

Moved by the glorious sea, Solvai had wanted to fly on her own for a while. In falcondrake form, she spread her wide brown wings at the head of the group beside Elle and Aurora. That left me alone with Brigan on Sniff's back.

"See that?" Brigan said, pointing southward with one hand as he gripped my tunic for security with the other. Heights still made him nervous, but I got the sense he very much preferred flying over water rather than land.

I squinted to see a lush mountainside of green dragonheart palms and white sandy beaches to our left. That would be Rengard's northern coast.

"Solhelm," Brigan confirmed. "That's home."

"It's beautiful," I said.

"Scorch, I miss it."

"We're flying right by. We could ask if there's time to stop?"

Brigan laughed. "Kai and his schedule would have a panic attack. Besides, it's too risky, what with my family there. I doubt my father would be sympathetic to our party."

I remembered the way Brigan's father had once spurned me for being a magi even while I was actively saving his life, and I had to agree.

"It was bad enough when I wrote to tell them I'd joined the Knights of the Torch," Brigan went on. "My father told me I'd disgraced our family, even threatened to cut me off. I convinced him to drop the matter for now, but I doubt he'll ever come around."

My heart went out to my friend. "I'm so sorry."

Brigan sighed. "He claims he only wants what's best for Rengard, but I can't help but think he's driven more by his desire to win social favor. But as for me? Gauntlet down: An alliance between the Knights and Rengard would be massively beneficial to both sides. Point one—The Knights would gain the aid of the largest of the eight keepdoms *and* one of the strongest armies in the realm. Their support could make all the difference in the war against the Gray. Point two—not to mention, it would stop the Canyonlands from falling into corruption while simultaneously bringing an end to Queen Ilona's ill-conceived war with the Dragon Isles. King Axel never wanted war, and if she keeps up like this, she'll lead the whole keepdom into ruin. And point three..."

Brigan trailed off as he gazed across the sea toward Rengard. Turning in the saddle, I saw sincerity in his warm brown eyes.

"Point three," he repeated. "I love the Canyonlands. I can't help but want to share the Knight's Code with it and do my part to bring its people the same peace and purpose I've felt. Not through compulsion, of course, but through opportunity."

I gave Brigan a nudge. "The realm needs more nobles like you, Brig."

There was a pause, and then all at once, Brigan was wrapping his arms more snugly around me, his arms folding around my waist to hold me close.

A jolt ran through me and I automatically froze, my body going as stiff as a board. A thousand thoughts flooded my mind as I came face-to-face with the reality that Brigan was making a move on me.

How *did* I feel about Brigan? Objectively speaking, he was the perfect guy—thoughtful, brilliant, skilled, handsome... Any girl would count herself lucky to be with him. We'd been through so much together, and it was hard to imagine what my life would be like if we hadn't met in basic training.

After what had happened back at Scorpio's Shadow, Brigan had become my rock more than ever. But while I cared for him deeply, there was something about our relationship that was... I don't know... *different* than my relationship with Jax had been. Different than my relationship with someone else might be.

My cheeks grew warm as I realized I was thinking about Asher. Involuntarily, I thought of the festival in Topaz Sierra and the silly dance Asher had done for me. He'd looked like an idiot, totally embarrassing himself, and he'd done it all just to make me laugh.

And drak, I needed that.

Oh, stars. Brigan absolutely sensed my hesitation. He quickly released his hold on me.

"I'm sorry," Brigan said, and I could hear the hurt in his voice.

The sound of it brought a lump to my throat. But the last thing I wanted to do was lead him on.

"*I'm* sorry," I replied. My two words communicated a thousand.

Silence stretched on and on, seeming to drive an emotional wedge between us. What was Brigan thinking? The rushing wind felt so loud in my ears.

Finally, I couldn't stand it anymore. I turned in the saddle to get a look at him.

Brigan's eyes were shut tight, his expression pained. Since he no longer dared hold onto me, he was gripping the back of Sniff's saddle so tightly his knuckles were white.

"You can still hold on, you know," I said timidly.

Brigan's reply was firm. "No. No, I can't."

I wanted to say more, but I knew he needed time. Hearts aching, we rode in silence until Elle called out:

"There it is!"

The clouds over the sea had parted enough to let us get our first good view of Skygard. I instantly understood why it was called the Cliffside Keepdom.

Waves crashed at the base of high rocks that jutted proudly over the water. The coastline stretched on, coming to a sharp point at the southern side. There, I could just make out the great stronghold of Orothion.

I'd heard lots of things about Orothion, but no description could compare to actually seeing it. Nine spires graced the stronghold, built to look like the spines along a dragon's back. The fortress had been built right up against the coast, with its tallest spire flush with the cliffs. A pyre with a reflector stood proudly atop that spire, used to guide ships at sea.

There was a strong outer wall, and from this high up, I could see that it was shaped like a nine-pointed star. The design was archaic, built during the Guardian Era.

"Orothion!" Asher cried, urging Thorn to go faster. The black wyvern obliged, zooming past us and exciting Sniff too. Sniff was about to hover-dash after them toward the castle when Kai cried out.

"Hold up! We're not going straight there! Keep flying—north, around the castle!"

For a moment, I hesitated. We were so close to where Kari and Akayto were being held prisoner. Part of me wanted to head straight to the stronghold.

But Kai's plan required waiting until the right moment to make our move. We needed to find a safe place to hide out for another week before Orothion would be hosting the big, splashy banquet that would cover our infiltration.

Thorn, Aurora, Sniff, and falcondrake Solvai swerved. We winged our way over a forest thick with some of the most enormous, red-barked trees I'd ever seen. It looked like the perfect place to set up camp so that we could finalize our plans for infiltrating Orothion.

But Kai waved us past the forest toward a far less idyllic place. The trees gave way to blackened foothills. The landscape was completely lifeless, the ground covered in what appeared to be craggy, ancient lava flows.

"No one will bother us here!" Kai declared as we searched for a place to land.

That was certainly true, but before too long, we spotted a large cluster of dragonhide tents set out on the lava beds. I instantly thought of the nomadic caravans I used to travel with alongside my parents. Could this be one of those?

"What's that?" Asher asked.

"It's a refugee camp!" Brigan called from behind me. He still held onto the back of the saddle rather than my waist, but his voice didn't betray his earlier sorrow. "People displaced by skyfalls!"

"Move past it!" Kai shouted over the wind, clinging to his map to keep it from blowing away. "There should be some secluded caves further west—"

"Can we stay in the camp?" Elle cut in excitedly.

"Are you kidding me?" Kai replied.

"That's a great idea!" Brigan said. "If they're all the way out here, it likely means these refugees were turned away by the keeps nearby. Gauntlet down: the refugees are likely to be receptive to Eliana and the Rebel Knights' cause."

"What do you think, Solvai?" I asked. My falcondrake friend roared her approval, diving toward the camp.

Even Kai couldn't argue with her, though he did grumble about how he'd have to use several complicated runes to secure illusions over Elle and Aurora until we were *certain* none of the refugees were going to run over to the Orothion Knights and alert them that we were here. But in the end, we all descended toward the camp.

Despite Kai's excessive concern, the camp welcomed us with open arms. Apparently, the leaders here were Rebel Knights themselves, with many of the refugees joining up with the cause every day. Once Kai removed the illusion from Elle and Aurora, eager folks surrounded the true dragon and the rider they'd heard so much about, singing the goddess's praises.

Even now, people followed behind us as one of their leaders led us through the camp. As we walked, this place felt even *more* like the nomadic caravans I'd grown up in. Each family unit had their own lavvu-style tent. Makeshift fencing corralled a few aldrakas and modest coops of drakehens. There were several cooking fires with stew pots over them as refugees cooked up dinner. Laundry hung from lines strung between tent poles and sturdy carts, several of which held what few possessions the refugees had. Nothing felt permanent.

A group of kids scuttled past us in pursuit of a rogue ball. What looked like a brother and sister dove for it at the same time, then entered into a heated argument about who'd reached it first.

Despite the fact that they were at each other's throats, I looked on fondly. Even with their home's stability frayed, they had each other. I'd had my parents, of course, but on those long, lonely days traversing the canyons, I'd have given anything for a brother or sister.

The Rebel Knight who led us through the camp was someone Kai, Asher, and Elle recognized from the first time they'd come to Orothion. Then, he'd worn red robes as he helped them through the Knights' golden initiation fire. Now, he'd exchanged the red robes for the black, belted ones of a Son of Streya. What's more, he had a large warsword on his back.

"I'll go back to red if the Knights ever get their scales in order again," the man, Rasec, said as we walked. He wasn't the only one who'd left Orothion after the schism—several soldiers, priests, and others helped run the camp, too.

"This whole schism is for the dreklings if you ask me," Rasec continued. "I can't imagine why anyone would stick with Vesta and the Orothion Knights—Especially after learning the truth about the Farseer."

"You know about the Farseer too?" Elle asked.

"The whole realm knows. Old Solrac's been forced to go underground—one of my contacts has said that not even the safehouse in the Mirror Forest is safe. Too many wild cards that might want to cash in on this."

Rasec shook his head. "It kills me. If Vesta hadn't taken over Orothion, Skygard would be the ideal hideout for Solrac right now. But as is, I hardly recognize the place. Orothion's always been a haven, the Knights inside willing to lay down their lives for the code. But now…." He glanced at the people in the camp. "Poor souls. Orothion promised them shelter in the city if they brought in enough skystone tribute. They did what they could—lost a lot of good men and women to wild dragons trying to get them from skyfall sites. But in the end, Vesta's patrols sent them packing anyway. Chased them out of the forest and into this wasteland."

Rasec kicked the dry, blackened ground. "I joined up here to see what I could do to help, but so many of these refugees are suffering from the shadow wasting. With supplies so limited, I hardly know what to do."

"Is there a sick bay here?" Brigan asked, his grip tightening on the strap of his medical bag.

"Right down there near the eastern caldera." Rasec pointed.

"I'd like to help," Brigan said, pulling out his supply of liquid light. "Can you take me there?"

"Stars," Rasec breathed. "They've been praying for a light-bringer for weeks down there in medical. Streya be praised."

Brigan hurried after Rasec without so much as a backward glance. I could hardly blame him for wanting to help and, at the same time, maybe take some time away from me.

As for the rest of us, we hurried to get set up in our tents. I knew the drill—It was time to make this place, however temporary, our home.

"There you go," I said, patting the dirt inside the little planter box. "That way, if you ever have to move on from the lava fields, you'll be able to take these with you."

The little girls excitedly picked up the repurposed wooden crates. I'd helped them seal the crates, fill them with dirt from the area nearer the forest, and plant seeds for coal beets and red cucumbers. Finally, I'd helped them label the boxes with their names. They'd had fun with that, and besides, it never hurt to mark your things when you lived in a group.

"Thank you, Meleya!" the oldest girl said. Then she nudged her little sister.

"Thank you!" the little one echoed.

I laughed. "Go on and show your parents what you made."

Eagerly, the girls scampered off, carefully carrying their garden boxes. I knew I wouldn't be around to see the plants sprout, but I hoped having them would help the girls feel like they had some roots.

An unexpected wave of sadness washed over me for all the years my younger self had longed for a real home. To stay in one place long enough to feel connected to it.

You were wronged, Meleya, a raspy voice suddenly appeared inside my head.

I jumped. I hadn't heard from Xan in a while.

It is not fair, Xan taunted. *Pushed around your whole life, bound by the restrictions a corrupt system laid upon you. But you do not have to continue to be a subject, Meleya. Not when you have the power to change things.*

Get away from me, Xan, I thought back. At those words, I felt her hold over my mind weaken.

But you know what I say is true, Xan pressed. *You deserved a home, and they denied you.*

"I said leave," I muttered out loud, clenching my fists.

Xan hissed on her way out of my head. I got the feeling she planned to lurk close by, but for now, I'd driven her off. After all, when I thought about it, she was wrong. Growing up, I may not have had a physical home, but I had something far more important:

A mother and father who loved me.

As I brushed the dirt off my hands, I couldn't help but picture Mom's face. Not the scarred, silvermarked face I'd always known, but the smooth, unmarked face I'd secretly—selfishly—resented.

Guilt pricked my heart. Mom's was the face of a woman doing her best to find meaning in a broken world. Despite her personal struggles, I'd never once questioned whether or not I was loved.

And how had I thanked her for it? For years, all I'd wanted was to have my family back together. Yet when we were finally reunited, I'd spent months avoiding her, so caught up in myself I never stopped to consider how difficult it must've been for her. She'd felt powerless to protect me, the same way I'd felt powerless against my wraith for so long. Mom and I weren't so different.

I swallowed. I should've said goodbye.

Absently, I headed through the camp back toward our party's tents. The three dragons were dozing outside, basking in the sunlight, and through the flap of the men's tent, I saw Kai. He was exactly where he'd been almost every day since we arrived at the camp, meticulously writing out the plans and backup plans for every possible scenario regarding our upcoming infiltration.

Just thinking about tomorrow evening's risky operation made me nervous. We'd been preparing nonstop for days now, rehearsing our roles and studying schematics until our ears hurt. Tonight, Kai planned on assembling our team to go over every detail of our rescue operation from start to finish.

Aside from all the planning, Kai had done a little research while here at the camp. With Rasec's help, he'd tracked down a couple of books taken from Orothion's library that made reference to some of the strange voidarchy we'd seen from the Mage Hunters throughout our travels.

"Shadestones," Kai had explained to our group the other day, pointing to a drawing of three gray rocks that looked just like the ones Jaira and Lothar had used to get wraiths to take over Leif the ursadon as well as Lord Scorpio.

"According to notes from the ancient philosopher, Theok," Kai went on, "shadestones are an old form of corrupted Rift anchor used to pull dark spirits into the physical plane."

"Gray Ones," I'd said.

Kai nodded. "Powerful, but severely limited Gray Ones. When the stone is dropped at the feet of a living creature, it releases the wraith. The wraith enhances the creature's power, but if the host is killed, the wraith dies with them."

"Like Leif and Scorpio," Elle said.

"How many more stones do you think they have?" Brigan asked. Nobody had an answer.

"Hopefully it doesn't matter," Kai forged ahead. "With any luck, Jaira and Lothar will stay out of Skygard. It's not a particularly Mage Hunter-friendly place. Maybe we've lost them for good."

I hoped Kai was right as I looked for something to distract me. As usual, Brigan was down at the medical tent, helping the victims of the shadow wasting. Too many people here suffered from gray wounds, bites from umbral creatures. Umbrals were rampant around the sites of skyfalls, they said, and getting commoner by the day as more and more towns fell to the dreklings.

Besides that, Brigan had told us about something the shadow wasting victims called 'the Haze.'

"What's a Haze?" Asher had asked the other night at dinner.

"I'm not sure," Brigan had answered. "From what they've described, it's as if certain parts of the land itself are being infected with the shadow wasting. Mostly in the areas around Kolbohr, they say."

"What do you mean 'the land is becoming infected'?" Elle frowned.

Brigan hadn't been able to give any more information on the Haze, but the idea of the land going Gray left us all with pits in our stomachs. Still, Brigan was doing wonders to help the sick, and his drake, Bolt, had even agreed to let Brigan break off several of her more ornamental scales from his ascension armor. He'd fastened them to vials to help create more liquid light. He'd been training the would-be medics on how to use it, losing himself in his work.

I'd tried going down to the sick bay to help out myself once, but Brigan had gently-but-firmly told me he preferred working alone for now. I got the message, and knew it would be best for him if I steered clear now, too.

I checked inside the women's tent for Solvai, but found it empty. Just before leaving the tent, I heard arguing outside and stopped short.

"Look, it was stupid, I openly admit that," Asher's voice penetrated the dragonhide.

"I'm not asking for an open admission," came Elle's heated response. "I'm asking for a promise to never try something like that again. Not when we need so badly to impress these people."

I could practically sense the melodramatic gestures Asher was making as he answered. "I, Asher of Steel Rim, solemnly swear never to steal Princess Eliana's tiara to use in a game of ring toss ever again. Happy now?"

"Not really, no."

"Me neither."

"Great!" I'd never heard sarcasm as strong as Elle's. Before I knew it, she was storming into the tent, practically barrelling into me as she headed for her pack. Furiously, she began rummaging through her things.

"You alright?" I asked hesitantly.

She looked at me and threw up her hands. "I'm so done." Grumbling, she found whatever she was looking for in her bag, then headed back for the tent door. "I'm going for a ride with Aurora. I'll be back for the meeting tonight."

"Okay."

Then she marched out of the tent.

Blinking, I couldn't help but wonder what had gotten into Elle and Asher lately. Ever since the festival at Topaz Sierra, something had been off between them. They'd gone out of their way to avoid each other most days, and this wasn't the first argument I'd overheard. I recalled the way Elle had spoken about her feelings for Asher while we'd been trapped at Lord Scorpio's mountain estate. Yes, she liked Asher, but she couldn't see a future between the two of them. I was finally starting to believe it.

I waited a few minutes before leaving the tent. When I did, I quickly spotted Asher using a ripple in the ancient lava flow as a bench. He sat with his elbows on his knees and his head in his hands, clearly frustrated.

Despite that, my heart gave a little flutter when he ran his fingers through his hair, messing up his fangknot so that his bangs fell over his eyes. Why did I like his hair messy like that?

Fully expecting him to tell me to get lost, I formed a portal and rifted over to his side.

"Copper mark for your thoughts?"

Asher didn't look up. "They're not even worth half a copper."

I took a seat beside Asher on the hardened-lava-flow bench. After a moment, I spoke.

"I've seen the beach now."

Slowly, Asher lifted his head to give me the most quizzical look he could muster.

I plowed ahead. "I've seen the beach. and it's beautiful, but too humid. I could tell when we flew over. That leaves the desert or the mountains, right?"

Understanding dawned in Asher's eyes as he remembered the conversation we'd had so long ago in the dragon stables of the Mage Hunter Academy. He almost cracked a smile.

"Right," he said. "So what's the verdict then? Desert or mountains?"

"Well, I love the desert since it's where I grew up. But there's something freeing about the mountains. Do I have to choose?"

"Yes."

"Hmm…" I trailed off as I noticed Asher's uncontrollably tapping foot. I chuckled.

"What?" Asher asked.

"You need to get out of camp," I said. "Stretch your legs. Something active."

Asher nodded. Then he sat up straight as he got an idea.

He turned to me. "Wanna spar?"

I raised an eyebrow.

"Your dad was training me a bit back at the safehouse," Asher continued, getting to his feet. "Helping me prepare for my duel with General Kheradok. The General—He's a Rifter, like you. Would you help me train?"

Soot, he was actually being sincere, not just messing with me.

He held out a hand to me. Heart inexplicably pounding, I took it as I replied.

"Sure."

CHAPTER 25: THE LAVA FIELDS

ASHER

C lang!

Tiny fragments of starglass flew across the hardened lava flows as my dragonhook spear met Meleya's seaxe. I'd summoned extra starglass to cover the edge of her seaxe, keeping it as blunt as my own weapon to make things a little more safe.

We'd put some distance between us and the refugee camp so that we wouldn't disturb anyone. There wasn't a sign of life this deep amidst the smooth ground of the ancient lava fields.

"Stars!" I said, grunting as I blocked her next strike. "You pack a hard swing when you're not distracted by the compulsive need to tidy up!"

Meleya narrowed her eyes as she remembered our altercation at Swan Spire. That felt like a lifetime ago.

"And you'd fight a lot better if you didn't feel the compulsive need to be clever all the time," she shot back.

I gave a melodramatic gasp. "Mel, you did it! You came up with a genuine, almost halfway-decent comeback! On the spot and everything!"

Meleya gave a growl as she tore open a portal, then thrust her sword arm through it to level her blade at my neck from behind.

"Like I said." Meleya's expression was confident.

I broke into a wide, crooked grin. Then I used my levitation to hover-duck away from her sword, hover-roll across the lava field toward her, and accelerate my spear toward her middle. She was good, but so was I.

And with my extra strength and speed, I was pretty sure I'd have had her beat in an etherarchy-free fight.

But there were no restrictions here. Not about to let me gain the upper hand, Meleya launched herself backward through a portal. I spun around, scanning the area as quickly as I could, trying to guess where she'd reappear.

Thunk!

Meleya's feet shoved against my back as she dropped through a portal straight above me. Just in time to avoid slamming face-first onto the lava rock, I activated my levitation to catch myself.

The spar continued as we tried to outwit and outmaneuver one another. I pulled out several of the moves I'd practiced with Ivar, plus a few I'd come up with since. My perfect execution of the 'fancy feet' left Meleya hopping like a mad drakalope to avoid taking my flurry of ether darts in the boots. We were both in stitches, and it took us a minute to get back into the fight.

But *stars*, she was skilled with those portals. Rifting herself in and out of gold-rimmed rifts, she was the first person I'd met who could keep up with my hover-dashing on the sparring field.

"I'm starting to see why they call you Snowstorm!" I called.

Meleya laughed, then said, "I'm not sure what the general will do in your duel, but I've got an idea."

"What's that?"

"What if *you* became the Snowstorm?"

From there, she helped me practice using my hover-speed to work her portals to my advantage. Each time Meleya opened a new portal, I'd flare my ether to hover-dash through it before she could. That put me right where she planned to go, leaving her vulnerable and giving me a prime attack position. It took a few tries to get it right, but soon I was as much a flurry on the field as Meleya was.

Our sparring went on. With this new snowstorm strategy, I kept gaining the upper hand.

I gave a triumphant shout. "Just call me Etherstorm!"

Meleya snorted. "I'm not calling you that."

Laughing, I sped through Meleya's next rift, only to find myself racing straight through another portal I *hadn't* planned on.

That portal turned out to be one that sent me in an endless loop, in and out of the same rifts over and over. It took me a second to figure out what was going on, and by then, Meleya was ready for me.

She used her seaxe to send my starglass spear flying. Instinctively, I burned ether to reform it, but I'd only finished the shaft by the time Meleya had me by the scarf, her blade against my throat.

"Guess the Snowstorm's a trick you want to keep close to your chest so the General doesn't catch on, eh, scarf-wearer?"

We were standing close, breathing hard. Her dark brown eyes were bright, her cheeks red from sparring in the summer heat. Maybe Meleya's choice of words got to me or something, because suddenly, without thinking, I was pulling 'the Snowstorm' closer to my chest.

Then my logic caught up with me. What was I doing? This was *Meleya*. She couldn't stand me... Right?

She must've sensed my hesitation because she suddenly drew back and awkwardly sheathed her sword as I released the starglass guard from its edge. Clearing her throat, she mumbled something about keeping hydrated, then opened her rift hold pantry and pulled out a couple of canteens.

After drinking my fill, I poured a big splash of water onto my face. The loop fell from my warrior's fangknot as I shook my head, water flying off the ends of my hair. Meleya cringed as some splattered onto her.

"Why?" she asked, more into the ether than to me.

"Hey Mel," I started as a random question popped into my head. "What would happen if you put an entrance portal *through* an exit portal?"

Meleya gave me a blank stare. "Why would I do that?"

I shrugged. "Aren't you curious?"

Meleya raised her eyebrow, then went back to drinking from her canteen.

"No harm in trying it out," I insisted. Now I really wanted to know.

"The Drekai general isn't going to put an entrance portal through an exit."

"Please?" I asked. "For science?"

I made an over-the-top pleading face, sticking out my lower lip. Meleya tried to roll her eyes, but I suspected it was to hide a laugh. Then, she runetraced.

At once, two gold-rimmed portals formed before our eyes. The entrance had a white interior while the exit was black within its golden edge.

Carefully, Meleya moved the two together so that the entrance was heading straight into the black center of the exit. I took a step closer in anticipation of what would happen when—

BOOM!

A pure white explosion blasted both Meleya and me backward. I landed hard on my back, coughing as I inhaled a mix of lava rock dust and etherdust. Meleya was close behind, falling halfway onto me.

"Oof," I said as the impact nearly knocked the wind out of me.

Meleya coughed too as she propped herself up on my chest. All at once, I recalled that we'd been in a similar position before—back on the Rise when we first met.

"Well," she said between coughs. "Now we know what happens. What's that move called, Mister 'For Science'?"

I gave my best crooked smile. "The 'eclips-plosion.'"

She could've gotten up right away. But she didn't.

As the thick ether cloud engulfed us, my senses went on high alert. I seemed to notice everything... Meleya's white hair matched the ether particles sparkling all around her head, contrasting with her deep brown eyes as they searched mine, double-checking that I was okay. She had a nice smell, too, like fresh bread.

Stars, the way she was looking at me... My grin vanished as my face went slack.

The sparring, the teasing, the pressure of tomorrow's operation... It all came to a head. All at once, Meleya was kissing me.

Her lips were soft but eager. Maybe even a little bit urgent, like she needed this. Honestly, maybe I did too. I started kissing her back, then froze. She was beautiful, of course, not to mention I felt a deep connection with her too. Meleya believed in me in a way few others ever had. She saw me as a bright, capable leader where others saw only a distraction.

But another part of me wasn't so sure. For some, a kiss might not mean much. But to me, it was a signal. Was I ready to send Meleya that signal?

My mind was racing. Before I could decide, she was gone. As she pulled away, she looked just as surprised as I was about what she'd just done.

"Uh..." She swallowed. "Better... camp, get back to. Start dinner... gotta... yep."

With that, Meleya took off through a portal, leaving me lying on my back in the middle of the lava field.

Rather than go back to the camp, I went for a walk around the rim of the lava fields to clear my head.

Unfortunately, my head was not in the mood for clearing.

My thoughts were as jumbled as the fragments of black lava rock crunching beneath my boots, bouncing between Meleya and Elle. Why had Meleya kissed me? Were things really over with Elle? Was I a bad person for not knowing how I felt about either of them right now?

Through my distant bond with Thorn, I thought I would feel at least a teasing burn of some sort, but he seemed to be giving me space to think this one through. Somehow that worried me even more.

Besides that, I couldn't stop worrying about tomorrow's risky mission to rescue my father and Kari. What if something went wrong? What if someone got hurt and it was all my fault?

I found myself wishing for another one of my strange, yet calming, mom-moments. Was she here in the spirit plane now, listening in? If anyone could help me organize my warring thoughts and emotions, it was her.

I was so caught up that I nearly jumped out of my skin when I heard the shriek echoing across the lava fields. I stumbled backward as a massive winged creature shot through the air in front of me.

"Soot," I swore, steadying myself. The creature seemed to have risen straight up from the ground, but I quickly realized it had come from over the edge of a high, sheer cliff face. I'd been so lost in thought that I'd nearly walked straight off it.

Peering over the edge, I realized I'd stumbled upon the roosting grounds for a colony of great, feathered falcondrakes. A dozen enormous nests sat tucked on ledges all along the broad cliffside. Several of the four-legged dragon birds with scaly bodies and earth-toned feathers flew between the nests while others lay curled up beneath their wings inside.

For a moment, I was afraid. Falcondrakes were wild, and these things were big enough to ride. I was just about to back away slowly when one falcondrake with rich brown wings alighted in front of me. Strange... this one's eyes seemed more intelligent than the rest, and were those gold marks glowing from its feathers?

Sure enough, a golden Wildshaper's mist engulfed the falcondrake, and before my eyes, Solvai reverted to her human form.

"Asher!" she said with an excited smile. "What are you doing here?"

"Wandering aimlessly." I shrugged. "You?"

Solvai chuckled. "I found this place not long after we arrived at the camp. It was like I could feel them out here. With Kai so busy planning the operation, I've been spending my time with my new friends."

To emphasize her point, one of the wild falcondrakes landed beside Solvai, pressing its large feathered head against her side. Solvai wrapped her arms around the large dragon bird. She was practically one of them.

"Valla says Wildshapers can form connections with animals, similar to dragon bonds," Solvai said. "It's no heartscale, of course, but there's something there."

That made sense. It was the same power that awful Lord Scorpio had used to command his army of winged terrors. I was glad to see Solvai using her power for light.

Solvai gestured my way as she looked into the falcondrake's eyes. "Say hello to Asher!"

The large, mottled cream-and-tan falcondrake took a few steps toward me. I tensed, ready to hover-dash away, but at Solvai's word, the falcondrake bent down in a sort-of welcoming bow before me. Unsure what else to do, I saluted the majestic beast.

"A pleasure to make your acquaintance, Swifty," I said.

Swifty gave a shriek. He must've approved of his name.

From there, Swifty gave another shriek before spreading his wings and diving over the edge of the cliff.

Solvai gave an excited squeak. "One of his fledgelings is about to fly for the first time! Come on!"

Gold mist covered her back as Solvai sprouted a pair of wings and dove off the cliff after Swifty. Not one to miss out, I used my levitation to skate down the cliffside after them.

We landed on a ledge beside one of the gigantic nests. Swifty was inside it, along with another falcondrake that must've been Swifty's mate. Together, they watched a tiny black falcondrake perch on the edge of the nest, his scaly tail twitching. He must've been afraid.

I could hardly blame the little guy. His wings looked so small and fragile compared to those of his parents. His mama used her beak to give him an encouraging tap, but otherwise kept her distance.

The young falcondrake squirmed. Leaning over to Solvai, I whispered, "Does he need help?"

"He's got this," Solvai assured me.

Finally, in what appeared to have been an accident, the young falcondrake slipped. He gave a small, helpless shriek as he plummeted down the cliffside toward the jagged rocks below. My heart stopped.

But then the little guy spread his feathery black wings. They were much wider than I'd originally thought, catching air and letting the young falcondrake soar for the first time. His parents shrieked with pride, and Solvai and I cheered.

"I was worried about him for a second there," I laughed.

"Well," Solvai replied, "when his choice is the rocks or the sky, I guess he'd rather do what he was born to do."

I felt a sudden warmth on my back, almost as if something—or someone—unseen was giving *me* a gentle nudge forward. But... what precisely had I been born to do? Distract people? Steal from nobles? Or something more?

"Hey," Solvai said, pointing to the setting sun. "We'd better get back to camp. You know what tonight is."

"How could I forget? Kai's only been reminding us about his big final meeting every day since we got here."

Solvai and I bid the falcondrakes farewell before we headed up the cliffside.

The only light in the dragonhide hut came from the low glow of the miniature illusion of the Orothion stronghold that hovered suspended between the six of us. Everything was eerily quiet—a result of the illusion of silence Kai had cast over the tent. Outside, our dragon bonds stood guard. An air of drama had settled over us.

Solrac would've been proud. But...

Undermining that drama were satisfying crunching sounds as we devoured a big platter of crispy cinnamon-sugar churros. Meleya had outdone herself making the tasty snacks for our final planning session before tomorrow's big operation.

"Scorch, these are good," Elle said.

"Thanks, Meleya," Solvai agreed.

"Seriously," I said. "We should start calling Mel 'Mmm-eleya.'"

Meleya glared at me, but I caught the light blush on her cheeks even in the low light. The memory of our kiss rose to the top of my mind and I felt my face growing warm as well. Absently, I touched my lips. I certainly hadn't told anyone about it, and I was pretty sure Meleya hadn't either.

The tent fell silent.

Elle instantly grew skeptical. Brigan raised an eyebrow. Solvai's eyes flicked between Meleya and me. Even Kai seemed to catch on that something had happened.

Was it just me, or had at least three Glints just crawled out of their hiding places to get a better seat?

"Nobody's being awkward," Meleya rushed, defensively answering a question nobody had asked. That got her even more deeply questioning looks from everyone sitting in the circle, and her blush upgraded to a full-on fire. I fought the urge to facepalm as I loudly crunched my churro. I glanced down at my Glint, who blinked up at me in silent innocence.

"Anyway," I said, mouth full, "anyone else impressed with the way Kai put together these little illusions of us? Just take a look at the excellent nose on tiny Asher. What a guy."

The group's focus returned to the central illusion. Standing before the illusory Orothion were six translucent, miniature humanoid figures and three dragons. Kai had nailed the details, down to the curl over Brigan's forehead and the scales on Elle's white armored dress.

"They look just like us," Elle said.

"Gauntlet down," Brigan said. "Kai's skill with illusions is second to none."

"Am I really that short?" Solvai frowned, pointing to her likeness.

"Yes," Kai said, and I thought I noticed a secret smile that said he liked Solvai's height. Then he turned to me.

"Speaking of your nose, Asher, I nearly forgot something," Kai said. He made a motion with his hand as one of the many golden runes over his forehead pulsed more brightly.

At once, the illusory avatar of me changed. My eyes went from dragonfire green to brown, my ears went from scaled and pointed to rounded, and to add soot to scorchmarks, Kai just had to go and tweak my nose too.

"Excuse me!" I complained. "You can't even recognize me!"

"That's the point," Kai said dryly. "Those of you infiltrating the castle will have to majorly fly under the watchtower. Asher, you've been to Orothion before and we don't want to risk anyone recognizing you."

I gave a vague grumble and took another churro.

"You'll survive," Kai assured me. "Besides, if all goes according to plan, I'll be able to ease up on the minor illusion you'll be wearing before too long. Now, for the plan."

Our infiltration involved keeping things simple: We would approach disguised as nobles ready to attend the fancy party the Knights were throwing to drum up more support for the war. Then we'd split up—Brigan and Meleya would go to dinner and a tour of the castle while Solvai and I would make our way to the dungeons to check for my dad. Once we found him, we'd meet back up near the skyforge where Kari was supposed to be and Meleya would rift us all back to Kai by way of a rift anchor at our base in the redwoods.

It was fun watching the little illusions of us run around the stronghold. Kai's overview was very straightforward, but I found myself missing Solrac at the head of the table. He'd always added a level of flair and drama.

Thinking of Solrac distracted me. When Rasec showed us that poster, I'd been blown away. But at the same time, Solrac being the Farseer just made sense. He'd always had a flair for the dramatic—something that would've made Kai's big final planning session that much more interesting.

Then Kai spent the next hour outlining backup plans one through ten. He also passed out little vials of silverbane to each of us as a precaution. We worked our way through the platter of snacks as Kai manipulated his illusions with sweeping gestures from his hands. He spent a long time showing us every detail of the castle, both inside and out. From the front gates to the dragon hold, all the way to the banquet hall, servants' hall, and the lower levels.

Finally, he focused on the skyforge. The illusion displayed a tremendous feat in architecture. The vast room was vaguely triangular in shape, featuring a central forge with metal ravines alight with green dragonfire. The ceiling was a dome held together with intricate golden arch-work. Between the framework was what appeared to be black starglass.

"It's amazing," Brigan commented, appreciating the design.

"It's the crowning feature of the castle, and one of the final building projects done by the original Evgardians, assisted by the Guardians themselves," Kai sounded like he was reciting from stuffy ancient texts word for word. Actually, I'd be surprised if he wasn't.

Various workshops faced the forge on the far walls, and Kai's illusion honed in on one of them. Inside was a pretty illusory girl with thick black curls and a heavy smith's apron. The sight of Kari made me wonder about what she'd say if she were here. She'd probably be gushing about how cute our little avatars were.

"This one's Kari's workshop," Kai said. "There's a twenty-nine percent chance we'll find her there. There's a seven percent chance she's being held in the dungeons below the castle with Akayto, but I believe—and my uh… my *visions* suggest to me the most likely place we'll find her is up here."

Kai snapped his fingers and the skyforge illusion took us on an interactive journey up a set of stairs. A door opened at the top of the staircase to reveal a large, open air terrace above the skyforge. The domed ceiling popped grandly out of the center, its golden framework catching the sunlight. A triangle-shaped wall surrounded the terrace, growing taller at one point into a slanted spike thrusting straight toward the sky. That section housed the grand lighthouse I'd spotted when we'd flown in.

I realized we were looking at the fortress's southernmost spire—the one overlooking the Scarlet Strait.

"The omens make me think that this terrace is where we're most likely to find Kari," Kai said. At this, a slight but noticeable tremor entered his voice. "It all comes down to this. Whatever happens in that castle tomorrow, by the end of the evening, you all *need* to be right here so Meleya can rift you all out of there—Kari and Akayto included. Got it?"

We gave solemn nods. A heaviness settled over the tent. All of the travel and preparation we'd done was finally coming together. We'd gone over every detail twice, then once more for good measure.

With ceremony, Kai held out his black notebook filled with tomorrow's plans. Then, he shut his notebook with a thud, at the same time letting his runes go out. The tent was plunged into shadow.

Well, soot. Maybe Kai had a little more drama in him than I'd given him credit for.

It was Meleya who ultimately broke the silence.

"I guess all that's left is for us to get some sleep. I've got a big breakfast planned so we can start the day off right."

Everyone started to get up, but I held up my hands. "Wait!" I said. "We forgot one of the most important things!"

"We forgot nothing, Asher. I'm ninety-nine percent sure of it." Despite his certainty, Kai couldn't help but crack open his journal once more.

"We forgot to give this operation an epic name," I said with a grin. "What would Solrac say?"

Kai and Elle gave knowing chuckles, but Brigan seemed confused.

"What do you mean?" he asked.

"Solrac names all of their operations," Meleya replied before I could. We all looked at her.

"How do you know that?" Solvai asked.

Meleya bit her lip, and I thought I noticed her absently fingering the quartz crystal on her belt.

"Uh," she started, "Jax might've mentioned it once back at Outcast Outpost." She looked at me, something unreadable in her eyes.

"A name?" Elle folded her arms. "Is that really necessary?"

"Lots of things are 'unnecessary,'" I replied. Though I tried to hide it, there was a slight edge to my tone. "Sugar in tea, morning walks, and dancing at parties to name a few. Even regular washing is technically unnecessary."

Elle's tone had that same edge. "That's debatable."

"Can we?" Brigan asked, excited. "Gauntlet down—"

"Enough!" Kai cut everyone off. "I already named the operation, anyway."

He lit up a simple illusion rune to form a glowing, golden sphere, which he used to cast light onto a page in his black leather journal. The sheet was filled with notes, and at its top were two words written in small, neat handwriting:

Operation O.

"Operation O?" I said indignantly.

"O for Orothion, of course," Kai explained.

I saw the others hiding chuckles as I let Kai have it. "That is the single most boring name you could've ever come up with!"

Kai shrugged. "Well, the original name was 'Plan Six'."

I blinked at him a few times before replying, "I stand corrected. Sorry guys, I guess we're stuck with 'Op O'."

"There's a subtitle, too," Kai said, pointing to a tiny row of words beneath the page's heading. "Operation O: Lie Low and Stay Away From Lady Vesta."

Kai's forehead runes pulsed as he formed a tiny illusion of a tall, scowling woman with a Geomancer's silvermark on her cheek.

Solvai jumped in. "Lady Vesta is the original Triarchy's Sentinel, the same position I hold among the Rebels. She pushed out Solrac and those who agreed with him in order to start the war with the Capital, and she's probably manipulating Zel and countless others into supporting her. She's the whole reason Kari and Akayto need rescuing in the first place. She's dangerous. So, while Kai's subtitle is on the cheesy side—"

"Hey!" Kai interjected.

"—please, stick to it like your lives depend on it, because they might. Lie low and stay away from Lady Vesta."

As we all nodded, a thick feeling of sobriety fell over us. While we'd been cracking jokes and sharing drinks throughout Kai's final preparation session, the gravity of what we were about to do hit me like a ton of scales. My father's life and Kari's depended on whether or not we could pull this off tomorrow.

"I've thought of a subtitle for the subtitle," I said. "Operation O: Lie Low and Stay Away from Lady Vesta: Goddesses be with us."

FRAGMENT: NO CHOICE

LANTHA

*T*hose who are great are at their greatest when they serve.

That had been one of the defining beliefs of Lantha's old bond, King Axel of Rengard, though Lantha was certain he hadn't meant it quite like this.

A wrenching sensation near Lantha's heart roused her from her sleep. Though she now served, she had no choice but to obey the command to arise. Such was the life of a dragon in a forced bond.

Lantha slowly rose up on her forewings, blinking in the dappled sunlight. All around her were the cliffs and the gigantic redwoods of keep Skygard. They had flown fast and far, her captors pushing Lantha as well as Luster beyond their limits in an attempt to keep pace with their skyskipping prey. The snowheaded Rifter they pursued was Meleya, the kindhearted soldier that had once been part of Axel's high guard. If it had been up to Lantha, she'd have left the poor girl alone or, better yet, helped her escape the cruel Mage Hunters' clutches.

According to Jaira's reckoning the night before, they should've been quite close now. Jaira had spent long hours chatting with the tiny silver dreamsnake she carried with them, using the familiar to communicate with Ilyan, the snake's creator. Ilyan was a Seer, and his omens told Jaira that they'd find their prey's traveling party in this very forest. Once they found them, Ilyan's snake would take care of the rest.

Lantha felt a tugging sensation again, and looked to the Mage Hunter that now held her heartscale. Lothar no longer wore his dusky blue cloak and silver pauldron, since Mage Hunters were not welcome in Skygard. But it wasn't the lack of uniform that made Lothar look like such a mess.

His outlander clothing was wrinkled and dirty. His red hair was bedraggled, his skin pale. Dark bags hung under his eyes. Lantha had noticed that Lothar had not been eating or sleeping well throughout their journey. Though Jaira hadn't seemed to notice, Lantha was certain it was a result of Lothar's conscience slowly eating away at him.

Though Lantha was the one trapped in a forced bond, it was Lothar she felt sorry for.

Lothar approached Lantha, looking apologetic. "Jaira and Luster are waiting for us down by the river. It's time."

Time to force more people to bend to your will? To sow more darkness in this realm as you pursue your ends?

"They're not my ends," Lothar replied, mechanically checking Lantha's saddle. He was completely devoid of emotion. Devoid of will.

You speak directly to my point, Lantha thought. *You are not like Jaira and the others.*

Lothar paused. It was now or never. Lantha would take her chance at freedom, and in so doing restore Lothar's own.

Leave, Lothar. Return my heartscale and abandon this foolish quest.

Lothar buried his face in his hands. "I can't."

Who tells you this? Your bond holds me, but what binds you?

Lothar looked up at Lantha with desperate, pleading eyes. "The High family... I owe them everything. Mason is my oldest friend... my *only* friend."

How does enabling his fall serve him?

Lothar met Lantha's gaze, his eyes wild and watery. "There's nothing else I can do! My meditations don't return an answer."

At least, not one you'll accept.

"Lantha, you don't understand!" Lothar stood, yelling now. "I'm in too deep. They'll kill me. They'll kill *Mason.* I believe they almost did once already, when he went north to slay the frostdrake. If I can't succeed on this mission, I don't know what they'll do."

Success will not save him, either—You know this as well as I do. Our enemy does not value life, only power.

Lothar was getting frantic. "I have no choice but to see this through!" Perhaps Lantha had pushed too hard.

Please, Lothar, take a moment to think. Meditate, center yourself.

Lothar was shaking. "No! Just stop talking. We have to go."

But if—

Crying out, Lothar held forth Lantha's heartscale once more, compelling her to silence. The once-great wyvern bowed her head, closing her eyes in resignation as Lothar climbed onto her back. She wished she could say more, but Lothar's will kept her mute as they made their way toward where Jaira and her own imprisoned dragon bond waited.

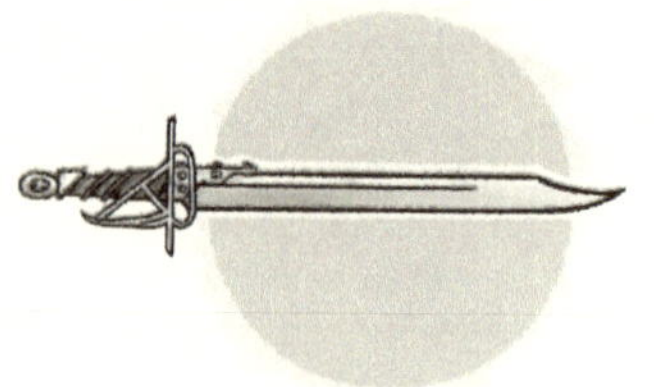

LIANA

"It just doesn't add up—I know my cousin. Vesta's no basket of sky-daisies, but she's no tyrant."

Queen Liana of Drakfell took her husband, Rodan's, hand. The pair alighted from the back of Rex, Rodan's proud white drake. Rodan wore his fine white ascension armor, and Liana had picked a lovely white dress to match. Both wore crowns distinguishing them as the King and Queen of the Badlands, with Drakfell tan gemstones in their centers.

"Her actions have made it clear," Rodan replied, keeping his voice low. "Vesta will stop at nothing to perpetuate this scorched war with Evgard, even if it means running the Knights of the Torch into the ground. I wonder why High King Magnus hasn't attempted a strike against Orothion already."

"Orothion *is* one of the most well-protected Keeps in the realm," Liana said.

Rodan gave a long, thoughtful sigh. Then he asked, "Was joining the Knights a mistake?"

"No," Liana said. "When we pledged Drakfell to the Knights, we did so under different circumstances."

"Perhaps," Rodan mumbled. "But now that choice is out of our hands."

When the Knights' schism first occurred, Rodan and Liana had hesitated. Their keepdom was on thin ice after turning their backs on Evgard in favor of the Knights of the Torch. They'd voted against Vesta's war with High King Magnus, but when she'd driven the Rebel Knights out of Orothion, she'd put Rodan and Liana in a tough position. For months, the king and queen had tried to avoid choosing a side. To back the Rebels would put them in danger of Vesta's wrath, essentially showing their house as turning traitor twice. But they couldn't in good conscience support her war, either. Most Drakfellian noble houses were following their lead, lying low rather than lending their aid to Skygard in their war efforts.

But ever since the king's brother, Aradan, had gone missing, Rodan and Liana felt they no longer had a choice. Rather than let harm come to his brother, Rodan had sent word that he'd changed his mind, accepting the invitation to attend Vesta's fund-raising banquet. After Rodan's acceptance, other nobles had done the same. Finally, Vesta was going to get the support of the Badlands, too.

Liana was surprised that Vesta would stoop to something like kidnapping. Rodan and the few advisors privy to the full story insisted it was absolutely in her aggressive nature. After all, she'd forced half of Orothion out of Skygard on pain of death.

Yes, Vesta came across as rather... intense. But Liana still believed that, beneath it all, her cousin was a true Knight of the Torch who valued the Code. Liana hoped she would get the chance to speak with her at the events over the next few days and find out why she was so desperate.

"Shall we?" Liana said, slipping her arm through Rodan's. Together, the pair began making their way through Orothion's outer city, set at the base of the hill leading up to the fortress. Liana and Rodan could have landed nearer the castle, but preferred to walk through the city where the people of Skygard could see them. Rodan saw it as a show of strength.

Sure enough, as they walked down the main street and up toward the castle, people stopped to watch the regal, white-clad couple and their noble third ascension drake. The people nodded, and Liana and Rodan nodded back. Liana even blew a few kisses. Where Rodan was stoic and dignified, Liana was all congeniality. Especially here in Skygard—her home keepdom.

"Oh, look!" Liana cried, pointing to a little streetside shop. "Signe's is still in business! We'll have to stop by for a new pair of shoes while we're here."

Liana gave an eager wave to the woman watching from the shop's porch, and the woman grinned widely. Liana had grown up in northern Skygard, but she and her cousins had visited Orothion many times before.

Speaking of cousins...

"Liana! Rodan!"

A couple wearing ruby-and-dragon-horn-adorned crowns suddenly engulfed Liana and Rodan in an embrace. Liana chuckled. The king and queen of Skygard had always been some of her favorite cousins. It seemed the pair of them had chosen to walk through the town rather than head straight to the castle too.

"Queen Ana and King Nik," Rodan said, sounding only slightly squashed. "How good it is to see you again. How is your family?"

The perfectly normal question seemed to take the couple off guard. The pair exchanged glances.

"The boys are fine," Nik replied vaguely as the two couples fell into step beside each other, heading toward the stronghold.

Liana arched an eyebrow. "And your daughter?"

Nik hesitated. "She's—"

"Fine too," Ana cut in. "At least, we hope. That is, she's out of the castle, but we're certain she'll be alright. She's off studying history with the Sisters of Streya."

Liana knew her cousin well enough to know that last part was a lie. But she didn't dare draw attention to it publicly.

Rodan, on the other hand, was none the wiser.

"Ah," he said. "We know what that's like. When Eliana went off to study with the Sisters, we didn't hear from her for the first month or so either. Don't worry, once the newness wears off I'm certain she'll write to you."

"Indeed." The king of Skygard nodded. "We're hoping Lady Vesta has heard from her. Annika was always close with her Auntie Vesta."

At the sound of Vesta's name, Rodan bristled. Liana squeezed his arm. Meanwhile, the other king and queen exchanged worried glances. They seemed strangely on edge, nothing like their normally jovial selves.

"And your family?" Queen Ana asked, trying to change the subject. "We've seen the wanted posters—It seems your daughter is causing quite the stir across the realm."

"That she is," Rodan replied with an almost imperceptible grimace. Liana knew how much Rodan hated the High King's bounty on Elle's head. He felt partially responsible—as if High King Magnus were exacting revenge on Rodan for his defiance in choosing the Knights of the Torch last summer.

"She's safe," Liana assured them. They hadn't heard from Elle in a while, or any of the Rebel Knights. But Liana couldn't think of any place safer for their daughter than the unfindable Rebel safehouse in the Mirror Forest. Not even Vesta and the other members of Orothion's Triarchy knew exactly how to get there. Liana only hoped Elle's true dragon rider training lasted long enough for all of this wanted poster business to blow over.

"Speaking of the Rebels—" Queen Ana lowered her voice, "I'm sure you've heard the news about the Farseer."

Liana and Rodan exchanged glances.

"Of course we've heard," Rodan said. "Solrac's face is plastered on every signpost, tree, and building in the realm."

"I still can't believe it…" King Nik stroked his thick beard with one hand while giving a wave to a group of bowing Skygardians with the other. "To think—the legendary, immortal Farseer was among us all along."

"Are you so sure he *is* immortal?" Ana added. "This is *Solrac*, Duke of Glacia, we're talking about. Not even his bardic songs are worthy of immortality."

"I find his songs amusing," Nik boomed.

"I, for one, think this revelation couldn't have come at a better time," Liana put in. "This makes the Farseer far more relatable. It humanizes the legend in unprecedented ways."

"And you see that as a good thing?" Ana asked.

"I do," Liana said confidently. "Granted, of course, that he's not caught and killed within the week."

"Goddesses be with him," Rodan said.

Nik turned to Rodan. "Does this mean the pair of you plan to throw your support behind the Rebel Knights?"

"Of course it doesn't," Ana said. "You wouldn't dare come here tonight unless you planned to support the Orothion Knights, right? When we heard you'd decided to come to the events this week, we assumed it was to sway the other Drakfellian nobles to fund Vesta's strike on the Capital."

"We…" Rodan trailed off. Liana could tell by the worried creases surrounding his eyes that he was thinking of his brother Aradan again.

"We plan to make our decision soon," Liana said, giving her husband's arm a reassuring squeeze.

Liana felt a twisting in her gut. There were so many unanswered questions, so many factors at play. What *would* they do when it came down to it? Was Rodan right, and Vesta was the monster everyone believed her to be?

As they arrived at the grand castle gate, one thing was clear. The window for choosing neutrality was over.

CHAPTER 26: OPERATION O

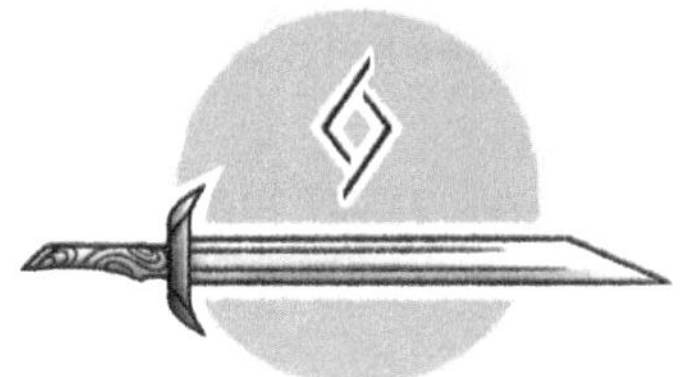

MELEYA

Growing up as a nomad-turned-soldier, I could count the number of times I'd worn a dress on one hand. And this one was by far the most expensive thing I'd ever worn.

Silky ice-blue fabric fell all the way to the tips of my toes and lovely, wildly impractical sleeves trailed just as long. Intricate beadwork wove along the dress's neckline and bodice, and though I hadn't quite filled it out when I'd first tried it on two days ago, a tailor living among Orothion's refugees had made Elle's gown fit me perfectly.

Elle had fixed my hair and done my makeup as well—nothing extreme, but she'd been rather proud of the way the tiny braids and soft white curls cascaded down my back. And I had to admit—It was kind of fun looking like a woman rather than a soldier for once.

Sniff was doing his best to behave like a proper noble dragon bond as well, smoothly alighting at the front gates that led to the Orothion stronghold with Brigan and I on his back. I could feel through our bond that despite wanting to throw in a little extra leap on our landing, he'd refrained. He held his pointed ears regally erect, walking as majestically as his four wings would allow.

My breath caught as I took in the splendor of the fortress from the front courtyard. The Orothion citadel was taller than the one back in Keep Rengard, and rather than white adobe walls, these were made from mottled gray and red stone. A row of increasingly tall spires rose like the spines along a dragon's back, starting here at the front door and ending at the southern tip where the castle met the oceanside cliffs. The mortar of the stone had a golden color to it, and I could see the golden gleam from the lighthouse that sat atop the highest tower. It wasn't hard to believe this grand structure was a remnant of the great Guardian Era.

Like the cabin in the Mirror Forest, ancient etherlocks safeguarded Orothion. I felt a shift when entering the citadel walls. Wild dragons wouldn't be able to sense my ether here, and my wraith wouldn't be able to get to me either.

Oh, won't I? Xan's voice rasped in my head. She seemed thrilled as she defied my expectations.

I froze. *How?*

Xan didn't respond. She just laughed. I got the feeling that even *she* wasn't sure how she'd been able to penetrate the barrier here, but she was certainly happy about it.

Through my bond with my dragons, I could feel the thunder of Blink's drum beats. They sounded strong, but somehow... strained? Moments later, Xan's whisperings grew distant, as if Blink was helping me push Xan from my thoughts.Whatever was going on, I felt grateful. Now wasn't the time to let my wraith distract me.

Iron gates loomed at the end of the path, and several nobles in clothing as fancy as mine stood in line ahead.

I nearly slid off of Sniff's saddle the way I normally did, but suddenly Brigan was on the ground, holding out a hand to me.

"Right," I muttered, taking his hand and dismounting with as much elegance as I could muster. Brigan had exchanged his travel clothes for traditional nobleman's garb, the small, pale blue gems along the seams of his jacket perfectly matching my dress.

Brigan didn't let go, instead tucking my hand through his elbow. Apparently, that was the way noble couples walked. Nervously, I glanced at the woven bracelets around our wrists. Fake marriage bracelets to complete our disguises.

When I'd first heard the plan, I'd been skeptical. Wouldn't Brigan and I look too young to pass as a married couple? But both Brigan and Elle had assured me that it was perfectly normal for the eighteen-year-old children of noble families to be newlyweds, going to events like this as they assumed more responsibility for their home keeps. If anything, our youthfulness strengthened the charade. And since Brigan was a Rengardian noble, there was very little chance of him being recognized, despite having been betrothed to Elle for years. They'd only seen each other in person a handful of times before the Rebel Knights brought them together, after all.

The whole idea made me feel uneasy. Brigan had just recently turned eighteen. Did that mean, if all had gone according to their parents' plans, that he and Elle would've been married within the next few months?

I accidentally stepped on the long hem of my dress and stumbled. Brigan had to stabilize me to keep me from hitting the dirt.

"Sorry," I muttered.

"Try using your other hand to pick up your skirts," Brigan whispered back.

I did and it helped, though I couldn't keep from noticing that Brigan hadn't looked me in the eye when he'd spoken. In fact, he'd barely glanced at me since the day we'd arrived in Skygard.

Guilt pricked my heart. I got the feeling he wished he'd been assigned a different task for this operation.

"Sorry," I said again, though this time for a different reason.

I was sure Brigan caught my meaning when after a moment, he turned to me with sincerity in his warm brown eyes.

"Don't be," he said. "It's not your fault you're not in love with me."

Awkwardness alarms seemed to blare inside my heart. I didn't know what to say, so Brigan had to settle for a jumbled array of miscellaneous mumbles.

"It's okay," Brigan said, quietly enough that nobody else could hear. "I just needed some time to process things. I know how hard it is for you to see others hurting, but I swear I'm alright. *We're* alright. Our relationship doesn't hinge on romantic love."

Relief washed over me like a cool gust of wind. "Gauntlet down," I said. "You're the best friend I ever could've asked for."

Brigan locked eyes with me and spoke with acceptance. "I know."

By now, we'd fallen into line behind several other noble couples waiting to be admitted into the castle. Asher and Solvai took their places just behind us, having ridden up on Thorn.

It was strange seeing Solvai in a dress too, though hers wasn't half as fancy as mine was. She'd be playing my maidservant today. Kai had tried several tricks with illusions to hide her Wildshaper's silvermark, but nothing had worked. The silver in the ink used on the blade that cut the mark made it untouchable by etherarchy. Fortunately, having a magi for a maidservant wasn't unheard of, especially since Drakfell joined with the Knights of the Torch. We'd just have to hope no one asked about it.

As for Asher, I did a double take when I saw him. I'd never before considered what Asher would look like with rounded, human ears and brown eyes instead of bright, dragonfire green ones. Plus, the way Kai had insisted on slightly altering his nose definitely made him look different, even if Asher wasn't happy with it. Despite those things, he looked undeniably sharp in his guard's uniform disguise complete with a Drakfell tan cloak.

A half-smile appeared on my lips when I saw that his hair had already begun its escape from the smooth ridgeknot Elle had fussed over this morning. As for me, I kind of liked the way those unruly black strands fell over one eye.

When Asher caught me looking, he gave me a wide grin. At least that scorching grin was still as charmingly crooked as ever.

For the hundredth time since yesterday afternoon, I thought of what had happened after the 'eclips-plosion' incident. I hadn't *meant* to kiss Asher, it had just sort of... happened.

And stars... It was kind of nice.

I hadn't told anyone, not even Solvai, about the kiss. Only Sniff and Blink knew, and they certainly had their own takes on the matter:

I like Asher! Asher's fun! Sniff thought through our bond.

Brrrum-ba-dum, Blink countered, letting us know she thought he might be a little *too much* fun. Blink liked Asher, but she still wasn't sure about the pair of us *together.*

Admittedly, I wasn't sure about us either. And I'd sensed that same hesitation in Asher out there on the lava fields. We were drawn to each other, yes, but deep down, I still wasn't sure *what* I felt for Asher of Steel Rim. Not yet. For now, all I knew was that I felt lighter, happier when I was with him, and something in my soul seemed to desperately need that.

But at the same time, he was still one of the most disorganized, obnoxious scarf-wearers I'd ever met.

On cue, Asher gave me a wink. I fought the urge to stick my tongue out at him. Ladies probably didn't do that.

I felt a squirm from the tiny mirror gecko inside my boot as the group mindlink bloomed to life. Kai had needed to duplicate his ethereal familiar a few extra times to accommodate all of us, though I knew that my Glint, Glint Eight-B, was only temporary. After the heist, Kai would dismiss her.

Part one is a go, Kai's thought sounded in my head. Along with it, I caught a mental glimpse of what Kai was seeing.

If I felt overwhelmed by the part I had to play in our risky rescue venture, I couldn't imagine what Kai must've been feeling. He sat in the center of a hollowed-out giant redwood tree. Before seeing the splendor of Skygard's southern forest for myself, I hadn't thought trees could grow this big.

Hovering around Kai on all sides were about a dozen shimmering illusions. Each illusion showed the point of view of a different member of our team, and among them I noted my own perspective displaying Orothion's front gates.

To keep himself from going completely insane, Kai had tethered each illusory burst to a different runemarked quartz crystal spread all around him within the tree hollow. Among the crystals I could see his black notebook open and ready, along with several papers bearing schematics of the castle. I noted a solid golden glow coming from all across the top edge of Kai's perspective—evidence that a lot of complicated runes were at play here.

Scorch, Kai thought to the group. *With my concentration split like this, I feel so vulnerable. I wish Flint were here.*

I recognized the name of Kai's stonescale dragon bond, whom we'd had to leave behind at Rhana's cabin. But it had already been a strain to have me skyskipping six humans and three dragons all the way here.

What are we, scrub kirin? Elle thought indignantly to Kai. Over the mindlink, I saw that her perspective showed the redwood forest just outside Kai's hideout.

I feel sorry for anyone who dares to try getting past us, Kai, Elle thought, and I saw a flash of her elegant saber in my head.

Of course, of course, Kai thought. *I'm ninety-six percent confident you and Aurora are perfectly capable of guarding me.*

You mean you think there's a four-percent chance we—

Kai mentally cut Elle off. *I just don't want to risk anything going wrong. The Rebel Knights are counting on us.*

It's true, Solvai put in. *Remember—Success today means crippling Vesta's war efforts. Behrfell will join us then and, with any luck, so too will others.*

Exactly, Kai thought. *We only need to get Kari and Akayto out. Just... Can I make one request?*

Several voices chorused in the affirmative.

Please be careful, thought Kai. *My sister's life is on the line.*

There was a solemnity that filled the mindlink at that. I felt Asher's worry as well—Not only was Kari like a sister to him, but his father was at risk too.

Before we knew it, Brigan, Solvai, Asher, and I had arrived at the gate.

My heart pounded as we made our way up the wide stone steps to Orothion's grand front doors. A pair of guards wearing calf-length cloaks in Skygard's red looked at us expectantly. Their hands rested casually on their dragonhook spears.

I squeezed Brigan's arm, trying to act as natural as possible while Brigan confidently addressed the guards.

"Lord Dolf and Lady Astrid of Naga Bay."

My heart was beating so loudly I was afraid the guards would hear it as they checked their list. After what felt like an eternity, one guard looked up.

"Didn't expect to see anyone from those parts here tonight," he said, his light northern accent coming through. "List says the royal family from Naga Bay weren't goin' to be able to make it on account of needin' to travel so great a distance."

"At first, we weren't going to make it in time, that's true," Brigan said. "But my lovely new wife here offered to speed up our journey using her abilities."

On cue, I turned my head so that the guards could get a better look at the Rifter's silvermark gracing my left cheek. Doing so made me feel vulnerable and a little afraid. Last time I was at a noble gathering, I'd done my best to hide my mark. But here in Skygard, etherarchy wasn't scorned.

"Hmph." The second guard eyed my cheek. "Rifter? Don't see many like you these days."

The first guard gave a little snort as he nudged his companion. "Took the Triarchy long enough to find the one we've got now, ain't that right?"

The second guard shot the first a look, then turned back to me with narrowed eyes. "Our records say nothing about you being a magi, Lady Astrid."

"You know how it was in Drakfell," Brigan jumped in, saving me from having to open my mouth. "Even for the upper class, it wasn't safe to be open about these things. At least, that's how it was before King Rodan made the excellent decision to align himself with Skygard. Now, with the honorable Knights of the Torch at the helm, Astrid is finally free to practice etherarchy openly."

Both guards seemed to accept this. Then, the first turned his attention on Brigan, eyeing his face with the same scrutiny he'd given mine.

"If you don't mind me askin', Lord Dolf," he began, "where'd you get that there nasty scar 'cross your brow?"

Brigan and I exchanged glances, a thousand unsaid words passing between us. After a tense pause, Brigan replied.

"A Mage Hunter gave it to me while I was trying to protect the woman I care for."

My gut twisted.

The first guard nodded with understanding, while the second eyed me, as if waiting for me to validate Brigan's story. I tried to give a ladylike nod, but suddenly got very self conscious. Soot, what did noblewomen do with their faces?

Not that, I hope, Elle's voice over the mindlink startled me. Oops. I hadn't meant to transmit that thought to the group.

Suddenly, I caught a glimpse of my own incredibly awkward face through Brigan's perspective over the mindlink. Drak—why couldn't I stop pursing my lips like that? Behind me, I heard Asher stifle a snort.

Try a smile? Elle suggested.

I did.

Over the mindlink, I heard a chorus of things like 'yikes,' 'scorch,' and 'stars above, someone put it out of its misery.' Likewise, the guards raised eyebrows and seemed to recoil slightly.

Great.

Never mind, Elle rushed. *Just... do nothing with your face, Meleya.*

Before I could somehow butcher even that simple request, Asher stepped in to save me, speaking with the authority of a high guard squad captain.

"It has been a long journey for my Lord and Lady. We trust that the great Lady Vesta and the other hosts here at Orothion will be pleased that representatives from Naga Bay were able to come in the end. We hear that nearly all the noble houses from Drakfell will be here over the next few days to discuss the coming assault on Keep Evgard, yes?"

The guards stiffened. "That's right," the first said. "Of course you may enter." Over the mindlink, I heard Kai mumble something about being glad none of them had recognized Asher so far. His illusory human disguise must've been working.

From there, the guards ushered Asher and Solvai down a corridor toward the servants' quarters. Meanwhile, Brigan and I headed straight toward the banquet hall.

See you all when this is over, Asher thought.

As I watched his and Solvai's retreating backs, I couldn't help but hope he was right about that.

The banquet hall was splendorous. Tall, peaked windows let in the light over the ocean, while beautifully painted panels depicted scenes from the history of the Knights of the Torch. Stars, the Farseer had been present during a lot of historical events. I couldn't help but think of Solrac and wonder whether these paintings depicted just him, or other Farseers throughout the ages.

As we joined the throng waiting to be seated, Brigan and I heard others wondering similar things. Solrac as the Farseer was the prime topic of gossip here at the banquet. Some insisted he was an immortal legend, while others were certain he was a mere showman and a fraud. Many whispered amongst themselves about whether Solrac's secret would affect Vesta's success this week in securing the nobles' aid in funding her strike on the capital.

"If Solrac truly is the Farseer," one man spoke quietly, "will that not sway more support for the Rebel Knights? Perhaps they will rise up against Vesta and those here at Orothion."

"Only if Solrac isn't caught and executed," another noble butted in.

"I'm waiting to hear what King Rodan says," said a third. "Where my king goes, I will follow."

"Hear, hear!"

Brigan and I were doing our best to lie low, seeking out seats at the far end of the table. All we had to do was quietly make it through this meal, then enjoy a lovely tour of the castle, ending in the upper terrace of the grand, ancient Skyforge. From there, we'd be able to grab Kari and rift back to Kai's tree before anyone knew what hit them.

"Excuse me, my lord and lady—" A servant tapped Brigan and me on the shoulders only seconds after we'd sat down. "Your presence is requested at the head of the table. Places have been set for you. If you'll just follow me."

"What? Why?" I blurted out.

Brigan rushed to cover my unsophisticated response. "Of course." We followed the girl along the long, long table, past men and women in fine jackets and silky dresses.

Hmm, Elle thought over the mindlink. *The head of the table is where the most important guests sit.*

So much for lying low, Asher added.

Who requested your presence? Kai's thought was skeptical, and I caught mental glimpses of him scratching more notes into his journal. *And why?*

"Presenting Lady Astrid and Lord Dolf of Naga Bay," the serving girl said to the guests.

The head of the table had three seats—one for each member of the Triarchy.

In the Archon's seat was a pleasant-looking, elderly gentleman with a Shadowbinder's silvermark on his left cheek. He had dragonfire green eyes and bright red scales on the tips of his pointed ears. He was a half-born, like Asher. That had to be Zel. He gave a little wave as we sat down.

The next seat was the Mystic's chair, the one that Solrac had filled before he had to flee Orothion. The man who occupied that place now was—according to Kai's notes—a Psion named Signus. He had wide, sharp eyes and sat with a hunched posture that reminded me of a ridgerat. I didn't like the way his left eye twitched as he observed each new arrival with a calculating gaze.

In the third seat, the Sentinel's chair, was the woman who was responsible for the loss of hundreds of lives in the Knights' war with Evgard. The tight-jawed, angry-looking woman silvermarked as a Geomancer. The one person Kai had specifically told us to avoid.

Lady Vesta.

And I was seated right beside her.

"Well, would you look at that," Lady Vesta said. "Guards at the door were right—The dragoncat *did* drag in a Rifter. Interesting. How very, very interesting."

The way she said it made my pulse race with fear.

Through the mindlink, I felt sheer panic from Brigan. He quickly dropped my hand.

But when I looked his way, it wasn't Lady Vesta who was eliciting calm, collected Brigan's distress.

It was the couple seated to his other side. A woman with long, dark waves and a white dress. A man with amber eyes and an ornate crown with a tan jewel in its center. Both were staring at Brigan as if they were seeing a ghost.

"King Rodan and Queen Liana," Brigan swallowed.

Oh no, Elle's voice thundered in our ears. *Oh NO!*

Impossible! Kai thought. *They sent word to Orothion multiple times that they wouldn't be attending! I triple-verified my sources!*

Soot, Asher thought. *Big, huge, messy soot.*

All at once, I realized what was happening here. King Rodan and Queen Liana... Those were Elle's parents.

"Hello there," Queen Liana said, one smooth eyebrow arched. "Lord *Dolf*, was it?"

CHAPTER 27: PRISONER

ASHER

I could hardly believe what I was seeing from Brigan and Meleya's perspectives over the mindlink. The two of them were seated directly beside *Elle's parents*. The very couple who'd nearly become Brigan's parents-in-law.

I may have been physically hurrying down the long, stone hallway that led to the servant's quarters with Solvai, but mentally, I watched the action unfolding in the banquet hall with equal parts concern and intrigue. Was it just me, or was the mirror gecko inside my boot squirming? I wondered what had her all excited.

"Oh, young Lord Dolf," Queen Liana said, as I could practically feel Brigan's mental tumult. "We were so disappointed when you weren't able to make it to our gala last summer! Weren't we, Rodan?"

"Uh…" King Rodan gave an unintelligible mumble.

"Now, Lord Dolf," Liana started.

"Yes?" Brigan replied, his voice cracking on the word.

Does she have to keep saying his name? Elle thought over the mindlink. *Come on, Mom.*

"Selene help us," Solvai muttered under her breath as we walked.

Meanwhile, in the banquet hall, Queen Liana wasn't finished. "The gala just wasn't the same without you, *Dolf*."

"Ah." Brigan cleared his throat. "Yes, you see, there's been so much to attend to back home."

"Of course! I'm sure you've been terribly busy, especially with your new bride."

She leaned past Brigan to get a better look at Meleya. Through Brigan's perspective on the mindlink, I saw her go white as parchment.

"Uh…" Now it was Meleya's turn to give an unintelligible mumble. She looked to Brigan with an expression that said 'help me.'

Lady Vesta's lip curled in disgust. "Yeesh. You newlyweds make me want to stick scales in my eyes."

Liana couldn't help herself. "Tell me, where did the two of you honeymoon? Rodan and I very much enjoyed our stay in Shard Shore. Or did you visit the Smoky Peaks—I hear they're lovely in the spring months. Then again, perhaps you celebrated on the gorgeous, balmy beaches of… *Keep Solhelm*. Ever been to Solhelm, darlings?"

Brigan and Meleya exchanged looks.

"Solhelm?" Brigan repeated. His voice was about an octave higher than usual. "Uh, no. That's a bit far from Naga Bay, you see."

"Oh, but you must visit sometime!" Queen Liana clapped her hands. "We know the royal family there quite well. Duchess Breona and Duke Brodrik are as charming as they come, and don't even get me started on their eldest son. A finer, more *honest* young man you'll never find!"

Brigan gave an uneasy laugh as the old man, Zel, chimed in.

"Quite right, Queen Liana! Solhelm has some of the loveliest beaches the realm over. And their fresh chili and lime oysters are to die for! Ah—speaking of excellent cuisine…"

At that moment, servants arrived with plates heaped with fantastic-looking cattledrake steaks, steamed vegetables, and buttery rolls. Through the mindlink, I noticed Meleya's instant distraction. I smiled.

What do we do? Kai was mentally muttering over and over again.

Get a Glint on King Rodan, I thought back as Solvai and I hurried around another corner, then began descending a set of stairs. *Let Elle talk to them before her mom asks Lord Dolf and Lady Astrid to kiss or something.*

Asher! Meleya mentally scolded.

I wouldn't put it past her, Elle thought.

That's actually a good idea, Asher, Kai thought, sounding a little more surprised than I would have liked. *Splitting Glint Eight-B now.*

Glint Eight-B? Meleya thought. *That's my—oh drak!*

Meleya's perspective played over the link as she glanced under the table, pulling back the folds of her pale blue dress to reveal a tiny gecko peeking over the top of her boot. Gold runes glowed from the gecko's scaly skin as her big, shiny eyes squinted with concentration.

Then, suddenly, Glint Eight-B sprouted another head.

I gasped with horror as another set of gecko forelegs grew, pushing off of the first Glint's back as a second body morphed out of it. Within a moment, two identical geckos crouched side by side within Meleya's boot.

By the scorching stars, Kai! I thought through the mindlink. *Your gecko just gave birth to itself!*

How did you think I made mirror copies of her?

I didn't think about it at all! There goes my innocence.

At least your leg wasn't the spawning grounds, Meleya thought.

That was *pretty graphic,* Solvai added.

Ah, Elle thought, *the miracle of life. Sort of.*

Everyone. Shut. Up. Kai's thought was strained. His mental bandwidth must've been under so much pressure. *And Meleya, stop looking before someone notices. I'm sending Glint Eight-B-Alpha to King Rodan now. Meanwhile, I'm isolating the mindlink channels so you all can focus. You'll all still be able to communicate with me, but you'll only be able to share thoughts with each other when you're intentional about it. Brigan, Meleya, your sole job is to get through this drakking dinner without completely blowing your covers. Okay?*

I didn't hear their replies. Kai must've already isolated their portion of the mindlink.

As for Asher and Solvai, Kai continued. *You're going to want to hang a left at the end of this hallway. There's no time to waste. Ugh! We're less than thirty minutes into the operation and already having to improvise.*

Just think of charts and numbers, Solvai thought, her mental tone soothing. *Neatly organized columns. Alphabetized lists.*

I chuckled as Solvai's tactic seemed to calm Kai down. Before me, Solvai shrugged.

"How did he find you?" I asked. Solvai grinned.

Over the mindlink, we caught a quick glimpse of my best friend's perspective as he looked over a painfully detailed map of the stronghold's inner schematics. *Head down this corridor then take a left, a right, then two more lefts,* Kai determined.

With Kai as our guide, Solvai and I made our way down the network of corridors. Lower and lower we went, down staircases and through secret passages.

Stars, I thought over the mindlink. *Orothion is a maze.*

Hang a right, Kai instructed. *And it's actually an incredibly sophisticated—left—ancient style of architecture—straight through this archway—typical of the Guardian Era—not that archway, the first one, back about twenty feet on the side—with built-in relics that far and away surpass modern etherarchical capacity—left again here.*

Okay, okay, I thought, getting slightly impatient, both with Kai's history lesson and his constant directions. Still, I followed without complaint. We'd reach the dungeons soon.

Hurry, Kai thought. *With so much going on in the banquet hall, I'd like you two to free Akayto three times more quickly to pick up the slack.*

Thanks for the warning, I thought back. *I was actually planning on freeing Dad really slowly, so it's good to know I'll need to work five times faster now.*

Solvai giggled. I could feel Kai rolling his eyes.

Only three times faster, moron.

I was just trying to come up with a clever retort when I felt a sudden tug in my core. To the side I saw a set of stairs.

Without thinking, I started walking down them.

Stop, Kai thought. *Wrong way.*

I knew Kai was right, but still... I felt something inside me compelling me downward. Intuition? Or something even stronger?

Asher...

I turned to Solvai. "Did you say something?"

Solvai shook her head.

Hello, Kai sounded impatient. *You're going to need to take another left down the next hallway, followed by another through a door. There's an eighty-one percent chance it's locked, but Asher's starglass key trick should be able to take care of that—*

"I think I need to go this way," I said, both out loud to Solvai and mentally to Kai.

No, Kai sounded annoyed. *That way leads to the armory. There's a whopping ninety-seven percent chance Vesta's keeping your father in the dungeon. We don't have time for useless detours!*

Grids, Solvai calmly thought to Kai. *Checklists. Standardized codexes.*

The plural is codices, Kai responded, sounding a little less stressed than before.

I bit my lip. Solvai must've picked up on my feeling through the mindlink, because while she calmed Kai, she was looking at me.

"Trust your gut," she said, nodding toward the staircase.

What? Kai thought, immediately breaking out of his happy place. *No. Asher's gut is a liability. We don't have time to waste.*

We'll split up, Solvai replied. *Asher can try the armory and I'll head to the dungeon. I have faith in Asher's instincts.*

Solvai and I exchanged a smile. This was why she was part of the Triarchy.

Ignoring Kai's mental protests, Solvai and I parted ways.

Kai's mental energy got pretty smug when the armory turned out to have nothing more than endless rows of weapons. Spears, long seaxes, and crossbows were everywhere. There was a section for specialty weapons as well, where I found some specialized crossbows that looked like they might shoot dreamweave bolts of some kind. I recognized Kari's fang-and-anvil signature burned onto them.

But then I found the well-hidden back door behind a wall of hanging shields. The lock on the door was insanely complicated—Vesta *really* didn't want anyone getting in here. It took several tries fiddling around with starglass inside the mechanism before I finally felt that satisfying click.

When I pushed the door open, I heard a faint snapping sound. Looking down, I realized I'd broken some kind of thin, black thread. Spydraweb, maybe?

I quickly forgot all about it because the brightness beyond the door nearly blinded me.

Skystone. It was everywhere, stacked in heaping piles all over the medium-sized room. Dozens of ether-filled crystals produced a palpable hum of pure power. For a moment, I wondered how wild dragons hadn't ransacked this treasure, but then remembered the etherlocks. They must've been working overtime to hide such a bounty.

Stars. Vesta was no better than the High Throne, hoarding skystone tribute from the people who risked their necks harvesting the skystone from skyfalls. I thought of the refugees on the lava fields who'd lost so much getting this very treasure. Vesta didn't care who she hurt in her efforts to get fuel for her Rifter prisoner.

And there he was. I'd nearly missed him at first, as thick, strangely shimmering black ropes bound him to iron shackles on the back wall. A sorry excuse for a cot stood nearby as did a tray with picked-over gruel and dry bread. The very sight of it all made my blood hot.

"Dad," I murmured. I could feel over the mindlink that Kai was surprised to see that my gut had, in fact, not been a liability. This time.

Without wasting another moment, I hover-dashed across the room to my father. He seemed dazed and almost panicked as I knelt beside him, his unseeing eyes darting back and forth.

"No," Dad said, his voice gruff. "Please, don't make me rift another army. It's too much."

"Dad, it's me," I said. He didn't have a Sight rune floating over his forehead, leaving him completely blind.

"Asher?" Dad's brow furrowed. "Is this a dream?"

"Nah," I said. "It's a Rebel Knight operation. We're gonna get you out of here."

As my eyes adjusted to the skystone's light, I realized Dad looked different. Not only was he clearly exhausted, but there were gold streaks in his hair and golden flecks in his irises. Gold, spidery lines like veins stood out against the skin on his forehead. It had to be evidence of how much ether Vesta was forcing him to use.

"Drak," I muttered. "What have they done to you?"

As I moved to free my father from his bindings, I realized that the ropes that bound him were made from thick, braided strands of shadowsilk. But when I saw that silver chain links—a repurposed Mage Hunter's whip, maybe—had been braided into the ropes, my anger with Vesta grew even greater. So that was why Dad didn't have the Sight rune going.

Not only that but... soot. The silver wasn't dissolving the shadowsilk into etherdust. That meant...

Someone's using voidarchy, Kai thought. *But that shouldn't be possible with the etherlocks. Drak—does that mean someone's tampered with the etherlocks somehow? What has Lady Vesta gotten Orothion into? If she's sided with the Gray... Soot, Meleya, nobility don't think about the rising time of bread loaves! Make your small talk smaller, please.*

I chuckled.

Oh, sorry, Asher, Kai thought. *I'm having a hard time keeping the different channels isolated. It's tricky etherarchy, even when I'm not stretched so thin. I swear, I've got so much going on in my head I can hardly—*

Kai's thought suddenly cut out. For a moment, the mindlink felt strangely muddled. An odd hissing noise momentarily overwhelmed anyone else's thoughts. Then, there were quick flashes of everyone's point of view, as if Kai were checking on each of us in rapid succession. I saw the stone halls of Orothion through Solvai's eyes on her way to the dungeon, then a goblet of tasty-looking dragonberry juice from Brigan's perspective. Elle's point of view showed the quiet redwoods outside our group's base camp, then, finally, the mindlink settled on what Meleya was seeing. For whatever reason, Kai seemed to be especially focused on her.

Queen Liana was no longer grilling Brigan. Rather, she and King Rodan seemed deep in thought as they casually ate their meal. With any luck, Elle was currently using the Glint network to bring them up to speed and ask them to please not blow our team's cover.

Meleya kept glancing nervously toward the head of the table where Vesta and Zel sat. Actually, just Vesta. Zel had just stood up as a servant whispered to him. Whatever the servant said got the old half-born man to give the table a quick wave.

"I'll be back in two flicks of a wyvern's tail," he assured them. "Just off to check that all is ship-shape at the front gates and that all our noble guests have arrived safely."

Vesta rolled her eyes as the elderly Triarchy member pitter-pattered from the banquet hall. "So, little Miss Rifter," she said, shifting her focus to Meleya. "You ever considered ditching the dismal drudgery of Naga Bay for the balmy beach breezes here in Orothion?"

"Beach breezes, hmm," Meleya replied with a vague nod.

"We could use more help from magi like you," Vesta went on, and I thought I sensed the beginnings of a threat in her tone. Was that why she'd asked Meleya and Brigan to join her at the head of the table? Because she hoped to use Meleya's rifting? I didn't like that.

That was when Meleya's perspective winked out. Kai must've fixed whatever was wrong with his runes, allowing him to isolate the mindlink channels once more.

Kai? I thought. *Everything okay?*

All is well, Kai responded. *Everyone, please, carry on with your assignments.*

Okay, Sir Formal, I thought back. The pressure of doing so much seemed to be getting to him. But Dad pulled my focus back to the armory's secret skystone room.

"Drakked Knights of the Torch," Dad murmured as I alternated between using Dad's old skyseeker dagger and silverbane to free him. "This is why I was skeptical of the whole lot of them right from the start. I finally trust Solrac and the rest and look where it got me."

I wanted to argue with Dad, but how could I? He was right. The Knights should have protected him, and Kari too. I'd grown up thinking Skygard would be a safe haven for my father, yet within months of his arrival, he'd become a prisoner. I knew that wasn't Solrac and the Rebels' fault specifically. Still, I found myself growing angrier with all the Knights with every passing second.

I was so lost in my thoughts that I nearly jumped out of my scales when I heard the door slam shut behind me. I hadn't quite finished freeing Dad yet, but I whirled around, already summoning my starglass spear.

Dad tensed, his voice betraying panic. "What is it?"

I frowned, gripping my weapon as my gaze darted around the room. "Nothing," I replied.

That response seemed to terrify Dad even more than if I'd said "a giant spydra."

"Scorch," he cursed. "He's here."

"Who?"

Asher! Solvai's voice burst onto the mindlink. I wasn't sure why, but it sounded like she'd been trying to get through to me for a while now. Come to think of it, the mindlink had gone strangely silent ever since Kai had re-isolated the channels.

Solvai went on, her thoughts fast. *You have to get out of there! I just got to the dungeon. Prisoners... Aradan, and others.*

Aradan? I recognized the name of King Rodan's brother.

Vesta's not the one—

There was another hissing noise as Solvai's voice cut out. I heard Kai once more.

Sorry about that, Asher, Kai thought. *It is not easy to keep your channels isolated. Carry on with your task.*

Kai, what's going on—

My thought faltered when black threads like spydrawebs appeared to grab my limbs. It was shadowsilk that quickly solidified into ropes around my wrists and ankles. Ropes intertwined with burning cold silver links. My starglass spear dissolved into etherdust on contact as screaming, ice-cold pain tore through me.

I cried out, and my fearful father called my name. My powers neutralized, I looked back and forth, searching for whatever had trapped me.

He materialized in front of us as he dismissed his Shadowbinder's invisibility. A deceptively pleasant elderly man with hundreds of wrinkles lining his smiling face, his eyes flashing as he used his Archonic power. Rather than gold, his power manifested with blue voidlight.

"Zel," Dad said, his tone dark. He tried to break free from his bonds—I'd gotten close to removing them—but with a flick of his wrist, Zel added thicker ropes to hold my father still. More black shadowsilk crept over my father's mouth to gag him.

Kai, I thought, strained, *Kai, please tell me you've got a backup plan accounting for this?* Thanks to the silver, my connection with the mindlink felt weak at best.

You're doing fine, Asher. Carry on. Kai's mental voice was distant and monotonous, as if he wasn't at all surprised to see Zel here. It was almost as if he was glad things were going so wrong.

Soot, Kai, what's wrong with—

I yelped as another person materialized beside me, then another and another. Pretty soon, a whole squad's worth of soldiers who'd been using Zel's invisibility had me surrounded, tugging on the ropes that held me.

I protested as they searched me. They must've known exactly what to look for, because when they found my mirror copy of Glint hiding in my boot, they didn't hesitate. I watched in horror as they pressed her against the silver chain links in one of the ropes. Glint Four disappeared in a little puff of etherdust.

"No!" I cried. I knew Kai could remake her, but the whole thing still made me sick. Besides that, the mindlink was gone.

To make matters worse, the next thing they took was the heartscale tucked under my neck scarf. As the cord snapped, I felt my bond with Thorn dull to almost nothing. My adrenaline raced—I was completely on my own now.

"Tsk tsk," Zel said. "Trying to escape with this silly Rebel, are we, Akayto? That wouldn't bode well for Kari."

Both Dad and I strained against the silvered ropes. I was still baffled by it. Zel? He was supposed to be the nice one. The kindly old man, as manipulated by Vesta as the rest.

"Now if we can keep this brief, I'd really appreciate it," Zel said, his bright, happy tone contrasting with everything going on around us. "You see, the King and Queen of Drakfell are upstairs, and I want to make sure they have a most splendid evening. If we can win them over, the others will follow, and our next strike will cripple the High throne once and for all! Hurrah!"

"I... it... what?" I stammered, wholly taken off guard by that overly jubilant 'hurrah'.

"Hmm..." Zel tapped his chin, taking little steps closer to me. I tried to lunge his way, but his squad of red-cloaked soldiers pulled more tightly on my ropes.

"How pleasant to find you here, Asher of Steel Rim," Zel went on excitedly. "Ever since I first laid eyes on you, I knew you were someone special. A man after my own heart."

Zel pointedly turned his head to show off the red tips of his pointed ears. He had a pair of short horns on his head, and his eyes were the same bright dragonfire green as mine.

"Us scale-skins have to stick together, eh?" Zel said, a trace of bitterness in his cheery tone.

"Half-borns," I corrected.

"Seaxe, sax." Zel shrugged as he gave the two distinct pronunciations of the same weapon. "It's all the same. To them, at least. That's why rather than lock you up, I'm going to offer you a chance to help the cause."

"You mean the Gray?" I spat. "Forget it! You're a voidmage. A traitor to the etherarchy you were born with."

Zel's bottom lip stuck out in a pout. "You want to talk about betrayal?" he said. "Alright, let's begin with the Knights of the Torch themselves. Asher of Steel Rim, they reject people like us. I'm certain you know exactly what I mean. A few pretend to care about us half-borns, but deep down even they resent us. We don't belong in the Isles. We don't belong in Evgard. We are not quite a part of either side. Have you not felt it?"

I wanted to say no. But the words of Rhana, Solrac, and others echoed within my mind.

Sit down, scale-skin!

Ah, a half-born.

Drekai and Evgardians don't really mix.

"That's why I chose the path of voidarchy," Zel continued. "It's not about dark or light ether, it's about power. The Gray... it's a power multiplier, Asher of Steel Rim. Those at the top, whether it's the High Crown *or* the Triarchy, wield their power selfishly. By using voidarchy, I balance the scales."

To emphasize his point, Zel dug deep to access his powers once more. His eyes flashed gold as a plume of black shadowfire burst from behind him like a terrifying, disintegrating glow. Even Zel's own soldiers shuffled backward.

As for me, I tried to take the opportunity to wrench free from their grip. Unfortunately, Zel saw it coming and thrust his hand my way, launching another cluster of shadowsilk at my feet to bind me more securely to the floor.

"Ah," Zel said, a ghost of a smile crossing his lips. "You remind me so much of him. Such spirit and skill, a real protégé with etherarchy. He... he even used to wear his hair like that to show off his drakked ears, same as you."

His expression looked so deeply sad, I had to ask, "Who?"

"My son," Zel said. "He was about your age when the High King's Mage Hunters took him. When I petitioned the leaders of the Knights of the Torch at the time, Amund, Rhana, even the Farseer, begging them to save my boy, what did they do? Nothing."

Zel winced. I felt a tug in my chest as well as he went on.

"They denied me, Asher of Steel Rim," he said. "They did it under the guise of not having adequate resources for such an operation, but we all knew the truth. They let my son die because he'd inherited *these*."

He gestured to his scaled, pointed ears and dragonfire eyes. With a sinking feeling, I recalled just how difficult it had been to get the Rebel Knights to agree to a quest to save my father. Had part of that been because of me? And if the scales had been swapped, would they have sent a crew to rescue me, or left me to die?

Doubt burned within me. In fact, once this mission was over, the Knights planned to send me off to my death in the Dragon Isles, a disposable tribute in an effort to gain information from the Drekai.

Deep down, I knew there was more to it, but at that moment, all I could see was red. Red cloaks as a reminder that the Knights would spill blood to serve their own ends, same as the High Crown and every sooty noble who'd ever wronged me.

"The Gray is the only side willing to put an end to all powers that be," Zel continued, his tone rich with sincerity and hurt. "It was far too easy to pit the Knights against the Capital. No matter the outcome of this war, I get to see *both* my son's murderers take each other down. It is too late for him, but it's not too late for you, Asher."

I chanced a glance at my father's drained, gold-marked face, his eyes empty of sight. Broken because of the Mage Hunters *and* the Knights. Wasn't Dad just saying how he'd never trusted them?

So what was I doing, playing Knight myself? I didn't want a part in these wars and battles with the Gray. I should've run away from all of it when I'd had the chance.

"Last chance," Zel said as his soldiers' grips tightened on me. "Join us, Asher of Steel Rim. See them all fall. We can rebuild a better, more forgiving world. No more Drekai versus Evgardian. No Knights versus Hunters. A perfect world, where everything is gray."

My mind plunged back to the moment in the island sanctuary before the quest. I'd stood before the statue of the Goddess Solei, lost. Ever since choosing not to kill the Black Valkyrie last summer, I'd been floundering, searching for my purpose.

Why am I here, Mom? I'd asked.

The contrast between Zel and my mother cut through my haze like a blazing beacon of light. Both were half-borns living in a world that told them they didn't belong. Zel had chosen bitterness, but Mom...

Mom had always chosen light.

She'd taught me to be proud of who I was. And now, I was a Knight of the Torch. A true Knight. No Knight was perfect—not those here at Orothion, not those from the past, not those branded Rebels, and certainly not me, especially considering how tempting I found Zel's proposal. But as long as I strove to drive out darkness, I had a purpose.

Zel had brought darkness into the very heart of the Knights. So what? It was up to my team and I to drive it out, and make a space where true Knights could still choose light.

Suddenly, I realized something.

It wasn't enough to rescue Dad and Kari and get out.

We had to take back Orothion.

With my bonds so tight I could feel myself beginning to go numb, I opened my big mouth.

"I'll never join the Gray, Zel," I said. "You'll have to kill me first."

Zel sighed, genuinely disappointed. "Very well then, if you're sure." He raised a hand, his eyes beginning to flash blue.

"Wait, wait, wait," I said. "Not here."

Zel cocked his head. His soldiers shifted, confused.

I gave my best crooked grin as my awful, wildly dangerous idea took shape in my mind. "The whole reason you invited all these Drakfellian and Skygardian nobles here was to demonstrate Orothion's might, right? Get them to fund your strike on the Capital?"

"That is correct," Zel said.

"But a big part of the problem is us scorching Rebels," I went on. "The nobility don't know whose side they're on, especially after learning Solrac is the Farseer."

"Indeed," Zel frowned, curious. Meanwhile, Dad was struggling against his ropes, shaking his head at me despite his gag. He didn't like where I was going with this.

I pressed on. "So make an example out of me. Show these sooty nobles that *you* have the power here. Isn't King Rodan himself always saying that the best way to win support is through a public show of strength?"

Dad was really fighting now, squirming so much that he slipped off his shadowsilk gag. "Zel, don't listen to him. He doesn't know what he's—"

"Hush hush hush." Zel put up a finger for silence.

I continued, my voice growing bolder with every word. "You know it makes sense! Make *me* the tour's finale. Execute me on the terrace above the skyforge in front of King Rodan and all the nobility gathered here tonight. He *will* be convinced. They all will."

Zel's fingers curled and uncurled eagerly as he considered my plan. I could tell he was having a hard time seeing a downside.

Meanwhile, all Dad could see were downsides.

"Don't do this," he pleaded. "I swear, I'll stay here and rift your armies until my soul gives out. Please, just spare my son."

Zel watched him with the gaze of a broken father. "They did not show me mercy, either," he whispered. Then he squeezed his eyes shut as if trying to reset his usual cheeriness. When he opened his eyes again, they were bright and smiling.

"Very well, Asher of Steel Rim," Zel said. "You shall get your ceremonious death, but I imagine it won't go the way you have planned." He turned abruptly. "Akayto, I'll no longer be needing your services."

Dad swallowed. "Why not?"

"My dear helper, Vesta, of course!" Zel said. "She is securing me a fresh Rifter as we speak. A younger, healthier one, too."

My heart froze. Meleya.

"Because of that," Zel grinned, "I'm not only going to execute you, scale-skinned Rebel Knight. I'm going to execute your father as well."

My stomach flipped. "Wait, you can't—"

"*And*—" Zel cut me off, reaching out a hand to one of his soldiers, who promptly tossed him Thorn's black-and-copper heartscale. Zel twirled it between his fingers as he went on.

"I know exactly how I'm going to do it."

Fragment: Liberator

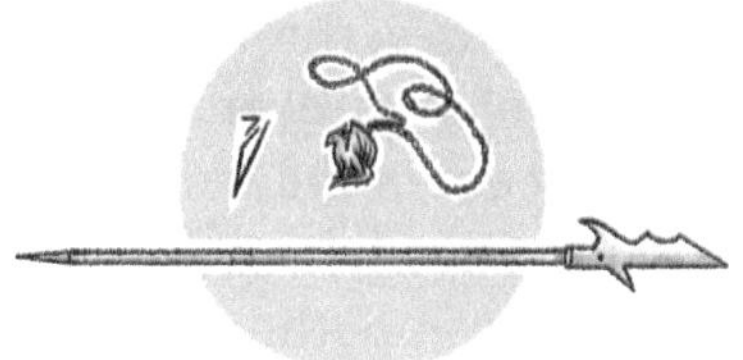

SOLVAI

Right after sending Asher to the armory, Solvai had gone to the dungeons as planned.

When she saw an entire squad of seven guarding the dungeon's entrance, she'd known something was afoot. Normally, only one or two were needed at the gates of prisons—at least, that was how they did it at Spydra Prison in Rengard. Something was fishy.

I'm going in, she thought over the mindlink.

Be careful, Kai warned. *You were supposed to have Asher as backup for this part. It's eighty-four percent more risky without him.*

Solvai fought a smile as she mentally asked, *Kai, you isolated the mindlink channels right?*

Yes. Unless I adjust my runes, you'll only be able to get through to each other with highly concentrated effort. Only I can hear your thoughts now. Why do you ask?

Oh, because I didn't want everyone else to hear me when I told you I liked your mind.

My... you what?

Your mind. Maybe it's a Sentinel thing, but through the mindlink, I can sort of sense how your mind works. It's orderly, like rows of books.

Kai paused. *And yours is like a...*

Solvai's heart began to flutter.

Like a... Oh soot, Kai suddenly thought. *Something's going on with Asher—one minute, Solvai. I swear I'll be right back.*

You'd better be. I need to know what you think my mind is like.

Kai's thought came through with equal parts nerves and excitement. *And I need to tell you.*

He cut out, and Solvai was alone with her thoughts again. She no longer needed Kai to guide her, so she figured she might as well move forward and get into the dungeon herself.

It wasn't hard for a small, nondescript bird to get past the guard squad as they played a rousing game of skyseeker's dice on the stone floor. From there, it was only a short way down the corridor and through a crack in the door to get into the area with all the prison cells.

She was just thinking of how smoothly that had gone when she heard an odd hissing noise inside her head. The mindlink bloomed to life, and Solvai caught quick flashes of multiple perspectives, from Brigan and Meleya at dinner to Elle outside in the redwoods to Asher surrounded by some sort of white glow. Then Kai's voice appeared.

All is well. Everyone, please, carry on with your assignments.

Just made it past the guard squad, Solvai thought. *So much for needing Asher, right?*

Kai paused for a moment before responding with a general, *Indeed.*

So, you ready to tell me, Kai? Solvai thought, a secret smile on her lips.

Tell you what?

That smile faltered. *Oh, just, you know. What we were talking about before? My mind is like a...?*

Kai paused again. *Would you mind focusing on your assignment? I am quite busy with the mindlink at the moment.*

At his words, Solvai wilted. Of course he was busy.

Kai went on to say, *Meleya, I need you to return to the redwoods base immediately.*

Solvai frowned. *This is Solvai.*

Scorch, Kai swore. *These isolated channels are difficult to maintain.*

I can't come back to base, Meleya's voice came through for a brief moment. *I need to be on the skyforge terrace to get everyone out.*

Plans have changed, Kai thought. *For your safety, we need you out of there.*

I'm not leaving, Meleya insisted.

Scorch, Kai cursed again. There was another hiss, and Solvai could sense him working to strengthen his runes and re-isolate the channels once more.

As he did, Solvai couldn't help but think that something felt off. While only a moment ago, his mind had reminded her of rows of neatly stacked books, it now felt distant and strangely pretentious. Besides that, Kai's go-to curses were 'drak' and 'soot.' He rarely said 'scorch.'

Then again, maybe Solvai was reading into things too much after feeling rejected. Kai was right, she needed to focus on her assignment.

Solvai crept deeper into the dungeons toward the cells and was surprised to find about a dozen people who looked far too noble to be run-of-the-mill prisoners. While they looked worried as they paced their cells, they all seemed well fed and cared for. The men wore fine jackets, the women silky dresses. Still, based on both their demeanors and the stacks of books, games, and even painting supplies inside the various cells, Solvai got the feeling that many of these prisoners had been here for a very long time.

None of them looked hostile, so Solvai risked reverting to human form. The golden mist that surrounded her drew every prisoner's attention.

"Stars above," one man whispered, immediately going to the bars of his cell to get a better look. "Who are you?"

"Are you working for him?" a different prisoner asked fearfully.

"They're coming for us," another added.

"Oh Streya, please, no."

"Hush," one girl whispered. "She's not one of them."

The girl's voice calmed the prisoners. She had dark curls and was dressed the nicest of them all. She was also the only prisoner bound in shadowsilk-and-silver cords—a sign that she was a magi of some kind.

"If she'd been one of them, her wildshaping mist would've been blue," the young woman said. Then she locked eyes with Solvai. "I'm Annika, Princess of Skygard."

Solvai put the pieces together. "You're the missing nobles Vesta is keeping as leverage. Drak, Solrac was right. "

"Solrac?" One man stood at the sound of the name. He had dark hair streaked with white, likely from snowhead heritage somewhere down his family line. He had topaz-colored eyes, a short beard, and the Drakfellian crest was embroidered on his jacket.

"Heard tell from the guards at the door that Solrac's the Farseer now," the man said. He reached a hand through the bars toward Solvai. "Any friend of his is a welcome sight."

Solvai grasped the man's arm at the elbow. "I'm Solvai, and I'm with Solrac and the Rebel Knights."

There was a din of hopeful relief from the prisoners.

"Thank the stars," the man with the Drakfellian crest said. "I'm Aradan, brother to King Rodan of Drakfell."

Solvai hoped Kai was seeing this over the mindlink, and sharing it with the rest of the team. This changed everything—this rescue was about far more than two people now.

"Thank the goddesses," the Princess of Skygard said. "My parents and Auntie Vesta will be so relieved."

"Auntie Vesta?" Solvai cocked her head. "But... Vesta's the one who kidnapped all of you so that she could get your families to back her war."

Princess Annika, Aradan, and the others shook their heads vigorously.

"Vesta's the face of this war because *he* wants her to be," Aradan said, his gaze darkening. "She's as much a prisoner as the rest of us. It's Zel who's brought the void to Orothion."

"Zel..." Solvai's eyes widened.

"Yes," Aradan said. "That son of a dragonmutt's part of the Coven of the Gray Ones."

At his words, a sense of cold dread filled Solvai. She'd fought the Coven at Outcast Outpost and again on Keep Rengard's Rise and knew they were ruthless killers.

But worse than that, Solvai knew just how manipulative Coven leaders could be. Before she was captured, Solvai's own mother had been the Liberator, the leader of the Coven of the Gray Ones in the south. For years, Lorelai had worked for the Gray Ones, trying to tear down the Rengardian government, lying to everyone, including her daughter. One of those lies had been to keep Solvai from the truth about her father. In the end, he hadn't been a valiant soldier who died on the field of battle. Rather, he'd been Torsten, an exiled, out-of-shape drunk. Over the course of one evening, Solvai's entire world had fallen apart, all thanks to the Coven.

But that experience had only hardened her resolve. Neither of her parents had turned out to be the heroes she'd thought they were. But that didn't mean Solvai couldn't become that hero herself.

"Zel is behind all of it," Princess Annika said. "He took all of us, and he's the one using that poor Rifter man in the armory, too."

"The armory?" Solvai repeated. "Akayto... Asher! Oh, soot."

Kai! Solvai thought. *Open the mindlink! Connect me with Asher.*

There was no response from Kai. Just more of that same pretentious, aloof energy.

Drak, Solvai thought. She mentally pushed harder, focusing on Asher's mind. She knew he was there somewhere, and hadn't Kai said before that highly concentrated thoughts could make it through?

Asher, Solvai thought, turning away from the prisoners and closing her eyes so she could focus. After a minute, she felt his distractible, energetic mind's presence in her head. The connection didn't feel particularly solid, so Solvai rushed to send her thoughts.

Asher! You have to get out of there! I just got to the dungeon. Prisoners... Aradan, and others.

Aradan? Asher sounded confused.

Vesta's not the one—

A sharp hiss made Solvai press her hands to her temples. Kai's voice in her head was harsh.

Focus on your assignment! I'll inform Asher, he ordered.

Solvai's natural response was to shrink back, shut up, and keep her head bowed. But she knew her position on the Rebel Triarchy required strength. Besides, her instincts were going crazy right now, telling her something was very, *very* wrong with Kai.

But right now, these people needed help.

Solvai looked around, hurrying over to a window on the far wall. The bars on it looked strong, but nothing she couldn't handle while in falcondrake form. Same with those on the prisoners' cells. The bigger problem was that the window overlooked the turbulent southern sea.

Solvai turned to their prisoners. "We have to get all of you out of here before Zel or any of his lackeys come back."

Aradan nodded. "I've got three dragon bonds in the dragon hold here. Two of them are flyers that can help get at least some of us out, at least if we manage to get their heartscales from the squad on duty just outside the cells here."

"What about the rest of us?" one prisoner asked.

Solvai took hold of the carved wooden charm hanging from a leather cord around her neck. It was the totem that allowed her to shift into a falcondrake. The one she'd been using all week to visit a whole colony of her new flying friends.

Solvai turned to the prisoners. "I'll take care of the guards and get Aradan's heartscales back. Then we're all flying out of here."

Even before Solvai and her small army of falcondrakes arrived at the hollowed-out redwood tree, they knew danger lay ahead. One of Aradan's dragons, a violet-scaled evren named Lyra who was a third ascension Seer, warned them.

I see a silver symbol... Mage Hunters, Lyra spoke to Aradan and Solvai's minds.

"Jaira and Lothar." Solvai's heart began to pound. "But where are Elle and Aurora?" She flew at the head of the group, not fully in falcondrake form herself, but with a pair of wings sprouting from her back.

Solvai tried to push through on the mindlink to reach out to Elle, but found herself mentally cut off from the others. Drak. If Jaira and Lothar were here, that meant Kai was in terrible danger. She had to get to him.

"Take the nobility somewhere safe," Solvai instructed Aradan. "I'll deal with the Mage Hunters."

Without waiting for a reply, Solvai gave a mighty flap of her wings and shot toward their redwood base like an arrow. When the tree came into view, sure enough, Elle and Aurora weren't at their post guarding Kai.

Instead, Solvai saw someone else.

She gasped at the sight of the sleek brown third ascension wyvern guarding the hollow where Kai hid. It was Lantha, the lovely dragon bond of the late King Axel of Rengard. The one whose heartscale was now with the Mage Hunters.

And not a moment too soon, either. Jaira and Lothar must've known Solvai was coming, and hoped to take the opportunity to take her down. Compelled through her heartscale, Lantha came for Solvai, claws raking.

Gold mist encompassed Solvai as she shifted into a mighty falcondrake. She wasn't as large as a third ascension dragon, but this way she at least stood a fighting chance.

The only problem was, Solvai didn't *want* to fight Lantha. She couldn't hurt the dragon she'd met so long ago in the stables at Keep Rengard, even if Lantha was trying to kill *her*.

Lantha's emerald eyes betrayed regret as she pounced on Solvai once again. Falcondrake Solvai rolled, dodging the strike, then darted under Lantha's wide wing and bolted toward Kai's hollow tree.

Drak, there he was. As Solvai suspected, something was *very* wrong with Kai. He seemed completely oblivious to the commotion going on just outside the tree as he stared straight ahead with vacant eyes, his irises covered in a violet sheen. Solvai's enhanced falcondrake vision let her see the tiny, silvery snake whose fangs were lodged in Kai's neck.

At the Mage Hunter Academy, Solvai had learned to recognize the signs of someone being mind-controlled by a Seer. Her gut twisted at the awful irony that now, the one using mind control was Ilyan, a Mage Hunter himself.

Solvai shrieked, racing toward Kai in her falcondrake form. At the same time, she mentally pushed through on the mindlink with all she had.

Meleya, Brigan, Asher, Elle! Solvai thought, her desperation enabling her to push through the mental barrier, if only for a moment. *The mindlink has been compromised—ditch your Glints, now!*

There was a brief moment of scattered, frantic thought. Then Solvai felt the mindlink go completely silent.

"Scorch you, bird girl!" Jaira's voice was harsh as the Mage Hunter appeared in the tree beside Kai. Lothar was beside her, looking sickly as he gripped Lantha's heartscale in one hand, his seaxe in the other. Soot, where were Elle and Aurora?

Behind Solvai, Lantha's claws lurched at her back, keeping her from reaching the tree. To make matters worse, she felt another set of claws rake along her wing. Turning, she saw Luster, the lightwielding wyvern who'd once belonged to Cenrik. With Jaira in control of his heartscale, his lightning crackled, and Solvai shrieked with pain. Even as a mighty falcondrake, Solvai knew she was no match for two third ascension dragons.

That was when, out of nowhere, a bramblevine launched toward them. The plant had a life of its own, lashing out to snare Lantha's draconic jaws before they could close around Solvai. More vines whipped toward Luster, dragging him away from Solvai.

Solvai craned her bird-like neck to see Annika, the Skygardian princess. Gold Sentinel marks glowed from her arms as she thrust her hands out toward the wyvern. More strong bramblevines obeyed the Woodweaver girl's command, winding around Lantha and pinning her to the earth.

Tighter and tighter Annika squeezed, eliciting painful moans from Lantha and Luster.

Quickly, Solvai reverted to human form. "Don't hurt them!" Solvai cried. "They're friends, trapped in forced bonds!"

Annika understood, loosening the bramblevines just enough so that they wouldn't crush them.

Meanwhile, Aradan arrived on Lyra's back, flanked by his other flying dragon bond, a wyvern named Glass. Glass was mythic too, an Astromancer, and he'd used his power to outfit Aradan with crude starglass armor and an oversized starglass warsword.

Aradan dismounted and the foreboding trio rushed to take on the Mage Hunters.

This clearly wasn't part of the Mage Hunters' plan. Both Jaira and Lothar blanched, cowering inside the hollow tree where the dragons couldn't get to them. Despite that, Aradan rushed in fearlessly after them, engaging Lothar.

But Jaira had another trick up her sleeve. Reaching into a small pouch, she hurled a small, gray stone through the hole in the tree.

Their third and final shadestone.

Before Solvai could stop it, the shadestone landed at Lantha's feet. Gray smoke poured from the stone, drifting into Lantha. Patches of gray soon tainted the beautiful wyvern's scales, and her intelligent green eyes turned void blue.

"Lantha!" Solvai cried, clutching a hand to her heart.

Her power enhanced, Lantha broke free from Annika's vines. Annika tried to stop her with more, but Lantha was too fast. Her thick, strong tail swung, knocking Annika to the ground.

Aradan's wyvern and evren swept toward Lantha, the three mighty creatures tangling in a flurry of scales and wings. Solvai wished there was a way to keep the dragons from hurting each other.

Meanwhile, Aradan sent Lothar flying from the tree to land in a heap. Jaira tried to flee, but Aradan engaged her just outside the tree before she got the chance.

It was obvious that Jaira was no match for the skilled swordsman and his great starglass blade, but she still had Luster's heartscale. Having also freed himself from Annika's vines, the lightwielding wyvern dove toward Aradan, lightning crackling all over his scales. Aradan cried out as it arced his way.

Solvai's body still ached from the dragons' prior attacks, but ignored the pain as she broke into a run, shifting back into a falcondrake as she dove between Luster and Aradan.

Her falcondrake form was far more nimble than a wyvern, and she did her best to dodge, block, or absorb Luster's strikes rather than make any aggressive moves toward the dragon. Still, she didn't know how much longer she could hold out against Luster's crackling lightning.

Then she realized that she didn't have to.

She was going about this all wrong. Solvai had been trying to face this like a fighter when what this situation really called for was a liberator.

Gold mist surrounded Solvai once more as she transformed into a ridgebacked wren. As such a small creature, it was far easier to evade Luster's erratic attacks.

Having gotten past the wyvern, Solvai dove toward Jaira's neck. In one swift motion, she used her sharp beak to snap the cord around her neck, freeing Luster's heartscale.

"Hey!" Jaira snapped, clawing at her collar.

But Solvai was already soaring away. No longer compelled by Jaira, Luster immediately backed away from the fight, relief evident in his tired dragonfire eyes.

Solvai was ready to free Lantha next. But upon glancing over, she saw that the great third ascension dragon already had Aradan pinned beneath her claws as she prepared a lethal blast of dragonfire.

The gray was strong within Lantha, the patches on her scales having become so large there was hardly any brown left. Her eyes burned with angry sapphire that made Solvai's heart wrench. Solvai knew Lantha's kind, careful nature. It must've been destroying her inside to do this.

Solvai considered shifting back into a falcondrake to try and redirect Lantha's flame. She had to do *something* to stop this, both for Lantha's sake and Aradan's life.

But she, Annika, and Luster all were too far away to help in time. Solvai's stomach dropped.

But then, with a *whoosh,* the gray suddenly retreated from Lantha's scales. The blue fled her irises, reverting to their natural emerald green hue. Light returned to Lantha, and she immediately backed away from the attack, redirecting her flame skyward.

Solvai's eyes went wide as she watched Lantha. What was happening? She remembered the research she and Kai had done while at the camp in the lava fields. The power-enhancing wraiths from shadestones only left their host when they were killed. But Lantha was still very much alive, so...

Just then, Solvai heard a pained grunt from back beside the hollow redwood tree. Lothar was there, lying on the ground. In his hands was a smooth, brown scale on a cord.

It was Lantha's heartscale. At once, Solvai realized he must've used it to force the wraith out of her. The heartscale had given him control of the wraith, just as he'd had control of Lantha.

But the wraith had to go somewhere. With horror, Solvai realized that Lothar had compelled the wraith to leave Lantha in favor of Lothar himself.

Swiftly reverting to her human form, Solvai ran to Lothar's side. Already, his skin was covered in inky gray splotches, his eyes unfocused as they glowed bright blue.

Soot, his wounds were worse than Solvai had realized. Blood soaked into his tunic, and his breathing was labored.

"Take it," Lothar managed, holding out Lantha's heartscale. Solvai grasped the bloodied scale, a lump rising in her throat.

"And... and..." Lothar stammered.

"Don't worry about talking," Solvai whispered. She wished she was more skilled in the Sentinel power of regeneration so that she could do something for him. But from the looks of things, not even Trickshot would've been able to save him now.

"No," Lothar insisted, then fumbled in his tunic until he produced a little quill pen, which he passed to Solvai as well.

"Give this to Mason," Lothar wheezed.

Solvai didn't plan on meeting up with Mason Drakeslayer anytime soon, but it wouldn't do Lothar any good to tell him that. Instead, she just gave a small nod.

A moment later, Lantha joined Solvai at Lothar's side. Lantha spoke her thoughts so they both could hear.

It was not too late for you to choose light, Lothar. Thank you.

At that, Lothar seemed to take comfort. Together, Solvai and Lantha watched his chest rise and fall for the last time. Luster and Annika, as well as Aradan and his dragons, stood reverently observing from a short distance away.

Emotion seemed to radiate from Lantha. Solvai sensed it, and she knew what Lantha was thinking. Lothar hadn't been bad—not really. Her heart went out to the young man who'd gotten caught up with such formidable darkness, becoming trapped by it until it consumed him.

Jaira, for her part, was nowhere in sight. She must've realized she was going to be overpowered and taken off into the woods without a second thought for her unfortunate companion. Lothar might've been against the darkness at his core, but Jaira embraced it.

Aradan and Annika joined Solvai beside Lothar's body. There wasn't time to do much for him at the moment, but Aradan suggested having Annika cover his body in vines until they were able to give him a proper burial.

As for now, their work was far from finished.

Solvai could feel her regenerative powers kicking in to begin healing her back as she got to her feet. Somewhat shakily, she climbed inside the tree where Kai was still staring blankly ahead, eyes filmy with violet energy. Ilyan's tiny, silvery snake still had its fangs stuck fast in Kai's neck.

Solvai cringed at the sound the fangs made as she yanked them from Kai's skin. She roughly tossed the ethereal familiar to the ground outside the tree, where Lantha pounced on it. It dissolved instantly into blue etherdust.

For the first several seconds, Kai's expression remained the same. Solvai's heart pounded.

"Kai?" Solvai said, carefully taking his face in her hands and trying to get him to look her in the eyes. "Can you hear me?"

Had breaking the snake's mind control somehow damaged him? No. She couldn't lose him like that. Solvai pressed on. "Think of logically ordered bookshelves. Chronological timelines. Completed tasks."

Slowly, the glassiness faded from Kai's eyes. He blinked a few times, and as Solvai's face came into view, he broke into a weak half-smile.

"A well," he said.

"A well?" Solvai cocked her head.

"That's what your mind reminds me of. A well, deep with thought, and filled with life-sustaining water. A source I can always turn to to feel refreshed. A well."

"A well." Despite everything, Solvai couldn't stop the smile from appearing on her lips. Instinctually, she took Kai's hand.

Solvai wished the moment could've lasted forever, but their friends were in danger. Quickly, Solvai caught an increasingly frantic Kai up on what had just happened, introducing him to Aradan, Annika, and the dragons, not to mention the nobility and falcondrakes straggling into the base now that the commotion had died down.

Naturally, Kai hadn't accounted for any of that in his plans and backup plans. Furiously, he scrambled to get the mindlink up and running again, ordering his Glint army to get back in contact with their assigned team member and report immediately.

Elle, where are you? Kai thought through the newly restored mindlink.

Aurora and I were on our way to the stronghold, Elle replied. *We were looking for a way in to get Meleya out like you asked us to, but we stopped when Solvai told us the mindlink had been compromised. Kai, what in the void is going on?*

I second that question! Meleya added, and Brigan agreed.

Apparently, under the Mage Hunters' influence, Kai had been harassing Meleya, employing all kinds of tactics to get her back to the base camp. No doubt they'd planned to overpower her using Lantha and Luster, then take her back to the Soul Reaper's lair so they could retrieve their precious voidshard.

Luckily, they hadn't counted on Meleya's stubborn desire to stick to the plan and get to the skyforge terrace so she could rift Kari and the others out of there. That was why the Hunters had needed to resort to sending Elle and Aurora.

Meleya and Brigan were currently touring the castle with the other guests at Orothion. They'd seen the throne room, the library, and several other highlights, and the evening was already coming to a close as they went through the skyforge.

Meanwhile, Solvai brought the others up to speed regarding the Hunters, the prisoners, and Zel's true nature. At first, they hadn't believed it. Vesta was innocent? But Annika and Aradan's testimonies confirmed it.

Aradan? My brother is with you? King Rodan's voice sent a ripple of surprise throughout the mindlink. Solvai and the others had clearly forgotten the King was currently set up with Glint Eight-B-Alpha, and having Elle's dad in on their group conversation felt somehow strange.

Still, Solvai rushed to assure him. *Aradan's with us. He's safe, along with the Princess of Skygard and a dozen others.*

Thank the stars. Rodan's relief flooded the mindlink.

Wait a second, Meleya suddenly thought. *Where's Asher?*

Stars, Meleya was right. With so much going on, Solvai hadn't even noticed that Asher hadn't been part of the conversation. There was a pause as, for once, everyone eagerly awaited Asher's inevitably goofy reply.

None came.

Asher? Kai asked. *Asher, say something!*

Don't you mean think *something?* Brigan needlessly corrected.

When Asher still didn't answer, Kai ran a hasty check of his Glints. Sure enough, Glint Four was unaccounted for. Someone had sent her back into the ethereal plane.

Oh soot, Kai thought. *Soot, soot,* soot!

Suddenly, a mental gasp from Meleya sounded over the mindlink.

What is it? Solvai asked.

No... Meleya thought. *Oh stars, please, no.*

What's happening? Elle echoed.

Brigan and I just got to the skyforge terrace, Meleya thought, notes of panic in her tone. *We know where Asher is.*

CHAPTER 28: CHOOSE LIGHT

MELEYA

I knew the plan was a wash the second I saw Asher and Thorn flying above the castle, tethered to Orothion's tallest spire like a living kite. Asher was bound in silver and, based on Thorn's excessively smooth flight pattern, someone—not Asher—had his heartscale.

This was *not* good.

The terrace above the skyforge was even more splendorous in person than it had been in Kai's illusion back at the refugee camp. Brigan and I stood with the other nobles, the great gold-and-black dome off to one side. Through the darkened starglass, I could see the skyforge's inner furnace while the intricate golden framework curved along the dome.

Atop the rampart was the lighthouse, which used a pyre and a large, reflective disc of metal to direct its light. A set of stone stairs led up to the lighthouse as it overlooked the ocean. There on the wall stood a double squad of red-cloaked soldiers holding an assortment of increasingly complicated-looking crossbows. Some sported dangerous-looking black-tipped bolts while others seemed to have no bolt at all, just rune-marked crystals that I thought might bear the rune for dream darts. They seemed ready at any moment to turn those weapons on Asher and Thorn as they flew above the tower.

At the head of the soldiers, on the tower's highest point, stood Vesta and Zel. When Solvai had told us that Zel was the one to watch out for rather than Vesta, I'd been certain she'd made a mistake. But I trusted my squad captain. After all, Solvai had received first-hand testimonies on the matter from King Rodan's brother, Aradan, as well as Annika, the Princess of Skygard. Besides, I figured that if someone as fearsome-looking as the Black Valkyrie could somehow keep a kernel of goodness hidden deep inside her core, then so too could a cheery, unassuming old man cover up his evil.

Beside them stood a young woman with thick black curls and a dirty metalsmith's apron. She looked so much like Kai, I wouldn't have even needed to have seen the illusory avatar of her last night to know this was Kari, the girl we'd been meant to rescue.

A man stood at Kari's side. He looked very much like an older version of Asher minus the scale-tipped ears and dragonfire eyes. He was gagged and bound in silver, and appeared utterly exhausted. This could only be Akayto, Asher's dad.

"Nobility of Skygard and Drakfell!" Vesta's voice rolled across the terrace as she caught the crowd's attention. "To finish off tonight's tour of Orothion, we've got quite the show in store for you. Trust us, when we're finished, there'll be no doubt that the Knights' forthcoming strike on the High Citadel will end in victory."

As Vesta's speech went on, I tried to make eye contact with Asher. He was so far away, and part of me wanted nothing more than to rift him out of there right away. But that would make a scene, and I'd risk losing my chance to get Kari and Akayto out too.

Not only that, but when I looked closely at the incredibly long, silky black rope that tied Asher and Thorn to the spire, I saw the way its silvery links glinted in the setting sun. I'd spent enough time around Mage Hunters to recognize a silver chain whip when I saw one. That would no doubt dissolve any portal I tried to send Asher through.

As I stared, I did a double take when it dawned on me that Thorn looked different. Larger and stronger, with antlers as majestic as an alpha stag. The scales that had once been a brassy copper color looked more gold, too. At once, I realized someone must've fed him enough skystone to get him to ascend. Thorn was on this third and final ascension. But why would they have...

The answer hit me like a ton of scales.

Asher and Thorn... *they* were the demonstration. They were meant to represent the third ascension Capital Riders, and executing them using those crossbows would be a show of the Knights' strength.

Oh soot.

I relayed my thoughts to the others on the mindlink, and Kai's response was so deafening I wanted to plug my ears from the inside.

DRAK, ASHER! Why do I bother?! I got the feeling Kai was violently chucking his notebook and all of its plans. I could almost hear Solvai working to calm him down.

Vesta was now introducing Kari, inviting her to 'explain her inventions or whatever.'

Kari stepped up to the edge to address the crowd. "Now, when I was first approached about creating an array of crossbows equipped to take down the legendary Capital Riders, I came up with several different variants, from the blackfire to the dreambolt repeaters. For weeks, I tested design after design..."

She's stalling, Kai thought over the mindlink.

Stars bless her, Solvai added.

Momentarily, the hairs on the back of my neck stood on end. I got the distinct feeling someone was watching me.

Trying to be subtle, I scanned the crowd. Soot, there were a lot of soldiers here, so many that they practically outnumbered the guests. As a trained soldier myself, I found it strange.

Then I saw him. I recognized the hunched posture and twitching eye of the third member of the Triarchy, the one called Signus.

His stare set my palms sweating, and I absently began to fiddle with my black stud earrings. After what had happened to Elle and me back in Lord Scorpio's shadow, I was more cautious than ever.

Up on the rampart, Vesta cut Kari off. "We've heard enough, inventor. Time to let these people see the crossbows in action. Specifically, to watch them take down a third ascension dragon and his rider."

Vesta stepped up, her voice carrying across the terrace as she gestured to Asher and Thorn.

"Nobility of Western Evgard, allow me to introduce you to the Rebel Knight thief we caught robbing the castle while all of you were at dinner!"

Even tied up as he was, I still caught an over-the-top wave from Asher.

Murmurs immediately began to ripple through the throng. The execution of a Rebel Knight was news indeed, especially with the revelation about Solrac being the Farseer.

Vesta pressed on. "For those of you who think *Solrac's* low-life Rebels stand a chance, let me assure you, they're nothing. Let this half-born and his traitorous father stand as an example."

My heart began to pound as the crossbow wielders took their positions.

We have to do something! Kai cried over the mindlink. *Elle, how close are you?*

Elle can't go in there, Solvai thought. *That would make the biggest scene of all!*

I'm not close enough anyway, Elle thought. *Maybe Meleya can try to rift everyone out despite the silver?*

That won't work either, Solvai replied logically, though I could tell she didn't have any better ideas of her own.

Besides, think of what a reckless escape attempt would look like to the assembly here, Brigan thought. *We would only prove the point Vesta just made: the Rebels are barbaric rogues. The optics aren't in our favor.*

I'm not risking Asher's safety for drakking optics! I thought, bouncing from foot to foot so much that Brigan had to stop me from drawing attention. Also, why was that Signus guy still staring at me?

What do we do, then? Elle thought frantically.

Scorch, I'm going to regret this... King Rodan's thought came through a split second before he stepped out in front of the crowd.

"Good people of Western Evgard—" King Rodan pulled the attention of everyone on the terrace, including Vesta, Zel, and the lineup of crossbow wielders on the parapet. "If I might say a few words."

Both the terrace and the mindlink went silent as we all waited to hear what the King of Drakfell would say.

Rodan cleared his throat, pointedly making the people wait so that his words would have an even greater impact. "We were invited here tonight so that the sitting Triarchy might win our aid in funding a strike at the heart of Evgard. High King Magnus must fall, they say. While I agree that things cannot continue as they are, I wish to make it known that Orothion *does not* have the support of me and my house. And if you know what is good for you, you will withdraw your support as well!"

That certainly got the reaction Rodan was hoping for. Execution momentarily forgotten, the throng burst into chatter.

Many nobles immediately began to voice their agreement, others their surprise, confusion, or discontent. But I was watching the faces of those on top of the wall. Vesta blanched, immediately looking to Zel. His normally cheery disposition flashed to anger, but only for the briefest second before he covered it up. He pressed his lips together, then leaned over to Vesta, whispering.

Stars, your majesty, Brigan thought. *Obviously, I agree, but that's not going to sit well with everyone here.*

My brother is safe, Rodan thought. *Those sons of dragonmutts don't have anything on me now. As much as I'd like to keep the peace, I'd rather do what's right.*

Rodan continued, fighting to be heard over the din. "While I agree the time for magi oppression must end, this is not the way! Sometimes the greatest show of strength is knowing when to show restraint. As King of the Badlands, I hereby declare that my soldiers will no longer be at Orothion's disposal."

The crowd swelled as several attendees turned accusations onto Rodan.

"Magi have suffered for too long! Magnus deserves to pay!"

"Striking at the capital is the only fair choice!"

"The blood they've spilt cries for justice!"

Brigan left my side then, unable to remain silent a moment longer. "King Rodan is right! It's not about justice, it's about *people.* A strike at the Capital won't make up for years of executions. It will only bring about more bloodshed."

"You're nothing but a child," one nobleman said. "You merely fear war!"

"I'm a soldier," Brigan replied. "I fought at the border of the Dragon Mists. I am not completely without experience—And my experiences have taught me to recognize that the *why* of war is vitally important. In this case, that 'why' is severely lacking."

Despite the protests surrounding him, Brigan plowed ahead. "This blind revenge against the mistreatment of magi... As Knights, our resources would be better spent seeking real solutions to the magi plight. Perhaps a deeper dive into the technology behind etherlocks rather than wasting our best minds on weapons designed to kill rather than save!"

That was when Vesta stepped up to the rampart. "King Rodan of Drakfell," she bellowed. "The soldiers who serve your keepdom aren't worth the boots that cover their feet. Your guard is in shambles and you know it! People of the West, we don't need the support of this unfit king!"

Drak, this is getting bad, Kai thought over the mindlink.

It's only a matter of time before they start making arrests, Solvai agreed.

They wouldn't dare to publicly arrest King Rodan, right?

They might, Rodan grumbled. *But scorch if I won't go down without a fight.*

"Executing the half-born who once saved my life will prove nothing!" King Rodan called out. "Long live the Rebel Knights, and long live the Farseer!"

The king's tone was firm, unafraid. It seemed that, between the kidnapping of his brother, finding out his daughter *wasn't* safely tucked away learning to ride her dragon, and all the political pressure of Orothion's plans to strike at the capital, he'd finally reached his breaking point.

The crowd roared. The soldiers shifted, gripping their weapons, ready to step in once someone gave the word. Though, I got the feeling many of them were increasingly unsure whose word to listen to.

King Rodan, I thought, only slightly nervous as I mentally addressed a king, *could you just tell the other nobles that their families are no longer hostages? That might make a difference.*

Well, that depends. Can we use these... Rodan mentally hesitated. *These... small intelligent lizards to prove it to the masses?*

Even if I did know of runes that could accomplish a remote projection of that magnitude, I'm so low on ether I can barely keep the mindlink going as is, Kai thought back.

Rodan's reply was sober. *Then it's too much of a risk. Some might believe without proof, but many would not. I certainly wouldn't. They might even think we're trying to manipulate them, which would only escalate things further.*

Why does Zel want to strike at the capital anyway? Elle's thought came through the mindlink. *If he's working with the Gray, and Magnus is too, shouldn't they be on the same side?*

It's because the Gray doesn't care who they use, I thought back, recalling the lesson I had with Vidya so long ago at the Academy. *They aren't on anyone's political side—They only want a weakened people. Chaos.*

You are not wrong, Meleya of Misthaven, Xan's raspy voice filled my head, adding to the growing tumult around me. *But now is your chance to use the chaos. Look.*

I felt Xan pushing me to look back up to where Asher and Thorn flew above the spire. Asher was squirming, only seconds away from freeing his hands from his silvery bonds.

But I wasn't the only one watching him. Zel had noticed as well, and even now I saw him whisper to Vesta, who barked something to the crossbow wielders. They took aim at Asher once again.

"No," I muttered. He was going to go ahead with it—Zel couldn't let Asher live, not now that he knew the truth about him. That he was working with the Gray.

I had to stop this.

But I'd only taken a few steps toward the spire when a man with hunched posture and a twitching eye appeared to stop me.

"Please, young lady," Signus said, his voice slick. "Things are verging on a riot here. Allow me to escort you somewhere safe."

I cringed as he not-so-subtly brushed his hands against a length of silver chain looped at his belt. A clear threat against me if I tried anything.

Not only that, but I caught a flash of gleaming black and bronze at Signus's collar. With dread, I realized he was the one wearing Thorn's heartscale.

Even with his silver, he does not stand a chance against the pair of us, Xan reminded me.

I tried to maintain my 'noble' guise as I replied, "I just... need some air." I quickly remembered that we were on an open-air terrace and quickly amended my statement. "Some air... over there." Drak.

Signus gave me a doubtful, almost pitying look. "I'm afraid I can't let you leave."

I looked for Brigan, but he was caught up in the debate. "I'll only be a moment—" I started.

"You misunderstand." Signus's eye twitched as he strummed the coils of silver chain. Despite being a Mystic, the silver clearly didn't affect him. That meant he was almost definitely part of the Coven of the Gray Ones, too.

"I've been given strict orders to ensure your safety," Signus continued. "You will not set foot outside the grounds, young Rifter."

My heart sank as memories of Scryer's Grotto suddenly assaulted me. The chilly stone ground. The hours spent in solitude. The way Mason had used me for my rifting, just like Signus, and presumably Zel, wanted to now. If they had me, they no longer needed Akayto.

There is only one option, Xan's whisper was strong, confident as she played off of my fear. *You must let me help you overpower him. Together, we can save your friends.*

The thunder of arguing all around me thundered in my ears. Angry nobles pushed back against Brigan and King Rodan from all sides.

"The only way we will ever end Magus's cruelty is through force!" one cried.

"Our force remains weak unless we are united! I stand with the Triarchy—We must stamp out the Rebel Knights!"

That had been the King of Skygard's booming voice, and many lesser nobles nodded their support of their ruling monarch. I remembered what Solvai had said over the mindlink—This man's daughter, the Princess of Skygard, was among those Zel had taken prisoner to use as leverage. No wonder the king was arguing so passionately. As far as he knew, his daughter's life was on the line.

Brigan bit back. "The Rebels aren't as weak as those here would have you believe. They thrive under the banner of Eliana, the true dragon rider!"

"My daughter!" Rodan pounded his chest. That got more people nodding for *his* side. Red-cloaked soldiers gripped their weapons, looking up toward where Zel and Vesta stood atop the rampart, just waiting for the order to step in.

Vesta… drak, Vesta was sweating, her finger on the trigger of a crossbow trained on Asher. Zel whispered in her ear, and she held up a hand for the other crossbow wielders.

Aradan, Kai, and I are on our way! Solvai thought over the mindlink. But there wasn't enough time for any of them. My heart threatened to thud out of my chest.

But when I took my next step toward Asher, I felt the icy stab of Signus's chain against my wrist.

"Don't be hasty, Rifter," he warned, eyes wild in a way that reminded me of my old squadmate, Bjorn.

His silver is nothing to us, Xan pushed deeper into my consciousness.

I'll never use voidarchy again! I thought back, desperation tight within my chest. I could feel Blink's drum beats thudding through our bond. Was she warning me against Xan's offer or encouraging me to take it? I was struggling to think clearly.

Vesta called to the crossbow wielders atop the wall. "Take aim!" The clicks of their weapons boomed in my ears.

Not even to save Asher's life? Xan asked. *There is no time! Let me in—become immune to silver and together, we will use the Soul Reaper's voidshard to destroy the wraiths of Signus, Zel, and any others who would threaten your friends. Use the darkness to drive it out.*

I trembled as I saw the logic in Xan's words. I could handle using voidarchy just once more, right?

Yes, Xan agreed. *There is no choice.*

"Three!" Vesta called, starting the countdown as she leveled her blackfire bolt crossbow at Asher. Thorn let out a low roar as Asher struggled against his bonds. Before me, Signus pressed the silver chain harder against my wrist. The mindlink was in chaos, no one able to do anything to stop what was coming. I felt the burden of protecting everyone weighing upon my shoulders.

"Two!" Vesta called, and I saw her shut her eyes as if she, too, couldn't bear to watch what she was about to do.

Xan's words echoed in my head: *There is no choice.*

"There's always a choice," I muttered aloud. Blink's drums swelled

Subtly, I traced a rune. *Two* runes.

Then, in one sudden motion, I leaped backward, away from Signus's threatening grip. At the same moment, two portals appeared. The first was directly behind me. The second was smaller—just big enough for my hand to reach through and yank the black-and-copper heartscale from Signus's throat.

Signus bared his teeth, snatching at my hand. But he wasn't fast enough to stop me as I vanished, Snowstorm-style, through the portal at my back.

I reappeared on the wall, amidst Vesta and the crossbow wielders. They jumped, and I heard Kai and Solvai over the mindlink.

Meleya, what are you doing? Kai asked.

Your portals won't work on Asher! Solvai thought.

I'm not going for Asher, I thought back. One more quick portal put me on the wall, directly between Asher and the end of Lady Vesta's crossbow. The word 'fire' was on the tip of her tongue, but when she saw me, she hesitated.

"What in the void—Out of my way, little miss Rifter!" she snarled.

But I didn't move. Instead, I offered three little words:

"Annika is safe."

Vesta's eyes widened, and I sensed the instant shift in her whole demeanor. In many ways, Vesta and I were as different as they come, but underneath it all, we were the same. We just wanted to protect the people we love.

Without a moment's hesitation, Vesta turned her blackfire bolt crossbow on a new target:

Zel.

She fired, sending Zel straight over the edge of the wall. He dropped like a stone, toward the churning sea far below. Screams sounded all across the terrace.

The heated debate exploded as the soldiers loyal to Zel turned on Vesta. Red cloaks swarmed her, but gold Sentinel patterns glowed to life across her skin. The mottled red stones beneath her feet rippled, the tremor knocking several soldiers backward. Those who managed to keep their footing found themselves facing a volley of arrow-shaped stones as Vesta hurled them their way.

"Eat schist, ghost-worshippers!" she cried.

Some of the soldiers seemed unsure what to do or who to follow, but the vast majority were ready to spring into action—Zel must've had them in his pockets. Vesta wasn't the only one they were after, either.

"Get the Rifter!" Signus's harsh tone reached the soldiers on the wall. They had me backed against the battlements. I glanced down toward the churning sea so far below, and my heart gave a trill.

"Nowhere to go," one soldier said.

In a move that I hoped would make Asher proud, I saluted the guards and leaped backwards, right off the edge of the tower.

The soldiers gasped and ran to the ledge to get a look. But rather than seeing me fall to my death, they watched as I soared through the skies on the back of my golden-yellow evren.

Trrring! Been waiting for you! Sniff thought through our bond as I secured myself in his saddle.

Sniff, you're my hero, I replied. *Now, come on—let's go get Asher!*

Sniff flew me close enough that I could easily rift myself onto Thorn's back behind Asher. I wasted no time in freeing him from his gag.

"About time you got here! I really thought you were gonna let me die—You trip on your fancy dress on the way to rescue me or something?"

I immediately moved to retie his gag.

"Kidding, kidding!" Asher said, squirming out of the gag as I worked to free his hands next. Soot, these silvered ropes hurt, but they were nothing my dragonmoose-antler backup dagger and a little silverbane couldn't handle.

Once Asher was free, I took Thorn's heartscale and reached around Asher to tie it carefully around his neck. I instantly realized I could've just as easily handed Asher the heartscale to tie on himself.

But when—possibly for the first time in his life—Asher held perfectly still, I was glad I'd done it. Time was of the essence, but part of me wished this moment could last. When I finished securing the cord, I let my fingers linger just a little longer than necessary on the back of his neck.

"Thanks, scale-in-the-mud," Asher said.

"You're welcome, scarf-wearer."

The words had no sooner left my lips than a great roar pierced the air. A hulking third ascension wyvern rose into the sky, its red scales matching the late evening sky. Its dragonfire eyes looked as wrinkled and old as those of his rider.

"Valiant Knights of the Torch!" Zel called to the people on the terrace. "Lady Vesta has gone mad! We must kill her and anyone who dares to oppose the Knights!"

That was enough for most of the undecided soldiers. Red cloaks surged toward Vesta.

"Soot," I cursed. "What do we do?"

"We're going to reclaim Orothion for the true Knights of the Torch, that's what," Asher said. There was a determined authority in his tone that I'd only glimpsed before. "True Knights will always choose light. We just have to show them the truth."

"How?" I asked, ready to follow the moment he told me where to stick my seaxe.

"We expose Zel for what he truly is: a voidmage. All we have to do is get him to use his powers, and they'll see."

I gave Asher a nod, then rifted myself back into Sniff's saddle. Side by side astride our dragons, I called out to Asher.

"So, are we gonna do this?"

"Absolutely."

CHAPTER 29: BURN BRIGHT

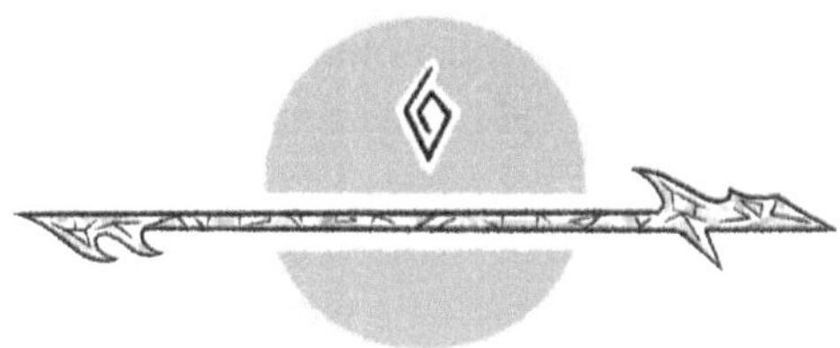

ASHER

What had started as political discontent on the terrace had turned into a full-blown fight. Some of the nobles cowered while others had drawn their swords. Many red-cloaked soldiers fought to take down Vesta, a few tried to stave off the fighting, and some just stood there in confusion. No one knew whose side to fight for. The lines between friend and enemy were too blurred.

It was up to us to change that.

"Let's go, Thorn!" I cried as I summoned my starglass spear and armor. Stars, it was good to have access to both my heartscale and my powers again. A sense of determination glowed between Thorn and I through our bond as my dragon activated his black and gold diamondoak armor. The armor was thicker than ever now that he was on his third ascension.

Together, Meleya and I swept through the sky toward Zel. His dragon bond may have been old, but he was clearly protective of his rider.

Meleya didn't have time to reach Zel before that creepy Triarchy dude with the twitchy eye, Signus, appeared atop the wall. He stood there, arms outstretched, runes hanging over his forehead. Psionic runes.

"I told you before, Rifter!" Signus cried out. "You're not leaving the stronghold!"

A long, silver chain telekinetically flew toward Meleya and Sniff, forcing them to dodge through a portal. I thought she had him beat, but Signus was fast, psionically sending out two more silver chains to block Meleya at every turn. The chains whipped their way through the air like serpents.

For a moment, I was confused. His runes were gold, so how was he performing etherarchy on silver? But then I remembered how the Black Valkyrie had used illusions to achieve the same effect last summer. Illusions may have been cloaking the blue light, but it was still voidarchy at its core.

"Mel!" I called out, ready to swoop in and help her.

But Meleya waved me back. "He needs me alive. Sniff and I can handle this. You go!"

I trusted her, so Thorn and I continued our flight path toward Zel. The sooner we revealed Zel, the sooner this would all be over.

Zel and his ruddy dragon didn't so much as flinch as Thorn and I zoomed their way. Even when I prepared a whole volley of ether blasts and launched them at Zel in quick succession, he merely phase-shifted through them. His eyes glowed blue, but it didn't get the visible response I'd been hoping for.

Still, that didn't stop him from *acting* like he'd been badly wounded.

"See the violence of the Rebel Knights!" Zel wailed, putting on a face that showed just the right amount of pain, shock, and disappointment. "Attacking a frail old man!"

His display convinced some of the undecided soldiers to turn their blades on Vesta and her supporters, as well as King Rodan. In fact, it seemed Rodan was fighting for his life here, grateful for the aid of Queen Liana's saber and Brigan's seaxe.

Thanks to Zel's gecko-murdering lackeys, I wasn't on the mindlink anymore. I could only hope that Kai had a brilliant backup plan that would hopefully include everyone coming to the terrace to aid us soon. We needed all the help we could get.

Before me, Zel's dragon gave a mighty roar before shooting a jet of flame at Thorn and me. My hands to his scales, I infused Thorn with my hover-powered ether. A white mist trailed after the pair of us as we flipped over the flames. I felt more in sync with my dragon than ever before as we twisted back around at lightning speed to face our foe. Stars, third ascension Thorn was agile! I felt warm embers of pride through our bond.

Friend! Thorn's voice sounded in my head, and I could tell he was channeling his thoughts toward the wyvern Zel rode. *Do you know that your rider serves the Gray?*

Yes, came Zel's mount's gruff reply. *But the Knights made my bond suffer. Now, they must suffer.*

The dragon shot another blast of fire our way, but we hover-dodged again. Disappointed in his fellow wyvern, Thorn launched his tail spike toward him. The spike regrew instantly.

It was the perfect shot, but Zel's dragon's scales went hazy as he phase-shifted through it. It seemed Zel's dragon was a Shadowbinder too.

Zel stubbornly refused to show off his voidarchy like he'd done in the armory before, letting his dragon do battle with us in the air above the terrace. Meanwhile, I caught sight of Meleya and Sniff as they alighted on the wall.

They landed near Vesta, Sniff's large, scaled body pinning several of the red-cloaked soldiers who'd been trying to take down the grouchy Geomancer. Signus was hot on Meleya's tail.

At least, he was until Vesta's geomantic earthquake stones swallowed him. I had to stifle a chuckle as she trapped him up to his neck in stone. I couldn't quite hear what biting remark she said to him next, but I hoped it was something along the lines of, "Looks like choosing gray doesn't pay, eh?"

Okay, maybe it was for the best that I wasn't feeding Vesta taunts.

I watched from the corner of my eye as Meleya and Vesta exchanged words, then took off together through one of Meleya's rifts. They portaled all around the terrace from person to person with Vesta directing Meleya on who to rift to next. I realized they were talking to the individuals Vesta knew weren't loyal to Zel, telling them the truth. Slowly, the tides began to shift as more people stood to protect Rodan.

It was a start, but I knew it wasn't enough. For every person who listened to Vesta, another tried to kill her for what they thought she'd done to Zel.

As for Thorn and myself, we were still pulling out every move in our arsenal, trying to provoke Zel into fighting back and displaying his voidarchy. Some blue-tinged fire would be much appreciated right about now. But he continued to phase-shift through our every attack, playing up the frail old man angle for all it was worth.

"This is what Solrac has pushed his Rebel Knights to be!" Zel cried, ensuring those on the terrace could hear him. "No better than Magnus! Aggressors, harming the innocent!"

"You're anything but innocent!" I shot back.

Zel gave me one of his cheery grins, then replied quietly so that only I could hear: "Prove it."

Zel could barely stifle his laughter as a squad's worth of his soldiers arrived on the scene. Dragon riders, like him, all bent on protecting their leader and taking me out.

Our hover-accelerated flying took us every which way to avoid claws, blades, and dragonfire. It took every ounce of concentration I had just to stay alive, forget attacking Zel.

There was a cracking sound as Thorn strengthened his diamondoak armor. A spray of crossbow bolts from soldiers on the wall bounced harmlessly off his flank.

"Nice one, Thorn!" I said.

He roared as he went head to head—literally—with one of the other dragons. Both had majestic, staglike antlers, and I had to hover-jump and levitate above Thorn's saddle to avoid getting thrown around, arming myself with starglass shields to absorb blows. It seemed my training with Boone, Rhana, and Ivar was paying off. The evidence being that I wasn't dead yet.

Unfortunately, some of the soldiers on the wall had gotten ahold of some of those dreambolt repeaters Kari had been showing off during her demonstration. We did our best to stop them, but with so many bolts coming at us, some slipped through the cracks. The violet-tinged bolts weren't lethal, but little by little, they started draining me of my stamina. Thorn got the worst of it as he tried to protect me, and I felt his wings droop as I landed back in the saddle.

"Soot," I said. "Let's avoid those ones, alright Thorn?"

You're a genius, Thorn replied. Drained as he was, his sarcasm was still as strong as ever.

But that was when I felt a light pulse from Thorn through our bond. It didn't completely overcome the effects of the dream darts, but I felt energized, the minor cuts and bruises I'd sustained so far vanishing in an instant.

Thorn... What are you doing?

My third ascension power, Thorn replied as his wing stabilized. *Enhanced regeneration—It seems I can share it, too.*

As if you weren't awesome enough, I thought back with a big, crooked grin.

Thorn and I continued to defend ourselves. Through the fray, I spotted Zel looking smug as he sat astride his dragon, calling encouragement to those on the terrace. I knew that even if I could land another hit on him, it would be useless. His ability to phase-shift kept him from needing to react in self-preservation, and taunting Zel into showing off his voidarchy hadn't worked, either. I needed a new plan.

Thorn and I were just hover-dashing out of range from another dragon's fiery breath when I saw her. A rider astride a white dragon, flanked by a flying force of dragons and falcondrakes, all carrying armed reinforcements on their backs.

"Elle!" I cried.

She and Aurora led the force into the fight. I recognized the colony of falcondrakes, with Solvai in falcondrake form flying at their head. Kai was on her back, looking reluctant and rather ether-drained, but ready to fight for the Rebels as well. They took on Zel's dragon rider soldiers, drawing the fire away from Thorn and me.

Aradan was there too, along with two of his dragon bonds. I recognized the violet evren he rode as Lyra, while his red wyvern, Glass, flew at their side with a young woman in a fine noblewoman's gown in his saddle. At the sight of the dark-haired girl, I heard a deep, resounding cry from the terrace.

"Praise the light, my daughter is safe!" cried the King of Skygard. At once, he switched sides, defending King Rodan alongside Brigan.

But those weren't all the reinforcements Elle had brought. She must've flown like the wind to reach the refugee camp at the lava fields, because I recognized Rasec flying in as well as several others of the Knights of the Torch who had been thrown out during the schism. They were all back, ready to help take back their stronghold.

I cupped my hands around my mouth and gave a loud, long whoop.

That got Elle smiling—the first real smile I'd gotten out of her since the night of the festival in Topaz Sierra.

"Asher!" Elle called as she and Aurora swooped in beside Thorn and me. "What's the goal?"

I pointed to Zel and his dragon. "We've got to reveal Zel for what he really is! But I can't get him to use his voidarchy!"

Elle got a look of concentration on her face, then said, "We don't have to. Watch my back!"

With that, she and Aurora took off toward the castle spire. Thorn and I followed close behind to ensure no rogue crossbow bolts or blasts of dragonfire reached her.

Elle was heading for the southernmost spire's great lighthouse. At once, I realized what she was planning.

At Elle's word, Aurora blasted the pyre with her dragonfire. Thorn and I were ready at the large, round reflector, rotating it at just the right angle. Besides that, I burned more ether to add extra, prism-like panels to each side to bend the light of the fire.

Aurora's firelight bounced off of the reflective metal round, and with the help of my starglass, it splayed all across the terrace in brilliant, green-and-violet ripples of light.

Aurora had infused her dragonfire with revealing power like lightwielder's torches used. The white true dragon's eyes flashed gold at the use of Archonic power, but I also saw some kind of mystic rune glowing from over her forehead. I recognized the rune and felt a surge of pride as Aurora imbued her fire with a touch of the Sight.

As the brilliant light beamed over the terrace, it revealed what was once hidden. The vast amount of Gray shadows was enough to send a chill down my spine. Wraiths lurked all around, some bound to soldiers while still others clung to nobles.

The most powerful, dominating gray mass of all lurked directly behind Zel, its bright blue eyes like cold, glittering sapphires. Zel looked on in horror as gasps and screams flooded the terrace.

"Voidarchy!" one noble called out, backing away from a wraith-bound soldier.

"The Gray is real!" another cried as he glanced from left to right.

Those who were bound to wraiths looked to Zel, unsure what to do next. Meanwhile, laughter rose from the wall.

It was Signus, gray smoke from his wraith curling all around him. He'd freed himself from Vesta's geomantic trap, and boldly pulled something out from within his robes.

It was a blank gray mask with white lettering scratched into it. The sight of it made my stomach drop.

Sensing that the time for obscurity was over, Zel and his dragon rose, seeming to suck all light away from the area immediately around them. Gray mist swirled as both Zel's eyes and those of his dragon burned bright blue, blue-tinged shadowfire bursting to life along Zel's arms.

Ah, *there* was the display I'd been looking for.

Already, Aurora's light had begun to fade, along with its revealing power, but Zel's wraith continued to fuel his grand display of voidarchy.

Spurred on by Zel, the soldiers loyal to him dropped their red cloaks callously to the ground. What was the point in hiding if everyone already knew?

From Thorn's back, with the green fire from the lighthouse pyre behind me, I called out to those on the terrace.

"Now you see who the *true* Knights of the Torch are!"

I saw the truth reflected in the eyes of both nobility and soldiers alike. Now, no one was undecided regarding which side to fight for.

"Light the way!" Elle gave the rallying cry.

Bearing arms with renewed resolve, the real Knights answered.

Chapter 30: Drive Out Darkness

Meleya

When Asher and Elle lit up the terrace with Aurora's revealing light, everyone else had focused on the wraiths.

As for me, my gaze had locked onto my spirit dragon.

Blink's silvery aura trailed behind her as she swept across the terrace, emerald green spirit-dragonfire shooting from her mouth. She fought alongside us against the wraiths, weakening them and causing them to hiss and shrink back. Her fire left the larger wraiths with golden scorch-marks while causing the smaller, weaker wraiths to burn away entirely.

When Blink saw me watching her, she gave a sharp, inaudible roar through our bond. She wanted to show me something.

It was difficult to see Blink as Aurora's light faded, but I traced a Sight rune of my own. Blink's translucent form beckoned to me, directing my gaze to a small object atop the skyforge's dome.

I let out a gasp—It was a voidshard!

The blue crystal was small, but even from afar I could feel its oppressive, far-reaching aura. Its cold, lifeless mist was like a hurricane all across the terrace—drak, all across the entire *stronghold*, with the glowing blue shard at its center.

The voidshard was embedded in the gold framework and must've been cloaked from physical eyes using some sort of shadowbinding that had burned away in Aurora's light. I couldn't be sure, but it seemed like some combination of metal and shadowsilk had fused it to the frame in a way I'd never be able to pry out with my sword. Whoever had put it there wanted to make sure it stayed put.

The voidshard, I thought. *It's corrupting the etherlock.* That's *what's letting the wraiths in!*

Brrrum-ba-dum! Blink agreed.

There wasn't a moment to waste. Strategizing, I let the Sight fade from my eyes. Vesta now had the support she needed as she and the other true Knights fought against Zel's Coven infiltrators. He'd managed to recruit so many, I wondered if he'd brought in outside support. The corruption ran deep through Orothion. In more ways than one, if my hunch about the voidshard in the skyforge dome was correct.

"Sniff, fly us higher!" I said, and my dragon bond obliged.

We cut through the sky, avoiding enemy fire as we hovered above the terrace. Sure enough, when I looked down at the dome, I noticed the pattern in the gold framework.

There were a lot of extra gold flourishes in the design. But amidst it all, I could still make out the large, central triangle with diamonds extending from each point.

It was the same pattern I'd seen at Rhana's safehouse. There was no mistaking it.

The skyforge dome itself was an enormous etherlock.

And Zel had used a voidshard to corrupt it. *That* was how Xan was able to speak to me here. How so many wraiths had infiltrated the once-safe stronghold.

I had to restore it.

But not me alone. I was done working alone.

Scanning the terrace, I spotted the dark-haired girl in her grease-smeared metalsmith's apron. Kari stood beside the now-free Akayto, who had a Sight rune glowing from over his forehead. Both of them had gotten ahold of some of those dreambolt repeater crossbows, and were doing their best to take down Coven soldiers.

"Kari!" I cried, rifting myself from Sniff's back to stand beside her. Sniff turned outward, sneezing a flurry of ether blasts at the Coven aggressors. Akayto nobly continued to do battle beside Sniff, though he looked like he could really use a long nap.

"Hello?" Kari said, clearly confused as to who I was and why I knew her name.

I hurriedly told them that I was here with Kai and the other Rebels, then proceeded to explain my hunch regarding the voidshard in the giant domed etherlock.

I could practically see the gears spinning in Kari's mind. "Of course… I've speculated regarding the gold in the framework being of significance before. Stars, the ancients were brilliant. To think, all along the skyforge has been Orothion's primary etherlock!"

"An etherlock Zel has corrupted," I said. "Will you help me get the voidshard out?

"Absolutely!" Kari nodded.

I pulled her onto Sniff's back behind me, and we swept toward the top of the dome. Sniff guarded us once more while we bent over the voidshard in its center. As I'd suspected, it was completely fused to the frame. The once-gold metal around the little shard had turned cool gray, and seemed to be slowly changing the very composition of the metal.

Kari squinted, muttering half to me and half to herself. "Fascinating. As for dismantling this and removing the… voidshard, did you call it? We'll need a tremendous amount of force. Shadowsilk as a binder is incredibly strong, especially since I suspect it's been forged using an alloy of iron and skystone in order to lock it more securely in place. This isn't going anywhere without some kind of etherarchically-charged chemical combustion."

"Did someone say combustion?" a young woman called up to us from the base of the dome. She wore a rather tight-fitting dress that showed off her figure, as well as a draccoon-skin cap atop her head.

"Who's that?" I asked.

Kari broke into a borderline maniacal grin. "Enya."

CHAPTER 31: LIGHT THE WAY

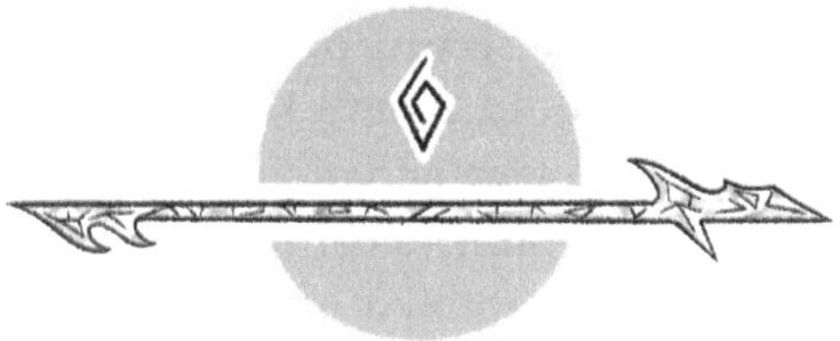

ASHER

Our reinforcements took care of the Coven, but it was up to Thorn and me to handle Zel.

And *stars*, Zel and his dragon were a lot to handle.

Zel was as precise with his shadowbinding as I was with my starglass. And with his wraith enhancing him, that shadowfire was deadly stuff. Blue-tinged black flame coiled through the sky at three different angles. Thorn and I dodged two of the streams, but I was running low on ether and the third hit us straight on.

I cried out, gripping the black burn on my arm as the shadowbinding essence broke through a segment of my starglass armor and began to eat away at my skin. I tried to activate my ascension bracers to heal it, but they sputtered out, completely drained. Thorn roared, activating his regeneration to help heal me directly. He wasn't sure how much longer he could keep it up though, since his ether well was draining fast too.

Meanwhile, I launched ether blasts, volleys of starglass shards like arrows, and came in swinging with my starglass spear. Thorn did what he could with his tail spike and claws, but Zel and his dragon were masters of phase-shifting. His wraith had to be assisting him.

"So much for being a frail old man!" I called.

Zel laughed as he prepared yet another jet of shadowfire. As Thorn and I zipped around the skies, we sought out backup. I knew that any of my friends would help me at the drop of a scale if I asked, but they were all pretty occupied with fighting the Coven soldiers. Elle and Aurora were like a beacon as they tangled with two riders at once, Elle's saber alight with Aurora's emerald-and-violet flame as it sent arcs of fire toward their enemies. Kai and Solvai were taking care of the crossbow wielders on the wall, and Brigan was still fighting alongside both King Rodan and King Nik against those on the terrace. As for Meleya...

What in the stars was Meleya doing with Kari and Enya atop the sky-forge dome? They seemed to be setting out jars of some kind of glowing, white substance. Was that liquid ether? Kari had been excited when I accidentally discovered the power-enhancing substance last year, using it in silverbane and no doubt countless other projects.

The three young women scrambled off the dome, huddling in a far corner. That was when Meleya traced a rifting rune. Two portals ripped to life just over the liquid ether concoction, and I saw Meleya carefully guiding the portals closer and closer together...

Oh stars. Oh *stars.*

"The eclips-plosion," I said under my breath as I realized what she was about to do. "Not bad, scale-in-the-mud, not bad at all..."

Continuing to keep Zel engaged, Thorn and I flew in a loop to draw him closer to the dome. Doing so let him get a better view of what was going on, and when he saw the two growing portals above the skyforge ceiling's golden framework, his face went ashen.

"What is she... stop! *Stop!*" he bellowed.

His eyes burning with blue light from his wraith, Zel seemed to have a breakthrough in his powers. Black and blue smoke trailed him as he and his dragon hover-flew to pass me up.

From there, Thorn and I flew upward and away from the path of the impending explosion as I drew deep into the last dregs of my ether well. I swung my starglass spear, launching an arc of ether toward Zel and his dragon and solidifying it to starglass as it hit them so that it weighed them down.

Zel plowed ahead, firing forth tendrils of silver-laced shadowsilk as he flew, reaching toward Meleya's portals in an effort to do something, *anything* to stop them.

Too late.

Meleya's entrance portal went through the exit.

In a fantastic flash of white and gold, the deafening explosion burst the bottles of liquid ether, amplifying the effects and sending out a wave of white etherdust that coated the terrace like snow. Nobles and soldiers alike braced themselves, and a couple of dragons and falcondrakes directly above the dome went spinning.

As for Zel, the eclips-plosion hit both him and his dragon the hardest of all. Thanks to a little starglass manipulation from me, they had almost been directly on top of it. Downward they fell, through the shattered dome and toward the fiery furnace in the skyforge below. There was too much ethersmoke to be sure exactly where they landed, but there was a great, pained roar, followed by a very promising *poof* of green dragonfire from the forge.

Not only that, but whatever Meleya had done seemed to cause a shift in the very air around us. Everything got a few degrees warmer and somehow brighter. Through the ether mist, I saw that the Coven fighters were significantly weakened, surrendering to their true Knight counterparts.

At once, I realized that Meleya had somehow done something to drive out the wraiths.

It started slowly at first, but pretty soon a cheer began to rise.

We'd done it—the Rebel Knights... *all* true Knights. Orothion was ours.

I looked around the terrace at the people. Vesta was embracing the noblewoman who'd flown in with Solvai and Aradan, and the King and Queen of Skygard were there with them, beaming. Elle was with her parents, hugging them as well, along with her Uncle Aradan. Kari and Kai had found each other, and my father was close by. Thank the stars he'd pulled through as well.

All across the terrace, people were embracing, clapping, and cheering. They were all a little battered and covered with etherdust, but in their faces I saw that hard-won hope had been restored.

I joined in the cry, and Thorn let out a mighty roar.

Well, as mighty as a totally exhausted, ether-drained wyvern could manage, anyway. He landed on the terrace, and I just had time to slide off his back before he curled up, resting his tired wings as his diamondoak armor receded back into his black and gold scales.

Meleya wasn't far from me. She was covered in white etherdust from head to toe, and I couldn't resist jogging over to her.

"You may think I'm the messy one," I teased, "but look what *you* did. This cleanup will keep you occupied for at least a few weeks."

Meleya looked me dead in the eyes. "I'd ask for your help, but I think you'll be busy at the infirmary. Hopefully they can give you something for your addiction to the sound of your own voice."

My jaw dropped at her top-notch comeback. The only problem was, Meleya's did too. She broke into a massive grin, which completely undermined her victory.

I gave her a light shove. "Not bad, Mel. I think we'll keep you."

Behind her, smoke was rising from the enormous hole that was once the skyforge dome. Curious, I made my way to its edge, stepping over bits of metal and fragments of ancient black starglass.

Meleya joined me as we peered over the side. She scanned the skyforge floor far below as if looking for something.

"The voidshard is still down there, I'm sure of it," she said.

"Voidshard?" I asked.

"Zel's voidshard, I think," Meleya said. "It was corrupting the giant etherlock. The eclips-plosion got it out, which is what forced the wraiths out. But the shard itself... I'm sure it's still down there."

"What do you think we should..." I trailed off as the smoke surrounding the forge below began to swirl.

Both Meleya and I paused, looking downward. What was going on?

Then there was a powerful *whoosh* as two red wings beat downward on the smoke. I gasped, getting between Meleya and Zel as he and his dragon shot upward through the shattered skyforge ceiling.

A few screams sounded from behind us. Zel and his dragon were both in very bad shape, bruised and completely disheveled. But it seemed they were back for one final, desperate hurrah.

In Zel's hands was a crossbow. It was big, and I thought I could make out Kari's mark on it, just like the ones they'd used during the demonstration. But this one seemed less refined, and had a fascinating crystal bolt locked into place.

At the sight of it, I heard Kari call out, "Not the Dreambolter!"

Everything happened so fast. I became aware of just how low my ether well was as Zel's lips curled into a totally sinister, cheery smile.

"You may have delayed my revenge, fellow scale-skin, but that doesn't mean I can't take at least a little now!" Zel said as he pulled the trigger.

Despite my nearly empty ether well, I summoned a starglass shield to block Meleya and me. Beside me, I saw her finger flying to runetrace. But that was the problem with Mystics—their etherarchy required time.

The Dreambolter's shaft pierced my shield, allowing the head of the bolt through. There was a flash as it released a massive conical wave of purple dreamweave energy that blasted both Meleya and me in the head.

Time seemed to slow. Screams rose from behind us. Aradan and his multiple dragons swooped in to take out Zel once and for all.

I felt my soul rip from my body. With horror, I watched—yes, *watched,* as my body and Meleya's fell through the void that was once the skyforge dome. Elle and Aurora shot forward, as did Thorn and Sniff. Would any of them make it in time to catch us?

As for me, I had other things to worry about. I heard a scream from beside me, and turned to find Meleya. Only, it wasn't Meleya, since I'd just watched Meleya fall into the skyforge.

Rather, I was staring at a translucent, shimmering ghost of Meleya, surrounded by crazy bluish-purple clouds. I looked down to see that I was just as translucent, with bright turquoise mists spinning all around me.

"Meleya," I said, unable to keep the panic from my voice. "What's going on?"

Meleya looked like she'd just seen a ghost. Oh soot—she *had* just seen a ghost. *Me.*

With grim terror, Meleya confirmed my worst fears:

"We're in Etheria."

MEMORY 3

Solrac's escape from Evyndara to Skygard had taken him through seldom-traveled passes, left him hiding in secret cellars, and running for his life from Capital Riders on more than one occasion. He was really looking forward to a hot meal, a nice warm bath, and a good night's sleep.

But of course, those things would have to wait.

The moment Solrac reached Orothion, a thousand different things required his attention. Countless Knights beset him, some bowing before the great Farseer. Others, like Vesta, brought him complaints. Surprisingly few came to Solrac with compliments regarding his well-trimmed, full beard. He'd grown out the goatee, partially for disguise purposes, but mostly because, as was customary, married men sported beards. Solrac wore his proudly.

Of course, there were slightly more important things to focus on than one's facial hair. Ever since Solrac's quest team of Rebels had reclaimed the stronghold for the light, things had been rather chaotic.

There was the Coven, Zel and his followers, to deal with of course. Zel wasn't the only magi among them, which meant they required round-the-clock watching down in the dungeons.

The whole of the Western Keepdoms had gone into lockdown. Magnus was growing desperate, and despite the end of Zel's revenge-fueled war on the Capital, tensions were brewing. Real war was on the horizon.

There was the enormous project of trying to rebuild the skyforge ceiling. Destroying it to eject the Gray from Orothion had been a stroke of genius, but, like most strokes of genius, it required a lot of cleanup.

Additionally, without the great skyforge etherlock in place, the effectiveness of Orothion's other etherlocks had diminished. The castle was still quite safe from wraithkind, but the etherlock networks' power to deter wild dragons would occasionally falter. The guard here worked tirelessly to ensure there were no tragedies, especially with such a high concentration of magi here giving off such a powerful ether signature. Well, that and the veritable hoard of skystone Zel had somehow managed to amass.

Solrac still couldn't believe he hadn't seen the kindly old man's betrayal coming. Was he the scorching Farseer or not? Solrac suspected that Zel's wraith must've given him access to some ancient form of shadowbinding, allowing him to keep his future hidden from prying eyes.

Besides that, Solrac had to admit he'd been distracted lately. Still, spending more time with his wife wasn't a decision he regretted. Vidya had been a lifesaver during the journey here, though some of the Knights had been understandably apprehensive about letting her into Orothion. Fortunately, being the Farseer did come with a certain amount of sway, and they eventually let Vidya through the gates.

What was more, rumor had it that Princess Eliana's dragon, Aurora, had miraculously healed a young girl of the shadow wasting. Solrac had asked Eliana to tell him every detail of what had happened in the obscure town, from the severity of the child's case to the white healing flames Aurora had created.

"Can she reproduce this fire?" Solrac had asked Elle.

But try as she might, Aurora couldn't replicate the white flame. Despite that, the tale gave Solrac hope, however flickering. Hope for the realm, and for Valla's dangerous quest northward. He worried for Valla—he hadn't heard from her in so long. No one had.

Solrac expected that things would get easier once Cenrik, Ivar, and Boone arrived with the bulk of the Rebel Knight—that is, the Knights of the Torch-forces. Their journey would be quite difficult as well, but ultimately, moving the base to Orothion would be for the best. Once again, the Knights would be a united front. Good thing too, since the Farseer was getting constant visions regarding the end of Evgard as they knew it.

Gray mists. A tall tower surrounded by dragons. The realm torn wide open. And, as always, the great gray dragon snapping up Solrac's head.

Solrac knew that bit was coming whether he liked it or not. Every day, he grew more certain. The dragon was the Soul Reaper, and the omen predicted Solrac's inevitable death.

He could not dwell on it now, though. Not when there was so much to do. Infinite things to prepare before the rest of the Knights arrived.

But first...

Solrac reached Orothion's medical wing. He breezed down the aisle, past several beds, some empty, some not, until he reached the two beds set up side-by-side at the far end. Light from the window streamed onto the two individuals lying eerily still upon the beds.

Asher of Steel Rim and Meleya of Misthaven breathed, but shallowly. Their eyes were closed, but Solrac noted the troubled expressions just beyond the surface.

As Solrac entered the room, Akayto roused from his place at his son's side.

"You made it, Solrac," Akayto said. "Or should I say, Farseer." A rune for the Sight glowed from over his forehead, which matched the new golden streaks in his hair. Scars from the ether overuse Zel had put him through.

Akayto had been one of the first to learn Solrac's secret. Solrac was grateful for his discretion—Even *he* hadn't been able to come up with a way to hide the truth from an incredibly skilled blind Rifter who used the Sight almost constantly.

"How are they?" Solrac asked.

"No change," Akayto replied grimly. "They're dead, but not *really* dead."

"No, they are very much alive," Solrac said. "For now. It is as I feared: They are afflicted by the same strange condition with which the late King Axel suffered. Unfortunately, I used up the last of my supply of the remedy on him, and the cure for Astral sleep is one that takes time to brew."

"Astral sleep? What does it mean?"

"It's technically a bit of a misnomer as their spirits are technically trapped in Etheria, the world of spirits, not Astra, the world of dreams. But it is an overabundance of dream energy that got them there."

Solrac's jaw flexed as he looked over Asher and Meleya. For longer than either of them knew, Solrac had been seeing them in his omenfires. Both were vital in the ever-nearing convergence of mythic stars. By their hands, the realm would rise or fall.

"We need to brew a remedy, and fast," Solrac said. "For very strange things can happen to a soul lost in the spirit plane."

CALYX

Lesser shades hissed, scattering before Calyx as he entered the conclave of the Elder Wraiths. Even the other Elders bowed their shadowy gray heads in reverence as he moved to the head of the circle.

The council stood together in the Soul Reaper's lair. Calyx could just barely make out the great telescope and other physical features of the room. True vision was something the wraiths only enjoyed when bound to a human host. Without a host, it felt like Calyx was trying to see through a thick, smoky haze.

But tonight's meeting would be worth leaving Calyx's soon-to-be host. There was much to be done if they were to be ready at the close of winter when the convergence came.

First, Calyx drifted past the lowest of the Elders, starting with Kalash, the Sower. Together with his chosen host, the half-born, Zel, Kalash had sown a great deal of discontent amongst the ancient enemy of the Gray Ones. That the Knights of the Torch had been weakened could not be denied.

And yet, Calyx could not help but think that Kalash had been sloppier in his performance this time around. Calyx had heard the news regarding what had occurred at Orothion and the way Kalash and so many others had been ejected from the Knights' headquarters. Perhaps Kalash had lost his touch. The Wraith King would not be pleased with this recent failure.

As Calyx floated past the lower ranks, he noted the Elders who had bound themselves to the High Crown. Mason and Magnus were men with powerful positions, prime choices for Elder wraiths. Both wraiths were performing their tasks well. Magnus's wraith lurked in shadows, but across the blank face of Mason's wraith was white writing, displaying the names, titles, and accomplishments taken from his past hosts. There were many, but not nearly so many as Calyx had collected.

Moving forward, Calyx passed Exusha, the Warrior. She and Calyx had worked together throughout many ages. Now, Exusha served the Wraith King by bending the great Black Valkyrie to her will. Unfortunately, Exusha had lost control of her host... For now.

Nearer the head of the council were the wraiths bound to Ilyan and Ilona, the twins who'd pledged to use their skill in etherarchy to serve the Surgeon. These wraiths were younger, with only a few names etched onto their blank, gray faces. They had not been part of the Gray's last attempt to overwhelm this land. But the Overseer and the Deceiver showed great promise, their drive causing them to rise quickly through the ranks.

At last, Calyx reached his own place at the right hand of the great Wraith King. Thick, gray smoke billowed all around Agnai, practically glowing with power. From his core, brilliant blue light glowed, matching the light burning within his eyes. His otherwise featureless face was etched with more names and deeds than anyone could count, and a great, smoky crown with nine points like claws tearing at the sky sprouted from his head.

Calyx had known Agnai throughout many ages. He had bound himself to countless hosts, always men of power, intelligence, and skill. Calyx had been surprised by the Wraith King's choice this time. But Agnai assured him that the Soul Reaper was the right man. His skill with soul surgeries would allow the Wraith King to become that which had destroyed them last time: A Guardian.

Agnai was the only wraith here so thoroughly bound to his host that said host was present here tonight. Agnai was clearly enjoying his physical form, his smoky gray hands aligned with his host's thin, corporeal ones as together they gripped a mighty sword. The long, silver blade had serrations along its lower back edge and was marked with ancient runes that seemed to glow with a purple light. Its starlike crossguard contained a swirling black hole at the crux. This was the weapon that would bring about their ultimate victory, said to have once belonged to the goddess Streya.

The Veilblade.

It seemed the meeting had already begun as the Wraith King berated one of the lesser Elders—the one bound to High Prince Mason.

We are disappointed, Agnai's doubled voice was harsh. *You still have not managed the simple task of retrieving our voidshard from that silly little girl.*

Forgive me, great one, the Elder bowed his shadowy head in submission.

Perhaps punishment is in order? The Wraith King used a churning, smoky hand to gesture to the turbulent mass of hissing shades behind him. The shades were hungry, and at the Wraith King's word, they would love nothing more than to consume the essence of one as powerful as an Elder.

Mason's wraith seemed to tremble. *I would remind the great Wraith King of all I have accomplished already. Were it not for me, Mason would not have ventured north to procure the Veilblade.*

Agnai seemed to consider this. *This is true,* he said. *But without the voidshard, the Veilblade will not serve us.* Indulgently, he dragged his fingers along the hilt of the sword, letting them linger in the empty space at the blade's base.

Mason's wraith hurried to pacify him. *Even now, Lightbane returns to my host at the Academy. We will regroup. Come up with a new, infallible plan to retrieve the shard once and for all.*

Actually, I believe I have the answer, one of the Elders said. If he'd had a mouth, Calyx was sure he would have held it in a self-satisfied smile. It was the Overseer, the wraith bound to Ilyan.

My host and I have had a vision, he spoke pridefully. *A powerful vision, so strong we believe its coming to pass is inevitable. Hundreds of stars fill the skies. The stars represent this very lair.*

The Overseer gestured to their surroundings as he went on. *Beneath the stars, the girl with the white hair, Meleya of Misthaven, holds her blade over the chest of the half-born, Asher of Steel Rim.*

At that, many of the Elders shifted uncomfortably. Even amongst wraithkind, this was not the first time the omenfires had burned with the faces of these two mortals. The Overseer claimed that they were to be key players in the coming convergence. Whether for the light or the Gray, it was too soon to tell.

When it comes to Asher and Meleya, the Overseer continued, *their fates are entwined. Where one goes, the other will follow. Do you not see? If we but capture Asher, we capture his bane. The voidshard will fall into our laps.*

There was murmuring among the Elders in the circle. Calyx found the Overseer arrogant, but he saw the sense in his plan.

We accept this plan, the Wraith King said. *Whichever among you brings me Asher will prove their loyalty. When the Gray Age at last commences, that Elder shall be my right hand.*

The murmuring around the circle gave way to eager hissing.

As for Calyx, he began to shift uneasily. That was *his* place.

But my King, Kalash murmured from the far side of the circle, *is not Asher too well protected? His* kalavira *is very strong.*

I do not fear any kalavira; *not even a human one.* Calyx radiated confidence. The others muttered their agreement, though Calyx sensed their hesitation.

The meeting went on as the Wraith King asked for reports from various Elders. He focused in particular on the account from the wraith bound to High King Magnus.

Calyx had never paid this Elder much attention before, but as he focused on him, he realized he'd never seen a wraith like him on the council.

He was not one wraith, rather, many lesser wraiths clinging together to form a greater whole. There were no eyes on their face. Instead, hundreds of smaller, dimmer eyes shone all across their form. With so many voices in his head, it was little wonder High King Magnus was struggling to hold the realm together.

The Horde spoke as one, reporting on the progress regarding the skystone tribute the High Crown took from the various keepdoms. Already the High King was preparing to receive the vast collection of skystone kept here in the Soul Reaper's lair. Housing so much of the ether-bearing stone would be risky, since it would undoubtedly draw every wild dragon the realm over.

At least, until Calyx corrupted it.

Very good, the Wraith King nodded to the Horde before turning his attention to Calyx.

And you, our dutiful Builder, he said. *Are you and your host prepared to perform your task?*

Calyx straightened. *I am stronger than ever, great Wraith King. My host's emotions are strong, and have fed me well. But he continues to resist me. He has not yet accepted my voidshard.*

A few judgmental murmurs rippled throughout the circle of Elders. Calyx felt a wave of shame.

The Wraith King replied with disappointed resolve. *Without your contribution, Calyx, we cannot succeed on the night of the convergence. Perhaps you have chosen the wrong host?*

No, Calyx rushed. *Jax is the one—He's strong, resilient, and skilled. I am certain I can break him. I just need to somehow push him over the edge.*

I have exactly what you need.

The new, raspy voice caught Calyx and the others off guard. Every Elder was already accounted for. Who would dare interrupt their meeting?

Lurking on the far fringes of the circle was Xan.

At the sight of her, there was a general din of discontent. Calyx heard the others muttering:

Low-tier shade.

Insubordinate.

Usurper.

She is no better than Skapa, the wraith of the Black Valkyrie, Exusha, whispered. *Just another arrogant rogue, desperate for power. Skapa fell to the power of the Wraith King, and you will too, Xan.*

The Elders hissed in agreement, and Xan hissed right back.

But Calyx recognized Xan's cunning. The fact that she'd been able to sneak into the conclave at all was evidence of how powerful she'd become.

Besides, the Wraith King encouraged jostling for power among his ranks, harnessing such ambition to strengthen his own aims. So long as no one dared to attempt to usurp his own position at the top, he didn't see a downside.

Speak, Xan, he said. *What do you know?*

Xan took this as an invitation to sweep boldly into the center of the circle, her misty gray body floating above the room's stone. She faced Calyx with confidence shining in her sly, glowing blue eyes.

I wish to break my chosen host as much as you desire to break yours. I have just the thing that will allow you to succeed—But it comes at a price.

There was a long, uncomfortable pause. Some of the Elders seemed unsure as to what Xan was waiting for, but not Agnai.

You are welcome to feed off of our shades, the Wraith King said, gesturing to the hissing conglomerate of shadows behind him.

Xan did not respond, a clear indication that she found such an offer wanting. Apparently, she felt that whatever information she had was worth far more than some measly shades.

The Wraith King rose, eyes burning with blue light as he floated above his ethereal host. For a moment, Calyx thought he would destroy Xan for her arrogance.

Instead, he gestured toward Kalash.

Zel's wraith let out a hiss of terror as the other Elders backed away, giving him a wide berth.

For a second, Xan and Kalash faced off. The Wraith King was testing the waters. Was Xan strong enough to take down one of the Elders?

In a sudden movement, Xan surged toward Kalash, her arm raised as she formed it into a jagged wraith-blade. The Elder tried to fight back, but Xan speared him with her blade, holding him in place as her gray and blue essence sucked away at the glowing blue light in his chest. It quickly became clear he didn't stand a chance.

A grim atmosphere settled over the lair as Xan finished devouring every last tendril of Kalash's essence. Her eyes glowed more brightly, her form more concrete than it had been before. Some of the lower-tier Elders shrank back, no longer confident in their mockery of the Usurper.

Only the Wraith King seemed unfazed.

You've had your payment, he said. *Now tell us what you know.*

Xan's laughter echoed like harsh winds across the lair.

Calyx found Jax exactly where he expected him to be in the dorm at the Mage Hunter Academy. Night had fallen, and the dorm was quiet but for the scraping sounds of Bjorn sharpening his jagged silver dagger as he perched like an animal on the balcony. A mid-tier Gray One clung to his soul.

Jaira was there, too, having just returned from her failed mission. Calyx could see minor shades nipping at the fringes of her aura, though she had yet been unable to draw another wraith strong enough to power the two dormant ether wells the Soul Reaper had stitched to her soul. But soon, there would be plenty of wraiths available to satisfy every willing—and unwilling—host in Evgard.

Jaira stood by, watching intently as Jax finished up his workout. As he wiped sweat from his brow, Jaira moved in, her fingers dragging along his upper chest.

Jax, once so easily swayed by such provocation, barely glanced her way. As he left the dorm, heading toward the men's sleeping quarters, he clung to the quartz crystal clipped to the side of his belt. Calyx knew the quartz reminded Jax of the only woman he'd ever *really* cared for.

Eagerly, Calyx followed Jax, drifting through the Academy walls like they were nothing. Jax sat on the edge of his bed, running his fingers through his thick, steely gray hair. It was late, and Calyx could tell Jax knew he ought to go to bed. But even sleep brought him little comfort lately. Jax's mind was a miserable, moldable space.

Calyx effortlessly slipped into Jax's consciousness. Jax's hands balled into fists as he sensed the shift.

"What do you want?" Jax asked aloud.

Only to help you, Calyx replied. And he meant it.

Next, Calyx felt another presence enter Jax's mind. A presence like a rumbling, mighty storm.

Calyx internally hissed. It was that dragon bond of Jax's again, trying to counter Calyx's mental attacks. She, too, had chosen Jax for his great potential, and was chronically making things more difficult for Calyx.

Her companionship strengthened Jax's will. "Get out of here," Jax said to Calyx.

Even those words were enough to push Calyx from Jax's mind like a stormy gale. But Calyx was determined.

He fought hard and slipped past the dragon bond's influence. He was an Elder Wraith, after all, the right hand to the Wraith King himself. Calyx would not be deterred.

I have something I must show you, Calyx pressed in on Jax's thoughts. *It is only fair you know the truth, after all.*

That piqued Jax's curiosity. *The truth about what?*

With satisfaction, Calyx latched more securely onto Jax's mind. Then he showed Jax the memory Xan had witnessed.

Meleya stood on an expanse of blackened, ancient lava flows. Her long, white braid swung, her dark eyes alight with energy as she swung her sword. Jax straightened at the sight of her.

"M," he breathed. Calyx had his attention now.

Meleya was in the middle of a sparring exercise. Her sparring partner, Asher. When Jax saw him, he tensed.

Meleya and Asher fought together on the lava fields, her seaxe meeting his starglass spear in the air over and over again. They laughed as they practiced, Meleya's bright smile cutting into Jax's soul like the edge of a blade. Jax watched as she taught Asher to use her portalling before she pushed a pair of portals into one another to create an explosion of etherdust.

Jax got abruptly to his feet when he saw Meleya and Asher collide on the ground. His knuckles cracked, his muscles bulging as Calyx forced him to keep watching the scene unfold.

Then, Jax saw Meleya kiss Asher.

Calyx relished the cumulation of Jax's white-hot anger, deep sorrow, and utter loathing for Asher. Calyx fed off of these delectable emotions like a leech.

No amount of calming from Jax's blasted dragon made an ounce of difference as Jax dropped to one knee, bracing himself against the bed. Agonized tears squeezed from the corners of his eyes.

It seemed Xan had been right about this memory's power and its effect on Jax. Kalash's sacrifice had been well worth it.

We must find Asher and make him pay, Calyx whispered to Jax.

"Find Asher," Jax mumbled.

But first, we will need to be stronger.

"Stronger." Jax was becoming more aligned with Calyx with every word.

Calyx made his move. On the floor before Jax appeared a thin blue crystal. On one side, Calyx's name. On the other...

Let me take away this pain, Calyx thought. *With your blood, seal our bond, and you shall feel nothing. I swear it.*

With trembling fingers, Jax took hold of the voidshard like it was a lifeline. Then, using the crystal's sharp point, Jax pricked his finger.

The bead of blood slid down the crystal's plane. In its wake, Jax's name appeared first in glowing red that quickly faded to white.

Eyes shut, Jax took a deep breath. In that breath, Calyx merged with his host.

Finally.

A thrill rushed through Calyx as he *felt* Jax's heartbeat thrumming in his chest. *Thump-thump. Thump-thump. Thump-thump.*

When Jax opened his eyes again, they were glowing sapphire blue.

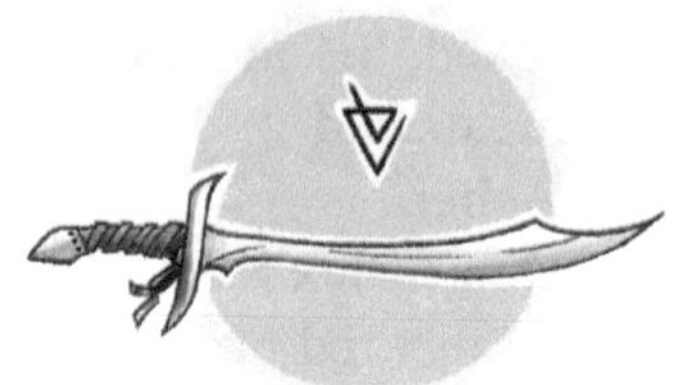

The explosion at the skyforge dome left everything so bright she almost missed him. *Taaket,* stars. Could it really be Asher? He and Meleya looked like a pair of lost dragonpups, scared utterly senseless.

They weren't dead like she was, that much was certain. Dead spirits didn't scream and point at one another, spinning around wildly and arguing about how to get back to their bodies. Zerana had watched enough spirits move through the first level of Etheria to know that death was typically a far more peaceful affair.

Besides, the fact that Asher and Meleya were still here and hadn't moved on yet tipped Zerana off that something was amiss.

Blessedly amiss.

Zerana took off running—or rather, floating—toward them, calling out for her son as she went.

"Asher!" She cupped her hands around her mouth. "Asher!"

Despite being only a translucent spirit, his dragonfire green eyes were bright as emeralds as he turned. All panic fled him as his whole being lit up, the mists of his turquoise aura brightening and swirling around him. A hundred emotions flew across his face. Confusion, shock, disbelief...

And pure, uninhibited joy.

Asher leaped toward Zerana, arms outstretched. He nearly knocked her down with the force of his embrace, and Zerana laughed heartily.

"*Vaaro,* careful, my *laaksi rakaai,*" she said, trembling as she held him. "You've gotten so much stronger since the last time I saw you! That is, since the last time I *really* saw you, face to face."

As they were both spirits, Zerana could feel Asher's arms around her in a way she hadn't in over three years. Whatever the spiritual equivalent of tears were cascaded down Zerana's cheeks.

Asher's one-word response left her spirit heart bursting. "Mom!"

End of Book 3

The story continues in The Skystone Chronicles, Book 4

A Brief Guide to EVGARD

By Blake & Raven Penn

the skystone chronicles

mystic
Mind

METHOD OF ACCESSING ETHER

- Mystic ether wells are located in their minds. They trace runes of golden etherlight in the air to achieve mythic effects. Mystics must know the correct runes and have the right intention behind them, and each rune requires a certain amount of ether. Once the rune is completed, it appears over the Mystic's forehead.

Runes can also be carved onto objects to save time. This is most commonly seen with runemarked wands or staffs. We once met a certain Mystic who'd even carved psionic runes onto a whisk. The meringue was delicious.

Seer

Seers are Mystics that can access telepathic runes. Some of the more basic runes enable them, to read minds or see omens of the future, while more advanced runes can enable mind control, precognition, and memory wiping.

SHARED POWER: DREAMWEAVE

All Mystics can access the Dreamweave. In the most basic terms, the Dreamweave deals with illusions.

This can manifest through simple runes to trick the eyes, or more advanced runes to trick the other senses. Some runes enable the use of dreamblades—weapons made of focused, purple dream energy that passes through physical objects, but drains the soul's vitality and the victim's stamina. Quite inconvenient when someone blasts you midway through a meeting about the end of the world.

Additionally, the Dreamweave can be used to make illusory bodies for ethereal familiars, which, for lack of a better term, are almost like a solidified imaginary pet.

Psion 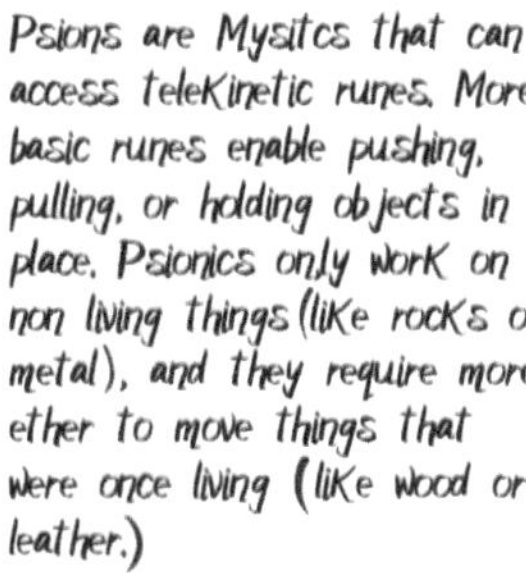

Psions are Mysitcs that can access telekinetic runes. More basic runes enable pushing, pulling, or holding objects in place. Psionics only work on non living things (like rocks or metal), and they require more ether to move things that were once living (like wood or leather.)

Rifter

Rifters are Mysitcs that can access teleportation runes. The most basic runes involve making portals through Etheria (the spirit plane), while more advanced runes allow them to make anchors, rift holds, and access the Sight to see into Etheria itself. Rifters can only open portals to places they can see or to an anchor.

the skystone chronicles

SENTINEL
Body

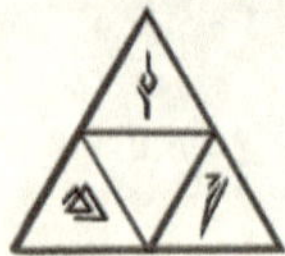

Method of accessing ether

Sentinel ether wells are located in their core, near the belly button. Their mythic powers are more instinctually driven, and generally require a physical totem of some kind for use. A Geomancer's totem might be a volcanic stone or granite, while a Wildshaper's might be a wolf's fang or a dragonhawk's feather. A Woodweaver's totem could be a leaf or a piece of amber.

When Sentinels access their ether, golden patterns appear on their bodies around whatever area is being affected.

WILDSHAPER

Wildshapers are fauna-based Sentinels. They can take on aspects of and transform into animals for which they have a totem. This is commonly used to enhance senses or gain a creature's strength or agility. Full transformations are typically accompanied by a cloud of golden ethermist. Careful—that desert finch perched on your sill might not be what she seems.

GEOMANCER

Geomancers are earth-based Sentinels. Using a totem take from a certain environment can grant them aspects of power related to that environment. A totem of sandstone might be used to make sandstorms, while a stalactites totem could grow into a large club. A common use we've seen is to make one's skin hard as stone, so try not to make any Geomancer enemies. Trust us, they know how to take a hit.

WOODWEAVER

Woodweavers are flora-based Sentinels. They can use their ether to manipulate and even generate plants based on what totems they have. Some use this power to keep an endless supply of freshly-grown arrows in their quiver or grow diamondoak armor. Others maintain their crops even throughout the winter months. Some have even discovered the secret to making plant servants, called Folians.

SHARED POWER: REGENERATION

All Sentinels share the power of regeneration. This enables them to use their ether to heal wounds. They can train to heal themselves more quickly or learn to heal others. Sentinel regeneration does not work on wounds caused by the anti-ether metal, silver.

THE SKYSTONE CHRONICLES

ARCHON
Spirit

Lightwielder

Lightwielders are Archons that manipulate light. Different forms of light carry different properties. Commonly, lightwielders use lightning for raw power or liquid light to heal. Lightwielding can reveal things hidden using etherarchy. Less commonly, these Archons can concentrate light into blades or barriers of a weightless, solid material called Luxite.

Method of Accessing Ether

Archon ether wells are located in their hearts. They achieve mythic effects through the will of their spirits. When they command ether, their eyes glow gold. When an Archon learns a new way to use their ether, it is typically through a "breakthrough" during a moment of intense emotion.

Shadowbinder

Shadowbinders are Archons that manipulate darkness. Solid darkness forms shadowsilk, while darkness in its plasmic form makes shadowfire that slowly disintegrates anything it touches. It's actually quite useful in sewer systems. Shadowbinders can even use their affinity for darkness to turn invisible and pass through objects.

Shared Power: Levitation

All Archons share the power of levitation. This entails Archons using their ether to manipulate how they move. It's most commonly used to make themselves lighter and faster, through hover-jumps and hover-dashes. Levitation has its limits, and in the past thousand years, we've only met one who learned how to use this ability to fly. An Archon manipulating their movement in this way leaves a faint trail of warped golden light behind them as they go.

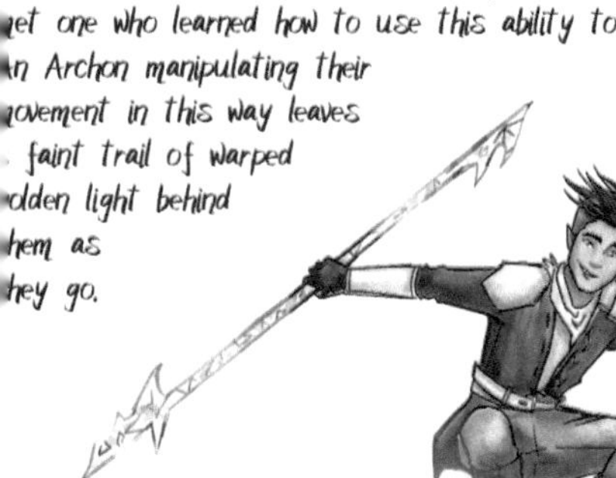

Astromancer

Astromancers use ether to manipulate ether itself. They can condense ether into starglass objects that will last a day, or blast ether directly. Ether leaves a white mark, and hurts both physical and ethereal creatures. It can stop dream energy as well. Some Astromancers can even sense where ether is, and what type is being used. Very few can give their ether away, and even fewer can take it from others. We think it's a latent astromantic sense in dragons that enables them to hunt magi by sensing their ether wells.

the skystone chronicles

True Dragons

True dragons are what your world generally thinks of as simply… dragons. They are great, intelligent, flying beasts with armored scales, four legs, two wings, and a tail. They vary in color, length, size, and style of horns. Every true dragons can command all nine types of etherarchy as well as breathe dragonfire, which produces an ultra-hot, emerald-green flame.

Since the Dragon Wars, true dragons are incredibly rare in Evgard.

Dragon Eyes

The eyes of dragons are a burning emerald green, just like their dragonfire. All dragons (as far as we know), even lesser dragons, share this trait.

A note on True Dragon Eggs

Usually no larger than a fist, True Dragon eggs harbor immense power. Their shell tends to be scaly, with a color matching the scales that the hatchling will have. Hatchlings are always bigger than the space the egg could have contained, which implies they must have some form of rift hold within them. The shell ought to be saved for its mythic properties.

Dragon Blood

While true dragons have gold blood, the blood of drakes, wyverns, and evren is more bronze or copper in color. Some like a few drops in their draquil, but it was a little acrid for our taste.

DRAGONS

DRAKES

Drakes are dragons with four legs and no
wings. They're commonly built like this
worlds panthers or tigers, but more
serpentine. They vary greatly in appearance,
though most are large
enough to carry
two human riders
in their first
ascension.

DRAGON BONDS

All dragons have a heartscale.
It's found on their chest,
near the heart. Dragons and
humans can forge a bond if
the dragon gives the human
their heartscale. This grants
the human power over the
dragon, while enhancing the
dragon's own cognitive abilities.

EVREN

Evren are dragons with four wings and no legs. They have small
claws on the joint of each wing which they can use to crawl,
but evren are much more suited to the air. They tend to have
more canine features, almost like this worlds flying foxes.
Evren prefer to sleep hanging upside down from trees or cliffsides, and are
usually only large enough to carry one human rider at a time until their second
or even third ascension.

WYVERNS

Wyverns are dragons with two wings and two legs. Their
wings have well-developed claws at the wing joint, allowing
them to navigate the ground far better than evren,
though not as well as drakes. They are the most
snakelike of the dragons, and tend to have
longer necks and tails. When it comes
to size, they're generally larger
than evren, but smaller
than drakes.

Ascension

Evgardian nobility jealously guard the
secret to dragon ascension. Still, we
suspect the trigger to a dragon's
ascension has something to do with
their hunger for ether. When a dragon
ascends, their ability to communicate
grows, and they advance in mythic power,
if they have any. Third ascension is the
highest level of dragon ascension that
we currently know of.

ETHER HUNGRY

Dragons love ether. They will take it from any source they can
find, even human magi. It is for this reason that magi are
outlawed in Evgard—their ether is what draws wild dragons to
the Keeps.

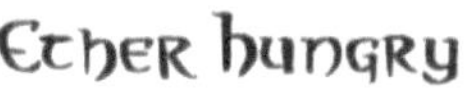

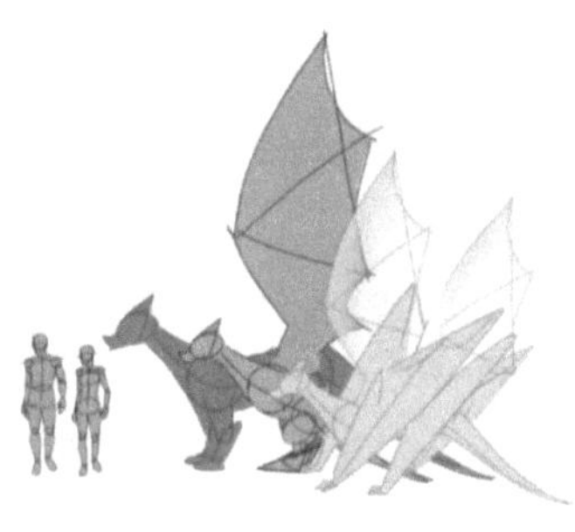

the skystone chronicles

Evgardian Creatures

Draconic Animals

There are countless draconic animals in Evgard. From draccoons to wyvernhogs to aldraka, the draconic lifeforms have supplanted most non-mythic animals. Some of our favorites are Kirin, which are draconic horses, and lutradons, which are large, scaly otters. There's nothing more fun than splashing around and riding a lutradon in the riverbank.

Ethereal Familiars

Ethereal familiars are not well understood. Born of etherarchy, these creatures act as an extension of the magi who created them. They develop their own distinct—and often strong—personalities as well (we once had rather an interesting encounter with a passive aggressive shrew). While all magi types technically have the capacity to create one, Mystics tend to do it most, using a complicated set of runes that manifest on the skin of their familiar.

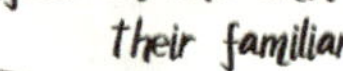

Umbrals

Umbrals are creatures corrupted by the shadow wasting. They fade until they become a smoky gray version of what they once were. They have lightning blue eyes. The bite of an umbral spreads the shadow wasting, though it will not turn humans or dragons fully umbral.

the skystone chronicles

Dragon Ascension

Dragons in Evgard ascend when they gain enough ether. This is why they seek after magi and skystone. They can indirectly gather ether from the sun, which we speculate might be part of why dragons sunbathe, since they are not cold-blooded.

* *Thorn is a more subtle example of the type of transformation one might expect from a dragon ascension.*

Tiers of Ascension

First ascension dragons are typically able to grow to the size of a large horse, and can generally serve as mounts for one to two people. If mythic, they tend to have access to only one type of etherarchy.

Second ascension dragons grow larger and usually become more vibrant in color. They gain more decorative scale ridges, fins, and horns. Mythic dragons will also gain a new expression of their etherarchy. All bonded dragons gain the ability to speak their bond's language with their minds.

Third ascension dragons are the largest and most grand. This ascension can vary the most from a dragon's initial form, though they will always be recognizable. Mythic dragons unlock a final expression of their etherarchy, and the telepathic speaking ability of bonded dragons becomes indistinguishable from human speech.

A Note on Bonding

All dragonkind can ascend, whether bonded or not, though bonding a human tends to increase the pace of ascension.

Ascension Armor

While ascending, dragons shed their old scales, leaving behind magically imbued scales that are typically used to make weapons and armor that are charged with the dragon's power.

the skystone chronicles

the MAGE HUNTER ACADEMY

Nestled deep in the Ridgeback Mountains of Evyndara, the Mage Hunter Academy stands as a monument to the High Throne's power. The building is embellished with silver from the inside out as a reminder that magi are the enemy. Here, cadets are trained to recognize, track down, and apprehend those born with etherarchy. It is also where those who have received the magi 'cure' go to convalesce.

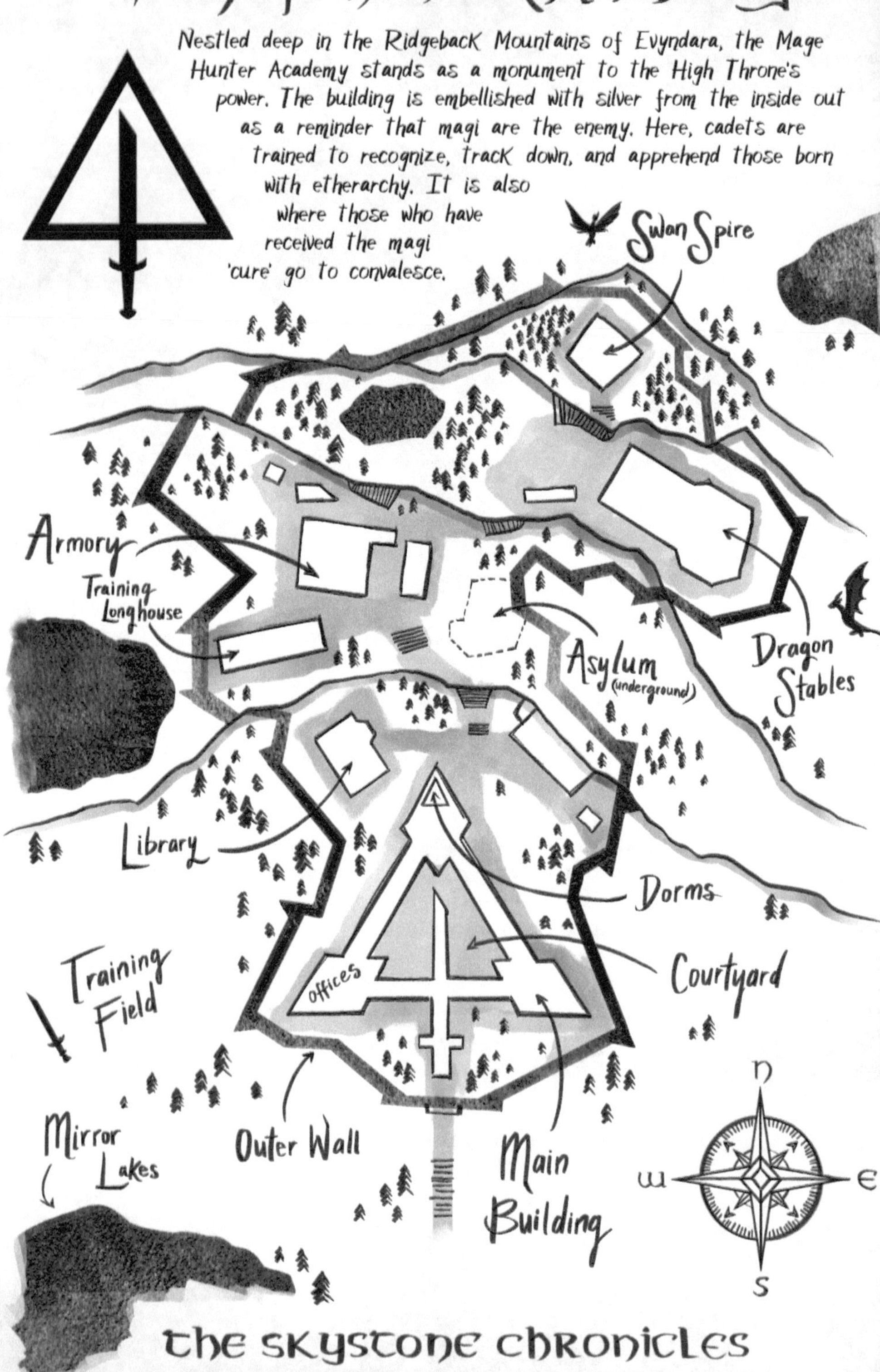

the SKYSTONE CHRONICLES

VOIDARCHY

Voidarchy is an ancient, mysterious form of power. It is essentially the opposite of etherarchy, and magi who use voidarchy draw not from ether wells, but from a darker source. Some say that source is the void itself. Others think it may be corrupted ether.

GRAY ONES

Information on the Gray Ones, or wraiths, is limited due to their mysterious, otherworldly nature. They are dark spirits, desperate to take charge of a body, as they feed off of negative emotions. Wraiths write a record of their achievements (names of prior hosts, titles, and accomplishemnts) on their otherwise featureless faces to distinguish themselves. They can also reshape parts of their bodies, commonly forming an arm into a 'wraithblade.'

Wraiths are locked in an eternal power struggle with one another. If they absorb enough of another wraith's essence, they can rise in power. The known tiers are as follows:

SHADES

Small wraiths with no voidcore that can only feed off of emotions.

ECHOES

Medium-sized wraiths with a core and the ability to speak. Can expend power to briefly interact with the physical realm.

VOIDSHARDS

Once a wraith has gained enough power through consuming enough negative emotions, or by defeating enough of their fellow wraiths, they can break off a portion of their core to form a voidshard with a willing host. When that voidshard is marked with the blood of their host, they form a bond similar to that of a dragon's. The wraith gains access to their host's senses and occasionally take control of their actions.

ELDERS

The most powerful wraiths. They can access some voidarchy of their own, though their reach in the physical realm is still limited unless bound to a host.

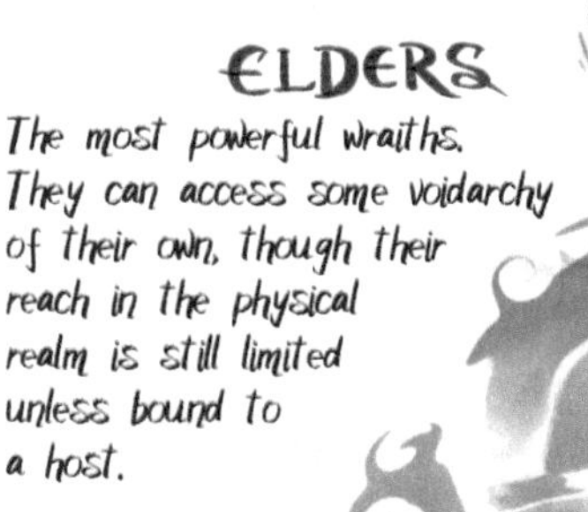

the skystone chronicles

the GLINT NETWORK

The following is a page recovered from the journal of Kai of Steel Rim. Obviously, the original was written in Evgardian, however, using illusion etherarchy, we were able to render an English approximation.

Number	Color	Assignment	Notes
Glint Prime (0)	Silver	me	—
Glint 1	Red	Solrac, Duke of Glacia (male, 40's, Psion)	Secretive & dangerously optimistic
Glint 2	Orange	Kari of Steel Rim (female, 19, non-magi)	My sister and expert inventor
Glint 3	Yellow	Jax of Blackfjord (male, 19, Psion)	Muscles, bandana, arrogant
Glint 4	Green	Asher of Steel Rim (male, 18, Astromancer)	Best friend and resident loose cannon
Glint 5	Blue	Boone of the Bramblewilds (male, 60's? Astromancer)	Superstitious, folksy sayings
Glint 6	Indigo	Ivar of Stonekeep (male, 40's, Psion)	Has a Kleptomaniacal draccoon familiar
Glint 7	Violet	Valla of White Cliff (female, 30's, Wildshaper)	Loyal, skilled, dangerous. Harbinger of weapons
Glint 8	White	Eliana of Drakfell (female, 18, non-magi)	Princess, true dragon rider

Orothion

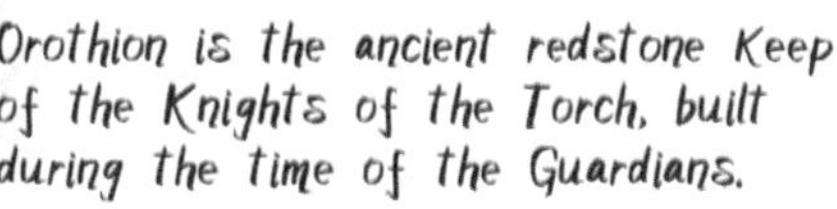

Orothion is the ancient redstone Keep of the Knights of the Torch, built during the time of the Guardians.

Etherlocks

Etherlocks are ancient guardian relics that can hide the ether signature of skystone and magi. They can also lock wraiths out of an area. There are other functions they appear to have, though they are currently a mystery to Evgardians. No smith has been able to recreate one yet.

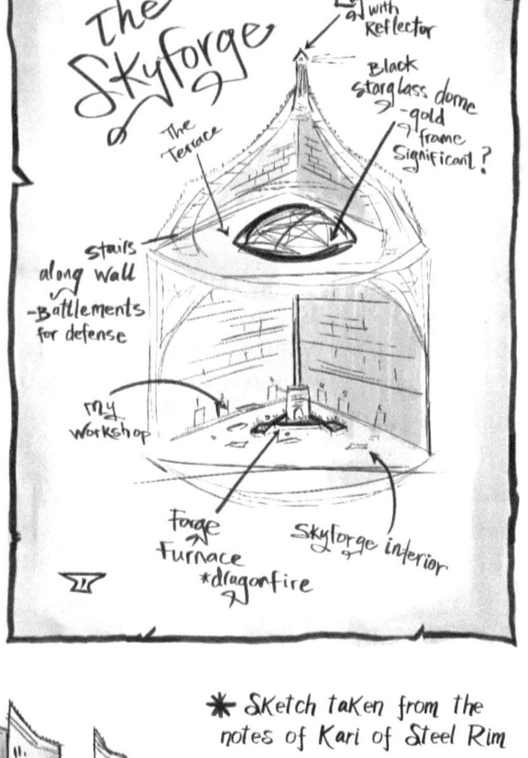

✳ Sketch taken from the notes of Kari of Steel Rim

Acknowledgements

Hey there, dragon riders! We've got a lot of fantastic people who deserve at least a thousand gold marks and a whole case of skystone for all they've done to help us bring the land of Evgard to life.

As always, we want to thank our parents for being our number one supporters through storm and skyfall.

Raven's mom, you've been right there at the top of the list of Skystone fans, laughing and crying through each draft right along with us. Not to mention the countless hours of babysitting you've given to make Book Three possible. Thank you. Raven's dad too! You were always ready and willing to distract the kids with epic car tracks and bubble machines so that we could get some extra writing in.

We couldn't have done it without Blake's parents either. Blake's dad, thanks for all the times you took the kids out on much needed 'adventures.' Blake's mom, your writing expertise rang in our ears on countless occasions, and we deeply appreciate every well-timed encouraging word that kept us going.

An enormous thanks to you too, kiddos. You put up with some pretty nerdy parents, and we hope you love these stories someday when you're old enough to read them.

Also, thank you Julia for watching our kids so often as well. You're literally watching them as we write this now.

As always, our beta readers deserve a special shout-out. Thank you for making this story actually work, Kimball, Amy, Brenden, Cathy, Elissa, Ella, Bjorn, Michaela, and Auriana. A special thanks to Michaela and Auriana for catching those last-minute typos! And Kimball, we are so sorry for what you had to go through after reading chapter fourteen.

One of the greatest members of Team Skystone is our brilliant editor, Nadav Laemmle. Seriously, this man makes it all come together. Thank you as always.

Last but not least, thank YOU for reading (or listening to) this book! We are thrilled to have you on Team Skystone. As indie authors, every reader makes a huge difference. If you liked Dragon Hunter, please let us know by leaving a review. That's the best way to get other readers to give these books a chance.

May you always choose light, burn bright, and drive out darkness.

Review Link

Blake and Raven Penn fought through epic battles and twisted love triangles to finally find each other. They both studied script writing in college, and now deign to turn their film and comedy experience into novel writing. Through sunshine or the dreaded Utah Valley inversion, they spend their days tending their wild offspring and dreaming of dragons. Aiming to write fantasy adventures that would keep their former teenage selves up reading long past midnight, Blake and Raven hope to brighten a world in desperate need of light.

To contact them, you can reach out via skystonechronicles.com or follow them on social media @blakeravenpenn. Also, be sure to join their mailing list and get a free short story set in the land of Evgard!